Harry Bowling was born in London, and left school at fourteen to supplement the family income as an office boy in a riverside provisions' merchant. He was called up for National Service in the 1950s. Before becoming a writer, he was variously employed as a lorry driver, milkman, meat cutter, carpenter and decorator, and community worker. He lived with his wife and family, dividing his time between Lancashire and Deptford. We at Headline are sorry to say that Harry Bowling very sadly died in February 1999. We worked with him for over ten years, ever since the publication of his first novel, CONNER STREET'S WAR, and we miss him enormously, as do his many, many fans around the world.

The Glory
and the Shame

and

Conner Street's
War

Harry Bowling

headline

THE GLORY AND THE SHAME first published in Great Britain in 1997
by HEADLINE BOOK PUBLISHING

CONNER STREET'S WAR first published in Great Britain in 1987
by HEADLINE BOOK PUBLISHING

First published in this omnibus edition in 2005
by HEADLINE BOOK PUBLISHING

A HEADLINE paperback

10 9 8 7 6 5 4 3 2 1

ISBN 0 7553 2653 9

Typeset in Times by Avon DataSet Ltd,
Bidford-on-Avon, Warwickshire

Printed and bound in Great Britain by
Clays Ltd, St Ives plc

Headline's policy is to use papers that are natural, renewable and
recyclable products and made from wood grown in sustainable
forests. The logging and manufacturing processes are expected to
conform to the environmental regulations of the country of origin.

HEADLINE BOOK PUBLISHING
A division of Hodder Headline
338 Euston Road
London NW1 3BH

www.headline.co.uk
www.hodderheadline.com

The Glory
and the Shame

To my family

Prologue

May 1941

More than a week had passed since the worst night of the Blitz, and on the Monday morning of the nineteenth they laid George Merry to rest. He had died a hero and his wife Lucy held her head up high as Father Dooley gave the eulogy. The spring morning carried a chill and the mist was slow to clear, but by the time the mourners arrived back in Totterdown Street the sun was shining.

Lucy Merry had no children of her own to share her grief, though her little terraced house was full of cousins, nieces and nephews, as well as the neighbours, who on the whole had had few kind things to say about George Merry during his lifetime but were singing his praises now that he was gone.

The Carey family spared Lucy Merry the hypocrisy and gathered instead in their own home, along with the Duggans who lived next door. The two families sat quietly talking over very welcome cups of tea, brewed ready for their return by Aunt Ellie, who now sat stony-faced in her high-backed chair by the hearth.

''E must 'ave bin goin' on seventy,' Martha Carey remarked. 'I remember Lucy Merry sayin' ter me 'ow worried she was about 'im takin' the night-watchman's job after all those years drivin' fer the firm.'

Mabel Duggan patted the bun of her dark hair and then folded her arms over her ample middle before replying. 'I didn't fink 'e looked 'is age. 'E was still very sprightly.'

'I feel sorry fer Lucy. She's all on 'er own now,' Martha went on. 'Shame she didn't 'ave any kids. They'd 'ave bin a comfort to 'er now.'

Aunt Ellie had heard enough, and after dabbing at her eyes she got up from her chair without a word and made her way to the sanctuary of her room on the bend of the stairs. The tears she shed and the pain she felt were not for George Merry. Her grief was for the man who smiled out of a framed photograph that stood on a small cabinet beside her bed.

Martha Carey gave her husband Joe a quick glance that spoke volumes as Ellie left the room and then she eased back in her armchair. 'I dunno where it's all gonna end,' she sighed. 'We can't take much more o' this bombin'.'

Mabel Duggan's daughter Pamela sat quietly listening to the conversation. At eighteen death should have been a stranger to her, but the Blitz had changed all that. At the funeral she had felt as cold as ice and she wept to see her mother weeping. She was blossoming into a beautiful young woman, with sparkling green eyes and red hair, but as she sat listening unobtrusively to the older women talking the colour had drained from her pretty face and she shivered involuntarily. She had hardly known George Merry but the solemn occasion had touched her deeply. As she saw her mother crying before her she was hardly expected to know that the tears she shed for other neighbours who had died during that terrible night, the elderly Simpsons, Flo Thomas, Hilda Moore and Granny Knight, were tears not only of sorrow but of shame.

Joe Carey and his old friend Charlie Duggan had taken their leave and gone into the backyard where they sat on upturned beer crates. The sun was warm now and the light ale tasted better than tea, but Joe was pensive as he watched the progress of a spider that was crawling down the underside of the tin bath hanging on the grimy brick wall.

'It was a nice piece in the *Bulletin* about ole George,' he remarked, still staring at the spider.

Charlie nodded as he ran his fingers through his thinning grey hair. 'Yeah, they did it well,' he replied. 'I expect it's a comfort ter Lucy.'

Joe eased his stocky frame against the wall and sighed deeply. 'Our Mo looked in early this mornin',' he said flatly. 'I was still in bed but Marfa was up. 'E didn't stop long.'

'Our Stan's callin'-up papers came this mornin',' Charlie said. 'It's the Navy. 'E's gotta report ter Chatham. Mabel 'ad a few tears but it's just as well 'e's goin'.'

'Yeah, it's a bad business,' Joe continued, noticing that the large spider was now running down the wall. 'In a way I wish our Mo was able ter go. It would 'ave bin the best fer all concerned. Mind you, Marfa wouldn't agree.'

'Nah, I s'pose not,' Charlie replied.

Joe Carey took a tobacco tin from his coat pocket and flicked off the lid, then he noticed the wry smile

3

on Charlie's ruddy face. 'Yeah, I know. I shouldn't be smokin' wiv my chest,' he said quickly. 'That's what our Marfa's always tellin' me.'

'I never said a word,' Charlie replied, his grin increasing.

Joe lifted his foot and brought it down quickly as the spider crossed the yard, only to see it scamper off under the toilet door. 'It ain't so bad this weavver. It's durin' the winter I suffer.'

For a few moments neither man said anything. ''Ave you 'eard from young Tom lately?' Charlie asked finally.

'We got a letter a few weeks ago but nuffing since,' Joe told him. ''E seemed ter fink 'is regiment was bound fer the Middle East but 'e couldn't be sure.'

'They're still only kids at eighteen.'

'Just like us. We were the same.'

'Yeah, an' if we'd 'ave only known.'

'Kitchener wants you! 'E would 'ave bloody whistled.'

'Be a lot different this time, it will.'

'That's fer sure.'

The two old friends were silent again for a short while then Charlie Duggan's grey eyes suddenly became sad as he tapped his pipe against the heel of his shoe. 'Best ter try an' put that business ter the back of our minds,' he said quietly. 'No use dwellin' on fings.'

'I make yer right,' Joe answered, nodding. He leant forward to lick his cigarette paper. 'We can never be expected ter ferget it, but as I said ter Marfa, we can't let it destroy us, an' it will if we let it.'

'We can start right now by promisin' ourselves

that we'll never mention it ever again,' Charlie said solemnly.

'Good as done. It's the only way,' Joe replied gravely.

Martha Carey had gone to Ellie's room and remonstrated with her. 'Look, I 'ope you ain't gonna sit up 'ere mopin' fer the rest o' the day,' she said sharply.

'I can't 'elp the way I feel,' Ellie replied with a long face.

'Well, pull yer bleedin' self tergevver,' Martha told her despairingly. 'I got enough ter worry about wivout you gettin' ill again.'

'I'm all right. I'll be down in a minute,' Ellie replied as she stared down at her crumpled handkerchief.

With the two families assembled once more Charlie Duggan did his best to raise a smile. ''Ere, did yer see what it said in the *Bulletin* this mornin'?' he asked.

Blank looks spurred him on and he picked up the newspaper. 'It ses 'ere that the government's asked the 'ead o' the 'Eavy Rescue Squad ter nominate some o' their men fer bravery medals, an' yer know what 'is reply was? "Medals? We don't want no effin' medals. The 'ole effin' borough deserves an effin' medal."'

'You mind your language in front o' young Pam,' Mabel said sharply.

Aunt Ellie's bottom lip quivered and she got up again.

'I fink I deserve one o' those bleedin' medals,' Martha sighed as she went to comfort her elder sister once more.

Chapter One

1947

The early days of April had been cold, but as the month wore on the weather had become more seasonal. This Saturday morning a heavy shower had died out and the sun was once again shining down on Totterdown Street.

The local folk were keen to make the most of the break in the weather, and now women hurried off to the market while the children went out to play in the quiet street. A few elderly people took the air at their front doors, and even Aunt Ellie Emberson stood on the doorstep of number 6 for a short while to peer along the turning, until she spotted the large and vociferous Bessie Woodward approaching. Ellie detested the woman and quickly went back inside.

Ellie Emberson was fifty-seven, four years older than Martha Carey, her married sister, whose home she had lived in ever since the day war was declared. Until then she had lived alone in two rented rooms supplied by the church, but the tenancy had been a little too near the river for Ellie's peace of mind. Drunken seamen and dock workers spilled out of the pubs every Saturday night at closing time and very often fights broke out. What was more, she had read a newspaper article back in the summer of '39 which, in her words, 'put the fear of God into me'. If war did break out London would be a prime target, and in particular the dock areas. The hack had gone on to point out that the German air force had won their spurs in the Spanish Civil War, and there was a picture of Guernica which had been totally destroyed by the Condor Squadron.

Martha Carey had been worried about her sister's lonely existence, and when she suggested that she move into Totterdown Street with them Ellie needed no coaxing. As Martha pointed out, she was family and at such times families should be together. Martha's husband Joe was a staid, homely man and he had raised no objections, though sometimes Ellie had the feeling he was merely suffering her presence in silence.

On the whole Totterdown Street was a good place to live, Ellie felt. It was a small turning leading off from Abbey Street and quite close to the large market in Tower Bridge Road. The cobbled turning had two rows of neat terraced houses with corner shops: Ogden's the tobacconist and newsagent and Field's baker's shop were at the Abbey Street end, while at the far end that led into Ship Lane John Raney ran an oilshop and opposite him was Kenward's the cobbler's shop. The street had survived the war intact, unlike Ship Lane, once a thriving industrial turning but now one huge bomb ruin, a ravaged wasteland hidden from view by corrugated sheeting that ran right along its length.

On that Saturday morning Ellie was feeling quite excited; a rare occurrence for her, admittedly, but today was a little special. It was her fifty-seventh birthday and Martha had had a cake made especially for the occasion. There had been cards too and presents from the family. The Duggans were calling in for tea that evening and Martha had insisted that Ellie look her best. She had done her hair for her and set it tightly in curlers, and at this moment she was collecting her best dress for her from the cleaners.

Sue Carey pushed her chair back and stretched leisurely. Saturday mornings were usually quiet at the *Bulletin*, and today was no exception. There had been very few callers and only a couple of messages to deal with, and time was dragging as it approached midday.

'Are you still here?' Paddy O'Brian said as he came out from the reporters' office. He was a large man in his mid-forties and he had amorous designs on the pretty receptionist, but he was sad to reflect, the young filly treated him like nothing more than a benevolent uncle. He could show her a good time, all the same, even though she was most likely quite worldly wise after her war years in the ATS.

'I was just about to switch off the phones,' she told him.

Paddy sat down on the edge of her desk and folded his arms. 'Why don't you let me take you to the flicks tonight?' he said. 'There's a good musical on at the Trocadera.'

'Sorry, Paddy, I'm all booked up,' she replied with a smile.

'P'raps another time then,' he said, not trying to conceal the disappointment on his pale flat face.

Sue reached down for her handbag, aware that his eyes were following her every movement. 'I'm afraid I'm spoken for,' she told him lightly.

The reporter shrugged his shoulders. 'All the best ones are,' he remarked, then he leaned towards her conspiratorially. 'By the way, did you hear the latest? There's a new reporter starting soon.'

Sue was fishing for her powder compact and she shook her head. 'I haven't heard anything.'

'Bit of a flash monkey if you ask me,' Paddy went on. 'I bumped into him when he came out of Spencer's office. Been with the *Star* and the *Evening News* as a cub reporter before the war and then he was involved with the services' magazine, according to Spencer's secretary. I wonder what's so attractive about coming to work for this rag? The way things are going we'll be lucky if we're still printing by the end of the year. Sales have dropped again and Spencer's walking around like a bear with a sore head.'

Sue had found the tiny silver compact and she looked at herself in the small mirror, quickly applying the powdered pad to both cheeks. 'He must have his reasons,' she replied.

Paddy got up from the desk and did up the buttons of his shabby coat. 'Well, I'd better be off,' he sighed.

Sue watched him leave. Poor Paddy, she thought. His weekend would be spent mainly at his local in Balham, and on Monday morning he would arrive late with a king-sized hangover and a crumpled shirt that he had slept in. There would be messages waiting for him, and Spencer on the warpath, but despite everything Paddy would survive. He was a good reporter for all his shortcomings and Spencer knew it.

As she hurried from the newspaper offices near London Bridge the young woman was looking forward to the weekend. Del Abelson had promised to take her dancing that evening which gave her an excuse to wear her new dress and shoes. There was Aunt Ellie's birthday party to get through first though, and there would no doubt be a few tears shed when the port took effect. Poor Aunt Ellie. Put into service as a young girl and then falling in love with the young man of the house. It could almost have been a fairy story, especially the way her mother had told it, but fairy stories have happy endings, and it hadn't worked out that way for Ellie and Charles Langley, son of Lord Langley and heir to the Langley wealth. The young man had joined the Royal Flying Corps at the beginning of the First World War and been killed in combat over France. Aunt Ellie had loved him dearly and there had never been any other man in her sad life. Now, on her fifty-seventh birthday, she would cut her birthday cake, take a couple of glasses of port and then feigning a headache she would retire to her room, to sit on the edge of her bed dabbing at her eyes as she stared at the sepia photograph of her one and only love, the handsome young airman Charles, who had been so tragically killed more than thirty years ago. How sad that she had never let him go.

Martha tutted as she worked at removing Ellie's curlers. 'Now keep still. They're nearly all out,' she said crossly.

'They were very tight. They've given me a bad headache,' Ellie moaned.

'Tight me arse,' Martha growled. 'Anyway they've gotta be tight or they won't curl yer 'air. Yer can 'ave a couple of Aspros. They'll soon shift yer 'eadache.'

'Do you have to be so common,' Ellie went on. 'There's no need for it.'

Martha smiled as she removed the last of the curlers. Ellie had adopted a refined accent during her days in service and it had been the subject of amusement ever since. 'I'm not common, Ellie,' Martha said with mock severity. 'I'm just a born-an'-bred cockney wot talks a bit rough, not wot like you do.'

'Now you're making fun of me,' Ellie retorted. 'You take Sue. She speaks properly and it sounds so nice. It puts that young man of hers to shame.'

'Don't you let Sue 'ear yer criticisin' 'er bloke,' Martha said quickly. 'Del's a smashin' feller an' 'e finks the world of 'er.'

'I'm not saying he doesn't. All I'm saying is . . .'

'Now shut up an' keep still or yer barnet'll never get fixed,' Martha ordered. 'I'm tryin' ter make yer look like Joan Fontaine.'

Ellie bent her head and suffered the discomfort as her younger sister combed out her thick greying hair. Joan Fontaine, she thought. And the ensemble were playing Strauss for the midsummer gathering, and the sweet aroma of honeysuckle scented the warm night air as the strains of the 'Blue Danube Waltz' carried out along the colonnade from the brightly lit ballroom. What a wonderful night it was, she recalled with a deep sigh.

'Darling, I had to see you,' he said with a tremor in his deep voice.

'Won't they miss you, Charles?'

'I don't care,' he replied passionately. 'My life is with you, not them. There's so little time and so much to say.'

'I do love you dearly, Charles, but I'm afraid,' she told him almost tearfully. 'We come from different worlds. I'm just a maid, a paid servant from a poor background, and you, you're the future Lord Langley, with a place in the history books. Let me go, darling. We can never be together.'

Ellie smiled to herself as she remembered her theatrical performance that summer night in the shadows of the arbour. How delicious the memory of his lips on hers, the pressure of his body and the sensation of his strong arms around her. That night it was as though the world stopped turning, and in the seclusion of the copse he had laid her down on the mossy slope and smothered her with his kisses. Her resistance soon melted away and she let him love her, urging him on with soft moans of pure ecstasy, grasping the too brief moments of passion before the imminent parting.

The next morning, as the mist rose off the lawns in the hazy dawn light, he left. Elegant in his tight-fitting uniform, his shoulders straight and proud, he took his leave of his family. He sat in the rear of the Daimler, the throaty roar of its powerful engine sending the sleepy birds skywards with protesting caws. She was waiting by the gate half hidden, but he saw her, saw her hesitant wave. His brief smile had turned her legs to jelly and kindled anew the longing in her aching heart, and cherishing the memory of his little clandestine gesture she had turned away, never to see him again.

'There we are. Yer look very nice,' Martha commented. 'Just let me put a bit o' rouge on yer face, it'll 'ide the paleness.'

'For goodness sake, Martha, stop fussing,' Ellie

complained. 'It's a birthday party not a coming-out party.'

Down in the parlour Joe was talking to his daughter. 'I 'ope our Tom ain't too sloshed when 'e gets in,' he sighed. 'Yer know 'ow Aunt Ellie gets wound up about 'im gettin' drunk.'

'Any chance of Mo calling in?' Sue asked him.

'I shouldn't fink so, though yer never know wiv 'im,' Joe replied.

'He is very busy, Pop,' Sue said in mitigation.

'No one should be too busy fer their family,' Joe said sharply. 'Tom'll make the effort, pissed or not.'

'Well, maybe Mo'll make the effort too,' Sue said hopefully. 'He is pretty fond of Ellie, despite her funny ways.'

Joe Carey eased his heavy bulk back in the armchair. 'I dunno, strike me if I don't,' he declared. 'There's our Tom earnin' a pittance at that poxy firm 'e's workin' for, an' not a care in the world, an' there's Maurice wiv a good business that's makin' a lot o' money, but is 'e 'appy? Is 'e 'ell.'

'Money's not everything, Dad,' Sue said a little reproachfully. 'Mo wanted to join up when the war started. He's always regretted not being able to do his bit. That accident changed him, we all know that.'

''E should remind 'imself sometimes that 'e was lucky it was only a smashed foot,' Joe said quietly. 'That poor sod on the back o' the bike was killed outright. The driver o' the car was badly 'urt too. 'E spent six months on 'is back. All right, so Mo couldn't join up, but there again it could 'ave bin a blessin' in disguise. 'E might not 'ave bin 'ere terday.'

Sue could never fathom the tension between her

father and her elder brother. Whenever they got together, which wasn't very often, they always seemed to argue. It was uncharacteristic of her father, who was normally very easy-going. He had been a bookkeeper with Napier and Sons, the Tooley Street wine firm, for almost sixteen years, and she felt that he was happy with his lot. Maurice seemed to rile him, however, and it was usually left to her mother to act as peacemaker.

The front door opened and slammed shut, followed by a shuffling in the passage. Tom Carey came into the room with a fixed grin on his handsome face. 'I'm not too late fer the party, am I?' he said with a slight slur. 'I've bin chattin' wiv the lads.'

'Mum's upstairs doing Aunt Ellie's hair,' Sue told him.

Tom slumped down in the vacant armchair and puffed loudly. 'I bin celebratin',' he announced.

'Celebratin' what?' Joe asked.

'A strike, that's what,' Tom replied. 'It seems we're all gonna be out on the cobbles on Monday mornin'.'

'I shouldn't fink that's anyfing ter celebrate,' Joe said curtly. 'Strikes never solved anyfing.'

Tom burped loudly and sat up straight in the chair. 'I dunno about that, Farvver,' he replied. 'We've bin tryin' ter get union recognition fer this new depot Brady's opened up in Barley Lane but 'e won't 'ear of it. Del Abelson's seein' 'im on Monday mornin' ter try an' talk sense into 'im, but I fink 'e'll be wastin' 'is time. Brady ses we're all gonna be sacked if we push the issue an' come out on strike.'

''E can't do that,' Joe said firmly. 'Men 'ave the right ter join the union.'

'You try tellin' ole Brady that,' Tom said with disgust.

'He could be bluffing,' Sue suggested.

'Well, if 'e is 'e's doin' a good job,' Tom told her.

Footsteps on the stairs halted the conversation and Sue smiled as Ellie walked into the parlour with Martha behind her carrying a small birthday cake. 'Your hair looks really nice, Aunt Ellie,' she remarked.

Ellie smiled and stood back while Martha set the cake down on the table. Tom got up and planted a quick kiss on his aunt's cheek. ''Appy birfday, Aunt Ellie,' he said, nearly losing his balance and quickly grabbing the back of the armchair to steady himself.

Martha gave him a blinding look and smiled at Ellie. 'Come on, luv, it's no good waitin' fer the Duggans to arrive,' she told her, 'let's cut the cake now.'

Ellie picked up the long-bladed knife. 'I decided against having candles,' she remarked as she slipped the edge of the blade into the soft icing.

'There'd 'ardly be room fer forty candles, Ellie,' Joe told her with a smile.

'You're just an old charmer,' she replied.

Just at that moment there was a knock at the front door and Sue went to let in Charlie and his wife Mabel, along with Pamela their daughter.

''Ere's a little somefing from the three of us, Ellie,' Mabel said, handing her a small parcel.

Aunt Ellie untied the string and removed the pink tissue paper carefully to discover a silver trinket box. 'It's really beautiful,' she said with feeling. 'Thank you all very much.'

'It's real silver. It's got an 'allmark,' Mabel told her. 'We know yer like pretty fings.'

16

'I do and it's just the right present,' Ellie said smiling.

Joe went to the sideboard. 'C'mon, let's open the port,' he said.

Sue gave her mother a quick glance and saw that she was trying to warn Joe against being too hasty, but she did not catch his eye quickly enough. Conversations sprang up between the families, and in the general chatter and joking that followed Tom and Pamela had slipped quietly out of the room.

'She'll be three parts pissed in no time,' Tom said with a grin as he stood with Pamela in the scullery.

'You are awful,' she told him with mock severity.

Tom smiled as he looked into Pamela's large green eyes. 'When are yer gonna ditch that no-good Bernie Catchpole an' come out wiv me?' he asked.

'Don't go talkin' about my bloke like that, Tom Carey,' she reproached him. 'Bernie's a nice fella, an' 'e's respectful. Which is more than I could say fer present company.'

'Yeah, but at least I'm straight. Wiv me what yer see is what yer get.'

'An' what's that s'posed ter mean?'

'Yer'll soon find out,' Tom said with a sly grin.

'D'you know somefing I don't?' Pamela asked quickly.

'Not really,' he replied, still grinning.

Pamela looked up at his dishevelled dark hair and saw the mischievous glint in his large brown eyes. 'Bernie wants us ter get engaged,' she said, looking back down at her feet.

'Don't do it, Pam,' he warned her. 'Yer'll be makin' a mistake.'

'An' goin' out wiv you wouldn't be, I s'pose.'

'Yer could do worse,' he said, becoming serious.

'I like yer, Tom, but yer don't seem ter take fings seriously. Wiv you everyfing's a joke. Bernie's got plans. 'E don't wanna stay a lorry driver all 'is life.'

'Will you two come in 'ere,' Martha called out. 'We're drinkin' a toast to Aunt Ellie.'

The two families gathered around the table to drink Ellie's good health and Tom let his free hand slide down to touch Pam's.

'I wonder if Maurice has forgotten it's my birthday,' Ellie said, looking at Martha.

'He'll be here soon, you'll see,' Sue told her kindly.

'Yeah – an' pigs'll fly,' Tom muttered to Pamela under his breath.

Chapter Two

The Palais de Danse at the Elephant and Castle was packed on Saturday night, though only a few couples were dancing. The slow foxtrot was not a particularly popular dance among the mainly young people, and they tended to sit around and watch the more adept and light-footed older couples as they glided confidently across the polished wooden dance area.

'Look at that bloody fairy,' one of the young men said resentfully to his friend. ''E only wants a number on 'is back.'

Billy Cuthbert smiled as he leaned over the balcony rail. 'She's a bit of all right though,' he replied. 'Wonder what she sees in 'im?'

'She's dance mad. Dance wiv the devil she would.'

'That scruffy-lookin' git can dance though.'

'Yeah I s'pose so.'

'One fing's fer sure, 'e won't be takin' 'er 'ome.'

'Nah I shouldn't fink so.'

The dance ended and the partners walked blithely from the floor, which provoked another snide remark from the envious Chalky White. 'Look at that smug look on 'is face. Really fancies 'imself.'

Billy Cuthbert was not a dancer, by his own admission, and like many of the young men present on that mild

April evening he only went to the Palais de Danse to 'pull a bint', as he put it. He could manage the waltz, and the quickstep with some difficulty, but his forte was standing at the bar above the dance floor and busily eyeing up the talent.

''Ere look at 'er. She's a stunner,' he remarked with a nudge.

Chalky glanced over to the nearby table and smiled at his friend. 'Yer better keep yer eyes off. She's spoken for.'

'Oh yeah?'

'That's Del Abelson's bird.'

'Well, I can't see 'im about,' Billy replied quickly. 'I fink I'll ask 'er fer the next dance.'

'It's up ter you but she'll only give yer a blank.'

''Ow d'yer know?'

'I've tried before.'

'Yeah but p'raps yer didn't use the right technique.'

'Let's see you try.'

Billy Cuthbert ambled over with a confident sway of his shoulders and smiled down at the young woman who sat alone at the table. ''Ello, luv,' he said. 'I bin watchin' yer dance an' I'd just like ter say yer very good.'

Sue Carey looked up at him and returned his smile, waiting for the inevitable follow-up.

'I wonder if yer'd care to 'ave a dance wiv me. I can only just about manage the waltz but I promise not ter step on yer toes.'

'I'm sorry but it's already promised,' she told him.

Billy frowned. 'Where's yer partner?'

'Getting the drinks,' Sue replied with a nod towards the bar.

'If 'e don't 'urry up the dance'll be over,' Billy said quickly.

'Then we'll do the next one,' she said, irritation creeping into her voice.

Billy flipped open his coat and slipped his hand into his trouser pocket, his face flushed as he grinned mockingly. 'I reckon yer feller's found anuvver partner,' he remarked.

'I've told you he's at the bar getting a drink.'

'So why don't you an' me get shufflin'. 'E won't mind.'

'No really, but thanks anyway.'

'C'mon, luv, be a sport,' Billy persisted. 'I'm a pretty good dancer really.'

Sue Carey suddenly glanced over his shoulder and Billy Cuthbert caught the look in her eyes. He straightened up and turned to see a tall, well-built young man standing behind him holding two glasses of beer.

'Sorry, mate, I was just askin' . . .'

'Askin' what?'

'If the young lady wanted ter dance.'

'Well, she don't.'

'Sorry, mate, I wasn't ter know.'

'Well, yer do now.'

Billy saw the steely look in the young man's eyes and attempted to ease the tension. 'No 'arm meant. I was just . . .'

'Piss off while yer still in front, will yer?'

Billy Cuthbert would normally have argued his corner but there was a cold look in the man's dark eyes that warned him not to press the issue, and he sloped off with a hostile backward glance.

Del Abelson set the two glasses down on the table

21

and sat down with a sigh. 'That monkey bin bovverin' yer?' he asked.

Sue looked at him with concern. 'He was only asking if I wanted to dance,' she told him quickly. 'There was no harm in it.'

Del glanced over his shoulder and then met Sue's eyes. ''Im an' that pal of 'is are a couple o' chancers,' he growled. 'One o' these days somebody's gonna sort 'em out.'

Sue lowered her eyes as she pulled the glass of beer closer to her, then she matched his angry stare. 'What is it with you, Del? You're like a bear with a sore head. You've been like it all evening.'

He sipped his beer without replying, which only served to irritate the young woman. 'Is it that union business? 'Cos if it is I wish you'd learn to leave it at home. It's Saturday night and we're supposed to be on a date.'

Del Abelson leaned back in his chair and his shoulders sagged. 'I'm sorry,' he sighed. 'Yer right, I just can't relax. I keep seein' Brady's ugly face an' that cocky grin. I'm sure 'e finks we're gonna swaller it an' back down.'

Sue reached out and laid her hand on his. 'Del, I know what the union means to you and I'm proud of the way you take on everyone's troubles,' she said quietly, 'but you've got to know when to switch off. Just now I saw that look in your eye and I was frightened. I'm sure that if that bloke hadn't moved off you would have hit him. It wasn't him you were seeing, it was Brady.'

The young man smiled, showing even white teeth, and his eyes softened. 'C'mon, Sue, let's dance.'

They stepped around the floor and the young woman

felt the strong yet tender grip of his arms around her and smelt his spicy aftershave as she rested her head on his shoulder. It was nice to be close like this, moving together with his hips tightly pressed to hers. They were gliding effortlessly, the sweet music instilling them both with a sense of well-being. Above them the ceiling was a blaze of coloured moving light, silvers and reds, yellows and gold, projected upwards from the revolving machines. The short clarinet solo followed by the roar of trumpets and the roll of drums sent a shiver of pleasure through Sue's body, and almost reflexively she caressed Del's neck with her fingers. In response he squeezed his arm around her waist and brushed his lips along her tiny ear. How delicious it felt, and how she wished it could go on for ever. He was all man, tender and loving, still to make her his, but how volatile, how dedicated in his beliefs, almost to the point of fanaticism, and with a sudden rush of anxiety she saw the dangers, knew that what they had together could all be washed away in bitter tears.

Pamela Duggan was dancing the quickstep, wrapped in the arms of the older man whose skill at the slow foxtrot had irritated the young men at the bar. She was a very good dancer and never off the floor, and her obvious enjoyment served to irk Billy Cuthbert even more as he stood idly with his friends. 'Why don't yer cut in, Bernie?' he growled. 'That scruffy git wants sortin' out.'

Bernie Catchpole looked unconcerned. 'I fink that sort over there fancies me,' he replied. 'She's bin givin' me the come-on.'

Billy glanced over at the group of young women

standing some way away and shook his head in puzzlement. Bernie must be mad, he thought. None of that lot could hold a candle to Pamela Duggan, and there he was letting her dance with that soapy git while he made eyes in all directions.

Chalky White nudged Bernie and nodded towards Billy Cuthbert. ''E got a blank ternight,' he chuckled. ''E tried ter chat up Del Abelson's bird.'

Bernie Catchpole's face took on a dark look. 'Don't talk ter me about that flash git,' he grumbled. 'If 'e 'as 'is way we'll all be out on the cobbles on Monday.'

'I 'eard 'e was a good shop steward,' Chalky replied.

'Who told yer that?'

'I just 'eard it.'

'Well, whoever told yer that was talkin' out of 'is arse.'

'Sorry I spoke,' Chalky muttered.

Tom Carey moved away from a nearby group and ambled over. 'Still 'avin' a moan, Bernie?' he said with a mocking smile. 'I couldn't 'elp over'earin'. I fink Del's done us proud so far.'

Bernie sneered. 'Can't you see what 'e's doin'?' he grated. 'We're just steppin'-stones as far as Abelson's concerned. 'E'll walk all over us ter get that full-time job wiv the union.'

Tom smiled calmly. 'Yer talkin' a load o' crap. Del's OK in my book, an' in most o' the ovver drivers' too.'

'Yeah, well yer would say that, wouldn't yer,' Bernie replied quickly.

Tom ran his fingers through his fair hair, his handsome face growing serious. 'What d'yer mean?' he asked.

'Yer wouldn't run 'im down, what wiv 'im datin'

yer sister,' Bernie sneered. 'Get wise, Carey. Del Abelson's only concern is feavverin' 'is own nest, an' your sister's gonna find out soon, just like everybody else.'

Tom Carey's pale blue eyes hardened and he clenched his fists angrily. 'You're all mouth, Catchpole,' he snarled. 'Why don't yer button it.'

Pamela Duggan had returned from the floor and heard the exchanges. 'C'mon, Bernie, let's dance,' she said, with a wicked glance at Tom.

'Nah wait a bit,' Catchpole said sharply. ''E's got a bee in 'is bonnet. What's yer problem, Carey?'

'I reckon you're a mouthy git who ain't got the courage of 'is convictions,' Tom replied coolly. 'You let Brady walk all over yer an' yer run down anyone who tries ter stand up to 'im.'

'C'mon, Bernie, I'm waitin' ter dance,' Pamela entreated him.

'Piss off an' let me be,' he shouted at her, turning back to face Tom. 'You want trouble?'

'I wouldn't mind puttin' me fist in that big mouth o' yours,' Tom threatened.

'Yer can try,' Bernie said, moving towards him.

'Right then. Outside. Me an' you.'

Bernie Catchpole's face had drained of colour and he gritted his teeth as he led the way down the back stairs to the street.

Pamela rounded on Bernie's friends. 'Why didn't anyone try ter stop 'em?' she shouted.

'Nuffink ter do wiv us, Pam,' Chalky said quickly. 'This 'as bin brewin' fer some time.'

'I'll kill that Tom Carey if 'e marks my Bernie,' she cried.

'Bernie ain't no slouch, gel,' Chalky told her. ''E can look after 'imself.'

'You're all useless,' the young woman yelled above the music as she hurried away.

The evening air was cool after the stuffy atmosphere inside the dance hall and Sue let herself relax in Del's strong arms. 'Promise me you'll try harder, Del,' she whispered. 'I don't like you when you're so screwed up.'

In answer he moved his fingers over her full lips and then delicately raised her chin, bending his head as he kissed her gently. 'I'll try. I promise,' he said quietly.

She looked up into his eyes and saw nothing to convince her. Instead that hardness was still there. He was his own person and nothing she could say or do would change that. She sighed in resignation, aware of her desire for him, wanting him so much to make love to her, but it had to be right and he had to be ready for her, not preoccupied with anything else. It was too important to her.

They were standing in an alcove at the side of the hall, in a paved area of tall plane trees, and suddenly Del stiffened. He gripped Sue's shoulders and pushed her from him as a group of young men spilled from the hall. He could see Pamela Duggan trying to pull Bernie Catchpole away from the group and then in desperation turn to Tom Carey who was following up. 'There's some trouble,' he said quickly. 'Your Tom's involved by the look of it.'

Sue glanced over and saw Catchpole take off his coat and pass it to a friend. Tom was trying to get away from Pamela and he looked furious.

'C'mon then, Carey. Don't let a woman stop yer,' Bernie snarled.

Tom loped up to his opponent still dragging off his coat and Bernie's rush slammed into him. Still entangled in one sleeve he fell to the ground and the heavier man sat astride him, pummelling punches down. Del Abelson reached them and grabbed Catchpole by the shirt collar, pulling him off and shoving him down into a heap. 'If it's gonna be a fight let it be a fair one,' he growled.

Tom struggled to his feet and slipped his arm from his coat. 'Right I'm ready,' he said breathlessly as he wiped blood from his split lip.

Sue Carey had hurried over and she placed herself in front of her younger brother. 'You make me sick,' she blurted out. 'You're all supposed to be workmates and you carry on like bloody animals. You too, Del. You're as bad as these two. Can't anything be said in anger without it getting settled by fists? God Almighty, won't you ever learn?'

Pamela moved in front of Bernie. 'She's right. You're like a big soddin' kid. Now put that coat back on. I wanna dance, not watch a fight.'

The incensed women seemed to have won the day as Tom bent down to retrieve his coat, but Billy Cuthbert had other ideas. 'Go on an' let 'em fight,' he shouted.

Del's right arm shot out and his fingers closed around the young man's neck. 'Shut yer noise,' he snarled.

Billy struggled free and looked shamefaced at the shop steward. 'I was only—'

'Well don't,' Del cut him short. 'Now let's get off before the coppers get wind of it.'

* * *

The last waltz was playing and Sue snuggled even closer to her partner. 'Del, I was proud of you tonight,' she whispered.

Pamela danced in the arms of the older man who could not believe his luck. 'Can I see yer 'ome?' he asked as they drifted across the floor.

'Sorry, luv, I'm booked,' she told him.

Up on the balcony the young men finished their drinks, and Bernie Catchpole's face was still dark with anger as he drained his glass. Some way apart Tom Carey stood with a few friends. He knew that he had not done anything to enhance his chances with Pamela Duggan. Quite the reverse. He also knew that on Monday knives would be drawn at Joe Brady's transport firm and the feud between him and Catchpole would be intensified.

That Saturday night the knives were already drawn in a pub not too far away from the Elephant and Castle. Joe Brady's large frame dwarfed the men beside him as he held counsel. He gripped a glass of whisky in his large fist and his bulging neck was turning red in anger. 'If it goes the wrong way I want Abelson's 'ead on a plate,' he said forcefully.

'Don't worry, Joe, we'll sort it out soon as we get the word,' the pale-faced man at his side replied.

Chapter Three

Totterdown Street was drying out after the night's rain and already Granny Minto had whitened her front door-step. She was an early riser and had strung up a clean, starched net curtain at her parlour window and swept the passage before first light. The old lady was very particular about her personal appearance as well as that of her house, and as she would be spending much of the day at her front door she wanted everything to be just right. That nosy fat cow Bessie Woodward was sure to notice things as she came past that morning on her way to get her winkles and shrimps, and Granny did not want to give her room to talk.

The little turning was coming to life by now and as Granny Minto leaned against the door-frame she saw the big woman coming towards her.

'Mornin', Mrs Minto. Nice day.'

'Mornin', Bessie. Goin' fer yer tea?'

Bessie nodded. 'Up early I see.'

'People die in bed,' Granny replied acidly.

Bessie Woodward smiled and walked on. Silly old mare, she thought. She'll never die in bed. More likely up against that door, the time she spends there.

Granny Minto watched her going down the street. I noticed her look at my windows, she said to herself.

29

Pity she doesn't spend as much time cleaning as she does rabbiting on about everyone in the street. Those front-room curtains of hers are a disgrace, and the windows need a good soaping. The only time they ever get done is when her old man does them, which is once in a blue moon.

At number 6 the smell of bacon cooking drifted up to Aunt Ellie's room and she glanced in the mirror of her small dressing-table before going downstairs. Her birthday party had been very nice, and the presents were nice too. Pity Maurice never showed up, she thought. Her sister Martha had made excuses for him as she always did but it didn't alter the fact that he had forgotten. Joe was a bit cut up about it, she could tell, although he never said much. Even the Duggans next door had remembered it was her birthday. There was no excuse for Maurice. Too busy running that business of his to spend any time with his family.

Martha was busy in the scullery and as Ellie looked in she smiled. 'Just in time. Take this in ter Joe will yer, luv. I got your egg boilin'.'

Aunt Ellie pulled a face as she took the plateful of bacon, egg and tomatoes topped with a thin slice of fried bread. No wonder he complains about his stomach, she thought. He'd be much better off with a boiled egg and toast.

Joe was sitting at the table in anticipation as his sister-in-law walked into the room with his breakfast and his face lit up. 'Just about ready fer this,' he said cheerfully.

Ellie noted that Joe's sleeves were rolled up over his elbows and his braces were off his shoulder. What's more he had not put on his collar, which irked her. It would never have been allowed at the Langley home. Even the groom and the gardener had to be properly dressed at the table. Mrs Grimshaw the housekeeper saw to that.

'Did you enjoy yer day, Ellie?' Joe asked with a mouthful of fried bread.

'Yes, it was very nice,' she replied. 'Shame Maurice couldn't get here though. After all it's only once a year. It might be my last birthday for all he knows. It wouldn't have hurt him.'

Joe sighed in resignation. It was going to be one of those days with Ellie. Anyone would think she was seventy-seven, not fifty-seven. 'Don't be silly, gel, you're only a young woman yet,' he said in an effort to make her smile.

'Well I don't feel it,' she told him in a miserable tone of voice. 'I don't think I had more than a couple of hours' sleep all night. I heard the rain coming down and then that rooster of Queenie's. Someone should wring its neck.'

'I don't fink Queenie would be all that 'appy to 'ear yer say that, Ellie,' Joe replied grinning. 'She's got a regular little farmyard out the back of 'er 'ouse. They get some nice big eggs from those chickens.'

Martha came into the room with Ellie's boiled egg and a plate of thin bread. 'There we are, luv. Sit yerself down at the table,' she said lightly.

Joe hid his distaste as Aunt Ellie set to work cracking the top of the egg with a teaspoon before cutting up the bread into thin strips. She was worse than a child in many ways, he thought. She was very finicky and proper, prone to tantrums and sulking sessions as well as feigning illness. Pity she hadn't got herself a good man instead of living with the dead. That's what it amounted to.

'Pass me the salt, Joe.'

'There we are. Want a cuppa?'

Ellie shook her head quickly as he reached for the teapot. He would only slop the tea on to the tablecloth, and she could never abide drinking out of a mug. 'Martha, have you seen my cup and saucer?' she asked as her sister came back into the room.

'Sorry, Ellie. There we are,' Martha said, taking it from the sideboard.

Joe finished the last of the bacon and proceeded to wipe the yolk of the egg from the plate with a hunk of bread, not looking up but willing to bet that Ellie was watching him. He knew that was another of her little dislikes, him wiping his plate clean. Well, she would just have to suffer it.

''Ave yer got enough bread?' Martha asked her.

Ellie nodded, dabbing at the corner of her mouth with the lace handkerchief that she held on her lap.

Joe glimpsed the strips of bread left on her plate and he glanced quickly over to his wife as he got up from the table. Soldiers, he thought scornfully. Have you got enough soldiers, she should have said.

Martha was reclining in the armchair and she gave Joe a furtive smile as she saw the look on his face. Ellie could be difficult at times, she knew, and many men would not have been as tolerant as Joe. 'Goin' fer the papers, luv?' she asked.

'Yeah, an' I'm gonna see if I can get Queenie Alladyce ter muffle that cock'rel of 'ers,' he said

grinning as he slipped his braces over his shoulders.
'It's woke our Ellie up again.'

'I shouldn't say anything to the woman,' Ellie
remarked quickly.

Joe had no intention of saying anything and his eyes
went up to the ceiling as his little quip misfired. Surely,
he thought to himself, there must be someone somewhere who could take the silly mare off their hands.

Tom came lurching into the parlour and sat himself
down at the table. 'Mornin', Muvver. Mornin', Aunt
Ellie,' he said in a croaky voice. 'Christ! I've got a
real right fick 'ead this mornin'.'

Martha glanced over at Ellie and saw the look of
disgust on her lean face. ''Aven't you washed an'
shaved?' she said quickly.

'I need a cuppa first, Muvver,' he groaned.

Sue breezed into the room and smiled her good
mornings before slipping into a vacant chair at the
table. She had got up early and had breakfast with
her mother while the rest of the household were still
asleep. 'I've a good mind to let you get your own
breakfast this morning,' she said firmly to her suffering
brother.

Tom was sitting with his head in his hands and his
bleary eyes came up to meet her unsympathetic gaze.
'Why? You always cook me breakfast on Sundays,'
he protested.

'Why? You know why,' she told him.

'Don't give me no grief this mornin', Sis. I'm feelin'
rough,' he croaked.

'So you should,' she replied with feeling. 'Who did
you think you were last night – Alan Ladd?'

Aunt Ellie had finished her soldiers and felt the

sudden need to leave the room before the bickering got under way, but Martha sat up straight in her chair to hear the rest. 'What's 'e bin up to now?' she asked with a frown.

Sue told her about what had happened at the dance hall and Martha shook her head sadly. 'I should 'ave thought you'd seen enough fightin' in the war wivout startin' trouble yerself,' she said sharply.

Tom leaned back in his chair and slowly turned his pounding head towards his mother. 'Take no notice of 'er, Mum,' he replied. 'It wasn't me what started it. It was that loudmouth Bernie Catchpole. She stopped me stickin' one on 'im, an' 'e deserved it.'

Sue filled his mug from the teapot and spooned sugar into the steaming brew. 'Drink that and then get a shave. You look disgusting,' she said, hiding a grin as he winced.

Martha too had to stop herself smiling as she saw the look on Tom's face as he sipped his tea. There was much love in the home, though a casual observer would have thought otherwise. Tom and Sue were very close, even though she was inclined to get on to him at times. They both seemed very fond of Ellie and managed to ignore her funny ways. How nice it was to have them both home and to hear the banter between them, she thought. During the war Sue had been in the ATS, serving on a gunsite in the south of England, while Tom had been fighting in the Middle East. How quiet the house had been then, with only Mo around. Now she and Joe hardly ever saw their elder son, and whenever he did call in he and his father always ended up arguing. Why couldn't they let the past stay buried instead of constantly resurrecting it? Nothing could be changed now. What had happened on that terrible night of the Blitz could end up destroying the family unless peace was made.

Despite her threats Sue had started to cook Tom his breakfast, and Martha got up to refill her teacup. Maybe it would have been better to have had a family conference about that night, she reflected, instead of keeping it from Tom and Sue. They must get upset at times seeing the hard feeling between Mo and their father. It was too late now though. The promise had been made and Joe was adamant that they stick to it. Charlie Duggan had never told his daughter about what happened that night and the two families had agreed to let the matter rest there. It wasn't that easy, however. People had died. Questions had been asked and fortunately the answers had been readily accepted. One day though it might all come out, for whatever reason, and that was the cross Martha and Joe had to bear, along with their neighbours Charlie and Mabel Duggan.

At number 4 Charlie Duggan was busy putting a polish on his best boots in the backyard and Mabel answered the knock on the door to find Sue standing there. 'She's upstairs, luv,' she told her.

Number 4 and number 6 were open houses as far as the two families were concerned and Sue smiled as she walked down the passage and climbed the stairs to the back bedroom. Pamela was sitting on her bed, her cotton dress pulled up high over her shapely legs as she applied a natural varnish to her toenails.

'That's not very ladylike,' Sue joked as she sat down beside her.

'Ter be honest I don't feel very ladylike this mornin',' Pamela replied with a weak grin.

'What's wrong?'

'Me an' Bernie got at it last night.'

'Did you enjoy it?'

'Don't joke, Sue, I don't feel like laughin',' Pamela told her.

'You had a row?'

'You could say that.'

'Over what happened?'

'What else?'

Sue shifted her position on the bed. 'Want to talk about it?'

'There's nuffink much ter tell, really,' Pamela replied. 'I called 'im an idiot fer startin' trouble an' 'e said it wasn't 'im it was Tom that started it an' I should mind me own business in future.'

'I think they were both as bad as each other to tell you the truth,' Sue remarked. 'Men always seem to think that a punch-up solves all life's problems.'

'That's what I said ter Bernie,' Pamela told her. 'Anyway we're finished.'

'No you're not. He'll come round, you'll see.'

'Not this time. I told 'im ter get stuffed an' 'e said I was a waste o' time. It was really nasty.'

'Lots of things are said in anger,' Sue replied kindly. 'It'll all be forgotten in a few days.'

Pamela shrugged her shoulder. 'Frankly I don't care, Sue. Bernie's always eyein' ovver gels up. 'E's got no intention o' gettin' serious.'

'Did you want it to get serious?'

'I dunno. I s'pose I did, at the beginnin', but 'e's changed lately. I can't seem ter please 'im, whatever I do.'

Sue leaned back on the bed. 'D'you mind if I ask you a personal question?'

Pamela smiled. 'I know what yer gonna ask, an' the answer's no. Me an' Bernie 'ave never slept tergevver. Ter be honest we've come close on a few occasions, but I can't bring meself ter let 'im go all the way. Don't get me wrong, I wanted to, but I was scared. I couldn't face me mum an' dad if I got pregnant.'

'You don't have to get pregnant, Pam. You could always use something,' Sue said quietly.

Pamela adjusted her dress over her knees and slid her legs under her. 'I know, but I'd still be worried. Anyway Bernie said those fings are not 'undred per cent an' 'e said it's like washin' yer 'ands wiv gloves on.'

'So you have talked about it?'

'Sort of, in a jokin' way.'

'Well, I'm no expert on such things but I can understand what a strain it is sometimes.'

'If the gel always ses no?'

'If she lets things get out of hand and then says no.'

Pamela looked sad as she traced a line on the coverlet with her forefinger. ''Ave you ever bin in a serious relationship, Sue?' she asked. 'When you was in the forces I mean?'

Sue shook her head. 'I thought I was once, but it was soon over.'

'Did yer go all the way?'

'I'm not a virgin, if that's what you mean.'

'Well I am, an' I intend ter stay that way till I get married.'

'Good for you,' Sue said smiling.

Pamela studied her fingernails for a few moments and then her eyes came up to meet Sue's. 'This is not a very 'appy 'ome this mornin', what wiv one fing an' anuvver,' she sighed. 'I got up early this mornin' an' there was Mum sittin' on 'er own cryin' like a baby. It would 'ave bin our Stan's birfday terday. It's four years now since 'is ship went down. We all miss 'im so.'

Sue saw the tears glistening in her best friend's eyes and she held out her arms to her.

'I can't understand me mum at times,' Pamela said as she rested her head against Sue's shoulder. 'This mornin' she said somefing about our Stan bein' well out of it. I asked 'er what she meant an' she just shook 'er 'ead.'

'I suppose she meant that nothing can hurt your brother any more, Pam. Life can be cruel at times.'

The younger woman sniffed and sat up straight on the bed. 'This is terrible,' she said with a brave smile. 'A weekend away from the factory an' there's me ballsin' it all up. C'mon, let's go downstairs an' 'ave a cuppa.'

At number 14 Granny Minto was standing over her lodger as he cooked his breakfast. 'Turn that bleedin' gas down a bit,' she moaned. 'You men can't boil an egg prop'ly.'

Albert Price looked up at his landlady. 'This ain't an egg, gel, it's a bleedin' fry-up.'

'Burn-up more like it.'

'Why don't yer go back ter the door,' he urged her. 'Yer might miss somefing standin' 'ere criticisin' me.'

Granny Minto allowed herself a brief grin. She was short and snappy with many of her neighbours, and there were some whom she totally ignored, but as far as she was concerned Albert Price was different. She thought him to be a lovely man, and he never gave her any reason to moan, though chide him she did, in a motherly sort of way. Albert had lived with her for a few years now and was always regular with his rent. He fed himself, cleaned his room and helped her with many of her chores. He had a dry sense of humour too, with a gift of summing people up to perfection. He could usually come up with a telling nickname. Benny Tracy, Queenie's lodger, had become 'Dick'. Wally Tucker became 'Soapy', and together with Jack 'Tubby' Saward, their ever-present drinking partner, Albert dubbed them 'The Three Musketeers'. There was no end to Albert's satirical talents, and Granny Minto spent many a happy hour just listening to his stories. He had been a horse carman for most of his working life and now, a short wiry man in his late sixties with thin greying hair, he still had a robust relish for life.

As Granny walked back along the passage his pale blue eyes twinkled, and with a look of defiance in her direction and a few mumbled words he turned the gas back up under the already crispy bacon.

Chapter Four

The Bell in Abbey Street opened at twelve noon, and after slipping the bolts the landlord Dave Ford stood to one side to avoid injury as his three elderly regulars almost charged through the door of the public bar. Dave was a big, jovial character with a paunch and a ruddy face, but even a man of his build could not have stemmed the stampede. Musketeers? More like barmy legionnaires charging towards an oasis, he thought.

The counter gained, the time-honoured ritual began.

'Right then, Tubby, what yer gonna 'ave?' Benny Tracy asked.

'The usual. No I won't. I'll 'ave a nice bitter.'

'That is yer usual.'

'No it ain't. I bin drinkin' stout,' Tubby Saward insisted.

'What about you, Wally?'

'I'll get these.'

Benny Tracy looked peeved. 'I'm in the chair. What yer 'avin' I said.'

Wally Tucker leaned his elbows on the polished counter. 'I fink I'll 'ave a mild an' bitter, Dick.'

'Oi watch it. Benny's the name. Don't you go

41

encouragin' that silly git Price. 'E's too fond o' taggin' people wiv stupid names.'

The landlord sighed as he pulled the pints. At least they had completed their order pretty sharply, he thought. Usually there was a lengthy and often heated discussion about who was going to buy the first round, not that it mattered. They all bought one before closing time.

'So 'ow yer keepin', Dave?' Tubby Saward asked him.

'Same as last night when you asked me,' the publican replied with a forced smile.

''Ow's the ole lady?'

'Bella's same as last night too.'

'Glad to 'ear it. 'Ere is that beer all right?' Benny remarked. 'It looks a bit froffy ter me.'

'Give it time ter settle, it's a new barrel,' Dave said indignantly.

'Well that's all right then,' Benny replied.

'Fancy a game o' crib?' Tubby asked his friends.

'Yeah all right. 'Ow much a peg?'

Dave Ford reached under the counter for the playing cards and cribbage board. ''Ere, if you blokes are gonna gamble, go over ter that far table away from the door, an' keep the money out o' sight. I got a licence ter fink of,' he growled.

Tubby grabbed the cards and Benny took the cribbage board and the three did as they were bid.

'What's the matter wiv 'im this mornin'?' Wally Tucker said, looking over his shoulder at the publican.

'I dunno. Got out the wrong side o' the bed I should fink,' Benny remarked.

Tubby shuffled the cards. ''Ere, I gotta tell yer. They reckon Brady's lot are goin' out on the cobbles termorrer.'

'Who told yer that?' Benny Tracy asked him.

'I was talkin' ter Charlie Duggan at the paper shop this mornin'. Apparently it's over non-union labour comin' in,' Tubby explained. 'We 'ad the same trouble when I was a carman fer Chas Walker. That was before I was an 'orsekeeper. They wouldn't tolerate the union. Caused a lot o' trouble it did.'

'Did yer go on strike?' Benny asked.

Tubby Saward ran a gnarled hand over his bald head. 'Nah. The blokes there wouldn't stick tergevver. The few that was causin' the ruckus got sacked, includin' me. That's 'ow I come ter be 'orsekeeper fer the railway. The ole Southern Railway was a good company ter work for at that time. Looked after their men. Not like that ole bastard Walker.'

'Joe Brady's a nasty kettle o' fish by all accounts,' Wally Tucker said, sipping his beer. 'I remember when 'e only 'ad two clapped-out motors. Used ter come ter the docks ter pick up timber. Always gettin' in scrapes wiv us dockers.'

'Look at 'im now,' Benny said. 'Biggest transport firm round 'ere.'

'Well, it's all gonna be off termorrer,' Tubby replied.

'C'mon, are we gonna play this game or what?' Wally asked.

The afternoon sun emerged from behind a cloud as Sue Carey strolled hand in hand with Del Abelson along the gravel path in Southwark Park, and they stopped at the bowling green as an elderly gentleman sent a polished bowl on a curving run along the soft cropped grass. It missed the clustered balls and stopped inches away from the smaller white jack and there was a polite smattering of applause.

Del sighed deeply and turned towards Sue. 'It's a peaceful scene don't yer fink,' he said smiling.

She nodded as she slipped her hand out of his and adjusted her shoulder-bag. 'An English Sunday. C'mon, let's go an' get a cuppa,' she said, taking his arm.

The two young people passed the tennis courts and made their way towards the small tea bar. They found a vacant table and sat looking over at the bandstand where a military band was performing. Children danced around on the large green behind the rings of seats and a few strollers stopped to listen to the music. The sun went in again and a mangy dog came sniffing between the iron tables.

'Are you worried about tomorrow?' Sue asked.

Del looked thoughtful. 'It's likely ter get nasty,' he replied. 'Ter be honest I can't see Brady backin' off wivout a fight. My main concern is whevver or not the men'll stand solid. If we don't get full backin' there'll be those that'll try ter go back ter work.'

'Cross the picket line?'

'Yeah.'

'You'll swing it, Del, I'm sure,' Sue said, touching his hand supportively. 'The men trust you, I'm sure they do. Apart from Bernie Catchpole of course.'

He gave her a brief smile. 'Bernie won't openly oppose the strike,' he replied. 'In fact knowin' 'im 'e'll most likely vote in favour of it, but it's the

44

nigglin', the moanin' if it goes on more than a few days. That's the danger. Brady'll try ter call our bluff, an' if 'e sees the strike's stayin' solid 'e'll try ter bring in scab labour.'

'Can you stop him doing that?'

'We can try, but it'll get nasty.'

'Can he win?'

'I dunno, Sue. It's in the lap o' the gods.'

'Why do you do it, Del?' she asked. 'Why do you put yourself up for all that abuse and aggravation?'

'Someone's gotta do it, or workers everywhere are gonna be nuffing but slaves ter the bosses,' he replied with a serious look on his face.

'Yeah but why you? What drives you?'

'You've asked me that before.'

'More than once, but you never tell me why, Del, you just give me that stock-in-trade answer.'

He stared down at his teacup for a few moments before matching her intense gaze. 'What ovver answer d'yer want?' he said finally.

'The truth,' she told him quickly. 'The real reason behind that passion you seem to have.'

He shrugged his broad shoulders and quickly ran a hand through his thick dark hair. 'I wish it was that easy to explain,' he said.

'Try. I'm listening.'

The young man leaned his arms on the table and looked down at his clasped hands. 'When the war started I expected ter go in the Army. I was lookin' forward to it. It was a chance ter do somefing really worthwhile, but when I went fer me medical they found that shadow on me lung. TB they said. So instead of goin' off ter fight fer me country I was packed off to a sanatorium. You know all that. I've told yer before. What I 'aven't told yer is what 'appened after I came out. I volunteered fer the Army straight away as a matter o' fact, but I was turned down again. They said I was still unfit because o' me medical 'istory. There I was, feelin' as right as ninepence an' doomed ter go back ter that poxy job drivin' up an' down the country while me mates were all in the services. I felt useless, an' what was more I was looked on as a draft dodger. You know the score. "You're fit. Why ain't yer doin' yer bit?" "I wish my son could 'ave managed ter get in a deferred occupation." Then there were the snide remarks about me name. "Abelson? That's Jewish, ain't it. You should be only too glad ter fight, wiv what's 'appenin' ter your people." Christ, Sue, I'm Church of England.'

'So the union business was a chance of doing something worthwhile, something you could get your teeth into.'

The young man's eyes came up to meet hers. 'There was a pal o' mine who lived a few doors away when I was in Weston Street. 'E was about my age an' when the war started 'e registered as a conscientious objector. I didn't agree wiv 'is beliefs, but I 'ad to admire the way 'e stuck to 'em, despite all the stick 'e took. I know fer a fact that 'e was beaten up more than once, but 'e never wavered. 'E ended up in the Fire Service drivin' the tenders an' as soon as the war ended 'e went ter work at Brady's. A few o' the drivers there were ex-service an' they got ter know about 'im bein' a conchie. They made 'is life a sheer misery, an' when Brady 'imself found out the poor sod was sacked. We weren't properly unionised at the time an' the shop steward there was in Brady's pocket anyway. Everyone knew it an' there were mumblin's o' discontent, but nobody actually challenged it, till the shop steward's re-election came round. I put meself up, an' much ter my surprise I was voted in.'

Sue smiled. 'So now the firm's fully unionised, thanks to you.'

He nodded. 'Since January. But the trouble is, Brady's openin' a new depot. 'E's got a big contract wiv the local food factories so 'e's started ter take drivers on, an' 'e's puttin' pressure on 'em. 'E wants that depot ter be non-union.'

'Can he get away with it?'

'If we don't stand up to 'im 'e can,' Del told her. 'Termorrer I've gotta try an' convince our drivers that if Brady does succeed then all our jobs are at risk. The way fings are at the moment 'e can play one depot against the ovver. Just fink about it. 'E could provoke a stoppage an' then simply give our work ter the ovver depot. In actual fact we'd be starved out of a job.'

'So this is not about wages?'

'No it's not,' he replied firmly. 'It's about jobs an' security.'

The band was taking a breather and Sue reached out and laid her hand on his. 'I'm glad you told me, Del,' she said softly. 'C'mon, let's take a stroll.'

The evening sky promised another fine day tomorrow as the two men strolled through the extensive garden. Behind them the stone house was swathed in shadow and the sweet smell of honeysuckle filled the air. The two were alike in build and stature, tall, lean and angular, though their clothes set them apart. The man dressed in country tweed looked thoughtful as they reached the stone arch, and once inside the rose-bordered flower garden Andrew Morrison motioned to a wooden bench set in an alcove. 'I come here when I need to think,' he said as he sat down with a grunt.

'It makes sense,' Ernest Spencer went on as he joined his employer on the seat. 'I've explained our position to Calkin and he's very much aware that the job could be for a limited period only. He seems very confident.'

'I like the idea of a war profile of Bermondsey. It could well increase the circulation, and God knows we need it. My one reservation is the young man's suitability. His track record doesn't inspire confidence I feel bound to say. Cub reporter on the *Star* and a junior post on that provincial rag.'

'He has had some wartime experience at the Ministry of Information,' Spencer was quick to add.

'I have read his application letter,' Morrison said brusquely.

'To be honest I was very impressed when I interviewed him, and he was keen to stress that he would stand or fall by his efforts.'

'So might the paper, Ernest.'

'Yes, Andrew, I'm only too well aware, and I feel this might be our last chance to survive.'

Morrison kicked a small twig to one side of the bench and clasped his hands together as he leaned back. 'My father started the paper on a shoestring,' he declared wistfully, 'and it rose in stature over the years. When I took over we were competing on favourable terms with both the *South London Press* and the *Kentish Mercury*. Now the *Daily Bulletin* is lower league. We need our advertisers back, and they won't reappear until sales increase. So it would seem that quite a lot hinges on our Mr Calkin.'

'I've every confidence in him, and you would too if you met him,' Ernest said firmly.

'How long have you run my paper, Ernest?' Morrison asked.

'Twenty years this September.'

'You've done a splendid job in all that time, old friend,' he said kindly, 'so I'm quite happy to go along with your idea.'

'Rather Calkin's idea, though I wish I'd thought of it first,' Spencer replied.

'Come along, Ernest, it's getting quite chilly. Let's drink to success.'

Two old friends sat together in the evening sunlight, their backs against the brick. A tin bath was hung up on the back wall beside them and upturned beer crates made do as seats.

'I took a stroll down Ship Lane this mornin',' Joe ventured to remark.

'Whatever for?' Charlie asked quickly. 'It's just a shell. There's nuffink left o' the place, except bomb ruins an' corrugated sheetin'.'

'That ware'ouse ain't bin pulled down yet,' Joe went on. 'There was a gap in the fencin' an' I could see it. It's still the same. Just the ground floor left an' all that rubble lyin' around.'

'What you tryin' ter do, persecute yerself, Joe?' his friend said with concern. 'We agreed long ago not ter talk about it. It's bin almost six years now. Can't yer let the 'ole fing rest?'

'Yeah I know,' Joe sighed. 'It was our Ellie's birfday that brought it back, an' I 'ad ter take a look.'

'I don't get yer,' Charlie said frowning.

'Our Mo never turned up an' Ellie got a bit upset, then I got ter finkin' about what drove the wedge between us two. Me an' Mo were very close at one time, 'im bein' the eldest, but now it's different. Now I never see 'im, apart from 'igh days an' 'olidays, an' even then we get at it.'

'You should make an effort, Joe,' Charlie told him. 'What's done's done. There's no goin' back, though I wish an' pray we could change fings. People died that night I know, but there would 'ave bin many more dead, if it 'adn't bin fer our efforts.'

'Yeah but those five people might 'ave bin alive terday,' Joe said quickly. 'It was all so unnecessary.'

Charlie Duggan looked at his friend with irritation creeping across his lined face and he eased his wiry frame on the crate. 'Look there's no use you goin' on about it,' he said. 'Let's do what we agreed ter do an' not mention it any more. We did promise each ovver, remember?'

'Yeah I'm sorry, Chas. It was stupid o' me ter go round there. Let's ferget it.'

'Yeah let's, but yer gotta try an' mend the rift wiv your Maurice. Until yer do the ghosts are gonna invade yer dreams, poison yer soul.'

'I know what needs ter be done, Chas, but it ain't easy.'

'What is.'

'Fancy anuvver light ale?'

'Why not.'

Chapter Five

Sue Carey swivelled round on her chair and reached for the in-house phone on the far side of her desk, knowing instinctively what the message would be.

'Susan, it's after nine-thirty. Has that idiot O'Brian not shown yet?'

She pulled a face and put on her best telephone voice for her employer. 'No I'm sorry, Mr Spencer. I'll give him your message as soon as he arrives.'

The mumbled reply was plain enough to convince her that Paddy O'Brian was in for a hard time when he did arrive. The *Bulletin*'s senior reporter was notorious for his Monday mornings. He was frequently summoned for a tongue-lashing over his lack of punctuality, and then he would set off from the office to redeem himself by producing very concise and readable copy for the Tuesday edition. It mattered not to Paddy whether it concerned a sewing circle or a major disaster in the area. He went out to investigate and to interview, and he did it very well.

At ten o'clock precisely he walked into the reception area and winced as he saw the look on Sue's face. 'I know. Don't tell me,' he groaned. 'Spencer's waiting. By the way, you look very nice this morning.'

'That's more than I can say for you, Paddy,' Sue replied with a smile. 'You look awful.'

The reporter rubbed a podgy hand over his forehead and leaned past her for the phone book. 'I need a number urgently,' he told her.

'There's no time for that. Spencer's fuming,' she said quickly. 'I'm to send you in as soon as you arrive.'

Paddy raised his hands in surrender and swallowed a burp as he went through into the main office. He saw that everyone was busy, heads down, typewriters tapping away, with one young man engaged in an animated conversation on the phone, and he managed to get a few sympathetic glances as he made his way to the far door. He could sense the customary anticipation around him as they waited for him to get inside, whereupon the air would turn blue and there would be much bellowing and issuing of imprecations before Paddy O'Brian re-emerged unrepentant.

On this particular morning the editor was busy on the phone, but instead of slamming down the receiver and invoking all manner of pestilence there was a brief look of recognition. Paddy waited for the tirade to begin, and when the phone call was over he was taken somewhat aback.

'It's about time. Now get down to Brady's Transport in Long Lane. On the double. There's a strike in the offing and it could get nasty,' Spencer told him with a wave of dismissal.

Paddy O'Brian came out of the inner sanctum with an expression of deliverance on his face. He had had a very heavy drinking session the night before and had been dreading yet another dressing-down. Now though his head was clearing and his astute mind was slipping into a working mode. 'Franny, see if you can get me anything on Brady's Transport of Long Lane, will you,' he said in a professional tone of voice.

Frances Miller detested being addressed as Franny but she tolerated it in Paddy's case. 'Like what?' she asked quickly.

'Like anything. History, community involvement, industrial relations. Anything. Go to it, girl. You know the drill.'

Frances was one of the few employees who actually had a soft spot for the dipsomaniac Irishman, and she gave him a quick nod and a smile as he hurried past her.

'Bad was it?' Sue said, grinning as Paddy came out from the main office.

'No time to stop,' he replied, feigning a serious expression. 'This could be a big one. By the way, Spencer was a pussycat this morning.'

Sue watched him leave and shook her head slowly. The man was driving himself into the ground with his drinking, but at least he never flunked a story.

Suddenly the door opened again and Paddy put his head back in. 'Sue, didn't you tell me once that your brother Tom worked for Brady's Transport?' he asked her.

'Yes. Are you covering the strike?'

'Threatened strike, my sweet.'

'Well, good luck.'

'I might need to have a chat about it later,' he said before the door closed.

Sue knew from experience that Paddy was an expert at fishing out snippets of information and she hoped he would not discover that the shop steward involved in the confrontation was her boyfriend. If he did find out he would pester her for some inside information, and it could well make things difficult for her.

Bessie Woodward was back from her early morning cleaning job and was already putting the story together, having first learned about the trouble at Brady's from her youngest son Patrick, who worked there as a mechanic. Bessie lived at number 9. Widowed and in her late fifties, she was a big woman with grey hair, piercing brown eyes and a freckled face, cutting in her manner at times, but with a heart of gold. She had been happy to see her eldest two sons married off, but Jeff and Patrick, who was the baby of the family at nineteen, were still living at home, and their weekly contribution was just about enough to cover their enormous appetites.

'I s'pose I'll 'ave 'im under me feet all day now,' she remarked to Martha Carey as they stood on the street corner outside Field's the baker's shop.

'Yeah, I'll 'ave it wiv my Tom as well,' Martha replied. 'They'll still want their food put in front of 'em though.'

'Too bloody right,' Bessie said. ''Ere, does your Sue know anyfing about what's goin' on at the place? Del Abelson's somefing ter do wiv the union, so 'is muvver was tellin' me.'

'Well, if she does she ain't said anyfing ter me,' Martha told her.

'It's like our Patrick,' Bessie went on. 'When I asked 'im about it 'e said it was no good discussin' it 'cos I wouldn't understand anyway. Bloody nice, ain't it?'

Like Bessie and several other women in Totterdown Street Martha did office cleaning, and she was keen to get back home and put her feet up for a while before starting the household chores. Seeing Bessie's best friend Nell Sharp coming along the turning made her heart sink and she decided to make her excuses and get away. Nell was a nice enough woman, she thought, but when she and Bessie got together for a natter you could watch the sun go round. 'Oh well, gotta go. I got fings ter do,' she said with a smile.

Bessie nodded her head in Martha's direction as Nell Sharp reached her. 'We've just bin talkin' about the strike at Brady's,' she said. 'She knows more than she's lettin' on. 'Er gel's bloke's the instigator. I could tell by what she said.'

'What she say then?' Nell asked.

'Just fings. Nuffink definite, but I could tell.'

'I reckon that Del Abelson's a bit of a Commie if you ask me,' Nell remarked.

Bessie nodded. 'It makes yer laugh. Those Communists start trouble over 'ere, but it wouldn't be allowed in Russia. They'd put 'em up against the wall an' shoot 'em, there.'

'Too bloody true.'

The Brady workforce of twenty drivers and two mechanics had attended an emergency meeting at seven o'clock that morning on a bombsite next to the transport yard, and after listening to what Del Abelson had to say they agreed to his request that they withhold their labour until certain answers were forthcoming. At seven-thirty, the normal starting time, the men remained gathered on the wasteground until they received some information.

At seven-forty-five Del Abelson came out of the yard looking very serious-faced and stood on a crate to address his workmates. 'I've spoken wiv Mr Brady an' 'is words were that the position at the Barley Lane Depot is as stands an' will remain so,' he told them. 'In ovver words, the new depot is ter be non-union.'

'Well, that's that then,' someone murmured.

'What d'yer mean that's that?' another driver sneered. 'If we don't fight this we might just as well all tear our cards up 'ere an' now.'

Del looked around at the angry faces and took some encouragement. 'Now listen ter me,' he said, holding his hands above his head for attention. 'Brady expects all you blokes ter walk in the gate this mornin' an' drive yer lorries out as though nuffing 'as 'appened, but I'm tellin' you that if yer do, yer might just as well do like the man said, tear yer union cards up. Then all the fings we've fought for over the last few months'll slowly get reversed. Let 'im win now an' it's curtains.'

' 'E's tryin' ter frighten us,' someone called out.

'Yeah, 'e's bluffin'. Let's show 'im.'

'I say we take a vote.'

Del held his hands up once more. 'All I want is room ter negotiate, an agreement from the management that they'll sit round the table wiv us. If I get that undertakin' then I'll tell 'em you'll all go ter work as normal while the talks take place. If the answer's no then I wanna be sure where I stand. I want you ter back me. Do I get that backin'? All in favour.'

The show of hands was unanimous and Del grinned and nodded his thanks.

Bernie Catchpole was standing at the rear of the group and he watched with a smirk on his face as the shop steward walked back into the yard. 'I tell yer now what the answer'll be,' he said loudly. 'It's gonna be piss off. Brady won't stand fer it.'

'Don't you be so sure,' one of the drivers told him sharply. 'That ovver depot ain't up an' runnin' yet. 'Ow's 'e gonna get 'is work done if we don't do it?'

'By bringin' in scab labour, that's 'ow,' Bernie replied quickly.

'Over my dead body,' the driver retorted.

'Yeah, that might just be the case.'

'We'll see about that,' a dapper man said, shaping up to the driver next to him.

'You can joke about it,' Bernie went on. 'Yer won't be so cocky when the 'eavy mob get 'ere.'

Del Abelson came out from the yard once more and climbed up on to the crate. 'The answer's no, lads,' he said loudly. 'As from this mornin' we're on the cobbles.'

Joe Brady shifted his position in his leather-bound desk chair and toyed with the gold ring on the second finger of his large hand. His bloated face was red with anger as Toby Lowndes the transport manager passed over the folder. 'What room 'ave we got ter manoeuvre?' he asked.

'Well, we can sub out the jobs I've underlined, at least for this week, guv, but the others are specialised. We've got two days at the most. Any further delays and we run the risk of serious contractual problems. The agreements are pretty watertight.'

Joe Brady brought his fist down angrily on the desktop and the blood rose in his face, giving it a purple cast. 'I won't be dictated to,' he stormed. 'I'm a born-an'-bred Bermon'sey boy. I started 'ere in Long Lane more than twenty years ago wiv one clapped-out lorry an' I built this firm up from nuffink. I'm the second biggest transport contractor south o' the river, an' I'm expected ter be dictated to by that power-crazed Commie bastard Abelson. Well, I won't stand fer it. D'you 'ear me!'

Toby Lowndes nodded dutifully. He knew full well that when Joe Brady was in this sort of mood it was best to be compliant.

'That depot in Barley Lane'll be runnin' by next week,' Brady went on. 'The contracts are fer food-stuffs. I don't need union men to 'andle foodstuffs. Why should I knuckle down ter demands? That depot is gonna stay non-union an' that's me last word on the matter. They'll be back ter work by midweek, you'll see. I'll give 'em a couple o' days ter let their actions sink in, then when they've 'ad time ter fink I'll screw 'em a bit more. I'll give 'em an ultimatum. Eivver they return ter work or I sack the bloody lot of 'em.'

The phone started to ring and as he picked up the receiver Brady ushered the manager from the room. He had been expecting the call, and when he rang off the transport contractor afforded himself a brief smile.

Paddy O'Brian was a very shrewd character and he saw little gain in joining the men on picket duty to hear what was going on. Instead he made his way to a nearby café and ordered a large tea and two slices of dripping toast. He knew full well that sooner or later some of the drivers would turn up at the place and they would be certain to chat together. Paddy felt it was a more civilised way of tackling the issue, but he was not to know what would transpire when the men did come in.

'It may go inter weeks instead o' days,' Bernie Catchpole remarked as he sat down clutching a mug of tea.

'So what? We gotta stand up ter the flash git,' one of his colleagues said as he joined the malcontent at the bench table.

'What d'yer mean, so what? Can you afford ter be wivout wages, 'cos I can't,' Bernie growled back at him.

'It's a matter o' principle,' the driver went on. 'It's always bin that way an' it always will. A man like Brady don't know what principle is, an' 'e finks we ain't got no bottle. 'E's got contracts to honour. If we don't drive those lorries the jobs don't get done. All right I 'eard what you said about scab labour, but scab labour never works. If Brady brings in the 'eavy mob the union'll see it as provocation an' they'll black 'is lorries.'

'Then we'll all be out o' work,' Bernie sneered. 'You talk a load of arse'oles. The trouble wiv you is, yer take fer gospel everyfing Abelson ses.'

The driver's face flushed up angrily and he leaned over the table in a menacing fashion. 'I've just about 'ad enough o' you, Catchpole,' he grated. 'You're the biggest arse'ole 'ere. Yer got no bottle, only a big mouth, an' if yer don't shut it I'll shut it for yer.'

Without warning Catchpole threw the rest of his hot tea in the smaller man's face and with a quick movement he reached over the table, pulling the man towards him by his coat lapels. As the driver's hands came up to grasp Catchpole's he was butted in the face right on the bridge of his nose and blood immediately spurted down on to his mouth and chin.

The elderly woman behind the counter screamed out in alarm and her cry brought out the shop owner who was busy cooking in the back kitchen. 'Get out of 'ere, yer bloody lunatics,' he shouted. 'This is a café not a bloody boxin' arena.'

Catchpole sauntered out of the shop with a cocky sway of his shoulders, casting a hard look at his wretched victim. The rest of the strikers followed on after, sympathising with the driver who was holding a badly stained handkerchief to his face.

'Catchpole went too far this time,' one said.

''E's a bloody guv'nor's man,' another driver added. 'I'll bet yer 'e don't take 'is turn on the picket lines.'

''E took me by surprise that time,' the injured man growled nasally. 'I'll get even wiv 'im, mark my words.'

The men walked off, watched by the *Bulletin*'s reporter who had followed them out of the café. Already he had something to work on, and he decided it was time to try and get a few words from Brady himself.

The picket line consisted of three drivers who looked a little sheepish as they stood talking at one side of the yard gates, and when Paddy walked up to them and introduced himself they gave him hostile looks. 'We can't talk about the stoppage, yer'll 'ave ter see the shop steward,' one said.

'So it's a stoppage not a strike then?' Paddy queried.

'Stoppage, strike, it's all the same. We ain't workin',' one of the others replied.

'Can you tell me the name of your steward?' Paddy asked.

'Del Abelson.'

'Can I have a few words with him?'

''E's gone down the union offices ter see the branch convenor,' the man said.

'Would you lads have any objections to me speaking to your employer?' Paddy asked them.

'We can't stop yer, but I 'ope yer'll listen ter what our shop steward 'as ter say before yer print the rubbish that no-good git Brady'll feed yer.'

'That's a promise,' Paddy O'Brian said with a disarming smile.

The yard was deserted as the reporter walked in and he glanced at the idle transport as he made his way to the office.

'I'm sorry but I don't think Mr Brady's available,' the solemn-faced secretary told him. 'If you'll wait here though I'll tell him you're here.'

Paddy took a seat and reached for the grease-stained copy of the *Picture Post* which was lying on the small table by his knees, thumbing through it with little interest.

'If you'll care to wait Mr Brady said he'll see you,' the secretary announced as she reappeared.

Paddy nodded and leaned back in the low, uncomfortable seat, letting his eyes take in the surroundings. The place was badly in need of a coat of paint and fresh wallpaper, he thought. The few pictures hanging round the room looked more suited to a parlour than a transport office. The secretary too seemed somewhat incongruous, and he started to hum quietly to himself as he waited.

After a while the door at the rear of the office opened and two smartly dressed men came out, followed by a big, ruddy-faced figure who Paddy guessed to be Brady himself. As he watched the two leave something suddenly clicked inside his head. He knew the face of one of them. It was some time ago now, but he felt sure that he had spoken to the man once. It would come back, he knew. His powers of recall usually got better as the day went on.

Brady was beckoning to him. 'I'll give yer five minutes,' he said curtly.

When Paddy O'Brian stepped out into the sunlight once more he had enough material to be getting on with. What was more, he had remembered the face, but it was rather queer. What would Joe Brady be doing consorting with that scum-bag, he wondered.

Chapter Six

Del Abelson lodged with the Coleman family at number 22, the end house next door to Albert Kenward's cobbler's shop. Rosie Coleman was a cheerful woman in her middle years who ran her home very efficiently, and her young lodger was happy to be living there. She provided a good table and kept the house spotless. The room she provided for him was nicely furnished and she encouraged him to spend time with her and her husband Jim during the evenings. The Colemans had never been blessed with a family of their own and they tended to treat Del as if he were their own son. Rosie ironed his shirts, pressed his suit and generally fussed over him while Jim, who worked as a machine fitter in a local metal box factory, took an interest in Del's union activities, feeling that his firm's workforce would benefit by having someone like him to represent their interests.

With tea over Jim Coleman leaned back in his chair and glanced across the table at the young man. 'So 'ow d'yer see fings progressin'?' he asked.

Del shrugged his shoulders. 'I dunno, Jim,' he replied. 'Brady's no fool. 'E'll let us sweat it out fer a few days. 'E'll sub out the main contracts ter cover 'imself an' 'ope that the strike crumbles.'

'What about the union? Won't they put pressure on 'im over that new depot?'

'Yeah they'll try to, but at the end o' the day it's down ter the new men,' Del explained. 'They can't be forced ter join the union an' Brady knows this. 'E's taken on a couple o' drivers straight out o' the nick by all accounts, an' there's a few more who were sacked from their last jobs fer one reason or anuvver. They're not in a position ter give Brady any grief, an' you can imagine the sort o' conversation that took place when they were interviewed fer the jobs.'

'So it doesn't look very good then?' Jim said as he took out a tobacco tin from his shirt pocket.

'Ter be honest it all depends on our lads,' Del replied. 'If they stay solid we've got a chance o' makin' Brady see sense.'

'I 'eard the bloke's a right nasty git,' Jim remarked as he rolled the cigarette makings between his fingers. 'Won't 'e try ter bring in scab labour?'

'I don't fink so, not just yet anyway,' Del told him. 'Brady knows it could get the firm blacked, 'specially at the docks. The dockers won't 'andle goods from firms who use scab labour.'

Rosie had been busy clearing the table and she gave her husband a reproving look. 'Why don't yer talk about somefing else, Jim,' she said quickly. 'Can't yer see the boy's worried enough as it is wivout you wantin' ter know the ins an' outs of a nag's arse.'

Jim lit his cigarette and caught the grin on Del's face. 'We're only discussin' fings, Muvver,' he answered lightly. 'Sometimes it's better ter talk about yer problems. Don't do anybody any good bottlin' fings up.'

'Just listen to 'im,' Rosie said, smiling at Del. ''E

sounds like that woman in the *Star* who answers readers' problems.'

'So what d'yer fink the union'll do then?' Jim went on regardless.

Once again Del shrugged his shoulders. 'The branch convenor's comin' wiv me ter see Brady in the mornin', but what'll transpire is anybody's guess.'

Rosie was beginning to get a little peeved at Jim's single-minded interrogation of the young man. 'Are you an' young Sue goin' out ternight, Del?' she asked quickly. 'If so yer'd better watch the time or 'e'll 'ave yer chattin' all night.'

'No, I've got some letters ter write, an' I'm seein' some o' the lads at the Bell later,' he told her.

Sue Carey went home from work that evening feeling worried. During the afternoon she had had a chat with Paddy O'Brian and what he had told her made her feel anxious for Del Abelson's well-being.

'Will you be seeing Del this evening?' she asked her brother as soon as she arrived home.

Tom nodded from the armchair. 'Yeah, we're meetin' at the Bell later. Why?'

'Well, you'd better warn him to be careful,' she replied in a quiet voice, glancing warily at the door.

The young man gave her a puzzled look. 'Why d'yer say that?'

Sue sat down facing him and kicked off her shoes. 'I don't want Mum and Dad to hear what I'm saying. I think Del could be in some danger,' she told him anxiously. 'Paddy O'Brian was covering the story today and he managed to get an interview with Joe Brady. While he was waiting to go in he saw two fellers come out of the office, and he recognised one of them. His name's Lennie Donald and he's a villain from Wapping. Paddy used ter work for a paper in the East End before the war and while he was there he met this Donald. Apparently the man was involved in a lot of dodgy goings-on over there. Paddy said he's a nasty character. He thinks Brady might have recruited him to cause trouble with the strikers.'

Tom leaned forward in his chair. 'From what you've told me, this Paddy O'Brian's a bit of an elbow bender. D'yer believe what 'e ses?'

Sue nodded emphatically. 'Paddy might like to get soaked more than's good for him but when he's working he's good,' she replied. 'That's the only reason he's tolerated at the *Bulletin*. I believe him and you should warn Del to be very careful. Tell him to warn the pickets too.'

Martha came into the room to lay the table and she looked at the two of them suspiciously. 'What's that about warnin' the pickets?' she asked.

'I was just saying that Brady might bring in outside labour and Del should warn the pickets in case there's trouble,' Sue said casually.

'You're on the picket line termorrer, ain't yer?' Martha asked, looking at Tom with a worried expression.

'Yeah, but there's no need ter worry, Ma,' he told her with a wide grin. 'I'm takin' an iron bar just in case.'

'Don't make light of it,' she said quickly. 'Strikes can get nasty. I've seen it before round 'ere. There was trouble outside the docks at one time while the men were on strike. They 'ad ter call the police. Blokes got beaten up an' Mrs Freeman's 'usband got 'is 'ead opened wiv a lump o' wood. In a bad way 'e was. They reckoned 'e'd never work again.'

'That was over scab labour,' Tom told her. 'Brady wouldn't be that stupid. Don't worry, Ma. We're peaceful strikers fightin' fer our rights. We ain't after causin' trouble.'

Martha did not look convinced and she sighed deeply. 'I dunno, I'm sure I don't. It's a bleedin' worry, what wiv one fing an' anuvver. C'mon, Sue, give us an 'and layin' the table. Yer farvver'll be in any minute.'

Granny Minto decided to take the evening air at her front door and she was joined by Albert Price. She sniffed loudly and gave him a disapproving look. 'What's that yer got on?' she asked him.

'It's called Target,' he told her with a grin. 'Cheap Jack was knockin' it out last Saturday so I got some. 'E reckoned it's the best aftershave on the market. 'E said the nobs use it all the time.'

Granny Minto narrowed her eyes. 'Yer did say after-shave, didn't yer? But you ain't 'ad a shave terday.'

'Nah but yer can still use it,' Albert replied. 'It makes yer smell fresh.'

'A bar o' Lifebuoy'd make yer smell fresher,' Granny told him.

Tubby Saward came out of number 18 and crossed the street to knock at number 15. Wally Tucker came out of the house and the two strolled off to collect Benny Tracy from number 8.

'There go the three musketeers,' Albert said grinning. 'They'll be in the Bell arguin' over who's gonna get the next pint an' whose turn it is at cribbage.'

'I fink Betty Tucker puts up wiv 'im well,' Granny remarked. ''E's always pissed when 'e comes 'ome. It's all right fer the ovver two. Tubby Saward's a widower an' that silly git Tracy's never bin married. They've only got themselves ter worry about.'

'Dick Tracy's all right,' Albert said in his defence. 'An' 'e ain't that silly. 'E's got a few bob put away.'

''Ow d'you know?'

''Cos 'e told me once.'

'Wally Tucker's only got 'is pension though,' Granny went on, 'yet 'e's up the pub nearly every night. I dunno 'ow 'e does it.'

'Those two married daughters of 'is see 'im an' Betty all right,' Albert told her. 'They're both good ter their ole mum an' dad. Soapy was tellin' me once.'

'You're anuvver Bessie Woodward, you are,' Granny said chuckling. 'Yer get ter know everyfing. You seem ter get where castor oil couldn't.'

'I was just listenin', luv,' Albert replied with a grin. 'It's surprisin' what yer do get ter know if yer just spend a bit o' time listenin' ter people. Fer instance, did yer know Queenie Alladyce 'as got a suitor?'

'Queenie Alladyce? She wouldn't wanna get spliced again,' Granny said with passion. 'She 'ad enough trouble wiv that ole man of 'ers. Dan Alladyce was the biggest boozer round 'ere at one time. Poor ole Queenie was left ter bring them four kids up on 'er own. All 'is wages went in the pub. I don't fink she grieved much over 'im when 'e died. It was the booze what killed 'im in the end.'

'Well, yer can say what yer like,' Albert replied nonchalantly. 'I'm tellin' yer Queenie's got a bloke.'

70

'Do I know 'im?' Granny asked.

Albert nodded towards the corner shop. 'It's John Raney.'

'Now I know yer pullin' me leg,' Granny said quickly. 'You must fink I just got off the boat. John Raney's a miserable ole goat. 'E ain't the sort ter want a woman in 'is life. 'E's quite 'appy ter be miserable on 'is own.'

'Well, you can scoff all yer like but I'm tellin' yer Queenie an' John Raney are keepin' company,' Albert said firmly. 'As a matter o' fact Queenie Alladyce is in that shop of 'is more times a week than you stand at this door. I'm tellin' yer.'

'Well I dunno what she sees in 'im,' Granny said haughtily. ''E reminds me o' Boris Karloff, 'e's got the same look about 'im. 'E fair puts the creeps up me whenever I 'ave ter go in the shop.'

Albert buttoned up his coat, his revelations complete. 'Well, I'm off fer a pint. Want me ter bring yer a Guinness back, luv?' he asked her.

'Yeah, that'll be nice,' she replied.

Albert strolled off along the small turning, smiling to himself at what Granny Minto might have said if he had told her about his own aspirations with regard to the new barmaid at the Bell.

Wally, Benny and Tubby were long-time drinking partners, and being a rather helpful and friendly trio they were always keen to lend a hand whenever they saw the need. Their neighbours had suffered as a result and the marks on Nell Sharp's piano bore testament to one attempt at neighbourly goodwill.

It had all started when she decided it was about

time she and Mick got themselves one of those modern radiograms, and consequently she began nagging at him.

'We ain't got no bloody room, what wiv that eyesore stuck there,' Mick growled.

'That pianer was me ole mum's, an' I ain't gonna sell it ter the totters fer next ter nuffink,' Nell told him adamantly.

Wanting to keep the peace Mick put the word around in the Bell, and when Wally got to hear he told his wife Betty, who happened to know that her friend Mrs Benjamin was after a piano for her daughter Connie. A deal was struck but Mrs Benjamin had no man of her own to help move it, and Mick Sharp had a bad back.

'It's no problem, me an' the lads'll shift it,' Wally said magnanimously.

'Yeah, we won't want payin',' Tubby chimed in. 'A pint apiece'll do.'

The job was arranged for Saturday morning, and after a beer to warm them up the three set to work. They managed to get the piano across the parlour without much trouble but then it became jammed in the doorway.

'Stand it on its end,' Wally puffed.

'Yer can't do that,' Nell told them quickly. 'The bloody insides'll fall out.'

'Look, luv, this ain't the first joanner me an' the lads 'ave shifted,' Wally assured her.

'It's the first one I can remember,' Benny muttered to Tubby who was already puffing like a train.

With great difficulty the piano was upended and swivelled round to face the front door, but then something clattered down inside the heavy instrument.

'I told yer didn't I,' Nell nagged.

Wally gave her an old-fashioned look. 'Mind yerself or yer'll get 'urt,' he growled.

As soon as the woman went back into the parlour Wally looked at his two confederates. 'Right, one big shove,' he urged them.

Granny Minto leaned against her doorpost, chuckling at the piano resting upside down on the pavement and Wally Tucker flat on his back outside Nell Sharp's house. 'That pianer'll be a bleedin' wreck by the time those silly gits are finished,' she remarked to Albert.

'Shall I go an' give 'em some 'elp?' he suggested.

'You stay out of it,' Granny warned him.

With much puffing and groaning the piano was finally righted, and the trio sat at the kerbside to catch their breath.

Suddenly Mrs Benjamin appeared with a tape measure, and after making a few quick calculations she shook her head regretfully. 'I thought that looked a bit too big fer my parlour,' she sighed.

'Yer mean yer changed yer mind?' Tubby said incredulously.

'Sorry, lads,' she told them with a sympathetic smile.

'I need a drink,' Benny groaned.

Nell came to the door. 'You ain't gonna leave it there, are yer?' she queried.

'We'll be back later,' Wally told her over his shoulder.

That night the badly battered piano was once again

resting in Nell Sharp's parlour, smelling of cat's piss and never again to utter a note.

'The trouble wiv us is, we're too easy,' Benny remarked as the three chastened musketeers walked home from the Bell.

'I don't remember anybody askin' us ter move the bloody fing,' Tubby replied.

'Nah, we put ourselves in the frame all fer a lousy pint,' Benny grieved.

'Sorry, lads,' Wally said humbly.

The saga of the unfortunate piano was long forgotten as the three musketeers huddled round their usual table, for there was another important plan to formalise.

'It ain't like the ole days,' Wally was going on. 'Them days people 'ad nuffink ter give. Fings are different now. I'm sure if we asked Vic Ogden 'e'd give us a couple o' packets o' fags an' I'm certain we could scrounge a few tins o' beans an' some biscuits from Ole Muvver Riley's shop in Abbey Street.'

'We could go round fer a collection,' Benny suggested. 'A few coppers 'ere an' there would 'elp.'

'I got an idea,' Tubby said quickly. 'Why don't we knock up a couple o' posters? We could march up an' down outside the yard wiv 'em.'

'What sort o' posters?' Benny asked him.

'You know. "Black Brady's Transport." "Join the union." "Brady's an ole git." Stuff like that.'

'I dunno,' Benny replied. 'The coppers might nick us.'

'I don't care if they do. At least it'd get some publicity,' Tubby told them.

'We'll bear that in mind,' Wally said. 'Let's draw up a list.'

'Good idea,' Tubby said. 'Anyone got a pencil?'

A shake of heads sent him off to the counter. ''Ere, Dave, got a pencil an' a scrap o' paper?' he asked.

'No I ain't. This is a pub not a stationer's,' the landlord growled.

Unabashed, Tubby went back to his friends. 'That dopey git ain't got one,' he told them. 'Never mind, we can remember the main points.'

A strategy to support the strikers was eventually drawn up, and at closing time the three staggered happily back to Totterdown Street. They had forgotten the main points, and the less important points too, but all three vaguely remembered that they had to meet the following day, for some reason.

Chapter Seven

Tubby Saward went into Vic Ogden's shop for his newspaper on Tuesday morning and listened while the elderly proprietor chatted to Queenie Alladyce.

'Is yer lad still out on strike?' Vic asked her.

'Yeah, there don't seem ter be any progress,' Queenie told him.

Something stirred in Tubby's mind, and when he called into Mrs Riley's grocery shop for a tin of steak and kidney pudding it all came back to him. ''Ere, luv, yer wouldn't mind givin' a small donation ter the strikers, would yer?' he remarked.

'Strikers? What strikers?' the gaunt-faced shopkeeper asked, peering at him over her glasses.

'Joe Brady's men are out on the cobbles, gel. Some of 'em live in our street an' we're supportin' 'em by 'elpin' out wiv bits an' pieces,' he explained.

'Joe Brady the transport contractor?'

'Yeah, that's right.'

'An' you want me ter give a donation ter the strikers?'

'Yeah, that's right.'

'Well let me tell you, Mr Saward. My 'usband an' Joe Brady are friends,' she said sharply. 'The last fing I would do is give support ter those lazy, good-fer-nuffing strikers. They should be only too glad to 'ave a job ter go to. Now if yer don't mind I'm busy this mornin'.'

Tubby glared at her for a few minutes while he gathered his thoughts. 'Right then. If that's yer attitude I don't see why I should give you me custom any more,' he declared indignantly. 'I'm gonna re-register wiv Perkins fer me rations. At least they're civil wiv their customers.'

'Well, you can please yerself. Now if yer don't mind.'

Tubby walked out of the shop fuming and decided there and then to remind his pals forthwith of the commitment they had made last night in the Bell.

By Wednesday the strike was beginning to crumble. Shorty Lockwood, the driver Bernie Catchpole had head-butted, was sporting two black eyes and a swollen nose, and he felt that he couldn't take a turn on the picket line looking the way he did. Bernie himself had not turned up to take his turn outside the firm's gates and those who did were beginning to grumble and lose heart.

'My ole woman's told me ter get back ter work or she's gonna 'ave ter pawn 'er ring,' one driver said.

'Well, I can't stand out 'ere much longer,' another moaned. 'I can't stand by an' see me kids go 'ungry.'

'I wouldn't mind if somefing was 'appenin',' a third remarked.

Tom Carey shook his head slowly as he listened to the dissent around him. 'You knew what you were doin' when you all put yer 'ands up ter strike,' he told them. 'We all made the decision ter go out tergevver an' we gotta stick to our guns. If we crawl back wivout a result Brady'll make it bad fer us, that's fer sure.'

'It's all right fer you, Tom,' the first driver said quickly. 'You've only got yer dick ter keep. We've got families.'

'Yeah, I know,' the young man said quietly. 'But can't you lot see that you're fightin' fer yer families as well as yerselves? It's the future you gotta fink of.'

'Yeah, that's what I am finkin' of,' the man replied.

Tom shrugged his shoulders. 'Look, there's a meetin' ternight at the Bell,' he reminded them. 'Let's wait an' see what the news is. Del's goin' in wiv the union convenor this afternoon. It may get us a result.'

'Yeah, well, if there's no news by Friday I'm puttin' it to a vote we go back on Monday,' the driver told him.

Sue Carey felt worried all day Wednesday. Paddy O'Brian had been out since early morning on a couple of assignments and she had not had a chance to ask him any more about the strike. She had refrained from telling him of her involvement with Del Abelson and now she wished she had done. After all, as far as Paddy was concerned the strike was old news, and he had no reason to know that what he had told her about the villain visiting Brady would concern her in any way. It was just chat on his part.

The report in the Tuesday edition of the *Bulletin* had been brief and without much elaboration, though Paddy had intimated to her that things could get rough and it might make a good story for the Friday edition. It was that throwaway remark that was worrying the young woman as she worked at the switchboard, took down messages and dealt with the usual stream of callers throughout the day. Her brother Tom had not been too forthcoming either. He had told her that he had had a word with Del about being wary, but he was dismissive of any possible flare-up. It was partly because he would not want to worry her, and mainly because he simply wouldn't see it as any big thing. Tom was like that. Sometimes he could be infuriating with his devil-may-care attitude to everything. But then he had been in a war, and after something as harrowing as that he would obviously see things differently now. To him the strike was merely an irritation.

Sue continued to worry, and on her way home from work that evening she called at Del's lodgings. Rosie Coleman invited her in and offered her a cup of tea. 'I've not seen anyfing of 'im all day, luvvy,' she said. 'I do know 'e's got some meetin' ter go to this evenin'. It's all a bit up the wall at the moment.'

Sue sat by the unlit fire sipping her tea. 'How's he seem, Rosie?' she asked.

'You know Del. 'E's full of it,' the older woman replied. ''Im an' my Jim were chattin' about union business again last night. I left 'em at it an' went ter bed ter tell yer the trufe.'

Sue smiled. 'That's Del all over. He's after making a career out of it.'

'Don't I know,' Rosie replied. 'You wanna put yer foot down an' make 'im give you some of 'is time. It ain't right the way 'e goes on, an' I've told 'im so more than once. I said to 'im only last night if 'e don't watch it 'e'll lose yer. I told 'im straight that 'e can't expect you ter play second fiddle ter the union.'

'And what did he say?' Sue asked smiling.

''E just fobbed it off,' Rosie told her. 'Mind you, 'e does fink the world of yer, I can tell. Del's a very nice lad, but I do worry about 'im sometimes.'

Sue put her empty cup down on the table beside her and gathered up her handbag from the side of the chair. 'Rosie, did Del say anything to you or Jim about him being in any danger, even jokingly?' she asked.

Rosie shook her head. ''E might 'ave mentioned it ter Jim, but certainly not ter me. Why? *Is* 'e in any danger?'

'I don't know, but I do know Joe Brady's got a few devious friends,' Sue replied. 'I wouldn't put it past him to get someone to sort him out.'

As she got up to leave Rosie laid a hand on her arm. 'Do me a favour, luv,' she said in a serious voice. 'Try an' get that lad to ease up a bit. Get 'im ter take you out a bit more. I wouldn't wanna see you two split up. You're good fer 'im, an' 'e should be made ter see it.'

'Rosie, you're a dear,' Sue said smiling. 'I must get home or they'll wonder where I've got to.'

Pamela Duggan was standing on her front doorstep chatting to Tom Carey as Sue came along the turning and she smiled sheepishly. 'Tom's bin tellin' me about the strike,' she said.

'That's more than he's told me,' Sue said with a frosty look at her brother as she let herself in.

'Is she all right?' Pamela asked.

Tom shrugged his shoulders. 'She worries too much,' he said dismissively.

'You won't take this business wiv Bernie an' that feller personal, will yer, Tom?' Pamela queried.

'Course not,' he replied. 'It was nuffink ter do wiv me. Me an' your bloke's got our own differences.'

She looked down at her feet for a few moments. 'Me an' Bernie's split up,' she said finally.

'Since when?'

'Since Saturday night.'

Tom Carey smiled, his white teeth flashing. 'So there's no reason why you can't come out wiv me ternight.'

'I dunno.'

'What d'yer mean, you dunno?' he said quickly. ''Aven't I bin askin' you fer months now ter ditch that no-good sod, an' now yer free of 'im you dunno. You 'ave really dumped 'im, ain't yer?'

'Course I 'ave,' she replied.

'Well then, what about it? There's a good picture up the Trocadera this week. C'mon then, say yes.'

'I thought you said you 'ad a union meetin' ter go to ternight,' she queried.

'It's not important, I can give it a miss,' he told her.

'Should you?'

The young man leaned his hand on the brickwork, his face close to hers. 'I like you, Pamela. I like you a lot,' he said in a serious voice. 'I'd much sooner be sittin' in the pictures wiv you than listenin' to a load o' codswallop at some union meetin'. Now is it gonna be yes, or do I ask Alice Dillon ter come wiv me?'

'She's nuffink but a trollop,' Pamela replied quickly.
'You wouldn't ask 'er, would yer?'

'Only if you say no,' he grinned.

'Oh all right. What time?'

'Make it about seven.'

'See yer then.'

'You bet.'

Dave Ford had been happy to make an upstairs
room available for the union meeting. It was the
room that the pub's football team normally used,
and as Wednesday evening was usually quiet he
was glad of the extra income. Wednesday evening
was also the night Dave's wife Bella took off and
the publican was anticipating making some inroads
with Angie Thomas, the new barmaid. She was an
attractive blonde in her late forties who knew how
to act the innocent, and with a husband locked away
in Pentonville for two years he felt that she should
be entitled to a little fun.

Albert Price had also found the new addition to
the Bell highly desirable, though he knew that he
was old enough to be her father. She made him
feel young again with her complimentary remarks,
and the street's jester had seen fit to spruce himself
up a bit. Granny Minto felt that he was going through
a second childhood and she had told him as much, but
Albert took no heed. If Angie Thomas wanted to flirt
harmlessly with him who was he to dissuade her.

On Wednesday evening Albert stood at the counter
chatting to Dave Ford, aware of Angie in the background. 'Yeah, I was workin' all the hours Gawd sent
an' she wasn't satisfied,' he was going on. 'There was

I drivin' meself intei the ground an' she was orf out at every opportunity. If we'd 'ave 'ad kids it might 'ave bin different, but there yer go.'

'So what 'appened? Did you leave 'er, or did she leave you?' Dave asked him.

'I kicked 'er out,' Albert said, pausing to sip his beer. 'Couldn't stand it no longer. One night I come 'ome late from the stables. We 'ad an 'orse wiv the colic yer see. Nobody knew what ter do except me, so I was cattled. It was Alice or the 'orse. Anyway I managed ter get it on its feet, yer got to wiv 'orses, an' then I finally got some jallop down its gullet an' it seemed ter work. Nearly ten o'clock it was when I finished, an' I ses ter meself, Albert, yer deserve a drink. Course, by the time I got 'ome Alice was fumin'. "Where the bloody 'ell you bin?" she said. "Takin' care o' the 'orse," I told 'er. "Well, you can go an' sleep wiv the 'orse fer all I care," she ses. That done it. I ses to 'er, "Alice, I'd get more lovin' from that ole mare than the one I got at 'ome."'

'An' what she say ter that?' Dave asked with a sideways glance at the amused barmaid.

'Well, ter tell yer the trufe she didn't say anyfing. She just went upstairs an' came down wiv 'er moth-eaten fur coat on luggin' a suitcase. "I'm off," she said.'

'Was that all?' Dave asked.

'Well, she called me a few choice names that I can't repeat in present company,' Albert replied. 'Anyway off she went an' I ain't seen nuffink of 'er since. Mind you, I did 'ear that she'd got 'erself 'iked up wiv a bookie. An' it's odds on 'e's 'ad enough of 'er by now.'

'Poor Albert,' Angie said sympathetically.

'I'm 'appy,' he told her. 'I got a good lady that I lodge wiv an' I get fed an' watered regularly.'

Dave looked up and frowned as he saw the two strangers come into the bar, and when Angie went to serve them he leaned on the counter close to Albert. 'I ain't seen them in 'ere before,' he remarked.

'They might be union blokes,' Albert suggested.

Dave Ford shook his head. 'I know the union blokes who are comin' ternight. They ain't union.'

The striking drivers were beginning to arrive and after buying drinks they made their way up to the room above. A little later Del Abelson arrived with Robbie Casey the union convenor and Will Smithson the branch secretary. Their appearance seemed to interest the two men and it began to worry the landlord. 'They look a right rough pair,' he remarked to Albert. 'I wonder what they're doin' 'ere.'

In the room above Del Abelson glanced around at the men, his broad shoulders hunched over the table. He saw that Bernie Catchpole had seated himself at the back while his victim Shorty Lockwood was sitting in the front row, but there was no sign of Tom Carey. 'Right, lads, I wanna make this as brief as possible, so listen carefully,' he began. 'We've got nowhere wiv Brady. 'E refuses ter budge an inch, an' I 'ave ter tell yer that as far as 'e's concerned, eivver we go back ter work by Monday or 'e'll sack the lot of us.'

Loud voices filled the room and Del held his hands up for silence. 'Now I'm gonna pass yer over ter Robbie, who'll spell it all out ter yer,' he said. 'Right, Robbie, yer've got the floor.'

The union convenor clasped his podgy hands together on the table and looked around the room, his dark eyes darting from one to another. 'If I was in your shoes,' he began, 'my first question would be, can 'e do it? So I'm gonna lay it straight on the line. Yes, 'e can.'

The murmur of angry voices was stilled when the convenor raised his hands. 'But yer gotta remember that we as a union can take steps ter dissuade 'im,' he went on. 'We feel that any sackin' of strikers would be tantamount ter suicide on Brady's part. We could stop 'im transportin' any goods to an' from union firms, an' as far as dock work went, 'e'd be blacked fer evermore. No, I fink Brady's tryin' the big bluff, though yer can never be one 'undred per cent wiv people like 'im. My advice ter you lads is ter stay strong an' let us continue wiv the talks. I feel sure we can make Brady see sense.'

'Yeah, but 'ow long's that gonna take?' a man shouted out.

'I can't answer that,' the official replied. 'It all depends on Brady.'

Will Smithson the branch secretary leaned towards Del Abelson as the men's voices were raised in an angry clamour. 'Yer gonna be 'ard pushed ter keep this lot from creepin' back ter work,' he remarked under his breath.

The convenor was trying to answer questions and his answers seemed to be doing little to pacify the men.

'I make yer right,' Del said out of the corner of his mouth.

Down in the public bar Albert Price was on the alert.

Angie had told him in a whispered aside that the two men sitting at the far table were trouble.

'Yer know 'em then?' he said, turning his back towards the strangers. Angie nodded. 'They use the 'Orseshoe in Tower Bridge Road,' she muttered. 'They used ter put the fear inter me when I was workin' there.'

Albert's mind began to work overtime. He had seen enough labour disputes in his lifetime to realise that those two villains were not socialising. They were there to do some damage. Maybe the union officials were their targets, but it was more likely to be Del Abelson, he reasoned. He had seen more than one strike leader beaten up in an effort to frighten the men back to work. From what he had heard about Joe Brady he wouldn't in the least put it past him to use strong-arm methods.

'Dave, can I get upstairs from the saloon bar?' he asked the landlord.

'Yeah. Why d'yer ask?'

'I'm sure those two are after sortin' Del Abelson out an' I wanna warn 'im,' Albert told him.

Dave Ford looked anxiously at the elderly man. 'Walk out casually as though yer goin' 'ome an' I'll slip in the ovver bar ter show yer the way up,' he said in a low voice.

'Well, g'night then,' Albert called out as he ambled to the door.

When he hurried into the saloon bar Dave was waiting. 'Through that door,' he said pointing.

Albert puffed loudly as he climbed the steep flight of stairs, and after a few words in Del Abelson's ear he came down feeling very pleased with himself.

The smile was soon wiped from his face, however. Dave was waiting for him. 'Angie said that as soon as you walked out the public those two followed yer,' he told him. 'I didn't know, I was in this bar, but Angie reckons they must 'ave clocked yer comin' in 'ere an' I make 'er right. They know yer warned Del, it's a dead cert.'

''Ave they come back in?' Albert asked quickly.

The landlord went through to the public bar and shook his head as he came back. 'They're gone, but they might be lurkin' outside,' he warned.

'I'm gonna take a gander,' Albert said with an exaggerated roll of his shoulders.

'Mind 'ow yer go,' Dave told him.

It was dead quiet in the street outside and Albert came back into the pub to report.

A few minutes later the meeting ended, and mindful of Albert Price's warning the men insisted on staying together until they were sure that their shop steward was in no danger. As they reached the corner of Totterdown Street they could see that the turning was deserted.

'Yer all right, Del,' one remarked.

'See yer on the picket line,' another said.

'G'night, lads,' Del said as he turned into the street.

A full moon shone down on the cobbles and his footsteps sounded loudly as he walked casually to the end house. Suddenly a car turned the corner and screeched to a halt beside him. The rear door opened and a trussed bundle was thrown out at his feet. 'Next time it'll be you, bruvver,' the driver growled as he accelerated away from the kerb.

The young man looked down in horror at the bound-up figure and heard a deep groan. He bent down and turned the body over, recoiling as he saw the battered face of Tom Carey staring up at him.

Chapter Eight

Sue Carey worked at her switchboard as though in a trance on Thursday morning. Before she left the house she had gone into Tom's room and felt physically sick at his appearance. He was propped up with pillows, still sleeping, and his face was almost unrecognisable. Both eyes and his nose were swollen and there was a large pad over his left eyebrow. She knew there were other hidden injuries too, and as she gently closed the bedroom door and hurried down the stairs her anger momentarily centred on Del Abelson. Maybe that was unreasonable she thought, checking herself. Perhaps Tom had brought these appalling injuries on himself in some way. He was a hothead at times, and too bold for his own good. When it came down to it, though, he had been encouraged to go on strike like the rest of the men and Brady had taken his revenge, she felt sure.

As she wrote down a phone message for Paddy O'Brian the young woman remembered what he had said about things getting rough. Did he know more than he let on, she wondered. Was he privy to any information? In any case she would have to talk to him now, tell him about her involvement with Del Abelson. Perhaps he would be able to piece a few things together and use them to expose Brady.

The morning dragged on and still Paddy had not made an appearance. He had left a message saying he was going to report on a new block of flats that the Council had just opened and would be in before lunch. He was a very unreliable sort and Sue became even more agitated as it neared midday. Perhaps she should take the afternoon off and go and speak to her brother Maurice, she thought. He had to be made aware of what had happened to his younger brother if nothing else.

On the stroke of twelve Paddy O'Brian walked into the office looking his usual dishevelled self. 'That bloody housing councillor could talk the jaw off a Donegal fishwife,' he growled. 'He was opening a block of flats for God's sake, not launching the *Titanic*.'

'Paddy, I need to talk to you,' Sue said, handing him the message she had taken.

'Urgent?'

'Yes it is.'

He threw the note into a wastepaper basket and smiled. 'Not here?'

'It's my lunchtime now. Can we go somewhere?' she asked him.

His face brightened. 'I know a nice pub with a few quiet corners,' he replied. 'We can be alone.'

Sue saw the way he moved his eyebrows and she gave him a hard look. 'Paddy, this is serious.'

He quickly became his professional self again. 'Say no more. Let's go,' he answered, holding the door open for her.

The junior whose job it was to operate the switchboard during Sue's lunch hour had already taken her place and she smiled to herself as she saw them leave together.

The small pub near the railway station was fairly packed but Paddy pushed his way to the counter and got the drinks. They found a vacant seat in the far corner and the Irishman took a large draught of his pint before glancing up at the young woman. 'Now what's the trouble?' he asked blithely.

Sue told him about her involvement with Del Abelson, and he was quite shocked when she told him how her brother had been bundled out of a car badly beaten up after the meeting. She reminded him of what he had said after the interview he had had with Joe Brady, and Paddy's face took on a serious look. 'I'd take a bet that it was Brady's doing,' he said quietly. 'In fact I'm sure of it. I just wonder why it was your brother Tom and not Del Abelson he targeted. Tell me, did your feller mention whether the people in the car said anything before they drove off? Anything that would tie it up with Brady?'

Sue shook her head and sighed. 'When I opened the door and saw Del carrying Tom in his arms I thought I'd die. My dad wanted to phone for an ambulance and the police but Tom was conscious by then and he wouldn't hear of it, so Mum ran up the street to phone the doctor. He wanted Tom to go to the hospital too but my brother's so obstinate. Anyway he took a good look at him and said there was nothing broken and no concussion as far as he could tell. He strapped Tom's ribs up and gave him something to make him sleep. He was coming again this morning. Tom was sleeping when I left so I don't know how he is.'

'He'll be feeling stiff and aching all over, that's for sure,' Paddy replied. 'So you're sure Del never said anything about who could have been responsible?'

'Not to me he didn't,' Sue told him.

Paddy took another sip from his beer. 'I'll need a statement from your brother and a comment from Del Abelson before I can print any of this,' he reminded her. 'Spencer would throw me out the office if I gave him speculative copy. It could be seen as libellous.'

'I understand what you're saying, Paddy, but I was hoping you could give me some information on this Lennie Donald you saw coming out of Brady's office. You said you knew him.'

'Yeah, I'd met him once, Sue, but it was a long time ago,' Paddy told her. 'The man might be straight now. He might have called in to see Brady on normal business. In any case there's no concrete proof that he was involved in what happened to Tom.'

'But you believe he was.'

'To be honest, yes, but where does that leave us? You said Tom wouldn't let anyone call the police.'

'I might be able to make him change his mind,' Sue replied.

'It would help,' Paddy said picking up his glass of beer. 'At least they could check out Lennie Donald. They might be interested in what he's doing this side of the water.'

Sue drained her half pint of light ale and Paddy picked up the empty glass. 'Let's get a refill,' he said.

The young woman watched him walk to the counter

and suddenly felt sorry for him. There was a new reporter coming to work at the *Bulletin* on Monday, and from the office tittle-tattle it appeared that Paddy would be relegated to covering minor events. It had even been hinted that the erstwhile senior reporter was on his way out. It would be a shame, she thought. He was good at his job, and would be even better if only he did not hit the bottle so often.

As though reading her thoughts Paddy smiled cynically as he sat down. 'Wonder Boy'll be starting on Monday,' he remarked. 'I wonder what Spencer's got lined up for him.'

'More to the point, what's he got lined up for you?' Sue said quickly. 'I should be careful. Don't give him any reason to get rid of you, Paddy.'

'Don't worry, I'm impervious,' he grinned.

They left the pub and strolled back to the office, Paddy chatting away about his bullying landlady while Sue half listened, preoccupied with what had happened to her brother. By the time they reached the newspaper building the young woman had made her mind up. She would feign a bad headache and go off early to catch Maurice at the arches before he left that evening.

Queenie Alladyce was the Careys' next-door neighbour, on the other side from the Duggans, but unlike them she was inclined to keep herself to herself. It wasn't out of cussedness, or that she was not a very neighbourly spirit. On the contrary, Queenie felt that she was allowing the Careys the privacy of their own home, and not turning it into an open house by popping in and out at all times of the day. The Careys were a nice friendly family, as were the Duggans, but the occasional chat at the front door was far preferable to daily tea parties in the parlour, she felt.

Being neighbourly was Queenie's prime concern on Thursday morning, when she went into her backyard and took two newly laid eggs from the straw. She had learned of what happened to Tom Carey when she saw Martha in the newsagents and had decided that a couple of eggs fresh from the hen would be the very thing for him, especially after Martha had described in detail her lad's facial injuries.

'Benny, I'm goin' next door if I'm wanted,' she called out from the passage.

Her lodger's mumbled reply prompted Queenie to poke her head into the parlour. 'What you doin' there?' she asked.

Benny had just finished rolling up the posters he had prepared and he gave her an embarrassed grin. 'They're posters fer the pickets,' he replied. 'Me, Tubby an' Wally are gonna give 'em a bit o' support.'

Queenie had had Benny Tracy as a lodger for a lot of years now and she had long since stopped asking him for explanations. He and his two pals were always up to something or the other and it figured that the local strike would have stimulated those peculiar three brains in some way. 'You mind you don't get inter trouble,' she warned him. 'It's not your fight.'

Benny nodded dutifully. 'We collected some bits an' pieces fer the lads in case they're out a long time,' he told her. 'Me, Wally an' Tubby are takin' 'em up ter the picket line.'

'Like what?'

'A few tins o' this an' that,' Benny replied, not wanting to let Queenie know that they had also collected money. He knew full well that the kind woman would want to put in a few coppers even though she was hard up that week after paying the tally man two weeks' money.

'Yer didn't ask me fer anyfing,' she queried.

'Well, I knew yer was—'

'I can spare a tin o' somefing,' she told him. ''Ere, there's a tin o' beans in the dresser, take it.'

Benny gave her a friendly wink. 'Fanks, gel,' he said, imagining that if he could have found a woman like his landlady a little while back he might have forgone his bachelor existence. 'Yer'll get yer reward in 'eaven.'

'Well, I sure won't get it down 'ere,' she remarked.

Martha Carey looked surprised when Queenie knocked and she was touched by her neighbour's kindness when she saw the two eggs. 'It's very nice of yer ter fink of us,' she said. 'I got the kettle on – why don't yer come in fer a cuppa?'

Normally Queenie would have politely declined the offer, but she felt that Martha might want to talk to someone after what had happened and she nodded. 'All right, if yer can spare the time,' she replied.

Martha led the way into her cosy parlour and quickly removed a piece of embroidery from a fireside chair. 'Sit yerself down,' she said. 'This is Ellie's work. She's just gone out fer 'er constitutional.'

''Ow is she?' Queenie asked.

Martha sighed in resignation. 'Still the same old Ellie,' she told her. 'This business wiv Tom's really upset 'er.'

'The lad'll be all right in a few days,' Queenie said. ''E's a tough 'un.'

Martha shook her head slowly. 'I can't get ter the bottom of it but it's got somefing ter do wiv that strike, I'll be bound,' she replied. 'Our Sue thought it might 'ave bin a come-back from what 'appened on Saturday night at the Palais. Apparently Tom an' Bernie Catchpole got at it over young Pam Duggan an' Sue reckons Bernie might 'ave got someone ter sort Tom out. Our Tom's very keen on Pamela yer know. As a matter o' fact she popped in a little while ago. She's still upstairs wiv 'im now.'

'She's a pretty little fing,' Queenie remarked. 'They'd make a nice couple.'

Martha excused herself to go and make the tea and she came back with a few biscuits on a plate. She noticed how her neighbour had her grey hair set in a soft perm and was wearing a rather fetching emerald green blouse with a high collar under her shabby coat. She was a big woman who sometimes seemed to carry the world's troubles on her shoulders but she always seemed to keep herself quite smart, and today she looked very relaxed. 'I like yer 'air,' Martha remarked as she tested the strength of the tea. 'That colour blouse suits yer too.'

It had been her latest acquisition from the tally man and Queenie smiled. 'We've gotta try an' keep up our appearances, 'aven't we,' she said lightly.

Martha was aware that Queenie had been on her own for a number of years, and she had also heard a few whispers recently about her and John Raney. She had discounted the gossip, imagining that after the hard life she had had with her late husband the woman would be loath to get entangled with another man. Seeing the way she looked this morning, however, gave Martha room for thought. Now that her four children were married off Queenie might have decided to make the most of her freedom. She could do a lot worse too. Raney was about her age, give or take a few years, and he was quite a presentable man, if he would only smile a little more. Perhaps Queenie would be able to help him in that department.

Martha poured the tea, aware that Queenie was staring at her fireplace. 'I gotta black-lead that grate this afternoon,' she told her. 'I gotta do me step before the weekend too. I must remember ter pop up the oilshop terday.'

'I gotta go up there later,' Queenie said as she took the cup from her. 'I can get yer whatever yer want.'

'I'll be much obliged,' Martha replied, beginning to think that perhaps the rumours were true.

Queenie sipped her tea, alone with her thoughts while Martha went to check on Tom. It was a small street where everyone seemed to know their neighbours' business, and it would soon get around about John Raney and her. After all, how many times a week would a woman need to go to the oilshop? With her it had become a daily trip, but she didn't mind. Far from it. John was a nice man, despite his gruff exterior. He had never married and had spent most of his adult life running the little shop like his father before him. His interest in lepidopterous insects had been the catalyst for the growing friendship between them, and Queenie smiled to herself as she recalled that particular morning when she learned of his secret passion.

She had gone into the oilshop to get a fly-paper and John Raney had seemed rather agitated. 'Give me a few minutes,' he said anxiously, disappearing into the back of the shop.

Queenie waited patiently until he returned, and seeing that he was a little flustered she asked him what was wrong.

'There was some chemical leakin' an' I 'ad ter transfer it to anuvver stone jar before I lost it all,' he told her.

'That sounds dangerous,' she replied. 'What chemical was that then?'

'Formaldehyde.'

'What's that for?'

'Preservin', amongst ovver fings.'

''Ere, you ain't got a dead body back there, 'ave yer?' she asked him jokingly.

'Sort of,' he said shortly.

Her look of shock produced a rare smile, and after a moment or two's pregnant pause he deigned to explain. 'I use the chemical ter preserve butterflies,' he told her. 'It's a sort of 'obby.'

'That's nice,' she said. 'Some butterflies are really lovely. The colours are beautiful. I remember seein' some preserved in glass cases at a museum when I was a kid. They were so beautiful.'

John Raney let his reserve slip a little. 'Would yer like ter see my collection?' he asked her.

Queenie recalled how impressed she had been on seeing the multicoloured specimens which had been pinned on to black velvet inside polished wood picture frames. They were hung all around his back room and there were more hanging in the passage.

'Did yer catch all these yerself?' she had asked him.

'Some. Some I acquired from second-'and shops an' market stalls,' he told her.

They were standing in the dimly lit passageway and he pointed to one particular frame. 'See that one? That's the Swallowtail an' it comes from the Papilionidae family. Yer'll only see that type on the Broads or the Fens. I caught that meself in Norfolk.'

Queenie saw the look of pride on his face and the mischievous glint in his pale blue eyes, and there and then she was taken by him. Behind that gruff, unfriendly exterior was a young adventurer, and she could picture him, his butterfly net extended, his face flushed with a rare excitement as he very slowly advanced on the elusive specimen that fluttered on a bamboo stem in the steamy jungle clearing.

He moved and broke the spell, the floorboards creaking under his feet as he glanced along the wall. 'It seems a shame,' he remarked almost to himself. 'These mountin's contain some o' nature's most beautiful creatures. They should be put up where everyone can see 'em, but 'ere they are, 'angin' in a dark passage in this grotty little shop.'

Queenie felt bound to reply. 'You've preserved 'em though, John,' she told him. 'In years ter come they could be part of a valuable collection an' on show in some gallery or museum.'

He had smiled briefly before his mask fell back into place. 'It was a fly-paper yer wanted, wasn't it?'

Chapter Nine

Pamela Duggan felt responsible for what had happened to Tom and she had taken the day off work to spend some time with him. Martha Carey was pleased by the concern she had shown, unaware of her guilty secret, and she smiled at the young woman as she ladled tomato soup into a bowl. 'I'll leave it ter you then,' she told her. 'Try an' get it down 'im, luv. It'll do 'im good.'

Pamela carried the tray up to the back bedroom and found Tom slumped against the pillows. 'I've brought yer some soup,' she said encouragingly. ''Ere, let me straighten those pillows.'

Tom winced as he leant forward in the bed. 'I feel stupid stuck in 'ere,' he groused.

'It's the best place fer you, Tom Carey. Now get that soup down yer,' she ordered him.

While he spooned up the soup Pamela sat watching him. His face was a mess, his handsome features swollen out of shape, but he seemed not to have lost his who-gives-a-sod attitude, she thought thankfully. If only she had not gone along to Riley's for that new pair of stockings, she would not have bumped into Bernie in Abbey Street, and would not have been so stupid as to try and make him feel bad by telling him

she was going to the pictures that night with Tom.
He had upset her with his womanising though and
she had been determined to get her own back. When
he told her he was sorry and asked her to go out
with him that evening, she could have just said no
and left it at that, but oh no. Instead she had acted
like a child, and in so doing been the cause of Tom's
injuries, however unwittingly. It was Bernie who had
organised it, it had to be. He and Tom had a score
to settle anyway and he would have been enraged
at the thought of his girl going out with his enemy.
He had certainly looked angry when she told him
about it. Why hadn't she realised something was
wrong when Tom called to tell her he had received
a message from Del Abelson to meet him at the
union offices right away? It had been delivered by
hand, by a complete stranger. That in itself should
have set the warning bells ringing, but to be fair it
had taken Tom in too. He had been as gullible as
she had.

The young man had emptied the soup bowl and as
she took it from him he smiled painfully.

''Ow d'yer feel now, Tom?' she asked with
concern.

'Like I've bin run over by a steamroller,' he
replied.

'It's all my fault,' she said, tears forming in her
green eyes.

'Don't be silly, 'ow's it your fault?' he said
quickly.

'Bernie Catchpole was be'ind what 'appened ter
yer an' it was all my fault,' Pamela told him, tears
starting to fall. 'I saw 'im in Abbey Street yesterday

evenin' an' 'e asked me ter make up, but I told 'im I was goin' out wiv you. Why didn't I keep my big mouth shut?'

Tom smiled through his battered lips. 'Yer fink Bernie Catchpole was the one who got me beaten up, do yer?' he said indulgently. 'Whoever done this were professionals. Bernie don't know those sort o' people. This was Brady's work, Pam, you take my word fer it.'

'I expected yer ter be angry wiv me,' the young woman said, wiping her eyes with a screwed-up handkerchief.

''Ow could I be angry wiv you?' he replied, reaching out slowly to touch her arm.

'You still wanna take me out?'

'Course I do, but not this week.'

She leaned over the bed, gently brushing her lips along his forehead. 'Get some rest, Tom. I'll look in later,' she told him softly.

That Thursday morning three elderly men marched purposefully along Abbey Street and crossed the Tower Bridge Road into Long Lane. Tubby carried a brown paper shopping-bag and Wally had a small parcel under his arm. Benny was carrying a long tube of white paper tied with string.

'I bet they'll be pleased ter get this,' Tubby remarked.

'It ain't much,' Wally replied.

'Every little 'elps, an' besides, it shows we care about our neighbours,' Benny reminded them.

When the three reached Brady's Transport gates they looked at each other in bewilderment. The strikers were nowhere to be seen. There was only one lorry in the yard and they could see a figure crouched on the mudguard with his head over the engine.

'That's Bessie's boy, Patrick,' Benny remarked. 'The bloody strike must be over.'

'Well, that's nice I must say,' Wally moaned. 'There's us bin sweatin' our cods off gettin' vittles fer the strikers an' the bloody turncoats 'ave gone back ter work.'

'P'raps they've got a deal,' Benny said.

'Well – what we gonna do wiv this lot?' Tubby asked them.

'My feet are killin' me,' Wally groaned, 'let's go an' 'ave a sit down.'

The three friends walked on to the wasteground next to the transport yard and sat down on upturned crates that had been left there by the pickets.

'Let's 'ave a look-see,' Tubby said, opening the shopping-bag. 'There's a tin o' peaches, a tin o' carrots, two tins o' baked beans an' a tube o' toofpaste.'

'Who the bloody 'ell donated that?' Wally asked incredulously.

'The same bloke who donated this I should fink,' Tubby said, pulling a small bottle from the bag.

'What is it fer Gawd sake?'

'Galloway's Lung Syrup.'

'I put it in there this mornin',' Benny confessed.

'Who the bloody 'ell donated it?' Wally persisted.

'Cheap Jack.'

'I might 'a' known.'

'One o' the strikers might 'ave 'ad a cough,' Benny said sheepishly.

'Yeah an' they might 'ave decided ter clean their teef while they was picketin' as well,' Wally growled.

'What about the money?' Benny asked.

'There's four an' a tanner an' two foreign coins,' Tubby announced. 'They look like Indian coins. I can't see prop'ly. I ain't brought me glasses.'

'Well, that'll just about buy us a pint each,' Wally remarked. 'Anyfing else ter declare?'

'Mrs Barton gave us these,' Benny said, reluctantly taking two small sachets from his coat pocket.

'What are they?'

'Beecham's Powders.'

'Beecham's Powders? I don't believe it!' Wally exclaimed. 'What wiv them, cough medicine an' toofpaste, all we want is Exlax an' we've got a full 'and.'

'Well, at least we did try,' Benny said quietly.

'Yeah, yer right, ole mate,' Wally replied. 'C'mon, let's go an' get a drink.'

'What we gonna do wiv this bag?' Tubby asked.

'Leave it 'ere,' Wally told him. 'Some ole tramp's gonna 'ave a pleasant surprise.'

''Specially if 'e's got a cough.'

'Or an 'eadache.'

'Shall I leave these banners 'ere as well?' Benny asked.

'Yeah if yer like,' Wally said. ''E might be able ter read.'

The Druid Street arches near Tower Bridge were leased out by the Southern Railway Company to small businesses, and it was there in the end arch that Sue Carey found her elder brother deep in conversation with a colleague when she arrived that afternoon. Maurice looked surprised to see her and he led her into the small office and found her a seat. 'What's the trouble, Sis?' he said as soon as he had closed the door.

Sue told him everything that had happened and Maurice's wide, handsome face took on a dark look. 'They should know better than ter mess Joe Brady about,' he said, sitting down on the edge of his cluttered desk. ''E's brought some muscle in ter break the strike, that's fer sure.'

'We don't know for certain if it is Brady's doing,' Sue replied. 'You know how quick-tempered Tom is. It might be Pamela Duggan's boyfriend who's responsible. Tom and Bernie got into a fight at the Palais on Saturday night and it would have got nasty if Del hadn't pulled them apart. Our Tom's keen on Pamela and Bernie knows it. He could have got someone to do his dirty work for him.'

Maurice gave her an old-fashioned smile. 'Come on, Sue, yer don't really fink Bernie Catchpole set Tom up, do yer?' he asked.

'Not really. But if it was Brady's doing why pick on our Tom?' she said quickly. 'Why not Del Abelson? After all, he's the shop steward. He's the one who's brought the men out.'

Maurice leaned forward, his dark eyes narrowing. 'Joe Brady's no fool,' he told her. 'It'd be too obvious fer 'im to 'ave your feller duffed up. With Tom it could be put down ter some private beef. Plus the fact that Tom's a bit Bolshy. Take it from me it's Brady's doin'. The rest o' the men are gonna bottle out an' creep back ter work after this, if they 'aven't already done so.'

Sue leaned back in her chair, eyeing her brother

keenly. 'You'll call in and see Tom, won't you, Mo,' she said a little gingerly. 'Maybe he'll tell you more than he's told us.'

Maurice nodded. 'Yeah, I'll call round this evenin',' he replied.

'And do me a favour, Mo,' she added. 'Don't get arguing with Dad again. Every time you call in it seems to end up in an argument. I just can't understand it.'

He smiled cynically. 'It takes two to argue. It's not always me that starts it.'

'I know,' she said sighing. 'Just don't pick Dad up on what he might say. He's worried enough about Tom without falling out with you again.'

'Just a moment,' he told her as he stood up and limped over to open the door. 'Stan? Is that order ready fer termorrer? Right. Can yer slip over the café an' get us two mugs o' tea.'

'I can't stop long, I've got to get home,' Sue told him.

Maurice hobbled back to sit down in his high-backed desk chair. 'You've got time fer a cuppa,' he replied. 'I don't see much of yer these days.'

'We don't see much of you, either,' she answered pointedly. 'I thought you might have called round last Saturday. It was Aunt Ellie's birthday and she was hoping you'd come.'

He pulled a face and smiled briefly, his strong white teeth flashing in the half-light. 'I wanted to, but I was out o' London on business,' he told her. 'Did it go off all right?'

'There were a few tears, but it wouldn't be Aunt Ellie if there weren't,' she said, smiling back at him.

'Poor Aunt Ellie. Is it too late fer a few flowers?'

'I don't think so. She'll be thrilled you didn't forget her.'

Maurice took two one-pound notes from his back pocket. ''Ere, get 'er some, an' a big box o' chocolates,' he said. 'Is that enough?'

'More than enough.'

He sighed and let the chair move back on its springs. 'I'll try ter come round more often,' he told her. 'I promise.'

Sue gave him an enquiring look. 'I wish I could fathom it all out,' she said quietly. 'Me and Tom often talk about the way you and Dad are when you get together. Every time I ask you about it you palm me off, and Dad's the same. It must have been something that happened between you two during the war, while me and Tom were in the services. Before the war we were a close family. Things were so different then.'

The door opened and Stan came in carrying two mugs of tea. 'There we are,' he said, smiling at Sue as he placed them down on the edge of the desk.

'Cheers,' Maurice said as he pulled one of the mugs towards him. 'By the way, Stan, get that tinned food order ready when yer get five minutes. They're comin' fer it this evenin'.'

'You seem very busy,' Sue remarked as she picked up her tea.

'Not enough hours in the day,' he replied.

'You will try to call in this evening?' she reminded him.

'I said I would, didn't I?'

She smiled briefly. 'I'll hold you to it.'

Maurice took another gulp from the mug and then

set it down on the desk. 'Yer know, Sue, you an' Tom were very fortunate in bein' able ter go in the services,' he said after a while. 'I only wish I could 'ave gone in. I would 'ave volunteered at the off. I fancied the Navy as a matter o' fact. This bloody foot o' mine certainly put the damp'ner on that.'

Sue eyed him sternly as she put her mug down on the desktop. 'Don't go getting all sorry for yourself again, Mo,' she said quickly. 'That injury could have been a blessing in disguise. You might have joined up and been killed in the war.'

''Ow many times 'ave I 'eard that,' he replied.

'Well, it's true.'

He nodded and then glanced momentarily at the sheaf of papers in front of him. 'What was that you said about gettin' 'ome?' he remarked with a comical grin.

Sue got up from her chair and gave him an indulgent smile. 'All right, I know when I've outstayed my welcome,' she told him.

'I'm a bit snowed under, Sis, but I will call in this evenin'.'

'You'd better.'

He smiled as he went to the arch door and stood watching as she stepped out along the street. It wasn't very nice that she and Tom were kept in the dark about that night during the Blitz, but the promise had been made. At least they had been spared the family shame and the heartache the tragedy had wrought. Maybe one day, in the future when they were all old and the war was just a distant memory, the truth would out. The passage of time would lessen the shock and make it easier to absorb.

Stan was waiting back in the office. 'What about that shipment due from the docks?' he asked. 'Brady's Transport are the carriers, ain't they?'

Maurice nodded. 'It should be arrivin' any minute now.'

'But I thought 'is drivers were on strike,' Stan said, looking puzzled.

'They were,' Maurice replied. 'I got a call an hour or so ago. They went back ter work this mornin'.'

Chapter Ten

A light was burning late on Thursday evening at the union office in Tooley Street. With the wharves closed and the thoroughfare deserted, only the rumble of a late tram disturbed the quietness. In the small cluttered room Robbie Casey folded his hands on the desk and waited patiently for a reply from his visitor. 'If yer wanna go 'ome an' sleep on it, Del, it's okay by me,' he said finally, 'but ter be honest I'd like yer answer 'ere an' now. Fings are movin' fast, an' wiv all this road nationalisation takin' place there's a lot ter be done.'

Del Abelson nodded. 'I understand what yer sayin', Robbie,' he replied. 'It's just that I feel like a rat leavin' a sinkin' ship. Wiv the strike crumblin' the way it did this mornin', Brady's gonna be crackin' the whip. You know the score. Any little upset or disagreement an' the man concerned is gonna find 'imself reportin' down the labour exchange.'

'An' you fink it'll be any different wiv you there?' Casey said with a cynical smile. 'Be realistic, man. Brady's confident that Tom Carey gettin' duffed up 'as put the fear inter those drivers. They won't be too keen ter walk out the door again. You'd be on a loser, an' before yer knew it they'd be votin' in anuvver shop steward, one who'd be in Brady's pocket. Take it from me, Del, yer'll be much more effective workin' full-time fer the union. This job is tailor-made fer you. Yer'll be able ter get involved in unionisin' the transport workers throughout the area an' yer'll be directly responsible ter me. We can work tergevver, son. You fink like I do, an' you 'ave the dedication. What's more yer can fight Joe Brady an' 'is ilk best by increasin' the membership. We'll 'ave strength in place o' weakness an' bad bosses won't dare use the sort o' tactics that were used on Tom Carey. They'd go out o' business.'

Del knew that Robbie Casey was making sense. The convenor had been right when he advised against the walkout, wanting more time to open up Joe Brady to talks on conditions at the firm as well as union recognition for the new depot. He had warned that the strike would crumble after a few days and he had been right. When Del had told the pickets first thing that morning about what happened to Tom Carey they had been visibly frightened and caved in, and nothing he could say would make them change their minds. Those on the picket lines had decided to return to work, and with one last attempt to make them change their minds he had called a meeting for ten o'clock.

The young shop steward recalled how bad he had felt having to walk through the gates to face Brady with the news that the men had decided to return to work. Fortunately he was spared the final indignity when Toby Lowndes the transport manager told him that Brady was away for the day. The return was less painful than he had imagined it would be, but it was obvious that Joe Brady would have a few words to say before the men took their lorries out of the yard on Friday morning.

'So what's it gonna be?' Robbie Casey asked, cutting across his thoughts.

Del looked up at the wizened face of the elderly convenor and smiled. 'I'll be ready ter start on Monday mornin',' he replied.

Robbie looked pleased. 'What about yer week's notice? Will Brady insist on it?'

Del's smile grew wider. 'I shouldn't fink so.'

Robbie Casey reached down into his desk drawer and took out a bottle of whisky. 'I fink we should drink to a successful partnership,' he said. 'Pass me those two glasses over, will yer?'

Del watched as the convenor poured out the spirit. 'What about Tom Carey?' he asked. 'Is there anyfing at all we can do?'

Robbie shrugged his shoulders. 'I'll be talkin' to our legal people, but it's very dicey,' he replied. 'All we've got ter go on is what those geezers said ter you. There was only Tom there ter back yer up an' yer said yerself 'e was out cold at the time.'

Del nodded, his expression hardening. 'I'm gonna be seein' a certain bloke when I leave 'ere,' he said with anger in his voice. 'Maybe 'e'll be of some assistance.'

The convenor looked worried. 'Don't go jeopardisin' yer position, son,' he warned. 'If you openly accuse Brady o' bein' responsible fer what 'appened yer leave yerself right in the cart, an' bang goes this job before yer even get yer feet under the desk.'

Del drained his glass before replying. 'Don't worry, Robbie,' he said, pulling a face as the whisky burned his throat. 'I'll be very careful.'

*   *   *

The late April evening had grown chilly and a fire had been lit in the Careys' parlour. Ellie Emberson sat with a woollen shawl draped over her thin shoulders as she worked at her embroidery. 'I've been feeling the cold lately,' she remarked. 'They say you feel the cold as you get older.'

Sue hid a smile. 'You're not old, Aunt Ellie,' she said kindly. 'In fact you don't look anywhere near your age.'

The spinster looked up over her glasses and allowed herself a brief smile. 'Well, I feel my age,' she replied. 'And these places are really draughty. That room of mine is like an ice box. God knows what I'm going to do next winter, if I live as long.'

Sue raised her eyes to the ceiling as her mother walked into the parlour. 'Have you seen how Aunt Ellie's embroidery's coming on, Mum?' she asked.

Martha realised that her daughter was trying to change the conversation, and she had a good idea why. 'It's really lovely. I don't know 'ow yer manage them tiny stitches, Ellie,' she remarked.

'Practice makes perfect.'

'I know, but I don't get much time ter practise.'

'Nonsense.'

'Anyway, me eyes wouldn't stand the strain.'

'Well, you should get them looked at.'

'I've got readin' glasses already.'

Ellie felt it was useless to pursue the matter, and putting down her embroidery she took off her glasses to clean them on the lace handkerchief she had tucked up the sleeve of her dress. 'It's no use you pottering around, he won't show up,' she said with conviction.

Martha looked peeved. 'Ellie, I'm only straightenin' the sideboard,' she told her quickly. 'I'm not doin' it fer Mo's sake, I'm doin' it because the sideboard needs it.'

Sue crossed her legs and massaged the sole of her foot. 'Mo'll be here, you'll see, Aunt Ellie,' she said. 'He promised.'

The spinster snorted. 'I've learned to take Maurice's promises a little lightly. I remember how he promised faithfully he wouldn't forget my birthday, but he did.'

'He told me he was sorry, Aunt Ellie, but he did send you those nice flowers, and the chocolates.'

'Almost a week late, but perhaps I shouldn't complain. The thought was there I suppose,' Ellie replied flatly.

Martha knew from experience that her sister was intent on depressing herself and everyone else around her that evening and she decided to use a little guile. 'Tell Sue about those parties you used to 'ave when you was in service,' she said, giving her daughter a surreptitious wink.

Ellie shook her head slowly as she gathered her thoughts. 'It was another world then,' she said with a distant look in her eyes. 'When I first went into service I was just a housemaid, but Mrs Grimshaw soon saw that I was eager to learn. She was the housekeeper and she ruled the servants with a rod of iron. She could be very hard at times, but underneath she had a heart of gold. She knew all our birthdays too and she would be sure to make us a nice cake on the day. There was always a little present too. Lord Langley allowed us the use of the music room whenever it was one of our birthdays and we used to gather round the piano while Constantia played a selection of popular melodies.'

Sue suppressed a yawn. 'Who was Constantia?' she asked.

'Constantia was Lord Langley's eldest daughter,' Ellie said in a voice that suggested Sue should have known. 'She had a wonderful touch and it always brought tears to my eyes. Anyway, on birthdays we were allowed the evening off. Mrs Grimshaw was very good in that way. Very motherly, she was, though she could be very strict. I remember when she overheard one of the grooms discussing Constantia's misfortune with a tradesman and she immediately got the man dismissed.'

'Did he take advantage of Constantia?' Sue asked, trying to sound shocked at the revelation.

'Did who take advantage?'

'The tradesman.'

Ellie puffed irritably. 'No, no. The groom was talking to the tradesman about Constantia.'

Martha sat down at the table and rested her chin in her cupped hand. 'About 'er misfortune.'

Ellie gave her sister a quick look. 'Yes. Anyway the groom went and the tradesman was told never to show his face there again.'

'What was Constantia's misfortune?' Sue asked.

'Her lover made her ill,' Ellie said solemnly.

''E gave 'er a dose,' Martha cut in.

Ellie glared at her sister. 'Do you have to be so coarse, Martha?' she remonstrated.

'In my book syphilis is a dose, an' that's what the dirty git gave 'er, accordin' ter you,' Martha said defiantly.

Sue swallowed hard in an attempt to stop herself laughing aloud. 'Tell me about that lover of hers, Aunt Ellie,' she encouraged her as soon as she had controlled herself. 'Was he a sailor?'

'He was a ship's captain,' Ellie went on. 'He was so handsome. All the servants used to swoon over him, and Constantia was besotted by him. He came to stay with the Langleys and it was then that they became lovers. It was obvious to us all.'

'An' that's when 'e gave 'er a dose,' Martha added.

Ellie did not look at her. 'That's when it happened,' she continued. 'The captain went back to sea and when his ship arrived back in Liverpool some months later Lord Langley was waiting on the quayside. Word had it that he challenged the captain to a duel but the police were sent for and it was all hushed up. If the papers had got word there would have been a terrible scandal.'

'You could 'ave made a few bob out o' that story,' Martha told her jokingly. 'I can see it now. "Maid's Revelations." Yer missed yer chance there, gel.'

Ellie was about to make an angry response but Sue intervened. 'What about Constantia? Did she get better?'

'Fortunately she was cured, but she was never the same after that ordeal,' Ellie said gravely. 'She ended up marrying a man much older than herself.'

Martha's eyes were beginning to droop as she leant on the table. 'A seventy-year-old undertaker,' she added wearily. 'I s'pose she thought she was pretty safe wiv 'im.'

'How terrible,' Sue said, stifling a yawn.

'That should teach yer a lesson, my gel,' Martha remarked. 'Never trust a sailor.'

Ellie was about to reproach her older sister for her flippancy when there was a knock at the door.

'That'll be Mo,' Sue said quickly as she got up from her chair.

The tall dark figure filled the parlour doorway as he stood there for a brief moment. He smiled as he limped over to Ellie and planted a kiss on her cheek. 'Sorry I couldn't get ter yer birfday, Aunt Ellie,' he said sweetly. 'Yer look very well.' Then he turned and laid a hand on his mother's arm. ''Ow's Tom?'

''E's not too bad, apart from aches an' pains,' she told him. ''E was awake a little while ago. Pop up an' see 'im.'

Ellie Emberson had a soft spot for Maurice, though she would have been the last to admit it, and Martha had noticed how she seemed to come to life whenever he did call on them. Tonight was no exception and Ellie was smiling as she looked up at the tall, handsome young man. 'Sit down first and catch your breath,' she bade him.

Sue gave up her fireside chair for him and he gave her a wink. 'Told yer I'd come round, didn't I,' he said as he made himself comfortable facing Ellie.

'What have you been up to?' the spinster asked him.

'This and that, Aunt Ellie,' he told her. 'And what about you?'

Before Ellie could get going Martha got up. 'I'll put the kettle on,' she said.

Sue followed her mother into the scullery. 'I can't listen to any more of Aunt Ellie's revelations,' she said, grinning.

Martha pulled a face as she lit the gas under the large

copper kettle. 'I wish Mo was as patient wiv yer farvver as 'e is wiv Ellie an' 'er rural rides,' she sighed.

Sue could hear her aunt's voice babbling on as she sat down at the small table. 'Notice Mo never asked where Dad was,' she remarked.

'I don't believe yer farvver went up the pub just because 'e knew Mo might be comin',' Martha replied. 'There's a darts match at the Bell ternight.'

'There's nothing stopping Mo looking in there later,' Sue said, frowning. 'I think I'll tell him if he does ask.'

Martha made the tea and took her son's favourite mug down from the dresser, filling it with the steaming brew. 'Take this up ter Tom, will yer, luv,' she said.

The invalid smiled painfully as his sister put the mug of tea down on the small cabinet beside his bed. 'Was that Mo's voice I 'eard?' he asked.

Sue nodded. 'Aunt Ellie's captured him,' she replied. 'He'll be up in a minute.'

'I'm surprised 'e's found the time,' he said with a sarcastic edge to his voice.

Sue gave him a searching look. 'Don't give him any grief, Tom,' she pleaded. 'It's bad enough as it is with him and Dad without you making him feel he's not welcome.'

Tom smiled reassuringly. 'Don't worry, I'll make 'im welcome.'

She sat down on the edge of the bed. 'What do you intend to do now, Bruv?' she asked him. 'You won't be going back to Brady's, will you?'

'Course I will,' he said quickly. ''E's not gonna frighten me inter leavin'. I'll chuck it in when I'm ready, as soon as I find a better job. If 'e wants me out 'e's gonna 'ave ter sack me, an' 'e'll need a reason.'

'He'll find one I'm sure.'

Tom winced as he reached for his tea. 'I thought yer'd be out ternight,' he remarked.

Sue shrugged her shoulders. 'Del's busy.'

Tom gave her a look of concern. 'Don't lay any blame at Del's door fer what 'appened ter me, Sis,' he urged her. 'Del's a good lad an' 'e's dedicated. If it wasn't fer people like 'im the Bradys o' this world would walk all over their workers.'

'Well, it hasn't stopped you being walked all over, has it?' she scolded gently.

He smiled at her concerned expression then his face became serious. 'If Paddy O'Brian was right an' Brady 'as recruited some muscle then it don't stay there,' he told her. 'A few more bosses might well follow 'is lead. It could get very nasty. I'm sure Del Abelson's aware of it an' 'e's gonna be on 'is guard. Be patient, Sue. Del's a diamond.'

Sue got up from the bed and gave him a warm smile as she paused in the doorway. 'I know, Tom,' she replied. 'I just wish I didn't feel like I'm losing him to that bloody union.'

Chapter Eleven

Del Abelson had mixed feelings as he left the union office and caught a tram to Rotherhithe. The aborted strike and what had happened to Tom Carey had left him drained and depressed, but he also felt a new sense of excitement building up inside him. Robbie Casey was right. He could do more working inside the union than merely representing a small and isolated group of workers. Now though he had to concentrate on the task in hand, be absolutely sure of what he was up against, and he needed answers.

The Rising Sun near the Surrey Docks catered for merchant seamen from the Russian and Scandinavian timber ships and its public bar was always packed. The saloon bar was comparatively quiet however, and when Del Abelson stepped down from the tram directly outside the pub and pushed open the door of the carpeted bar he saw Toby Lowndes immediately. He was sitting alone, a full pint at his elbow.

'It's bin a bad day, Toby,' Del said as he walked up to the table.

Brady's transport manager looked up in surprise. ''Ello, Del. What you doin' down this way?' he asked.

'We need ter talk,' the young man told him. 'What yer drinkin'?'

Toby shook his head. 'I'm okay.'

Del went to the bar and came back with a pint of bitter. 'I need some information,' he said as he sat down facing the older man.

Toby frowned. 'Information? What sort of information?'

Del leaned forward over the table, his eyes glaring. 'I wanna know about those visitors Brady 'ad. Who were they?'

Toby Lowndes looked down at his glass. 'Brady gets a lot o' visitors. I don't ask who they are, it's none o' my business,' he replied.

'You know who I'm talkin' about,' Del said quickly. 'Two men called in at your office on Monday an' one of 'em 'appens ter be a villain from over the water by the name of Lennie Donald.'

'I s'pose they were after doin' some legit business. I wasn't included in the conversation,' Toby told him.

Del's face took on an angry cast. 'The only business they were on was thuggery,' he growled. 'I know that Joe Brady recruited 'em ter break the strike. They were responsible fer Tom Carey's beatin', but I can't prove it.'

'So what d'yer want from me?' Toby asked directly. 'Yer don't expect me ter give yer the proof yer need, do yer? I couldn't, even if I wanted to. I work fer Brady the same as you do. 'Ow long d'yer fink I'd last if Brady found out I'd bin sittin' 'ere talkin' ter you?'

Del leaned back in his chair and sighed. 'Yer've always bin fair wiv me an' the men, Toby, an' yer've sometimes gone out of yer way ter keep the peace,' he said mollifyingly. 'I feel I can trust yer, an' this conversation is strictly between us two. I've bin offered a full-time job wiv the union startin' on Monday, an' I've accepted it, but I wanna know just what I'm up against. I'm pretty certain that what 'appened ter Tom Carey ain't gonna be a one-off. I've got this gut feelin' that Brady's linin' up wiv certain employers in the area who are all opposed ter their men joinin' the union, an' 'e wants muscle ter back 'em. If that's allowed to 'appen the union'll be fightin' a losin' battle, unless it's all exposed.'

Toby puffed loudly. 'I shouldn't be tellin' yer this, Del,' he said quietly. 'This is big, very big. We're not talkin' about a few 'ard men, we're talkin' about organised crime. The little I know about it 'as bin frew keepin' me ears an' eyes open, the same as you. Brady was in the East End terday, that much 'e told me, an' I can only assume it was ter do wiv that meetin' in the office on Monday. There's bin a lot o' phone calls lately, before the strike. Brady's bin doin' a lot of entertainin' as well. But I've said enough already. I've got no desire to end up in the river.'

Del Abelson nodded. 'I wanted ter know I was on the right track, an' what yer've just said reinforces it. I appreciate it, Toby, an' don't lose any sleep over it. I never met yer ternight.'

'Too true. That way we'll both stay alive a little longer,' the transport manager said with a weak smile.

Totterdown Street was much like any other Bermondsey backstreet, with good neighbourly folk, busybodies, and others who tended to keep their personal lives private. It also had its share of animosities and feuds, and there were families who for one reason or another spent most of their time at each other's throats.

The Sloans and the Barlows came into the last category. They were blood relatives, and had lived in the same slum buildings in Dockhead until a German bomb flattened them at the height of the Blitz. The people who had been living there were saddened in many ways. Most of them had been in the nearby shelter when the buildings were hit, and although they were happy to have survived they knew that they would be rehoused in other parts of the borough, separated from their neighbours of long standing in many cases. Things would be different now. Never again would they hear the cry, 'The Barlows and the Sloans are at it again.' Never again would they look over their balconies and out of their windows on Saturday nights after the pubs had turned out to see Annie Barlow and Minnie Sloan having a set-to on the cobbles. No more would they witness the sight of Alf Barlow and Micky Sloan squaring up to each other after a heavy drinking session and struggling to keep their feet.

Annie and Minnie were first cousins but they had never been able to agree on anything since they were kids, and though it was generally agreed that blood was thicker than water, it did not stop them from fighting like alley cats whenever the mood took them, which was pretty often. Their husbands Alf and Micky drank together, shared a joke and generally got on well, until the womenfolk fell out. Being loyal to their spouses the men got at it too, but fortunately they were usually too drunk to cause each other much harm. In fact when one fell over, which was usually through the drink rather than a blow, the other would stretch out a helping hand, and then the shaping-up would resume.

When Annie Barlow was interviewed for resettlement after the buildings were flattened it just so happened to coincide with a bad period of family relations. Annie was sporting a bruised lip at the time and she was adamant. 'I don't care where yer put us, as long as it's as far away from that scatty mare Minnie Sloan as possible,' she growled.

Her warring cousin was just as firm. 'Yer can put us where yer like, as long as I don't 'ave ter see that ugly cow Annie Barlow every day,' she said with venom.

The rehousing officer was hard put to it to find any accommodation at all, what with the ever-growing list of homeless, and the special needs of the sort presented to him cut no ice. His assistant felt compelled to point out, however, that as the Sloans were earmarked for number 19 Totterdown Street it might be imprudent to house the Barlows at number 20. 'After all, next-door neighbours are supposed to get on,' he remarked.

The rehousing officer was not to be swayed. He happened to know that in Totterdown Street the numbers ran in evens on one side and odds on the other. At least they wouldn't be sharing a wall that they could both bang on, he decided. The fact that the two terraced houses faced each other across the street was of little concern to him. With thousands of homeless people desperate for a home Minnie Sloan would have to put up with seeing 'that ugly cow Annie Barlow' every day.

So it came to pass that in the spring of 1941 the Sloans and the Barlows were installed as Totterdown dwellers, and at the very beginning the two families did their best to create a good impression on their new neighbours by observing a truce. They felt that apart from Granny Minto, who only talked when she felt like it, and Bessie Woodward, who talked incessantly, the Totterdown folk seemed a very nice crowd. It wasn't very long, however, before the fragile ceasefire was broken and hostilities recommenced. The Barlows and the Sloans were at it again.

The warring families soon gained the same old name in their new surroundings, though their neighbours got on with them very well on the whole. The battles were always confined to the two cousins and their spouses and outsiders were never involved. What was more, they were all getting older, and the battles had become less frequent since the end of the war, though occasionally on a Saturday night the war cry went up. Very soon, however, the combatants were destined to enjoy some fame, which would serve to bond them together – for a time.

On Friday morning before the daily work sheets were given out at the Brady Transport yard the men were summoned into the hangar-like lorry shed. They stood around for a few minutes before Joe Brady sauntered in, his bulky frame dwarfing the transport manager who stood at his side.

'Right now, lads, the strike's over an' done wiv,' he began, 'an' as far as I'm concerned there's no ill feelin'. Yer've got work ter do an' there'll be a bit of overtime goin'. As fer yesterday, I've decided ter pay you all a full day's money as a show o' goodwill. Yer'll also know that there's a vacancy fer a shop steward. I'm quite prepared ter let yer pick a replacement fer Del Abelson, an' provided I agree wiv yer choice there'll be no problem. One fing more. I understand from Toby that Tom Carey's off sick after bein' set about, an' I wanna make it clear that despite what yer might 'ear ter the contrary, what 'appened to 'im 'ad nuffink whatsoever ter do wiv the strike. It was a private matter an' no concern o' this firm. Let me tell yer 'ere an' now that 'is job's still 'ere fer 'im, an' I'd like yer all ter know that Toby's gonna be 'oldin' a collection fer the lad. Yer can put a few coppers in as soon as yer get yer wages ternight. I'm sure it'll be appreciated. Right, that's all. Now let's get back ter work.'

As Brady and his dutiful transport manager walked out of the shed the murmur of voices grew.

'Who the bloody 'ell's gonna put 'imself in the frame now?' one driver growled.

'That's a bloody disgrace what 'e said,' another man said angrily. 'Whoever we pick as shop steward 'as gotta be okayed by 'im.'

Del Abelson smiled as he listened to the angry comments. 'My advice ter you lot is, pick the man yer feel can do a decent job for yer, an' if Brady gives yer any grief get on ter the union straight away,' he told them firmly. 'Remember, you 'ave the right ter pick who yer want, not who 'e wants.'

'An' if Brady gives us any grief what do we do, go out on the cobbles again?' the first driver said sarcastically.

'We're cattled an' Brady knows it,' the second man grunted.

'It's a bad time fer you ter leave us roastin',' another driver said resentfully, rounding on Del.

The young steward raised his hands for attention. 'Now look, listen ter me,' he said calmly. 'You all voted fer a strike, but as soon as yer found out about Tom Carey gettin' beaten up yer couldn't wait ter run back ter work. Anyfing that 'appens to yer now yer brought on yerself. By lettin' yerself be bullied inter submission yer've undone a lot o' good. I only 'ope Brady don't decide ter bring in a few o' those non-union geezers from Barley Lane. What yer gonna do then? Yer gonna work alongside 'em, or make a stand? The choice'll be yours. Make the wrong decision an' yer'll be lookin' fer work in no time at all.'

The men left the shed looking a little crestfallen, and as Del Abelson made to follow them Bernie Catchpole called him back. 'You an' me never got on very well, but there's a few fings that need ter be said,' he remarked. 'In the first place, I want yer ter know that it wasn't any o' my doin' that Tom Carey got sorted out. I know me an' 'im 'ave got a private score ter settle, but that's strictly private, I fight me own fights. Brady's bin gettin' all the news from one o' the drivers. 'E knew that Carey was right be'ind yer, an' 'e knew as well that we'd 'ad a bust-up. As fer the strike I was dead against it. Don't get me wrong, I ain't 'appy wiv what Brady's gettin' away wiv, it's just that I knew this bottly crew wouldn't last five minutes on the cobbles.'

Del looked at him with contempt. 'Don't you fink they might 'ave felt the same about you?' he countered. 'You didn't encourage anyone wiv the way you was mouthin' off.'

Bernie shrugged his shoulders. 'I dunno. Maybe you're right. Anyway I'm out of 'ere as soon as I get somefing else. No 'ard feelin's. Best o' luck wiv the new job.'

Del clasped Bernie's outstretched hand. 'In the meantime why don't you put yer name down fer the shop steward's job?' he suggested with a brief smile.

'I'm not that stupid,' Bernie growled as he walked away.

Frances Miller had worked for the *Bulletin* for more than twenty years now and she was worried about its decline. She remembered how vibrant the office had once been, and how she had been kept busy dealing with the constant demands for advertising space. Large firms had used the paper to promote their business, and private individuals called in to place personal messages in the columns. Now though it was all so different. Most of her time was spent running errands and doing research for the reporting staff. The basement where the old copies of the paper were stored had become a glory hole for her. Everyone in the office knew that if she wasn't at her desk she could be found in the basement, surrounded by the past.

On Friday morning Frances Miller was gathering together all the information she had promised Paddy O'Brian, and as she sat at a dusty table beneath a bare light bulb she fretted. She was turned forty and still single. There had not been many men in her life, and the few who had dated her had soon been frightened off by her obstinate, spiteful mother, who had seemed intent on keeping her only daughter tied to her apron-strings for the rest of her life. Frances was quite aware that she was no oil painting, but she felt that she had much to offer in other ways, if only one young man could have braved her mother's tirades. She was a home-maker, and she could have loved a man fully, if only it wasn't too late.

Paddy was always asking her to find something or other and he was always very nice about it. She suddenly found herself thinking how wonderful it would be if he came down into the basement while she was alone there with the musty, dusty files and sundry records. Maybe then she could tell him how much she liked his articles, how much she admired him and how lovely it would be if they could share their thoughts over a quiet drink one evening. After all, Paddy liked a drink, and he lived alone. He was about her age as well, give or take a year or two. She was willing to wager too that he would want to see her again, once he learned a little more about her and her desires and aspirations.

Frances put the paper clippings into a large envelope and sealed it. There wasn't much of importance, she had to admit. The Brady Transport firm was an old-established concern with nothing to excite or intrigue about it. Maybe Paddy would spot something to assist him, but in any case she had done his bidding and she was happy to have done so. Maybe she should be more forthright. Perhaps she should copy Josie Willard who greeted all the men by fluttering her eyelashes and giving them one of those toothy smiles that they all seemed to like. Maybe then he would show some interest in her, instead of merely using her as his fetch and carry person.

When Paddy O'Brian walked into the office Frances gave him a broad smile and fluttered her eyelashes a little, which caused him to frown. 'Something in your eye, Franny?' he asked.

'There's what you asked for,' she said curtly, wanting to scream at him.

Normally he would give her a brisk smile and hurry over to his outrageously cluttered desk, but this morning he dallied. 'Franny, have you ever had the feeling that the Sword of Damocles was suspended over your head?' he asked her after a moment or two.

Her look of puzzlement made him go on. 'According to legend it was supposed to have hung by a single hair and it threatened the most prosperous. Now yours truly is not prosperous in a monetary sense, but I consider myself prosperous in that I have a job which I enjoy doing and people around me like your good self who do my bidding willingly. Therein lies my good fortune, but I fear that very soon that single hair will suddenly snap.'

'You mean when the new reporter starts work?' she answered.

'You've got it in one.'

'I think you're being a little premature,' Frances told him, feeling that maybe fluttering her eyelashes had worked a little after all.

'I think I'm for the chop, like a side of beef in a butcher's shop, dear lady,' he said smiling.

Frances sighed inwardly. It wasn't her eyelashes, it was the drink, she decided. Nevertheless her chance had come and she had to take it. 'If you feel that you need to talk to someone about it I'm a good listener, but not here,' she replied, aware that her heart was starting to pound.

'Tonight then, after work,' he said quickly, his eyes widening theatrically as he moved away from her desk.

Frances could not decide whether to burst into tears or scream out in frustration. He was mocking her, ignoring the shoulder she had offered him. Well, good riddance should the sword fall on him.

It was then that she noticed he hadn't taken the envelope. She looked over towards his desk and saw him leaning forward with his head buried in his hands, and she reached into her handbag before going over to him. 'There's the envelope you wanted urgently,' she said sarcastically, and then with some feeling she added, 'here, take these. They're good for headaches.'

Paddy nodded his thanks and turned to watch her walk back to her desk. Nice legs, he told himself. Pity about those awful stockings she wears. Heart of gold though. Shouldn't think she has much of a life, according to what Josie Willard has said. Never mind, he would go over and speak to her sensibly, not in riddles. The poor woman must have thought he was losing his marbles.

'Franny, would you do me the honour of having a quiet drink with me after work?' he asked her in a serious tone of voice.

'Yes, of course,' she said as her heart leapt.

Chapter Twelve

Sue Carey moved closer to him in the darkness of the back row as the screen lovers embraced and Del's arm tightened around her shoulders. The kiss lingered as the music increased and someone sitting nearby sighed.

'Take me away from all this, Joel,' the heroine pleaded as she looked into the cavalry officer's dark, smouldering eyes.

The fêted star of the silver screen stepped back a pace, his eyes slowly surveying the line of bodies beside the wagon, then he looked down at her, his face a dark mask. 'They'll be back soon. We must stay and fight,' he said in a deep, resonant voice, obviously untroubled by the wound to his forehead which had been expertly bandaged.

'But we are the only ones left,' she sighed. 'The whole wagon train slaughtered. Everyone gone.'

Sue was sure that one of the bodies lying in the sun had suddenly moved and she had to stop herself laughing aloud.

'They're coming back. Quick, behind the wagon,' the hero ordered as he slipped his arm around her waist. 'Don't worry, my dearest. I won't let them take us alive. I'll save two bullets for us.'

Sue was getting more and more irritated and she

puffed heavily. 'There are only six bullets in that gun,' she whispered in Del's ear, 'and look at those Indians coming over the rise. There must be thousands of them.'

Del hushed her, ready for the climax as the officer opened fire. Sue counted ten shots and straightened in her seat, only to see the Red Indian braves stop in a line some way from the overturned wagon.

'What's the matter with them?' she whispered. 'Why don't they finish the job?'

Suddenly the screen was full of galloping horsemen as the Fifth Cavalry charged into view and the Indians rode off. The hero laughed hysterically, Sue thought, and the heroine swooned in his arms. The young woman sitting nearby sighed loudly again and Sue giggled as the hero swept the maiden up into his arms and carried her towards the wagon. Del turned and grinned. 'What a load o' rubbish,' he said as the credits started to roll.

They left the cinema and Sue clung on his arm. 'I wish we'd gone dancing instead,' she told him as they crossed the road.

'Let's get a drink,' he suggested.

They sat together in the quiet pub and after taking a sip of her gin and lime Sue glanced around the bar. 'This is a dead and alive place for a Saturday night,' she remarked.

Del shrugged his shoulders. 'We wouldn't 'ave got a seat if we'd 'ave gone back ter the Bell.'

'At least it's lively,' she replied a little pointedly.

Del gave her a quizzical look. 'Are you all right?' he asked her. 'You seem a bit on edge ternight.'

'I'm not on edge. I'm just a bit fed up,' she replied.

'Is it somefing I've said?' he asked quickly.

'No it's just me, just the way I feel.'

'Is it somefing I've done?'

'Del, will you leave it,' she told him, her voice raised slightly.

'All right, there's no need ter get shirty,' he said sharply.

'Who's shirty?'

He took a gulp from his glass of beer and then met her gaze. '''As this got anyfing ter do wiv me takin' that job at the union?' he asked.

'Look, Del, this is getting stupid. Just leave it, will you.'

'I need ter know,' he told her.

She took another sip from her glass and set it down on the table carefully. 'How long have we been going out together, Del?' she asked.

'I dunno. Two months, three months.'

'It's four months to be exact,' she said coolly. 'We seemed to be getting close, but for the past couple of weeks we've just been marking time. I've hardly seen anything of you during the week and then we spend Saturday night watching a stupid film. What's more, we come in a dump like this and sit arguing. We're getting nowhere fast, Del.'

He stared down at his glass for a few moments then he looked up at her. 'Yeah, I s'pose you're right,' he conceded. 'It's just that I've bin very busy wiv one fing an' anuvver lately. I feel a bit jaded.'

'It shows,' she answered.

'Would yer prefer it if we didn't see each ovver fer the time bein'?' he asked.

'No I wouldn't,' she said firmly. 'I want us to get

back to where we were before all this union work got
in the way. When we first started going out together
I had to fight you off. Now, I can't get you to hold
me properly, to even kiss me the way you did at the
beginning.'

'I'm sorry,' he said with a sad look in his dark
eyes.

'Tell me, Del. Do you honestly still want us to be
together? Do you still fancy me?'

'I fink yer know the answer wivout me spellin' it
out ter yer,' he said quietly. 'Of course I want us ter be
tergevver. When we're apart I can't stop finkin' about
yer. Yer always in me thoughts.'

'Then let's get away for a few days,' Sue said
impulsively. 'Let's spend some time together without
having to worry about anything except us.'

He reached his hand across the table and closed
it over hers, his handsome face coming alive with
a smile. 'Let's do it soon, very soon.'

They left the pub and Sue slipped her arm through
his as they walked slowly along the New Kent Road.
On each side of the wide thoroughfare large plane
trees partially hid the night sky, their leafy branches
full of sleeping starlings. Trams and buses lumbered
by and up ahead they could see the Bricklayers Arms
junction.

They had both been quiet for a while and suddenly
Del gave a little chuckle. 'Bernie Catchpole pulled me
aside yesterday,' he remarked. 'Wanted ter make sure
I knew that it wasn't 'im who sorted your Tom out.
As if I 'ad any doubts. 'E couldn't even sort 'imself
out. I told 'im 'e should apply ter be the new shop
steward. That'd be a laugh.'

Sue sighed in resignation. 'There you go again, Del,' she replied. 'You can't seem to get work out of your mind, not even on Saturday night.'

He brought his free hand round to touch her fingertips. 'I'm sorry. I won't mention work again this weekend, I promise.'

She squeezed his arm in response and gave him a smile. 'I want to be part of what you're doing, Del, I really do,' she told him, 'but I don't want it to take over our lives. You do understand, don't you?'

He nodded and then his face relaxed into a wide smile. 'I wonder if that Fifth Cavalry caught those Indians.'

She giggled. 'Would you have saved two bullets for us?' she asked him.

'Certainly.'

'I'd sooner we rode off into the sunset.'

'Wiv two 'undred Indian braves at our backs,' he chuckled.

They reached the junction and crossed into Tower Bridge Road. The shops were shuttered and piano music drifted out from a corner pub. Loud voices could be heard singing 'Comrades' and Del looked at her with a smile. 'That was me farvver's favourite tune,' he remarked.

'What was he like?' Sue asked.

''E was a good man so I was told, but I never got ter know 'im very well,' Del told her. ''E died when I was eleven years old. It was 'cos o' the First World War. 'E was gassed on the Somme an' 'is lungs were burned.'

'That's terrible.'

He nodded sadly. 'I do remember once when me

dad came 'ome on leave, just before 'e went ter France. I remember 'im tellin' me the story about the lemonade sea.'

'Lemonade sea?'

Del smiled. 'Once upon a time – it was always once upon a time, wasn't it? Anyway, once upon a time a young lad got 'is wish when 'e released a genie from a bottle. 'E was transported on a carpet ter fairyland, an' the lad discovered that the pavements were made o' chocolate squares an' the roads were glazed wiv Glacier mints. A long road led ter the sea an' on the way 'e stopped at a little shop owned by a wizard who gave 'im a very large bagful o' sweets fer a penny. At the end o' the road the lad saw the sea an' sand. The sand was made o' sherbet dip, an' when 'e took a swim 'e found that the sea was lemonade.'

Sue saw amusement in his eyes and smiled. 'Well, go on then. What happened next?'

'Well, when the boy came out o' the lemonade sea 'e saw a boatman beckonin' to 'im an' 'e climbed aboard,' Del went on. 'The boat set sail an' took 'im to a desert island, an' on this island white chocolate bars an' peppermint sticks grew on the slopin' palm trees, an' there was a spring where ginger beer splashed out o' rock that was made o' caramel. Arrowroot biscuits an' chocolate creams grew everywhere an' the lad decided that 'e'd stay there ferever.'

'And did he?'

Del smiled. 'When the boatman called at the island the followin' week the little lad was very tearful an' feelin' very sick, an' 'e begged the man ter take 'im back 'ome, ter where water came from a tap, where there were shops which sold fresh crusty bread, an'

where white fluffy snow fell at Christmas. By the time
the lad finally reached these shores 'e'd realised that
gettin' what yer wanted wasn't always such a great
fing an' 'e was a very contented little boy.'

'Your father must have been very wise,' Sue said
as she smiled up into the young man's face. 'It was
his way of preparing you for the future.'

He nodded. 'Mind you, at the time I still 'oped I'd
find a genie corked up in a bottle.'

'But after the story your dad told you would you
have pulled the cork?' she asked.

He shrugged his shoulders. 'I'll never know now.'

They had reached the deserted Ship Lane, and in
the shadows of a derelict factory doorway he took her
into his arms. They heard the muffled sound of a tug
whistle and the rattle of loosened corrugated sheeting
caught in the rising wind, and as storm clouds rushed
to cover the crescent moon they kissed.

'I want you all to myself, very soon,' she whispered
as he pulled her tightly to him.

'Very soon,' he said, squeezing her slim waist.

She pressed herself even closer against him, her back
arched slightly as she waited for the kiss. He lowered
his head, tantalising her as his lips brushed her open
mouth and then nuzzled her tiny ear. She closed her
eyes and sighed deeply as a delicious feeling flooded
her whole body. 'Very soon,' she gasped as his lips
found hers.

Granny Minto had been feeling off colour for a few
days and on that Saturday morning she had decided to
have a lie-in, which surprised her lodger Albert Price
when he came down and found that the kettle was cold.

His first thought was that she must have died in her sleep and he made to go back upstairs to check, but then common sense prevailed. If she was dead there was nothing he could do anyway except phone her panel doctor, who would most certainly be sleeping off a heavy night of drinking. Better he boil the kettle and take the old lady a cup of tea, he decided, realising that taking her up a cuppa had its risks. As long as he had lodged there Granny Minto had risen before him, and the shock of him delivering the morning tea might be enough in itself to kill her off.

At eight o'clock Albert tapped on her bedroom door, and getting no reply he went in. She was snoring loudly and it took some gentle shaking before she roused herself.

'Bloody 'ell! What time is it?' she asked.

'Eight o'clock on the dot,' he replied cheerfully, only to be tutted at.

'What 'appened ter you? You ain't shit the bed,' 'ave yer?' she asked him.

'I 'ad me sleep out,' he replied, holding the cup of tea while she sat up and arranged the bedclothes round her body.

'I couldn't sleep,' she told him. 'Pacin' the floor 'alf the night I've bin. I'm sure I've got kidney stones. Anyway I took a Beecham's Powder wiv a drop of 'ow's yer farvver, an' it must 'ave sent me off into a deep sleep. I always know when I've slept 'eavy 'cos I got a poxy 'eadache.'

Albert glanced at the bottle of Booth's gin on the bedside cabinet and saw that it was empty. 'Yer shouldn't drink that stuff, gel,' he warned her. 'Yer know 'ow depressed it makes yer.'

'I was depressed before I 'ad any,' she replied quickly. 'By the way, where's me biscuit?'

'We're out of 'em,' he told her.

'There's a ten-shillin' note under the clock. Go an' get me a nice crusty Vienna loaf an' a packet o' broken biscuits from Field's will yer, Albert? An' while yer goin' out will yer get me shoes from Kenwards? You should 'ave enough money. I've only 'ad 'em 'alf soled an' 'eeled. Oh, an' while I fink of it, will yer get me two fly-papers an' anuvver tin o' condensed milk? That one I bought last week's full o' dead flies.'

Albert sighed in resignation. 'Anyfing else yer want?' he asked.

'Only a pound out the till,' she chuckled.

Granny Minto finally climbed out of her bed at two o'clock that afternoon, and as the day wore on she became more and more miserable and depressed. 'Gawd knows what Bessie Woodward's said about me dirty doorstep,' she groaned. 'She must 'ave noticed it. An' them winders o' mine are a disgrace. I bin too queer ter do me curtains an' the place needs a good sweep-out.'

Albert volunteered to iron her curtains and whiten her front doorstep but Granny shook her head. 'I wouldn't live the shame down if anybody should spot yer doin' my work,' she told him.

'Well, at least let me sweep the place out,' he said.

'All right, as long as yer keep that front door shut,' Granny warned him. 'That Bessie an' 'er crony Nell Sharp's bound ter nose in if the door's open. I don't want them seein' yer sweepin' up, is that clear?'

'Yeah,' Albert grunted.

During the afternoon Granny Minto sat in her fireside chair bemoaning her situation and sinking more and more into herself. By teatime she was almost catatonic and Albert had become quite worried. The last time she had been that way she ended up nearly gassing herself by mistake. Of course she wouldn't admit it when he told her that she had been dozing in the chair with an unlit gas jet hissing away in the scullery, preferring him to think she had intended doing away with herself.

Albert went to the fish shop and got them both a large portion of haddock and chips, which Granny hardly touched. She was now descending into one of her black moods and he knew that that was when she was most likely to do herself some harm, intentional or otherwise.

''Ow about a nice cuppa?' he suggested.

'Yeah, if yer like,' she said glumly.

When she had finished her tea Albert went to wash up, only to be called back crossly. 'Leave them fings,' she ordered. 'There'll be plenty o' time fer washin' up after I've gone.'

'Gone? Gone where?'

'I'm goin' upstairs ter put me best coat on, then I'm gonna chuck meself orf Tower Bridge,' she announced.

'I shouldn't do that, gel,' Albert replied. 'Yer could well catch yer death o' cold.'

'Don't sit there grinnin' like a polecat,' she said angrily. 'I'm serious.'

'Cheshire cat yer mean.'

'I know very well what I mean,' the old lady grouched. 'Anyway, there's me 'ousekeepin' money in the tins an' yer'll find me ovver purse in the wardrobe next ter me best 'at. Queenie Alladyce can 'ave the 'at. She always passes a remark every time I wear it.'

'C'mon, Granny, the joke's over, let's 'ave anuvver cuppa,' Albert pleaded.

'Nah, it's time I made a move,' she told him adamantly.

Knowing it was useless to argue Albert decided to play along. 'Well, if that's yer final word there's nuffink I can do ter stop yer,' he said coolly.

Granny Minto looked very determined as she put on her best coat, brushed the front of it with a stiff brush and then carefully put on her summer hat.

'I thought yer left that ter Queenie,' Albert queried.

'Nah, that's me ovver one,' she replied. 'Well, goodbye an' look after yerself.'

'Cheerio then. All the best, gel.'

The old lady tottered along towards Tower Bridge, occasionally glancing over her shoulder, and when she reached the first span she stopped and stared down at the foreshore. A patrolling policeman was in the middle of the bridge and he started to walk towards her. If she was going to jump, he reckoned, she would surely make her way further on to the bridge, considering that below her at that point was just thick mud. He stopped as he saw the man approach her and smiled to himself as the couple turned and walked slowly away.

'Why d'yer do it, luv?' Albert asked her kindly. 'Why d'yer put me to all this worry?'

''Cos I felt like it,' she said quickly.

They walked back along Tower Bridge Road and suddenly Granny Minto turned off the main road.

'What yer goin' this way for?' he asked her. 'We'll 'ave ter go frew Ship Lane.'

'That's me intention,' she told him curtly.

As they turned into the deserted byway they could see the row of corrugated fencing, and the derelict warehouses looked Satanic, like ghosts of brick and darkness in the fitful light of the moon. There was a shuffling sound up ahead and then a couple emerged from a deep doorway. The unconcerned young lovers walked off, the man slipping his arm around the girl's waist.

'Stop 'ere a minute,' Granny ordered.

'What now?' Albert asked impatiently.

'In there,' she mumbled. 'That's where it 'appened.'

Albert peered through the gap in the fencing and saw the ruined factory, now reduced to the first-floor level. ''Ow could I ever ferget it,' he said quietly.

Granny Minto sighed. 'Mr an' Mrs Simpson, an' Flo Thomas, 'Ilda Moore an' poor ole Granny Knight. All gone.'

'We could 'ave all gone that night, luv,' Albert reminded her.

'It was a bad business,' she said, nodding her head slowly. 'I don't fink the real trufe o' the matter'll ever come out. I just know that somefing wasn't right. Those poor people should never 'a' died that night.'

'C'mon, luv, let's get goin',' Albert urged her. 'This place gives me the creeps. I'm bleedin' shiverin'.'

'Yeah, there's a presence 'ere,' the old lady said reverently with an otherworldly look in her eyes. 'It's the spirits o' the poor souls who met their end 'ere that terrible night. Unquiet spirits.'

Chapter Thirteen

Sue Carey had just made herself comfortable at her desk on Monday morning when she saw him come in. So this was the new reporter who was going to turn the paper round, she thought with some amusement. He looked presentable enough. He was young, fair, in his thirties and of medium height, with a decent grey suit on and a tie casually knotted over a light blue shirt. He smiled easily as he walked to the desk.

'The name's Calkin, Sam Calkin, and I've to report to you,' he said in a quiet voice.

'Pleased to meet you,' she replied as she reached over to the intercom link. 'I'm Sue Carey. I'll tell Mr Spencer you've arrived.'

The editor's voice sounded enthusiastic as he answered her message and she smiled up at the young man as she replaced the receiver. 'Will you please go through. You know where his office is?'

He nodded. 'Yeah, I know where it is. Thank you, Sue,' he replied. 'You don't mind if I call you Sue?'

Her smile broadened. 'Of course not. Everyone does.'

As he pushed open the door leading into the main office he gave her a quick wink as he held up his crossed fingers and she grinned to herself. He was handsome in a rugged sort of way, she decided, and he had a lot of confidence, despite his show of apprehension. If the office tittle-tattle was anything to go by Sam Calkin was going to do wonders, or, as a few sceptics were quick to remark, fall flat on his face. It was a bit silly to dramatise it in such a way, she felt. He was coming to work at a local newspaper that was fighting to survive. He might be instrumental in increasing the twice-weekly sales, as Spencer seemed to expect, but nevertheless it was asking a lot. Time alone would tell, and if the latest distribution figures were anything to go by there wasn't a lot of that left.

Earlier that morning Tom Carey had climbed out of bed and surveyed his face in the mirror which hung above the washstand in his bedroom. Most of the swelling to his face had gone down, but there was still some bruising around both eyes. The cut over his right eye was healing nicely but his ribs still felt tender to the touch. He smiled mirthlessly as he rubbed at his stubble. From what Del Abelson had told him Joe Brady was being the whiter-than-white boss ready to welcome his black sheep back into the fold. Well, two could play at that game. He would walk through the gates as though nothing had happened and bide his time. His day would come and Brady was going to be sorry.

Before he dressed Tom took a roll of crêpe bandage from his bedside cabinet and bound it tightly round his sore ribs. It felt better, he decided, guessing that he wasn't going to be shown any favours today. Toby Lowndes the transport manager would obviously have received his orders from Brady and he was willing to wager that he was in for a hard day's work. There would also be Bernie Catchpole's hostile attitude to deal with. Matters would be even worse between them now that Pamela had finished with Bernie and was going out with him. The bloke wouldn't be too pleased about that to say the least. All in all it was going to be a very interesting time, Tom thought as he carefully put on his overalls and went down to hurry his breakfast.

At nine o'clock on Monday morning Joe Carey walked into his place of work at Napier and Sons in Tooley Street and seated himself at his desk. The dingy office of the old-established wine merchants had not changed in the long years he had worked there. Even during the war it had not been any different, apart from the protective strips of brown paper over the windows and the buckets of sand placed about the large room. The same two big lightshades hung from the shadowy high ceiling and the floor was covered in the same dark green linoleum. The desks were still placed too close together and the flimsy hatstand in the corner near the wide doors still somehow managed not to topple over beneath the weight of coats and hats and Mr Darnley's crumpled old umbrella.

Joe Carey had to concede that everyone looked that little bit older, but their habits hadn't changed. Darnley the chief clerk still coughed nervously at regular intervals, and Mrs Gates still styled her hair in the same fashion she had always done. Now though it was grey and she had put on some weight. Fredericks and Baxter still exchanged banalities and wore shirts two sizes too big, which Joe thought made them look like animated matchsticks. The other occupant of the office, Norman Wilson, had looked like an old man when Joe first went to work there and he alone had not seemed to age, which would have been hard to envisage anyway. His thin face was lined deeply beneath a bald skull and he had a way of hunching himself vulture-like over his desk as though he were engaged in some very secret operation.

Joe finished checking the rows of figures he had entered on Friday and tallied them successfully. Then he opened the large ledger he had brought from the rack in the far corner of the office and entered the day's date on the top of the page. Darnley coughed again and Baxter tittered after a brief exchange with Fredericks, which made Joe scowl inwardly. They were like naughty schoolchildren secretly passing obscene notes, he thought. He looked up at the wall clock and immediately glanced at the door. It was exactly nine-thirty. Was he becoming neurotic, he wondered? Were the habits and idiosyncrasies of his fellow clerks finally driving him over the edge?

By the time it reached twenty minutes to ten there was a distinct feel to the office. It seemed to Joe as though everyone was waiting with bated breath. Darnley coughed twice in quick succession, Baxter and Fredericks kept glancing up at the door and even Mrs Gates deemed it pertinent to cluck as she realised she had made a typing error. At nine-forty-five she brought the completed invoices over for Joe to enter in the ledger and she frowned as she glanced at the door. 'Whatever could have happened to Mr Coombes?' she whispered.

'I was just beginnin' ter wonder meself,' Joe replied. 'It's so unusual fer Mr Coombes ter be late.'

At ten minutes to ten the door swung open and the tall, gangling office manager entered. He mumbled a 'Good morning all' as he removed his hat and mackintosh and hung them on the hook reserved for him, then he placed his umbrella in the well of the stand and looked over his gold-rimmed spectacles at the gawking staff. 'Blasted train was cancelled due to industrial action,' he almost spat out. 'I don't know what this country's coming to, really I don't.'

Joe watched him walk over to the large desk in the corner of the office and go through his exaggerated preliminaries. Drawers opened and closed, pencils were produced and the blotting-pad was repositioned, the phone cord was unravelled and the in-tray moved slightly, then with a sigh that could be heard throughout the office Mr Coombes began to polish his glasses. Darnley coughed, Baxter gave Fredericks a furtive glance and Mrs Gates appeared to increase her typing speed suddenly. Joe picked up his pen and dipped it in the inkwell, as he had so many countless times before. Time and custom were beginning to wear him thin, he thought with sudden concern. If he wasn't careful he would soon be coughing nervously at frequent intervals and involving himself in the idiocies of Fredericks and Baxter. God! He might even stoop to passing rude notes to Mrs Gates. How much he envied Charlie Duggan. His old friend was a true working man. He used his brawn with an acquired skill in a practical way. Laying gas pipes and installing gas stoves and heaters had to be preferable to recording the sale of magnums of Moët & Chandon to the Sir William Fazackerleys of this world.

'Mr Carey, I'd like to see the figures for the twenty-fifth of January if you please. There seems to be a discrepancy somewhere. Mrs Ashley-Groves has written in about her outstanding account.'

Joe had not seen Coombes come over, and taken by surprise he blotted an entry. 'I'll bring the ledger over, Mr Coombes,' he said quickly, irritation building up inside him. The office manager had taken to creeping about now, he thought as he went to the ledger rack. Why couldn't he get the bloody ledger himself? Wasn't he capable of carrying it? It wasn't that heavy. Perhaps he was still suffering from the trauma of being late getting to the office. No doubt he would be fuming inside. The strikers were all Marxists, hellbent on destroying the fabric of the country. Make the likes of Mr Coombes late for work, that was it. Treason. Upset the capitalist system, and let Mrs Ashley-Groves wait for a response to her query. Insurrection! Joe gritted his teeth. Christ, he thought. I'll have to pull myself together or I'll end up in the loony bin before Darnley.

'Ahh. I see. Umm. Yes, I see. Thank you, Mr Carey.'

Joe carried the ledger back to its resting place and sighed deeply as he took his seat. That was another thing, he reflected. How long had they all worked together now? Long enough for a little relaxing of formalities. Instead the atmosphere had grown more stuffy than ever. How nice it would be to arrive in the morning and ask, 'How are you feeling this morning, Beatrice?' and, 'What sort of a journey have you had, Matthew?' He might even get to understand the workings of the minds of Fredericks and Baxter. 'Have you heard this one, Felix?' and, 'Did you hear that programme on the wireless last night, Victor?' Even Darnley might forget to cough once in a while.

Suddenly the figures in front of him started to dance. An ink stain spread out to form the shape of a kidney, and as he reached for the blotting-paper Mr Darnley coughed again.

Mr Coombes looked up in surprise. 'Yes, Mr Carey?'

'I'm sorry, Mr Coombes, but I need ter get out in the air fer five minutes,' he said in a heavy breath. 'I'm not feelin' too good.'

'Well, if you must,' Coombes replied, looking rather shocked.

Mrs Gates stared over her glasses at him as he passed by her desk, and Fredericks and Baxter lowered their heads over the piles of invoices. Darnley forgot to cough as he gawped unbelievingly at the sight of someone other than Mr Coombes leaving the office during working hours.

Tooley Street was a hive of industry as Joe Carey walked slowly along towards the Bevington Statue. Carmen stood in little groups at the kerbside waiting for their call into the wharves and cart-horses blew into their nosebags. Trams rumbled by and a steam wagon chugged past with a violent mechanical din. Two dockers were exchanging crude obscenities outside a coffee shop and up ahead a stream of traffic moved in fits and starts across the Tower Bridge intersection.

He reached the statue and sat down thankfully on an unoccupied bench, wheezing loudly as he strove to regain his breath. It was stupid, he realised. He had needlessly got himself into a state of panic. Maybe it was more than work that was getting to him once more. It happened now and then but he usually managed to fight it off. Charlie had always been a calming influence, but even he had seemed preoccupied that weekend at the Bell, and later as they sat together in Charlie's backyard. People often said that time was a great healer, but in this case it was different. The wounds were constantly being opened. A chance remark, the name of one of the shelter victims mentioned in a conversation, and the raw reminder of the derelict warehouse in Ship Lane that stood there crumbling on the wasteground like an unburied skeleton. It seemed to Joe that the tragedy of that night in May would stay to haunt him for the rest of his life.

'Got a fag, mate?'

Joe looked up into the grubby face of a tramp. 'Only a roll-up,' he told him.

'That'll do nicely, pal.'

As he took out his tobacco tin the tramp sat down beside him. 'Out o' collar?' he asked.

'Nah, just takin' a breavver.'

The down-and-out watched while Joe shaped the makings for him, and as Joe licked the cigarette paper the tramp put his tongue out, unconsciously aping him.

'There we are,' Joe said, handing the roll-up to him.

'Bloody 'andsome,' he said as Joe flicked his cigarette lighter into flame. 'First one since Friday. Bin tryin' ter pack 'em up.' And he suddenly broke into a fit of coughing.

Joe rolled another cigarette and lit it. 'So 'ave I. I know the feelin',' he replied.

The tramp crossed his legs to display a pair of boots held together with string. His face took on a look of pure pleasure as he dragged on the cigarette. ''Ad it all once, but look at me now,' he said after a while. 'I'm down ter poncin' fags an' pushin' rotten stinkin' fish barrers up the 'ill fer a few poxy coppers. Yer wouldn't 'ave known me a few years ago. Anyway it's not your concern. Andrew's the name. Andrew Walker.'

Joe looked down at the filthy hand held out to him and he hesitated momentarily before clasping it. 'Joe Carey.'

'Ring a bell does it?' the tramp asked, smiling through his long beard.

''Fraid it doesn't.'

'Finest legal brain in the country at one time, so they reckoned,' the man went on. 'I represented Crippen, only a junior counsel yer understand, but it was the case I cut me teef on. Seen quite a few black caps go on too. Not a very nice fing, 'specially if you're standin' in the dock at the time. Remember Roger Casement? Called 'im a traitor they did, but 'e denied it. Asked fer me ter represent 'im. Too risky though. The evidence was overwhelmin'. 'E might 'ave got away wiv a life sentence if I'd 'ave took the case, so they said, but I couldn't take the chance. After all, I 'ad me career ter fink of.'

'So 'ow come yer on the streets?' Joe asked, hiding a smile.

'I flipped me lid. That's right, I went doolally-tap. Stone mad they said I was when they picked me up orf the railway line. I'd 'ad enough, yer see, so I decided to end it all. Trouble was I picked a disused sidin'. Never bin used fer years. The only way I'd 'ave ended it all there was frew starvation. Pressures o' work they said it was. Mind you I'm better now. Totally cured the specialist told me. That's the reason I walk the streets. There ain't no pressures involved in livin' rough, ole pal, 'cept where yer gonna doss down or where the next crust is comin' from. You should try it some time. Yer'd be surprised 'ow much better yer'd feel.'

'Yeah, I might just do that,' Joe said with more conviction than he would have liked.

The tramp took a last drag on his stub and ground it under his foot. 'Well, it's nice to 'ave met yer,' he said with a serious look. 'Got ter get goin' now. Got fings ter do. I'm defendin' Martin Bormann next week. Yeah, that's right. They picked 'im up down Petticoat Lane last Sunday mornin'. Workin' on a stall 'e was by all accounts. It makes yer fink.'

Joe shook his head sadly as the tramp ambled off. How thin the line for us all, he thought as he set off back along Tooley Street.

Chapter Fourteen

Frances Miller was feeling like a new woman as she set about tidying up her desk on Monday morning. It had been a wonderful experience last Friday evening as she sat alone with Paddy O'Brian in the Old Coach House. He had been so attentive and sympathetic as she poured out her life story to him. Other men would have been more interested in telling her all about themselves, bragging about their accomplishments, but not Paddy. He had listened intently as she explained how her elderly mother had totally dominated her and prevented her from having any life of her own. He had sympathised too when she told him how difficult it had been after her mother died last year and she had had to make all the necessary adjustments. Her home in Lambeth had been transformed now and she had felt disposed to describe in detail all the changes she had made.

What had worried her at the time was the realisation that he was the first person she had actually confided in, and she had been afraid that he might be bored with her going on so. Far from it though. He had actually asked her to meet him on Saturday evening and they had spent a very pleasant few hours together. The musical at the Lyric Theatre was very good and afterwards they strolled through the West End and along the Embankment to Waterloo Bridge. They stopped there for a short while to gaze down into the dark water and she reminded him of the film *Waterloo Bridge* where Robert Taylor met Vivien Leigh beneath a gas lamp on a foggy night and kissed her passionately. Paddy had smiled and then unexpectedly kissed her gently on her cheek before they left to catch the tube train home.

The office was buzzing with conversation after the new arrival had made his way past the desks to the end office and Josie Willard in particular had a lecherous smile on her face. He certainly looked a very nice young man, Frances thought, but she had eyes only for Paddy O'Brian, and he was still to arrive. He had better not be too late this morning. With the new reporter in place Spencer might decide it was time Paddy was shown the door. She prayed not. He had stirred her dormant feelings and made her feel like a young woman again. The office wouldn't be tolerable without him now.

Spencer came out of his office followed by Sam Calkin and the formal introductions took place. Josie put on one of her little-girl-lost smiles and the male staff nodded briskly as they shook hands with the new arrival.

'Sam, I would like you to meet Frances Miller,' he said, smiling at her. 'Frances has worked here for over twenty years and she's a mine of information. In fact, she looks after our glory hole. You'll have the opportunity of seeing just how organised it is. We couldn't possibly manage without Frances.'

Sam Calkin smiled as he held out his hand. 'Very

pleased to meet you, Frances,' he said cheerfully. 'I was hoping you could show me how the system works. I need to get started right away.'

Ernest Spencer looked pleased and he lowered his glasses on to the tip of his nose. 'Well, I'll leave you in very capable hands,' he said, laying on the syrupy charm that Frances abhorred.

'If you'll follow me,' she told him a little stiffly.

'I'm sorry to be taking up your time,' Sam said with a smile. 'Once I've been shown the layout I'm sure I'll be able to manage quite well.'

Frances bit back a sharp retort. The glory hole had been hers to manage and organise for many years now and she did not relish anyone disrupting things by rummaging about. 'This is it,' she said as they walked down the flight of stone steps into the dingy basement.

'Have I your permission to study the files and look for information, or should I leave it to you?' he asked quietly. 'I will promise to replace everything where I find it.'

Frances was mollified somewhat by his considerate manner and she nodded. 'As long as everything goes back where it should be I'll be happy to let you search for things yourself,' she replied.

'I do appreciate it,' he said, his easy smile making her feel less antagonistic.

'If you need any help . . .'

'I'll know just where to come, but I don't want to be a nuisance,' he told her. 'You must have quite enough to do without nursemaiding me.'

Frances was won over and she gave him a friendly smile. 'Well, good luck. I hope you get to like working here,' she said.

As she started to climb the stairs the young man smiled up at her. 'Thanks, Frances.'

'You're very welcome,' she replied.

Granny Minto had recovered from her bout of depression and she looked chirpy as she stood at her door enjoying the feel of the morning sun on her face. Bessie Woodward had passed by and remarked on how well she looked, and Nell Sharp had bothered to stand and chat for a few minutes. Albert Price was busy chopping firewood in the backyard as promised and Queenie Alladyce had stopped to say hello, which was unusual for her. Normally she would just nod as she walked by. Perhaps Albert was right about Queenie, Granny thought. She's been in that oilshop for ages and nobody ever spends much time in there. John Raney was never one to chat with his customers anyway. Sometimes it was as much as he could do to serve anyone. Strange man, but then it takes all sorts. Whatever Queenie Alladyce could see in him though was beyond her. After the way her old man had behaved it was a wonder the woman could even look at another bloke.

'Well, that's finished,' Albert said as he joined Granny at the front door.

'Did yer chop it up in little pieces?' she enquired. 'Last time it was too big ter get in the fire.'

'Just as you ordered,' he said with a grin.

'Albert, will yer take those curtains down in yer room some time terday. I got yer clean ones all ready.'

'Yeah, okay.'

'By the way,' she said with a ghost of a smile. 'I

saw Queenie go in the oilshop ages ago an' she ain't come out yet.'

'There we are, what did I tell yer,' Albert replied. 'There's definitely somefing goin' on between them two.'

The old lady suddenly nudged him in the ribs. ''Old tight, 'ere she comes.'

Queenie walked across the street and smiled at her. 'Very nice mornin',' she remarked. 'Makes yer feel good ter be alive.'

'The papers forecast rain later,' Granny told her.

'Yer can't take no notice o' what the forecasters say,' Queenie replied. 'I'm gonna put me washin' out anyway.'

''Ow's ole Raney?' Albert asked over Granny's shoulder.

''E seemed all right ter me. Why d'yer ask?'

''E looked a bit under the weavver on Saturday an' I saw yer go in there earlier.'

Queenie smiled briefly. 'An' yer saw me just come out. If yer must know, 'e's fine. I was talkin' to 'im fer quite a while as a matter o' fact. Did you know that some butterflies 'ibernate? What's more, did yer know that the Small Copper 'as three broods a year?'

'We live an' learn,' Albert said, giving her a strange look.

Granny too was secretly perplexed but she did not bat an eyelid. ''Ow many does the large one 'ave?'

Queenie smiled indulgently. 'John Raney's very interested in butterflies. 'E catches 'em an' mounts 'em.'

'That's quite an undertakin',' Albert remarked, hiding a grin.

''E don't catch 'ouse-flies, does 'e?' Granny asked sarcastically. 'I got some 'e can 'ave.'

Pearls before swine, the younger woman thought. 'Well, I'd better get me washin' out,' she said.

Albert laid his hand on Granny's shoulder. 'If she's Madam Butterfly John Raney must be the Mikado,' he chuckled.

The *Bulletin* was a twice-weekly publication, the main edition going out on Friday mornings while the smaller Tuesday edition was mostly taken up with advertising. Of late the pages had dwindled as the business calls became fewer, but today Ernest Spencer was feeling optimistic as he put down the phone. Sam Calkin had promised him earlier that the first of the articles would be on his desk by Wednesday evening, which would allow time for inclusion in the Friday edition, and Spencer had inserted an introductory piece on the front page of the Tuesday's paper to make readers aware of the new weekly articles by Sam Calkin.

FRONTLINE HEROISM IN BERMONDSEY.

[Starting this Friday.]

During the Blitz Bermondsey was a frontline borough, and while its emergency services were highly praised by the Government many acts of selfless sacrifice and devotion to duty went unsung. Now you can read for the first time the hitherto untold story of the heroic deeds by the people of frontline Bermondsey. Don't Delay! Order Your Copy Now!

As an added incentive the *Bulletin*'s editor had initiated a cut-price advertising offer and the phone lines were busy as his team set to work.

Alf Barlow was in his early fifties, and like his friend and neighbour Micky Sloan he had been just beyond the age limit for conscription when the war broke out. Wanting to do their bit, however, both volunteered for the Heavy Rescue Squad and were immediately accepted for training. Alf Barlow was a scaffolder by trade while Micky Sloan worked as a builder's labourer, and their acquired skills working at heights and at times in dangerous conditions were an asset. During the Blitz their prowess and courage were put to the test and they lived dangerously, worked hard, and sometimes reluctantly fought each other to protect the good name of their wives, but behind their rough, tough façade both men were self-effacing and unobtrusive. They were happy to live their lives in harmony with their neighbours and friends, which unfortunately could not be said for their respective spouses.

The problem was, Annie Barlow was a very determined woman, reluctant to lose an argument, and her cousin Minnie was of a similar temperament. It was inevitable that the two should fall out occasionally, and it was usually over something trivial.

There had been an extended truce, frayed at times, lasting since the end of the war, but hostilities commenced again after Annie Barlow's youngest son Steve, who was twelve years old, got into a difference of opinion with Minnie Sloan's youngest son Patrick, who was eleven.

163

'When I leave school I'm gonna be a scaffolder like me dad,' Steve declared.

'When I leave school I'm gonna get a barrer an' sell fings in the market,' Patrick replied.

'Ain't yer gonna work on the buildin's like yer dad?' Steve queried.

'Nah, me dad said I gotta get a decent job.'

'Bein' a barrer boy ain't a decent job.'

'It's better than workin' on the buildin' sites.'

'Who ses?'

'I say.'

Steve traced a line along the gutter mud with a short stick as they sat at the kerbside then threw it across the road at a passing dog. 'Scaffoldin's a good job. Better than bein' a buildin' labourer any day.'

'I 'spect it is, but I'm still gonna be a barrer boy when I leave school,' Patrick avowed.

The mangy dog had grown quite used to having objects thrown at it and it trotted over unperturbed. Steve Barlow felt sorry for trying to brain the animal and he started to stroke it. 'I reckon it's 'ungry, don't you?'

Patrick nodded. 'It's always moochin' round 'ere. I fink it's a stray. Shall we find it somefing to eat?'

'There was 'alf a pork pie left on our table,' Steve remarked. 'I wonder if it's bin chucked away yet.'

Patrick took over stroking the scruffy animal until his friend returned.

'Nah, it's gorn,' Steve said.

'I'll see if there's anyfing in our 'ouse,' Patrick replied.

A few minutes later he came back with a slice of brawn, which the thankful dog devoured in one gulp.

'The bloody fing's still 'ungry by the look of it,' Steve laughed. 'Was that all there was in yer 'ouse?'

'Well, it was more than you 'ad,' Patrick told him, looking aggrieved. 'Anyway your dad earns more than my dad.'

'Well, my dad's a skilled worker. Your dad's just a labourer.'

'Anybody can do scaffoldin'.'

'Well, why don't your dad do it then?'

'I dunno. P'raps there's no jobs goin' as scaffolders.'

'My dad said yer gotta be brainy ter be a scaffolder,' Steve said forcefully. 'Not anybody could do it. Yer gotta be strong too, carryin' all those 'eavy great poles up ladders.'

'My dad could do it,' Patrick replied quickly.

The dog decided it wasn't going to get any more to eat and ambled off, dodging the group of children who were playing football with a battered tin can. The two lads decided to forget their differences and joined in the game, unaware of what was going on at number 19.

'Where's that bloody brawn gone to?' Minnie asked as she went into the scullery.

''Ow the bloody 'ell should I know?' Micky replied.

'Well, I've only bin up ter change the beds an' it was 'ere then.'

'Well, I ain't shifted it,' Micky told her.

'I saved that slice fer yer sandwich termorrer,' Minnie said puffing, hands on hips.

Just then Patrick came in for a drink of water and Minnie captured him. 'Did you touch that brawn on the dresser?' she asked him.

The lad nodded sheepishly. 'I thought yer was

gonna chuck it away so I took it fer this dog that was 'ungry.'

'Gawd 'elp us!' Minnie exclaimed. 'There's me tryin' ter save a few coppers an' you take the food out yer farvver's mouth ter feed all the stray dogs in the area.'

'It was only one dog, Mum.'

'There was only one slice.'

'Steve Barlow went ter see if there was anyfing goin' in 'is 'ouse an' there wasn't, so I took the slice o' brawn,' Patrick went on.

'Don't worry, I'll 'ave some cheese,' Micky said defensively. 'Yer got cheese ain't yer?'

'No I ain't,' Minnie said sharply. 'In fact I'm out of everyfing. I'll 'ave ter pop round ter Mrs Riley's an' see if she can let me 'ave a few fings on tick. The money don't seem ter go anywhere these days.'

'Never mind, luv, there'll be some overtime next week on that new job we're startin',' Micky said supportively.

'Why don't yer be a scaffolder, Dad?' Patrick asked. 'Yer clever enough, an' yer strong enough.'

Micky chuckled. 'Yer don't 'ave ter be brainy ter be a scaffolder, son, but yer gotta be strong though.'

'Steve Barlow said yer gotta be brainy.'

Minnie's ears pricked up. 'I bet they've bin talkin' about us. What else did Steve say?'

''E said 'is dad was a skilled worker an' you was only a labourer,' the lad replied. 'When I took the brawn out ter the dog 'e said, "Is that all yer've got in your 'ouse?"'

'An' what did you say?'

'I told 'im it was more than 'e 'ad in 'is 'ouse.'

'I gotta take that sugar back I borrered. I'll 'ave a word or two wiv 'er while I'm there,' Minnie growled.

'Fer Gawd sake, don't go upsettin' 'er,' Micky pleaded. 'It's bin nice an' peaceful lately.'

Minnie put on her coat to go to Mrs Riley's grocery shop in Abbey Street and Micky slumped back in his chair. If he was not mistaken it was going to get a little bit lively in Totterdown Street very shortly.

Annie Barlow was feeling at peace with the world when Minnie knocked. She had finished her ironing, washed up the tea things and was enjoying a nice cup of tea which Alf had unexpectedly made for her. 'See who that is, luv,' she called out.

Alf was putting a quick polish on his shoes in the scullery, prior to asking Annie if he could borrow a few bob out the jug to go for a pint, and he hurried to the front door.

'I won't come in. There's the sugar I borrered,' Minnie said offhandedly.

Annie frowned as she came out of the parlour. 'Anyfing wrong?' she asked.

'Not so's yer'd notice,' Minnie answered sharply.

'I wasn't waitin' fer the sugar,' Annie said lightly.

'I believe in payin' me debts back. Mind you, if my ole man was as brainy as your ole man I wouldn't 'ave ter come poncin' off you, would I,' Minnie said cuttingly.

'What you talkin' about?' Annie demanded, her hackles up.

'You know very well. Your Steve told my Patrick that yer gotta 'ave brains ter be a scaffolder,' Minnie sneered. 'Where'd 'e get that from? From listenin' ter you an' that brainy bastard o' yours, that's where. I s'pose yer boy told yer there wasn't any food in our 'ouse as well.'

'No 'e never.'

'Well, I don't believe yer.'

'You can believe what yer like.'

'Yer fink yer so 'igh an' mighty, just 'cos your ole man earns more than my Micky.'

'Now come on, gels, don't let's 'ave a barney,' Alf pleaded.

'Shut yer row, you,' Annie shouted at him. 'Just keep out of it.'

'That's right. She shouts shit an' you jump on the shovel,' Minnie jeered.

'Don't you talk ter my ole man like that,' Annie said menacingly.

'I'll talk to 'im 'ow I like.'

'Oh no yer won't.'

'Who's gonna stop me?'

'I am.'

'You ain't big enough, yer boss-eyed cow.'

'I'm bigger than you, yer skinny prat.'

Suddenly Minnie grasped Annie Barlow by her hair and pulled her out on to the street and as Alf tried to intervene he was sent sprawling by Annie's backhander.

'What's goin' on 'ere?' Micky shouted as he hurried across the road and grabbed Minnie round the waist.

Alf climbed to his feet and shook his head to clear his senses. 'That scatty cow o' yours come causin' trouble again,' he growled.

The two women were holding on to handfuls of hair as they swayed to and fro and Minnie kicked backwards to make her husband let go of her waist. The blow caught him on the shin and he howled in pain.

The fracas had brought neighbours to their doors, and when Albert Price saw the action from his bedroom window he ran down the stairs to let Granny Minto know what was going on. 'The Barlows an' Sloans are at it again,' he shouted. 'Those two women are pullin' chunks of each ovver's 'air out.'

Granny was enjoying a nap and she sat up straight in her armchair. 'Someone should chuck a bucket o' water over 'em,' she said irritably.

Albert thought it was a very good idea and he chuckled evilly to himself as he dragged out a galvanised pail from under the scullery sink. Minnie and Annie were locked in combat when he stepped out into the street with the brimming receptacle, and ignoring Alf Barlow's raised hands and horrified expression he swung it forward and threw the cold water over the two of them.

'Bloody maniac!' Minnie said, gasping for breath.

Granny Minto had come to the front door and she cackled. 'If it'd bin me yer'd 'ave got the pail as well!'

Chapter Fifteen

The Monday evening ruckus was the main topic of conversation in the street but Joe Carey had other things on his mind when he called in on his next-door neighbour on Tuesday evening. 'Did yer see this in the *Bulletin*?' he asked.

'Yeah, I did,' Charlie replied. 'Mabel pointed it out ter me when I got in from work.'

'I don't like the sound of it,' Joe said, looking worried. 'This could bring it all up again.'

Mabel patted her bun the way she always did when something was troubling her and pinched at her bottom lip. 'I said the same ter Charlie,' she sighed. 'Why can't they leave fings alone instead o' draggin' up the past. People don't wanna be reminded about the bloody war an' the Blitz.'

Joe shook his head slowly. 'That's just the point, luv. People do,' he told her. 'It's bin six years now an' people still talk about the Blitz as though it was yesterday. They'll all be buyin' the paper ter see who's in it.'

'D'yer fink they'll mention the Ship Lane shelter?' Mabel asked.

'They'll get round to it I'm sure, 'specially after what 'appened,' Charlie replied.

'They'll most likely send a reporter round ter see us,' Joe puffed. 'Me an' our Marfa are worried sick in case they start delvin' inter fings. You know the way they are.'

'Now listen, Joe, if we do get a visit we just gotta keep it simple,' Charlie said, raising his hands in a calming gesture. 'What we said at the time is down on record. We can't tell 'em ter piss orf if they come to interview us, that'll look like we've got somefing to 'ide. We'll tell 'em exactly the same as we told that inquest. The reporter who's doin' these articles would 'ave seen the report anyway I'm sure.'

'You even got commended by the coroner,' Mabel reminded them.

'Well, we did what we could an' no one could 'ave done more,' Charlie said as he reached for his tobacco pouch.

'P'raps they won't get round to it,' Joe suggested without conviction. 'After all, there's a lot of ovver fings ter write about.'

'Well, it's in the lap o' the gods,' Charlie shrugged. 'I just 'ope they don't go troublin' Mrs Merry.'

'So do I,' Mabel cut in. 'The poor cow ain't bin 'erself lately an' she 'ardly goes out o' the 'ouse.'

'I shouldn't fink they'd do anuvver story about George Merry,' Joe remarked. 'They did a nice piece at the time. What else can they say they 'aven't already said?'

'I dunno,' Charlie replied. 'Once they get talkin' ter Mrs Merry they could open a can o' worms.'

Mabel had heard enough and she got up with a deep sigh. 'All this is worryin' the bleedin' life out o' me. I'm gonna go an' 'ave a chat wiv Marfa.'

As soon as she had left the house Joe turned to his old friend. 'Our Marfa's beside 'erself too,' he said sighing. 'If the trufe o' that night ever got made public she'd die o' shame.'

Charlie's face grew tense. 'I fink we all would,' he replied.

Benny Tracy had never given up hope that one day his landlady Queenie would come to see him as more than just a paying lodger, but he realised with regret that he had done nothing to encourage her in any way. He saw himself as the eternal gentleman, always willing to help about the house and always most proper in his behaviour. He had never married, and now in his autumn years he gave much thought to his life. There had been women but nothing had come of the liaisons, and he had decided that he would most probably die a bachelor. Such independence had suited him really. He could go for a drink when he liked and meet his friends without hindrance. He had a few pounds put away too and a decent suit for special occasions.

Lately however, his life had begun to seem rather empty and lacking. True he had his friends, but there was no one special to share his private moments, share his bed, and almost without him realising it his eye had started to wander, albeit not very far. Queenie was still an attractive woman whose children were all married off. She had more time on her hands these days, and now that she was free from her brute of a husband she could cast her net if she so desired. Benny realised that he should not have given too much credit to what she said about not wanting another man in her life. Instead he should have staked his claim with subtleness and panache, advancing his desire while continuing to be the perfect gentleman. Now it was too late, he sighed sadly as he polished his shoes. Queenie had suddenly found a man and she appeared to be doting on him. There was nothing he could do about it, short of beating John Raney to death with a hammer, and he resigned himself to a few drinks at the Bell with his old pals.

As the three musketeers sat together in the public bar Wally Tucker was holding court. 'My Betty was only sayin' yesterday 'ow sad it was,' he went on. 'That poor ole cow Lucy spends all 'er time sittin' in that 'ouse of 'ers an' she 'ardly 'as anyone call on 'er. If it wasn't fer our Bet she could be dead an' nobody would be any the wiser.'

'Queenie runs a few errands for 'er now an' then,' Benny reminded him.

'Yeah but she 'ardly ever goes out the 'ouse,' Wally insisted.

Tubby looked thoughtful. 'I s'pose we could ask 'er ter come out fer a drink wiv us one night,' he suggested.

'That's a good idea,' Wally replied. 'Why don't yer pop in an' 'ave a chat wiv 'er? She might like ter come out. When George Merry was alive they was always in 'ere. Lucy loved a drink.'

Tubby shook his head. 'I can't ask the woman,' he said. 'She might get the wrong impression, me bein' on me own like 'er.'

'Yeah, I s'pose yer right,' Wally said nodding.

'I couldn't ask 'er neivver,' Benny told them. 'I'm a single man an' it wouldn't look good.'

'Well, I couldn't neivver,' Wally said as he picked up his pint. 'She might get the wrong impression about me. Fer all she knew I might be tryin' fer a bit on the side.'

'We could all go tergevver,' Benny suggested.

'It'd scare the daylights out of 'er,' Wally said shaking his head.

'I know,' Tubby said quickly. 'Why don't yer get your ole woman ter go an' see 'er? She could tell 'er the lads wanted ter give 'er a night out.'

Wally stroked his stubbled chin. 'It wouldn't 'urt would it. Right, I'll do it.'

'When?'

'Termorrer.'

'What, get 'er out termorrer?'

'Why not?'

'Better make it Thursday.'

'Why's that?'

'Well, the cockle stall's 'ere on Thursday,' Tubby reminded them.

'Good finkin',' Wally said nodding. 'Ole Lucy loves jellied eels. She always used to 'ave a bowl o' jellied eels in 'ere on Thursdays.'

The three musketeers looked pleased with themselves as they sipped their pints. It was another chance to be neighbourly in their own special way, and as Benny put it, 'If yer can't 'elp yer neighbours who can yer 'elp?'

Earlier that evening Del Abelson sat alone in the Colemans' house, scanning through the list of local transport firms, and he ringed two. They were both experiencing labour troubles and their respective shop stewards had reported a hardening of attitude on the part of the management. The workforces had reacted and confrontation was looming. It seemed to be the pattern, he thought. There was a lot of work to be done to keep the criminal element from muscling in any further.

The young man quickly closed the folder and slipped it behind the cushion when he heard the knock. The clock showed seven-thirty and he cursed himself as he hurried along the passage. He had promised to call on Sue at seven.

'I was worried something was wrong,' the young woman told him, looking peeved.

He gave her a mortified smile. 'I'm sorry, Sue, I've bin workin',' he said as he stood back for her to come in. 'I didn't realise it was so late.'

Sue walked into the parlour. 'The clock seems to be working all right,' she remarked sarcastically.

Del made a grab for his coat. 'We've still got time, 'aven't we?'

Sue sat down on the settee and leaned back. 'Yes, if you want to walk in halfway through the first picture, which I don't,' she answered abruptly.

Del hung his coat back on the door and came over to sit beside her. 'I'm really sorry, Sue,' he told her. 'I just got involved wiv what I was doin'.'

Sue leant forward and reached behind the cushion. 'I wondered what I was leaning against,' she said. 'Is this what was taking up your time?'

Del took the thick folder from her and put it down beside him. 'I need ter make a good start an' there's so much ter read up on,' he replied.

'Perhaps I shouldn't have called,' she sighed.

'No I'm glad yer did,' he said quickly. 'We could go fer a drink if yer like.'

She shook her head. 'Where's Rosie and Jim?'

'They've gone ter the pictures,' he answered.

'Have you thought any more about what we discussed?'

'Of course I 'ave.'

'Well?'

He could see the mocking glint in her eyes and he leaned across and laid his hand on her shoulder. 'I'll sort somefing out soon, I promise.'

She turned slightly towards him, noticing how his eyes moved as she crossed her legs and adjusted her cotton dress. 'How soon, Del?'

He looked slightly irritated as he met her gaze. 'I can't say, not till I find out about when the public meetin's are due ter take place.'

'At weekends?'

'Yeah.'

It was Sue's turn to be annoyed. 'So now you'll be working at weekends too.'

He sighed as he saw the look on her face and turned fully towards her, drawing one leg up on the settee. 'I've got a chance ter really make somefing o' this job,' he said with a passion in his voice. 'It's what I've always wanted. It's an important time, Sue. Fings are movin' fast an' I can't tell yer 'ow important it is.'

'You could try me,' she remarked. 'I'm listening.'

'I thought yer didn't want me ter keep goin' on about the union,' he replied.

'Well, if I'm not going to be seeing much of you from now on I'd like to know what I'm up against,' she said firmly.

He picked up the folder and held it up. 'It's all in 'ere,' he told her, dropping it on the settee between them and laying his hand on it. 'Ter start wiv, the union wants ter get all the transport workers ter join. A lot of local transport firms already 'ave union drivers, 'specially those that do dock work. Dockers often want ter see the drivers' union tickets before they load an' unload the lorries. That's why Brady's drivers 'old tickets, but as yer know from Tom this new depot 'e's opened up won't be involved in dock work. They'll be solely food factory contracts.'

'What about the loaders at the factories? Couldn't they do what the dockers do?' Sue suggested.

'They could, if they were unionised,' Del explained with a smile. 'Our union is transport an' general, which allows labourers ter join. That's what we're about. If we can get full membership at the factories as well as the transport firms we'll 'ave a lot o' clout, an' the likes o' Joe Brady won't be able ter take any more liberties.'

'What about all this villainy?' she asked.

'I've just bin readin' about the union troubles in America,' he went on. 'Recent communications we've 'ad from over there show that the Teamsters Union an' the Longshoremen – their equivalent of our dock workers – 'ave been infiltrated by organised crime. The reports sent from the States ter the Transport and General Workers' Union are full o' cases where workers' representatives were bein' victimised an' the men themselves threatened wiv violence unless they knuckled down ter certain rules an' regulations. It could 'appen 'ere too before very long, if nuffing's done about it.'

'But why should someone like Brady pay the villains?' Sue asked. 'Surely it'd be easier and a lot cheaper to work with the unions instead of trying to fight them all the time?'

'It goes a lot deeper than union membership,' he told her. 'Just consider the implications. Your bruvver Mo wants transport ter move 'is stuff from A ter B. At the moment 'e can pick the firm that suits 'im. But if the villains got control only transport firms who pay their dues could get the work. Firms outside the cartel would be squeezed out. What's more, transport firms who do dock work would 'ave shop stewards who were in the pay o' the cartel an' the drivers would be levied. No pay-off, no work. It's started to 'appen in the States.'

'Surely the unions are too powerful in this country to let that happen?' Sue queried.

'Unions are only as strong as their members,' Del replied. 'If the men don't back their representatives it all falls down. The Brady fiasco is proof o' that.'

'So how can you stop the villains taking control?' she asked.

'Bringin' it all out inter the open,' he said with a look of determination. 'Our union wants solid evidence ter give ter the newspapers. Proof o' corruption, proof of intimidation, an' what the implications can be if union members don't stand tergevver ter fight it. That's why those planned public meetin's are so important. I fink Trafalgar Square's gonna be the first venue, an' there'll be speakers from all over the country. Union officials from Liverpool, Manchester, Glasgow, Southampton an' Bristol, as well as campaignin' MPs. It'll be a start, Sue.'

She could see the fire in his eyes and hear the passion in his voice and she moved towards him. 'I'm sorry if I sounded so negative,' she said quietly. 'I understand a lot better now. You must go to those meetings, Del. Stand up and tell them what's going on.'

He chuckled. 'I'm just a minor branch official. I won't get the chance ter do any tub-thumpin', but it's important I go though.'

She moved even closer, her hand resting on his chest. 'You did say the Colemans have gone to the pictures, didn't you?'

In answer he slipped his arms around her and found her eager lips, and she ran her fingers through his thick dark hair as she moulded herself hungrily to him. He moved above her and she sank back as he stroked his hand along her thigh and up to clasp her firm breast. Her heart was pounding as his lips brushed her neck and her ears and then pressed down over her open mouth. Firmly, gently he caressed her willing body and she knew that the time was now. They were alone together in the warm and it had to be now, she thought as her heartbeats seemed to shake her body. She moved to accommodate his searching hands and felt the roughness of his fingers as he reached beneath her dress and gripped her bare thigh. She could hear his breathing coming faster and she moaned softly as his hand strayed upwards. Suddenly he moved back as though checking himself and took her hand as he struggled from the settee. He pulled her on to her feet, wrapping his arms round her as he kissed her passionately, then he led her out of the room, into the dark passage and up the steep flight of stairs. His desire was every bit as urgent as hers, she could tell, and as they walked into the small bedroom he swept her up into his strong arms and carried her to the bed. Her cotton dress was up around the tops of her thighs as he hovered over her and she saw the hot desire in his handsome face. No more waiting, she wanted him now and he knew. With a quick movement he pulled her knickers down over her shapely thighs and then as she looked up at him he loosened the front of his trousers. He pressed down on her and she gasped as she felt his stiff sex enter her hot wet body. It was furious and rapid, the tensions and frustrations of unsatisfactory fumbling in doorways now released, redeemed in a sharp, sudden flood of ecstasy, and they savoured it like long-famished creatures as they lay locked in each other's arms.

Chapter Sixteen

Tom Carey had walked through the gates on Monday morning with his head held high, and after a few backslaps and handshakes he was presented with an envelope containing two pounds seven and sixpence which had been collected on his behalf. Bernie Catchpole was lingering in the background and after a brief hard look he climbed into his lorry and drove out of the yard. Tom was given his delivery notes by a stone-faced Toby Lowndes who told him that Joe Brady wanted to see him right away. He was surprised to find that his day's work entailed picking up a load of cased machinery from Dockhead which had to be delivered to Maidstone. It could have been worse, he thought. The cases would be lifted on and off by crane and all in all it would be a comfortable day's work.

The young man climbed the exterior iron staircase and saw that Brady's office door was open. The man was sitting behind his desk, biting on the unlit stub of a cigar. He smiled to show a gold tooth as Tom walked in. 'Take a seat, son,' he said amiably. ''Ow yer feelin'?'

'Pretty good,' Tom told him with a deadpan look.

Brady removed the cigar stub from his mouth and aimed it into a wastepaper basket. 'I just wanted yer ter know what I told the rest o' the drivers,' he said, fixing him with his stare. 'What 'appened ter you was nuffink ter do wiv this company. You got yerself into a bit of a scrape an' yer seem to 'ave come out of it all right. But that's over an' done wiv. Glad ter see yer back. By the way, yer know that Del Abelson's left us?'

'Yeah, so I 'eard,' Tom said nodding.

Brady shuffled some papers and then looked back up at the young man. 'They'll be votin' somebody else in,' he went on. 'I want it ter be somebody I can work wiv. What about you puttin' yer name forward? I'm sure me an' you could work tergevver. The men all get on wiv yer an' they'll listen to a cool 'ead. You could do well by it too. I'm pretty generous ter those who look after my interests.'

Tom Carey felt the anger rising inside him and he stared back hard at the heavy-jowled man behind the desk. 'Like you said, guv'nor, what 'appened ter me is over an' done wiv,' he replied in a measured voice, 'but that don't mean I'm changed in any way. On the contrary. If I accepted that shop steward's job I'd most likely be every bit as militant as Del Abelson was. One fing's fer sure, I wouldn't be in anyone's pockets, the guv'nor's or the union's. As it 'appens I'm not interested anyway. As far as I'm concerned I'm 'ere ter do a day's work fer a day's pay.'

Brady nodded slowly, only his eyes betraying his displeasure. 'All right, son, yer better get started then.'

Early on Tuesday morning an official from the union called in to oversee the appointment of a new shop steward and Bernie Catchpole was voted in unopposed.

'Of all the people ter be a shop steward,' one of the drivers growled. 'When we was out on the stones 'e was the first ter start moanin'.'

'I make yer right,' another scowled. 'We won't get much joy out of 'im.'

Shorty Lockwood was more scathing. 'The bloody git's an out-an'-out guv'nor's man. 'E'll be takin' a back'ander ter keep the peace, that's fer sure.'

Tom Carey smiled cynically at the comments made around him. Bernie Catchpole was disliked by most of the men but he had been voted in regardless. The show of hands would have indicated to him just who were opposing his appointment and as expected very few were bold enough to keep their hands in their pockets; apart from himself, Tom noticed only one abstainer, Shorty Lockwood. It would be interesting to see how Catchpole tackled the job. It was obvious that Joe Brady had had words with him but Catchpole was unpredictable, and as much as he disliked him Tom Carey could not totally believe that the new steward would take a backhander. Some of the other drivers felt differently however, and only time would tell, he told himself as he climbed into his lorry to pick up a consignment of Danish cheese from Mark Brown's Wharf.

On Wednesday morning Minnie Sloan had a visitor, and while he was there she ran across the turning to get Annie Barlow. Later that morning the two women walked to the market arm in arm, to the disgust of Granny Minto.

''Ere, Albert. Come an' take a gander at those two prats,' she called out.

Albert hurried to the front door. 'Don't it make yer wanna spit,' he said shaking his head as he saw them walk out of the street. 'On Monday evenin' they was at it 'ammer an' tongs, an' now they look like a couple o' love-birds.'

'Yer should 'ave seen the look on their faces,' Granny went on. 'I dunno about love-birds, they looked more like pigs in shit ter me.'

Nell Sharp came into the turning and spotted Granny and Albert talking together. ''Ere, I've just seen those two silly mares. Arm in arm they was,' she said breathlessly. 'I couldn't believe it.'

'I was just sayin' the same to Albert,' Granny replied. 'I wonder what's goin' on wiv them two.'

'Gawd knows,' Nell said shaking her head. 'I just can't understand it. I remember 'avin' a set-to wiv that Mrs Burroughs who used ter live next door an' we never spoke fer months afterwards.'

'Yer know what I fink,' Albert interjected. 'I fink they've battered each ovver stupid over the years. I mean ter say, when yer talk to 'em yer don't get any sense out of 'em.'

Nell Sharp chuckled. 'I 'ad ter laugh when yer chucked that pail o' water over 'em.'

Queenie Alladyce came out of her house and waved to them as she hurried towards the corner shop. Granny Minto smiled as she waved back, then turned to Nell. 'I'm sure she wants 'er 'ead examined. She was on about butterflies the ovver day. I fink that Raney's bin fillin' 'er brain wiv a load o' rubbish.'

'D'yer fink there is anyfing goin' on between them two?' Nell asked.

'Well, she don't go in there fer whitenin' or blacklead

186

every day, that's fer sure,' Granny remarked. 'Still, it's 'er life. If she makes 'er bed she's gotta lie in it.'

''Is bed yer mean,' Nell said grinning.

Betty Tucker walked round the corner carrying a laden shopping-bag and was soon able to throw some light on the strange behaviour of the two viragos. ''Ere, there's somefing very strange goin' on in this turnin',' she told them.

'What d'yer mean?' Granny asked her.

Betty rested the shopping-bag against her leg and rubbed her aching hands. 'Well, this mornin' I was cleanin' me windersill, an' I saw this bloke come in the turnin'. 'E gave me a smile. Good-lookin' chap. Quite smart too.'

'Go on then,' Granny said impatiently.

'Well, I stood watchin', an' I saw 'im knock at Minnie Sloan's door. She invited 'im in an' then a few minutes later, just as I was dustin' me doorstep, I saw Minnie run across to Annie Barlow's an' back the two of 'em come. I thought ter meself, what's goin' on there then, like yer would. Anyway what d'yer fink I saw just now?'

'Annie an' Minnie arm in arm,' Granny answered.

Betty Tucker looked disappointed at having her punch line stolen. 'Grinnin' all over their faces they was. Gawd knows what's goin' on between them two but I bet that bloke who called on Minnie 'as got somefing ter do wiv it.'

Albert was getting a little tired of the hen meeting. 'Well, I'm orf ter get me *Sportin' Life*,' he announced.

'We've just bin talkin' about Queenie,' Nell said after Albert had strolled off. 'We fink there's somefing goin' on between 'er an' John Raney.'

'I've 'eard the same,' Betty replied.

'We was just sayin', what would she be wantin' in that shop every day?' Nell went on. 'I only ever go in there fer me whitenin' an' blacklead. Once a month if that, 'cept if it's very warm an' I need fresh fly-papers.'

At that moment Queenie came out of the shop carrying a bundle wrapped in newspaper. 'Just bin fer me whitenin',' she called over as if mocking the three. 'I fergot me blacklead. I'll 'ave ter go back later.'

A block of old buildings in Dockhead was being renovated. New windows were being installed and scaffolding had already been fixed up. Normally there would be nothing going on which would inspire people to stop and stare, but today passers-by had stopped to take notice. One of the scaffolders was having his photo taken and he leaned out precariously from high up, prompted by a man on the ground holding a large camera. The onlookers then saw another man climb up a ladder with a filled hod resting against his shoulder, and he stopped halfway up to smile down at the photographer. At that moment Minnie and Annie arrived arm in arm.

'Did the reporter come an' see yer?' Annie yelled up.

''E's just left,' Alf shouted down, still feeling bemused by the sudden publicity.

''E seemed a nice feller. Did yer tell 'im all about it?' Annie called back.

The photographer had already been informed that the two wives would be arriving at the building site to have their photos taken at their husbands' place of work and he puffed loudly. 'Do you mind if I take these pictures, ladies?' he said with some sarcasm.

'What's goin' on?' one onlooker asked.

'Gawd knows,' the man next to him replied.

'That's my ole man up there,' Minnie said nudging him.

'An' that's my Alf up on that scaffoldin',' Annie told him.

'Why are they 'avin' their pictures taken?' the man asked.

'Just get the *Bulletin* on Friday,' Minnie said with a wink.

'Yeah, yer'll be able ter read all about it,' Annie added.

More people had gathered and Minnie took the opportunity to wave. 'All right, luv?' she called out.

Alf Barlow was enjoying the sudden fame and he leaned further out.

'You be careful now, luv,' Annie shouted up.

The photographer had finally taken the necessary photos of the two men and he turned towards the women. 'When you're ready, ladies,' he said with a smile.

Minnie pulled Annie towards him. 'C'mon, gel, let's get our pictures taken,' she said loud enough for everyone standing round to hear.

One of the onlookers scratched his head. 'What was that she said ter you?' he asked the man next to him.

'She said it'll be in the *Bulletin* on Friday.'

'What will?'

'Search me.'

Annie slipped her arm around Minnie's shoulders and looked very stern at the photographer.

'No, don't fold your arms, luv. Put your arm round her waist,' he said to Minnie. 'That's right, now let's have a big smile. C'mon, look at me.'

'We are,' Annie said just as he took the shot.

'I'll need one more,' he said, mumbling under his breath as he focused the camera.

Minnie decided to look proud and she stuck out her ample bosom and pouted. Not to be outdone Annie turned to wave at Alf just as the camera clicked.

The photographer was beginning to feel that he was dealing with a couple of halfwits. 'I think I should take just one more,' he told them. 'Now please look at the camera this time and keep still. Right then, big smile.'

'I 'ope they come out all right,' Annie said as he put the camera into its case.

If they do it'll be a bloody miracle, he thought, smiling at her reassuringly.

Sam Calkin was busy that afternoon putting the finishing touches to his first article, and he felt that barring any disaster with the photo shoot all the material would be on Spencer's desk by five o'clock. Beside him on the desktop was a folder of news cuttings he had brought up from the glory hole and already the next article was shaping up in his mind. The editor would want a few pointers on what was to come to insert in the Tuesday edition and Sam wanted to get ahead. He leaned back and stretched leisurely, glancing over to Frances's desk. She had been gone for some time and he guessed where she would be. He gathered up the folder and returned Josie Willard's big smile as he passed her desk. The light was on in the basement and as he reached the bottom of the stairs he saw Frances standing beside Paddy O'Brian. Her face looked flushed and she gave him an embarrassed smile. 'We were just looking for something,' she said.

Paddy cleared his throat and ran his hand through his dishevelled hair. 'How's it going?' he asked.

Sam hid a smile. 'Fine, thanks.' He turned to the custodian. 'I've finished with these, Frances. I just came down to put them away.'

'Just leave them on the table, I'll do it. It's no problem,' she replied, still looking nervous.

Sam decided not to argue. He had obviously interrupted something and it seemed prudent to beat a hasty retreat. 'Thanks, Frances,' he said, chancing a quick wink.

Back at his desk he sat pondering. The article he had just prepared concerned a rescue operation that had taken place in Dockhead, and when he first followed up the brief report he had salvaged from the archives he had discovered that the two men involved were now living in Totterdown Street. By a coincidence the subject of his next planned article had lived there too. The original piece in the paper six years back had stated that the man had died a hero and had left a wife to grieve over him. He would need to call in to the street first thing tomorrow morning and make some enquiries.

Sam took his coat from the back of the chair and slipped it on as he made his way out. 'Sue, in case I'm wanted I'm off to chase up some photographs,' he told her. 'By the way, I'll be going to Totterdown Street directly from home tomorrow morning.'

'That's where I live,' she said, giving him a smile.

'Well, then you may be able to help me,' he replied.
'If I can.'

He leaned on the raised counter. 'Does George Merry's wife still live in Totterdown Street?' he asked.

Sue nodded. 'Yes, she does. Number twenty-one, but she's a semi-recluse these days. She hardly ever goes out. Tell me, are you doing a story about George Merry?'

Sam nodded. 'I wonder if she'll see me. Do you think she would?'

'It's hard to say,' Sue replied. 'She may need some prompting. One or two of her neighbours pop in to see if she needs anything. They may be able to help.'

Sam stroked his chin. 'Actually I found the piece on George Merry in the files but it was very brief. I want to get an insight into what the man was like, how his wife managed to cope after his death, you know the sort of thing. I want to make it a human interest story. I hope she'll agree to see me, but if not maybe I could talk to her neighbours.'

'Well, there's Mrs Betty Tucker who lives at number fifteen,' Sue informed him, 'and sometimes the woman who lives opposite her at number twenty-two calls in to see her. It's Mrs Rosie Coleman.'

'That's smashing,' Sam said giving her a wide smile. 'Thanks, Sue.'

'I wish you luck,' she told him. 'I'll be interested to see how you get on.'

'I promise I'll let you know,' he said buttoning up his coat, and as he reached the door he added, 'don't forget to read this week's piece.'

The three musketeers had enjoyed a lunchtime drink

in the Bell, and for want of something better to do they ambled along to sit in the flower garden behind the old Bermondsey Church. While in the pub they had discussed the state of the world in general and occasionally things had got a little heated, but now in the more serene surroundings it was time to reflect on local issues.

''Ere, while I fink of it,' Wally said suddenly, 'I told Betty about what we 'ad in mind fer Lucy Merry an' she thought it was a very good idea. As a matter o' fact she went in ter see 'er last night an' told 'er that we'd like ter take 'er out fer a drink on Thursday evenin'. When she found out the poor ole cow shed a few tears.'

'Whatever for?' Benny asked.

'She was overcome, that's why,' Wally told him. 'She told my Bet 'ow nice it was fer people ter fink of 'er.'

'So is it on fer Thursday night then?' Tubby Saward asked.

Wally shook his head. 'Nah. Lucy slipped over in the scullery a few days ago an' sprained 'er ankle. Our Bet said it was up like a balloon. Apparently Rosie Coleman went in ter see 'er that night an' she 'ad ter fetch the doctor. 'E bandaged it all up an' told 'er ter stay off it fer a week at least.'

'Couldn't we get a wheelchair for 'er?' Benny suggested.

'Where we gonna get a wheelchair from?' Wally asked.

'What about if we ask the 'ospital ter lend us one.'

'They won't lend 'em out. They're short of 'em as it is,' Wally told him. 'Remember when they tried ter borrer one fer Mrs Benjamin that time she 'urt 'er back? They couldn't get one fer love nor money.'

The problem seemed insoluble and a lengthy silence ensued while the three friends watched a gardener hoeing a nearby flower bed. Suddenly Benny's face broke into a big grin.

'I know. Why don't we borrer Sharkey's barrer? We could put a cushion on it.'

'We'd 'ave ter carry 'er out the 'ouse,' Wally remarked.

'Well, there's three of us.'

'I s'pose we could.'

Tubby seemed less enthusiastic. 'I dunno. It ain't very nice bein' pushed up the pub on a barrer, is it?'

'I s'pose it all depends 'ow much she fancies a drink,' Benny replied.

'I tell yer what,' Wally said. 'Benny, you go an' see Sharkey an' make sure we can get the barrer an' then give us a knock. I'll tell our Bet ter tell Lucy that we've laid transport on for 'er. She won't be none the wiser till we call round. Then we lift 'er up an' plonk 'er in the barrer. She won't 'ave time to argue.'

'Right, leave it ter me,' Benny said, replacing his cloth cap to hurry off to the market straight away.

'I just 'ope we're doin' the right fing,' Tubby remarked.

Chapter Seventeen

When Sam Calkin knocked at number 21 just after nine o'clock on Thursday morning there was no answer, and just as he was about to walk away from the door Rosie Coleman came out of her house opposite and crossed the street. 'Can I 'elp yer?' she asked him.

'You might be able to,' he replied with a disarming smile. 'My name's Sam Calkin and I'm from the *Bulletin*. I just wanted to have a few words with Mrs Merry.'

'As a matter o' fact she can't get ter the door. She's got a sprained ankle,' Rosie told him. 'I'm just poppin' in ter see if she wants anyfing at the market.'

'I'd appreciate it if you'd tell her I've called,' he said.

Rosie nodded as she let herself in and a few moments later she came back to the front door. 'Mrs Merry said it's all right ter go in,' she told him.

Sam followed her into the spotless parlour and saw that the frail old lady was sitting with her bandaged ankle resting on a cushion.

'This is the gentleman, luv,' Rosie said. 'I'll leave you to it while I slip down the market.'

Lucy Merry nervously brushed her hand down the

front of her clean apron. 'Would yer like ter sit down?' she asked.

The young man unbuttoned his coat and took the armchair facing her. 'Thank you for seeing me,' he began. 'I'm Sam Calkin and I'm doing a series of articles on the Blitz for the *Bulletin*. Do you get the *Bulletin*?'

'Rosie brings it in for me on Tuesdays an' Fridays,' the old lady replied. 'Nice woman that Rosie Coleman. So's Nell Sharp. She's the lady who lives a few doors along the turnin'. I dunno what I'd do wivout them two. Mind you the rest o' me neighbours are quite nice. They've bin a comfort to me since I lost my George. I don't go out much yer see. The noise o' the traffic frightens me, an' now o' course I couldn't move if I wanted to. I gotta stay like this fer a week, so Dr Wells told me. You 'ave ter take notice of 'em don't yer.'

Sam smiled in sympathy, allowing the old lady to gain confidence by chattering on. 'It's best to do as the doctor says, Mrs Merry,' he agreed.

'My George used ter like ole Dr Wells,' Lucy went on. 'Mind you, 'e did warn George about 'is drinkin'. George liked a tot o' whisky yer see an' Dr Wells said that if 'e didn't ease up 'e was gonna suffer later.'

'I read about your husband and what he did that night, Mrs Merry, and I'd like to do another piece, if you'll agree,' Sam told her slowly.

Lucy Merry eased herself in her chair and then she fixed him with pale watery eyes. 'I've no objections,' she said quietly. 'So long as it's nuffing bad. I couldn't bear that. George was a good man an' it wasn't fair what some people said about 'im afterwards.'

'The piece the *Bulletin* did was very good, I think you'll agree,' Sam said.

'I've no quarrel wiv the paper,' Lucy replied. 'It was the whisperin' that went on. It soon got back ter me, as yer would expect in a small neighbour'ood like this. It made me ill at the time.'

Sam leaned forward in the chair and gently laid his hand on the old lady's arm. 'As far as I'm concerned your husband died a hero, and I wouldn't dream of putting anything in the article that would upset you or blacken his memory. That's a promise.'

'Fer that I'm grateful,' Lucy said, reaching into her apron pocket for a handkerchief as her eyes filled with tears. 'Yer see, my George loved 'is drink, but I 'ave ter tell yer 'ere an' now that 'e was never abusive wiv it.' She paused to dab at her eyes. 'My George was 'ard-workin'. 'E spent more than firty-five years wiv Moxen's the lead mills in Ship Lane. 'E was a driver there fer all o' that time, an' after 'e got put off at sixty-five 'e was at a loose end. That's when 'e started drinkin' heavy. George was always in the Bell an' a lot of 'is ole mates at work used ter treat 'im. Anyway, just before the war started the ole night-watchman at Moxen's died an' they offered George the job. 'E was turned sixty-seven at the time but still sprightly. I remember 'ow 'appy 'e was ter be back at work, even though it meant leavin' me on me own at nights. I didn't mind, if it made 'im 'appy.'

'Are you feeling up to this, Mrs Merry?' Sam asked with concern. 'I don't want you to upset yourself.'

'Yeah I'm okay,' the old lady replied with a quick nod of her head. 'I can never ferget that night, when it 'appened. May the tenth it was. It'd bin quiet fer a while, wiv only a few night raids, nuffink ter speak about, then that night it was like 'ell itself. They say it was the worst raid ever an' I believe 'em. Everywhere was burnin' an' the loss o' life was terrible. It wasn't only them there 'igh explosives, it was incendiaries as well. That was the night the ware'ouse in Ship Lane copped it an' them poor souls from this street were killed. Anyway. Ter start at the beginnin'.' She paused for a moment and sighed. 'It was about one o'clock in the mornin' accordin' ter the reports when an oil bomb landed on Moxen's. The 'ole place was blazin' an' they 'ad two lorries in the yard beside the mills. My George used ter be in the yard office an' when the bomb landed it set the yard alight. Now the back lorry was already loaded fer the next mornin', a load o' solder sticks I believe they said it was, but the lorry nearest the gates was empty. George drove it out o' the yard an' went back ter try an' save the loaded one but 'e never made it. They found 'is body by the lorry next mornin'. It was under a load o' rubble. They said the side wall fell on top of 'im. George could 'ave saved 'imself but 'e was a conscientious worker. All 'e was concerned about was gettin' that loaded lorry out the yard. Goin' back in there cost 'im 'is life. As a matter o' fact the guv'nor o' the firm called round ter see me the next day. 'E was very nice. 'E said some nice fings about George, 'ow conscientious 'e was an' such like. The terrible fing about it all though, it was all in vain. I 'eard later that the lorry George drove out inter the street outside was burned out when the ware'ouse opposite copped it.'

'The warehouse where the people died?' Sam queried.

'That's right,' Lucy went on. 'They said George died

an 'ero, an' I s'pose it's true. It must 'ave took a lot o' guts ter go back in that yard wiv the place on fire an' bombs fallin' everywhere. Everybody said 'ow brave 'e was an' all the neighbours turned out ter give 'im a nice send-off. There was also that nice piece in the paper, an' it should 'ave bin left at that, but no. People can be wicked at times. It wasn't long after the funeral when the rumours started.'

'What rumours were they, Mrs Merry?' Sam prompted her.

'It was said George left the yard fer a drink that night an' 'e ended up blind drunk,' she told him. 'Accordin' ter the rumours 'e was out on 'is feet an' two o' the blokes from the Bell 'ad ter carry 'im back ter Moxen's. They said that 'e couldn't 'ave pulled that lorry out the yard the state 'e was in, an' ter be fair I wouldn't 'ave argued, if it was true about 'im bein' sloshed. When George got drunk 'e was 'elpless, but I knew 'im. 'E would never 'ave left that yard unattended, no matter 'ow much 'e fancied a drink.'

Sam Calkin nodded slowly. 'I'm certain you're right, Mrs Merry. I'm going to make some more enquiries before I write the piece. I'd like to be able to scotch those evil rumours once and for all. At least when I do write the article I'll be able to add a bit about you and how the neighbours have rallied round since George has been gone, if you've no objections.'

'That would be very nice, young man,' the old lady said smiling. 'I'm sorry I've not bin able ter make yer a cuppa.'

Sam stood up and squeezed Lucy's hand gently. 'It's all right. It's been a real pleasure talking to you. I hope I'll have the opportunity of calling again before long.'

Martha Carey brushed a strand of hair from her forehead with the back of her hand as she stirred the bubbling contents of the stewpot. Tonight was a night she had prayed for and she was anxious that everything should be just right for the occasion. She added another stock cube, letting it crumble between her fingers and stirring it in with the large wooden ladle. Meat stew and dumplings was Mo's favourite meal and tonight she would be able to watch his face as he ate it.

It had come as quite a surprise, really. That morning Maurice had called in to find out if Tom would be available for a chat during the evening and she had managed to coax him into coming for tea. He had declined at first, saying that it might save any upset if he called later, but she had been insistent. Maybe it was the tears she was very obviously fighting back which had swayed him, or the promise that his father would be threatened with all sorts if he started an argument. Whatever the reason Mo had finally agreed to come for a meal and she was going to make it special.

'Mum, come and see if this is all right,' Sue asked as she looked into the scullery.

Martha followed her daughter into the parlour and smiled appreciatively. The best white linen tablecloth showed off the olive green dinner service and the silver cutlery gleamed in the light. Chairs were placed around the table and the best china teapot stood in the middle on the square of cloth Aunt Ellie had painstakingly worked on with needles and cotton for the past few months. 'It looks lovely,' she said clasping her hands together. 'That cloth really sets it off.'

Aunt Ellie looked up from her usual place beside the fire and nodded, feeling that her sister was being a little patronising. Not much could be seen of her handiwork with that ugly teapot standing on it, but never mind, Mo was coming to tea, and that in itself was comfort enough.

The well-used enamel teapot was standing on the back of the old iron gas-stove, the tea brewing ready for when Joe got home from work. Everything was under control, Martha thought. First she would sit him down with a strong brew in his favourite mug and then he would be warned in no uncertain terms to keep the peace. Tonight was special and neither he nor anyone else was going to spoil it.

'Who's comin' ter tea, the archbishop?' Tom said as he looked into the parlour.

'Mo's coming,' Ellie told him with a smile.

'Where's the ole feller goin' fer 'is tea, the fish shop?' the young man joked.

Ellie hid a smile. Tom could be very flippant and even crude at times and she wouldn't encourage him. 'Mo wants to see you, and your mother persuaded him to come for tea. I just hope there's no upsets. I don't think I could stand it,' she sighed.

Tom sat down in the armchair facing her and started to unlace his working boots. 'Don't you worry, Aunt Ellie, I won't let anyfing upset this evenin',' he told her. 'If Farvver starts, me an' Mo'll chuck 'im out in the yard like 'e used ter do ter me when I was a kid.'

Aunt Ellie dabbed at her nose with her lace handkerchief. 'Tom, shouldn't you take those boots off in the scullery? They smell awful.'

'It's only vinegar,' he replied with a grin. 'I 'ad ter do a delivery ter this vinegar firm over in Poplar an' the poxy place was swimmin' in stale vinegar.'

Ellie looked at him with disgust. 'Is there any need for that sort of talk?' she said.

Martha had heard the exchange. 'Tom, don't take those boots off in the parlour,' she called out to him.

The young man shuffled into the scullery with the laces trailing. 'I was only windin' Aunt Ellie up,' he said grinning.

'Well don't,' Martha told him sharply. 'Leave 'em in the yard, they smell terrible.'

Just then Joe Carey walked in, and after peering into the parlour to greet Ellie he came out to the scullery. 'What's goin' on?' he asked with a frown.

Martha had filled his mug as soon as she heard the front door go and she placed the tea down on the small table. 'There you are,' she said.

'Did you 'ear me?' Joe said. 'I asked what was goin' on.'

'Nuffink as far as I know,' she replied.

'What's the table laid for?'

Martha sat down facing him. 'Now listen ter me, Joe,' she said quietly. 'I've invited our Mo fer tea an' I don't want no upsets. 'E called in this mornin'. 'E wanted ter see Tom ternight, so I thought it'd be nice fer us all ter sit down to a meal tergevver, the way we used to.'

Joe sipped his tea. 'I've no intention of upsettin' fings,' he replied with a frown, 'but I'm not gonna be tagged wiv bein' the villain o' the piece neivver. What's bin said 'ad ter be said, an' you know it. You agreed wiv me at the time.'

Sue came into the scullery and looked from one to the other. 'What's going on?' she asked.

'It's all right, luv, I'm just gettin' the riot act read out ter me,' Joe said, giving Martha a placatory grin.

Sue sat down facing him. 'I wish I knew what it is with you and Mo, Dad,' she sighed. 'None of us ever see much of him and on the rare occasions he does call there's an atmosphere. You can cut it with a knife. Tom feels the same way as I do. It seems to us as though a bomb's waiting to go off the way you two carry on. It's not right. We're supposed to be a family. I wish you'd tell us what it is.'

Tom had gone into the backyard as asked, and as he came back into the scullery in his stockinged feet he gave Sue a quick glance before going through to sit with Ellie. Martha got up again to give the stew another stir, glancing furtively at Joe as he put down his tea. What could he say, she thought. He had been put in a corner and she could almost see the cogs racing in his mind as he searched for a reply.

'I make yer right, luv,' Joe began. 'We are a family, an' we always will be. Sometimes though fings 'appen in families an' it causes tensions an' ructions. Often fings can be put right, but in ovver cases there's somefing that can't be undone. Bad words an' fings that 'appen sometimes cut ter the quick an' it can destroy the closeness in families. If what's said an' what's transpired can never be forgotten then all yer do is bury it away an' try ter forget. That's what I'm tryin' ter do, an' in 'is own way that's what Mo's about. I just 'ope that fings'll improve an' we can be a close family again. I 'ope an' pray we can.'

Sue wanted to ask him what had really happened or been said, and why it was so bad that he was avoiding telling her, but it seemed inappropriate to pursue it at that moment and she nodded her head slowly. 'I hope so too, Dad, I really do,' she said with passion.

Martha came over and laid a hand on Joe's shoulder. 'Go an' get washed, luv,' she said affectionately. 'Mo'll be 'ere soon.'

The early June sun had long since dipped down below the rooftops and now the copper sky was tinged with purple dusk. Outside a breeze was getting up, promising night rain, but the backyard at number 6 was sheltered and offered a little privacy as the two brothers sat talking.

'Didn't yer 'ave any inklin' at the time?' Mo asked.

'I s'pose lookin' back on it I should 'ave, but on the spur o' the moment it just seemed normal,' Tom replied. 'Fings were 'appenin' an' when I saw the message I 'ad no reason ter fink it wasn't from Del, so off I went.'

'An' yer say yer didn't get a look at any of 'em?'

'Not really, it all 'appened too quick,' Tom said shaking his head. 'I was grabbed from be'ind just as I got near the union office an' this bag was put over me 'ead. It was a sack as a matter o' fact. Then I was bundled in the van an' driven around fer what seemed like an eternity. There was two geezers in the back wiv me, I could 'ear 'em talkin'. They trussed me up quickly an' one of 'em sat on me. I was bloody uncomfortable I can tell yer.'

'Was yer scared?' Mo asked with a smile.

'You bet yer life I was scared,' Tom said emphatically.

'So go on then.'

'Well they finally pulled up an' it must 'ave bin near the river, 'cos I could 'ear tug whistles quite plainly. I thought they were gonna chuck me in the water ter be honest but it must 'ave bin a place they could wait wivout anyone gettin' suspicious. Anyway, after what seemed ages I 'eard this car screech to a stop an' then voices. I was dragged out o' the van on ter the ground an' they started steamin' inter me. I was 'elpless. The way I was bundled up I couldn't even turn over. I must 'ave passed out. The next fing I remember was Del talkin' ter me. That was when 'e got me to our front door 'cos I 'eard Mum scream out. Then I must 'ave blacked out again. When I woke up next I was tucked up in bed.'

'Well, it seems like they 'ad it all worked out,' Mo remarked. 'They knew about the union meetin' an' they were waitin' round the corner in Ship Lane wiv you in the car fer when Del Abelson come down the street.'

'Del told me what they said to 'im as they frew me out the car,' Tom scowled. 'I wish I could get me 'ands on those bastards. They'd get more than a kickin'.'

Mo smiled as he took out a packet of Goldflake from his shirt pocket. 'Ferget it, Tom, yer'd be out o' yer depth,' he said quietly.

'So I'm s'posed ter say, "All right, fellers, no 'ard feelin's,"' Tom growled.

Mo eased his heavy bulk on the upturned beer crate and leaned towards his younger brother. 'Listen, Tom,' he began. 'I've got a good business goin', an' occasionally I do deals wiv some very shady characters. I get ter learn a lot about what's goin' on amongst the local villains an' I can tell yer that they're not very 'appy at the moment. It seems that a mob from over the water are tryin' ter muscle in. Joe Brady started it all by askin' fer their 'elp ter break that strike an' 'e's bin after settin' up some sort of employers' federation that'd fight the unions. I got that from a good friend o' mine who runs a small transport concern a few arches from me. 'E was approached by Brady. Accordin' ter what 'e told me, this so-called federation would be like a closed shop wiv strong-arm enforcement be'ind it. I don't need ter spell it out ter yer. Suffice it ter say that if that 'appens we'll all suffer. I'll be told what I can an' can't do as well as you.'

Tom nodded slowly. 'Why should Brady go over the water fer 'elp?' he frowned. 'Surely 'e knew it'd cause trouble wiv the local mobs.'

'That I don't know, but I'll find out,' Mo assured him. 'I do know that a lot o' people 'ave started askin' questions.'

'This Lennie Donald who was seen wiv Brady,' Tom remarked. 'What d'yer know about 'im?'

'After Sue told me about 'im I checked it out,' Mo replied. 'Lennie Donald's a front man fer this East End mob. The geezer wiv 'im was probably Frank Swain, a right nasty character. It was most likely Frank Swain who set you up. Don't worry though. This business 'as brought the local teams tergevver. They've put their differences ter one side fer the time bein'. Donald an' Swain are gonna be spoken to, if yer get the drift.'

'I'll look forward ter that,' Tom grinned.

*   *   *

Inside the house Aunt Ellie reclined in her armchair reading the evening paper. Normally she had an aversion to learning about all the terrible things going on around the world, as she was prone to make clear, but tonight was different. Mo was here and the evening meal had gone off without any acrimony. In fact, Joe had been a little more talkative than she could have expected and Mo had nodded occasionally, instead of sitting there with a blank expression. The meal was excellent too, Ellie thought, though with a little too much salt in the seasoning, if she were totally honest.

Martha was feeling happy as she sat repairing a tear in Tom's overalls. For once the family had been united and the meal had been trouble-free. Even Ellie had been complimentary and had refrained from her usual small criticism. The fact that she had remained in the parlour in preference to her room said something too. Mo was undoubtedly her favourite nephew and she was so different when he was around. How quiet and peaceful now, Martha reflected contentedly, with Joe next door gossiping to Charlie Duggan, Sue off to see Del and the two boys chatting in the yard. Whatever they were talking about was for their ears alone, but she was willing to bet it was something serious. She just hoped they weren't hatching any plots after what had happened to Tom, but then tonight was not the time to dwell on such things. It would only serve to spoil a very pleasant evening.

Chapter Eighteen

Benny Tracy slipped into the Bell early on Thursday evening and as soon as he got his pint he informed the landlord that tonight Lucy Merry was coming for a drink.

'I ain't seen anyfing of 'er fer ages,' Dave Ford told him. ''Ere, Bella, Mrs Merry's comin' in later.'

'Goodness me, that'll be an event,' Dave's buxom wife remarked. ''Ow did yer manage ter coax 'er out, Benny?'

'Me an' the lads got talkin',' he replied. 'We thought it'd be nice for 'er. All she ever does is sit in that 'ouse mopin'. Trouble is, the poor ole cow's got a bad foot so we've 'ad ter get transport for 'er.'

'A taxi?'

'Nah, a barrer.'

'Yer mean ter say yer gonna bring Lucy up 'ere on a barrer?' Bella said incredulously. ''Ere, Dave, did you 'ear that?'

'What's that?'

'Them three maniacs are bringin' Lucy on a barrer.'

'Barrer? What barrer?'

'Sharkey's.'

'What, the fishmonger's? Yer can't do that,' Dave

209

said derisively. 'It'll reek o' fish. She won't stand fer that.'

'She won't be standin', she'll be sittin',' the musketeer replied with a grin.

'Well, sooner you than me,' Dave said shaking his head.

Benny took a sip from his glass. 'I'm gonna go round an' collect the barrer soon's I've finished me drink,' he told them. 'An' don't worry about it woofin', Sharkey said 'e'll give it an 'ose-down in 'is yard.'

'I'm not worried, it's your problem,' Dave remarked.

Bella gave him a look that would have killed a lesser mortal before she went off into the saloon bar and the landlord leaned forward on the counter. 'You three are always up ter somefing or the ovver,' he said grinning. 'I just 'ope this little escapade's gonna work out all right.'

'Course it will,' Benny assured him. 'We know what we're doin'. By the way, you ain't got a cushion you could lend us, 'ave yer?'

'If you fink I'm gonna lend you a cushion ter stick on that poxy fish barrer yer got anuvver fink comin',' Dave scoffed.

'Suit yerself,' Benny said, draining his glass.

Lucy Merry was feeling a little nervous as she waited. She had put on her best coat and hat, and had used a little rouge to brighten up her pale cheeks. Rosie Coleman had been in earlier and tonged her hair and Nell Sharp had popped in too to see if she wanted anything. How nice it was for people to fuss over her, she thought. It was going to be fun riding in a taxi, even if it was only a short trip. She could not remember the last time she had ridden in a taxicab.

Outside at the corner of the turning a heated conversation was going on. Benny had collected the barrow but it did not meet with his friends' approval.

'' 'Ow the bloody 'ell we gonna coax the poor ole cow ter ride on that?' Wally said with disgust.

'I did tell 'im ter swill it down first,' Benny replied defensively. 'It ain't my fault. Sharkey 'ad ter go out an' get somefing apparently an' 'e didn't 'ave time.'

'Well, we ain't got time ter clean the poxy barrer now,' Tubby said, scratching his balding head.

'We could chuck somefing over it,' Benny suggested.

'Like what, a gallon o' lysol?'

'Nah, I mean a sheet o' some sort.'

'Who's gonna give us a sheet?'

'I'll pop in an' see Queenie,' Benny told them.

'Silly as a box o' lights,' Tubby growled to Wally as their friend hurried into the house.

'' 'Ere, this'll do,' he said triumphantly as he emerged a minute or two later. 'This is Queenie's ironin' blanket. She's not in but I know she won't mind.'

'What about a cushion? We'll need a cushion fer Lucy ter sit on,' Tubby reminded them.

'I thought yer'd 'ave asked Dave in the Bell,' Wally said, glaring at Benny.

'I did, but 'e as good as told me ter get stuffed.'

'Well, yer can't blame 'im, can yer,' Tubby chipped in.

'I know what,' Benny said. 'We'll bring 'er out in 'er chair.'

'Yer can't do that,' Tubby told him. 'The bloody

legs'll fall down the gaps. The poor ole cow's got a sprained foot already, she don't wanna end up wiv a broken 'ip.'

'Well, I dunno what we're gonna do,' Benny replied irritably.

'We'll just 'ave ter borrer one o' Lucy's,' Tubby decided.

When the three musketeers knocked at Mrs Merry's door the old lady reached down and picked up her handbag. 'Push, it is open,' she called out.

Tubby led the way. 'Your transport's waitin', yer majesty,' he said grinning widely.

'I'm afraid I can't put any weight on me foot,' Lucy told them.

'Don't worry, we'll carry yer out, gel,' Wally said with a smile. 'Right now, if you an' me make a fireman's lift, Wally, Benny can steady 'er.'

With a bit of manoeuvring they lifted the old lady from her chair and out into the passageway. Benny had grabbed the cushion from beneath her and as he pulled the front door wide open Lucy spotted the barrow. 'I ain't gonna ride on that!' she shouted.

'It's only a short distance, Lucy. You'll be okay,' Benny tried to reassure her.

'Up yer pipe,' she snapped. 'Put me down. Put me down this instant!'

Benny took the initiative for once and placed her cushion on the edge of the barrow midway between the shafts. 'C'mon, put 'er on 'ere,' he said quickly.

Lucy wanted to pummel her abductors but was frightened to take her arms from around their shoulders. 'I've never felt so embarrassed in me 'ole life,' she wailed as they set her down on the barrow.

'Right then, 'old on, gel,' Tubby said as he took up the shafts.

Lucy responded by kicking him in the rear and thumping Benny with her fist as he tried to steady her. 'Yer'll pay fer this, I swear it,' she wailed. 'Whatever must I look like!'

'Good ole Lucy,' Albert Price shouted out from his front door.

'I'll be up there meself in a few minutes,' Granny Minto called out to her.

''Old on tight, gel,' Nell Sharp shouted.

'She's got some pluck,' Mrs Benjamin said to her daughter, loud enough for the old lady to hear.

Vic Ogden came from behind the counter to see what all the fuss was about and he and his wife Coral stood in the shop doorway as the barrow came along. 'Well done, Mrs Merry,' he called out.

'Yeah, that's the spirit,' Coral added.

Lucy Merry had decided it was useless to protest any further and she sat upright with a stern expression on her thin face as Tubby pulled the barrow into Abbey Street. Passers-by stopped to look and one or two waved. A taxi honked and a carman cracked his whip over his head as he drove by. Up ahead the old lady saw a little group gathered outside the Bell and she began to settle down slightly. She was being fêted and everyone was being very nice, she thought.

'Get that door open.'

'Careful, lads, mind 'ow yer go wiv 'er.'

'Yer'll be all right, luv.'

Lucy Merry allowed herself a brief smile. 'If yer drop me I'll 'ave the bloody pair of yer fer breakfast,' she threatened.

Tubby and Wally managed to carry her into the public bar and sit her beside a table which Dave Ford had reserved for her.

'Right then, gel, what yer fancy ter drink? This one's on the 'ouse,' the landlord told her.

'I'll 'ave a nice milk stout then,' Lucy said, looking round haughtily.

People came up to pay their respects and one old lady sat down at the table facing her. 'I'm Elsie Robbins from Anchor Buildin's,' she told her. 'Yer don't remember me do yer, but I remember you. You was only a kid when they pulled those buildin's down.'

'Yeah, I remember yer, course I remember yer,' Lucy said, laying her hand on the older lady's arm. 'I remember that ole bastard of a caretaker too.'

'Fred Dunkley, that was 'is name,' Elsie replied. ''E got killed in the Blitz. I'm eighty-seven yer know.'

'Well, I wouldn't 'ave thought it.'

'I am. Eighty-eight next month,' Elsie said chuckling. 'Mind you, it's the 'ard life we 'ad wot keeps us goin', I'm sure of it. Good food too, not like terday. Everyfing's in tins now.'

Wally brought Lucy her drink and she tugged at his coat sleeve. 'Oi, wait a minute. I wanna get Elsie a drink,' she said, fishing into her purse. 'While yer at it yer better get you an' those ovver two silly gits a drink. I s'pose yer've earned it, but I still ain't gonna ferget the way yer tricked me.' She turned to her new-found friend. 'There's me expectin' a taxi ter call fer me an' they turned up wiv a fish barrer, would yer believe. Talk about shame an' embarrassment. I didn't know where ter put me face.'

'Well, you're all right now, gel,' Elsie told her,

patting the back of her hand. 'They'll be bringin' the jellied eels round soon. I do love jellied eels.'

The piano struck up and Lucy quickly forgot the rough ride and the embarrassment as she chatted away to Elsie. Fresh drinks were sent over to her table, and as the public bar filled with customers more drinks began to arrive. Dave Ford and Angie the barmaid were kept busy, and when the jellied eels arrived at ten o'clock that night Lucy Merry and Elsie Robbins were inebriated.

The three musketeers were feeling pleased with themselves, and as they stood at the counter and watched the two old ladies getting steadily drunk they were reminded that the night's work was not finished yet. They still had to get Lucy Merry home.

'She's pissed,' Wally remarked.

'D'yer fink we should get 'er 'ome now?' Benny wondered.

'Nah, let 'er finish the night out,' Tubby said chuckling. 'The poor ole cow ain't bin out since Gawd knows 'ow long.'

Lucy Merry said a fond farewell to Elsie Robbins when the old lady's two chaperons came over to take her home, and as the pianist played the introduction to 'The Miner's Dream of Home' she was prompted, and felt able, to give a rendering. She leaned back in her chair, her hat askew as she drew breath, and her high-pitched, melodious voice rang out as the first bars sounded.

'I saw the old 'omestead an' faces I loved,
I saw England's valleys an' dales,
I listened wiv joy, as I did when a boy,

Ter the sound of the old village bells.
An' the lamp was burnin' brightly,
'Twas there ter banish all sin,
An' the bells were ringin' the old year out an' the
new year in.'

Her face had become very red with her efforts, and as
she slumped down in her seat Wally nudged Tubby.
'C'mon, mate, let's get 'er 'ome,' he said.

'Nah, I'm all right, I ain't ready yet,' the old lady
slurred.

'It's gettin' late, gel,' Benny said kindly.

'Piss orf an' leave me alone,' Lucy growled. 'Anyway, I ain't finished me drink yet.'

Wally looked at Tubby and nodded towards the
door. 'Get 'er up,' he said firmly.

The pianist started up with 'Show Me The Way To
Go Home' and the customers all joined in. Dave Ford
shook his head in amusement as the pair managed to
get Lucy out through the door and on to the barrow,
and people spilled out on to the street to witness the old
lady's undignified departure. Benny was following up
with the cushion and Queenie's ironing blanket under
his arm. ''Ang on a minute,' he called out. 'Nah, don't
lie down yet, luv, let's get this blanket under yer.'

Lucy Merry was past caring as she stretched out,
and Benny managed to put the cushion under her
head and the blanket over her before Wally lifted
the shafts. As the improvised transport trundled back
along the cobbles a few of the neighbours stood at
their front doors, and Granny Minto was reminded
of the days when drunks were carted away to the
police station to sleep it off on a similar-looking

contraption. 'She's gonna suffer in the mornin',' she chuckled.

''Er coat's gonna stink to 'igh 'eaven,' Albert added as they watched Lucy being transferred with much difficulty into her house.

Fortunately Rosie Coleman and Nell Sharp were on hand to get the old lady settled in her bed, and finally, after the three musketeers had exchanged self-congratulatory handshakes, Benny sneaked Queenie's ironing blanket into the house under his coat.

Chapter Nineteen

Annie Barlow and Minnie Sloan hurried down to Vic Ogden's papershop very early on Friday morning, and they could hardly wait to get back into Annie's house to read the article and see their photos.

'Put the kettle on then,' Minnie said excitedly as she made herself comfortable in the parlour.

'Wait, sod yer, I'm gonna read this first,' Annie told her.

''Ere, look at us. Don't we look good,' Minnie enthused. 'Shame about that face yer was pullin'.'

'It's a bloody sight better than that silly grin yer got on your face,' Annie countered.

The argument would most certainly have developed but for the fact that each of them was agog to read the account of her husband's bravery. Annie always became emotional when she thought about it and this morning was no exception. She dabbed at her eyes as the words swam before her while Minnie sat serious-faced with the *Bulletin* open on her lap.

''Ere, yer wanna read what it ses about yer?' Annie called out to the scullery.

Alf was having a shave and he grunted a reply which was lost on his wife.

'I better get goin' before Mick leaves fer work,' Minnie told her.

'Come over once 'e's gone an' I'll make us a cuppa,' Annie replied.

Joe Carey read the account of the rescue before he left for work and he felt troubled as well as surprised. The piece was very well done, he thought, and it had certainly cast the two Totterdown families in a new light. He had never heard about the act of bravery described in the article and he doubted very much whether others in the street had known about it either. Alf Barlow and Micky Sloan were both nice blokes who generally kept a low profile, except when those biddies of theirs set about each other and they were forced to intervene. They would be looked up to now regardless of their public squabbles, and there was the rub. What if the Ship Lane shelter tragedy was selected for a future piece? True it had been a desperate operation to free the people in that warehouse shelter and he and Charlie Duggan had received quite a bit of praise for the way they had handled it, but after the brief account in the *Bulletin* at the time people had started asking questions, and subsequently a few rumours had circulated. Fortunately nothing had come of it but people remembered, and it could well do more harm than good to resurrect interest in the tragedy.

When Martha read the article she went next door to see if Mabel Duggan had seen it.

'Yeah, I've just read it,' her friend told her. 'It just shows yer, yer never know about people.'

Martha nodded, feeling that Mabel had said more

than she intended. ''As your Charlie seen it?' she asked.

'Yeah,' Mabel sighed. ''E didn't say a lot but I expect 'e's finkin' all the more.'

Martha's antidote to worry was a cup of strong tea and she was grateful when her neighbour reached for the teapot.

Albert Price had bought the paper and while he sat reading it Granny Minto came into the parlour. 'What's me stars say?' she asked him, and got no answer. 'Oi, deafy. I asked about me stars.'

''Ang on a minute, gel, I'm just readin' about Alf Barlow an' Micky Sloan,' he told her.

'What about 'em? 'Ave they bin done fer murderin' their wives?' Granny chuckled.

'Nah, it's about the war when they were in the 'Eavy Rescue,' Albert replied. ''Ere, read it fer yerself.'

'I ain't got me glasses, I've left 'em by me bed,' Granny said. 'You read it out ter me.'

Albert ran his eye down the column, skipping the build-up which would only serve to irritate the impatient old lady. 'It ses 'ere, "While the rescue team searched the ruins of the buildin's fer survivors they 'eard a child's faint cry, an' Michael Sloan burrowed 'is way inter the rubble while 'is colleague Alfred Barlow used 'is shoulders ter support a large joist that was in danger of collapsing on ter the tunnel. Above them a side wall rocked precariously but despite the risks involved the two men refused to abandon the rescue operation. One hour later four-year-old Mary Goodhew was brought out injured but alive. Mary now lives in Kent, and on Wednesday the ten-year-old made a special trip ter Dock'ead ter fank the two men." There's a photo below of the little gel standin' between the two of 'em. Ain't that nice.'

Granny screwed up her eyes to see the picture. 'Who'd 'ave guessed about them two,' she said shaking her head. 'I took 'em ter be a couple o' Dopey Dicks.'

'Yer never can tell wiv people, can yer,' Albert remarked.

'I bet the street won't be big enough fer them two scatty mares now,' Granny growled.

'P'raps now they'll stop tryin' ter knock six buckets o' shit out of each ovver,' Albert said folding up the newspaper. 'An' then again . . .'

Sam Calkin was deep in thought as he stepped from the eight-forty-nine at London Bridge Station. He had been intending to write the George Merry story for the next Friday edition, but after visiting his widow he had decided to hang fire and substitute another episode which had taken place in Dockhead at the start of the Blitz. There was something about the events in Ship Lane which troubled him and he could not put his finger on it. Lucy Merry had spoken about her husband's heavy drinking and the rumours that had surfaced after his death, and he felt he needed more time to look into it, maybe talk to people who knew the man well, before he wrote something that could be discredited.

As he walked into the *Bulletin* office Sue was waiting. 'Sam, there's been a call for you. A Mr Button. He wouldn't leave a message except to say he'd call back later.'

Sam glanced at the slip of paper Sue handed him and shrugged his shoulders as he slipped it into his coat pocket. 'Is Frances in?' he asked.

'She beat me in this morning,' Sue told him with a furtive smile. 'Paddy's arrived too, about five minutes ago. You're not stepping on his toes, are you?'

'Heaven forbid,' Sam said grinning lopsidedly.

'By the way, congratulations on the article,' she told him. 'It was very good.'

'You're too kind, m'dear,' the young man said in a low-voiced impersonation of Clark Gable.

'No really. It was very nice,' Sue insisted. 'As a matter of fact I read it when I got in this morning. I was very surprised and I expect everyone in the street was too. We're getting quite a bit of publicity, and talking of which, are you intending to do the other one, the—'

'The George Merry story,' he cut in.

Sue nodded. 'You did go to see her, didn't you?'

Sam leaned on the counter. 'Yes I did, but I need more time to work on that one.'

The young woman noticed the sudden change of expression on his face and she frowned. 'Is there anything wrong?'

He shrugged and then scratched his ear. 'Sue, can I ask you a big favour?'

'Fire away,' she invited.

'You live in Totterdown Street, and you'd know what was what,' he said in a serious voice. 'Can I ask you a few questions? It is important.'

'Yes of course,' she replied as the intercom phone buzzed.

He waited, taking the opportunity to study her as

she leant across her desk. She was an attractive girl, he thought. Her fair hair was cut short and styled around her ears and her pretty face reflected good health. She had large, expressive blue eyes, and her figure was trim and shapely, her firm bust prominent under the tight blue jumper she wore.

She looked up at him and pulled a face as she spoke into the receiver. 'Yes, Mr Spencer, he's just arrived. Yes, I'll tell him to come in right away. Yes, okay.'

Sam raised his hands in a gesture of surrender. 'His master's voice?'

Sue nodded smiling. 'You were asking me about the street.'

'Can I talk to you later, if it's all right?'

She nodded as he pushed open the inner door and he rewarded her with a friendly wink.

Now in his early seventies, Billy Button had led a chequered life. As a young man he had served with the colours, first in India and then in East Africa, where he picked up a nasty infection which would have been enough to finish the average squaddie. Billy was one of life's survivors, however, and he recovered sufficiently to serve out his time. When the First World War started he volunteered to serve his country again; his knowledge and training were sufficient to land him a post on the Isle of Sheppey as gunnery instructor, and when the war ended Billy finally retired from the Army with the rank of company sergeant major. Between the wars he spent some time in the Corps of Commissioners, but was compelled to resign after giving a dressing-down to a disrespectful visitor to the Ministry of Defence while on duty there, unaware at the time that the recipient of his sharp tongue was none other than the retired Brigadier Knox, MC.

Finally out of uniform and getting on in years, Billy Button survived on his wits, and as he sat waiting in the London Bridge Hotel for the reporter to arrive he was hopeful of a nice little earner. Money had been in short supply ever since he first made the acquaintance of John Barleycorn, and at the moment he was slowly beginning to pull himself together after the most recent drinking bout which had lasted longer than he cared to remember. The shakes had gone now and he was eating at least one square meal a day, but he was under no illusions. It was inevitable that very soon he would once again tempt providence and succumb to another extended bash with his good old friend and enemy. And why not, he thought offhandedly. Drink blocked out the memories he wished to forget, and eased the pain of the loneliness he had felt ever since the summer of thirty-nine when his beloved Diana passed away. At least she had been spared the horror of the Blitz, he often told himself, but it did little to assuage the inconsolable blackness in his heart . . .

This would be the reporter, Billy thought, as the broad-shouldered young man sauntered confidently into the large public bar and looked around.

'Mr Button?'

Billy stood up and took the outstretched hand. 'You spotted the button'ole then. Mr Button wiv the button'ole.'

Sam smiled. 'Can I get you a drink?'

Billy stroked his chin for a few moments. 'I'd like a shandy if yer please.'

'Nothing stronger?'

'I'm on the wagon,' Billy told him, 'fer the time bein' at least.'

Sam brought over a shandy and a double whisky, and when he had made himself comfortable at the table he fixed the old soldier with his dark eyes. 'Well, Mr Button, you said on the phone you had some information that might be of value. I'm listening.'

'Call me Billy.'

'Righto then, Billy.'

The frail-looking man touched the faded flower in his coat lapel and smiled. 'I was waitin' wiv interest ter see the sort o' fings you was gonna write about after seein' that introduction piece in Tuesday's paper,' he began, 'an' I 'ave ter say that first article was good. If the rest are like that one I'm sure it'll sell yer papers. People never tire of it, do they? They like ter read all about themselves, an' the more scandalous it is the better.'

'You could hardly call that first article scandalous,' Sam said frowning.

'No, but I was just makin' the point,' Billy said, picking up his drink.

Sam waited till the old man put his shandy back down on the glass-topped table. 'Tell me, Billy, what exactly have you got that I could use?' he asked patiently.

Billy smiled slyly. 'Are you familiar wiv the Ship Lane shelter affair?'

'I've come across it while I've been researching,' Sam told him.

'Are you intendin' writin' about it?'

'It's quite likely.'

'Yer probably know already that five elderly people

lost their lives that night when the Ship Lane ware'ouse copped it,' Billy went on. 'Well, I can tell yer 'ere an' now that it should never 'ave 'appened.'

'All those Blitz deaths should never have happened,' Sam said quickly.

'Yeah, but in that particular case it was criminal,' Billy replied, his eyes widening.

'Criminal? You mean negligence?'

'You could call it that.'

Sam drained his glass and then looked closely at the old man. 'What is it you've got, Billy?'

'What I've got is big stuff, an' I fink your paper would be 'appy ter pay fer that information,' Billy said folding his arms.

'I'm not so sure,' Sam replied. 'My articles are centred around the heroic deeds that ordinary Bermondsey people performed during the Blitz. This is something quite different.'

'Like I just said, people love ter read scandalous fings, an' you know that as well as I do,' Billy continued calmly. 'What 'appened that night was murder. I know 'cos I was there.'

'In the shelter?'

'Nah, I was in the lead mills opposite.'

Sam looked at him intently. 'Were you on your own?'

Billy shook his head. 'I fink I've said enough fer the time bein',' he replied with a mocking glint in his eye. 'If yer want the story it'll cost yer.'

'What are you asking for?'

'I want a pony down an' anuvver pony when yer publish,' he answered.

'Fifty quid's a lot of money. I don't know.'

'Well, yer can take it or leave it, son, it's up ter you.'

'I'll need to speak to my editor, it'll be his decision.'

'Fine. I'll be waitin'.'

'Just a moment, Billy,' the young man said quickly. 'I can't just go in with that assertion on its own. I'll need something more.'

Billy thought for a while. 'It's not an assertion, son, it's what 'appened. All right, what about robbery?'

'At the lead mills?'

'Nah, the ware'ouse.'

'But I understood the warehouse was used for storing furniture from bombed-out homes.'

'So it was, but it was bein' robbed when those poor sods copped it.'

'Are you willing to back this up?'

'If the money's on the table.'

Sam nodded slowly. 'All right, but I'll need a few days. Can you meet me here the same time on Tuesday?'

'Sure fing.'

As the old man got up to leave Sam reached out and caught his arm. 'One more question. Did you know a George Merry?'

Billy smiled. 'Until Tuesday then.'

Chapter Twenty

Sue Carey was intrigued by what Sam Calkin had said to her and she felt disappointed when he hurried from the office building without saying anything more. It was almost lunchtime and still he had not returned. As she dealt with the morning's visitors and telephone calls her thoughts shifted to Del Abelson. Since Tuesday night she had hardly seen anything of him, apart from Thursday evening when she looked in on the Colemans. She had wanted to say so much to him, how special it had been for her when they made love and how much she was looking forward to the romantic weekend they had talked about, but it was impossible. That evening Del was wrapped up in a discussion with Jim Coleman and she had spent most of the time chatting to Rosie in the scullery. Del's goodnight kiss on the doorstep seemed almost perfunctory, his mind presumably still on the intense and passionate conversation he had been having with Jim. The coming weekend looked as though it was going to be a very quiet one as far as she was concerned. Del was attending a union conference on Saturday afternoon, and on Sunday there was the first of the rallies at Trafalgar Square. Maybe she could commandeer him on Saturday evening and get him to take her dancing. She might even be able to rouse his passion enough for him to recognise that she was the woman who loved him and wanted him.

As she gathered up her coat, handbag and a small paper shopping-bag Sam Calkin walked back into the office. He looked a little thoughtful but gave her a brief smile. 'Off to lunch?' he asked.

Sue nodded. 'There's two messages,' she said, handing him the slips of paper.

Sam glanced at them and screwed them up in the palm of his hand, missing the wastepaper basket with his cricket bowl. 'Where do you go for lunch?' he asked casually.

'Well, as it's a nice day I might take a stroll along Bankside and sit in the cathedral gardens,' she told him. 'It's nice and peaceful there, and I've got a sandwich.'

'Would you mind if I joined you?' Sam asked.

'No of course not,' she replied.

They strolled over into the bustle of London Bridge Station and crossed the busy concourse, taking the flight of stone steps which led down to Southwark Cathedral. The gardens were full of colour, the well-cared-for lawn a soft bright green as it led up to the ancient gravestones at the foot of the lofty edifice. Workers seeking solitude and respite strolled along the gravel path or sat on wooden benches shaded by trees.

'Shall we sit here?' Sue suggested.

Sam joined her on the vacant bench and looked up at the brilliant sunlight that spangled through the leafy canopy above their heads. 'This is nice,' he sighed as he leaned back.

Sue rummaged into her paper bag and took out a packet of sandwiches. 'It's only corned beef but you're welcome to one,' she said.

'No I couldn't.'

She unwrapped them and held them out to him. 'Go on, take one. I can't eat the two.'

Sam smiled as he relented. 'Usually I go in a pub for a drink and a cheese roll but I have to say this is much nicer,' he told her.

'The food or the company?' she teased.

'The company, definitely. I'll get back to you about the food.'

They ate the sandwiches and Sam ran his tongue over his lips. 'That was really nice. Now would you let me buy you a drink?'

'That's taken care of too,' she told him, slipping her hand into the carrier bag. 'I take it you like coffee?'

Light wisps of cloud passed high up in the azure sky and the bright sun felt pleasantly warm. From somewhere behind the tall stained-glass windows of the ancient cathedral they could hear choristers in practice, and then abruptly the singing was drowned out by a passing train.

'You were going to ask me something,' Sue reminded him as she sipped her hot coffee.

For a moment or two he looked down at the dregs in the plastic cup he was holding. 'When I called on Mrs Merry,' he said finally, 'she told me about the rumours which started to circulate after her husband was killed.'

'About George Merry being a heavy drinker?'

'Yes.'

'I was away at the time,' Sue told him, 'but I do

know there were stories doing the rounds that George Merry was blind drunk and couldn't have driven the lorry out of the yard.'

'You were away?'

'In the ATS.'

'Really?'

'Yes, I was in a gunnery section. I spent most of the time stationed on a gunsite near Dover.'

'That must be a whole load of stories in itself,' Sam said with a smile, resting one arm on the back of the bench as he turned towards her. 'Where was I? George Merry, yes. His wife told me that he liked a drink, and occasionally he did get drunk.'

'That's right,' Sue replied. 'It was common knowledge, but no one made much of it. He never bothered anyone.'

Remembering what had transpired in the pub that morning Sam decided to tread softly. 'It must have been terrible in London during the Blitz,' he remarked. 'I've been going through all the material I could find in the glory hole and I read a piece about the Ship Lane shelter tragedy.'

Sue nodded. 'My father and Mr Duggan who lives next door to us were on duty there at the time.'

Sam looked surprised. 'Of course, Mr Carey. I honestly didn't make the connection. God, that must have been a night. I read that five people died there.'

'They all lived in Totterdown Street,' Sue said frowning. 'Mr and Mrs Simpson who lived at number three. They were both in their late seventies, and Hilda Moore, she was a nice old lady who'd been widowed for years. Then there was Flo Thomas who was once a matron at Guy's Hospital, and Granny

Knight who lived at number seven. They were all asphyxiated.'

'How did it happen?' Sam asked her.

'My dad never talks about it,' she replied quietly, 'but I gather that the warehouse got a direct hit from an oil bomb and the smoke from the burning furniture and bedding that was stored there went through the air vents into the cellar shelter. It was one of those building shelters, you know the sort, reinforced with concrete pillars, and there was an emergency exit which unfortunately got blocked when the lead mills opposite took a direct hit. My dad and Mr Duggan finally managed to clear the burning debris away from the rear door but by then it was too late for those five poor souls. As I said, my father never talks about it, but I did overhear him saying once that he'd never forget the screams that came from behind that iron door while he was trying to get it clear.'

'Was the place used for anything else other than people's belongings?' Sam queried.

'No, it used to be a leather firm but they moved out at the beginning of the war,' Sue told him. 'The council took it over as a store place when the Blitz started.'

'And your father was the shelter warden?'

'Actually it was Mr Duggan who was the warden in charge but my dad did fire-fighting,' she explained. 'He used to do his fire-watch duty on the roof of the warehouse and he shared the shelter work with Mr Duggan. They're old pals as well as living next door to each other. They were both in the First World War and they never stop talking about it when they get together.'

'May the tenth, nineteen forty-one,' Sam said almost

in reverence. 'It must have been hell on earth that night.'

Sue nodded slowly. 'Everyone was on duty, and our guns were red-hot as the planes flew over towards London. I can never forget the deafening drone of their engines, and then the din as we opened up on them. We could see the red glow in the sky and we knew London was getting a bad pasting. I remember hearing about the raid on the wireless next morning and soon as I could I tried to phone the firm where Dad worked to find out if they were all right, but I couldn't get through. I was in a real panic till I finally managed to get connected. I can't tell you how relieved I was to hear Dad's voice.'

'I can imagine,' Sam said quietly.

'What about you?' she asked him. 'Were you in the services?'

He shook his head. 'I was a cub reporter over in the East End, and the year before the war I landed a job with the *Evening News*. I'd just about got my feet under the table when I was called up. At the time the Government were setting up an information office and I got recruited. I led a very unexciting life in the propaganda section. The office was based in Hertfordshire as a matter of fact. Far enough away from London to be reasonably safe yet near enough to hear the nightly bombs and see the red sky, like you saw.'

'So what brought you to a local newspaper?' Sue asked intrigued.

Sam smiled as he leaned back on the bench. 'I'd been pursuing a career and doing well at the *Standard* and I had visions of being their top crime reporter.

After the war I went back there and found myself covering road accidents, fires and society weddings. I got disenchanted with it all so I decided to make the break. I felt that I needed a challenge. I wanted to write about things I felt passionate about, and I got this idea. I researched Bermondsey's war and then I did a piece which I thought would be suitable for publication and took it to the *South London Press*. They liked it but I told them it wasn't for sale. I wanted a job and that piece was my intro. Then I came to the *Bulletin*.'

'And Spencer liked it,' Sue cut in.

Sam smiled. 'Yeah, and I got the job. It's only a temporary situation though. He explained that the paper's fighting for survival and he couldn't guarantee me a secure future.'

'So this is a stepping-stone.'

'Not necessarily. It depends what happens to the paper.'

'I'm sure you'll be successful anyway, if that article you wrote is anything to go by,' she said encouragingly.

Sam smiled appreciatively. 'As a matter of fact I'm thinking of doing the Ship Lane shelter piece soon. Do you think your father would allow me to speak to him about what happened?'

Sue shrugged her shoulders. 'I really don't know, but I suppose I could ask him, if you'd like me to.'

'I'd be very grateful,' he replied. 'Oh and while we're on the subject, is there anyone you could suggest I talk to about George Merry? I was thinking about old friends, people who he would have drunk with, the publican maybe . . .'

'I'll speak to Mum and Dad,' Sue told him. 'They may be able to suggest some names.' She glanced at her wristwatch. 'I'd better be getting back to work,' she said with a sigh.

'It's been very nice,' he answered. 'Thanks for letting me share your company, and your lunch.'

'It has been nice,' Sue replied, giving him a friendly smile as they stood up.

The young man took her arm gently as they climbed the steps and crossed the busy road. 'I hope you'll pardon the audacity, but is there a lucky man at the moment?'

She nodded. 'Yes, but I'm currently sharing him with the Transport and General Workers' Union.'

Sam chuckled. 'Dedicated?'

'And how,' she said ruefully.

The office building loomed up ahead and she broached the question she had wanted to ask him earlier. 'What about you? Are you married?'

For a brief moment he hesitated. 'There was someone, once, but we both had a change of heart and we broke off the engagement.'

'I'm sorry,' Sue said with feeling.

'It was a long time ago,' he replied.

They entered the building and Sam smiled as Sue took her place at the reception counter. 'We must do it again some time.'

Jean Kenny the office junior gave up her seat, convinced that half the staff at the newspaper were involved in private liaisons, including Sue Carey now. If Josie Willard found out she wouldn't be pleased, since the girl hardly ever stopped talking about how handsome the new reporter was and how she was hoping he would very soon get to know her a little better.

As Sam opened the door for her and stood back with a friendly smile, Jean Kenny's face reddened slightly.

On Friday lunchtime two men visited the Bell and Dave Ford immediately felt uneasy. He recognised them as the two men who had been there the night of the union meeting and he remarked on it to Bella.

'I shouldn't worry, luv,' she told him. 'P'raps they like the pub.'

The pair sat in a far corner and for some time seemed to be discussing something intently, then they walked to the counter, ordered two more large Scotches and downed them quickly.

'When's the next union meetin', pal?' the larger of the two asked with a trace of a smile.

'There's none planned as such,' Dave told him. 'You after joinin'?'

'We might at that,' the man replied as he turned on his heel.

'They're trouble-makers them two, I can smell 'em a mile off,' Dave muttered to Bella.

'You worry too much,' she said dismissively.

''As Monty Groves bin in lately?' he asked her.

'Last night, why's that?'

'Is 'e due in ternight, would yer say?'

'Gawd knows.'

'If 'e does pop in, give us the wire,' Dave told her.

'What d'yer want wiv 'im?'

'Those two geezers 'ave got me finkin' an' I wanna talk ter Monty about it, that's why.'

'Why Monty Groves?'

''Cos Monty's pretty fussy about who drinks in 'is local, that's why.'

''E don't run the pub, you do,' Bella reminded him.

'Yeah, but I like ter keep on friendly terms wiv people like Monty.'

'Well, don't go causin' trouble fer no reason, that's all,' she warned him.

'All I'm gonna do is mark 'is card.'

'Make sure that's all yer do.'

'Bella, it's nearly closin' time, get Wilko ter collect those empty glasses.'

She sighed and shook her head in resignation. Dave seemed to be getting very awkward in his old age, she thought.

Chapter Twenty-One

Monty Groves had been doing business in a drinking club for most of the afternoon, and satisfied with the outcome he decided to call in at the Bell on his way home. The saloon bar would be empty and peaceful after the rowdiness of the club, he thought, but when he pushed open the door the villain's eyes popped. 'What the bloody . . . !' he gasped.

'Someone's paid me a visit,' Dave Ford said flatly.

'What wiv, a tank?' Monty growled as he glanced around the shattered bar.

The landlord was still shaking as he poured Monty a whisky from the near-empty bottle in front of him. 'I was just openin' up an' before I knew it these two geezers charged in,' he puffed. 'They 'ad pickaxe 'andles an' they just started smashin' up the place. I tried ter stop 'em but what could I do on me own? One of 'em belted me then 'e smashed a glass an' 'eld it up ter me face. I just 'ad ter stand an' watch. Look at it. They've done me mirrer, the optics an' every glass an' bottle they could lay their 'ands on. Just look at me pumps an' the counter. It'll cost a fortune ter put this right.'

Monty carefully brushed splinters of glass from the counter before easing his heavy frame down on to a stool. 'Who was it?' he asked, looking around in disbelief.

'Gawd knows,' Dave groaned. 'They were in 'ere at lunchtime an' before they left one of 'em asked me when the next union meetin' was. I said ter Bella at the time they was trouble-makers.'

'Is that the first time they've bin in 'ere?' Monty queried.

'Once before,' Dave replied. 'There was a union meetin' goin' on upstairs an' they were sittin' by the door. They left just before the meetin' broke up.'

The villain scowled. 'It figures. Tell me, what did they look like?'

Dave shrugged his shoulders. 'They were both on the big side, booted an' suited. The one who belted me 'ad a zig-zag scar on the side of 'is face. They'd be in their mid-forties I'd say.'

Monty Groves nodded slowly. 'I got 'em. They're from over the water. Lennie Donald an' Frank Swain, that's the one wiv the scar.'

'What's it all about, Monty?'

'They're tryin' ter muscle in over 'ere.'

'Yer mean they're after protection money?'

'Not at the moment, but it'll come, if nuffink's done about it,' the villain told him. 'Right now they've got ovver priorities, like warnin' you against lettin' the union 'old their meetin's 'ere.'

'Who's payin' 'em?' Dave asked quickly.

Monty Groves drained his glass and breathed out with a grimace. 'Don't worry about this, Dave,' he replied, ignoring the question. 'Those two ponces are gonna be sorted out soon as we can locate 'em. All the local crews are tergevver on this one.'

Dave looked relieved. 'I 'ope yer find 'em quick. I don't want no more o' this sort o' fing. Our Bella's in a right state. She's upstairs shakin' like a leaf.'

Monty suddenly glanced up at the glass rack. 'Did they get my mug?' he asked.

'Yeah.'

His florid face darkened. 'That's a fing I'll be takin' up personally wiv them two bastards,' he growled. 'D'you know that George Raft drank out o' that mug once?'

'Yeah, so yer told me.'

The villain watched as the landlord filled his glass. 'By the way, 'ave yer seen Winkle since 'e's bin out?'

Dave shook his head. 'I didn't know 'e was out.'

'Last week,' Monty informed him. 'I thought 'e would 'ave bin in by now. Do us a favour, will yer. Soon as yer see 'im tell 'im I was askin' after 'im. Tell 'im ter look me up in 'ere, okay?'

'Will do.'

Monty picked up the brimming glass and studied it for a moment before draining it in one gulp. 'Tell Bella not ter worry,' he said, pulling a face as the spirit burned his throat. 'I don't fink you'll be seein' any more o' those two monkeys.'

As soon as the villain had left Bella walked into the bar. 'I s'pose we'd better start clearin' this bloody mess up,' she said sighing.

'Monty's just bin in,' Dave told her.

'Yeah, I was listenin' from the back room,' Bella replied. 'I 'eard 'im mention Winkle.'

'Winkle's just out an' Monty wants ter see 'im,' Dave explained. 'I s'pose 'e's got a job fer 'im.'

Bella picked up a large shard of glass and laid it down on the counter. 'I dunno where ter start,' she groaned.

'Just leave it, I'll pay a couple o' the lads ter do it,' he told her. 'I fink me an' you are gettin' too old fer all this aggro. I reckon we'll 'ave ter seriously consider takin' a nice little country pub down in Kent.'

Ellie Emberson looked up over her glasses as Sue sat down facing her. 'Aren't you out tonight?' she asked.

Sue shook her head. 'Del's at a branch meeting.'

'He takes his work seriously, doesn't he,' Ellie remarked as she reached down at her side for some more cotton thread. 'You two should go out more. All work and no play isn't good for anyone.'

'You try telling Del that,' Sue said sighing.

Tom loped into the room with his shirt collar pulled up. 'Sue, do us a favour, will yer,' he said puffing loudly as he struggled to knot his tie. 'I need a button sewed on me coat.'

'Give it to me, I'll do it,' Ellie offered.

Tom took it down from behind the door. 'Fanks, Aunt Ellie,' he said smiling at her. 'You're a diamond.'

'Where's the button?'

'I dunno.'

Ellie sighed as she rummaged through her sewing-box. 'I don't know. There's you dashing about everywhere and your sister sitting on her hands every night.'

'Not every night,' Sue corrected her, with a brief look at her younger brother.

'I'm in demand, Aunt Ellie,' he said grinning. 'The gels are just queuin' up fer me.'

'I hope you're not leading young Pamela Duggan on,' Ellie said sternly. 'She's a very nice girl and I wouldn't like to see her hurt.'

'Don't worry, Aunt Ellie,' the young man replied as he finally fixed his tie. 'Me an' Pam are goin' steady an' I'm bein' the perfect gentleman. D'you know, last night we went up the Bell, an' when she'd got the drinks in I told 'er that I was a changed man.'

'When she got the drinks?' Ellie queried in a shocked voice.

'As soon as she put the pints down on the table.'

'You mean that you let the girl go and get the drinks?'

'The two pints, yeah.'

'She drinks pints?'

Tom grinned as the remark hit home. 'She only drinks about four. Pam's not a big boozer. Anyway the place was packed an' there was nowhere fer 'er ter sit, so I offered 'er my seat, but she wouldn't. She's a real sport is Pam.'

'You were sitting and you let her stand?' Ellie said with a look of horror.

'Yeah, but I was tired yer see.'

'Don't take any notice of him, Aunt Ellie,' Sue cut in. 'He's having you on.'

Ellie snapped the cotton and passed the coat over to her nephew. 'I wouldn't put it past him,' she remarked.

Tom gave her a swift peck on the cheek, which only served to irritate her and she pulled a face.

Sue looked up at the clock as her brother stood parading himself. 'You're going to be late,' she told him.

He gave her a quick wink as he made for the door. 'Pamela don't mind waiting,' he said, hiding a smile. 'She knows 'ow lucky she is.'

Ellie snorted, at a loss for words, and Sue gave her a sympathetic smile as the front door closed. 'You shouldn't let him rile you, Aunt Ellie,' she told her. 'After all it's only a joke. Tom really cares for Pamela.'

'Well, I just hope he doesn't get the girl into trouble,' Ellie replied.

Sue rested her head against the back of the armchair and closed her eyes. She recalled the chat she had had with Pamela not so long before when her friend had told her that she was determined to go to the altar pure. It wouldn't be easy. Tom had been out with quite a few girls since he came home from the war and he wouldn't be backward in coming forward, as the saying went. Maybe he was serious about Pamela. Perhaps he had changed. In any case time would tell.

'I think I'll go upstairs,' Ellie said, interrupting Sue's thoughts. 'I've got a couple of letters to write.'

The young woman watched with puzzlement as her aunt left the room. She hardly ever ventured out and there she was off to write more letters. Whoever to? Was there a secret beau? Did she have a pen-friend whom she preferred to keep under wraps? Poor Aunt Ellie. She only seemed to come alive when Mo was around.

The small room at the bend of the stairs was warm, heated by a gas fire, and Ellie found it made a nice change to the evening chill of the parlour. She could be alone with her thoughts here, and her secret. It had to be that way, for the present at least. One day it would be known to everyone, if she ever dared to make it public, but for now there was much work still to be done and tonight she felt inspired as she reached into the cupboard and took out a bundle of papers.

The stableman was not young, not in years, but his attitude to life and his vitality made him appear young to the chaste young girl, Ellie decided as she turned the page. Yes, that would seem right. Now for the seduction. Was it as powerful, yet as tasteful, as it could be? Maybe not, but how else could she have described the fateful event, the taking of a virgin, and in such a way as to ruin her for life? It had to be made poignant, heart-rending and tragic. Tonight, come hell or high water, she would finish the chapter she had struggled over for so long and then the story would flow. Another few months and the novel would be completed, and then the momentous decision. Would the manuscript gather dust and be discovered after her death, or would she have the courage to send it off to a publisher?

Ellie started to work, her avid labours fuelled by unmentionable thoughts which could only be allowed to surface fully in the privacy of her room and in her writing. She was the virgin, young and beautiful, and the stableman? Dare she pursue it? She must, if the novel was ever to get finished. He was very tall, broadshouldered and darkly handsome. He worked hard at his calling, with a sense of pride, but deep down he simmered, forever cursing the day when fate had intervened to change him into a shuffling cripple. Now, in the lonely dell, with the full moon emerging from thunderous clouds, he could vent his spite, and with a sound that roared up from deep down inside him he lowered himself over the young maiden and with a ferocity that was terrifying he ravaged her young body.

Ellie paused to massage her temples, while the heat in her blood cooled to embers. It was madness, she thought as she took up her pen and scratched out the lines. She was baring her soul. No, he would have to be fair, short and stocky, and he could never be anything other than physically sound.

Joe Carey put down the evening paper and rubbed at his eyes with his thumb and forefinger. 'Are yer not goin' out ternight?' he asked.

Sue shook her head. 'Del's busy,' she replied.

Joe looked up at the chimer on the mantelshelf. 'Yer mum's bin gone some time.'

'She's only next door, Dad,' Sue said testily.

He nodded and forced a smile. 'Yeah, she does like a chat, 'specially when 'er an' Mable get tergevver.'

The young woman smiled back, wondering whether it was the right moment to broach the subject. 'I was talking to that reporter who did the piece about Alf Barlow and Micky Sloan,' she said casually. 'He wants to do a piece on Ship Lane.'

Joe's eyes widened angrily. 'Ship Lane? Why Ship Lane?'

'Well, it is the sort of thing he's interested in,' she replied quickly.

'Why they can't leave fings alone I'll never know,' Joe said disgustedly. 'What can be achieved by it? All it does is rake up the past an' cause people 'eartache. Don't yer fink those people who lost friends an' relatives should be considered? Nah, all they're interested in is sellin' newspapers.'

Sue leaned forward in her chair. 'I don't dispute what you're saying, Dad. It's all about selling papers, but people do like to read about themselves, and it is about them more than the people they lost. The important thing is that the articles are done with discretion. Sam Calkin, the man who's writing them, is very careful not to offend anyone. That's why he wants to talk to people who were involved before he goes ahead.'

'Are yer sayin' 'e wants ter talk ter me an' Charlie Duggan?'

She nodded. 'That's right, Dad.'

'I don't wanna talk to 'im,' Joe said sharply.

'But you and Charlie were heroes that night,' Sue replied. 'If it wasn't for your quick thinking more people would have died. It said so in the newspapers, and the coroner said it too. Surely you haven't forgotten.'

'Forgotten? How could I ever forget that night?' he said in a raised voice.

'I'm sorry, I didn't mean it like that, but you and Charlie have a right to be in that series Sam Calkin's doing,' Sue told him firmly.

Joe slumped back in his armchair, suddenly mindful of his discussions with Charlie about such an eventuality. To refuse would raise questions. He took a deep breath and puffed. 'Did this Calkin bloke actually say 'e wanted ter write about Ship Lane?' he asked.

Sue nodded. 'Yes, but he can't very well do it without you and Charlie's say-so. If you refused to see him he could only repeat what's already been said. These articles of his are about the survivors, what they're doing now, their own recollections.'

Joe stared down at the unlit grate for a few moments, then he looked up at his daughter. 'I'll 'ave ter speak wiv Charlie first,' he said quietly.

'Look, Dad, don't do it if you're not both up to it,' she urged him. 'Just remember that you deserve some recognition for what you did that night. A lot of people have got you two to thank for them still being here.'

'I fink we'll be able ter go along wiv it,' he replied frowning, 'provided we get the reporter's assurances that what we tell 'im don't get twisted. You know 'ow reporters tend ter twist fings. Soon as yer muvver comes back I'll go an' 'ave a word wiv Charlie. I don't want 'er ter know yet a while. I'd sooner break it to 'er gently, an' in me own time.'

Sue saw what she took to be fear in his eyes, and it set her thinking. Something had happened that night which had never come out, that she was sure of. It wasn't natural to refuse to talk about it, unless there was something he and Charlie were ashamed of. Did they blame themselves for the deaths? Was it some form of negligence? Did they feel that they took too long to clear the emergency exit? The reports on the tragedy had had nothing whatsoever to say about negligence or any other failing on their part. It was baffling, and unless she was very much mistaken the secret, whatever it was, would most likely die with them.

The damage to the Bell public house soon became news in Totterdown Street and it was not very long before it reached Wally Tucker's ears. His wife Betty heard the story when she called in at Mrs Riley's grocery shop, which was only a few doors away from the pub. On the way into the turning she bumped into Nell Sharp and Nell just happened to see Albert Price when she called in to Vic Ogden's for her evening paper. Albert told Granny Minto, and while she was standing at her front door the old lady relayed the news to Queenie Alladyce.

'We'll 'ave ter pop up there,' Wally told Betty.

'We?'

'Yeah, me an' the lads.'

'Don't you get involved,' Betty warned him sharply. 'Whoever done it must 'ave 'ad reason. If they see you an' those two dopey mates o' yours interferin' they might take it out on you.'

'Don't be so bloody melodramatic,' Wally scoffed. 'All we're gonna do is offer our sympafy. We're regulars, an' it's only right.'

'I shouldn't fink the Fords'll want yer sympafy,' Betty replied. 'They'll need a bit of 'elp ter clear the place up.'

'I ain't got time to argue the toss,' Wally said as he put on his coat.

Benny Tracy had already heard the news from Queenie and he was busy debating what to do when Wally knocked. Tubby Saward meanwhile was dozing in his warm armchair in ignorance of what had happened, until the loud knock made him jump with fright.

'Get yer coat on, Tubby, there's bin trouble at the Bell,' Wally told him in a very serious tone of voice.

'Yer scared the bloody life out o' me, knockin' like that,' Tubby growled.

'If I'd 'ave tapped on yer door yer wouldn't 'ave 'eard it, yer silly git. Now get yer coat on,' Wally told him once more.

The three musketeers hurried along the turning, observed as usual by Granny Minto who called out to Albert to come and look. 'They're up ter no good, I can tell by the look on their faces,' she remarked.

'I know where they're off to,' Albert told her.

'Up the Bell that's fer sure,' Granny replied.

Tubby was having some trouble with his arthritic hip and he struggled to keep up with his two pals. 'What's the bloody rush?' he moaned. 'The pub ain't alight, is it?'

Dave Ford looked at the three with a gleam in his eye as they almost fell into the public bar. ''Ello, boys, 'eard the news?'

Wally nodded. 'Yeah. Sorry to 'ear it, Dave. Who was it?'

'Gawd knows.'

'Anyfing we can do?'

'That saloon bar's a right poxy mess,' the landlord replied. 'There's glass everywhere. Me an' Bella's gonna clean it up, when we get time.'

'We could do that for yer,' Tubby said. 'We wouldn't mind, would we, lads?'

'Certainly not,' Benny chimed in quickly, glancing suggestively at the beer pump.

'Much obliged,' Dave said smiling. ''Ave a drink on the 'ouse first.'

Wally leaned on the counter watching while the landlord filled three pint glasses. ''Ere, I saw Winkle yesterday,' he remarked. ''E's 'elpin' out on Sharkey's stall. I didn't know 'e was out.'

'No nor did I, till Monty Groves told me,' Dave replied. 'Monty wants ter see 'im.'

'I'll tell 'im,' Wally said, licking his lips in anticipation as the brimming glass of beer was placed in front of him.

'Ask 'im ter look in 'ere,' Dave instructed him.

'Will do.'

The public bar was beginning to fill with curious customers who had heard the news, and having downed their drinks the three musketeers set to work in the shattered saloon bar.

'Winkle should be careful who 'e consorts wiv,' Tubby remarked as they scoured the heavy carpet for glass. 'The rozzers'll be markin' 'is card after the last turn-out.'

'Seven years 'e got, didn't 'e?' Benny queried.

'Yeah, don't time fly.'

'They say Winkle's the best in the business,' Benny declared.

'If 'e's so good 'ow did 'e get caught? That's what I'd like ter know,' Wally cut in.

''E wasn't caught on the job, 'e was grassed,' Tubby said.

'Yer can't trust anybody these days,' Benny growled as he picked up a large sliver of glass.

Chapter Twenty-Two

Lennie Donald and Frank Swain were enjoying a game of pontoon, and between them they had managed to relieve the other four players of most of their stakes.

'I'm cleaned out,' Bonny Harper said with a sigh as Swain turned over an ace and a king. 'I'm goin' out fer a bit of air.'

Two of the other three players were innocent victims of the card sharps, while the third had his suspicions but dared not accuse the villains of using marked cards. Bonny Harper's position was a little different. He had been sent with twenty pounds in his pocket and told to make sure he was cleaned out by nine o'clock and then cry poverty.

As he lit a cigar on the front steps of the old Victorian house in Rotherhithe Bonny saw movement across the street. He took a large drag and puffed a cloud of smoke skywards before making off at a quick pace. He was a con man, quite willing to resort to trickery but unable to stomach any form of violence, and he knew that serious violence was on the cards tonight.

The three dupes were pushed aside as the team burst in, taking the two villains by surprise. Swain was floored with one blow from a pickaxe handle before he could move and Donald had the chair kicked away from under him as the boots went in. One hour later, Frank Swain regained consciousness to find himself upside down, suspended over the river by his feet. The water seemed a long way below him and he twisted in terror, suddenly seeing Lennie Donald hanging alongside him still out cold. He tried to move his hands but realised that they were tied securely behind his back. There was a strip of plaster over his mouth too and his head was throbbing with pain.

'Right then, let's put 'em in the picture. Pull 'em in,' ordered a tall shadowy figure.

The hydraulic crane raised the two captives quietly, and when their heads were hanging level with the wharf loop-hole the man in the shadows spoke again. 'Take the plaster off their mouths.'

Lennie Donald started groaning as he came to, while Frank Swain tried to see just who it was who dared to put him through such an ordeal. 'What's this all about?' he growled.

'Shut it an' listen,' the tall man said harshly. 'I need a few answers to some questions, an' if you co-operate yer might just walk away from this. If, on the ovver 'and, you choose ter keep yer ugly traps shut, then I'm afraid you'll be goin' down ter the eels. They'll be fightin' over yer, wiv all the blood comin' out o' yer froats. The choice is yours.'

'I dunno what yer on about,' Swain grunted.

'Speak when yer've somefing o' value ter say or don't bovver,' the obscured figure said calmly.

'What you after? Tell me, fer Chrissake!' Swain shouted.

'It's simple. I want names. I wanna know who's

payin' yer an' what's yer reasons fer crossin' the water. Yer've got five minutes ter decide. Eivver yer spill yer guts or my lads'll attach chain balls ter yer feet an' dump yer in the river. I'm goin' out fer a smoke, an' I'll be gone fer five minutes. Make the right decision, boys.'

A dark cloud covered the moon as the two captives swung like lumpy pendulums, and when the five minutes were up the tall man stepped back into the wharf chamber. 'Well, 'ave they said anyfing?' he asked.

'Nah, they seem resigned ter bein' fish food,' someone said.

'Right, lads, do the business an' then cut the ropes. I'll see yer termorrer.'

Ernest Spencer felt a little more at ease than when he last visited Melfield, and he had been pleasantly surprised to find the *Bulletin*'s proprietor in an accommodating mood.

'Well, it's very early days yet, but at least some of our advertisers seem to be returning to the fold,' Andrew Morrison remarked as he poured the claret.

'Calkin's first article seems to have been well received, but as you say it's too soon to gauge,' Spencer replied.

Distant thunder and a sudden flash in the night sky lit the large study momentarily and Morrison got up to draw the curtains. 'Tell me about this minor hiccup you've had, Ernest,' he said. 'It sounded very mysterious when you phoned me.'

Spencer smiled self-effacingly. 'I couldn't say too much over the phone,' he replied as he picked up the glass of wine. 'There were still some enquiries to be made.'

'Well?'

'The man who contacted Calkin was William Button, a retired Army sergeant major,' the editor explained. 'India, Africa and all that. He's an alcoholic and down on his luck, but according to Calkin he has something.'

'But could we use it?' Morrison queried.

'No, it would be too counter-productive running in tandem,' Spencer said quickly.

Andrew Morrison smiled as he put down his glass. 'Now come on, Ernest. You haven't travelled all the way to Melfield just to drink my claret. What's on your mind?'

The editor stretched out his long legs towards the log fire. 'Sam Calkin was intending to put the George Merry story in his series, but after talking to this Button character he feels that he can't use it. Apparently there's been a major cover-up.'

'How so?'

'George Merry, the old night-watchman at the lead mills, died a hero trying to salvage his firm's vehicles,' Spencer went on. 'On the same night of bombing the warehouse opposite was destroyed by an oil bomb. In the basement of that warehouse ninety people were sheltering. All hell broke loose when they tried to evacuate the shelter. The emergency exit was blocked by falling debris, and in the delay while it was cleared five elderly people died of smoke inhalation. Tragic as it was the story only rated a few lines of newsprint at the time, which was not unusual, bearing in mind that London was being systematically destroyed by nightly air raids and people were dying everywhere. What was unusual, and criminal, if the informant is to be believed, was that at the very moment the warehouse in Ship Lane took the direct hit it was being robbed.'

'Good Lord!'

'What's more,' Spencer continued, 'George Merry, the night-watchman at the lead mills, was thoroughly drunk and incapable of removing the lorry, which somehow found its way into the lane, only to be destroyed by fire.'

'Good grief!'

'The mystery deepens,' Spencer said for effect. 'The warehouse was a council store for furniture and the belongings of people who had, and were, losing their homes during the Blitz. What are we talking about here? Antiques? Paintings? Persian carpets? No, these were items of little value, except of course to those poor people who had been bombed out of their homes. So why the robbery? And how could it have taken place without being discovered by the shelter warden, and the fire watcher, who were on the roof of the warehouse at the time?'

'Go on,' the proprietor urged.

'Mr William Button stated that he was at the lead mills, in George Merry's company that night, and he witnessed the robbery at the warehouse. His assertion that the night-watchman was drunk and incapacitated could well be the truth, when we consider the rumours which circulated after the tragedy about George Merry having to be assisted back to his place of work by friends after drinking at a local pub. Even his widow admitted to Calkin that sometimes her husband used to drink himself into a stupor.'

'How much is Button asking for this information?' Morrison enquired.

'Fifty pounds. Half up front and the other half on publication.'

'Does he realise the implications?'

'Calkin did point out that there would be repercussions,' Spencer replied. 'The man was quite aware of it. Calkin seemed to feel that he was looking forward to the publicity.'

'Pay him what he wants,' Morrison decided. 'This could be the biggest exclusive since that gas-works explosion we covered in thirty-seven. Just one question. How will you handle it?'

'I've sounded out Calkin and I have to say that he concurs with my idea of a Friday lead-in, in the form of a postscript to the heroes article, and the exposure in the following Tuesday's edition.'

'Goodness me. Can you manage it?'

Spencer smiled slyly. 'We'll need the extra page but the cost can be traded off with some cut-price advertising space. It's a gamble I know, but we are engaged in a battle for survival.'

'Good man, Ernest,' the proprietor said enthusiastically. 'Go to it, and the best of luck.'

Spencer sighed with satisfaction as he picked up his claret. If the plan for a Tuesday exposure worked then the advertisers would flood back, he thought. Maybe now that Morrison had okayed it he could reconsider his decision to sack that drunken sot Paddy O'Brian.

A room had been set aside at Monty Groves's favourite drinking club in Walworth and the lights burned into the night.

'Lennie Donald was near ter shittin' 'imself an' 'e spilled 'is guts, but yer gotta give that bastard Swain credit,' Monty said. ''E never flinched till 'e saw the game was up. Anyway we got what we wanted. Nosher an' Darbo took 'em over the water an' dumped 'em outside the Queen Anne in Whitechapel Road. Trussed up like a couple o' chickens. They'll be a long while livin' it down.'

The tall man nodded. 'We'll need ter call everyone in. Monty, can yer get 'old o' Winkle?'

'Word's out.'

'We'll need 'im soon. Put 'im on a retainer.'

'S'posin' 'e don't wanna know?'

''E will, if the shekels are right.'

''Ave we got anyone we could use inside the union?' Monty asked.

'Leave that ter me,' the man replied.

''Ere we don't gotta get union cards, 'ave we?' an ex-boxer enquired.

'You'll be all right, Ben. They'll give you a free pass,' Monty chuckled.

The tall man rapped the table for silence. 'Now listen carefully,' he urged them. 'I want none of yer strayin' over the water fer any reason. Yer face might be known an' the East End teams are gonna be 'avin' their little get-tergevver after this, just like us. Keep yer wits about yer an' put the word out ter the publicans an' bookies we know ter watch out fer strange faces on the manor.'

'D'yer reckon they'll try an' come at us?' one of the gathering asked.

'Not yet a while,' he replied. 'We're gonna scotch 'em anyway. Once we get what we need an' it goes public someone's gonna pull the plug. After that there'll be no finance an' no mileage in them comin' over this side o' the water. Fings'll be the way they always were. They'll take care o' their patch an' we'll take care of ours, an' like the poet said, never the twain shall meet. Well, that's all, lads. Monty, 'ang about will yer. I need ter go over a couple o' fings wiv yer.'

A light was burning late in the union office in Tooley Street and Robbie Casey resisted the urge to refill his glass. His ulcer had been playing him up for the past week and his doctor had warned him about the whisky. It was good for the nerves though, he told himself as he stared down at the phone. He should have reminded the doctor. 'A burst ulcer or a heart attack. What a choice,' he snorted as he reached down for the bottle.

When the phone rang the elderly convenor snatched at it, spilling some of the whisky over his blotting-pad in the process. 'Casey speakin'.'

The conversation was soon over, and the union official was still wrapped up in his thoughts as he walked along the dark and deserted Tooley Street. Shadowy doorways and tall gloomy wharves lent the place a ghostly atmosphere, and it was not an area for the faint-hearted to roam, but for Robbie Casey it held no fears. This was home. This was where the men came together in strength and where the business was done, and as he walked to the railway station he forgot the nagging pain of his aggravated ulcer.

Chapter Twenty-Three

Sue Carey rested her chin in her hands and stared disconsolately at the telephone. It was close to ten o'clock on Saturday morning and Del had still not rung. He had promised faithfully that he would try to find out how long the union conference was likely to take and let her know by nine-thirty. He's a selfish pig, she thought. Didn't he realise that she wanted some sort of life outside of work? Probably not. Now that he was working for the union it would take him over body and soul. It was what he had really wanted and nothing else mattered. Well, if he thought that she was going to sit about on Saturday evening waiting for him to arrive home then he would be sorely mistaken.

Paddy O'Brian came into the office and leaned on the counter. 'And how's my little toffee apple?' he said grinning.

Sue smiled at him, glad of the chance to trade a joke or two before she became totally depressed. 'Don't you let Frances hear you say that, Paddy,' she told him with a maidenly expression. 'I don't want her scratching my eyes out.'

'I can see that the latest office gossip for idle minds has reached you,' he replied, rolling his eyes. 'Frances and I are just good friends.'

'Of course,' Sue said quickly, the smile still lingering on her face. 'But anyone can see that Frances thinks a lot of you, and she can be possessive.'

Paddy beamed. 'It shows, does it?'

Sue looked at him closely and it cheered her to see the change in him. He was clean-shaven, his dark hair neatly parted and his white shirt crisp and fresh, and he sported a loud tie that somehow suited his personality. How different from his slovenly appearance just a short time ago. She felt happy for him and could not resist letting him know. 'Well, all I can say is, Frances Miller's a changed woman lately, and look at you. You look nice enough to eat.'

Paddy's face grew a little serious. 'Frances and I do seem to have got close, Sue,' he remarked. 'It's funny how things happen, isn't it? I've known her a few years now and we've always got on well together. In fact she's been a little treasure in getting me all the information I need, but there was always a cut-off point. Neither of us had the urge to get too familiar and we never even chatted unnecessarily, but suddenly things seemed to change.'

'Haven't you figured it out?' Sue asked with a sly smile.

'I think she feels sorry for me all of a sudden,' Paddy said unconvincingly.

'It's not that at all,' Sue replied quickly. 'She's being protective.'

He looked disappointed. 'You think so?'

'Don't get me wrong,' she told him. 'It's because she's very fond of you that she's allowed her defences to slip, now that there's good reason.'

'You mean since Sam Calkin's arrived?'

'Exactly,' Sue said. 'Frances is a very nice person, but she's been on her own for a long time and become set in her ways. Now she realises that the person she cares for is under threat, so she overcomes her reserve and begins to let you know that she's around. She's always been there for you, Paddy, but she's not been able to tell you, up until now.'

He nodded slowly, then his eyes lit up. 'We're going to see *King Lear* at the Old Vic this evening. Frances likes Shakespearian plays.'

'Well, good for you,' Sue said smiling.

'And so to work,' the Irishman declared, giving her a debonair wink as he pushed open the main office door.

Sue sighed as she slumped down on her desk, then jumped nervously as the telephone rang. The caller wanted some information on obtaining press photos, and after she had explained the procedures she put the phone down and slipped back effortlessly into her Saturday morning blues. How inconsiderate Del was. There must have been phones at hand. Surely he could have gleaned some idea of how long he was going to be there. Perhaps she should have been less generous with her favours. Maybe then he would have been more inclined to spend a little more time with her instead of that stupid union.

Tom Carey drove his empty lorry over Tower Bridge and swung left into Tooley Street. It had been a reasonable morning considering, he thought. He had managed to squeeze into Smithfield meat market and unload the stinking offal baskets without much delay. It wasn't the best of loads, true, and the lorry needed swilling down and disinfecting before he could clock off for the weekend, but he had time to look in on his brother Mo.

Maurice Carey was standing outside the arch when the lorry drew up and he pulled a face. 'What you bin cartin', fer Chrissake?' he asked as Tom climbed down from the cab.

The younger man grinned. 'Offal baskets.'

Mo led the way into his office just inside the arch and looked enquiringly at his brother. 'What's up?'

Tom leaned back in the tatty armchair and crossed his legs. 'What makes yer fink there's somefing wrong?' he answered.

Mo sat on the edge of his desk and folded his arms. 'Yer look a bit worried,' he replied.

Tom's face relaxed in a smile. 'That's not worry yer seein'. It's fatigue. I'm courtin' strong.'

Mo grinned back at him. 'Pamela Duggan?'

'The same.'

'I see. So this is just a social call.'

Tom picked at the torn arm of the chair. 'Actually I was finkin' about what yer said when yer called round the ovver night.'

'What did I say?'

'You know, about talkin' ter Swain an' Donald.'

'They've bin spoken to,' Mo told him with a ghost of a smile on his fine-featured face.

'Mo, you are an aggravatin' git at times,' Tom said in a deadpan voice. 'Gettin' anyfing out o' you is worse than tryin' ter find a fry-up in a synagogue.'

'So what d'yer want me ter say? D'yer want me ter go inter details?'

'It'd make a change.'

Mo got up and limped over to light the gas under a small tin kettle. 'Swain an' Donald were 'ung up ter dry, or ter get wet, an' they saw good sense as it 'appens,' he said as he checked the gas jet. 'They gave us names an' info. I don't fink they'll be seen this side o' the water in future.'

'So yer didn't duff 'em up then?'

'Nah, we just scared the crap out of 'em.'

'Yer should 'ave given 'em a bit of a smack at least,' Tom growled. 'So what 'appens now?'

Mo spooned tea-leaves into a battered pot and took two large mugs out of a cupboard before answering. 'Swain an' Donald were, as we suspected, front men fer an East End crew run by the Duke bruvvers. They're small-time but they do cause quite a bit of aggravation in the Whitechapel area. We've managed ter find out that this team 'ave bin recruited ter cause trouble wiv the unions.'

''Ang on a minute,' Tom said quickly. 'This is gettin' above me. Yer said "we". Are you involved personally?'

'Yer could say that,' Mo replied. 'I told yer the ovver night I got friends amongst the local villains. Any trouble from over the water is likely to affect me an' a lot of ovver small businesses.'

'But why should somebody pay a tuppenny-'a'penny mob like the Dukes ter come over 'ere chuckin' their weight about?' Tom pressed him.

The kettle started to boil and Mo filled the teapot. 'Look, Bruv, if I tell yer what I know I want your promise that it stays between us two, is that understood?'

'It goes wivout sayin',' Tom replied nodding his head vigorously.

The older man stirred the tea and filled the two mugs, adding milk and sugar while his brother waited impatiently. 'Durin' the war me an' a lot like me made money while you young bucks went off ter fight the battles,' he began as he handed over a mug of tea. 'It wasn't my choosin' ter stay be'ind, you know that, but that was 'ow it was an' there was nuffing I could do about it. Anyway, there was money ter be made buyin' an' sellin'. The black market was rife an' yer just 'ad ter be in the know. Since the war ended though, fings 'ave changed. Servicemen like yerself comin' back ter civilian life were in no mood ter take any ole shit an' they wanted certain rights as workers. There was gonna be no more doffin' the cap an' bowin' an' scrapin' ter the employer fer a day's work, an' then puttin' up wiv starvation wages. The way out was ter get organised, which upset quite a few bosses.'

'Look, I know all this,' Tom said puffing. 'Don't ferget I've bin out on the cobbles, an' suffered for it.'

Mo smiled indulgently. 'I'm gettin' to it, if yer'll just listen,' he replied. 'Business people like meself can live wiv the unions. The few workers I employ get a good deal, an' that's the way it should be, but in some quarters trade unionists are seen as bein' a load o' Bolshy bastards 'ell-bent on destroyin' the country out o' spite. What's more, these mad bastards seem ter fink the unions are in the pay o' the Commies an' ready ter bring the country to a standstill when Russia gets round to invadin' us.'

'I know about all that,' Tom cut in. 'There's bin bits in the papers about it. It's bin ridiculed anyway.'

'Well, let me tell yer there's a group of very influential people who've banded tergevver, an' they call themselves the Crusaders. They're out ter ruin the unions an' at the same time they're after formin' an association o' businesses. Puttin' it simply, if yer in the warm yer get the contracts, an' yer stay outside at yer peril.'

''Ow the bloody 'ell d'you know all about this?' Tom asked.

'Do you know Robbie Casey?' Mo asked him.

'Yeah. 'E's the union convenor at Tooley Street,' Tom replied.

'Robbie's an ole pal o' mine,' Mo told him. 'I was in a position ter do 'im a favour once an' 'e put me on me guard when this Crusader business started up.'

''Ow did Casey get ter know about the Crusaders?'

'That's not too 'ard ter figure out,' Mo said smiling. 'Robbie Casey's also a member o' the local Labour Party an' 'e's very well respected. Apart from top union officials 'e sometimes finds 'imself rubbin' shoulders wiv politicians. That's where the whisper first came from. Yer remember that MP who blew 'is brains out a few months ago?'

'Patrick Cox.'

'That was 'im. Apparently 'e was one o' the founder members, an' when they turned ter the criminal fraternity fer 'elp Cox threatened ter spill the beans. Word from a reliable source suggests that 'e was murdered, though nuffing could ever be proved.'

Tom took a large gulp from his mug. 'Well well,' he said, shaking his head slowly. 'If someone else 'ad told me you an' the union was 'and in glove I'd never 'ave believed 'em.'

'Don't get me wrong,' Mo cautioned him. 'I'm a businessman not a trade unionist, but it don't mean ter say I can't 'ave friends in both camps. As I said, me an' Robbie go back a long way.'

'You're full o' surprises,' Tom said grinning. 'What next, now yer got the names yer want?'

'You ain't bin listenin' properly, 'ave yer?' Mo told him gruffly.

'Yer said Swain an' Donald talked,' the younger man replied, looking puzzled.

'So I did, but they only told us what they knew, who they were workin' for an' that it was a job o' work their mob was bein' well paid for. People like those two knuckle-scrapers are never allowed ter know too much. They're just sent ter do the aggravatin', or at least they were.'

'So what next?'

Mo drained his mug. 'Some'ow, some way, we've gotta find out the names o' those so-called Crusaders, then they've gotta be exposed. They're dangerous people.'

'That could be a very dodgy undertakin',' Tom remarked, looking at his older brother closely.

Mo read the sign. 'Don't worry, this 'as brought the local teams tergevver an' they all know what the upshot'll be if this Crusader business is allowed ter flourish. Don't ferget there's a lot like me, wiv members o' their families in a union. Saul Kemp runs the Elephant mob an' 'is farvver an' bruvvers are stevedores, an' then there's Monty Groves from Rovver'ithe. Monty's two bruvvers are shop stewards in the print union. That's apart from Monty an' Saul's own business involvements.'

'So what can I do to 'elp?' Tom said with enthusiasm.

'Just keep out o' trouble,' Mo said grinning.

The young man got up to leave, remembering that he had a lorry to wash down before he could clock off. 'Well, I'll keep an eye out, an' an ear ter the wall,' he said. 'Maybe Joe Brady might let somefing slip some time.'

'Yer never know,' Mo said, slipping his arm round his brother's shoulders as they walked through the arch to the street.

That Saturday morning in Totterdown Street was no different from any other Saturday. Granny Minto stood at her front door, very selective about who she would speak to and who she would ignore. Albert Price stood at her shoulder for part of the time, and Nell Sharp stopped as usual to have an extended chat with Bessie Woodward. Along the turning Annie Barlow chatted with Rosie Coleman, while opposite Minnie Sloan dutifully cleaned her windows. Queenie Alladyce went to the oilshop for a tin of Zeebo, so she said, and had still not emerged when Nell Sharp finally got away from the gabbling of her neighbour.

'I can't understand what the silly mare sees in 'im, strike me if I can,' Granny Minto growled. 'I mean ter say, 'e ain't no oil paintin', is 'e.'

'I dunno,' Albert replied. ''E's got a sort o' mysterious look about 'im.'

'Mysterious me arse,' Granny said in disgust. 'Yer'll be sayin' I look like Greta Garbo next.'

'Come ter fink of it there is a likeness,' Albert said with a straight face.

'Piss orf up the pub if yer goin',' Granny told him. 'An' bring me back a milk stout, if it's not too much trouble.'

At number 4 Charlie Duggan sat in the backyard scraping dried mud from his working boots, watched by his worried-looking next-door neighbour. 'Like I said, there's no sense in tryin' ter put the bloke off,' he went on. 'We'll just keep it simple, an' don't let 'im draw yer out. Those reporters can be very devious gits at times.'

Joe Carey nodded. 'Yeah, yer right, Chas. We've got nuffink ter worry about.'

Charlie banged his boot down on the paving-stone and straightened his back with a grunt. 'Your Tom an' our Pam seem ter be 'ittin' it off,' he remarked.

'Yeah,' Joe agreed. 'They make a nice couple.'

'I never could stand that Catchpole feller,' Charlie added. 'Too cocky.'

'Our Tom said 'e's the shop steward at Brady's now,' Joe told him.

'I can't see 'im doin' any good at the job.'

'No, nor can I.'

'Pass us that ovver boot, pal.'

''Ere y'are.'

'Fancy a pint ternight?'

'Yeah, if yer like.'

'Don't worry too much about it, Joe.'

'I'm not worried over much,' Joe said almost to himself, though there was no denying it. It had been a bad week as it was, and then Sue had sprung it on him about the reporter wanting to do the shelter piece. It was as if his worst fears were being finally realised. 'In fact I'm not worried at all.'

Chapter Twenty-Four

The two young couples boarded the number 68 tram in Tower Bridge Road and climbed the steep flight of steps to the upper deck. Pamela Duggan looked at Sue as they slipped into a hard seat. 'Are yer sure my 'air looks all right?' she asked, giving it a little pat with the palm of her hand.

Sue nodded reassuringly. 'It's really nice, honest.'

The two young men took the seat behind their partners and Tom pulled out a handful of change for the fare. 'I thought I was never gonna get rid o' that bloody smell,' he groaned. 'Me muvver stuck all me clobber in the copper an' I 'ad ter go round the baths fer a scrub.'

Del Abelson smiled. 'That's what yer get fer bein' militant,' he remarked. 'Yer not likely ter get any o' the plum jobs, 'specially now that yer ole pal Catchpole's the steward.'

Tom shrugged his shoulders. 'Ter be fair it ain't bin as bad as I expected,' he replied. 'Takin' it all round I don't get any more bad jobs than the rest, an' as fer Bernie 'e just seems ter give me the elbow.'

'D'yer fink 'e's takin' a bung?' Del asked.

'I dunno really, but I'd say not,' Tom replied. ''E's already 'ad a few run-ins wiv ole Toby Lowndes.'

'You surprise me,' Del said.

Sue turned round in her seat. 'Can't you fellers forget work for five minutes,' she said sharply. 'This is supposed to be a Saturday night out.'

Tom grinned and leaned forward in his seat. 'I'll make a bargain wiv yer,' he suggested. 'You two stop chattin' about clothes an' make-up an' we won't talk about work.'

Pamela turned to give Tom a look of disapproval but the smile playing in the corner of her small mouth gave her away. Tom pouted his lips and she turned her head back quickly. Sue meanwhile was fishing into her small handbag and she found her silver powder compact, opening it carefully and glancing down into the mirror while she used the tip of her little finger to wipe a trace of lipstick from the edge of her mouth.

The tram clattered over the track intersection at the Bricklayers Arms and turned into the New Kent Road where it pulled up with a jolt.

'That's Billy Cuthbert getting on,' Pamela remarked. ''E's got that 'orrible Chalky White wiv 'im.'

'They're like Darby and Joan those two,' Sue replied.

'I'm not gonna dance wiv 'im any more, offend or please,' Pamela said firmly.

'Who, Billy Cuthbert?'

'Nah, Chalky White. 'E's all 'ands an' 'e's real clumsy wiv 'is feet.'

'It's just as well,' Sue replied in a low voice. 'You know how quick-tempered Tom can be.'

'I wonder if Bernie Catchpole'll be there ternight,' Pamela said, looking a little concerned. 'I couldn't stand any repeat o' last time.'

'If he is just ignore him,' Sue told her.

The conductor had not come up to the upper deck to collect the fares and Tom held the copper coins in his hand as the tram slowed down at the Elephant and Castle. People were milling around as the vehicle ground to a stop and he grinned as he watched the conductor busily talking to a passenger at the front of the lower deck.

'Well, that was a cheap ride,' he said triumphantly as they jumped down and crossed the busy junction.

The evening sky was turning red as they walked up to the Palais de Danse, where the band could be heard already playing and familiar faces were milling around outside. In front of them Billy Cuthbert was chatting to a young girl who had her hair piled up on the top of her head while Chalky White stood back leering.

'They don't waste no time, do they,' Pamela snorted.

Del Abelson got the tickets and the two couples entered the ballroom. 'I'll get the drinks while you find a seat,' Tom offered. 'What'll it be?'

Del noticed that Bernie Catchpole was standing at the bar in the company of a shapely blonde and he smiled as he nudged Tom. 'He looks suited,' he remarked.

The two young women were looking around the dance floor and suddenly Pamela touched Sue's arm. 'Look, there's Fred Astaire over there,' she said quickly.

'Fred Astaire?'

'Yeah, 'im wiv the brothel creepers on.'

Sue chuckled. 'You've got a lovely turn of phrase.'

'Everyone calls 'im Fred Astaire,' Pamela went on. 'It's a shame really. 'E's a lovely dancer but 'e never gcts ter take a gel 'ome. Not ter my knowledge anyway.'

Sue watched as the middle-aged man whisked his partner across the floor. The tall brunette looked to be enjoying it and her face contrasted with his stern look of concentration. 'He might be lucky tonight,' she remarked.

Pamela shook her head. 'That's Billy Cuthbert's sister. Billy would 'ave 'is guts fer garters.'

Tom stood at the bar waiting for the drinks and he exchanged a brief nod with Bernie, who appeared to be in a relaxed mood as he chatted with his new girlfriend. Del came up to help carry the drinks to the table and he leaned on the counter. 'Tom, I might not get a chance to ask yer later, but would yer be prepared ter meet wiv a feller I know?'

Tom looked at the taller man with a frown. 'What's it about?' he asked.

'Info.'

'What info?'

The drinks were ready and Del picked up the women's. 'I'll tell yer later, but if I don't get the chance can yer call in at my place termorrer mornin'?'

'Yeah sure.'

When they reached the table Tom glanced at his sister. 'Where's Pam?'

'She's dancing with Fred Astaire,' she told him.

'Who?'

'The one with the brothel creepers,' Sue said chuckling.

'Well, what's good fer the goose is good fer the gander,' he said smiling. 'I'm gonna ask that gel over there fer a dance.'

As he sauntered over towards two young women who were looking a little nervous Del turned to Sue. 'I'm sorry about ternight,' he said quietly.

Sue gave him a brief smile. 'It's forgotten,' she replied.

Del sipped his drink. He had arrived home from the union conference at six o'clock and had been content to spend an evening at the Bell but Sue would have none of it, and he winced inwardly as he recalled her sharp rejoinder. 'No, I was wrong an' I apologise,' he said quietly once more. 'I was bein' selfish. But tell me. If I'd 'ave refused ter come dancin', would you 'ave really come on your own?'

'I meant it, Del,' she replied. 'We can go to the pub any night. This is more lively. And besides, you need to relax too.'

'I could 'ave relaxed at the Bell.'

'So you say, but how many times have we gone there on a Saturday night and you've got involved in union talk with those clowns?'

'Okay. Point taken,' he said with a wide grin. 'As long as I'm forgiven I won't mention anyfing ter do wiv the union.'

'Come on, it's a waltz,' Sue said as the band struck up.

She slipped into his arms as they reached the floor and let him guide her round. He could smell her perfume and the scent of her fair hair and feel her warm body pressing against his, and he sighed contentedly. She was all woman, vibrant and loving, and she deserved more from him. Soon, he thought. Very soon he would get some free time and take her to a pleasant country inn for a romantic weekend.

She felt his arm tighten around her waist and she responded by nuzzling his ear as they danced. 'You're very desirable,' she whispered.

'That's s'posed ter be my line,' he replied.

'Well, say nice things to me then,' she urged him.

'We're alone, wiv a log burnin' in the fire, an' I take yer up in me arms an' carry yer over ter the bed.'

'Go on.'

'I lay yer down an' slowly . . .'

The music had stopped and the couples began to walk off the floor.

'I'll tell yer the rest later,' he said smiling.

She squeezed his hand in hers. 'Don't tell me, just do it.'

The evening was getting under way, drinks were flowing and tobacco smoke hung in the warm air around the bar area, and gradually more couples were chancing the floor. Pamela was dancing with a young man and Sue had been asked for a dance by a very courteous young man who had first sought Del's permission.

'So tell me about this meetin',' Tom urged as he picked up his drink.

Del looked around quickly then leaned forward over the table. 'Would you be prepared ter give the lay-out o' Brady's ter this feller?'

Tom's forehead creased in a puzzled frown. 'What's this all about, Del?'

'We need ter get inter Brady's safe,' Del told him.

'Yer gotta be kiddin' me.'

'It's no kid. I'm serious, Tom.'

'Whatever for?'

'We need ter find out a few fings.'

276

Tom Carey put his drink down with slow deliberation and looked through narrowed eyes at the union man. 'D'yer know somefink. I'm gettin' a little bit sick of all this cloak-an'-dagger stuff,' he said crossly. 'Terday I looked in on me bruvver Mo an' 'e was all mysterious as well. Are you involved wiv 'im?'

Del Abelson raised his hands in a conciliatory gesture. 'I spoke wiv Mo. 'E told me 'e saw yer.'

''Ow could 'e 'ave told yer?' Tom queried quickly. 'We're talkin' about this mornin', an' you was at a union conference all afternoon.'

'Mo was there.'

'At the union conference?'

'It wasn't exactly a strict union conference,' Del corrected him.

'Well, p'raps yer better tell me exactly what it was then.'

'Apart from Mo there were representatives from the local mobs, or teams as I prefer ter call 'em,' Del explained. 'Some top union men were there as well, in fact, an' the meetin' was 'eld at the union 'eadquarters in Finsbury. Basically it was all arranged by a few MPs who are concerned about what's 'appenin'. I understand that Mo put yer in the picture about this Crusader business.'

Tom nodded. 'So you wanna get inter Brady's safe ter see if there's anyfing that could give yer names?'

'Right first time.'

'What makes yer fink Brady might 'ave the info yer need?'

''Cos 'e's bin the link man,' Del told him. 'We know that Brady's bin attendin' meetin's wiv ovver bosses on both sides o' the water an' we reckon 'e's bin paid ter do it.'

'When d'yer want me ter meet this geezer?' Tom asked.

'Termorrer night.'

'What time? Where?'

'I'll let yer know termorrer mornin'.'

The women were returning from the dance floor and Del picked up his drink. ''Ere's ter success, Tom.'

'Too bloody true,' the young man said grinning.

In the small, dimly lit room behind the oilshop Queenie Alladyce sat looking around while John Raney took the seal off a bottle of Johnny Walker. She had to admit that under normal circumstances the room would have been off-putting to say the least. It was clean, true, but the heavy drapes up at the window were not to her liking, nor were the flattened cushions on the armchairs and the heavy brocade tablecloth. The kitchen range and fire grate were sorely in need of blacklead, and the glass shade hanging from the centre of the ceiling severely restricted the light. Around the walls there were some awful pictures, she felt, one of which made her cringe every time she looked up at it. An eagle with outstretched wings and extended talons was swooping down on an unsuspecting lamb and the predator's eyes seemed to burn out of the frame.

Nevertheless Queenie felt a sense of peace here, a sense of tranquillity, and she refrained from casting her eyes up at the picture. He was a good man, John Raney: simple and unassuming, educated and knowledgeable about a lot of things, and he made no demands upon her, other than to crave her company.

'It's just a small one,' he said, handing her the drink.

Queenie smiled. 'You do know everyone's talkin',' she said.

'It's not important,' he replied.

He was easy to talk to, although she felt that often his answers begged more questions. 'Why did yer never marry?' she asked.

John sat down facing her, holding his drink carefully. 'I s'pose the simple answer is that I never met the right woman,' he replied.

'Do many of us ever meet the right partner?' she remarked.

He sipped his whisky. 'There was a time though. She was nice. Pretty as a picture. The sun was shinin' an' she smiled over at me.'

'Go on,' Queenie urged.

'It was a Whit Sunday an' there was a fair up at Black'eath,' he said wistfully. 'I was a young man, just twenty. Thirty-five years ago, an' I can still see that smile. I was wiv a couple o' friends an' we were strollin' amongst the stalls. There was this tall contraption, I don't know what it's called but you 'ad ter strike the padded piece wiv a large mallet, an' if the blow was strong enough it rang a bell an' yer got a prize. My two pals tried but they couldn't ring it an' then they dared me ter try. I felt a bit silly but anyway I raised this mallet over me 'ead an' brought it down as 'ard as I could.'

'An' you rang the bell?'

'No, I missed the pad completely,' he said smiling sheepishly.

Queenie laughed aloud. 'Poor lad.'

John Raney twirled the glass he was holding. 'I walked away in disgust an' then I saw 'er. She was dressed in a long gown of the time an' 'er fair 'air was done in those long plaits the young women favoured. She was wearin' a small summer bonnet an' she seemed ter drift along. She was so pretty.'

'Go on, John.'

'She must 'ave seen my pathetic effort ter ring the bell 'cos she looked over an' gave me the most lovely smile. I was too frightened ter respond an' I remember turnin' away in embarrassment. I walked on frew the fairground, past the stalls an' rides, then I saw 'er again. She was ridin' the merry-go-round an' 'oldin' on as though terrified she was gonna fall off. I just stood an' watched, an' every time she floated past I saw that look of fear. She 'adn't noticed I was there, an' then when the ride stopped an' she climbed down she spotted me. 'Er eyes went up ter the sky, as though tellin' me 'ow frightenin' it was, an' then I plucked up courage an' smiled back. I remember it well. She was carryin' one o' those lace-edged parasols, an' as she moved away from the ride she accidentally dropped it in the mud. I wanted ter retrieve it for 'er but I found meself rooted ter the spot. Suddenly an 'eavily built young man stepped forward, picked it up for 'er, an' gave it back wiv a flourishin' bow. They started talkin', an' ter my dismay they walked off tergevver. I was the nearest person to 'er when she dropped 'er parasol but I was too slow to act. 'Ad I bin quicker I might 'ave ended up marryin' the gel, who knows.'

'Did yer see 'er again that day?' Queenie asked. 'The man might 'ave left.'

John Raney shook his head. 'Every year after that

until the war broke out I went ter the Whitsun fair in the vain 'ope of meetin' 'er again,' he went on. 'Last year the fair was back again an' I went along once more, believe it or not, just like the old days. I'd bin walkin' past the stalls an' rides an' then I felt tired, so I found a seat just across the way an' this old lady sat next ter me. She looked very tired too an' I was sure there were tears in 'er eyes. Then she looked round at me. "I used ter come 'ere every Whit Sunday when I was a young lass," she said. "So did I," I told 'er. "I met my late 'usband 'ere," she went on, an' then she gave me a smile. There was no mistakin' it. It was 'er.'

'Good gracious!'

John sipped his drink. 'I was dumbfounded an' I just looked at 'er in disbelief. Then she said, "I nearly met a nice young man at the fair one year. 'E was eyein' me an' I was sure 'e was interested, so I dropped me brolly in the mud on purpose but 'e never picked it up. I fink 'e was goin' to but the man who became my 'usband beat 'im to it."'

Queenie brought her hand up to her mouth in surprise. 'What a sad, strange story,' she said. 'That's fate for yer.'

John Raney gave a little chuckle. 'I don't like fairs. Never 'ave done.'

'Yet yer went every year.'

'No I never. It was just a fairy story.'

Chapter Twenty-Five

The Ferry Inn at Dockhead had a veranda overlooking the Thames, and it was there that Tom Carey met the Winkle. Del Abelson had described him well and there was no mistaking him, Tom thought as he introduced himself.

'Nice of yer ter take the trouble,' Winkle said as they re-emerged from the bar after getting their drinks. 'It's quieter out 'ere. Too many ear'oles in there fer my likin'.'

'I understand yer gonna do a job o' work,' Tom said, treading softly.

The thin-faced little man smiled slyly, showing a row of tobacco-stained teeth. 'People'll tell yer that Larry Fields is the best in the business,' he replied, 'though they might add that I'm not the luckiest o' people. That's 'ow I got caught, yer see. Sheer bad luck. Strange as it may seem I didn't get me moniker 'cos o' me size. They call me Winkle 'cos o' me passion fer shellfish an' winkles in particular. Take no notice o' me prattlin' on though. I'm just tryin' ter give yer a clear picture o' meself. After all, us people who rely on each ovver should know these sort o' fings.'

'I make yer right,' Tom said grinning, taking an instant liking to the talkative character.

'Mind you, I don't gabble on about what I do, ovver than ter me partners in crime so ter speak,' Winkle went on. 'By the way, were you in the services?'

'Infantry.'

'A PBI, eh? Good fer you,' he said with a grin. 'You've seen action an' men like yerself don't bottle it very easy. Nice ter do business wiv yer.'

Tom felt that the man was being a little premature but he let it pass. 'You are actually gonna do the safe then?' he asked in a low voice.

'That's what I'm bein' paid for,' Winkle replied. 'Now what I need from you is the exact lay-out. I can't expect yer ter give me any details o' the make an' size o' the peter but I need the location o' the office, if there's any night-watchman an' such like. Got me drift?'

Tom nodded and took a pencil and a piece of paper from his coat pocket. 'It's not gonna be easy gettin' in there,' he began as he spread the paper out in front of him. 'Fer a start the Brady yard gates are directly opposite a block o' flats. Yer'd be spotted gettin' over. Besides, they're about eight feet tall. Yer best bet is round the back, but yer gonna need 'elp.'

'Sorry, son, I always work alone,' Winkle cut in. 'It's better that way.'

Tom shook his head as he picked up the pencil. 'Round the back in Nelson Lane there's a bomb ruin surrounded by a wall. Like the gates it's over eight feet tall. Yer gonna need a ladder. Once up the wall yer'll 'ave ter pull the ladder up after yer an' lay it across the gap between that wall an' the back wall o' the yard. The gap's about ten feet so yer won't be able ter jump across. Once in the yard there's the Alsatian ter take care of.'

'Whoah! Wait a minute,' Winkle said in alarm. 'I can't stand dogs, let alone Alsatians. The bloody fings terrify me. I s'pose it's runnin' loose as well.'

Tom smiled as he nodded. 'That's why I was sayin' yer'll need 'elp.'

'Who yer got in mind?' Winkle asked quickly.

'Me.'

'You?'

'Yeah me.'

'I don't fink the boyos are gonna agree ter that,' the little safe cracker replied. 'They don't like ter be piss-balled about an' I've already agreed a price.'

'I'm not askin' fer payment. Let's say this is retribution,' Tom told him with a wicked smile.

'Got a score ter settle 'ave we?'

'A week in bed wiv cracked ribs fer starters,' Tom growled.

Winkle sipped his beer in silence and then met the young man's eyes in a hard stare. 'What about the dog?'

'I'll sort the dog out,' Tom replied. 'It knows me an' it won't come at yer if I'm wiv yer. I often feed it so it'll make a fuss o' me. I'll give it a bone ter gnaw an' I'll tie it up ter the kennel. It's always tied up durin' the day anyway so it shouldn't start barkin'. The office yer need is up an outside flight of iron stairs an' the door leadin' into it won't be 'ard ter force open. A jemmy should do it.'

The safe cracker watched as Tom drew a plan of the yard. 'What's on the sides?' he asked.

'There's a factory ter the left an' anuvver bomb

ruin ter the right,' Tom said as he sketched the details in.

'I don't s'pose there's any chance o' gettin' in via that ruin is there?' Winkle asked.

Tom shook his head. 'Nah, it's a sheer brick wall. It's the back o' the office.'

'I see.'

'Right then. Inside the door at the top o' the stairs there's a small corridor an' Brady's office is the second door on the left,' Tom went on. 'Ter be honest I can't 'elp yer wiv the safe. I've seen it though. It's a big one an' it stands by the end wall.'

'Facin' the door?'

'No, the side o' the desk.'

'That's a pity,' Winkle said pulling a face.

'Why's that?'

'Blast effect.'

'Yer mean yer gonna blow the safe?'

Winkle looked surprised. 'What d'yer fink I'm gonna do, pick the lock?'

Tom grinned. 'I thought yer'd use a stethoscope an' spin the tumblers like we see on the films.'

'That's a load o' cobblers, if yer'll pardon me French,' Winkle said with a snort. 'Spinnin' the tumblers is okay wiv little wall safes but those large office safes are built ter prevent that sort of entry. Besides, it can take quite some time ter get it right. Nah, jelly's the fing. Quick an' sure. Mind you, yer gotta know what yer doin' or the explosion can ruin the contents. I gotta be extra careful too 'cos we're after papers. Draw me a plan o' the office.'

When Tom had finished the rough sketch Winkle pored over it. 'So there's the winder be'ind the desk an' the front o' the safe is side-on ter the door. As I said it's a pity. If the safe was facin' the door it'd minimise the blast effect. As it is the partition wall could go an' then the bloody roof could cave in. So we gotta be careful.'

'Yer said we. Does that mean yer takin' me wiv yer?'

'It seems I got no choice,' Winkle said with a grin. 'I can't stand dogs an' I ain't up ter bein' savaged by a poxy Alsatian, not fer a fousand smackers.'

Tom looked happy as he picked up his drink. ''Ere's to a successful venture.'

Winkle smiled. 'I'll drink ter that,' he said lightly. 'By the way – the safe. Any idea 'ow big it is?'

'I'd say it's about two foot wide an' three foot tall.'

''Ow deep?'

'About two feet.'

'Now can yer remember if there's any markin's on the front o' the safe? A name or a pattern?'

'I've not bin in the office much, ter tell yer the trufe,' Tom replied, 'but I seem ter remember there's a scroll mark on the front. It's sort o' raised if I remember right.'

'Sounds like a Union 420. That'll be no problem,' Winkle said with a confident smile.

'So when do we go in?'

'Around two o'clock on Wednesday mornin'.'

'Any special reason fer the timin'?'

'From my experience it's the time when fings quieten down an' the night-beat bobbies get their 'eads down fer a while,' Winkle explained. 'Besides, the bang's gonna be 'eard an' it'll rouse people. By the time they come lookin' we'll be gone. Precious minutes, son. Precious minutes is what we're gonna be needin'.'

Tom drained his glass and stood up. 'Same again?'

'Nice of yer,' Winkle replied as he pulled out a battered briar and tobacco pouch.

By the time Tom came back with the drinks Winkle was enveloped in a cloud of rough shag smoke. ''Ere, by the way. Will there be any tarpaulins lyin' around the yard?' he enquired.

'In the shed,' Tom replied.

'Accessible?'

'Yeah. Why d'yer ask?'

'We can use the tarpaulins ter deaden the noise an' save the winders goin' out.'

'Anyfing else?'

'Yeah, there is as a matter o' fact. What about the ladder?'

Tom smiled. 'Leave that ter me,' he said with a wink. 'I got a pal who's a winder cleaner an' 'e'll let me borrer one.'

'We can't carry it frew the streets at that time in the mornin',' Winkle said quickly.

'I know that,' Tom replied. 'I'll arrange ter meet 'im termorrer an' I'll 'ide it on the ruin be'ind the yard. It should be okay there till we need it.'

'This winder cleaner. 'E ain't got 'is name plastered on the ladder 'as 'e?'

Tom shook his head. 'Can yer fink of anyfing else?'

The safe cracker shook his head slowly and then looked up at the young man. 'Are you sure that dog knows yer?'

'Don't worry,' Tom told him. 'If it does give me any grief I'll slit the mangy fing's froat.'

'Can yer meet me in 'ere at six o'clock on Tuesday evenin', just ter make sure we got it all off pat?' Winkle asked.

'Yeah, I'll come straight from work,' Tom replied. 'I gotta go now. I've promised me girlfriend a trip down the river this afternoon.'

Billy Button rolled on to his back and realised that he was soaking wet. He thought at first that it had been raining during the night but looking around he saw that the pathway was dry and realised it must be the dew. It wasn't very sensible to fall asleep on the grass, he told himself, even if it was under a tree. He must be getting senile. Never mind. He had a few coppers for a mug of tea and a meat pie from the coffee stall and the sun was getting up. Soon he would be dry, and in a few days he would have a nice wad of notes in his pocket as well. Things were not that bad, he thought as he struggled to his feet and put the tree between him and the park policeman who had just come into view.

An hour later Billy Button was dried out and enjoying a hot steak and kidney pie at the stall across the road from the park gates. Hard times make hard men, he recalled the old saying going. Anyway, poor old George Merry was dead and gone and wherever he was now he would understand the predicament. At least George would know that his old drinking partner was telling it just like it happened. There would be no veneer of heroics or glamorisation. It wasn't Billy Button's style.

The old soldier ordered another mug of tea to wash

down the last of the pie and then he made his way down Blackheath Hill. Loners and old soldiers like himself would be gathering at the gardens behind the lodging house in Deptford and there would be the chance of a chat about better times, and some relief from the sorry state of affairs that was his lot at the moment. At least it would be better than sitting by himself all day long.

Billy marched down the hill still deep in thought. George could not be hurt now, but his wife could be, and would. It was his only regret, but his decision to make the truth known was brought about by a strong survival instinct, and survive he must for a little longer. One day the drink would kill him, but until then . . .

Chapter Twenty-Six

On Monday morning Ernest Spencer leaned back in his large leather chair and bit on the arm of his spectacles as he faced the young reporter. 'Look, Sam, I've got the go-ahead to pay the money,' he told him, 'but I'm relying on you to substantiate this information as best you can. We don't want to be left with egg on our faces.'

Sam Calkin nodded. 'I'm seeing Mr Button tomorrow morning and in the meantime I'm going to take a look at Ship Lane. By the way, I'll have this Friday's Rotherhithe piece on your desk by this evening.'

Spencer afforded himself a rare smile. 'I can see you've been busy.'

'I wrote the piece up over the weekend,' Sam told him. 'I need to make time. I've a feeling this coming disclosure is going to involve a lot of leg work.'

The editor nodded and replaced his spectacles. 'I'm counting on you, Sam. I'll need the full story as soon as possible. We're talking about survival here. A good spread in a Tuesday edition will certainly boost the sales. As a matter of fact I was with Morrison last Friday evening and he feels that without a thirty-per-cent increase in sales we'll go under.'

'Did he indicate a time limit, Mr Spencer?' Sam asked.

'Three months at the outside.'

The young man stood up. 'I'll get to work then,' he said with a faint smile.

Josie Willard flickered her eyelashes at him as he passed her desk and Frances Miller gave him her customary smile. 'Was the Rotherhithe material suitable?' she enquired.

Sam rested his hands on her desk and gave her a saucy wink. 'Do you realise you kept me busy all weekend,' he said with mock severity.

Frances looked pleased with herself. 'I'm so glad you found it interesting, but weekends,' she tutted. 'I was saying to Paddy O'Brian he should get out more at weekends. Relax a little.'

'I hope you'll make him see the error of his ways, Frances.'

She caught the humorous slant of his lips and the glint in his eye and flushed slightly. 'I'll do my best.'

'Good girl. Paddy's a lucky feller.'

As he walked away from her desk Frances knew that it was useless to pretend any more. The secret was out of the bag and she felt a sense of relief. She was in love with Paddy and the world could know it for all she cared.

Sam glanced over his shoulder and smiled to himself as he picked up his coat from the back of the chair. He felt that he had made a little contribution to the happy fund and he ran his fingers through his dark hair as he sauntered out of the main office.

Sue looked up as he came into the reception area.

'Sam, I've talked to my dad and he's willing to see you,' she told him.

'I'm very much obliged,' he replied with a warm smile. 'Maybe I should be briefed first though. Would you care to have lunch with me?'

'Well I . . .'

'Look, I know a nice pub at Bankside,' he went on. 'It's a lovely day and we could sit out on the terrace overlooking the river. Say you'll come.'

Sue nodded. 'You've talked me into it.'

'Roll on lunchtime,' he said, giving her a wink that was slowly becoming his trademark.

Sue watched him leave and twiddled with her pencil thoughtfully. Was she doing the right thing, she wondered. Would he read something into her agreeing to meet him for lunch? No, she was being silly. He was just acting friendly, and it did make good sense for him to learn a little about her father and Charlie Duggan before he actually met them. Anyway, it would be nice to sit by the river and chat in the warm sunshine. He was a refreshing character with self-assurance and an easygoing attitude. He seemed to be a good listener too, and he knew that she was going steady.

The telephone rang and then there were a few callers to deal with, but the morning seemed to drag past. Paddy O'Brian made a brief appearance, hurrying off to cover a mayoral function and looking very spruce, and then it grew quiet again, leaving the young woman alone with her thoughts. Saturday night had been a pleasant enough evening, she reflected, but Del had seemed tired and jaded, try as he might to conceal it. When they danced together she had felt an intimacy and mutual desire and had tried to encourage him with sensuous movements and meaningful glances, but the moment had seemed to fade. The goodnight cuddle in the shadows had left her feeling that Del was going through the motions of a ritual. He had caressed her and his kisses were loving, but there was something lacking. It seemed as though he was holding back when it should have been she who had to call a halt. Maybe she was being too predictable and it was putting him off. He had a vocation now and was totally committed, but he was a man after all, and he had needs the same as she.

The clock above her head said eleven o'clock and she sighed as she filled the notepad in front of her with abstract designs and meaningless scribble. What would the eggheads make of this, she thought as she screwed up the page and consigned it to the wastepaper basket. Did Del see her as a woman who couldn't wait to drag him down the aisle and have his children? Was she smothering him with her demands and excessive desires? No, it wasn't that way at all. They had never discussed marriage and they weren't even engaged. They had only made love once, and that was a hurried, physical thing. It was not as if she had been a gullible virgin either. Perhaps she should have been a little more guileful and called a halt when he became aroused. Maybe then he would have realised that she was not a convenience, an object there for the taking.

Paddy came into the office with a look of frustration on his broad face. 'The bloody mayor was indisposed and that dozy Councillor Franklin opened the block of flats,' he growled. 'He cut the tape on the second attempt, almost tripped over his own feet and then declared the place open. No speech, no words of thanks to the builders, no nothing. This'll take me five minutes to write up. Heaven preserve reporters from the Franklins of this world.'

Sue smiled at his animated indignation. 'Paddy, you've just saved me from wallowing in self-pity,' she told him.

'I'm not sure if that's meant to be a compliment but I'll take it as one,' the Irishman said grinning.

'Be sure, Paddy. It is.'

'Well then, I won't ask for details.'

Sue returned his smile. 'Did you enjoy *King Lear*?'

He looked uncertain. 'Yeah, it was very good, but frankly I prefer a good review or a musical.'

'Paddy, am I frumpish? she asked him suddenly. 'Do I come over as being a domineering cow?'

'Darling, you're delightful and I'd marry you tomorrow if you'd have me,' he said with a lilt in his voice.

'That's just your Irish blarney,' she said laughing aloud. 'But thank you anyway.'

'Do I suspect a lovers' tiff?'

'No it's just me. I'm a bit down in the dumps,' she sighed.

'Well then, don't take in *King Lear*. Stick to the reviews,' he said, waving his finger for effect.

Frances came out from the inner office at that moment carrying a folder and her eyes lit up when she saw Paddy. 'I, er, I was just going to let you see these,' she told Sue. 'They're cuttings from the Ship Lane shelter report. Sam Calkin wanted me to dig them out for him. Mum's the word, but I think he's planning a write-up. There's a nice piece there about your dad but I expect you've kept the paper anyway.'

Sue glanced at the cutting Frances pointed out and nodded. 'Yes we have,' she replied.

Frances tucked the folder under her arm. 'Well, back to work,' she said, glancing at Paddy. 'I've some more cuttings to look for.'

Sue hid a smile. The glory hole was Frances's domain and she was now more than happy to share it with Paddy. Good for them. Paddy had changed out of all recognition, and Frances seemed to have gained a new lease of life. She looked up at the clock and saw that it was nearing midday, and almost without thinking she reached for her powder compact.

Joe Carey took down the heavy ledger and blew the dust from it. 'Doesn't the cleaner ever fink o' dustin' the shelves,' he grumbled under his breath.

'It's a nice day,' Fredericks remarked to Baxter.

'Very nice,' Baxter replied without looking up from the pile of invoices in front of him.

Joe carried the ledger over to his desk and let it fall heavily, startling the grey-haired Mrs Gates into looking up quickly. He was waiting for some reaction from Darnley the chief clerk, but the thin-faced figure remained as though wrought into shape with his head bent and his shoulders hunched. The elderly Norman Wilson looked up, feeling able to contribute something to the morning. 'They say there's going to be a drought,' he remarked.

Darnley coughed at last and Wilson lowered his head quickly.

'Bad for the roses,' Baxter said.

'Brings out the greenfly,' Fredericks added, not wishing to be upstaged.

Darnley coughed again and the office became quiet. Joe Carey could not make any sense of the figures and he leaned back in his chair to rub at his eyes. What was going wrong with him? he fretted. His concentration was lacking and he was constantly becoming preoccupied. Maybe he should take a few days off, once he got the ledgers sorted out for the previous week. When was the last time he went sick? It was during the flu epidemic in forty-four. Three years without a day off, apart from his annual week's holiday.

'Mr Carey? Mr Carey, did you hear me?'

Joe looked up suddenly. 'I'm sorry.'

Darnley had come to life. 'Can I have the figures for the Bulestine account if you please?'

'Comin' up,' Joe replied jauntily, which made Mrs Gates glance over at him.

'Might I have the Bulestine invoices from April onwards?' the chief clerk commanded.

'Certainly, Mr Darnley,' Baxter told him in a businesslike tone of voice.

Mrs Gates did not look up this time but Fredericks smiled to himself in anticipation.

Joe went over to the shelf and took down what he thought to be the appropriate ledger and ignored the film of dust. 'There we are,' he said as he laid the thick book down in front of Darnley.

The chief clerk coughed again and looked with distaste at the dust on the cover. With Mr Coombes the office manager out of the building that morning he felt obliged to show his vested authority. 'This ledger's filthy,' he remarked over his glasses.

'Yeah, I think we should let the cleaner know,' Joe told him coldly.

Mrs Gates looked up in surprise while Baxter and Fredericks exchanged secret smiles. Norman Wilson buried his head down even lower into his papers and hummed to himself. Darnley opened the ledger and ran his eyes over the figures, glancing up to observe that Joe was still standing there. 'That'll do, Mr Carey,' he said with a dismissive wave of his bony hand.

That's it, I'm going on the panel for a week, Joe told himself as he went back to his desk.

It became deathly quiet as Mrs Gates stopped typing to change the ribbon, and Joe glanced over and saw Darnley apparently deep in thought. The ticking of the wall clock seemed to grow in volume and even the scratching of Baxter's pen began to grate on his jagged nerves.

'Mr Carey?'

'Yes, Mr Darnley?'

'I wonder if you'd be good enough to bank the cheques while Mr Baxter's sorting the invoices?'

'Certainly,' Joe replied.

The noise of the traffic and the smell of fresh horse droppings as Joe made his way up on to London Bridge was a welcome relief from the oppressive atmosphere of Napier's office. Down below the muddy waters swirled and eddied and to his right he could see the majestic square structures of Tower Bridge. City office workers with their dark suits, bowler hats and the inevitable rolled umbrellas came past from both directions, while beneath the New Fresh Wharf a banana ship from the Canary Islands was being emptied of its cargo. In midstream a tug fussed around a tramper flying the

Danish flag and another tug sounded its whistle as it came into the Pool towing a brace of barges. As he passed above the banana ship Joe glanced over the balustrade and watched two dockers engaged in a good-natured slanging match, and he smiled to himself. Here was life, the pulsating heart of the capital and he could feel its quickness around him. How different from that morgue of an office with its cryptful of walking zombies. God! He was slowly rotting in the place. His mind was beginning to moulder and crumble in that airless tomb and he was rapidly reaching the point of no return.

He crossed into Gracechurch Street and walked into the lofty marble hall of the Commercial Bank, returning a nod from an attendant who was dressed in an olive-green uniform and sporting a top hat. He handed in the cheques to a baby-faced teller and waited while the receipt book was stamped and signed.

'Good day, sir,' the attendant said pleasantly, touching his waxed moustache.

Out in the sunlight again Joe Carey looked around him as he strolled leisurely back through the City streets. The scars of the Blitz were still very much in evidence but the spark of life was pervasive and infectious. He walked on to the bridge and saw the stevedores sweating in the ship's hold and high above them the crane driver lording it as he controlled the monster to perfection. It was a short walk back now to the tomb of the living dead, and he was willing to bet his weekly pay packet that he had been the sole topic of conversation. It was obviously the reason why he had been elected to bank the cheques. They wanted him out of the way while they put their heads together.

Joe walked down the steep flight of stone steps into Tooley Street and took a few deep breaths before going into the office.

'Ah, glad you're back, Mr Carey,' Darnley said with uncharacteristic courtesy. 'Mr Coombes would like to see you after lunch.'

Joe looked over at the empty desk in the corner and then back to Darnley.

'Mr Coombes will be back at two o'clock,' the chief clerk informed him.

At twelve o'clock Joe Carey did something he hadn't done for years. Instead of the homely café he usually went to he chose to take his lunch break in the Station Tavern, and after a cheese roll and two and a half pints of bitter he felt he was suitably prepared for the worst.

When he walked back into the office ten minutes after one o'clock he found difficulty making eye contact with the staff. They were purposely avoiding him. Well, sod the lot of them, he thought as he took out his crumpled edition of the *Daily Mirror* to catch up with the day's news.

For the next fifty minutes there was an atmosphere of barely contained excitement as the loyal and dutiful staff awaited the arrival of their manager. As the second hand clicked into the upright position on the large wall clock Mr Coombes made his entrance. As always his mackintosh was deposited smartly on the stand and his Homburg and rolled brolly followed suit. 'Ah, Mr Carey. If you will,' he said in his reedy voice.

Joe followed him back out into the corridor and across to the very rarely used office room opposite.

Coombes took a seat at the desk, leaving Joe standing in front of him like a recalcitrant schoolboy.

'Yes, Mr Coombes?'

'I, er, to get to the point, Mr Carey, I'm concerned about your work of late,' Coombes began a little hesitantly. 'Mr Darnley has had to make adjustments to your balances and there are one or two omissions which have caused this company some embarrassment. I'm a little concerned too about your general attitude. As an old and well-established company we do have high standards and frankly you appear to have flouted these lately. I'd like to hear what you have to say about it. Are you ill?'

Joe looked hard at the tall, gaunt office manager and anger boiled up inside him like a volcano ready to erupt. He leaned forward over the desk, his hands clenched into tight fists. 'Sixteen long years I've worked in that morgue you call an office an' you ask me if I'm ill. Yes, I'm sick. I'm sick an' tired of Darnley's poxy cough. I'm sick of Baxter an' Fredericks playin' silly buggers. I'm sick of Mrs Gates's 'olier-than-thou attitude, an' I'm sick o' watchin' poor ole Wilson bein' ridiculed day after day. But d'you know what sickens me the most? It's you. It's that sanctimonious way you've got of lookin' down yer nose at us like we're shit on yer shoes.'

All the time Joe was speaking Coombes sat open-mouthed, his eyes popping, and as he was about to make a reply Joe shut him up with a finger pointing in his face. 'D'yer know what? That office in there needs a good disinfectin' fer a start. Then that poxy coat rack wants goin' on a bonfire along wiv that filfy carpet. The place wants a gallon o' paint an' you lot

301

want puttin' in a bag an' bein' given a bloody good shakin'.'

'Have you quite finished?' Coombes gulped.

'Yeah I'm finished,' Joe told him, shaking with anger. 'I'm pissin' off 'ome. I'll be in first fing Friday mornin' fer me cards. Make sure they're ready.'

Coombes's Adam's apple bobbed up and down like a floundering cork as he struggled to pull himself together. He dabbed at his sweating forehead and sat staring at the door for a few minutes after Joe Carey slammed it shut behind him.

'The man's gone completely mad,' he gasped as he finally climbed out of his seat.

'Is anything wrong, Mr Coombes?' Darnley asked him.

The office manager searched through his desk for an aspirin, and failing to find one he made what was for him an unprecedented decision. 'I'm going home early, Mr Darnley,' he said in a shaky voice. 'As a matter of fact I'm feeling a little under the weather. Take care of things, will you.'

Chapter Twenty-Seven

Upstream from London Bridge and the Pool of London the river was comparatively quiet. There were a few laden barges moored at the riverside warehouses and wharves, but the unloading had ceased for the time being and the quiet Thames was dropping on the tide to expose the sour-smelling mud. Across the narrow lane from the ancient public house a veranda overlooked the eddying water, and there by the river Sue Carey and Sam Calkin sat chatting together.

'Tell me about your dad,' Sam said, folding his arms on the wooden table.

'Well, he's about your height and pretty stocky,' Sue replied. 'He'll be sixty in November. He was gassed in the First World War and it affects him in the winter, but he's still pretty lively, considering.'

Sam smiled encouragingly. 'You were telling me that during the war he was a fire watcher, and he was on the roof of that warehouse in Ship Lane the night it took a hit.'

Sue nodded. 'As I said then, Dad never talks about it so it might be difficult getting him to volunteer much more information.'

'I understand,' Sam told her. 'I've got the original report from the wardens' control post and the newspaper cutting. What I really want is a comment or two and maybe a photo of him and Mr Duggan. It'll follow the pattern of the series, hopefully. You know the thing – where are they now, what do they remember of that particular night, little anecdotes.'

'Well, I'll try to prepare him, and Mr Duggan,' Sue replied, 'but as I say, it won't be easy.'

Sam sipped his beer. 'It's nice here, isn't it?'

Sue looked over at the sun-kissed dome of St Paul's Cathedral and along the waterside towards Blackfriars Bridge and she sighed. 'I love this river,' she remarked. 'It's dirty, smelly and it's dangerous, but could you imagine London without it?'

'It wouldn't be London, would it?' he replied.

Sue toyed with her glass of shandy for a few moments then she looked up to find him gazing at her intently. 'Do you like working at the paper?' she asked, trying to hide her sudden embarrassment.

'Yes, I do.'

'If the sales do increase would you consider staying on?'

'I don't really know. I'm hoping this subject that I'm researching will act as a stepping stone to something like crime reporting, which I've always been interested in.'

'Maybe the nationals are better suited to that.'

He laughed aloud, his white even teeth flashing. 'Sam Calkin, chief crime reporter of the *Daily Whatever*.'

'And why not,' she said, smiling back at him.

Sam followed the progress of a police launch fighting the current as it travelled upstream, then he turned back to the young woman. 'What does your dad do for a living?'

'He's a bookkeeper at a wine merchant's in Tooley Street,' she replied. 'He's been there quite a few years now.'

'What about Mr Duggan?'

'He's a gas fitter.'

'You said they were old pals.'

Sue nodded. 'Charlie Duggan and my dad are both old soldiers and they're always chatting together about those days. They get on very well as a matter of fact. Charlie lost a son in the war. He was in the Navy.'

'Has he got any other children?'

'A daughter, Pamela,' Sue told him. 'She's a striking redhead, very pretty. She's going out with my younger brother Tom.'

'Do you think I could call round tomorrow night?' he asked.

'I don't see why not. I'll speak to my dad this evening.'

Sam leaned back on the bench seat. 'How are things with you?'

She shrugged her shoulders. 'Not too bad.'

'You don't sound too convincing,' he pressed. 'Union troubles?'

'Union blues I'd say,' Sue replied with a sad smile. 'Del was at a meeting for most of Saturday, and yesterday he was at a union rally in Trafalgar Square.'

'And what did you do?'

'What does a woman do at such times? I washed my hair.'

'Pity. I could have shown you my boat,' he said smiling.

'You've got a boat?'

He nodded. 'It's a small cabin cruiser. It's a wreck at the moment, but I'm doing it up.'

'Where do you keep it?' she asked, intrigued.

'On the Medway in Kent,' he replied. 'It's a bit of a story.'

'I'd like to hear it,' she told him.

'Would you really?'

'Really.'

Sam grinned self-consciously. 'When my mother died in thirty-seven my father sold his small printing business and moved down to Burlingford,' he began. 'It's a tiny hamlet right on the Medway between Rochester and Maidstone. My dad loved the river and he was always messing about in boats in his spare time. He had this small cottage which he got for a song and he spent a lot of the time doing it up. He also managed to buy a cabin cruiser which became his pride and joy. He'd just about finished working on the boat by the time the war started. I used to go down there to lend a hand, whenever I got the chance. Then came Dunkirk, and when the call went out for volunteers with small boats my father never hesitated. He was nearing seventy but it made no difference to him and he sailed off to a rendezvous at Sheerness.'

Sam paused to take a sip from his glass. 'It must have been a fantastic sight. There were thousands of small boats like his, as well as larger craft and pleasure steamers. They all sailed from Sheerness to the Channel ports and then across to Dunkirk. Dad brought twenty soldiers back in that boat of his and he towed a lifeboat behind him which was crammed full of troops. Not satisfied with that he made another trip, but halfway across he was hit by machine-gun fire. He died instantly.'

'How terrible,' Sue said with a sad look on her face.

'The boat was towed back by the Royal Navy and my dad was posthumously awarded a George Medal. That boat is the very same one that I'm working on. One day soon it'll be ready to launch once more.'

'I'd love to see it,' Sue told him.

'Why don't you come down to Burlingford with me?' he said quickly, his eyes sparkling.

'When?'

'This weekend.'

'I don't know, it's a bit tricky.'

'The boyfriend?'

Sue nodded. 'Del may be free this weekend. I've been nagging at him to take some time off.'

'Well, let's leave it open,' Sam suggested.

Sue smiled. 'I'll try and let you know in good time,' she said.

They finished their drinks and he took her arm as they walked down the steep steps to the cobbled lane and strolled slowly back in the warm sunshine through the now deserted Borough market and out into the busy thoroughfare. 'I've enjoyed our chat,' she said as they neared the newspaper office.

'So have I,' he replied, looking into her eyes. 'We must do it again soon.'

The three musketeers were having a lunchtime drink in the Bell and Benny Tracy looked decidedly glum.

'Cheer up, fer Gawd's sake,' Tubby exclaimed. 'Yer givin' me the 'ump just lookin' at yer.'

'Leave 'im be,' Wally said, hiding a smile. 'Our Benny's got woman trouble.'

'I don't believe it,' Tubby replied. ''E don't 'ave nuffink ter do wiv women.'

'Who don't?' Benny said gruffly.

'You don't.'

'I bin wiv a few in me time.'

'That's as it may be, but yer still a bachelor.'

'So what?'

'Well, why yer gettin' all screwed up about a woman?'

'I didn't say it was a woman.'

''Ere, it ain't a feller is it?'

'Don't be stupid, Tubby.'

'Why don't yer come clean, Benny,' Wally told him.

'I told yer not ter say anyfing,' Benny moaned. 'I won't tell yer anyfing next time.'

'Well, please yerself.'

''Ere, what the bloody 'ell's goin' on?' Tubby growled. 'Am I bein' left out o' somefing?'

'Tell 'im, Benny.'

'You tell 'im.'

'Somebody tell me, fer Chrissake.'

Wally took a large gulp from his glass of beer and set it down on the table. 'Benny's bin settin' 'is cap at Queenie an' she's give 'im a blank,' he explained.

'All I did was ask 'er out fer a drink,' Benny added.

'An' she said no?'

'Yeah.'

'What's the matter, don't she like our company?' Tubby said sharply.

'I didn't ask 'er ter come up 'ere,' Benny told him. 'I asked 'er out up West.'

'It seems reasonable enough,' Wally remarked to Tubby. 'Queenie's on 'er own an' so's Benny. I fink they'd make a nice couple, provided 'e bucked 'imself up a bit.'

'What d'yer mean?'

'Well, you are inclined ter moods at times.'

'What sort o' moods?'

'Bad moods.'

'I'm as cheerful as you.'

'Not just now yer not.'

'Well, I ain't feelin' particularly bloody cheerful just now, that's why.'

'This conversation is gettin' us nowhere,' Wally complained.

'Trouble is, Queenie's fell fer that scruffy git in the oilshop,' Benny grumbled.

'Who, ole Bela Lugosi?' Tubby said. 'It's only rumours.'

'Nah, she 'as,' Benny went on. 'Ter be honest I thought I was in wiv a chance, till she got in wiv Raney.'

'I don't fink there's anyfing in it,' Wally said reassuringly. ''E ain't Queenie's sort.'

'There's no accountin' fer taste.'

'Benny boy, just trust me,' Wally said, trying to look serious. 'You're more Queenie's sort.'

'Yeah, if only 'e bucked 'imself up a bit,' Tubby cut in.

'Don't you start,' Benny warned him.

Wally held his hands up for attention. 'Now listen ter me,' he told them. 'What Benny's gotta do is make 'imself noticed.'

''Ow d'yer mean?' Benny asked him with a frown.

'Well, fer starters yer gotta 'ave a shave every mornin', an' put a bit of aftershave on. Then yer gotta do little bits an' pieces round the 'ouse. Clean 'er winders an' do the doorstep. Anuvver fing. Take 'er up a cuppa in the mornin'. Women love a mornin' cuppa in bed.'

'I daren't do that,' Benny said looking horrified. 'She'd fink I was after givin' 'er one.'

'Well, you are, ain't yer?'

'In good time.'

'No time like the present,' Tubby said.

Wally held his hands up again. 'Apart from all those little fings, yer gotta shock 'er inter noticin' yer.'

''Ow do I do that?'

'Do somefing outrageous.'

'Like what?'

'I dunno. Start wearin' one o' them fancy silk scarves an' use a fag-'older.'

'I'd look like a bloody ole poof.'

'You do talk arse'oles at times, Wally,' Tubby said scornfully. ''Ow can 'e use a fag-'older wiv roll-ups?'

'I was only puttin' suggestions to 'im,' Wally replied frowning, 'but 'e does need ter get 'imself noticed. What about if we set somefing up?'

'That sounds a better idea,' Tubby said, nodding.

'Right, let's put our finkin' caps on then.'

Benny got the drinks in and the three of them sat deep in thought without uttering a word, which did not escape Dave Ford's notice. ''Ave those three 'ad a row?' he remarked.

'Nah, I fink they've just run out o' steam,' Albert Price told him.

The silence continued, until Wally got an idea. ''Ere, I know what,' he said suddenly. 'Why don't we work a fast one, like ole Bonzo Norris did?'

'Who the bloody 'ell's Bonzo Norris?' Tubby asked.

'You remember 'im, Tubby. That skinny bloke who lived at number twelve before the war.'

'Can't say as I do.'

Wally leaned forward on the table, ignoring the solemn-faced Benny. 'Bonzo's ole woman used ter lead 'im a dog's life. You remember 'er. Maggie she was called. She was a big fat woman, boss-eyed wiv ginger 'air an' a face like the back of a bus.'

'Yeah, I remember now,' Tubby said nodding.

'Well, this ole cow 'ad a long-standin' upset wiv the Brannigans next door at number ten,' Wally went on. 'Maggie was always complainin' about the noise yer see. Nobby Brannigan's ole woman was ferever bangin' away on the pianer an' 'e used ter 'ave this squeeze-box. Maggie kept on at Bonzo ter go an' tell 'em ter keep the noise down but the trouble was Nobby Brannigan was a stevedore wiv a bull neck an' arms like tree trunks, while poor ole Bonzo's arms 'ad muscles like sparrers' kneecaps. Anyway, ole Brannigan used ter get on very well wiv Bonzo an' 'e knew 'ow 'en-pecked 'e was, so the pair of 'em worked out a little plan. This night the Brannigans made as much noise as they could an' when Maggie banged on their door an' gave 'em an ear'ole-bashin' Nobby Brannigan told 'er ter piss orf, then Bonzo stormed up an' grabbed Nobby by the scruff of 'is neck an' offered 'im out on the cobbles fer a punch-up. Maggie was still rantin' off an' Bonzo glared at 'er. "Shut yer noise, before I belt you too," 'e told 'er. Then 'e shook

Nobby an' raised 'is fist. "Don't whack me, I didn't mean no 'arm," Nobby ses, cowerin' down wiv 'is 'ands up to 'is face. "Let that be a lesson then. Now I want no more of it. Understand?" Bonzo shouts at 'im. That boss-eyed ole cow of 'is was so shocked she clammed up straight away. An' you know what? Maggie Norris was a different woman after that episode. Never raised 'er voice to 'im again. In fact they got ter be like a couple o' love birds.'

'So what yer got in mind fer Benny?' Tubby asked, looking puzzled.

Wally sipped his drink, looking very pleased with himself. 'We'll 'ave a word wiv Masher,' he said confidently. ''E'll do anyfing fer a few drinks.'

Tubby nodded his head slowly as he finally realised what Wally was getting at. 'Benny an' Masher on the cobbles?'

'If you two fink I'm gonna challenge that bloody big gorilla to a scrap yer got anuvver fink comin',' Benny growled. ''E was an ole bare-knuckle fighter.'

'Now this is what we're gonna do,' Wally said.

Chapter Twenty-Eight

Billy Button had scraped together enough for a room at the working men's hostel in Deptford and at last he had a much-needed bath and a shave. Next morning he felt reasonably well as he made his way to the pub near London Bridge, and he bought a newspaper and folded it under his arm as he strolled into the public bar. This was a business transaction after all, he thought. Might as well look businesslike.

Billy was halfway through his first pint when Sam Calkin walked in and he nodded casually. ''Ave yer got the money?' he asked as the reporter came up to his table.

Sam nodded. 'First things first though.'

'Mine's a bitter,' Billy told him.

The sound of the traffic was muted by the bottle-bottom windowpanes as the two men faced each other across a small table in one corner of the large, lofty bar. 'Okay, Billy. Shall we make a start?' Sam said, taking out a notepad and pencil from his coat pocket.

'I'll never ferget that night. May the tenth, 1941. One o' the worst nights o' the Blitz,' Billy began with a heavy breath. 'I was well on the booze around that time. Me wife 'ad bin dead fer less than two years an' I was still missin' 'er. Me an' ole George

313

Merry got friendly. We used ter drink tergevver in the Bull at Dock'ead. George knew I was down on me luck an' 'e used ter stand me a few drinks now an' then. Sometimes I'd go an' see 'im at the lead mills after the pub turned out. I'd take 'im a pint o' stout an' we'd sit chattin' away in the office. 'E let me kip down there sometimes if I couldn't get in the doss-'ouse. There was always two lorries parked in the yard an' I'd stretch out in one o' the cabs an' be away at first light. George didn't mind, besides it was company for 'im.'

Sam looked up from his notes. 'Did George ever leave the yard to go to the pub?' he asked.

'Sometimes 'e'd slip out fer a couple o' pints an' leave me ter look after the place,' Billy replied. 'There wasn't anyfing ter do really, 'cept make sure nobody climbed over the gates. The factory itself was well secured. It 'ad ter be, what wiv all that lead an' solder layin' about. They made sticks o' solder there, yer know.'

'Were the lorries loaded on that particular night?' Sam asked.

'The back one was, but the one in front was empty,' Billy told him, sipping his drink. 'Anyway, I'd got a double up on the dogs that night. Twenty-seven an' six it was, so I took a quart bottle o' beer round ter the mills ter celebrate. It was George's birfday too an' 'e was well sloshed when I arrived. 'E'd bin on the piss all day, so 'e told me. Anyway we sat chattin' tergevver in the office fer a while then 'e told me a few pals were callin' for 'im ter round the night off, an' would I 'old the fort till 'e got back. I didn't mind, after all I 'ad nowhere else ter go. Then George said a funny fing. 'E asked me if I could be trusted. I told 'im that I could be trusted wiv anyfink an' 'e just nodded. About an hour later some people came. Two of 'em climbed up in the front lorry an' started it up an' George opened the gates. They drove the lorry out o' the yard an' George shut the gates again. There was two more blokes there an' they took George off fer a drink.'

'Where were you when all this was going on?' Sam enquired.

'George 'ad already primed me up ter stay out o' sight, an' when the blokes knocked on the gate I got up in the back lorry an' laid down on the seat so they couldn't see me,' Billy explained. 'I was well sloshed meself at the time but I still 'ad me wits about me. They never knew I was there.'

'Go on, Billy.'

The elderly man sipped his pint of bitter. 'There'd bin a few nights wivout air raids an' it was all quiet so I decided ter settle down fer the night. I remember George comin' back. It didn't seem as though 'e'd bin gone five minutes. These two fellers 'alf carried 'im inter the yard an' stuck 'im in the office. Poor ole George seemed out of 'is tree. Anyway the two geezers didn't stop an' I kept me 'ead down. Then the siren went. Bombs started ter fall an' the guns in the park opened up. I remember sittin' up straight in the cab an' then as I looked over the top o' the gates I saw somefing that made me rub me eyes. From where I was I could see the top floors o' the ware'ouse opposite, an' there was a bloke standin' on the fire escape passin' down a rolled-up bundle. As far as I could see it looked like a carpet. Then 'e went back inter the ware'ouse an' brought out anuvver one an' passed it down.'

'Could you see who he was passing the bundle to?' Sam asked.

Billy shook his head. 'As I said, I could only see the top two levels from where I was sittin'. The bloke was on the second one from the top. Anyway, just then there was a big flash an' a loud bang. The ware'ouse 'ad copped it. Chunks o' debris came rainin' down in the yard an' it was only by good luck that the roof o' the cab I was sittin' in wasn't stoved in. Some o' those chunks o' concrete were pretty big I can tell yer. The 'ole place was burnin' an' I couldn't see what 'ad 'appened ter the bloke, there was too much smoke. All of a sudden there was a noise which I can only describe as rattlin' corrugated iron, then a terrible bang. The lorry I was in seemed ter lift up in the air an' come down wiv a great jolt, the windscreen shattered an' I was showered wiv glass. I thought me end 'ad come. I could see the mills was burnin' an' I suddenly remembered George. I climbed out o' the cab an' then I saw that the gates 'ad gone. They were lyin' in the street. I rushed inter the office an' dragged George out. 'E never stirred, an' as I laid 'im down in the yard I could see that 'e was gone.'

'You were sure he was dead?'

'Listen, young man, I've seen a few stiff 'uns in me time an' I can assure yer George Merry was as dead as a doornail,' Billy said firmly. 'Anyway, just then there was anuvver loud bang an' the side wall come down. I managed ter get clear but George was buried under a big slab. I could see 'is arm stickin' out. It was terrible.'

'What did you do then?'

'I scarpered.'

'Did you see anything happening over at the warehouse when you left?' Sam pressed.

Billy shook his head. 'That ware'ouse was burnin' an' there was black smoke pourin' from everywhere. I just put me 'ead down an' run off before I was buried under the fallin' debris.'

'Where did you go to?' Sam asked.

'I dunno,' Billy replied. 'I remember someone grabbin' me arm an' pullin' me into a shelter, an' there I stayed till mornin'.'

'So you honestly believe that there was a robbery taking place when the warehouse was hit?'

'I saw what I saw,' Billy said adamantly. 'That ware'ouse was definitely bein' robbed.'

'You'd swear that what you've told me is the truth.'

'May I drop dead this minute if I'm lyin',' Billy said with passion.

Sam reached into his pocket and pulled out a sealed envelope. 'There's twenty-five pounds as agreed,' he told him. 'If you'll just sign here for it. As stated, the other twenty-five is payable on publication.'

Billy signed his name with a flourish on the slip of paper Sam passed to him and then he looked up at the young reporter. 'I get no great pleasure out o' doin' this, Mr Calkin,' he said quietly. 'George Merry was like a bruvver ter me. I know that when you print the article it'll make people see 'im in a different light, but it can't 'urt 'im now. In fact I'd be willin' ter bet that wherever George is now 'e's 'avin' a little chuckle over this. I'd say the only person it can 'urt is George's wife, an' I've got a good idea that she never really believed 'er 'usband died an 'ero.'

Sam got up to leave. 'Sleep easy, Billy,' he said with a smile. 'I think you're right.'

The Honourable Walter Miles-Strickland MP, QC had had a privileged upbringing. The only son of Gerald Miles-Strickland the shipping magnate, he had gone through Charterhouse to Oxford and a distinguished career at the Bar before going into politics. Now in his late fifties he had become disenchanted. His two marriages had not produced an heir, and furthermore his second wife, Elizabeth, had left him.

Had the Honourable Gentleman's liking for young prostitutes been kept apart from his affair with the bottle, and brandy in particular, he would have been able to indulge his passions without being found out, but to become befuddled enough to take a teenaged prostitute into a hotel where he was known was 'crass', as he later described it. Elizabeth was informed of his misdemeanour by 'a good friend' but was persuaded not to talk to the press, at a price. Walter gave her his stud farm in Dorset, where she retired with her long-time lover Bernard Devonish, who until then had been her husband's private secretary.

As for Walter, he began to devote more of his time to furthering the aims of the Crusaders. Their campaign was a heaven-sent opportunity to damage others with his anger and disgust instead of himself, and feel jolly happy doing it too. The good standards and traditions of the country and its prestigious position in the world were being compromised by upstarts representing the working classes, and they were getting too powerful.

Walter Miles-Strickland had been a go-between on a number of occasions and he had been exceptionally generous with regard to the financial well-being of the Crusaders Society. They now had money to spend, and some of it had been used to set the working class upon themselves, as Walter had noted with satisfaction. 'They're like a pack of baying wolves,' he once told an invited audience. 'Shoot one and the rest will turn on it. Put our resources into strike prevention and we shall see the frustration and anger turn inwards. Let the rabid animals unite and batter the bastions and citadels of civilisation with their infernal cry for betterment and we shall see the demise of everything we stand for. A totalitarian state controlled by Moscow will replace our land of hope and glory, our green and pleasant land, and we will have a red flag flying over our revered institutions and our beloved monarch butchered, buried in an unmarked grave. Is that what we want?'

As was usually the case at such meetings, much shaking of hands and passionate pumping of hearts accompanied the appearance of cheque books and the appropriation of decent sums of money from self-appointed defenders of the realm who had been roused to the outermost reaches of jingoistic indignation by the oratorical powers of Walter Miles-Strickland, the patriot of patriots, whose prime aim now was the presidency of the movement. Never again must he be caught up in any scandal or licentious carryings-on, he realised with a shiver of fear. In future, everything in the way of pleasure must be conducted with the utmost discretion and secrecy.

Such considerations jarred the cogs of Miles-Strickland's mind into top gear in the reception area of the Royal Standard Hotel in London's West End when he bumped into a beautiful woman with long shapely legs, an hourglass figure and raven hair that danced on her shoulders when she moved.

'I'm so sorry, do forgive me,' she said shyly, and the Crusaders' president-in-waiting had no time to reply as she hurried off, her body swaying deliciously. Later that day, after the meeting of like minds had volunteered funds to the tune of five hundred pounds, Miles-Strickland saw her again. She was sitting alone at the bar dabbing at her eyes, and intrigued, he approached her, only for her to slip gracefully off her stool and hurry away. Was he ever going to speak to her, he wondered.

That night, with the hotel bar packed and most of the tables taken, Miles-Strickland saw her again. She was sitting with a distinguished-looking elderly man and as he watched, the man got up and gently kissed her hand before leaving. Lorna glanced around her in a coy manner and took out a tiny lace handkerchief to dab at her eyes before finishing her drink.

Strickland could not pass up the chance and he went over to her. 'I do beg your pardon,' he said in a chivalrous manner, 'but we have met before.'

'I'm sorry,' she smiled weakly, 'I don't recall.'

'I nearly knocked you over in the lobby this morning,' he told her with his best smile.

'I remember,' she replied, smiling back more warmly now. 'It was my fault. I was in a state.'

'I saw you at the bar this afternoon,' Strickland continued. 'You were distressed by the look of it. I wanted to enquire, but you hurried off.'

The young woman's shoulders sagged as she sighed. 'It's all so depressing.'

'Look, do you mind if I sit here?' he asked. 'Can I get you a drink?'

'I don't usually accept drinks from strange men,' she replied.

'Walter Miles-Strickland. At your service, madam,' he declared.

'Lorna Mae Lawrence. Pleased to meet you.'

With the introductions over and fortified with a pink gin, Lorna Mae Lawrence told him her sad story. 'During the war I was an Army nurse,' she began. 'I was posted to a military hospital in Singapore, and when the island fell I was interned in Changi Jail. Later we were sent up-country to a women's internment camp and there I made friends with three women in particular. We became very close, and then the last year of the war we were all split up. I never saw them again, but we had arranged that if ever we survived captivity we would all meet up in London on the first anniversary of the end of the war. I gave them the address of my Uncle Rufus who lived in Sussex. He was here with me tonight.'

'Yes I noticed,' Strickland said with a rapt expression. 'The tall grey-haired man.'

Lorna nodded. 'My friends never got in touch and I could only assume that they never survived. My Uncle Rufus had been trying to find out what became of them and he has only just managed to get at the truth. All three died of cholera in that last year. The difficulty was compounded by my friends being Australian and it meant a lot of letters travelling back and forth.'

'How terrible,' Strickland said shaking his head. 'Are you staying at the hotel?'

'No, my uncle and I arranged to meet here,' Lorna told him. 'He's travelling back to Sussex tonight.'

'Do you live in London?' Strickland asked.

'I've just moved here from Norfolk,' she replied. 'I've taken a flat in Bayswater. I don't know a soul here and apart from the feeling of being totally alone there was the sad news from Uncle Rufus. It was just too much.'

'Well at least you know someone now,' Strickland said, calling the waiter over.

After more pink gins and a good deal of prompting, Lorna Mae Lawrence told him quite a lot about herself. Strickland was in a devil-may-care mood himself after his brandies, and when she invited him back to her flat for coffee he accepted with courtesy and enthusiasm. His evening had only just begun, and for the next two hours the Honourable Member for East Graveney was indulged with a feast of sexual arts which were unsurpassed, even by his standards. Finally, as he lay totally spent and watched the beautiful nymph flitting into the bathroom, Strickland closed his eyes and grinned, feeling very pleased with himself.

Lorna Mae Lawrence was also feeling pleased as she slipped on a large towelling bathrobe and stared at herself in the mirror. 'That wasn't a bad performance, even if I say so meself, Maisie me gel,' she murmured to her reflection.

The photographer in the next flat would have agreed with her. He had it all on film and he had to admire her ingenuity in positioning herself and Walter for best effect during their love-making.

Maisie Lawrence the high-class prostitute from Camden Town was expecting her fee to arrive by post the following day, and she smiled into the mirror. Fortune favours the brave, she thought. Who knows, I might even give this acting lark a chance.

Chapter Twenty-Nine

Benny Tracy had had his doubts when Wally's scheme was finalised on Monday afternoon in the church gardens. Masher Wilkins could usually be found there after a lunchtime session at the watermen's club in Dockhead, and when the trio approached him with their proposition he pulled on his cauliflower ear and rubbed his flat nose. 'Yer mean yer want me ter give 'im a pastin'?' he asked.

'Nah, pay attention, Masher,' Wally told him. 'All yer gotta do is let Benny give yer a right-'ander an' flatten yer.'

'I dunno,' the ex-bruiser said, shaking his head. 'I got me reputation ter fink of.'

'It'll be seen as a lucky punch,' Wally coaxed. 'After all, yer did take a few lucky punches when yer was boxin'.'

'Yeah, but that was against quality opposition, not against a skinny-lookin' git like Benny.'

''Ere, d'you mind,' Benny replied with a hurt tone in his voice. 'I might be on the lean side but I was pretty nifty wiv me fists when I was a young sprog.'

Masher chuckled. 'I dunno about that. I've never 'ad ter climb in the ring wiv a rasher o' bacon.'

'Will yer do it?' Wally said puffing. 'We'll all buy yer a pint each if yer'll say yes.'

'All right, all right. Now leave me alone,' Masher growled. 'I wanna get me 'ead down fer ten minutes.'

'Let's just go frew it wiv yer then we'll leave yer in peace,' Wally urged him.

Now, as Benny washed up the tea things on Tuesday evening, he was glad of the opportunity to let Queenie see that he was in the frame for her attentions. 'That bloody ole git Raney's turned 'er 'ead,' he grumbled aloud, not for the first time.

Queenie looked up from her copy of *Butterflies of Great Britain* and pulled a face. 'Is that you mumblin' ter yerself, Benny?' she shouted from the parlour.

'Nah, I'm just singin',' he called back.

'D'yer want me ter dry?'

'Nah, I can manage it.'

'Put the kettle on while yer there.'

It was Benny's turn to pull a face. He was beginning to feel like a servant. Do this, do that. It's only been this way since she took up with that oil-rag Raney, he thought. Never mind, just let her wait till he finished the washing up. She was going to be in for a shock.

'Did yer make the tea?' Queenie enquired as he walked into the parlour.

'Yeah, it's drawin',' he told her.

'Why ain't yer brought it in?'

'I left it on the gas stove ter keep warm,' he replied.

'Ain't you 'avin' a cuppa?'

'Nah, I gotta see somebody,' he told her. 'There's somefing I 'ave ter take care of.'

Queenie frowned. 'Right now?'

'Yeah, right now.'

'Is it important? I mean, won't it keep?'

'Nah.'

'You look upset. 'As somebody upset yer?' she asked with concern.

'Yer could say that,' he replied, warming to the part.

'Yer don't normally keep fings from me,' she went on. 'Ain't yer gonna tell me what's the matter?'

'I would, but it might upset yer.'

'I fink yer better tell me.'

'It's Masher.'

'Who?'

'Masher Wilkins who gets in the Bell. 'E's an ex-boxer. 'E used ter be pretty good, so they say, but 'e don't scare me.'

'What you on about, Benny?' Queenie sighed in exasperation.

'Nah, it's better I don't say anyfing.'

'Well, please yerself,' she said, picking up her book.

'Masher was shoutin' 'is mouth orf in the Bell last night.'

'Yeah?'

'Yeah.'

'What was 'e goin' on about?'

'You.'

'Me?' Queenie started, dropping the book in her lap.

'Well, sort of.'

'Are you gonna tell me or am I s'posed ter guess?'

Benny sat down facing her. 'Me an' the lads were talkin' about fings, like we do, an' your name come up.'

'Oh yeah?'

'It come up regardin' lodgers, an' I told 'em that I get treated very well,' Benny went on carefully. 'I told 'em that I 'ad nuffink ter complain about.'

'I should fink not. I've always looked after yer, ain't I?'

'Course you 'ave. Anyway, Masher come over an' 'eard what we was talkin' about. 'E's always pokin' 'is nose in an' 'e asked me about you an' John Raney.'

'What the bloody 'ell's it got ter do wiv 'im?' Queenie said indignantly.

'That's what I told 'im,' Benny replied. 'Masher said that 'e 'eard you an' Raney were, yer know . . .'

'No, I don't know.'

'Masher said 'e 'eard that you an' Raney were at it.'

'Well, if it's any consolation we're not at it, not that it's anybody else's business anyway.'

Benny looked down at his hands for a few moments. 'Masher started goin' on about widders an' their lodgers an' I took umbrage. I told 'im that as far as you was concerned you was a decent woman an' I wouldn't dream of takin' advantage of yer.'

'Yer'd better not,' Queenie cut in sharply.

'Anyway I told Masher ter shut up or I'd give 'im a clout an' 'e laughed,' Benny said rolling his shoulders. 'Little does 'e know I used ter be the junior flyweight champion o' Bermon'sey.'

'So yer gonna 'ave it out wiv 'im,' Queenie said, shaking her head in disgust.

'We're goin' on the cobbles be'ind the Bell at seven sharp,' Benny told her solemnly.

'I don't believe it,' she puffed. 'You gotta be jokin'. You're not a young man, Benny, nor's 'e.'

'Well 'e shouldn't 'ave took yer name in vain.'

'The pair of yer are gonna end up 'avin' an 'eart attack fightin' at your age.'

'Don't you worry about me,' Benny replied quickly. 'I keep meself in trim. I can still punch me weight.'

'Now you just pour out that tea an' let's 'ear no more of it,' she ordered him, 'd'yer understand?'

'Sorry, Queenie. No can do,' Benny told her as he reached for his coat behind the door. 'Masher's gone too far this time. I ain't 'avin' anybody talkin' about you like that.'

'Benny, come back this minute. Come back, d'you 'ear me?' she shouted as the front door slammed shut.

'Bloody fool. 'E'll be the death o' me,' she said aloud as she slipped her shoes on.

Albert Price leaned on the counter and looked round the public bar as he waited for Dave Ford to fill the glass. 'I'll take a pint o' milk stout fer Granny while yer at it, Dave,' he said.

Masher Wilkins was sitting in the far corner reading the early edition of the *Evening News* and Albert took his pint of bitter over to his table. 'Wotcher, Masher. I ain't seen yer around fer a while. Everyfing all right?'

'Yeah I'm fine, Albert. 'Ow about you?'

'Mustn't grumble.'

'Backed any winners lately?'

Albert shook his head. 'Nah, I don't 'ave a bet these days.'

'Don't go tirin' 'im out wiv yer chattin',' Dave called over with a smile on his face. 'Masher's got a fight comin' up shortly.'

'What's this, an eliminator?' Albert joked.

'Ain't you 'eard?' Dave went on. 'Benny Tracy's challenged Masher to a scrap.'

'I've 'eard everyfing now,' Albert said with a shake of his head as he came over to collect Granny's stout.

The door opened and Winkle walked into the public bar. 'Give us a double whisky, Dave,' he asked.

'You're startin' early,' the landlord remarked.

'I 'ad a good day terday,' Winkle replied. 'I 'ad a oncer on a ten-ter-one outsider an' it obliged.'

'Well done, son,' Albert told him. ''Ere, yer should see what odds yer can get on Masher while yer on a winnin' streak. 'Im an' Benny Tracy are gonna 'ave a set-to ternight.'

'I don't believe it,' Winkle frowned.

'That's what I said.'

'Masher'll murder 'im.'

Wally had just walked into the bar and he heard the comment. 'Don't you be too sure,' he said quickly. 'Benny used ter be a tasty flyweight when 'e was a nipper.'

Winkle looked over at the ex-bruiser and saw him gulping down his beer. He'll be too drunk to fight if he keeps on at that rate, he thought, and he turned to the landlord. 'What odds will yer give us on Benny?'

'It's gotta be about ten ter one.'

'There's ten bob on Benny ter floor Masher.'

'I don't like takin' yer money, Winkle, but if you insist,' Dave said, smiling as he picked up the note.

Suddenly the door crashed open and Benny Tracy stepped in looking like he meant business. 'When yer ready, Masher,' he growled out of the corner of his mouth.

The small piece of wasteground next door to the Bell was not much bigger than a boxing ring and Benny made good use of it as he went through his warming-up exercises.

'Ain't yer gonna take yer coat off?' someone asked him.

'It won't last that long,' the confident challenger replied.

Wally and Tubby had been hard at work putting the word around and they were looking towards a good turn-out. Masher meanwhile had decided to keep his opponent waiting while he took another drink, and when he finally walked on to the wasteground he found quite a few spectators already assembled. Someone had provided two beer crates as stools and Albert Price stood holding a bar cloth.

'Stop this nonsense at once!' an angry voice shouted out.

Everyone turned to see Queenie Alladyce standing there with arms akimbo.

'It's too late now, missus, the bets are down,' someone told her.

'Stop it. D'you 'ear me?' she said regardless.

No one took any notice of her and Albert pushed Masher down on to the stool. 'Right now, son, yer gotta watch 'is right 'and,' he said, playing to the crowd.

Wally stood over Benny. 'Now let 'im move around yer an' then give 'im the ole one-two,' he instructed him.

The beer he had drunk and the atmosphere of expectation conspired to take Masher back to his younger days, and as Albert massaged his shoulder muscles the years fell away from him and he was there once again. The Blackfriar's Ring was packed with fight fans and they were shouting his name. Boy Dunkley was up and coming and Masher knew that he had a fight on his hands.

'Go easy on 'im, Masher,' someone called out as the old boxer stood up and stiffly shuffled his feet. That night the young Boy Dunkley had dropped him on to the canvas twice in the first round and again in the second before the referee stopped the fight. That was last time though, and tonight Dunkley wouldn't be so lucky. He's gonna be on the receiving end of a classic Wilkins come-back, Masher thought as he lumbered up. One more for the cooking pot, lads.

'Right, way yer go then,' Wally bade them.

'Stop it this minute!'

'Shut up, yer silly mare.'

'I'll give you silly mare.'

''Old 'er, somebody, she's bit me bloody 'and.'

With both arms held securely Queenie had little option but to be an unwilling spectator as the two combatants slowly circled each other, their clenched fists stuck up in front of their faces. Suddenly Masher feinted with his left then threw a quick right which missed Benny by a mile. Thinking he had been given carte blanche Benny jumped forward with his arms going like windmills. Masher could hear the crowd roar and their chants and he gritted his teeth. It was now or never, he thought. A short right from the shoulder hit Benny in the chin and he dropped like a stone.

'Yer've killed 'im, you ugly great brute!' Queenie screamed.

'Nah, 'e's just stunned,' her captor told her.

'Let me go, d'you 'ear,' she ranted.

'Get up, Benny,' Wally barked as he bent over the supine figure.

''E's out cold,' Tubby said.

'Get a bucket o' water somebody.'

Queenie had struggled free and she went over to Benny, concern etched on her face as she bent over him. 'You silly ole sod,' she remonstrated.

Albert handed Masher his coat and the ex-bruiser sat down on the beer crate looking bewildered. 'I wasn't gonna chuck the fight this time,' he muttered.

'Nah, course not.'

'I could 'ave bin up there in lights but they made me chuck the fight. I swore ter meself then that I wouldn't let it 'appen again.'

'I fink yer'd better go 'ome an' get a good night's sleep,' Albert advised him.

As the old fighter shuffled off Benny sat up and blinked. 'I 'ad 'im goin' till I got careless,' he groaned. 'Next time I'll know better.'

'There ain't gonna be a next time,' Queenie told him firmly. 'Now let's get you 'ome.'

'Well, what d'yer reckon?' Wally asked.

'I dunno, it's early days yet, but yer gotta admit, it does look promisin',' Tubby replied.

As soon as Sam Calkin arrived that evening Martha Carey made her excuses and went next door to her old friend. 'I've left 'em to it,' she said. 'I couldn't sit listenin' to it all again, it makes me so depressed.'

Mabel Duggan handed her a cup of tea and then sat down facing her. 'Are you all right?' she asked with concern.

Martha nodded. 'I feel a bit better than I did last night.'

'Did yer get any more out of 'im?' Mabel asked.

Martha sipped her tea. 'Yeah but I 'ad ter nag it out of 'im,' she replied. 'Apparently they'd bin blamin' 'im fer some mistakes in the books an' 'e blew 'is top. Sixteen years 'e's worked there an' shit's 'is fanks.'

'I don't fink my Charlie could 'ave stood it in an office,' Mabel told her, 'in fact I know 'e couldn't.'

'Joe often talks about 'ow 'e wishes 'e 'ad a job like your Charlie's,' Martha went on. 'Ter be honest I fink 'is nerves 'ave bin on edge lately, what wiv one fing an' the ovver, an' this business wiv the books was the last straw.'

'I bet 'e gave 'em a right mouthful,' Mabel said.

''E just told the manager that it might be better if 'e parted company wiv the firm.' Martha shrugged. 'Mind you I can't believe Joe took it that easy. 'E's got 'is pride.'

'What'll 'e do now?' Mabel asked as she sipped her tea.

'Gawd knows,' Martha replied. ''E ain't a young man any more. Tom said 'e should try ter get a job round the Council. They take older men on at times.'

'It's a worry,' Mabel said shaking her head.

'As if I ain't got enough trouble,' Martha sighed. 'There's Ellie moochin' about in 'er room all evenin' too. Last night I went up ter see if she was all right an' I noticed that she was writin'. She told me it was a letter to a friend. What friends? She never goes out wiv friends, an' there's never any letters come fer 'er. I fink she's goin' round the twist, in fact I'm sure of it.'

'What did she 'ave ter say about Joe puttin' 'is notice in?'

'Not a lot. She just said 'e knew best.'

Mabel put her empty cup down on the table. 'Pamela an' your Tom seem ter be 'ittin' it off,' she remarked.

'Yeah, they do don't they?'

'What about your Sue?'

'I dunno,' Martha sighed. 'She puzzles me at times. She never goes anywhere durin' the week. That feller of 'ers is always workin' from what I can gavver. I said to 'er last night she should put 'er foot down but she made excuses for 'im. Don't get me wrong, I like the feller, but 'e should be more considerate. If 'e keeps on the way 'e's goin' 'e's gonna lose 'er.'

'I'm sure 'e will,' Mabel replied. 'She's a very attractive young woman an' there's always someone on the sidelines.'

'I could see the way that reporter looked at 'er when 'e called ternight. 'E's a nice-lookin' feller too.'

'Anuvver cuppa, Marfa?'

'Yeah, go on then. I don't wanna go back while 'e's still there.'

Winkle went back to the Bell in the company of two friends and they sat in a corner playing cards for a while. As the evening wore on they became more noisy and Dave Ford began to get a little anxious. 'Winkle's bin on the turps all day by the look of it,' he remarked to Angie the barmaid. 'Ter be honest I dunno 'ow 'e's still managin' ter put it away.'

A short time later Winkle got up to use the toilet and fell over, and it was not long before he started singing in a loud voice.

'Don't you fink yer've 'ad enough?' Dave said quietly.

'Just one more fer the road an' then I'll be gone.'

'I fink yer'd be better goin' off now,' Dave persisted.

'Dave, yer a brick, but yer don't know when I've 'ad enough,' Winkle told him in a slurred voice. 'I know. An' that's why I want one more fer the road.'

'Just one.'

At ten o'clock Winkle's head dropped on the table and his two friends lifted him up by his arms and half carried him out of the pub. A minute later one of the men came back. 'Dave, can yer phone a cab fer us?' he asked. 'Winkle's out cold.'

When the cab pulled up outside the safe cracker's lodgings in Rotherhithe the driver was given a large tip and the two men carried Winkle into his bedroom.

'I don't like 'im comin' in this way,' Mrs Freeman moaned. 'It gives the place a bad name. Six lodgers I've got, an' 'e's the only one who gets this way.'

'Winkle's bin celebratin', luv. It's 'is birfday,' one of the men told her. 'Anyway we've tucked 'im up in bed. Yer won't get a peep out of 'im till mornin'.'

Chapter Thirty

Tom Carey lay awake in his bed as the minutes ticked slowly away. When he had met Winkle in the Dockhead pub as arranged the little safe cracker seemed very calm and cheerful. The ladder had been hidden on the bombsite in Nelson Lane and it was now a question of waiting. There was only one thing bothering Tom and he had mentioned it to Winkle that evening. It wasn't every day that a company's safe got blown open and the police would know where to start their enquiries. Winkle had shrugged it off, insisting that it was all a question of having a watertight alibi, and he would not be drawn any further.

Ten minutes after one o'clock in the morning Tom dressed quickly and sat on the edge of his bed for a few minutes. The house was silent and he reminded himself about the stair that creaked outside Aunt Ellie's room. She was a light sleeper, and as she often pointed out, the slightest noise would wake her. There was also the problem of getting to the transport yard unnoticed. Very few people walked the streets in the dead of night and any passing policeman would be sure to make a mental note of his appearance. He might even be curious enough to start asking questions, which would jeopardise the operation.

As he crept down the stairs Tom saw that there was a light coming from under Aunt Ellie's bedroom door and he gritted his teeth as he gently closed the front door after him. She was a strange woman, he thought as he hurried along the deserted turning and out into Abbey Street. Whatever could she be doing at that early hour?

A crescent moon slipped behind a cloud as he crossed the Tower Bridge Road into Long Lane. So far so good. He was sure he hadn't been seen and he crossed his fingers as he turned into a side street and took a left into Nelson Lane. A cat jumped down from a dustbin and scurried off as he walked silently towards the bomb ruin. Winkle would be waiting there, he hoped.

He slipped in through a gap in the corrugated fencing and picked his way over rubble and into the ruins of a roofless house, where he spotted the long ladder propped up against the chimney breast, pointing up at the star-filled sky. There was still no sign of Winkle and Tom decided to move the ladder to the edge of the bombsite while he was waiting. Mindful of leaving his fingerprints about he pulled out a pair of gloves from his coat pocket and put them on, and as he carried the ladder out of the ruined building he suddenly saw a shadowy figure shift behind a pile of bricks. 'Winkle?' he said in a low voice.

The safe cracker came up to him carrying a small carpet-bag. 'We ready ter go?' he asked.

They set off across the desolate wasteground and

Tom grunted with the effort as he propped the heavy ladder against the high wall that ran along the rear of the bombsite. 'Right, I'll go first,' he said.

Once atop the wall he held the ladder steady and took the bag from Winkle while he clambered up after him. The moon had emerged from behind a cloud and they could see the exposed cellar floor more than twenty feet below.

'Christ Almighty!' the little man gasped as he looked down. 'If we fall down there we'll never get out.'

'If we fell down there we'd be dead,' Tom replied soberly.

Winkle sat rigid on the wall while Tom pulled the ladder up and let the end of it fall into place on the facing wall.

'Right then, away we go.'

'Are you sure?' Winkle said gulping with fright.

'Wait till I'm across,' Tom hissed. 'This ladder won't take both our weights.'

Once he had reached the other wall Tom held the end of the ladder while Winkle crawled over holding the bag. Suddenly the Alsatian dog dashed across the yard and started to bark.

'Quiet, Lady,' Tom called down urgently.

The dog cocked her head and watched while he pulled the ladder over with some difficulty and lowered the end into the yard.

'Is that mutt all right?' Winkle asked fearfully as he followed Tom down toward the ground.

'Stay close ter me an' yer'll be okay,' the young man told him as he pulled the ladder down to conceal it from the road.

They crossed the yard with the dog at their heels

and Winkle pulled at Tom's sleeve. 'Can't yer tie it up?' he hissed.

'If I did it'd start barkin',' Tom told him. 'Let's get on wiv it.'

When they reached the top of the iron staircase Winkle took over. He reached into his bag, took out a crowbar and quickly prised open the door. 'Get us a couple o' tarpaulins while I sort out the safe, an' don't leave that bloody dog up 'ere,' he growled, reaching back into his bag. ''Ere, give 'im these.'

'What is it?' Tom asked as he took the blood-stained newspaper parcel from him.

'Pork chops,' Winkle told him. 'I got those in case that mutt took a fancy ter me.'

The two men worked fast. While Winkle fixed the explosive to the safe with adhesive tape Tom carried two tarpaulins up the stairs and placed them against the windows. The fuse lead was fed out into the passageway and then Winkle held up his crossed fingers. 'Once the safe goes we won't 'ave a lot o' time,' he said. 'Take that dog over ter the kennel an' tie it up. The barkin' won't matter once that fing blows.'

Tom nodded. 'Good luck, pal.'

'Get that ladder ready,' Winkle said quickly as he took a box of matches from his coat pocket.

A split second after the bright flash a loud explosion rocked the yard and slates flew from the roof of the office. The Alsatian started to bark loudly as it strained against its leash and Tom shouted at it from the foot of the ladder, willing Winkle to appear. Smoke started to pour from the doorway and still there was no sign of the little safe cracker. Realising that something was wrong Tom dashed across the yard and bounded up the stairs.

The smell of cordite burned his nostrils as he entered the passageway and saw the damage. The force of the explosion had brought down part of the passage wall and Winkle was struggling to pull himself out from beneath a pile of rubble.

'Let's get ter that safe quick!' he cried out as Tom helped him free.

Most of the smoke and dust had been sucked out through the gap in the roof and Tom could see that the door of the safe was hanging open. Winkle pushed past him and grabbed a folder of papers, ignoring a bundle of money. 'I'm on orders, more's the pity,' he hissed as he put the folder into his small carpet-bag. 'C'mon, let's get out of 'ere.'

As they reached the top of the wall they heard a police car bell and a squeal of brakes. Tom pointed across the bombsite as headlights lit up Nelson Lane. 'It's too late!' he cried. 'They're surroundin' the bloody place!'

'Well, we can't stop 'ere,' Winkle growled.

'There's only one chance,' Tom shouted as torchlights began to move towards them over the rubble.

Winkle followed the young man back down into the yard. 'What yer doin'?' he hissed. 'They'll catch us 'ere.'

'Foller me,' Tom ordered him.

Winkle dashed after the young man and jumped up behind him into the cab of a lorry that was parked facing the gates. As the engine roared into life Tom gritted his teeth. 'Brace yerself!' he shouted.

The lorry charged forward and hit the gates like a hammer, throwing the splintered wood across the two police cars which had just drawn up. Tom swung hard on the steering-wheel as the heavy vehicle bounced over the wreckage and then as it careered at speed along Long Lane he braked hard, drove it at a near-skid into a narrow turning and pulled up. Winkle could see why his partner in crime had chosen that particular street as he clambered out of the cab. It narrowed into an alley which snaked off into a warren of backstreets.

'Round 'ere quick!' Tom shouted as he dived into a cobbled lane, leaning against a lamppost to regain his breath. 'We've gotta split up,' he gasped.

Winkle held up the carpet-bag. 'This is a dead giveaway,' he said panting.

'Give it ter me,' Tom told him.

'What yer gonna do wiv it?' he asked, hesitating.

'Turn left 'ere,' Tom said snatching the bag.

As they turned into another narrow lane the young man suddenly threw the bag over into a locked yard. 'It'll be all right there,' he told the shocked safe cracker. 'That's where I borrered the ladder from. I can pick it up later.'

Exhausted, they walked to the corner of the lane, and when they leant against the wall to recover Winkle held out his hand. 'Yer done us proud, son,' he said with a grin.

Suddenly they heard footsteps and Winkle grabbed at Tom's coat lapel. 'It could be a rozzer,' he hissed.

They hurried away from the sound of the heavy tread and turned into a street with a row of bomb-damaged houses.

'We'll 'ave ter 'ole up in 'ere till daylight,' Tom said quickly. 'It's too risky ter stay on the streets.'

They clambered in through an empty windowframe

into a rubble-filled room and Tom felt his way into the passage with Winkle holding on to his coat. 'This'll do,' the young man said as they stumbled into a small back room.

They settled down facing the window opening with their backs against the bare brick wall, and for a while they sat silently staring out at the waning moon and the few bright stars.

'I nearly ballsed it up,' Winkle remarked after a time. 'That safe was a Union 520. They take a lot o' bustin' but I used too much jelly. I nearly blew the 'ole place up.'

'Never mind, we got the papers,' Tom replied. 'That money though. There was a nice bundle there. I was surprised yer left it.'

'Like I said, I was told in no uncertain terms ter leave any money that might be there,' Winkle reiterated. 'This Brady geezer's gonna sweat. 'E'll know that 'e's bin rumbled.'

Tom nodded, and his face broke into a wide grin. 'I bet those rozzers were surprised when we drove out o' the yard. I fink we made a mess o' those two cars.'

Winkle chuckled, then he grew serious again. 'I'll need ter get back ter my digs soon as I can. The landlady gets up at 'alf six.'

'Does she give yer a mornin' call?'

'I get a cup o' tea every mornin' at a quarter ter seven.'

'Won't she know yer was out?'

'Last night I did me little party piece in the Bell,' Winkle said grinning. 'I was seen ter get drunk by the landlord an' the rest o' the customers. What they didn't know was that most o' the booze got tipped away. I bet that aspidistra plant's got an 'angover. Anyway I got took 'ome in a taxi by a couple o' pals an' they carried me inter me lodgin's. They told me landlady they'd tucked me up fer the night. So when the rozzers start makin' enquiries I got a few witnesses that'll say I was in no fit state ter go safe-breakin'.'

'What about if they suss it was you an' raid yer digs before yer get back there?' Tom asked anxiously.

'I don't fink they'll be that quick,' Winkle replied. 'All right they know I'm out, but they don't know I'm lodgin' in Rovver'ithe under anuvver name. They'll raid me 'ouse in Peckham first an' then when they realise I ain't bin back there they'll put the word out an' do the rounds o' the local pubs. Anyway, if the worst comes ter the worst an' they do visit me digs before I get back they're gonna be waitin'. If that 'appens I'll tell 'em I just went fer a walk ter clear me 'ead.'

'I 'ope they believe yer,' Tom said smiling.

Winkle shuffled his feet and yawned. 'Those papers need ter be delivered as soon as possible.'

'It's a bit risky you doin' it, in case yer get picked up,' Tom remarked. 'Why don't I get my pal the winder cleaner ter do it?'

'Can 'e be trusted?' Winkle asked. 'I wouldn't like any cock-ups to 'appen after what we 'ad ter do ter nick 'em.'

''E's a good lad. 'E'll do it, no sweat.'

Winkle reached into his trouser pocket and took out a five-pound note. 'Give 'im this fer the ladder,' he said, 'an' tell 'im ter take the papers ter number ten Druid Street an' ask fer Maurice.'

Tom looked at the little man in surprise. 'That's my bruvver.'

'Yeah, I know,' Winkle said smiling slyly. 'It's a small world, ain't it.'

At five o'clock that morning the two conspirators left the ruined building and set off in different directions. Tom managed to get back into his house without detection while Winkle caught the early morning tram to Rotherhithe and climbed in through his bedroom window.

Before getting into bed the safe cracker took a large swig of whisky and then sprinkled a liberal amount over his chest. Mrs Freeman was going to be disgusted with him, he thought, but she would get over it.

Chapter Thirty-One

Sam Calkin came into the newspaper office early on Wednesday morning and greeted Sue with a smile. 'I hope I didn't cause any problems last night,' he said. 'I thought it went off very well.'

Sue smiled back at him. 'They both seemed happy enough about it,' she replied.

'Any messages?'

'Mr Spencer wants to see you.'

'Right. I'll see you later.'

Paddy O'Brian strolled in a short while later and after a few minutes he came back out of the main office. 'Things are looking up, my girl,' he said making big eyes. 'I've got something to get my teeth into at last. Apparently the Brady Transport establishment had visitors last night.'

'Burglars?'

'Someone blew the safe.'

'Really?'

'Our revered editor saved this one especially for me, would you believe,' Paddy told her, his eyebrows raised haughtily.

'There's hope yet,' Sue said grinning.

'I hope so, but there's mischief afoot, if I'm not mistaken,' he replied with a collusive wink. 'Mr Spencer and our star reporter are locked in deep conversation even as I speak.'

Sue chuckled at his comical expression and then lowered her eyes slightly. 'That's a smart tie you're wearing,' she remarked.

'It was a present from Frances.'

'She's got good taste.'

'That's what I said to her the first time we went out together,' Paddy replied.

'Paddy, you're incorrigible.'

'I know, but it's nice.'

'It won't be if you don't hurry after that story,' she told him.

'I'm away to make my name,' he declared as he reached the door.

'You as well?'

Paddy raised one eyebrow quizzically. 'Should I read something into that remark?'

'No.'

'Well, I'm off then.'

The phone lines grew busy as the *Bulletin* came to life, and Frances Miller wore a businesslike expression as she went down to the glory hole on an important mission. It was all here, and if it was available she would find it, she told herself as she scanned the titles on the box files.

Inside the sanctum Ernest Spencer leaned back in his leather-bound chair and listened intently as Sam Calkin made his report.

'Carey and Duggan are both respected family men and they came over as being very modest about their achievements that night,' he recounted. 'What they told me ties in with the original *Bulletin* piece. They were both commended for their actions in saving lives and I find it hard to relate that to what Billy Button told me.'

'You think Button might be lying?'

'That's the puzzling part,' Calkin went on. 'He didn't come across as a liar, and his assessment of George Merry backs up the rumours about Merry leaving the lead mills to go to the pub and being prone to drinking heavily.'

'You've not told Carey and Duggan about Billy Button, have you?' Spencer queried.

'No, of course not.'

'So where does that leave us?'

'My hunch is that there was a robbery taking place just before and during the air raid,' Calkin replied. 'It's quite possible that Carey and Duggan would not have known. The warehouse had a lot of floor space and the two men were ensconced at one end of the flat roof in an observation shed reinforced with sandbags. The fire escape was situated at the other end of the warehouse. For a start it was out of their line of sight, and there was also a blackout. Mr Carey told me that they took it in turns to patrol the roof during the raids watching for incendiary bombs and scanning the immediate area. He said that one of them was always manning the phone link to the warden's post.'

'I've read the reports of that night,' Spencer said, removing his spectacles. 'Apparently the basement shelter was filled with smoke which came down through the lift shaft after the oil bomb fell on the warehouse, and when the people inside tried to get out through the emergency exit they found it blocked by debris from the lead mills opposite, which had also had a direct hit.'

Sam Calkin nodded. 'Mr Carey told me that the oil bomb made a large hole in the roof and blew out the side wall above the shelter entrance. He said he looked down into Ship Lane and saw that the wall had collapsed over the entrance of the shelter, completely blocking it. Then Mr Duggan said that when he tried to get through to the shelter by phone and got no reply he and Mr Carey went down the fire escape at the other end of the building and heard banging coming from behind the emergency door. It was blocked with rubble and timber and it took them a few minutes to clear it. By that time five elderly people in that shelter had been asphyxiated by the smoke.'

'So if there was a robbery taking place the thieves would have made their getaway as soon as the warehouse was hit,' Spencer said, scratching his chin.

'From what Mr Button said, one of the lorries had been taken from the lead mills yard earlier that evening, so it's quite possible that it was used in the robbery,' Calkin continued. 'Also it was only a minute or two after the warehouse got bombed that the lead mills copped it. In that short time the robbers must have made their getaway or the lorry would have been caught under the debris. As it was it was found burned out at the end of Ship Lane, trapped there by burning debris from another warehouse.'

'So it follows that the stolen articles were on that lorry when it burned out,' Spencer added. 'What I can't figure out is, what were they stealing? Carpets? It doesn't make sense. We're talking about working people's belongings. Very few if any would have had carpets worth stealing.'

Sam Calkin leaned forward in his chair. 'Mr Button said that he saw what appeared to be a rolled-up bundle being passed down the fire escape. He guessed it was a carpet, but it could have been something else.'

'Like what?'

'I've asked Frances Miller to do a search,' the reporter replied.

'What's she supposed to be looking for?'

'Any unsolved local robberies which took place around that time.'

'I'm not with you.'

Sam Calkin sat back in his chair. 'Let's say that some expensive carpets had been stolen locally and they needed to be stored until a buyer could be found. Where better than with other carpets, and at a Council storehouse?'

'But that would mean complicity.'

'Both Mr Carey and Mr Duggan had sets of keys to the warehouse,' Calkin said pointedly. 'They had to have them in case of incendiary bombs going through the roof.'

'So one or both of them could be implicated,' Spencer replied.

'The keys could have been borrowed and copied without their knowledge,' Sam Calkin suggested, 'though they were kept in the roof shed in a locked box.'

The editor stroked his chin thoughtfully for a few moments. 'All we have here is the word of an admitted drunk against the word of two respectable family men,' he said. 'We'll need more than that, Calkin.'

'Yes I know,' he replied quickly. 'I need a few more days and then I think I can prove it one way or the other.'

'Are you going to let me into your plans?'

'I'd prefer to wait, if you agree.'

'Right then, get to it, young man, and the best of luck. I think you're going to need it.'

Sam Calkin came out of the office to see Frances waving to him and he walked over to her.

'This might be of assistance,' she said with a smile.

Sam read the newspaper cutting quickly and then gave her a big grin. 'Frances, you're an angel.'

She looked very pleased with herself and sighed with satisfaction as he strolled through to reception.

Larry Fields, alias the Winkle, was pulled out of bed at ten o'clock on Wednesday morning and bustled into a police car.

'What the bloody 'ell is all this about?' he said angrily as he faced Inspector Robinson across the table.

'I'll tell you what all this is about,' the inspector replied. 'Early this morning the Brady Transport firm in Long Lane had their safe broken into and the job carries your trademark.'

'I dunno what yer talkin' about,' Winkle said calmly. 'I done me time an' now I'm on the straight an' narrer. Anyway, what would I be doin' blowin' a transport firm's safe? There wouldn't be enough money in there ter make it werf me while.'

'Who said anything about blowing the safe?'

'Well, yer said it 'ad my trademark on the job,' Winkle replied. 'I used ter blow 'em, as well you know.'

'What were you after, Winkle?'

'I wasn't after nuffink.'

'We've got some nice dabs, and as soon as we get the match you won't be acting so calm and collected,' Robinson scowled at him.

'I might seem calm but I'm not, believe you me,' Winkle assured him. 'When yer got a record like mine yer bound ter feel scared when yer get pulled in. All I can say is what I said just now. I'm on the straight an' narrer an' that's gospel.'

'Why don't you come clean, Winkle,' Robinson urged him. 'You'll make it easier on yourself. We're gonna have you dead to rights soon.'

The little safe cracker knew that the policeman was bluffing. He had never gone on a job without wearing gloves and his alibi was sound. 'I'm innocent, inspector,' he said.

'Who were you with last night?'

'Jumbo Ellis an' Arnie Watson.'

'On the job?'

'Nah, in the Bell.'

'Don't sod me about, Winkle,' the policeman growled.

'Look, inspector. Those two pals took me 'ome an' stuck me in bed, so me landlady told me this mornin',' he said earnestly. 'I was out o' me brains. Then you come bargin' in. It's enough ter give a bloke an 'eart attack.'

'Who paid you to blow that safe?'

'Nobody paid me.'

'They must have done. Papers were taken and the money left behind.'

'You know I always used ter work on me own,' Winkle replied.

'Not this time.' Inspector Robinson leaned back in his chair. 'Why are you not living at home in Peckham?'

'Woman trouble. My ole lady was naggin' me narrer so I upped an' left.'

'Your wife wasn't at home when we called there.'

'Well, she must 'ave pissed orf then.'

'We're going to nail you good and proper,' Robinson sneered.

'Look, I'm gettin' just about sick of all this,' the little man said defiantly. 'Eivver charge me or let me go.'

'We'll be making more enquiries and when we're ready we'll come to get you, so don't leave the area,' the policeman told him with a threatening look.

'I'm not plannin' on goin' anywhere,' Winkle said as he got up.

Sam Calkin walked into the deserted Ship Lane on Wednesday afternoon and pulled the collar of his mackintosh up around his ears as light rain fell from a leaden sky. He stood looking for a few moments at the ragged corrugated fencing in front of the ruined warehouse and then he squeezed through a gap and crossed the rubble. Like many of the bombed factories and warehouses in war-torn Bermondsey, the Ship Lane building had been demolished down to the first-floor level and the rubble piled up inside the lower walls for safety reasons. The black shelter sign was still visible over an iron door which was almost buried behind huge concrete slabs.

Sam cast his eye along what was left of the building and saw the rusted iron base of the fire escape at the far end. He picked his way over the rubble and stood looking at the scene. To the left of what was once the emergency exit a few steps led up to the top of the wall at an angle, and he realised from having studied a photograph of the warehouse that the fire escape originally led up to doors on each of the four floors. For a while he stood looking, trying to visualise the carnage and panic that night as people tried desperately to get out from the smoke-filled shelter beneath the building. He moved forward to the rusted iron door and suddenly noticed two oblong black marks on the brickwork, one on each side of the door at the same height. He could see that they resembled bitumen and he took a small penknife from his pocket and prodded at the substance, removing a small piece which he slipped into his top pocket.

Sam Calkin's next visit was to Moxen's lead mills which had moved to Rotherhithe Street, and the transport manager there was very accommodating when Sam explained the reason for his visit. 'I knew old George Merry very well,' he said. 'It's nice that he'll be remembered. A very brave man was George. Such a sad business.'

'Do you still use the same make of lorries?' Sam asked him.

'No, they were Albions,' the manager replied, looking puzzled. 'We use Fodens now. Very reliable vehicles.'

'Are they out at the moment?'

'One's being loaded now.'

'Would you mind if I took a look at it?'

'No, of course not,' the manager said, looking even more puzzled.

Sam followed him down into the yard where men

were stacking bundles of solder on to a large, drop-sided vehicle which was backed up against a loading bank.

'They carry a lot of weight and the bodies have to be reinforced,' the manager pointed out.

Sam looked down at the gap between the bank and the rear of the lorry. 'Where are the bodies made, at Foden's?'

'No, most heavy vehicles come with just the chassis and the body is built to individual requirements,' he was told.

'Who built this body?'

'Westbury Body-builders in Northampton.'

'What about the Albions you used to run?'

'The same body-builder.'

Sam nodded thoughtfully. 'Thank you for your time and trouble,' he said, holding out his hand.

'This all seems very mysterious,' the manager remarked.

'Once I get the information I need I'll be in touch,' Sam replied.

'I can't wait,' the manager said, smiling.

Chapter Thirty-Two

Tom Carey had delivered a consignment of cheese to a provision merchant's in North London and on the way home he stopped off in Druid Street. He found his older brother Mo sitting with his feet up on the desk talking on the phone and he nodded towards the tatty armchair. Tom grinned as he sat down and rubbed his hand along the split arm.

'You're gettin' ter be quite a regular visitor,' Mo said as he put the receiver down.

'I'd come 'ere more often if yer'd do somefing about this poxy furniture,' Tom joked. 'It's a bloody disgrace. What must the customers fink.'

'The sort o' people I do business wiv ain't worried about the decor,' Mo told him.

'Yeah, yer right I s'pose,' Tom replied. 'By the way, did yer get the papers?'

'Early this mornin'.'

'Are they any good?'

''Ow the bloody 'ell do I know?' Mo said bluntly.

'All right, keep yer 'air on,' Tom retorted.

Mo grinned. 'I've passed 'em on. They're mainly copies of letters to an' from various companies but there were quite a few from one company named Bartlett Enterprises.'

'What were they about?'

'Just business jargon mainly,' Mo told him. 'One letter was interestin' though. It referred to a consortium meetin' an' there were quotes from the minutes. I expect the people concerned will be able ter make somefing of it.'

'This is all above me,' Tom said puffing.

'That's the way it is, Bruv,' Mo replied with a smile. 'Just let the interested parties deal wiv it.'

'Who are these people?'

'I've told yer. Union leaders, MPs, activists. It's an impressive list.'

'I bet it is,' Tom growled.

''Ave yer got time fer a cuppa?' Mo asked him.

'Yeah, get that kettle on.'

'I understand our little friend made a mess o' that office,' Mo remarked as he lit the gas under the battered tin kettle.

'Yeah, I 'ad ter pull 'im out from under a wall that 'ad fell on 'im,' Tom replied, grinning.

'You was wiv 'im?'

'Yeah, I 'ad to.'

'What d'yer mean, you 'ad to?'

'The Alsatian. Winkle was terrified o' the mutt.'

'You bloody fool,' Mo said angrily. 'Why risk your neck?'

'Why not? You're takin' chances,' Tom countered quickly.

'It's different wiv me,' Mo said sharply. 'I run wiv the villains, you don't.'

'I do now,' Tom said, chuckling, 'unless yer don't consider Winkle ter be a villain.'

'Take a tip from me, Bruv. Stay well out of it in

future,' Mo warned him. 'The business 'as bin done as far as we're concerned. It's in the 'ands o' the big league now.'

'Mo, the kettle's boilin',' Tom remarked with a grin.

Martha Carey looked across the dining-table at her husband as he put down his knife and fork. 'Wasn't it nice?' she asked with concern.

Joe rubbed his hand across his middle. 'I'm just not 'ungry,' he replied.

Tom and Sue exchanged glances while Aunt Ellie seemed to be toying with a cube of beef on the end of her fork.

'Don't tell me you're not 'ungry eivver,' Martha said to her with a sigh of exasperation.

'I can't help it if I've got no appetite,' Ellie whinged.

'It looks like I've bin wastin' me time sweatin' over that meal,' the matriarch moaned.

'No you 'aven't, Muvver,' Tom told her as he wiped a hunk of bread round his plate.

'No, it was very nice,' Sue said in support as she pushed her empty plate away.

'It seems a bit strange blowin' the safe,' Joe remarked, resuming the conversation they had been having before Martha served the meal. 'I mean ter say, there wouldn't be that much in there surely.'

'They might 'ave bin after somefing else,' Tom suggested as he wiped his plate clean.

'Like what?'

'Papers, documents.'

'Just as long as they don't suspect you 'ad anyfing ter do wiv it,' Martha cut in.

'Why should they suspect me?' Tom asked.

'Well, you said it was yer lorry that they used ter get away.'

'It was just that my lorry was nearest the gates,' Tom told her casually.

Ellie looked up at the young man with a question in her eyes and then lowered her head again over her plate. 'It's frightening,' she mumbled.

'What was that, Ellie?' Joe asked her.

'I said it's frightening, what with one thing and the other.'

'It's nuffing fer you ter worry about, Aunt Ellie,' Tom said reassuringly.

'Nothing to worry about? You get beaten up, then your firm has its safe blown open?' Ellie replied quickly. 'What's going on?'

'Search me,' Tom said with a shrug of his shoulders.

'I fink I'll try the Council termorrer,' Joe announced.

'I don't want you workin' outside, not wiv your chest the way it is,' Martha told him.

'Beggars can't be choosers,' Joe sighed. 'Anyway they might 'ave a vacancy in one o' the offices fer a bookkeeper.'

'We've got a few bob put aside so there's no immediate rush fer a week or two,' Martha said as she got up to clear the table.

'That's our 'oliday money. We decided to 'ave a week in Margate.'

'Sod the week in Margate, Joe.'

Aunt Ellie gave her sister a critical look. 'Joe's right. You need the break.'

'Well, we'll see,' Martha replied in a tone of voice which indicated that the subject was closed.

'Are you and Pamela going out tonight?' Sue asked her brother.

'Not ternight,' Tom said as he got up from the table. 'She's got fings ter do. We're goin' down ter Brighton fer the weekend.'

Joe and Martha glanced at each other while Aunt Ellie looked somewhat disapprovingly at the young man. Sue caught his eye and gave him a faint smile. 'Lucky for some,' she remarked.

'That's what you an' Del should do,' Martha told her. 'You two never seem ter go anywhere tergevver.'

'I don't think it's right,' Ellie declared as she found her usual armchair. 'It's putting too much temptation young people's way. It wouldn't have happened in my day.'

'Ellie, it went on all the time,' Martha said. 'Anyway, if they're gonna get up ter mischief they wouldn't need ter go away fer the weekend. They could do it in a doorway.'

'Martha, you can be very crude at times,' Ellie said with a look of distaste.

'Well, I'm right.'

'Yes I know, but you don't have to be so blunt.'

'I'm gonna slip in an' see Charlie later,' Joe told them.

'I think I'll get an early night,' Tom said, yawning.

Ellie gave him another quick glance and this time Tom noticed. Had she heard him go out early that morning? he wondered.

'I think I'll go and see Pamela for a chat,' Sue added to the family schedule.

'Is Del workin' late?' Martha enquired.

'I don't know, but I'm fed up with knocking for

him,' Sue told her with irritation in her voice. 'He should be calling for me.'

'Well, that's you lot sorted out,' Martha said. 'What about you, Ellie?'

'I've got a letter to write,' Ellie told her.

Martha and her daughter carried the piled-up crockery into the scullery and Joe followed them out of the parlour.

As soon as they were alone Ellie looked over at her nephew. 'I heard you about early this morning,' she said pointedly.

'Yeah, I couldn't sleep,' Tom said with a smile.

'I thought I heard the front door go,' Ellie probed.

'It was probably the wind.'

'There wasn't any wind last night.'

'Most likely the yard door.'

'I think I know the difference, Tom,' she replied quickly.

'Look, Aunt Ellie. I couldn't sleep, so I put me coat on an' went fer a stroll.'

'At two o'clock in the morning?'

'Yeah.'

'Tom, you weren't involved in that business at your firm, were you?' she asked, looking very worried.

'Course I wasn't.'

'Your mother can do without that sort of trouble. She's got enough on her plate with your father at the moment.'

'Don't you worry, Aunt Ellie,' Tom said quietly. 'I 'ave bin known ter go walkies in the middle o' the night. Last night was just a coincidence.'

Ellie sighed. 'It's all right, everyone here thinks I'm

a silly old woman, but I notice things. I understand a little more than I'm given credit for.'

'I don't fink yer a silly ole woman,' Tom told her kindly. 'I fink yer very shrewd, an' very mysterious.'

'What makes you say that?'

'All those secret letters you write. All that burnin' the midnight oil. I've noticed the light under yer door many times.'

Ellie's face flushed slightly and she smiled to cover her embarrassment. 'I might be writing a book for all you know.'

'I thought you might be,' Tom replied, smiling back at her.

Ellie glanced at the door quickly and then leaned forward in her chair. 'I am, but not a word to anyone.'

'Aunt Ellie, my lips are sealed,' Tom said with a flourish. 'By the way, is it a steamy romance?'

'That would be telling,' she replied.

Joe's footsteps in the passage ended the conversation and Ellie picked up her embroidery. Just a silly old woman. But they'll all be surprised one day, she thought.

Lorna Mae Lawrence had received a bouquet of flowers that morning with an invitation to a party at the Ritz Hotel, and as she soaked in the bath she felt pleased with her progress. Walter Miles-Strickland had taken the bait, hook line and sinker, and if she played her cards right very shortly she would be able to earn the promised bonus.

That evening Lorna attracted much attention as she walked into the private reception on the arm of the Honourable Gentleman, but her eyes were for him only as champagne flowed and toasts were drunk. Later, with the names of many of the guests imprinted in her mind, she and her escort left the Ritz in a taxi which took them to his flat in Bloomsbury. There, after a brandy and coffee supplied in the lounge by an effeminate valet, Strickland showed her into his private study. 'I shot that in Kenya back in thirty-three,' he told her, pointing to the antelope's head trophy over his large ornate desk.

Lorna hid her repulsion with a forced smile. 'This is so intimate,' she remarked, hunching her shoulders for effect.

'You're privileged,' he told her. 'A man's den is no place for a woman, but in your case I make an exception.'

'I'm very flattered,' she replied, giving him one of her most seductive smiles as he moved towards her. 'But I don't want to know the secrets of your private domain. It wouldn't be right.'

'Secrets?' he said, raising his eyebrows.

'You know. In films the villain presses a button or moves a lever and the bookcase slides back to expose a secret hiding-place.'

He laughed aloud as he reached out to her. 'That's only in films.'

'You disappoint me, Walter,' she replied in a baby voice. 'No hidden love nest? No secret cache?'

His eyes flickered quickly as he pulled her to him. 'Our love nest is ready and waiting,' he said huskily. 'But first I'll get William to take the night off.'

Lorna allowed him to kiss her and then she gently pushed him back. 'Remember William,' she said.

Strickland took her arm and led her from the study

into the lavishly furnished lounge and she squeezed his hand encouragingly. She had been very perceptive while in the study and the slight movement of his eyes had made her feel confident that his cache was a wall safe hidden behind a picture of a snow-capped Kilimanjaro. Yes, things were progressing very well, she congratulated herself.

Robbie Casey put the phone down and smiled with satisfaction. 'Fings seem ter be movin' very nicely,' he said. 'Wiv a bit o' luck the workman can go in soon.'

'That's good news,' the young man replied. 'D'you want me ter contact Mo Carey?'

'No it's gettin' late, I'll give 'im a ring termorrer,' Casey told him. 'We've gotta be very careful. I don't want anyone pointin' a finger at the union. To all intents an' purposes we've got nuffing whatsoever ter do wiv it. Now let's 'ave a drink, son.'

Del Abelson watched as the elderly convenor poured out two liberal measures of whisky. 'You've bin knockin' that stuff back a bit by the look o' that bottle,' he remarked.

Casey passed over the glass, ignoring his nagging ulcer as he downed his drink in one gulp. 'It's bin very busy this last two weeks,' he replied. 'We've got anuvver big meetin' this Saturday as well as the demo on Sunday.'

'You can give those two a miss,' Del suggested.

'No way. This is what the job's all about,' Casey said grinning. 'I'd only be sittin' about frettin'. What about you? You've bin strongin' it lately. You give it a miss.'

Del shook his head. 'I'll take a few days off after the meetin's.'

Casey got up and reached for his coat. 'C'mon, son, let's get off 'ome.'

The two union men parted company at the corner of Tooley Street and Del Abelson walked off towards Abbey Street. Sue wasn't going to be very happy, he thought, but she would understand. The pressures would ease up very soon and then he would be able to give her the time she so deserved. Maybe a weekend at Brighton, or Hastings. In the meantime she would have to be patient. Surely she could understand that this was his big chance. Robbie Casey was a good teacher and his opinion counted for a lot in the higher echelons of the union. The door of opportunity was ajar at the moment, and one day soon Del Abelson was going to open it wide.

Chapter Thirty-Three

Sam Calkin took a return call from Northampton at ten minutes to twelve on Thursday morning, and with the phone resting against his hunched shoulder he furiously jotted down notes. A few minutes later he left the office and made his way to the Bull in Dockhead. The little waterfront pub had just opened and the landlord was busily getting ready for the invasion of rivermen. An elderly man sat smoking a clay pipe, a pint of beer in front of him, and two old ladies chatted together as they enjoyed their morning stout. The bar was grimy and smoke-stained and there were old pewter pots hanging from the oaken beams and framed photographs spaced along the roughly plastered walls.

'Expecting a rush?' Sam asked the landlord.

'Yeah, they won't be long,' he replied with a friendly grin. 'They're busy this week wiv the bacon ships.'

'Have you been here long?' Sam enquired as he paid for his beer.

'Six months.'

The reporter took a sip from his drink. 'I'm with the *Bulletin*,' he said. 'I was hoping to find out a little bit about a George Merry. Apparently this was his local.'

'Sorry I can't 'elp yer,' the landlord replied, and he pointed to the old man sitting alone. 'That's the gent yer want. Griff's bin a regular 'ere fer donkey's years, so 'e's always quick ter remind me.'

Sam smiled gratefully and went over to the table. 'Mind if I join you?' he asked.

'It's a free country,' Griff said curtly.

'I was wondering if you could help me.'

'I know yer was.'

'I beg your pardon?'

The old man took the stained clay pipe from his mouth and laid it down on the table. 'Why should yer wanna sit next ter me wiv all those empty seats, unless yer after somefink?' he said with raised eyebrows.

'I need a bit of information, but can I get you a drink first?' Sam offered.

'I only drink one o' those a day.'

Sam smiled to himself, realising that the ancient gent was trying him out. 'What about a short?'

'Now yer talkin'.'

'What'll it be?'

'It depends 'ow much info yer want,' Griff said with a sly grin.

'What about a double?'

''E does Johnny Walker's 'ere.'

'Right then, Johnny Walker's it'll be.'

When Sam came back with the whisky the old man placed it beside his pint of beer and studied it for a few moments. 'Fire away, son,' he said.

'Did you know a George Merry?' Sam asked him.

'Yeah, I knew 'im,' he replied. ''E was killed in the Blitz.'

'I work for the *Bulletin* and I'd like to do a bit about him,' Sam explained.

'A reporter. Don't get many o' them in 'ere,' Griff remarked.

'I understand George used to drink with a friend called Billy Button,' Sam prompted.

'Yeah, I knew 'im. Old Army man by all accounts.'

'That's right.'

'Billy still about? I ain't seen 'im in 'ere fer Gawd knows 'ow long.'

'Yes, he's still bright and breezy.'

'Billy used ter run the outin's,' the old man said as he carefully picked up the whisky. 'We used to 'ave some good outin's at one time. Don't 'ave 'em now though, not since this bloke took over. 'E's all right I s'pose, but not a patch on ole Bert Franklin. Lovely fella 'e was. Nuffing was too much trouble fer 'im.'

'What happened to him?' Sam enquired.

'' E retired after the pub got blasted durin' the Blitz,' Griff told him. 'It was shut up fer ages, an' when they opened it again after the war they put a manager in. Bloody useless 'e was. Always pissed, an' sarky wiv it. This guv'nor's more cheerful but 'e don't encourage pub outin's like ole Bert used to.'

'These outings were before the war, I take it?'

'Yeah. Sometimes we went ter Margate an' we used ter go down the 'op fields on ovver occasions,' Griff went on. 'The last one we went on was the summer before war broke out. There's a picture of it on the wall over there. The one nearest the karsey. Go an' fetch it.'

'Will the landlord mind?'

'Nah. Go an' get it.'

The old man filled his clay pipe and packed the dark tobacco down tightly into the bowl as he stared down at the framed photograph. 'That's Billy Button wiv the trilby on, an' that's George Merry standin' next to 'im,' he pointed out. 'That's Mickey Flynn an' there's Bonky Williams. Loved a piss-up 'e did. That's Nobby Vine an' there's young Stan Duggan. 'E was only eighteen there. Poor sod got killed in the war.'

Sam glanced up quickly at the old man. 'Charlie Duggan's son?'

'Yeah. That's Charlie in the back row, next ter Bonky. That's Maurice Carey at the end. 'Im an' Stan Duggan were the best o' mates.'

Sam scanned the faces. 'Did Maurice Carey's father ever go on the outings?'

'Joe Carey yer talkin' about. Yeah, Joe used ter go, but 'e wasn't on that outin'. 'E was in 'ospital at the time. Perforated ulcer I believe it was. Can't be sure now though.'

'Did George Merry have any special mates apart from Billy Button?' Sam asked.

'Bonky Williams an' Nobby Vine. They used ter go up ter the lead mills where George was night-watchin' an' fetch 'im down fer a drink. Funny ter watch it was. Sometimes 'e used ter get paralytic an' they'd 'ave ter carry 'im back. Gawd knows what would 'ave 'appened if 'is guv'nor 'ad found out. The state George used ter get in anyone could've robbed the bloody place blind. 'E would 'ave bin none the wiser.'

Sam got up to replenish the drinks. The pub was starting to fill up by now, and when he returned the old man seemed to be deep in thought as he puffed on his pipe.

'I read that bit in the *Bulletin* about those two blokes in Totterdown Street,' he said after a while. 'Did you write it?'

'Yes, that was me.'

'Yer won't mention anyfing about George Merry gettin' pissed that night, will yer?'

'I wouldn't dream of it,' Sam told him. 'Was he pissed that night?'

'Paralytic.'

'He did well then in getting that lorry out of the yard.'

'All I can say is, 'e made a quick recovery,' Griff replied, chuckling.

'I'm thinking of doing a piece about the Ship Lane shelter,' Sam said, probing.

The old man looked at him intently. 'Strange business that one.'

'Strange?'

'There was a lot o' talk at the time.'

'What sort of talk?'

'People died in that shelter. It don't do ter go delvin' too much inter fings like that.'

'Sometimes we have to delve. Sometimes it helps to uncover the truth.'

The old man puffed out a cloud of tobacco smoke and took the pipe out of his mouth. 'Let me tell yer somefing, son,' he began. 'There was a lot o' people died round 'ere in the Blitz. Some died 'cos they wouldn't use the shelters, an' ovvers died while they were fire-watchin' an' on air-raid warden's duties. Young lads got killed runnin' messages backwards an' forwards ter the wardens' posts, an' there was those who copped it fightin' the fires, but people didn't expect ter get killed in air-raid shelters unless they got a direct 'it. Five elderly people died in Ship Lane shelter, an' there was those who said it shouldn't 'ave 'appened. All right, the exit was blocked up an' it 'ad ter be cleared, an' that was understandable, but somefing was goin' on there that night what shouldn't 'ave bin.'

'Like what?'

'I dunno,' Griff replied with a shrug of his thin shoulders. 'Billy Button got pissed 'ere a while ago an' 'e was mumblin' on about it. 'E kept on about the poor bleeders in that shelter bein' sacrificed. Bonky an' Nobby warned 'im ter shut 'is row up an' it nearly come ter blows. In the end they bundled 'im out o' the pub, but by that time everybody 'ad 'eard what 'e said. People were sayin' that Bonky an' Nobby shut 'im up fer a reason.'

'What reason?'

'Gawd knows, but I remember finkin' that they couldn't get Billy out o' the pub quick enough.'

Sam glanced down at the photograph once more. 'Do most of those fellers still use the pub, pop?' he asked.

'Charlie Duggan don't, nor does the Careys, but most o' the ovvers do,' Griff replied.

Sam finished his drink and got ready to go. 'I'll leave you a tot over the counter, pop,' he said. 'Maybe we can have another chat later.'

The old man nodded as he puffed away on his pipe. 'Any time, son.'

On the way back to the newspaper office Sam Calkin

stopped at Ship Lane and made his way over the rubble to the ruined warehouse. He took a cloth tape-measure from his pocket and made a few calculations. It was gradually dropping into place, he realised. What happened that night was slowly becoming clear, but there was still a lot to be done before he could confront the persons responsible for the five deaths.

Queenie Alladyce had not had any inkling that her lodger felt the way he did towards her, until the débâcle on the wasteground beside the Bell. Now she was feeling a little bewildered. She wondered whether she should have made it clear to Benny that there was nothing romantic in her association with John Raney the oilshop man and she wasn't in the market for a new man in her life. As it was she had been very secretive and childish in the way she had acted and Benny felt threatened. It was quite understandable really. He might well be afraid that he would be asked to leave should she decide to marry Raney.

'Ow's yer jaw?' she asked as Benny struggled with his meal.

'It's still a bit stiff, but I'll survive,' he said melo-dramatically.

'Well, I've got no sympathy wiv yer,' Queenie told him firmly. 'Men of your age fightin' like a couple o' schoolkids was stupid.'

'It wasn't much of a fight, was it,' Benny said self-pityingly as he put down his knife and fork. 'One punch an' it was all over.'

'Yer gotta remember you ain't a violent man an' that big ape is,' Queenie said kindly. 'I'd prefer a nice gentleman sooner than a loudmouthed bully.'

Benny looked a little more happy as he picked up his mug of tea. 'What about you an' John Raney?' he asked tentatively.

'What about us?'

'Well, are yer – you know?'

'No I don't.'

'Are you finkin' o' marryin' the geezer?'

'We're just good friends, Benny, not that it's any business o' yours.'

'I've 'eard that one before.'

'Well, it's up ter you if yer believe me or not,' Queenie replied sharply. 'But fer what it's werf, I ain't got no intention o' marryin' Raney or any ovver man. Once was enough fer me.'

'If yer married me I'd look after yer, an' I wouldn't be nuffink like that ole bastard you 'ad before,' Benny said passionately.

Queenie felt a lump rise in her throat and she got up quickly to hide her emotion. 'You look after me?' she said with a brisk smile as she began to collect the dirty crockery. 'You need lookin' after yerself. Gawd knows what'd 'appen if I was laid up. Yer'd starve.'

'Oh no I wouldn't. I can cook, if I 'ave to,' Benny replied quickly.

Queenie picked up the pile of plates and cups. 'Let's see what yer like at dryin' up,' she said with a mocking smile.

Benny followed her out into the scullery. 'I'm only a few years older than you,' he went on.

'You're knockin' on seventy an' I'm only fifty-eight,' she replied.

'Yeah but I keep meself fit, an' I could still do a day's work if I 'ad to,' he told her.

'Benny, you're a nice man an' I've never 'ad any reason ter regret takin' you in as a lodger,' Queenie replied, 'but I don't want fings complicated by you finkin' that I'm out ter get married again. Let's just leave fings the way they are.'

'Are yer goin' over ter Raney's this evenin'?' he asked.

'I might do, an' on the ovver 'and I might not.'

'I thought yer might like ter come up the Bell fer a drink,' he said gingerly.

'I wouldn't be seen dead in that pub, not after the turn-out there,' she replied quickly.

'We don't 'ave ter sit wiv my pals,' Benny went on. 'We could sit in the corner, or go in the saloon bar.'

'Benny, the answer's no. You go up the pub an' I'll go over an' 'ave a chat wiv John.'

'Would you stop in if I did?'

'No.'

'Women. I'll never begin to understand 'em,' he grumbled.

'You're not meant to, Benny,' she chuckled.

Chapter Thirty-Four

Joe Carey bought the Friday edition of the *Bulletin* and saw that a Heavy Rescue team from Rotherhithe were featured in the weekly article.

'I wonder when our piece is goin' in there,' he said as Martha handed him a cup of tea.

'Give 'em time,' she told him. 'It might be next week's story.'

'I only 'ope it don't start people's tongues waggin' again,' he sighed.

'Joe, yer gettin' on my wick wiv this business,' Martha said irritably. 'What can they say, ovver than what yer told that reporter? Charlie's not bovvered about it, why should you be?'

'That's a lot you know,' Joe rounded on her. 'Charlie's worried sick.'

'Not accordin' ter Mabel 'e ain't.'

'She wouldn't admit it anyway.'

'Now listen 'ere,' Martha replied firmly as she sat down facing him. 'Sixteen years yer worked at Napier's, an' then yer go an' chuck the job in. Why? All right, I know it was gettin' yer down after all that time an' the people there weren't your sort, but it ain't like you ter let that type o' fing bovver yer ter that extent. I fink this business wiv the newspaper stories

375

'as upset yer nerves. Yer've bin a right misery lately. Even Ellie's noticed it.'

'What's she said?'

'Not a lot. Just that yer seem worried an' on edge lately.'

'She's the last ter talk,' Joe replied quickly. 'She sits up in that room of 'ers fer hours on end, supposedly writin' letters. I fink she's the one 'eadin' fer a nervous breakdown.'

'I'm not goin' inter that,' Martha said dismissively. 'I'm concerned about you. We all are.'

'I'll be all right, once I get a job sorted out,' he told her.

'Why don't yer try the Council?' she suggested.

'I'm goin' this mornin'.'

'Yeah, an' I've gotta get me shoppin' in,' she said, glancing at him as she got up.

Outside, the street seemed to be alive with speculation as Martha left for the market. Bessie Woodward was chatting to Nell Sharp and Marie Benjamin, and further along the turning Queenie was talking to Rosie Coleman and Minnie Sloan.

''Ello, gel,' Bessie said as Martha crossed the street. 'I've just bin tellin' Nell. They wanna talk to us about the shelter trouble.'

'Who does?' Martha asked.

'This reporter from the *Bulletin*, the one who's doin' the bits on the war.'

'What's 'e wanna know?'

'About what it was like that night.'

Martha felt her heart sink. Joe was going to be more on edge than ever when he found out, she thought.

'The reporter's comin' round ter Bessie's this afternoon,' Nell told her. ''E wants as many people as possible ter be there.'

'You'll come, won't yer, Marfa?' Bessie asked.

Martha nodded. 'Yeah, I'll be there.'

Bessie looked pleased. 'Yer'll 'ave ter lend me a few cups an' saucers, Nell. Now let's see. There's Granny Minto, Rosie Coleman, the scatty pair, you, me, Marie an' Marfa. Who else?'

'Queenie.'

'Gawd 'elp us, we mustn't ferget the Queen o' the May.'

Nell chuckled. 'That wouldn't do, would it.'

'What time's 'e comin'?' Martha asked.

'Four o'clock, so 'e said.'

'I'll tell Mabel,' Martha replied as she left for the market.

Sam Calkin walked into the office and nodded to Sue. 'I spoke to Mrs Woodward and she's fine about it,' he told her.

'I thought she would be,' Sue replied. 'She loves organising. I expect she'll have the whole street there.'

'The more the merrier.'

The phone rang and while Sue dealt with the caller Sam leaned on the counter patiently. 'I'm going down to the boat this weekend,' he remarked when she put the receiver down. 'Why don't you come with me?'

Sue wanted to say yes but held back. 'I don't know. I had arranged to go out.'

'The weather's going to stay fine by the look of it,' Sam said, smiling expectantly. 'It'll make a change to get away for the weekend.'

'Del is busy this weekend,' Sue said, weakening, 'but I'm supposed to be meeting some friends.'

Sam folded his arms on the counter. 'Look, I've got transport and the spare bedroom's all finished. I can pick you up early tomorrow morning and we can be in Burlingford in a couple of hours.'

'You've got transport?'

'Yeah, a BSA five hundred. You're not frightened of motor bikes are you?'

'But I'd need clothes and things.'

'All you'd need are your overnight things and a warm jumper,' he told her. 'I've got a leather coat you can wear for the journey, and goggles, and your toiletries can go in the pannier. So there's no problem.'

'Yes but . . .'

'I think you're looking for excuses,' he said, smiling broadly.

'No I'm not, but . . .'

'But nothing. Say you'll come.'

Sue thought about the alternative. With Del busy all weekend and Pamela away at Brighton with Tom the prospect of doing anything at all was remote. 'Yes, all right then.'

Sam punched the air enthusiastically. 'That's wonderful. I can show you the boat, and there's a nice little pub we can eat in. You'll love it.'

'What time will you pick me up?' she asked.

'Nine o'clock?'

'Look, it may be better if you meet me somewhere,' she told him. 'You understand.'

'Of course,' he replied. 'What about the station forecourt?'

'That'll be fine.'

The phone rang once more and as she reached for it Sam gave her a big smile before he went into the main office.

Frances Miller had been very busy in the glory hole, and when the young reporter appeared she waved him over. 'There was nothing whatsoever about where that business moved to after it was bombed out,' she said, reaching for a file. 'But I have found something,' she told him in a low voice. 'This explains why you couldn't find the firm in the phone book. It was tucked in amongst a stack of cuttings about birthdays and celebrations. I came across it by accident. Here it is.'

Sam took the cutting and read the article beneath a photograph of an old man sporting a large white beard and a monocle:

Nathan Goldberg celebrates his eightieth birthday today. Still hale and hearty despite his advancing years, he was in fine fettle when our reporter called on him at his home in Ilford. He wishes to be remembered to all his friends and business associates in Bermondsey where he traded for many years. During his working life Nathan Goldberg was very active in his support of various charities and institutions, as well as the Jewish Ex-servicemen's Association.

Although enjoying his retirement, Nathan still keeps in touch with the family business now run by his eldest son Emmanuel, who was there for his father's birthday celebrations. Emmanuel told our reporter that despite the restrictions imposed by clothes rationing, Goldberg Clothiers, now trading under Emmanuel Fashions, remains healthily solvent and a new factory in Bermondsey is planned for next spring employing fifty more workers.

'How do you do it, Frances?' Sam asked with a huge grin.

'It was pure luck,' she said coyly.

'You're too modest. Spencer should give you a rise immediately.'

Frances reached across her desk and picked up a slip of paper. 'There's the address and phone number of Emmanuel Fashions,' she told him.

Billy Button had been able to afford a room at the Deptford Men's Hostel and he was feeling quite opulent as he ordered a drink in a nearby pub. He had decided that his new-found wealth entitled him to the room for the next two weeks while he waited for the final instalment to be paid him, and he had also phoned the *Bulletin* with the hostel's telephone number. Things were certainly looking up, and it would be interesting to see how the article was written.

Billy sipped his drink thoughtfully. Once the proverbial hit the fan he might be called upon to give more details to the papers, and quite likely the police, if any action was to be taken, but as far as he was concerned they could whistle. He had no intention of doing anything of the sort. They would have to find him first, which would be very unlikely.

The old soldier finished his drink and walked back to the hostel, looking forward to an afternoon nap. Being a paying guest at the establishment was quite a different matter to begging for a bed for the night.

There was a certain dignity attached to being a patron with a few coppers in your pocket.

'Mr Button, there's a message for yer,' the porter told him.

'Who from?'

'A Mr Calkin. 'E phoned this mornin'. I tried ter catch yer but yer'd just left. 'E wants yer ter meet 'im at the same place at two o'clock this afternoon.'

Billy glanced up at the large clock over the reception desk. Ten minutes past one. Just enough time, he thought.

The walk to Creek Road took him fifteen minutes and there he had no trouble catching a tram to Tooley Street. At five to two Billy walked into the station pub and saw Calkin sitting at a table with a pint at his elbow. He bought a drink and sauntered over. 'It's a nice day,' he said casually.

'Billy, I want to check on something you told me,' Sam began keenly.

'Fire away.'

'That night those men came to take George Merry for a drink. Did you know them?'

'Nah, they were complete strangers.'

'What about the two who drove the lorry from the yard. Did you know them?'

'Nah, like I said, they were strangers.'

'Do you know Nobby Vine and Bonky Williams?'

Billy shook his head. 'Can't say as I do.'

'Well, I've got news for you, Billy,' the reporter said leaning forward over the table. 'I saw a picture of you yesterday. It's hanging up in the Bull at Dockhead. An old chap there told me you used to run the men's outings.'

'Yeah, that's right.'

'And you still say you don't know Bonky Williams or Nobby Vine?'

'I might know 'em by sight,' Billy replied defensively. 'It was a long time ago.'

'The summer of thirty-nine as a matter of fact,' Sam reminded him. 'Eight years to be exact. You can remember six years back though. Your description of that night in May was pretty good.'

'What yer gettin' at, son?'

Sam stared at him, his eyes hardening. 'What I'm getting at, Billy, is that you've not been exactly truthful. It's hardly credible that you'd drink in the Bull regularly, organise the outings, and yet not know any of the customers who went on them.'

'Some I knew, some I didn't.'

'Bonky Williams and Nobby Vine were George Merry's drinking partners. They were the two who collected him from the lead mills and took him back from the Bull on that night in May, weren't they?'

'I can't remember.'

'Did you know Maurice Carey or Stanley Duggan? Don't lie to me, Billy,' the reporter told him sharply. 'They were in that photo of the last outing in thirty-nine.'

'Yeah, I knew 'em,' Billy said hesitantly.

'I'm putting it to you that Maurice Carey and Stanley Duggan were with the other two men and it was those two who collected the lorry from the lead mills that night. You saw them, didn't you, Billy?'

'I told yer, son, I didn't see nuffink. I was told ter keep me 'ead down, remember.'

'People died that night,' Sam said darkly. 'They died

because they couldn't get out of that emergency exit in time. Why? I'll tell you why. The lorry that was taken from Moxen's Lead Mills was blocking the exit, that's why. It was backed up against the wall, and I can prove it. You must have seen the lorry parked in that position when you ran out of the mills. Christ, man! It was right opposite. You must have seen it.'

'I already told yer,' Billy whined. 'There was smoke an' flames everywhere. I just ducked down an' run out o' the lane as fast as I could. I didn't stop ter look around.'

'Give me names, Billy,' Sam pressed him. 'You saw the man on the fire escape. You know who it was.'

'If I did know I couldn't tell yer,' Billy said shaking his head. 'They'd get me. They'd 'ave me 'ung, drawn an' quartered.'

'Who would?'

'That's all I'm gonna say.'

'We had a deal, remember,' Sam said pointedly.

'I've kept my end o' the deal. I told yer what I know.'

'I can't print part of the story,' Sam told him. 'It wouldn't be right.'

'You don't 'ave ter print names,' Billy countered. 'Yer could say the information was anonymous.'

Sam leaned back in his chair. 'Tell me something, Billy. Why did you bother to contact me in the first place? You must have known I'd check out the facts, make enquiries.'

'I was desperate,' the elderly man replied with a sigh. 'You don't know what it's like ter be down on yer luck wiv no roof over yer 'ead. I need the money. I didn't expect yer ter go into it the way yer did. You're not a reporter, you're a bloody Sherlock 'Olmes.'

'If I withhold your name the police'll be down on our newspaper like bats out of hell,' Sam told him.

'All right, print me moniker, but don't expect me ter name names,' Billy said firmly. 'I didn't see who it was an' I didn't know 'em. That's what yer gotta print. Anyfing else an' I'll deny it. That won't do yer poxy paper any good, will it.'

Sam nodded slowly. 'Okay, Billy. I'll make do with what I've got.'

'When will I get the money?'

'Soon as the story gets into print.'

'When will that be?'

'Maybe next week, but certainly by the following week.'

Billy took a sip of his drink. 'I'm sorry I couldn't 'elp yer any more, son, but you know 'ow it is. It's a question o' survival.'

Sam buttoned up his coat. 'When I leave here, Billy, I've got to see a group of women who were in the Ship Lane shelter that night. It was a question of survival for them too. More to the point, five elderly people died there through a criminal act, and I'm committed to exposing it, come hell or high water. You could help me, and you'd be protected. Think on it.'

Billy Button watched with a solemn face as the young reporter walked out of the pub. He had already made his decision.

Chapter Thirty-Five

Sue Carey was feeling guilty as she made her way up the steep flight of steps that led from Tooley Street to London Bridge Station. As far as her family were concerned she was going to spend the weekend in Broadstairs with Frances Miller and her sister. Tom had given her a cheeky look when she mentioned the trip to the family and Aunt Ellie was predictably critical, mumbling on about the tendency of modern young women to go gallivanting all over the place without any fear. Her mother though had seemed pleased. She felt that Del Abelson was too wrapped up in union business for his own good and it would serve him right if she found someone else.

Sue smiled wryly to herself. Sam Calkin was a very handsome young man with ambitions of his own, though she was not quite sure in which direction they were pointing at this particular moment in time. In any case she could look after herself. It was going to be a weekend away from the grime and smoke of London, and there were no strings attached, she reminded herself.

She saw him standing beside the motor cycle with his goggles pushed up on to his forehead and she walked up to him with a smile.

'I've got you a leather coat to wear,' he said unfolding it. 'You'll need it. As a matter of fact it used to belong to my ex-girlfriend. She was about your size.'

Sue looked at him quizzically as she tried it on. 'A souvenir?'

Sam shrugged his shoulders. 'It just got left behind. I don't think she'd need it now anyway. She married a City gent and last I heard of her she'd moved to Croydon. Can you imagine him travelling up to London in his pin-stripe suit and brolly on something like this?'

'No, not really,' Sue laughed as she buttoned up the coat.

'Put these on,' Sam said, handing her a pair of thick goggles.

She squeezed them down around her eyes then pulled the coat collar up over the back of her fair hair. 'You won't drive too fast will you?' she said in a nervous voice.

Sam laughed. 'You don't drive a motor bike, you ride one. Anyway I won't go too fast, I promise. Have you ever been on the back of a bike?' Sue shook her head. 'Well, the thing to remember is, hold on tight and move with me. When I lean the bike over on bends you lean with me. It's simple really.'

Sue stood back while he kick-started the machine and she looked hesitantly at him.

'Well, come on then, get on,' he said as he lowered his goggles over his eyes.

She gathered up the ends of her long leather coat and got astride. 'I'm ready,' she shouted above the noise of the engine.

'Hold me round my waist. It's all right, I won't bite you,' he shouted back.

They set off, and as Sam twisted the throttle and the machine surged forward Sue felt a sudden burst of exhilaration. They weaved in and out of the morning traffic and gathered speed as the road ahead widened, the young woman all the while holding on very tightly. Sam called out something over his shoulder but it was lost on the wind and she turned her head and rested it on his broad back. The traffic thinned out to a car or two and soon they were roaring up the steep hill to Blackheath. Sue felt a prickly tingling in her cheeks and she dared to look over her shoulder as the built-up areas were very soon left behind. The noise of the machine was now a steady throb as it ate up the miles, and she was glad of the leather coat and goggles as the wind rushed past her ears and stung her face.

'We'll stop up ahead,' Sam shouted over his shoulder.

Sue was glad to stretch her legs when they pulled into a parking area that boasted a small tea cabin. 'It was really exciting,' she enthused as she ripped off her goggles.

'Yeah, there's nothing like it, when the weather's nice,' Sam replied.

Armed with mugs of sweet tea and cream buns, they went and sat at a rickety table on the veranda.

'Did the meeting with the women go off all right?' Sue asked.

Sam nodded. 'You were right. Bessie Woodward loves to organise. She had them all sorted out by the time I got there. Old Mrs Minto wasn't too forthcoming at first, but once she got started she was very open.'

'Did you get everything you wanted?'

'Almost.'

'Will you be seeing them again?'

'I'd like to see Albert Price if I can,' Sam told her.

'Wasn't he there yesterday?' Sue queried. 'I thought Granny Minto would have nagged him into going. He was in the shelter that night.'

'Mrs Minto told me that Albert wasn't up to sitting with all the women. Apparently it was he who led them to the emergency exit.'

'It must have been terrible,' Sue said sadly.

Sam nodded and took a sip of his tea as he thought about what he had gathered so far. The whole thing was becoming clearer now and it troubled him. Joe Carey and Charlie Duggan were implicated in some way, he felt sure, but it was also obvious that Sue was completely in the dark. She had been very helpful in suggesting the names of people who might be able to help him and she had never shown any reluctance to assist in any way she could. It was hardly the behaviour of someone who was guarding a family secret.

'Penny for your thoughts,' Sue said smiling.

'Oh, I was just thinking about yesterday.'

'What about yesterday?'

'When you asked me what transport I had and I told you it was a motor bike. Your face was a picture.'

'I was surprised, and a bit scared,' Sue replied with a smile.

Sam waited for the young woman to finish her tea and bun and then he picked up his goggles from the table. 'Half an hour and we'll be there,' he told her.

The sun was climbing high in a crystal blue sky as they rode on to the Maidstone Road and accelerated. Trees and fields flashed by and Sue felt the wind clutch at her hair and a sensation of wild freedom welling inside her as their speed increased. They hurtled along for about half an hour and then Sam suddenly eased back on the throttle and leaned the machine over to slip into a side road. It was quiet now, with no other vehicles around, and the young man slowed a little further as they passed under an archway formed by leaning birch trees. He veered to the left and Sue caught a glimpse of the signpost that said Burlingford two miles. She could taste the salty tang in the wind now, and when Sam finally turned into what seemed little more than a path and pulled up she could only stare.

'Well, this is it,' he said cheerfully as he tore off his goggles.

The small cottage was situated in a little clearing. It had a roof of thatch and vines clung to the old walls and almost hid the wide, low door. Tubs of geraniums and sweet peas were spaced along the frontage, and to the left there was a chopping-block with an axe embedded in it. Overhead the sky was still cloudless and the silence was so deep it could be felt.

Sue got off the motor cycle and looked around as she stretched her legs. 'It's so quiet,' she said reverently.

'That's what Dad liked about the cottage,' Sam told her. 'It is pretty isolated, although the river's only a short way along the lane.'

Sam unlocked the front door and stepped back to let Sue go in. Her heart leapt when she saw the wide open fireplace piled with logs, the low-beamed ceiling and the roughly plastered walls which were crossed with dark-stained wood. The armchairs and settee were covered in a chintz fabric and there was a low coffee table in the middle of the small room, complete with a flowering plant in a pewter pot. A few pictures of river scenes were arranged around the walls and over the fireplace a blunderbuss and a pair of foils were hung from large dark nails. Coconut mats were spaced about the polished wooden floor, and to the left of the door was a large carved sideboard. A solitary picture frame stood on the polished top and Sam reached for it. 'That's my dad,' he said proudly.

Sue studied the portrait of the white-haired man wearing a naval cap at a jaunty angle and then looked up at Sam. 'I can see the likeness,' she remarked. 'You've got his eyes.'

Sam took the picture from her and replaced it on the sideboard. 'Let me show you where you'll be sleeping,' he said.

The steep stairs creaked, the landing seemed to lean and Sue was aware of the distinct smell of lavender. Sam opened the far door. 'This is the room I've just finished,' he said, standing back for her to enter. 'You'll be quite comfortable in here.'

'It's lovely,' she gasped.

'You can just see the river from the window,' Sam told her.

Sue moved forward and eased back the lace curtain as she peered out.

'Look, over there, just above the tree line,' Sam said, standing close to her as he pointed.

The young woman could smell leather and feel his arm against hers and her face grew hot. 'I can see it now,' she told him.

'I'll show you the bathroom and when you're ready I'll take you down to the boat,' he said as he moved away. 'There's a little inn by the river. We can have our lunch there if you like.'

'It sounds lovely,' Sue said smiling.

Sam went down to the sitting room and took off his leather coat before sinking down into the deep cushions of an armchair. Was this a good idea after all? he wondered. He had contrived to spend a weekend with a very pretty young woman who he hoped had a liking for him, while at the same time he was trying to uncover a secret which could well have disastrous consequences for both her and her family. It was bordering on stupidity, if not wilful cruelty. He had allowed his feelings for her to obscure his better judgement, but she had got to him. She had captured something inside him the first time he spoke to her and he had been unable to get her out of his mind.

Footsteps on the stairs interrupted his thoughts and he stood up as Sue bounced into the room.

'I'm ready,' she said with a big grin.

Sam looked at her as she stood in the doorway and he was taken by her beauty. Her face was flushed and her large bright eyes seemed full of expression. She had tied her soft fair hair back with a narrow ribbon and she looked slim and shapely, her firm breasts prominent under her flowered summer dress. He wanted to take her in his arms there and then and taste her sensuous lips but instead he just smiled quickly, reached for a windcheater and then took her arm as they walked out of the cottage and strolled along the narrow lane.

As they rounded a bend Sue saw the river, shimmering like liquid silver in the bright sunlight, and Sam laid his hand on her shoulder as he pointed. 'That's Burlingford. You can just see the pub. Beyond that there's two shops, a crumbling church and a few cottages. I think it was forgotten when they built the new road system. It's like going back in time.'

They walked towards the river and Sam nodded. 'There she is.'

The boat was propped up on a gantry on shingle near the water's edge, and it looked tiny by comparison with the other craft which were moored along a wooden jetty further on. An old man was sitting fishing at the end of the landing and Sue sighed at the idyllic peacefulness of the scene.

Sam picked up a short ladder from under the gantry and set it against the hull. 'I'll go up first,' he said.

Sue gingerly followed him up the steps and he grabbed her around the waist with both hands to set her down on the deck. The cabin was tiny and they had to duck their heads as they entered. 'I'm going to raise this,' he told her. 'My dad was only five foot two.'

Sue could smell the river, and as she listened to the soft sound of water washing over pebbles she sighed deeply. 'It's intoxicating,' she said almost breathlessly.

Sam was standing close to her and his eyes lingered on hers for a few moments. 'You're intoxicating,' he replied in a low voice.

Sue felt her face getting hot and she stepped out of the cabin. 'When do you hope to get the boat finished?' she asked.

He shrugged his shoulders. 'There's so much to do. This decking needs work on it and the engine needs stripping down. I've got to work on the hull too. I'd say a year, at the rate I'm going.'

They climbed down from the gunwale and strolled

leisurely along the water's edge until they were almost opposite the little inn. Sam picked up a pebble and skimmed it over the water, then he turned and faced the young woman. 'I'm glad you agreed to come with me, Sue,' he said quietly. 'It gives us the opportunity of getting to know each other better. There are so many questions I'd like to ask.'

'A woman has to preserve some mystique,' she replied, mocking him with her smile as she moved across to an upturned rowing boat and sat down on it.

He followed her over and stood with one foot resting on the hull of the damaged craft. 'Are you going steady with that feller you told me about?'

She nodded. 'Steady, yes, but as I've already said before, it's a question of sharing Del Abelson with his work. I feel a bit neglected. I don't know, maybe I'm being too possessive, but it's the way I am.'

'Del Abelson's a fool,' he said with feeling. 'If I were in his place I'd make sure you weren't neglected.'

'I believe you would, Sam,' she said quietly.

He rested his arm on his knee and leaned towards her. 'I like you, Sue. I like you a lot, and I hope you come to feel the way I do.'

'I do like you, Sam,' she replied. 'That's why I agreed to come here with you.'

'Did it cause any problems at home?' he asked.

'They think I'm with Frances Miller. We're supposed to be staying in Broadstairs with her sister.'

Sam smiled. 'Very devious.'

'Sometimes a girl has to be,' she told him.

'Are you a close family?' he asked.

'Yes we are. My brother Tom still lives at home and our elder brother Maurice calls round sometimes.

Oh and there's Aunt Ellie. She's not married and she's been living with us since the beginning of the war.'

'It must be nice to have a close family,' Sam remarked. 'I've missed out on that.'

'Isn't there anyone in your life?' she asked.

He shook his head. 'No, but I'd like there to be.'

Sue looked up at him. 'At least you've got this place to come to, and your boat. It must be nice to have a haven to flee to whenever the mood takes you.'

'Those sort of things are meant for sharing, Sue,' he said with a longing in his eyes. 'I mean with someone special.'

Sue got up and stretched herself. 'It's a lovely day,' she sighed.

'We could get something to eat, and then we could walk to the crossroads and catch the bus to Maidstone,' he suggested.

She turned to face him. 'Tell me, Sam. If you were alone today what would you do?'

'I'd have lunch and a pint,' he replied as he took her arm and led her across the shingle towards the pub, 'then I'd lie in the sun for a while, then when I was good and ready I'd set to work scraping the hull of my boat.'

'Then that's what we'll do,' she said resolutely.

After a lunch of bread and cheese with pickles which they washed down with bitter shandies, they strolled back along the water's edge and then rested in the shade of the boat with their backs propped against the gantry timbers.

'I think I'll make a start,' Sam said after a while. 'Why don't you make yourself comfortable on deck. I've got some cushions in the cabin.'

'I was in the ATS remember,' Sue replied quickly. 'You give me a scraper and I'll lend a hand.'

Sam climbed into the boat and threw a pair of dungarees down on to the shingle. 'Try those on,' he said.

Sue scrambled into the large overalls and stood with her arms outstretched for effect. Sam tried to remain straight-faced but he ended up shaking his head and laughing as she paraded in front of him. 'They are a bit large,' he remarked, still grinning.

'I'll fix 'em,' she said, turning up the trouser bottoms and the sleeves. 'There we are. Now, where's that scraper?'

They set to work with a vengeance on the flaking paint, Sam humming tunelessly, and they rested their aching arms occasionally as they admired their efforts. Neither was aware of the time until long shadows had crept across the shingle and a cool breeze stirred.

'It must be getting on for teatime,' Sam remarked.

They spent the next half-hour rubbing down the woodwork with sandpaper and then he called a halt. 'There's been more work done on this boat today than in the past six months,' he told her. 'C'mon, let's go back and clean up.'

'Is there anything I can cook for tea?' Sue asked as they made their way back to the cottage.

Sam chuckled. 'I brought a few things down in the pannier. I'm going to demonstrate my cooking skills.'

'I can do it,' Sue volunteered.

'I wouldn't hear of it,' he replied, reaching his hand down to clasp hers. 'You can relax in your room for a while, you've earned it. I'll give you a call when tea's ready.'

The evening sun had sunk down behind the trees, leaving a marbled sky of red and purple flame as Sue stretched out on the bed to ease her aching back. A gentle breeze drifted in through the wide open window and rustled the lace curtains. It had been a day to remember, she sighed.

A soft tap on the door startled her and she realised that she must have fallen asleep.

'Tea's ready.'

Sue could smell cooking as she got up and brushed out her hair before going downstairs. When she walked into the sitting room she could hardly contain her surprise as she saw the candle burning in a wax-coated bottle in the centre of the table.

'Table for two, madam,' Sam joked as he led her over and pulled a chair back for her.

'This is lovely,' she sighed.

'I'd try the food first,' he said out of the corner of his mouth as he went back to the kitchen.

The candle flickered, the sole light in the low-ceilinged room, and while they ate Sam told her of his plans to finish the boat by the autumn. The meal itself was a simple grill of eggs, beans and sausages, but they were ravenous from all their hard work and quickly cleared their plates. After the warmth of the day it was becoming chilly and Sam lit the fire as they moved over to the settee. The logs crackled and the aroma of bubbling pine sap permeated through the room as the first heavy spots of rain began to fall.

Sam had been talking about the intricacies of river navigation with his arm resting on the back of the settee, and then in the pregnant silence that followed and with a suddenness that surprised the young woman he slipped his arm around her shoulders and leaned over to kiss her gently. It was not a fiery, passionate kiss, more a spontaneous gesture of gratitude for her being with him, but as their lips touched she pressed herself to him. This was not real, she thought, heedless of the danger. She was in control, unconcerned that she was deceiving Del Abelson. He wasn't here with her, but Sam Calkin was.

A log rolled in the fire, sending a shower of sparks upwards as Sam pulled her from the settee and took her hand to lead her from the room, up the creaking stairs to the darkness of her bedroom. She could feel his body pressing against hers, feel his roused passion as his hands sought the buttons of her dress. This was unreal, a brief moment in time, and she wanted to savour it to the full. Her trembling hands unbuttoned his shirt as he fumbled with her brassiere, and then she pulled him down on to the bed, his lips closing over her firm nipple as he slid her panties down over her thighs. He raised himself above her, his face flushed in the darkness, his breath coming fast, then he lowered himself to meet her lips, letting her guide him into her hot desiring body.

The night breeze rustled the curtains and somewhere in the woods a creature screamed as Sam moved on her, slowly and deliberately at first, then with a deep, rhythmical stroke which quickly grew in intensity. She eased her hips forward to meet his thrusts, gasping as the delicious feeling grew into a flood of passion, groaning as she struggled to hold on. She could sense he was ready now, and as his body shuddered she let the waves of wild desire cascade.

They lay together still locked hungrily, his lips

tasting hers, their arms wrapped around each other, and a crescent moon rose above the trees to send a cold light into the room. The moment was theirs to savour, a moment out of time to remember, and somewhere in the darkness a lonely creature of the night cried out once more.

Chapter Thirty-Six

Maisie Lawrence took the powder compact from her handbag and passed it over to the grey-haired man sitting opposite her in the hotel lounge. ''Andle it wiv care,' she said smiling. 'I took me bleedin' life in me 'ands gettin' that.'

The man returned her smile and gingerly opened the silver compact. 'You did very well,' he said as he studied the impressions in the wax.

'The small one's the alarm key,' she told him. 'The control panel's just inside the front door ter the right at eye level.'

He nodded and reached into his coat pocket. 'There we are, my dear, and be careful,' he said as he handed her a sealed envelope. 'You know his haunts well enough by now, so take my advice and stay well away.'

'Don't worry,' she said smiling confidently. 'I can look after meself.'

'If you do need any help, feel free,' he told her. 'It might be an idea to take a short holiday until this business is finished.'

'I might just do that,' she remarked.

The man got up to leave. 'One more thing, Maisie. The photos. We don't intend to use them unless we have to.'

'I understand,' she replied.

'Goodbye, my dear,' he said, extending his hand. 'We're all indebted to you.'

She watched him leave and smiled to herself as she took out a small flat case from her handbag and selected a gold-tipped cigarette. They were indebted, he had said. She was the one who was indebted. The chance to be a part of Miles-Strickland's downfall had been too good an opportunity to pass up, and it would surely be a comfort to her very good friend Janice. She still bore the scars of that unspeakable monster's depravity and as a result would be unable to work for a long time yet.

Maisie looked across the wide lounge and saw that the young man was still looking in her direction. He was a visitor to London, she guessed. He looked very nice, and well heeled too judging by the cut of his clothes. Maybe he needed some company. She cast a glance towards him briefly then she lowered her head, dabbing at her eyes with a lace handkerchief. He was coming over now and she sighed sadly for effect.

'I hope you don't mind the intrusion, but I noticed you seem upset,' he said in a cultured voice. 'Is there anything I can do?'

Lorna Mae dabbed at her eyes once more. 'The gentleman who's just left happens to be my uncle,' she told him, 'and he's just brought me some bad news.'

Winkle was roused from his sleep early on Monday morning by the impatient Monty Groves. 'Get yer bloody strides on an' let's get goin',' he barked.

'All right, all right,' the little man complained. 'Give

us a chance ter wake up.'

'It's bloody nigh dinnertime,' Monty told him. 'C'mon, move yerself, they don't like bein' kept waitin'.'

Winkle grumbled under his breath as he scrambled into his clothes. 'Is this the ovver job I bin told about?' he asked as they hurried from the lodgings into a waiting taxi.

'Yer'll get the proper s.p. when yer get there,' Monty replied, giving the safe cracker a sideways glance as the taxi drew away from the kerb.

'Where we goin'?' Winkle asked as Tower Bridge loomed ahead.

'Over the water.'

'I can see that. Whereabouts over the water?'

'We're goin' ter the Cumberland 'Otel. I just 'ope they let you in. Yer look like a poxy tramp,' Monty growled.

'We could always go in the tradesmen's entrance,' Winkle said, grinning.

'You just do as yer told,' the villain replied. 'I don't want you givin' me any grief.'

Winkle folded his arms over his chest as the taxi swung into the City. 'I wouldn't dream of it, Monty.'

When Tom Carey walked into the transport yard on Monday morning he saw a few of the drivers talking to Bernie Catchpole, their shop steward. 'What's up?' he asked.

'We're 'avin' a quick meetin' before we go out,' one of the men told him.

Tom looked over to the small cabin which was serving as the temporary office and he could see

Joe Brady talking to his transport manager in the doorway.

The shop steward led the way over to a lorry shed and raised his hands for attention. 'Now we gotta make this quick,' he told them. 'Brady's given us ten minutes ter make our minds up. It seems that the ovver depot's a driver down an' Shorty Lockwood's bin told ter go over there fer the day.'

'I told Toby I wasn't gonna work wiv scabs,' Shorty cut in.

'All right, let me finish,' Bernie said impatiently. 'I've bin ter see Brady an' 'is answer was, eivver Shorty goes over there or 'e can collect 'is cards.'

'That's bloody outrageous,' one of the drivers growled.

'Brady's gettin' too flash,' another remarked.

'So what do we do, Bernie?' Tom asked.

The shop steward looked around at the gathering. 'I fink we should call Brady's bluff.'

'We gotta stick tergevver this time,' one of the drivers said loudly.

'What about the rest of yer?' Bernie asked.

The nodding of heads encouraged him to go on. 'Anyone against backin' Shorty? Right then, wait 'ere. Shorty, come wiv me.'

'Times seem to 'ave changed,' Tom remarked to the driver standing next to him. 'It wasn't so long ago that Bernie 'ammered that little feller an' now they look like ole buddies.'

A few minutes later a dejected-looking pair walked back to the shed.

' 'E give me me poxy cards would yer believe,' Shorty announced to the assembled drivers.

'Toby wants yer, Tom,' the steward told him.

The young man sauntered over to the cabin. 'What's up?' he asked.

'Nuffing's up,' Toby replied. 'You're workin' out o' the ovver depot terday.'

'I don't fink so,' Tom said with a shake of his head.

Brady looked up from his desk. 'It's eivver that or yer cards,' he declared with an edge to his voice.

'Shorty got it about right,' Tom replied. 'We don't work wiv scabs.'

'Give 'im 'is cards,' Brady growled.

'Yer better get the rest o' the lads' cards ready while yer at it,' the young man told him with a cold smile.

'You never learn, do yer,' Brady snarled at him.

Tom fixed him with a hard stare then he cast his eyes around the cabin. 'I could say that about you,' he replied before walking out into the yard.

Bernie Catchpole looked serious. 'You too?'

Tom nodded. 'I just 'ope they'll all back yer.'

Bernie pulled a face. 'I'm goin' back in there an' 'avin' it out wiv 'im.'

'I know we've 'ad our differences, but I wish yer luck,' Tom said, holding out his hand.

Bernie smiled generously. 'I've learnt a lot since I've bin the shop steward 'ere,' he said, clasping Tom's hand. 'There's no 'ard feelin's, mate.'

Martha Carey was wondering how Joe was getting on at the Council that morning as she gathered up the potato peelings in the newspaper and slipped them into the dustbin under the sink. Maybe a change of job would be no bad thing at his time of life, she thought. He had not been happy at Napier's and from what he had told her about the people working there he was better off out of it. She lit the gas under the kettle and went into the parlour.

Ellie looked up with a smug expression on her thin pale face. 'I bet you're wondering who those two letters are from,' she said.

'Well, ter be honest it did cross me mind,' Martha replied, 'but I wouldn't wanna intrude on yer privacy.'

'They're both from publishers,' Ellie told her with a sly smile.

'Publishers?'

'Yes, publishers.'

'Well?'

'I sent them both an outline of the story I'm writing. This publisher wasn't interested, but this one's more enthusiastic,' Ellie said, waving the letter. 'They said they'd like to see the first few chapters.'

'You mean ter tell me yer writin' a book?' Martha queried with an incredulous expression on her face.

'Yes I am.'

'So that's why yer've bin up all hours scribblin' away.'

'Two years I've been working on it and it's almost finished,' Ellie told her proudly.

'Well, I never did,' Martha replied with a slow shake of her head. 'Just fancy. Our Ellie, writin' a book. D'yer realise yer could be famous? 'Ere, what's it about?'

'It's a romance.'

'Your romance?'

'Certainly not,' Ellie said firmly.

'We'd better drink ter your success,' Martha remarked. 'I'll go an' make the tea.'

A few minutes later Tom came in. 'Any tea in the pot, Muvver?' he enquired.

'What you doin' 'ome at this time o' the mornin'?' she asked.

'We've all got the sack,' he replied.

'All of yer?'

'Yep.'

'What for?'

'It's a long story, Ma.'

'You ain't goin' all secretive on me too, are yer?' she enquired. 'Yer Aunt Ellie's just told me she's writin' a book. Apparently she's bin at it fer two years would yer believe.'

'Yeah, she told me a couple o' days ago,' Tom replied as he sat down at the small table.

'Yet she didn't tell me,' Martha said with irritation. 'Did she fink I'd laugh at 'er?'

'You know Aunt Ellie.'

'Yeah, don't I just. Anyway, what's all this about you gettin' the sack?'

'It's over scab labour.'

Martha shook her head slowly. 'First yer farvver an' now you. I dunno, it's like everyfing's turned upside down lately.'

'Don't worry, Ma,' Tom said kindly. 'There's plenty o' jobs fer drivers, an' Dad won't be out o' collar fer long.'

'I 'ope not,' Martha sighed. ''E's bin worryin' me lately.'

There was a knock at the front door and when Martha opened it she found Mabel standing there with a worried look on her face. 'I'm just off down the market,' she said. 'I thought I'd better tell yer. My Charlie's just bin in. 'E was doin' a fittin' job in Abbey Street this mornin' an' 'e bumped inter Griff Morley. Griff told 'im that reporter was in the Bull askin' 'im questions about George Merry, an' then it came up about Ship Lane. Apparently the bloke seemed very interested in what 'appened that night. Anyway, Griff said that 'e didn't entertain 'im, but it makes yer fink.'

Martha sighed deeply. 'I dunno, it's all worry, what wiv one fing an' anuvver. Are yer sure yer won't come in?'

'No, I gotta get goin',' Mabel replied. 'Just thought I'd let yer know.'

'All I want now is fer Sue ter tell me she's pregnant, God ferbid,' Martha mumbled to herself as she walked back down the passage.

Chapter Thirty-Seven

Sam Calkin was shown into the well-furnished office at Emmanuel Fashions in Whitechapel and was received cordially by the managing director. He was a heavy-set man in his mid-thirties with thick dark hair, dressed in a pin-stripe suit and immaculate shirt and tie. As he came from behind his desk and held out his large hand Sam caught a glimpse of the heavy rings he was wearing and he smiled amiably. 'Nice of you to make the time to see me, Mr Goldberg,' he said.

'I was intrigued by your phone call to be honest,' the clothier replied as he motioned the reporter into a chair. 'Our firm's always had a good rapport with the *Bulletin*.'

'I'll get straight to the point,' Sam said. 'As I told you on the phone, I fully believe that the robbery from your factory in Bermondsey was linked to the shelter tragedy, and I felt that I should talk to you about it before we went to print.'

'It was certainly a shock,' Goldberg replied. 'Obviously I'd like to help you, but I don't see how. The robbery was reported in the *Bulletin* at the time but nothing came out of the police investigation. Anyway I'd be interested to know how you made the connection.'

'I have an eye witness who actually saw a robbery in progress at the Ship Lane warehouse,' Sam began, 'and he thought that there were carpets being removed. It was only after going through old paper cuttings that I came across the robbery from your factory which had taken place a few weeks earlier. I couldn't find any further information and I had to assume you never recovered the rolls of cloth.'

'No we never did,' Goldberg confirmed. 'The van was found empty in Rotherhithe, which as you know is only a short distance from the factory we had in Tower Bridge Road. We lost ten rolls of satin and a couple of rolls of best quality silk, as well as five rolls of navy blue serge. It was quite a haul. As a matter of fact we'd only just taken delivery of the satin and silk.'

'Could it have been an inside job?' Sam asked.

'It's possible I suppose, but I prefer not to think so,' the clothier replied. 'My father was running the business at the time and he was very well liked. All our employees were loyal and hard-working. Some of them came over with us when we opened up in Whitechapel. Actually we're planning to open another factory in Bermondsey next spring. Our original premises in Tower Bridge Road were destroyed the same night as the Ship Lane warehouse.'

Sam stroked his chin thoughtfully. 'From what you said about only just getting delivery of the cloth I feel that it might well have been an inside job,' he went on, 'and to sell that amount on the black market would need some planning. Where better to hide the cloth for the time being than at a Council store, amongst rolls of carpets, bedding and the like salvaged from bombed-out homes.'

Goldberg nodded. 'Our driver always filled in a log book, and by checking the end-of-day mileage the police established that the van only travelled three miles. It's two miles from Tower Bridge Road to where it was recovered in Rotherhithe. The cloth had to be dropped off locally, but where? It was like looking for a needle in a haystack. The warehouse in Ship Lane could well have been the place.'

'I'm sure of it,' Sam replied. 'Working-class people from Bermondsey could not be expected to have expensive carpets, certainly none worth taking such a risk for.'

'So you hope to make this public?'

'Yes I do,' Sam told him.

'You explained on the phone that you were writing articles about the heroic deeds of Bermondsey people during the Blitz,' Goldberg reminded him. 'Is this to be an independent article?'

'In one respect,' Sam replied. 'But with the glory comes the shame. I hope to prove that it was the warehouse robbery which cost the lives of five elderly people, and I'm almost there.'

'I look forward to reading your article,' Goldberg remarked.

'I'll be glad to send you a copy,' Sam said with a warm smile as he got up to leave.

'I'll see you out,' the clothier told him. 'I've got to go down to the cutting floor anyway.'

As they reached the ground-floor level and walked along the passageway Sam's eye was taken once again by the big bronze plaque hanging on the dark wall. 'That's rather impressive,' he said to Goldberg.

The clothier nodded. 'My father decided to have that

done, in memory of the five workers of ours who lost their lives while on active service.' Sam glanced up at the plaque and saw engraved towards the top of the list: Leading Seaman Stanley Duggan, R.N.

Sue Carey found it hard to concentrate her mind on the job in hand after the glorious weekend at Burlingford and she was feeling nervous about seeing Sam again. He had not come into work that morning and the message she had was that he was out doing interviews and would not be in till late afternoon. Saturday night had been wonderful, she thought with a sigh, and Sunday too. She had risen early and was standing by the window when Sam came to her. He took her by surprise, pulling her back against him to kiss her neck and her ears, filling her whole body with delicious sensations, and as the warm rising sun dissolved the morning mist she gave herself to him once more. There had been no promises of undying love, nor whispered words of young infatuation. It was purely a stolen dalliance for both of them, she reminded herself. She could not, dared not allow it to develop into anything more. They were grown adults who had merely enjoyed a brief liaison.

'Are you busy, Sue?' Paddy asked as he put his head round the door.

'Not really,' she told him.

He looked hesitant. 'I wondered if – no, perhaps it might be better if we talked later.'

'Paddy, you've not been a naughty boy, have you?' Sue said smiling.

'I wish,' he replied with raised eyebrows. 'No seriously. How are you fixed for lunch?'

'I've no plans, but what about Frances?' she queried.

'She's going to the wool shop in the market for a knitting pattern,' Paddy replied. 'I told her I was going to invite you to lunch.'

'And she doesn't mind?'

'She thought it was a good idea.'

'This sounds very mysterious.'

'Will you come?'

'Of course.'

Granny Minto rested back in her favourite armchair and folded her arms. 'Well then?' she said impatiently.

'Well what?'

'Yer go out ter meet that reporter bloke an' then yer come back 'ere wiv not so much as a kiss me arse.'

'I was gonna tell yer,' Albert replied. 'I thought yer was asleep.'

'Nah, I was just lookin' frew me eyelids,' Granny said with a toothless grin. 'So go on then. Tell me.'

'There ain't much ter tell really,' Albert remarked. ''E bought me a drink an' then 'e asked me about that night.'

''E asked us a lot o' questions an' Bessie Woodward told 'im about 'ow she fell over poor ole Granny Knight's body,' the old lady recalled. 'I told 'im about you an' 'e said it was a shame yer didn't go along.'

'I couldn't face sittin' there wiv you lot,' Albert told her. 'Anyway I've seen 'im now an' I answered all 'is questions.'

'Well? Go on then.'

'Bloody 'ell, woman, yer wanna know the ins an' outs of a nag's arse,' Albert grumbled. 'I told 'im just

411

like it was. I said that I'd bin down wiv bad bronchitis an' I wasn't up ter doin' fire-watchin' so I went ter the shelter wiv you when the air-raid siren sounded. I told 'im when the bomb caught the ware'ouse we was all shook up an' then everybody began screamin' when the smoke started comin' in frew the lift shaft.'

'I never screamed,' Granny said emphatically.

'You was the only one then,' Albert growled. 'Anyway, I said that I tried ter get frew on the phone ter Joe an' Charlie up on the roof but the line was dead. So then I told you all ter foller me.'

'Yer did no such fing.'

'Oh yes I did.'

'Oh no yer didn't.'

'Are you gonna let me tell yer, or what?'

'I'm listenin'.'

'I told the reporter that I led the way up the stairs ter the back door an' pushed on the 'andle but the door only moved a tiny bit,' Albert went on. 'I said it was like somefing was stoppin' it.'

'Yeah, there was,' Granny Minto interrupted him. ''Alf the bloody ware'ouse.'

'No it wasn't. It was bricks an' timbers from the lead mills opposite.'

'Go on then.'

Albert gave her a hard look before continuing. 'I told 'im I could 'ear Charlie an' Joe shoutin' fer us to 'old on an' not ter push on the door till they'd cleared the debris. Then when they shouted out it was clear I pushed the door open an' fell out inter the open air.'

'Did yer tell 'im yer fainted?'

'I didn't faint.'

'Yes yer did.'

'No I didn't. I was just exhausted, what wiv me complaint.'

'Was that all?'

''E asked me a funny fing then,' Albert said, stroking his chin.

'What was that?'

''E asked me if I 'eard a lorry pull away while I was waitin' fer the rubble ter be cleared. I told 'im that bombs were fallin' an' the guns in the park were blazin' away. I asked 'im 'ow I could be expected to 'ear a lorry engine wiv all that racket goin' on.'

'Was that all?'

'Yeah, that's about the strength of it,' Albert told her.

Granny Minto looked thoughtful. 'It seems ter me this reporter bloke's takin' a lot o' trouble over this story,' she remarked. 'That scatty cow Minnie Sloan told me it didn't take 'im more than 'alf an hour ter get the story about 'er ole man an' Alf Barlow.'

'Yeah it makes yer wonder what 'e's up to,' Albert replied.

Sue Carey and Paddy O'Brian sat together on a gantry overlooking the Thames as they ate crusty cheese rolls and sipped cool shandy.

'I don't want this to be seen as sour grapes, but I feel Sam Calkin's going well over the top on this story about Ship Lane,' Paddy was saying.

'In what way?'

'Frances told me that Calkin's been delving,' he explained. 'He wanted reports on any robberies which took place about the same time. He's also following up some information Frances supplied him with about a firm that was robbed of bales of cloth.'

'I don't see that as being unusual,' Sue replied. 'He could be working on something else at the same time.'

Paddy shook his head. 'No, it's all tied together in some way. This I got from Frances, and she's got Calkin's attention. She's been in and out of that glory hole like a ferret down a burrow.'

'It's interesting I grant you, but frankly, Paddy, it's none of my business,' Sue told him.

The Irishman took a sip of his drink. 'Listen, darling. I've been a reporter for a lot of years,' he said quietly, 'and I've learned to follow my instincts. I'm sure that this obsession Calkin's got with this particular story can only lead to a lot of heartache and worse. I say this to you because I know that your father and his good friend Charlie Duggan are going to be the subjects of the Ship Lane story.'

'You're not suggesting that my father and Charlie Duggan were involved in any underhand business, are you, Paddy?' Sue replied a little indignantly. 'Sam Calkin spoke to them both and they told him exactly what happened that night, just as they told the coroner. They spoke the truth. I know they did.'

Paddy O'Brian nodded his head slowly. 'I don't think for a minute that they had any reason to lie, nor that they would,' he said. 'The problem is that sometimes a reporter can be sucked in over his head, and then there's a risk that sensationalism replaces constructive and informative journalism. When that happens comments and statements often get twisted to support and fit the story.'

The young woman looked out across the fast-flowing river and saw the eddies swirling at the foot of Southwark Bridge. A barge had become detached from its towing line and was drifting sideways on the tide, while a lighterman struggled laboriously with a long pole in an effort to bring the barge around. The deceptively calm river scene had at first made her think of the weekend, but now all at once she sensed an intimation of dangerous currents lurking unsuspected beneath the placid surface of things and her heart sank. Was Paddy right? Had Sam become so disorientated that he could no longer differentiate between fact and fiction, or was there something darker at work?

Paddy was quiet, his grey eyes staring out over the river, and she touched his arm. 'You were right to let me know,' she said kindly. 'I do appreciate it.'

He nodded a little awkwardly. 'I talked it over with Frances before I asked you out for lunch,' he told her. 'She's worried too. She thinks a lot of you, and like me she's concerned for you and your family.'

Sue finished her drink and gathered up her handbag. 'We'd better be getting back,' she said.

They walked through the empty wholesale market and into the milling crowd, each immersed in their private thoughts. Sue could not rid herself of the nervous ache in her stomach. She had been only too pleased to help Sam Calkin in his enquiries and the knowledge nagged away at her. Had she unwittingly been party to something which could eventually destroy her family? There were important questions that needed answering and the place to start was at home.

Chapter Thirty-Eight

When Del Abelson walked into the Tooley Street union office he found that there was a heated discussion taking place between Robbie Casey and shop stewards from the dockers' group. The elderly convenor was trying to pacify the men and he glanced over briefly at the young official to acknowledge him. 'Look, lads, the best I can do is to 'ave a word wiv the employers' rep later terday,' he told them. 'I can't get away fer the moment, we've got a strike brewin' over at Brady's Transport an' there's a dispute down at Chamber's Wharf.'

'Well, yer better get round an' sort this mess out or there'll be anuvver strike on yer 'ands,' the shop stewards' leader warned.

'Leave it wiv me,' Robbie said as the men left mumbling discontentedly.

Del followed the convenor into the small office and took a seat. 'You look a bit under the weavver, Rob,' he remarked.

The elderly man sat down at his desk and pulled a face. 'This bloody ulcer o' mine's playin' up an' all 'ell's breakin' loose,' he growled. 'I've 'ad Bernie Catchpole in 'ere first fing. Apparently Brady's sacked the lot of 'em this mornin'.'

417

'What for?' Del asked, frowning.

'Brady wants integration wiv the new depot an' the men told 'im they won't work wiv scabs,' Robbie explained.

'I suppose you've promised ter sort that out too,' Del said, shaking his head slowly.

The elderly convenor nodded then suddenly he winced and leaned forward with his hand held to his midriff. 'I need a drink,' he gasped.

Del got up quickly and gripped Robbie's wrist. 'Nah, yer don't,' he said bluntly. 'Yer need ter get that seen to.'

'It'll pass.'

'It's gettin' worse, Robbie,' the young man told him firmly. 'I'm takin' yer ter Guy's.'

'Oh no yer not,' Robbie muttered as he doubled up in pain.

Del put his head out of the door. 'Jamie, phone fer a cab, will yer. Not in a minute, now.'

'Yer makin' a fuss over nuffink,' Robbie gasped.

'That ulcer'll burst if yer keep on neglectin' it an' then it'll be too late,' Del told him plainly. 'Don't worry, I'll sort the Brady business out, an' we've got enough people in ter look after any ovver business.'

Robbie Casey's face had drained of colour and he gritted his teeth as the pain in his stomach increased. 'Lean on Brady, son. Lean 'ard on the bastard,' he said with difficulty.

The cab arrived and the elderly official was helped into it.

'Go wiv 'im, Jamie, an' stay wiv 'im fer a while,' Del told him. 'I've got some urgent business to attend to.'

* * *

Larry Fields, alias the Winkle, was briefed by a tall, scholarly-looking man in gold-rimmed spectacles who spoke in a cultured voice that could well have graced a lecture hall or two. Drinks were provided and the diminutive safe cracker nodded constantly, occasionally glancing in Monty Groves's direction for support.

'You'll wait here until the taxi arrives at three o'clock,' the tall man instructed him. 'Mr Groves will have all the items you've requested, including your tools. You'll put the overalls on in the taxi and go in the tradesmen's entrance. If you happen to be challenged you're investigating a reported gas leak. The occupier of the flat is out of London today so you won't be disturbed. The taxi will drive around, passing the block of flats at regular intervals of ten minutes, so plan your exit accordingly. And remember, only papers and documents are to be removed, is that understood?'

Winkle nodded his head vigorously. 'I've got yer.'

'One last thing,' the man said. 'On the way to the flats you'll be handed two keys. The larger of the two affords entry and the smaller one de-activates the burglar alarm. You will also be given a sealed envelope. After you've completed the task you will fix the contents of the envelope on to the safe door, or in the immediate area so that it won't be missed. This is very important, so don't forget. One last thing. As before, you are on your own, should you be apprehended. I don't need to remind you that your future good health will depend on your silence.'

Winkle nodded his head vigorously once more, casting a quick glance at Monty.

'All yer need ter know fer the moment is that steps 'ave bin taken ter prevent yer bein' pulled in by the rozzers fer this job,' the gang leader told him. 'So long as yer carry out yer instructions ter the letter.'

Winkle downed his drink and looked expectantly at his two companions.

The tall man called a waiter over. 'Two large gin and tonics, and a lemonade if you please,' he ordered, then turning to the safe cracker he muttered, 'you'll need a clear head.'

The yard was filled with parked lorries as Del Abelson walked through the gates and made his way to the temporary office.

'I was expectin' Casey not 'is boy,' Brady said with malice.

'Robbie Casey's got more important matters on 'is mind at the moment,' Del replied icily.

Brady leaned back in his desk chair and folded his arms. 'I'm in my rights 'ere,' he declared. 'Any driver I send over ter the ovver depot gets the same wages as the drivers already workin' there. I can't see what their argument is.'

'Well then, yer gotta be more fick than I thought yer was,' Del growled. 'You know the men's argument. They won't work wiv scabs.'

'Then they don't work fer me,' Brady growled back at him.

'Are their cards made up yet?' the young man asked him.

'They'll be ready at five o'clock.'

Del leaned forward over the desk. 'You've got a couple of hours ter reconsider,' he said. 'I should give it some thought if I were you.'

'Well, you ain't me,' Brady replied angrily, his face flushing up. 'This is my business an' I ain't about ter let the union dictate terms. I run it the way I see fit.'

'All I can see are idle lorries,' Del remarked sarcastically. 'And by termorrer night this'll be what it looks like in yer ovver depot.'

'Don't you believe it,' Brady sneered. 'I don't 'ave union problems over there.'

Del Abelson straightened up and smiled condescendingly. 'Wilson's Biscuits, Bentley's Paints, Cookson's Meats, ter name a few o' your contracts,' he replied. 'My union 'as got assurances from those companies' shop stewards that as from termorrer the loaders there'll be askin' fer union cards before they let your transport in. No cards no contract, so think on that.'

'Don't you try bluffin' me,' Brady shouted, rising out of his chair. 'The loaders at those firms are non-union men.'

'They were, but not any more,' the young man told him with satisfaction. 'While you've bin consortin' wiv scum we've bin talkin' ter the men at those factories. They didn't go a lot on your strong-arm tactics.'

'What d'yer mean by that?' Brady spluttered.

'I'll tell yer what I mean,' Del replied. 'Certain papers came inter the union's possession recently an' they've bin 'anded over ter the appropriate authorities, but not before we took a good look at 'em. Yer on yer own now, pal. Those two gooks yer got ter duff up

Tom Carey 'ave bin sorted out an' they spilled their guts. It's all out in the open now. So let me regale yer wiv a few words o' wisdom. Give us the okay ter talk ter the drivers at yer ovver depot an' reinstate yer men at this depot right away, or yer'll be scratchin' fer work, an' I mean scratchin'.'

'Piss off out o' my yard,' Brady ordered as he slumped down at his desk.

'Don't worry, I'm goin',' Del told him with a smile. 'I've told Bernie Catchpole ter give me an update at five o'clock. I'll expect the men ter be workin' as usual termorrer.'

Ernest Spencer took off his glasses and polished them carefully as he glanced over the desk at Sam Calkin. 'So it's all finalised?'

Sam nodded. 'It's all here,' he declared, laying a folder down on the desk. 'All the interviews I've done, notes and comments.'

Spencer picked up the folder and quickly turned the pages. 'I can go over this later,' he said. 'Let's hear your conclusions.'

Sam Calkin took a deep breath. 'I think I should start at the beginning, if you can spare the time,' he replied.

'Go ahead. I'm listening,' Spencer said.

'It all began when I went to see old Mrs Merry,' Sam told him. 'She was unhappy about the stories that had circulated suggesting her husband was drunk that night and could not have pulled the lorry from the yard. Then while I was wondering how I should write up the story Billy Button contacted me. His information about witnessing a robbery at the warehouse backed up the rumours of George Merry being incapable that night. I was sure at the time he was telling the truth, and nothing I've found out since has made me change my mind. I spent a lot of time pondering over it and the more I thought about it the more convinced I became that somehow the robbery had a direct bearing on the deaths of those five people.'

'The proverbial gut feeling?' Spencer cut in.

'That, or a reporter's intuition. Anyway, I went to take a look at the warehouse in Ship Lane,' Sam continued. 'I'd checked local records and found out that it used to be a tannery with the tanning pits at the front of the building. After it fell into disuse the Council took the property over and got rid of the pits for public health reasons. They widened Ship Lane over them, which left the warehouse in a recessed plot, and because the iron fire escape that had once led down into the tannery yard now ended on the public highway they built a brick lean-to at the base with a locked gate to prevent anyone from using it unlawfully.'

Sam took a small piece of hard black substance from his pocket and laid it on the desk. 'I dug that out from the brickwork at one side of the emergency door. A friend of mine who works at a laboratory did a test for me. It's melted rubber compound. There's a deposit of that substance on each side of the door at exactly the same height. Now bearing in mind what Billy Button told me I checked with Moxen's the lead mills and got the name of the coach builders of their lorries. They told me that they fitted rubber stops on the rear of their vehicles as standard practice. I got the specifications. The stops were fitted exactly forty inches from the floor, the same height as the two deposits on the walls of the warehouse.'

'So the lorry was backed on to the door while it was being loaded?' Spencer queried.

'Yes, and if you were to take a look at the location you'd understand why,' Sam went on to explain. 'The iron staircase slopes upwards from ground level at forty-five degrees over the top of the emergency exit door from the left-hand side, and because the brick lean-to juts out further it was easier to back the lorry up to the door than to manoeuvre it side-on. There was another consideration that struck me too. Ship Lane narrows further along and leads into a maze of narrow backstreets, whereas the other end leads out directly into Dockhead. After the lorry was driven out of Moxen's yard and over to the warehouse for loading it would have to be turned round anyway. It would make sense to back the vehicle up to the door under the fire escape for ease of loading and to be ready for a quick getaway.'

'Yes it makes sense,' Spencer agreed.

'Now the question's posed. What was it that was being stolen?' Sam continued. 'As we've agreed, it was hardly carpets and bedding. So I got Frances to do some checking. Three weeks before the warehouse robbery there was a consignment of cloth stolen from Goldberg Clothiers in Tower Bridge Road. The firm's vehicle was later found empty in Rotherhithe but the rolls of cloth were never recovered. It's my belief that they were hidden in the Ship Lane warehouse while a buyer was sought.

'Now the big question. Who were the people involved? Both Joe Carey and Charlie Duggan the wardens at the warehouse held keys to the place. Furthermore, both their sons used the Bull public house, the same pub that Billy Button and George Merry used. In fact Button ran the outings there before the war and he knew all the regulars very well. Understandably in the circumstances he swore that the men who called that night to take George Merry to the pub were strangers to him, although it was common knowledge that two regulars from the Bull were in the habit of collecting him. Button also swore that the two men who took the lorry that night were unknown to him. I feel sure that the two in question were Maurice Carey and Stanley Duggan, the wardens' sons.'

'I suppose it's quite possible, considering that they knew George Merry well and could have persuaded him to let them use the lorry,' Spencer said, stroking his chin.

'There's one other thing which convinces me it was Maurice Carey and Stanley Duggan who did the robbery,' the young reporter told him. 'Frances Miller found out that Goldberg Clothiers is now run by Nathan Goldberg's son Emmanuel and trades under the name of Emmanuel Fashions in Whitechapel. I went to see Emmanuel Goldberg and we discussed the possibility of the theft of the cloth being an inside job, considering the fact that the firm had just taken delivery of expensive rolls of silks and satins. Goldberg felt it was possible but unlikely. He felt his staff were a very loyal bunch, and before I left he showed me a plaque his father had put up in memory of employees of the firm who'd died on active service. One of the names was that of Leading Seaman Stanley Duggan.'

'Good Lord!' Spencer exclaimed.

'Failing positive identification by Billy Button it's all circumstantial,' Sam said with a sigh. 'But it's damning nevertheless.'

'So in actual fact the death of those five people that night was directly due to the exit door being blocked by the lorry,' Spencer summed up.

Sam nodded his head slowly. 'I spoke to the elderly man who led the shelterers to the exit. He said that the door had a push bar and it only opened a fraction. He heard Carey and Duggan shouting to him to hold on for a few seconds while they cleared the rubble away but in actual fact it was to move the lorry. I asked the man if he heard a lorry start up but he said that there was so much noise from falling bombs and guns firing from the park nearby it was impossible to hear anything else.'

'What about the lorry?' Spencer asked.

'It was parked further along the lane completely burned out.'

'Along with its load of cloth.'

Sam nodded once more. 'During that night two firemen lost their lives fighting a fire in Abbey Street. I'd like to do a tandem piece headed, "The Glory and the Shame". On Friday the firemen's story and on the following Tuesday the Ship Lane tragedy, with your front-page editorial.'

Spencer picked up his glasses from the desk and slipped them on. 'You realise that we're legally bound to hand all this information over to the police,' he remarked.

'Yes I know,' Sam replied. 'I realise too that if the police catch up with Billy Button he could well deny the story's true, saying that he'd made it up with the intention of getting money from the newspaper. Should that happen we could look foolish. That's why I followed everything up. At first Billy Button was all we had, but now we have a folder of information, interviews, et cetera, which support his story.'

'We need to conduct two more interviews before we go to print with this,' Spencer reminded him.

'Carey and Duggan,' the reporter finished for him.

'We have to, on moral grounds if no other,' the editor went on. 'If we're going to act as public prosecutor the accused have the right to defend themselves. Then we print the facts as we know them and let the readers decide for themselves.'

'The police could oppose our making the story public till they complete their own investigations,' Sam commented.

'I'd oppose that all the way through the press council to the courts,' Spencer said firmly. 'But in any case we'll have to meet with Duggan and Carey before we can draw any final conclusions.'

Sam nodded, feeling suddenly drained. The story was one which he had committed himself to follow up, and he had persevered with it doggedly and ambitiously, but he had been wrong to dally with Sue Carey's affections. She had been very helpful from the beginning and he had ingratiated himself and used her. What had happened that weekend had complicated things and he should never have allowed his feelings to get in the way of what he had to do. Now he was to become quite possibly the agent of her family's destruction and the knowledge weighed heavily on his shoulders.

'I'll need to okay everything with Morrison,' the editor concluded. 'Now let's see. You're taking a couple of days off.'

'I intend to see Carey and Duggan on Wednesday evening,' Sam told him. 'I'll have the finished article ready for Thursday morning.'

'Good,' Spencer replied. 'We'll meet first thing on Thursday then.'

In a more opulent part of London another drama was unfolding. Entry to the flat had been achieved without a hitch and the alarm was switched off. As expected the wall safe was hidden behind the hinged picture of the mountain and Winkle smiled to himself. A Denton XB. Hardly a problem for an old professional, he thought. No sense in using jelly on that piece of old iron. A stethoscope, a feather touch and a bit of patience would be enough. A four figure number and clumsy tumblers were the Denton's main features, Winkle recalled smugly. If he wasn't out in twenty minutes he would be very surprised.

The little safe cracker blew his nose hard to clear his sinuses then he put the stethoscope into his ears and listened. He could hear the faint scraping sound as the tumblers spun and then the sudden click. After the fourth click he crossed his fingers and pulled on the handle. The safe door opened smoothly and he reached inside. The papers were in one bundle tied with a ribbon, and beside them was a velvet-covered box. Winkle opened it gingerly and stared down at an exquisite row of pearls. For a moment he was sorely tempted, but he resisted the urge with a deep sigh of resignation. These were big people he was employed by and it would not do to disobey their orders.

He gathered his things together then took the envelope from his pocket and tore it open. The black and white picture of the naked young woman and her older companion left nothing to the imagination and Winkle whistled to himself as he used the attached sticking plaster to fix it to the safe door. Disgusting, he told himself. Disgusting but necessary, evidently. So that was what Monty Groves had meant about keeping the police out of it.

Chapter Thirty-Nine

As Sue Carey walked home through the evening bustle her mind was in a turmoil. After what Paddy O'Brian had told her that lunchtime she had urgently wanted to confront Sam and ask him outright exactly what his intentions were, but there had been no opportunity. He had come into the office late that afternoon while she was engaged on the phone with a caller waiting to be attended to and gone straight in to see Spencer. She had thought about hanging on for him after work but decided against it. He was still with the editor and she was anxious to get home and try to bring the whole thing out into the open. There were too many questions remaining unanswered, too much fobbing off, and it couldn't go on. Not now.

When she walked in everyone was in the parlour and her father was talking about his new job.

'I expected ter be put on a broom with the rest o' the casuals, ter be honest,' he was saying, 'but the foreman asked me if I could read an' write would yer believe.'

'You mean road sweeping?' Ellie queried.

'Yeah, that's what the casuals do ter start wiv,' Joe explained. 'Anyway, when I told 'em I was a bookkeeper they stuck me in the weigh-bridge office.

431

I 'ave ter weigh the lorries an' book 'em in an' out. It's a doddle really.'

'I'm glad,' Martha said smiling. 'Maybe yer'll be a little more even-tempered now. You ain't exactly bin one o' God's little sunbeams this last week.'

Joe leaned back in his chair and grinned. 'I fink I struck lucky,' he said. 'Mind you I was prepared ter go on the broom.'

''Ave they got any more vacancies in the office, Farvver?' Tom asked smiling broadly.

''E's bin on strike again terday,' Martha remarked to Sue, rolling her eyes.

'Brady give us all notice would yer believe,' Tom told his sister. 'We 'ad ter go back this afternoon ter pick up our cards, but Del got it sorted. 'E done a good job.'

'He would, wouldn't he,' Sue remarked icily.

'Well 'e certainly put Brady in 'is place,' Tom replied defensively.

'I can't sit 'ere chattin', I gotta put the veg on,' Martha said, getting up.

'Wait a minute, Mum,' Sue said quickly. 'We need to talk, all of us.'

Ellie frowned at her niece. 'I think I'll go up and . . .'

'No, this concerns you as well, Aunt Ellie,' Sue told her firmly.

'What is it?' Martha asked, glancing briefly at Joe.

Sue sat down at the table and looked from one to the other. 'There's been certain things we can never get to the bottom of in this house, and I think it's about time Tom and I were given some straight answers,' she began in a clear voice.

'What exactly d'yer mean?' Martha asked.

'Whenever we ask you about that night those people died in the shelter you clam up,' she replied. 'It's the same whenever Mo's name comes up. Neither of you have told us why our brother hardly ever comes round to see us, and why there's always tension on the rare occasions he does call.'

'It's no big mystery. We just don't see eye to eye, that's all,' Joe said quickly.

'And what about that night the people were killed?' Sue pressed. 'When Tom and I came home from the services you didn't even want to show us the newspaper cutting. We got more from outsiders than from you. You and Charlie Duggan were heroes that night, Dad, and people owe their lives to you, but you acted as though you were guilty of some crime.'

'Yer dad an' Charlie were very upset about those poor people that got killed an' they don't like ter be reminded,' Martha butted in. 'That's why we decided ter try an' ferget it, not talk about it.'

'But it won't go away,' Sue persisted. 'Sam Calkin's determined to do the story and I've been giving him some help, putting names forward for him to go and see.'

'So it was you who told 'im who was in the shelter that night,' Joe said gruffly.

'Sam Calkin wanted to meet some of the people who were there so I told him to speak to Mrs Woodward, that was all,' Sue countered. 'There was no harm in it, and why should there be?'

'That reporter's bin nosin' around at the Bull so I was told,' Joe went on.

'That's the pub Mo an' Stan Duggan used before the war,' Tom said.

'Why should 'e go in there askin' questions?' Martha fretted.

'I don't like this one little bit,' Joe growled.

'I'll tell you something else too,' Sue said in a measured tone of voice. 'Frances Miller's been doing some research for him and she found something which he seemed very interested in. It was a newspaper cutting of a robbery that took place a few weeks before the shelter got hit.'

The blood drained from Joe's face and he looked at Martha in despair. 'I knew it,' he groaned. 'Why can't they let the past stay buried?'

Sue looked at her brother quickly and saw by his narrowed eyes that he too was shocked by their father's reaction.

'What's a robbery got to do with what happened at the shelter that night?' Ellie wanted to know.

'Yer'd better tell us everyfing, Farvver,' Tom said quietly. 'We're s'posed ter be a family. Me an' Sue 'ave a right ter know.'

Joe and Martha's eyes were locked together and she nodded slowly in answer to his unspoken question. 'It 'ad ter come out some time,' she sighed. 'I fink deep down inside we knew it.'

Joe nodded his head slowly then he rested his forehead in his hand for a few moments. 'All right then. Like yer say, yer've got a right ter know,' he sighed, and he hesitated for a second or two.

'It 'ad bin quiet fer some time before that bad night an' when the siren went off me an' Charlie opened up the shelter as usual. We both thought at the time we were gonna be in fer a bad time of it. There was a full moon, an' what was more the river was at its lowest. It was what yer call a spring tide. The fire service used ter pump water from the Thames ter fight the fires an' we expected it ter be an incendiary raid. The Germans seemed ter know the right time ter come over. Anyway, me an' Charlie went up on the roof an' kept a look-out. It was quiet fer a while, an' then we 'eard the roar as the planes come over. All of a sudden it was like 'ell itself. Bombs were fallin' everywhere an' a lot o' the factories an' ware'ouses were coppin' it. We phoned frew ter the warden's post ter report the fires an' Charlie phoned down ter let the people in the shelter know that we were doin' our bit. It used ter make 'em feel better if they knew we were on 'and.'

'Me an' Aunt Ellie didn't go ter the shelter that night, as it 'appened,' Martha cut in. 'She was in bed ill wiv quinsies so I stayed 'ere wiv 'er.'

'It was terrible,' Joe went on. 'I was worried about yer muvver an' Aunt Ellie, I was worried about the ware'ouse coppin' it, an' then it got really bad. Me an' Charlie thought about gettin' off the roof, that's 'ow bad it was, but anyway we stayed put. All of a sudden a bomb fell smack bang on the ware'ouse. We 'eard it comin' down. It sounded like somebody rattlin' corrugated iron. That's 'ow yer knew it was gonna be close. Me an' Charlie dived down on the floor an' then there was this almighty crash. It was an oil bomb an' it went in the ovver end o' the roof, right over where the people were shelterin'. We picked ourselves up an' ran over ter the 'ole it 'ad made. The floor below was burnin' fiercely an' we could see that all the stored stuff was alight. Part o' the wall on that floor 'ad blown out an' we run over ter the roof edge ter see if the debris 'ad fallen down over the emergency exit. The top-floor door was open an' smoke an' flames were pourin' out. There was a bale o' cloth lyin' on the iron staircase, an' as the smoke cleared a bit we saw young Stanley Duggan goin' down the fire escape carryin' our Mo over 'is shoulder. Mo was unconscious. 'E'd bin caught by the blast. Then the smoke cleared a bit more an' we saw the lorry below us. It was backed right up ter the emergency door an' there must 'ave bin about a dozen bales o' cloth on the back of it.'

'You mean to say that Mo and Stan Duggan were robbing the warehouse?' Sue gasped.

Joe nodded. 'Flames were startin' ter come up all round the lorry an' I followed Charlie down the fire escape as quick as I could. I was worried in case the petrol tank blew up. I saw Stan Duggan lay Mo down in the lane an' Charlie dragged 'im out o' the way o' the lorry as Stan jumped in the cab. Then suddenly I 'eard bangin' on the ovver side o' the door an' people screamin' an' shoutin'. I couldn't tell 'em there was a lorry blockin' the door, could I, so I just shouted out fer 'em ter stop pushin' against it till me an' Charlie cleared the rubble away. It all 'appened so quick. Anyway, Stan managed ter drive the burnin' lorry along the turnin' an' then the people came out. They never knew the difference, but by the same token we'll never know whevver those five people would be alive terday if that lorry 'adn't bin blockin' their escape. Yer see, the shelter was already filled wiv smoke from the lift shaft. Bessie Woodward told us that one ole lady, Mrs Knight it was, collapsed as soon as the smoke poured in, before Albert Price led the way ter the exit.'

Sue and Tom both had agonised expressions on their faces and Martha dabbed at her eyes.

'So that's why Mo's estranged from the family,' Sue said quietly.

'I can't fergive 'im, Gawd 'elp me I can't,' Joe said, his voice breaking.

'Did our Maurice an' Stanley Duggan steal the rolls o' cloth from that firm?' Tom asked.

Joe nodded. 'Stanley worked there an' 'e told Mo about the delivery of expensive silk they'd just 'ad, an' they decided ter nick it. The problem was, they needed a place ter store that amount. It was too much ter sell off in bits.'

'Did you know? Did you allow them to store it at the warehouse?' Sue asked.

'I never knew. May I be struck down this minute if I'm tellin' a lie,' Joe swore.

'What about Charlie Duggan?' Tom asked.

'Charlie was as shocked as me.'

''Ow did they get ter store the cloth then?' he frowned. 'They'd need keys ter get in.'

'Stanley used ter bring us jugs o' tea an' sandwiches up ter the roof,' Joe told him, 'an' the box where the keys were kept was always open durin' air raids. It would 'ave bin simple fer 'im ter get an impression o' the keys. In fact 'e knew where we kept the key ter the box. 'E could 'ave gone up there an' borrered the keys durin' the day. We never found out. Neivver o' the boys would say anyfing. Mo moved out after that an' Stan went inter the Navy very soon after.'

'Why were we kept in the dark, Dad?' Sue asked him. 'We're a family and we're supposed to share our troubles.'

'You were always very close as kids,' Martha reminded her. 'It was bad enough us knowin', wivout you two carryin' the guilt around as well.'

'I know it was a terrible fing to 'appen, but Mo an' Stan weren't ter know that the ware'ouse was gonna get bombed,' Tom said. 'It was just a terrible twist o' fate.'

'Did they cause those five people ter die, that's the question,' Joe replied. 'We can't answer it. Only the Lord knows.'

Aunt Ellie had been very quiet while Joe was relating what had happened and suddenly she lowered her head and sobbed loudly. 'May God forgive you, Mo,' she cried out in anguish.

Martha got up from her chair and put her arm round her sister's shoulder, which only served to make Ellie wail all the more.

'C'mon, luv, pull yerself tergevver,' she told her.

'I need to go to my room,' the spinster croaked.

Tom looked down at his clenched hands while Sue studied her father's solemn face. Sam Calkin had somehow linked the two incidents, but how? she pondered. Someone must have said something, planted the seed. She would have to confront him to get to the bottom of it or she would never rest. She would also make a point of letting him know what a despicable man he was. He had traded on her friendship to further his own ends, and then slept with her, knowing full well that when the story broke it would destroy her family. They would have to face their neighbours of many years and they would be compelled to move away with every chance that their guilt would follow them wherever they went.

Martha came back into the parlour and slumped down heavily in the armchair. 'Ellie's taken it bad,' she sighed. 'Mo's always bin 'er favourite.'

'If only I'd known,' Sue groaned. 'Maybe I could have put Calkin off.'

'It was destined to 'appen one day,' Joe told her quietly. 'You couldn't 'ave prevented it, luv.'

'Gawd knows what's gonna 'appen now,' Martha said, tears welling up in her eyes. ''Ow can we look our friends an' neighbours in the eye?'

'Don't give up,' Sue said firmly. 'It's not printed yet. There may still be time.'

Joe was staring down into the empty grate. 'I just can't understand 'ow that Calkin bloke linked the robbery from that clothes factory wiv what 'appened at the shelter, unless someone saw what was goin' on at the ware'ouse an' told 'im. Even then it's a mystery 'ow 'e linked the two fings tergevver.'

'That's just what I'll be asking him tomorrow,' Sue told him.

'I don't fink they'd dare print a story like that unless they've got proof,' Martha remarked. 'Mo would never say anyfing an' young Stan's dead.'

'There's the police ter fink about,' Joe added. 'They'll be round askin' questions, that's fer sure.'

'What a terrible mess,' Martha said, dabbing at her eyes.

'Mo's gonna 'ave ter know,' Tom reminded them. ''E'll 'ave ter be put on 'is guard.'

'You'd better talk to 'im,' Martha told him.

'I'm just wonderin' what 'is reaction'll be,' the young man said. 'You know 'ow volatile Mo is.'

''E might frighten Calkin off,' Joe suggested hopefully. ''E knows it means prison fer 'im if it's proved.'

'I fink I'd better go an' tell Mabel,' Martha decided. ''Er an' Charlie need ter know what's in front of 'em.'

Sue looked up at the clock and sighed. The tea had been forgotten for the time being and she doubted whether any of them could stomach a meal that evening. What she really needed right now was a comforting arm around her and a few soft words, and the person she needed to turn to was Del Abelson.

Chapter Forty

Del Abelson walked into the ward at Guy's Hospital on Monday evening and found Robbie Casey propped up in bed looking very pale and drawn.

'This is a bloody fine mess I must say,' the reluctant patient growled.

'Yer in the best place, Robbie,' Del told him firmly. 'The only booze yer'll get now is a Guinness.'

Robbie pulled a face. 'Can't stand the stuff. Ain't no chance o' smugglin' me in a drop o' tiddly, is there?'

'Certainly not.'

'Nah, I didn't fink so.'

'I got a phone call from Mo Carey just before I left the office,' Del remarked. ''E sends yer 'is best an' told me ter tell yer that the job went off like a dream. 'E said it's a bit early yet, but the signs look very good. There's some stuff that'll open a few eyes at least.'

'That's good news,' the elderly convenor replied. 'Maybe now our friends'll 'ave enough ter blow the gaff. That evil mob 'ave got ter be stopped some'ow. None of us in our business could afford ter stand by an' see all what we've fought for go down the poxy drain.'

'All right, ole pal, take it easy,' Del said quickly as Robbie's face flushed with passion. 'Yer preachin' ter the converted. Anyway yer in 'ere ter get sorted out yerself, not ter run the union from yer bed. Leave the business ter the rest of us.'

'Yeah, yer right,' Robbie said with a sigh. 'Jack Watson'll take over while I'm away. 'E's a good man, yer'll learn a lot from 'im.'

'The Brady trouble got sorted by the way,' the young man grinned.

'Yeah, I thought it would,' Robbie nodded. ''E was just tryin' it on. Make no mistake about it, Brady knows the score. Eivver that ovver depot gets unionised or 'e'll find 'imself scratchin' fer work.'

'I told 'im exactly those words,' Del replied.

The elderly convenor looked closely at the younger man. 'You look a bit jaded yerself,' he remarked. 'Take my advice an' nick a few days. Yer don't wanna end up wiv what I've got.'

Del nodded. 'Yer right, Robbie. I've bin neglectin' a few fings lately an' it's time I did somefing about it.'

'Fank Mo Carey fer 'is concern,' Robbie said. 'Tell 'im I'll 'ave a drink wiv 'im soon as I get out of 'ere.'

'I will do,' Del replied. ''E was upset when I told 'im you was in 'ere.'

'One nice feller 'im,' Robbie said, easing himself up on the pillows. 'Very shrewd too. 'E's got a lot o' respect amongst the local villains, which makes 'im powerful. A good man to 'ave on your side. The fing wiv Mo is, 'e's kept clean, though I know fer a fact that 'e sails close ter the wind at times. I remember the time I was convenin' in a dispute at the brewery an' the lads were out on the stones. A group o' publicans got tergevver ter fetch their own beer from the depot an' they brought a load o' muscle ter back 'em up. It looked like all 'ell was gonna break loose an' I was earmarked fer a good pastin' I felt sure. Anyway I spotted this young bloke wiv the publicans. 'E seemed ter be one o' the ringleaders an' I went up to 'im. I told 'im straight that the lads'd fight if their picket line was broken then I asked 'im ter give me anuvver day's grace. I was convinced the trouble could be sorted out an' I told 'im so. I remember 'im lookin' right at me, as though weighin' me up, an' then 'e smiled. "Yer got twenty-four hours," 'e said. Fortunately that's all I needed an' a battle royal was averted. That was me first dealin' wiv Mo. Like I said, 'e's a good man to 'ave on yer side.'

'I'll bear that in mind, Robbie,' the young man told him. 'Now I'd better get off. There's a few fings I gotta take care of.'

The current meeting of the three musketeers was being conducted with all due seriousness and the main item on the agenda was introduced by Wally Tucker. 'The next story in the *Bulletin* is gonna be about the Ship Lane shelter, it stands ter reason,' he began.

'Well, I would 'ave thought so,' Benny cut in. 'That reporter's bin talkin' ter the women in the street an' Bessie Woodward told me 'e was askin' 'em loads o' questions.'

''E's bin talkin' to Albert Price too,' Tubby Saward said.

'Gawd knows what that silly git told 'im,' Wally

growled. 'Anyway, the point I'm makin' is that we should be prepared fer it.'

'What d'yer mean?' Benny asked.

Wally took a swig from his glass and wiped a large hand over his lips before replying. 'We gotta do somefing ter show our appreciation,' he explained. 'Joe Carey an' Charlie Duggan were bloody 'eroes that night an' a lot more people would 'ave died if it wasn't fer them two.'

'We never done anyfing fer Alf Barlow an' Micky Sloan,' Benny remarked.

'Yeah, but those two families ain't bin in the street as long as the Careys an' the Duggans,' Wally replied.

'An' what they did wasn't nuffink ter do wiv the people in our street,' Tubby said.

'So what yer got in mind?' Benny asked.

'I was finkin' of askin' the mayor ter make a presentation,' Wally declared.

'What sort o' presentation?' Benny enquired.

'A bravery certificate.'

'That's a good idea, but you don't know the mayor.'

'What bloody difference does that make?'

'None I s'pose.'

'I should fink 'e'll be only too glad ter give out a certificate,' Tubby cut in. 'Mayors like doin' fings like that.'

'We could get 'im ter do it 'ere,' Benny said grinning. 'Then we could 'ave a good ole piss-up.'

'I've already spoke to our Bet about it an' she finks it's a very good idea,' Wally went on. 'She told Bessie Woodward an' Bessie told 'er she knows someone who could do a certificate wiv all that coloured writin' on.'

'A luminated address,' Benny informed them.

'Nah, a few words o' praise wiv a nice coloured border,' Wally replied.

'A few words o' praise? Sounds more like a church service now,' Tubby remarked.

'I'm tellin' yer it's called a luminated address,' Benny insisted.

'Well anyway, Bessie's gonna see this woman an' ask 'er if 'er ole man'll do it,' Wally said as he picked up his pint.

'We could ask the Salvation Army ter bring their band along ter the street an' play a few patriotic songs,' Benny suggested.

'Now yer goin' over the bleedin' top,' Wally growled. 'We don't wanna make a poppy show out of it.'

'We could all go an' see the mayor, I ain't never spoke to a mayor before,' Benny chuckled.

'Right then. All agreed ter my plan?'

Benny and Tubby nodded, which brought a satisfied smile to Wally's round face. 'I'll tell Bet ter give Bessie the okay,' he said. 'You two stay posted. By the way, it's your turn ter get the drinks, Benny.'

Rosie Coleman opened the iron door of the oven and carefully lifted out the covered plate. 'Don't touch it, it's very 'ot,' she warned.

Del looked pleased as he picked up his knife and fork. 'Beef stew, my favourite,' he said smiling.

Rosie removed the cover and awarded him a brief smile. She had been growing more and more irritated by her lodger's lack of consideration for mealtimes and she was constantly worried that the gravy would crust up before he made an appearance, but to give him his due he always complimented her on her cooking, and as far as he was concerned everything she cooked him was his favourite. 'I was gettin' worried,' she told him. 'Yer did say yer'd be in early this evenin'.'

'Yeah I'm sorry, Rosie, but I 'ad ter go in 'ospital an' see Robbie Casey,' he explained. ''E was rushed in wiv 'is ulcer. I fink it's perforated.'

'That's what'll 'appen ter you if yer don't ease up,' she warned him.

'Yeah, that's what Robbie said,' he replied as he grabbed a thick slice of bread.

'I don't wanna go on, but yer'll 'ave ter give that gel o' yours a bit more consideration,' Rosie told him. 'If yer not careful she's gonna ditch yer. There's plenty o' lads who'd be glad ter take 'er out.'

'Yeah I know,' he replied. 'I'm gonna take a few days off an' spend a bit more time wiv 'er.'

'Good fer you. Now get on wiv that food before it gets cold,' Rosie said firmly.

Jim Coleman had been reading the evening paper and he looked up to give the young man a smile. 'She's a proper ole fusser, ain't she,' he said light-heartedly.

'Good job I am wiv you two,' she replied as she brushed her hands down her clean apron.

Del dipped a hunk of bread into the gravy. 'I'm finkin' o' buyin' Sue a ring,' he announced, 'but I don't know 'er size.'

'Well, that's simple. Take 'er wiv yer,' Rosie told him.

'I want it ter be a surprise.'

'An engagement ring?'

'Sort of.'

'What d'yer mean, sort of? Eivver it is or it ain't.'

'Yeah, it is.'

'Are yer gonna pop the question?' Rosie asked wide-eyed.

'I reckon so.'

'About bleedin' time.'

'I bin very busy.'

'Do tell me about it.'

''Ow can I get 'er size wivout tellin' 'er?' Del asked.

'Leave that ter me,' Rosie told him.

'She'll find out,' Jim cut in. 'Our Rosie's as canny as they come.'

'That'll be enough from you, Jim Coleman,' she said in feigned disgust.

Del finished his meal and sat back contentedly. 'I fink I'll see if Sue wants ter go ter the pictures,' he remarked.

'D'yer remember where she lives?' Rosie replied sarcastically.

'Give it a rest, Muvver,' Jim butted in.

''E knows I'm right, an' not so much o' the muvver.'

Jim went back to his paper, and when Rosie started clearing the crockery Del got up to help her. 'C'mon, I'll dry up,' he offered.

'Are you feelin' all right?' she asked with a saucy grin.

They set to work in the scullery, and as he carefully

447

wiped a plate the young man looked pensive. ''Ow d'yer propose ter find out what size ring Sue takes?' he asked.

'I got a few ole bits o' jewellery in me box upstairs,' Rosie told him. 'I'll get 'em out an' show 'er. There's a nice ruby ring me gran'muvver passed down frew the family an' I'll ask 'er if she finks it's very valuable. I got a few ovver rings as well an' I'll get 'er ter try 'em on. She won't suspect anyfing.'

At that moment there was a knock at the door and Rosie came back into the scullery looking a little worried. 'It's Sue,' she said. 'She's in the parlour. She looks upset, Del.'

The young man went through and kissed Sue on the cheek. 'I was callin' round later,' he told her. 'Is anyfing wrong?'

'I need to talk, Del,' she said flatly with a deep sigh.

Rosie had followed Del into the parlour and she snapped her fingers at Jim. 'Oi, Jimbo. Let the young ones 'ave a bit o' privacy fer a few minutes,' she told him. 'Come an' 'elp me finish the washin' up.'

As soon as they were alone Sue told him what had happened and he looked shocked. 'Can't 'e be persuaded not ter print the story?' he asked.

'I'm intending asking him first thing tomorrow,' she replied.

'I'd 'ave thought the paper would contact yer dad an' Charlie Duggan fer their version before they print the story,' Del said. 'It's the least they can do.'

'They might,' Sue replied. 'All Dad an' Charlie can do is deny it.'

'What a mess,' Del sighed. ''Ere, couldn't Mo put the frighteners on that Calkin feller?'

'Tom's going to see him tonight,' Sue told him. 'The only problem is, it's as good as admitting guilt trying to suppress a story.'

Del slipped his arm around her. 'I'm very sorry, Sue,' he said gently. 'It must be terrible fer you an' yer family.'

She leaned her head on his shoulder. 'I had to come and see you, Del,' she whispered. 'I've missed you so.'

'I've missed you too,' he replied in a quiet voice. 'Fings are gonna change from now on though. I realised somefing terday when I went ter see our convenor in 'ospital. They took 'im in wiv a suspected perforated ulcer an' I got ter finkin'. Is that gonna be me in the future? Poor ole Robbie Casey's spent 'is life wiv the union an' now 'e's sick an' frail. I reckon 'e gave too much of 'imself ter fightin' fer ovver people. I'm not gonna make that mistake.'

Sue stood up straight and faced him, her pale blue eyes fixed on his. 'It's a question of finding the right balance,' she replied. 'You're a good man, you've got principles. You're at your best sorting other people's problems out and you care passionately about what you do. It's a laudable thing, but just remember I care for you. I want some of your time, and I want your love, Del. I don't want us to drift apart.'

He reached out and took her by her shoulders. 'Listen ter me,' he said, his voice thick with emotion. 'There's never bin anyone else fer me. I care fer you the way yer care fer me, an' I need your love every bit as much.'

She leant forward, her lips finding his, and as she savoured his tender kiss and felt his strong arms around her a sense of guilt twisted sickeningly in her stomach. She had betrayed him. She had given her love to a man who wasn't fit to walk in his shadow. He would never know of her infidelity, but the shameful memory of it would serve as a spur to make her cherish him and love him all the more.

'You need cheerin' up,' he said as they moved apart. 'There's a good film on at the Elephant. Gimme a minute ter get ready.'

Rosie Coleman did not consider herself to be a snoop, nor an interfering sort, but there were times when contingency demanded a more pragmatic approach, and she marked time on the spot at her vantage point in the passage before entering the room. 'Are you two off out?' she asked innocently.

'I'm takin' Sue ter the flicks,' Del told her.

'Well yer better 'urry up an' get ready then, or yer'll miss the start,' she replied. 'By the way, Sue. While that feller o' yours is sortin' 'imself out could yer spare me a minute? I'd like your advice. I got this old ring yer see, an' . . .'

Chapter Forty-One

When Bessie Woodward agreed to speak to her friend about getting the bravery certificate printed up, Betty Tucker had a few words of advice for her. 'This is gotta be kept secret, so don't go givin' the game away,' she warned her. 'An' be careful what yer say ter Nell Sharp. I know she's yer friend, but she talks a lot ter Marfa Carey an' she might let somefing slip, yer know 'ow she is.'

Bessie nodded her head frantically. 'I won't say a word,' she replied.

Nell Sharp met Bessie that morning in the market and was promptly told of the plan to present the street's heroes with the certificate. 'Yer can trust me, luv. I wouldn't breave a word,' she said with her hand on her heart.

Nell Sharp passed Granny Minto on her way to the oilshop later that morning, and knowing the old lady's thirst for gossip she told her about the plan in confidence. 'I'm not s'posed ter say anyfing,' she whispered, despite the fact that no one was within earshot, 'but I know yer can keep a secret.'

Granny Minto was pleased to be entrusted with it. 'I understand, gel. I wouldn't tell a soul,' she said, shaking her head for effect.

A short while later when Albert Price came back with the morning paper the old lady gave him the news. 'Now don't go tellin' anybody,' she warned. 'If yer mention anyfing it'll get back ter those three silly gits an' they'll know where it came from.'

'I'll stay well out o' their way so they won't 'ear anyfing from me,' he promised.

When Martha Carey came into the turning that morning she was surprised to see Granny Minto go in and shut her door. Normally she would exchange a few pleasantries with her when she passed on her way home. Across the street Bessie Woodward was chatting to Nell Sharp and Martha looked over ready to nod a greeting, but the two seemed oblivious of her presence. It was very strange, she thought. Betty Tucker was at the market and she had appeared very preoccupied with what was on Cheap Jack's stall. Usually she was only too glad to chat for a while.

The women of the street were taking their vow of secrecy very seriously, and none of them wanted to be seen talking to either Martha Carey or Mabel Duggan for fear of being labelled the one who let the cat out of the bag. But in her ignorance Martha grew scared that malicious rumours were starting, pre-empting the *Bulletin*'s article, and she was being ostracised. It had to be someone who knew the truth, and she said as much to Mabel Duggan.

'It's funny you should say that,' Mabel told her. 'I saw the Sharp woman in Abbey Street this mornin' an' I'm sure she saw me but she made out she never.'

'Why do they listen ter gossip?' Martha sighed.

'They'll soon 'ave somefing ter get their jaws round, that's fer sure,' Mabel replied as she poured out the tea. 'This 'ole business is worryin' the life out o' me. My Charlie's took it bad. 'E put on a brave face while you was 'ere but later 'e came over all shaky. 'E told me 'e reckoned 'e 'ad a chill comin' on but I knew different. Twisted an' turned all night 'e did. It's unlike 'im. Normally 'e's asleep soon as 'is 'ead touches the piller.'

'Joe's the same,' Martha told her. 'I've never seen 'im so pent up before. I'm worried about what our Mo might do as well, though. Tom said 'e took it quite calm when 'e told 'im. 'E said they'd need positive proof before they could make anyfing stick an' no one was gonna come forward ter swear it 'appened.'

'It's all right fer Mo, 'e don't live round 'ere, but I couldn't stay 'ere once the trufe's out,' Mabel said as she sipped her tea. 'We'd be like lepers.'

'I said the same ter Joe,' Martha replied.

'All we can do is pray fer a miracle, an' they don't 'appen very often,' Mabel sighed.

'I'm not givin' up 'ope till our Sue gets 'ome ternight,' Martha told her. 'She might be able ter persuade Calkin not ter print it.'

'I wouldn't 'old out much 'ope o' that,' Mabel replied. 'Yer know what newspapers are like.'

The letterbox flap sounded and Mabel frowned. 'That can't be the postman again this early,' she said getting up.

Martha drained her cup and put it down on the table, looking up to see Mabel standing in the parlour doorway frowning at an unstamped letter. 'It must 'ave bin delivered by 'and,' she said as she tore it open and stood there looking at it. 'It's from the *Bulletin*. 'Ere, read it.'

Dear Mr Duggan,

Following our meeting concerning the Ship Lane shelter tragedy on the night of May 10th 1941, I have to tell you that certain things have come to light which you should be made aware of. In furtherance, it would be in your interest to agree to see me on Wednesday evening. I suggest seven o'clock. I will hold the planned article in abeyance until we have spoken. Should you feel that a further meeting will serve no purpose I would be grateful if you could contact the *Bulletin* on the number above.

I have to tell you, however, that should you decide against seeing me I will have no option left other than to print the article as it stands.

Yours faithfully,

Samuel Calkin.

'There'll be one frew my letterbox too,' Martha remarked as she handed the message back.

'All they can do is listen ter what's bein' said an' stick ter their story,' Mabel said as she slumped down in the armchair.

'Yeah, yer right, luv,' Martha sighed dejectedly. 'Like our Mo told Tom, they need proof, an' if nobody comes forward it'll be down ter who's ter be believed, the *Bulletin* or our fellers.'

Mabel was suddenly overcome and she cried bitterly into her handkerchief. 'This'll ruin us, all of us,' she sobbed. 'I wish I was dead.'

'Don't talk so silly,' Martha said sharply as she rose to put her arm around her old friend's shoulders. 'We're not finished yet, not by any means. Now c'mon, pull yerself tergevver. Yer can't let Charlie see yer in this state. Don't ferget 'e's gonna need your support.'

Outside in the little street word was spreading, and while Queenie Alladyce went to the oilshop to tell John Raney what she had just heard from Albert Price the three musketeers were making their way to the Council chambers to request an audience with the mayor himself.

Sue Carey had left early that morning determined to have it out with Sam Calkin. He would have to listen to her, regardless of his day's commitments. Two families were involved, their future welfare and happiness depending on her, and she had to make him see sense.

Frances Miller was already in the reception area taking a call when Sue walked in and as she finally placed the receiver back on the stand she gave the younger woman a smile. 'All right for some,' she remarked. 'That was Sam Calkin. He was phoning from Burlingford, wherever that is. He said he won't be in today but he'll be in tomorrow evening before the office closes. Something about doing some inter-views.'

Sue slumped down in the chair and sighed deeply. 'I've got to see him, Frances,' she said. 'It's very important.'

The older woman laid a hand on her shoulder. 'I don't know what's going on here but I don't like it,' she replied with concern. 'Paddy's worried about you and so am I.'

Sue reached up and patted her hand. 'I can't say

anything just yet, love, but I will as soon as I can. In the meantime I must see Calkin.'

'He'll be in tomorrow evening.'

'That's too late. I need to see him this morning.'

'But he's at Burlington.'

'Burlingford,' Sue corrected her.

'You know where it is?'

'Yes I know. It's near Maidstone. Calkin has a boat there.'

'Look, if it's that important go and see him right away,' Frances told her. 'I'll say you phoned in sick. Now get out of here before anyone else sees you.'

'Frances, you're a treasure,' Sue said with a big smile as she gathered up her handbag.

The sun was high overhead now, its heat shimmering down from an almost cloudless sky. The river curled past peacefully towards the sea, its waters lapping the shingle as Sam Calkin set to work with a sanding block. Soon the boat would be ready for painting, and then he would be able to launch it once more. It was a welcome break, he thought gratefully. Spencer had agreed to him having some time away from the office to get the article written up, and everything was moving smoothly. This evening he would complete it, apart from the final piece, and that would be added after the meeting tomorrow evening. Spencer had got the go-ahead from the newspaper's proprietor and once he got the completed write-up on Thursday morning as promised he was going to give the police a copy before going to press the following Tuesday.

As he worked on the carvel planking Sam could not help dwelling on the past weekend he had spent here in the company of the beautiful young woman who would now very soon come to hate him. It was a bad mistake to trade on her friendship, but things had moved so fast and it was too late now to change anything.

At first he ignored the sound of footsteps on the shingle, but as they grew nearer he turned to see Sue Carey coming towards him.

'I thought I'd find you here,' she said, her face unsmiling.

'This is a surprise,' he replied, feeling his cheeks flush up.

'Frances told me where I'd find you,' she said, moving the strap of her handbag further up on to her shoulder. 'I must talk to you, and it can't wait.'

'Yes I know,' he said quietly.

'Why, Sam? Why did you let me believe everything was fine, when all the time you were putting a story together which will destroy my family, and the Duggans too?'

'It's not finished yet, Sue,' he reminded her. 'There's still your father and Charlie Duggan to see. They have the right to defend themselves.'

'Well, that's very big of you I must say,' she retorted angrily.

'A letter went out this morning to each of them,' Sam told her, lowering his eyes. 'I've asked them if they'll meet me tomorrow evening.'

'They might not want to see you,' Sue said sharply. 'In any case you don't really expect them to change their account of what happened that night, do you?'

'Yes I understand that, but I have to give them the opportunity.'

'You've still not answered my question,' she told him furiously. 'Why didn't you at least warn me what you were doing? I could understand it if you hadn't gone so far as to bring me down here with you. You just used me, didn't you?'

Sam met her malevolent stare. 'I can't understand that myself,' he replied helplessly. 'I was strongly attracted to you from the first day I saw you, and it never registered with me that I was using you. Whatever you feel towards me and whatever happens now, that weekend together was very precious to me.'

'Well then, don't do it, Sam,' she pleaded. 'Don't destroy us. Please don't print that story.'

He looked into her eyes and sighed heavily. 'God, I wish I hadn't started it,' he said forlornly.

'Then tear it up,' she urged him. 'I'll do anything you ask, just tear it up.'

Sam leaned against the upturned boat and for a few moments his eyes searched the wide blue sky. 'Before I got embroiled in all this I had a dream,' he remarked in a quiet voice. 'It was my father's dream too. I was going to sell the cottage and take this boat down to Cornwall. There's a little place near Land's End called Lamorna Cove. It's a fishing community and the crabs caught there can't be bettered anywhere. I intended to ride out the winter at Lamorna and then exchange this boat for a small fishing smack. I had it all planned. There are quite a few old stone cottages dotted along the cliffs overlooking the cove which used to belong to the tin miners and I was going to buy one. I had this idea of fishing for crabs to eke out a living. I wouldn't need very much in the way of money or possessions. A well-stocked boat and I'd have peace of mind and live a good, worthwhile life. But that was just a dream. I can't live that dream. None of us can. The harsh realities of life just won't allow it.'

'It's a beautiful dream and the best dreams are meant for sharing,' Sue said, looking into his sad eyes. 'I'd come with you. Together we'd make it work, if you'll only tear up that story.'

'You'd do that for me?'

'I'd come to love you,' she said softly. 'I'd have peace of mind too, and I'd feel safe in the knowledge that my family could continue living their lives amongst the people they grew up with. We'd be able to visit them in London from time to time too.'

'Let's walk back to the cottage,' he said.

They made their way along the shingle and crossed the river road into the winding lane. Trees shaded their path and ahead Sue saw the old stone house again as they turned the bend. Sam was quiet and she refrained from interrupting his thoughts. They walked into the cool sitting room and Sam went over to the oaken desk and picked up a folder. 'It wouldn't work, Sue,' he said quietly. 'You can't turn love on and off like a tap. After a few weeks you'd come to detest me and you'd see me as the person who took you away from the people who love you.'

'No, I'd see you as the person who had enough compassion, and courage, to make a decision which saved two families from being destroyed.'

Sam put the folder back down on the desk. 'Last Sunday morning you were at the window staring out at the morning mist,' he told her. 'You didn't know I was lying awake and watching you. I could see your cheek was wet and you were clasping that locket you wear round your neck. I knew you were thinking of the young man who gave it to you. I knew then that you couldn't fall in love with me. By the same token I know full well that you couldn't learn to love me, Sue.'

'I could, believe me I could,' she said with feeling.

Sam shook his head slowly. 'What you're doing is offering yourself up as a sacrifice for your family,' he said quietly. 'You'd sacrifice everything for them.'

'I've told you, Sam, I'd do anything it takes,' she replied.

He picked up the folder and stared down at it for a moment, then he looked up as he held it out to her. 'Take it. Destroy it,' he said. 'This has come to haunt me, and if I printed it now I'm sure it would destroy me as well.'

Sue took the folder and suddenly threw herself into his arms. 'You're a lovely man,' she cried.

He smiled sheepishly, hiding his sadness. 'You'd better be going,' he said. 'I'd give you a lift to the station on the bike but I think you'd prefer a taxi. C'mon, we'll phone for one at the pub.'

The sun was still high overhead as she leaned out of the taxi window. 'Keep the dream, Sam,' she said smiling.

'God help me,' he replied, smiling back at her. 'I just hope Lamorna Cove will be far enough away.'

Chapter Forty-Two

The Duggans had a tiny shed in their backyard where Charlie kept his tins of paint, nails and screws and other bits and pieces he could not bear to throw away. Whenever Charlie wanted privacy or time to think he would disappear into the shed, and that was where Joe Carey found his old friend on Tuesday evening. 'Where's Mabel?' he asked.

'Up the fish shop,' Charlie replied.

'We need ter talk about the letter we got,' Joe told him.

Charlie banged a congealed paintbrush down on the bench, seeming not to hear. 'I've 'ad this brush fer donkey's years an' soon as I let 'er use it the bloody fing's ruined,' he moaned.

'Seven o'clock 'e's comin', so it ses 'ere,' Joe reminded him.

'I 'ad a box o' tin-tacks, I know I did,' Charlie grumbled. 'I'll 'ave ter stop 'er comin' in 'ere. She moves everyfing about.'

'Charlie, are you listenin' ter what I'm sayin'? We should talk about this,' Joe said sharply.

'I wanted those tacks ter pin the lino down but the bloody fings 'ave disappeared. It means I gotta buy more.'

'I got some yer can 'ave, Charlie.'

'It ain't the point. She shouldn't mess about wiv my fings,' Charlie went on. 'I know just where I put everyfing an' then when I come in 'ere I can't find a fing.'

Joe Carey looked at his friend anxiously. 'Come in an' sit down a minute. We gotta talk.'

'Yeah all right. You go in. I won't be a minute.'

Joe went through and sat down in the parlour. Charlie was certainly acting strange, he thought. Mabel would never go in the shed. For one thing she hated spiders, and she'd never dream of touching any of his things.

The clock on the mantelshelf ticked loudly and Joe became impatient. Finally he went out to the backyard and found his neighbour sitting on an upturned beer crate with his head in his hands. 'Are you comin' in or what?' he asked.

Charlie looked up. ''Ello, mate, I was 'opin' yer'd call in,' he said.

Joe frowned. 'I bin sittin' in there waitin' for yer,' he replied irritably.

'Right then,' Charlie said, getting up.

'The way I see it, we can't afford ter change our story, no matter what,' Joe remarked as they stepped into the parlour.

'Is that bloody clock stopped?' Charlie said, frowning.

'Nah, it's still goin'. Can't you 'ear the tickin'?'

Charlie went over to the sideboard and seemed to be searching for something. 'Look I'm a bit pushed at the moment,' he said. 'Can yer come back later?'

'Yeah sure. 'Ere, are you all right?'

'All right? Course I'm all right,' Charlie replied quickly.

'Sorry fer askin',' Joe growled as he walked out.

'Sue's not 'ome yet,' Martha said as he walked into the parlour.

'Somefing's wrong wiv Charlie,' Joe told her. ''E's actin' very strange.'

'Mabel told me 'e's not bin ter work,' Martha replied. 'Apparently 'e's bin sittin' in the church gardens all day. I always thought Charlie was the one who didn't worry.'

'Make no mistake about it, Charlie's worried like everyone else,' Ellie said, looking up from her embroidery. 'He'd be a fool not to.'

'Sue's late,' Joe remarked as he settled himself with the evening paper.

'I expect she's talkin' ter Calkin,' Martha replied.

Tom began to snore in the armchair and Ellie reached out her foot and tapped his ankle. 'He sounds just like a pig,' she said disgustedly.

Martha had just set to work tidying the scullery when Sue came in. Her face was beaming as she went to her mother. 'It's going to be all right, Mum,' she said smiling widely. 'Calkin's not going to do the story.'

Martha threw her arms around her as everyone gathered around them. 'Well done, gel,' Joe told her, matching her smile as he patted her back.

'Bloody brilliant,' Tom shouted.

Ellie managed to keep some of her reserve but she too displayed a smile of relief. 'Thank God for that,' she said.

'I must go an' tell Mabel an' Charlie,' Martha said excitedly as she took off her apron. 'They'll be so pleased.'

At that very moment there was an urgent banging on the front door, and when Tom answered it he saw Pamela with her arm round her mother's shoulders. Both women were distraught.

''Elp us fer Gawd's sake!' Mabel pleaded.

'Whatever's wrong?' Martha asked as she led the two of them into the parlour.

'We've just got in from the fish shop an' 'e was gone,' Mabel sobbed. ''E left me this.'

Martha grabbed the slip of paper Mabel was holding in her hand. It read: 'Sorry love, but I can't take any more. Forgive me. Love, Chas.'

'Where could 'e 'ave gone?' Pamela cried.

''E could be anywhere,' Mabel said, dabbing at her eyes.

''E couldn't 'ave got far,' Joe replied. 'I was wiv 'im a little while ago.'

'I know where he's gone,' Ellie remarked. 'It was in my dream.'

'What are you talkin' about, Ellie?' Martha chided her.

'I tell you it was in my dream. I saw it plain as day.'

'Will you please make sense,' Martha almost shouted.

'Ignore me if you will, but I know where he's gone.'

'Where, fer goodness sake?!'

'Two nights ago I had this awful dream,' Ellie told them. 'I saw a man walking along Shad Thames and he threw himself into the water from Coxen's

Steps. It was an omen. That's where Charlie's gone. Coxen's Steps.'

Tom quickly grabbed his coat from the back of the parlour door. 'It's as good a place as any ter start I s'pose,' he said.

'I'm comin' too,' Pamela told him.

Tom grasped her hand and they hurried out with Ellie's words ringing in their ears. 'It'll be high tide soon.'

Joe Carey turned to Sue. 'I need ter go to 'im,' he said. ''E'll listen ter me.'

'I'll come with you, Dad,' she replied, reaching for her coat.

As they left the house Tom and Pamela were already halfway along Abbey Street. They crossed the quiet thoroughfare into Dockhead and up ahead Shad Thames veered off towards the river. The narrow cobbled lane that ran alongside the river was deserted and as they reached Coxen's Steps they spotted Charlie standing at the bottom of the ancient stone stairs with dark ripples lapping over his feet. Tom pulled Pamela back into the thickening shadows. 'If we scare 'im 'e'll jump,' he whispered.

'Talk to 'im, Tom,' she gasped as she choked back tears.

Tom started to hum tunelessly, his voice slowly getting louder as he moved out of the shadows. ''Ello, Charlie,' he said casually. 'What you doin' 'ere?'

Charlie looked over his shoulder quickly. 'Leave me alone,' he growled.

'Everyfing's gonna be all right, Charlie. Calkin's not gonna write the story,' Tom told him calmly.

'Don't lie ter me,' Charlie shouted.

'It's no lie, it's the trufe.'

'Piss orf an' leave me alone,' Charlie snarled at him.

'I got some ovver news too,' Tom said as he eased forward to the first step.

'What news?'

'It's your Pam. She's pregnant,' he said blithely. 'Yer gonna be a gran'farvver.'

Charlie raised his arm as Tom took another pace. 'Stay away from me or I'll go in,' he shouted.

'C'mon, Charlie, yer scarin' Pamela. Just climb up the steps an' we can all go 'ome.'

'Yer'll 'ave ter grab 'im,' Pamela said quickly.

'One false move on our part an' 'e'll jump,' Tom hissed. 'I couldn't 'old 'im up in that water, we'd both be sucked under.'

'Dad, did you 'ear what Tom said?' Pamela shouted down to him. 'Yer gonna be a gran'farvver.'

'No I'm not. It all ends 'ere,' Charlie called back.

Pamela pulled on Tom's arm. 'Yer dad an' Sue's 'ere,' she told him.

Joe Carey sat down on the top step. 'It's yer ole pal, Charlie,' he called down into the gathering gloom.

'Don't try an' grab me, Joe, or I'll take yer wiv me,' Charlie warned.

'That's not very nice,' Joe said calmly.

'It'll soon be over, then yer can all go 'ome.'

'Not wivout you we won't.'

'I'm finished now,' Charlie said in a gruff voice. 'There's no way I'm gonna end me days in prison.'

'Don't be silly, Chas, it ain't gonna come ter that,' Joe replied. 'Our Sue's persuaded Calkin not ter publish the story. That's right, ain't it, Sue?'

'It's true, Charlie, I swear it,' she said urgently.

'It makes no difference now,' he replied. 'I caused those poor sods ter die. It was me.'

'It wasn't you, ole pal,' Joe told him kindly.

Charlie swung round and looked up at Joe. 'It *was* me. I told Stan 'e could store the stuff at the ware'ouse,' he confessed with a break in his voice. 'I gave 'im the key. It was *me*, d'you 'ear?'

'Yes I 'ear, but it's over an' done wiv,' Joe replied.

'My Stan 'ad a buyer but I told 'im 'e could get a better price if 'e 'ung on,' Charlie explained. 'I said they could store the stuff in the ware'ouse, Gawd fergive me.'

'Our Mo never said a word,' Joe told him.

'That's Mo for yer,' Charlie replied with a ghost of a smile. ''E kept quiet about it 'cos 'e knew it'd cause trouble between me an' you.'

Tom moved down another step and Charlie raised his arm again. 'Come any closer an' I'll jump,' he threatened.

'Yer better wait till that police launch goes past then,' the young man told him.

As Charlie Duggan turned to look out across the river Tom leapt the remaining gap between them and grabbed him. For a moment it seemed as though both men would go into the water but Joe sprang forward to grasp them and they fell in a heap on the slippery stone steps.

The hour was late and Aunt Ellie stifled a yawn as she stood up. 'Well, it's been a tiring day,' she said. 'I'm off to bed.'

'She's a strange woman,' Tom remarked as he sipped his cocoa. 'Fancy 'er knowin' where ter find Charlie frew that dream she 'ad.'

Martha smiled knowingly. 'She never dreamed about it. It was just 'er bein' melodramatic,' she told him. 'Ellie knows very well that Coxen's Steps was a notorious spot fer suicides at one time. If I remember rightly it was Charlie who told 'er.'

Epilogue

The Wednesday evening meeting at the *Bulletin* did not turn out to be the fiery confrontation Sam Calkin had envisaged. In fact Ernest Spencer seemed somewhat relieved that there would be no story. Frances Miller had already advised him that Sue the receptionist was indeed Joe Carey's daughter, and the family disgrace would weigh heavily on her young shoulders. As she pointed out, it was hardly the way to treat one of the *Bulletin*'s loyal employees.

Spencer did see fit to challenge Calkin's motives for withholding the story, however, and finally it was mutually agreed that the next article would be the last, allowing the bright young reporter to seek pastures new.

When the three musketeers saw that the Friday edition of the *Bulletin* did not carry the story of Ship Lane they were very disappointed. Their attempts to involve the mayor in their little scheme had been unsuccessful too, with the doyen of the borough crying off through other more pressing commitments. Undeterred, and with their customary panache, the intrepid threesome decided on another course of action. They knocked at number 6 first, and Wally acted as spokesman. 'We

469

know yer must be very disappointed Joe an' Charlie didn't make the *Bulletin*, Mrs Carey, so we decided ter get this certificate done for yer,' he announced. 'Both yer 'usbands' names are on it so yer'll 'ave ter share it. I 'ope it won't cause no problems. It's a pity that miserable bastard the mayor couldn't get off 'is fat arse an' come down too. Still never mind, try not ter fink about it. Maybe they'll do anuvver bit in the paper soon.'

Over my dead body, Martha thought to herself as she smiled graciously.

'Well it's bin nice talkin' to yer,' Wally said. 'We're gonna knock next door now an' give the Duggans our commiserations. C'mon, lads.'

'There's nobody in,' Martha replied quickly. 'I'll be 'appy ter pass yer message on though.'

'Rightio. Tell the chaps we're proud of 'em, even though the bloody *Bulletin* chose to ignore 'em,' Wally told her.

Martha shook her head slowly as she watched them walk away in the general direction of the Bell. They're getting worse, she thought.

Good as his word Tom Carey made Pamela pregnant, despite her vow to go down the aisle chaste, and the wedding was planned for the autumn.

Another autumn wedding was averted when Queenie Alladyce said no to John Raney after he told her that he intended selling his business and buying a small place in the country. Queenie was happy with her freedom, but her lodger Benny Tracy still lived in hope that one day she would change her mind.

*   *   *

Robbie Casey recovered from his perforated ulcer and was one of the specially invited guests at a private dinner in the union headquarters. Larry Fields, alias the Winkle, was also invited, and along with Mo Carey, Del Abelson and a few local 'faces' they heard the speaker, Warren Simpson MP, declare that following adverse publicity, coming hard on the heels of the tragic death of Walter Miles-Strickland MP, QC whilst fox hunting, and the retirement through ill health of Lord Chief Justice William Waterfield, the Society of Crusaders had decided to disband, with all monies derived from assets going to deserving charities.

Winkle wondered whether or not he would qualify, considering that he was now a legal proposition eking out a living with his seafood stall on Sundays, but on reflection he thought not.

The Duggans and the Careys had picked up with their lives once more, though Joe and Charlie still confined their backyard chats to light-hearted matters and the vagaries of the horses.

In September Sue Carey received a postcard from Sam Calkin in Cornwall, telling her that he had completed his long coastal trip and was now establishing himself as a fisherman. She read the message twice, and as she turned it over once more to look at the picture the solitary diamond in her engagement ring flashed in the light. Her heart was as light as a feather and there were no regrets when she dropped the postcard into the fire.

In November the *Bulletin* closed down, and two weeks later Paddy O'Brian and Frances Miller were married.

Conner Street's War

To Shirley, Stephen, Sharon and Sally

Prologue

An old man walked slowly past the shuttered shops that spread along the base of the building on the Riverside Estate, and took the walkway to Conner Point. The wind caught the door of the high rise building as he opened it and slammed it behind him as he crossed the hall. As he waited for the lift, the door again creaked open and slammed behind a woman carrying a bulging shopping bag. She put it down and pulled up her coat collar against the cold wind that whistled through the glassless window panel beside the door. A plastic sheet had been crudely nailed to the frame and it flapped fiercely. The woman held a hand to the middle of her back. "'Ello Mr Bowman," she said, glancing up at the light above the lift which had remained on above number ten. "It's them kids wot do it. They press all the buttons."

Bob Bowman looked at her and grunted.

She stabbed at the lift button impatiently. "I keeps on tellin' the porter, though a fat lot o' good 'e is."

The old man nodded and looked up at the light that had now started to move along the numbers. At last there was a clunk and the lift door slid open. The two entered the lift and the woman's face screwed up as she noticed the puddle at the rear. "Bloody kids. They don't even live on the Estate. 'Arf of 'em are gyppos' kids."

Bob Bowman was getting irritated. He pressed the button marked fifteen and the woman reached across and pressed the button above. Bob noticed that she had a tic. Her eyes blinked and her nose twitched like a rabbit's. A grin ghosted over Bob's hawkish features and his pale blue eyes twinkled. "Coffins," he said, and the lift stopped at the eleventh. He pressed the correct

v

button and the lift moved up.

The woman looked at him blankly.

"That's right yer know. These lifts were made ter take coffins. Saves slidin' 'em down the apples." The woman's nose twitched. "Well, coffins an' stretchers," he added as the lift stopped on the fifteenth. He alighted grinning, aware of her stern gaze boring into the back of his head.

There was a numbered door at each corner of the hallway. He made for the one to his right and put his evening paper under his arm as he started to search for his key. The door opened suddenly and Brenda his daughter stood in the doorway. "I heard the lift, Dad. We were getting worried."

The lights below spread out into the distance. They twinkled, a myriad earthbound stars. A twin row of lights arced away, tracing the path of the Old Kent Road. Eastwards, a square of lights lit the railway station. A commuter train slid along toward the dark hills of suburbia, its carriages coughing out blue flashes. Immediately below, the grassed area looked clean and deserted in the light from the tall concrete lampposts.

Brenda sat in an easy chair, a sewing basket at her feet. She held a needle and cotton out at arm's length, her eyes squinting as she sought to threadle the needle. On her lap lay a pair of torn trousers. Her husband Joe sat facing her, his back to the window. He had the evening paper spread out over his crossed legs as he tried to interest himself in the news. Right then sleep seemed to be the better proposition, and his eyes started to close.

Bob Bowman sat by the window. The curtains remained open, for as his daughter often remarked, "only the birds can look in". The young woman studied her father's face as he sat hunched in the high-backed chair. Concern showed in her eyes. She had noticed the change in him since he had moved in with her and Joe just over a year ago. His shoulders sagged more of late, and his sure stride had become slower, more deliberate. His eyes were now growing glassy and faded. Worse still, he had started to mumble to himself on occasions. He was doing it now. Brenda thought about their impending move down to Sevenoaks. Her father had flatly refused to leave dockland. "'Ere I was born, an' 'ere I'll die," he'd said.

The council had promised her father a bedsit in the old people's dwellings near the river, and the old boy was looking forward to it, but as yet there was nothing definite. Brenda hoped that once he got away from the tower block and among people he knew, her father's health would improve. Brenda felt helpless. Her husband's firm was moving, and there were houses made available for the staff. If only she did not feel so worried about her father. She turned to Joe but her husband was lost to sleep. His head hung to one side, his mouth gaping open.

Down below a car turned into the estate, its headlights scything a path before it. The car revved along the road and the muffled sound of its engine was lost on the old man. He had heard a different sound, the deep, throaty sound of a river boat as it dragged its charge toward the Pool. The tug belched again; a long hoot, then a shorter one. The familiar sound stirred his memories. He was back once more amongst the river men: stevedores, dockers, cranemen, like himself, and lightermen. He could almost taste the river, with its pungent-smelling, greyish mud, its sudden fogs that crept up from the Estuary and spread inshore, swirling over the quayside and into the narrow, cobbled dockside streets. He remembered the muffled sounds of the chugging workhorses of the Thames, the tugs that sat low in the oily swell and hauled and fussed at the complexities of moorings. He remembered the dangerous climb up the cold iron ladder that took him high above the quay, up into a space above the sheds, where he was powerful, where he lorded it over the men below, yet was attentive to their every signal and gesture. Up here he pulled and pushed the levers that moved the monstrous crane jib and arm, which hoisted, swung, lowered, and set down rope-slung cargoes gently onto the quay. Up here the smells drifted, smells of sweating wine casks, ripening fruit, and sour mud.

There were other sights that the old man's memories surveyed. He saw Tower Bridge rising and he sighed deeply. He saw again the cantilevers rise and sink, the slender part reaching high for the bridge towers, the bulk sinking into the giant stone bastions. He heard the warning bell and saw the large vessel as it slipped slowly and silently out from the Pool of London, toward the Estuary and the oceans beyond. He saw once more the scene down river, the rotting boatyards where ships were once made of stout English oak. He saw the riverside taverns, where long ago corsairs hung to rot, their popping, sightless eyes meat for the crows, and a terrible warning to returning mariners.

Bob Bowman raised his shoulders and let them sag again. The river ache was in his bones and he looked down below. The scene changed. He saw the little back-street and felt its heartbeat. There was the iron lamppost, its light spreading over the cobbled stones. A looped rope hung from the ladder support and at the bottom of the rope a coat was folded to make a seat. A young girl occupied the seat. She swung slowly, her feet scraping over the cobbles. Above her the hiss of the damaged mantle sounded and the escaping flame burned blue in the cold evening air. A small boy stood inside the lighted area, his face stained with the juice of the half orange that he held in his dirty grasp. Bob Bowman looked down into the dark backyard. A door opened and a shaft of light caught the rusting wringer with its dry wooden rollers that had started to split. He saw the long bathtub and the dartboard hanging from the whitewashed wall. The door shut and the darkness reclaimed its secrets.

Iron wheels sounded on the cobbles as the horse-cart rounded the turn. A carman sat, his shoulders drooping in fatigue, while his eager horse was struggling home to its hay-filled stall. Bob Bowman, sitting by his window in the sky, saw the lights all go out. A terrifying wail reached his ears as the generator on the police station roof started up. As the scream of the siren died so another familiar sound reached him. It came from the dark sky, and Bob stiffened in his chair. He watched as the pencils of light danced about the heavens and then converged on a tiny silver object floating in the light. The object drifted on. There was a loud swish and a louder roar as mortar and bricks flew skywards and the rush of flames engulfed the wharf. A whole wall toppled into the Thames and the water burned. The old man's head was held sideways, his ears straining for the sound. It floated up to him, "There's an old mill by the stream." Softly, then more loudly, "Nellie Dean," it said, and he looked down, his eyes searching for the place. There it was, the mound of earth, like some prehistoric barrow. From the bricked vents on top of the mound, the voices were now loud and clear. The song went on, "Where I used to sit and dream."

Another roar, and the urgent shout of "Oil bomb on the factory!" Burning contents from the building spewed over the mound and the earth burned. Gun flashes lit up the street and the running feet as the men raced to the shelter. They dived down into the gutter for safety, then jumped up and ran faster. One man stayed still, his life-blood draining out and down into the sewer.

There was a shout "The warden, get the warden!"

He was running; steel helmet held down by the tight strap under his chin. His hands were blackened and cut. His chest was heaving and his coat scorched and torn. He saw the faces; grey, dust-caked and pleading, "'Elp us, Bob! ... Don't leave us, Bob! ... Gawd bless yer, Bob." Bob Bowman shuddered and sank back into his chair, his eyes closed.

A voice, nearer and louder, came to him. "Dad. Dad." He felt the hand on his shoulder. "There's your tea, Dad. Was you dreaming?"

Bob sat up, shook his head and clasped the mug of steaming tea. "Sorry girl, must've dozed orf."

His daughter looked out of the window at the full yellow orb floating in the night sky. "It's a full moon," she said.

"Bomber's moon we used ter call it, once upon a time."

Chapter One

The early morning light had filtered very rapidly into the velvet sky, and caused the elevated signal box at Bermondsey Crossing to stand out in sharp relief. The white painted weatherboards around the four sides of the cabin had lost some of the grime after the night storm, and the water had run down on to the six feet high bricked base, which had absorbed the moisture like a sponge. The storm had laid the dust and the air was crystal. The rows of track glistened, and seemed to forge into a silver strip away into the distance. Westwards, the track bent, a long arc that reached the London Bridge terminal. One track split from the sweep and took an opposing curve into the goods depot, a half mile from the station.

Inside the cabin Joe Harper yawned and stretched his aching back. The first of the morning trains was due, the Kent milk train.

A bell sounded; a shrill ring that told the signalman the 'milkman' was on time and he responded by throwing over the heavy lever that controlled the bisection of the track. He then pulled on an adjacent lever that dropped the signal-arm into the 'clear' position. Joe glanced down the track to check that the green light showed, then wiped his hands on a piece of cotton waste. The kettle rattled as the blue gas flame licked around its sides. A steam ring popped from the spout and enlarged as it floated upwards. Joe carefully counted out four heaped spoonfuls of tea leaf from a battered canister into a brown enamel teapot. A minute later the milk train clattered past and the cabin became enveloped in steam. Rivulets of the condensed vapour ran down the windows and the cabin shook. The kettle started to boil and Joe Harper filled

1

the teapot to the brim, stirring the brew thoughtfully. Fred Harris, the day man, was due soon and, as was the custom, the shift always started and ended with a strong brew.

Joe put the filled teapot under a ragged looking cover and stretched again, his fingers reaching around for the offending ache. There was a stained mirror taped onto the wall and Joe Harper looked at his reflection. The wide spaced eyes, grey-green and tired, stared back at him. He studied the thick dark hair that had started to recede and the square chin that had sprouted a black stubble. He looked at his broad nose and noticed how the skin was becoming loose around his neck. He sighed and pulled a face at his reflection, then walked over to the window facing down the track. He grinned to himself as he saw Fred Harris limping towards the cabin. The day man carried a canvas bag that was slung over his shoulder, his thumb crooked around the strap. Fred's limp was the result of a shell splinter, obtained on the Somme in '15. Pieces of the metal had been removed by doctors, and by Fred himself over the years, as tiny pieces worked their way to the surface of his leg. Fred was convinced that the steel portion still embedded was going rusty. "Stan's to reason, don't it? Wiv all the rain we get."

The two men were lifelong pals. They had run the streets as boys, and marched out of those backwaters to fight in France. They took the 'King's Shilling' and suffered the mud and slush of the trenches, and they both returned. Fred Harris limped back on crutches and his pal returned with his lungs blistered and scarred from the evil vapours of the mustard gas.

Fred Harris climbed the wooden steps up to the cabin and walked in. "Mornin' mate, quiet night?"

"Not too bad, Fred, got two extra early on. One looked like a troop train."

Fred sat down and rubbed his leg. "It's the bloody rain, bin givin' me 'ell all night," he complained. Joe grinned, handed a mug filled with red-coloured tea to Fred, and sat down on a tall stool. "That'll oil your rusty leg, me ole mate."

2

Fred sipped the hot tea noisily. "Rained all night, so my little woman tells me."

Joe nodded and he took a swig at his tea. "Left off around four this mornin'. 'Eavy too."

Fred Harris rubbed a large hand over his eyes. "My Sara woke me up just about then. Said she could 'ear the water drippin' in. I said to 'er, wadja s'pect me to do, shin up the drainpipe wiv a load o' slates? Go back to sleep I told 'er."

Joe laughed and finished his tea. He collected Fred's empty mug and washed them both under the running tap. There was a large calendar hanging on the wall which depicted a young lady in tennis clothes and sporting a large green eyeshade. She smiled down into the room. Joe tore the date slip off to expose the new date. It read Sunday 3rd September, 1939.

"Well I'm away 'ome, mate, take it easy."

"See you, Joe," Fred replied.

The night man paused by the door. "I'm goin' to stay up for the speech, it looks bad."

Fred nodded. "Don't see no way out now, wot wiv the Czechs, an' now the Poles."

Joe opened the door of the cabin. "Gawd 'elp us if it does start. Be a sight worse than the last lot."

A flock of pigeons flew over the pickle factory as Joe Harper walked along the empty street. Birds were singing and the sun had started its journey into the sky. Joe was feeling a sense of uneasiness as he walked on. The sound of iron wheels on cobbles reached his ears, and from around the corner Taffy Davies appeared, struggling to get his heavy milk-cart on an even course as the wheels slithered over the cobbles. The empty milk bottles on top of the cart rattled in their containers and two small metal churns swung together on the side rail. Taffy leaned forward against the weight, his head down and his neck muscles straining. Joe nodded a greeting but the Welshman ignored him. Joe stood for a moment watching as the cart resumed a straight course, then he turned into Tanners Alley, a cobbled pathway that led to Conner

3

Street. The alley was flanked on one side by the high wall of the leather factory, and on the other by a row of pretty little cottages. The local kids had named the place 'Door Knocker Alley' — and for good reason. On every door there were the most hideous-looking door knockers. One was of a lion's head, snarling; another, the grinning face of the devil. A mailed fist warned from one door, and many other leering, threatening monstrosities confronted the passer-by.

It was as though someone had looked at the pretty cottages, with their ivy-covered walls, their colourful flower-boxes that hung below the shuttered windows, and had decided to exact a penance. This someone had looked at the front doors that opened onto the cobbled path and maliciously concluded that a reminder would hang there. Beauty had no place in such an area; for how could any tranquility exist with the grimy wharves and warehouses, the noisy grind of the leather factories, the belt-driven machines and the steam presses that thrashed and thumped, the ugly arches and cold iron bridges that carried the railway, and the run-down streets and tenement blocks, stained and covered with sulphur and carbon. Why should there be such a place in the morass that was dockland?

The knockers were fitted, and the perpetrator stood back to ponder. He was not pleased, for the ugliness of his work was partly concealed, subdued by the flowering beauty that grew from the window boxes, and from the wall-rooted vines. Yellow primrose, and bright red geranium calmed the ashen iron. Shades of begonia and pansy and the white of the doorsteps soothed the trepidation of the passer-by and he breathed more easily. Young children walked the alley without fear as they leered back at the faces, and they gave the place its name.

Joe Harper heard the gurgle of rain water running beneath the drain grill as he walked along the path and into Conner Street. At the point where the alley opened into the Street was an iron hitching post. It stood upright and embedded in the path. The post was once the barrel of a Crimean war cannon. But now its muzzle was

4

plugged and faced the sky. Joe touched the cold, smooth surface as he passed by and thought it strange that he had never really recognised the significance of the harmless looking piece of ironmongery, until this morning. But then this particular morning was different.

The signalman turned left, and strolled along the quiet street towards number 22. As he passed the Flannagan's house at number 30, he heard the new baby yelling, the loud shout from Patrick, then the soothing voice of Bridie as she no doubt satisfied the belly pains of the child. The Flannagans were a large brood. Bridie fussed over them all like a mother hen over her chicks. She also kept a firm hold over her huge husband, although she barely reached his shoulder. Patrick worshipped them all, but there were times when the strain, and the din, would force him to seek the peace and quiet of the 'Eagle', a little pub on the corner of Conner Street.

Joe reached his house and pulled on the door string. He walked into the dark passage and entered the tiny parlour. His lodger, a wizened looking old man, followed him in and stood waiting as Joe sat down heavily into his favourite chair.

"Like a cuppa, Joe?"

"I could do, Skip," replied the younger man.

The old man blew his nose on his large red handkerchief.

Joe started to take off his boots. "Is Rosie awake?"

The old man poked the handkerchief into his back pocket. "I took 'er up a cup, gone back to kip," he answered.

"You're up early this mornin', Skipper."

"Couldn't sleep for the rain, and that wind. Reminded me of those storms we used to get at sea."

Joe licked his lips and grinned. "I'd really like a cuppa, Skip."

The lodger pointed his long boney finger at him. "Comin' up."

Joe Harper knew the man well. If he allowed the old seaman to get started on a subject concerned with the sea, then the chances of a quick cuppa would evaporate.

There were nights, when the wind howled and the fire burned bright, when Joe and Rosie listened with interest as the old seafarer spun his yarns from the oceans. On this particular morning, however, and at this early hour, he was not inclined to listen.

Skipper was in his mid-seventies, a dapper little man, with a full mane of snow-white hair that hung over his coat collar, and defied the comb. He had spent his youth walking the piers of the world and sailing the oceans under canvas; in the coal-fired tramps, from Yokohama to Lisbon, from Valparaiso to San Francisco. He'd weathered the storms and suffered the food, until the pains in his bones and the hardships became more than he could bear. He had said goodbye to the feel of the wind and spray and settled for the lodging room near the docks. That way, he could still walk near the ships, and meet the like of himself, men that smelt of the sea and talked of the ships. For a time the old seaman moved around, then he found the Harpers and he loved them like his own. They were a real family, and they cared for his needs. He'd seen the girls grow into women and marry. He'd been around when the eldest's two were born. Yes, this was his home, his family.

Joe sat back in his chair and lit a cigarette. Skipper came in with the tea. "'Ere we are, son," he said.

"Thanks, Skip," Joe answered, looking quizzically at the other's fluffy white hair. "Wot you been doin' to your barnet?"

The old man ran his fingers through his mane. "Rosie got on to me to get it washed, said I was goin' lousy, so I used some of them there Lux flakes."

Joe smiled. "Looks like a pile of candyfloss, mate."

Skipper growled and sat down.

Rosie came into the room. She had her dressing gown wrapped tightly around her ample figure.

"Mornin', luv, busy night?" she asked.

"Not so bad, bit of extra traffic." he replied. "Did you sleep okay?"

"Didn't 'ear a thing, I was that tired out."

Joe puffed a cloud of cigarette smoke ceilingwards.

Rosie started to remove the wire pipe-cleaners which served as curlers from her hair. "I'll get you some breakfast," she said.

"No rush, luv, I'm staying up for the news anyway."

Rosie looked into his pale eyes. "Bad ain't it?"

"Yeah, it is, an' there's no use sayin' otherwise. There's goin' to be a war, my love, an' it's goin' to be a nasty one."

Rosie pulled up a chair and sat down at the table. She placed a small mirror in front of her and started to comb out her hair.

Skipper took out his pipe and greasy tobacco pouch then proceeded to fill the blackened bowl. When he'd packed the 'Nosegay' strands down tight, he struck a match and drew on the stem. Sparks flew onto his dirty waistcoat and he quickly brushed them off. Rosie gave him a cold stare. "One of these days you're goin' to set yourself alight."

The street was coming to life. Footsteps sounded as folk went for their Sunday papers and their usual weekend supply of winkles and shrimps. Near Tanners Alley, the old rag-and-bone man leaned on his battered barrow and called out his unintelligible cry. On the pavements, the children played at hopscotch and with their coloured glass marbles along the kerbsides. They cracked their whips and sent the wooden tops skidding along pavements and in amongst the cobbles.

Two girls slowly turned a skipping-rope as a smaller girl hopped in and out of range of the thudding cord, singing a ditty as she went. The sun shone down from a cloudless sky, and at the end of the street the ice-cream man fixed the canopy above his stall.

Skipper had gone for the morning papers and Joe sat with Rosie in their tiny parlour. The woman looked up at the framed photograph sitting on the mantelshelf. "I'm worried over 'em, Joe, what with them children bein' so young. I've told Josie to try an' get out of London, get 'em into the country somewhere."

Joe looked at her. "Listen Rosie, Josie nor Brian would let them kids be evacuated. Brian will be called up

7

soon and as for Mary an' Bob, well, Bob's bin mobilised now, an' Mary's workin' at the 'ospital. It's goin' to be difficult."

Rosie looked down at her hands and studied her nails. "Mary's takin' it well, but young Josie seems upset," she said.

"I've noticed 'ow our Josie's got lately, seems jumpy with the kids," replied Joe.

Rosie's eyes filled with tears and her husband leaned forward, taking her hands in his own and gently squeezing them as he planted a kiss on her forehead. Rosie dabbed at her eyes and stood up. "I'd better get those breakfast things washed up," she said.

The door latch slid over against the pull of the string and Skipper came into the parlour and dropped the papers onto the table. He had his clay pipe held in the corner of his mouth. Joe ignored the papers and lit another cigarette. Skipper sat down by the empty fire-grate and reached for a pipe-cleaner. "Rosie looks upset, Joe."

"Yeah, it's the girls, an' the two little ones. Rosie wants 'em to try an' get away from London."

Skipper threaded the pipe-cleaner along the stem of his stained pipe and worked it back and forth. He then tapped the bowl gently against his foot and blew hard down the stem. "If it does start we're goin' to get a pastin' aroun' this area. Stan's to reason, there's the docks, an' railways. The bastards are gonna go them sort of places."

Joe stood up. "I'm goin' for a breath of air."

The signalman leaned against the door post, his gaze wandering up and down the street. A large woman was having an argument with the ragman, "You want to get that there contraption fixed. It must come to more than that," she exploded.

"I've 'ad this spring balance for donkeys' years, it's right to the penny," the man said with conviction.

"Looks like it could do wiv a drop of oil," she replied, not wishing to be outdone.

The rag man counted out a few copper coins and dropped them into the woman's hand. She turned without another word and marched off. The man tucked the spring scale into his belt and threw the bundle of old rags onto the near-empty barrow.

Joe's gaze took in the row of terraced houses opposite. The sulphur and black carbon stains on the bricks were somewhat toned down by the white-laced curtains and the clean white-stoned front door steps. The grey slated roofs sloped down to meet drooping gutters and above, perched precariously, were the brick stacks, supporting red earthenware chimneypots.

Almost directly across from the Harpers' house was a newly erected structure. The design was of a hump-shaped tunnel with a thick wall placed down the centre to divide the space into two separate caverns. The roof was at ground level, and to get inside a path had been provided that sloped down to the entrance. The whole thing was covered by a thick layer of rubble and earth, making it invisible from the air. The path was flanked by metal railings and a gate closed the entrance. Just inside the iron gate there stood a wooden post set into the ground. A square board was nailed on top of the post and the square was painted a dull green. Beneath the painted part a sign was hung which said: 'In the event of a GAS ATTACK the paint will change colour'. What the notice did not say was which colour the board would take, nor did the sign inform the curious that, should they wait around to see the miracle happen, they also would change colour.

Joe looked over at the shelter and noticed that the padlock was missing and the gate ajar. He pondered over this and went into his house. The loud ticking clock on his parlour mantelshelf said ten forty-five.

A few miles away, in a room overlooking the quiet Westminster street, last minute preparations were taking place for the broadcast that was to change the lives of the folk of Conner Street. In fact it would never be the same again for millions of people throughout the whole world.

Chapter Two

The long, wide Tower Road stretched from the wharves and docks to a junction, and from that junction main arteries led away to tidy suburbia, to large homes and to well kept gardens. The arteries led away to open green areas and to places with large smart shops. Tower Road had shops, but they were not smart, and the only greenery in Tower Road poked out from the boxes and bloomed from the barrows and stalls in the market. The dockland market was famous, for it was said that if an item could not be purchased there, then it wasn't made.

The Conner Street folk were proud of their market, and when they walked up the street, and dodged across the busy road between the clattering trams, they found themselves right in the middle of the kerbside trading.

The bone-shaking trams squealed to a stop at the beginning of the market and disgorged stern-faced, basket-carrying women who hurried into the trading place. The trams also transported idlers, who came to be part of the bustling scene and who strolled along the line of stalls at a leisurely pace.

Early each weekday morning a number 68 tram brought Stanley Nathan to Tower Road market. Stanley walked through the area at a brisk pace, for he had a business to attend to and by nature he was punctual and conscientious. The stall-holders acknowledged him as he passed by and Stanley returned their salutations with a nod and a grin. Stanley Nathan was well-liked and a respected member of the market fraternity. He had been a 'market man' for as long as he cared to remember, as his father had before him. The bustling scene and the smell of the place never failed to stimulate him and as he walked to

10

his particular place of trading his face took on a cherubic expression. Stanley had had his share of sadness, however, and sometimes he dwelt upon it, but this was his home and he experienced a feeling of contentment when he looked about him.

Fruit and vegetables were piled high on the stalls, and there were barrows stacked with odd clothes, salads and toiletries. There was a fish barrow, and a live eel stall, where the children peered into the galvanised tanks to watch the squirming, sliding snakes of the sea. There was a 'Cheap-Jack' stall, where cards of buttons, thimbles, needles and pins, and blocks of coloured dyes were heaped together with cough mixture, soap and soda. When the pile started to diminish, Cheap-Jack would tip another box of mysteries onto the heap. One day, Mrs Wallace stopped to search for some shirt buttons and, delving into the pile, she discovered a bottle of patent cough cure. The label was dirty and stained, but she was able to read about the miraculous qualities of the tar-black contents. As her husband had a racking cough, Mrs Wallace took the bottle home.

It didn't cure her husband's cough, but it did turn the spoon green and a small drop burnt a hole in her only tablecloth.

Spaced about the market were solemn-faced hawkers, who stood over their open suitcases displaying bundles of boot and shoe-laces, cards of collar studs, and razor blades. They sold dusters, handkerchiefs and cheap brooches, little celluloid dolls and rubber ducks. The hawkers stood in the gaps between the stalls, alongside the traders, their backs no more than a couple of feet from the passing trams.

One character stood between the eel stall and a salad barrow. He wore a dirty, faded raincoat with a row of campaign medals pinned to the lapel. A strap slung around his neck supported a tray, which contained matches and shoelaces. A ginger-tinged moustache grew down over his lower lip. The man never, ever, spoke, nor did he ever seem to move his eyes. He stared ahead, like a sentry, protecting the space between the stalls. Even when

11

a passing baby, held over the mother's shoulder, grasped a packet of laces the man's eyes remained perfectly still.

The smells of the ripened fruit and the fresh fish hung in the air, and were carried on the wind into the little backstreets, so that the inhabitants became aware of the market the moment they opened their front doors. The sounds too carried into the backwaters, above the noise of the clattering, rocking trams.

The market had shops that faced the stalls and barrows, and if an item was not available at the kerbside then it could more than likely be found in one of the shops.

The fame of Tower Road market spread afar, so that one day a lady in a moth-eaten fur coat came to the market to buy a parrot. She went away with a fine specimen, a talking parrot in a tall round cage. It was Cheap-Jack who told the story when he'd attracted an audience around his stall: "True as I'm standin' 'ere," he said. "This 'ere lady takes this lovely parrot 'ome, an' stan's it on 'er sideboard. Well the bleedin' parrot won't say a word. So back she comes an' gives ole Silas an earful. Anyway, the ole man knows what's wrong, an' 'e sells the lady a little mirror. It turns out that parrots like to see 'emselves, it perks 'em up. 'That'll make the cow-son talk,' 'e says. Anyway, next week, back come this 'ere moth-eaten lady. 'That bleedin' parrot's not said a word yet.' 'P'raps the thing's short-sighted,' 'e says. 'E sells 'er a little silver bell, an' 'e says that when the parrot 'ears the tinkle it'll answer." Cheap-Jack cleared his throat and a customer who had just stopped at the stall asked him how much was a packet of collar studs. "Just a minute lady, I'm tellin' 'em about this parrot. Anyway, the lady goes away an' sure enough, back she comes the next week an' gives ole Silas a right mouthful. 'The bleedin' parrot's dead,' she says. Silas can't understand it. 'Didn't it say anythin'?' 'e asked 'er. 'Well', this lady said, 'it did try to mumble a few words before it croaked it ...' 'Well, go on,' Silas almost shouts at 'er. The lady dabs 'er eyes cos she's a bit upset. 'It sounded like it tried to say food ... food.'"

The customers erupted in laughter, and the woman

holding the card of collar studs asked him again about the price.

"Just a minute, lady, I'm nearly finished. Ole Silas went berserk. 'You mean to stan' there an' tell me you never fed the bleedin' thing? Strike me pink, lady, it only needed a sprinkle o' birdseed.'" The customers were laughing, and Cheap-Jack went on, "Ole Silas was raving. 'E reckoned the lady should 'ave known 'ow to look after pets, she 'ad enough of 'em on 'er bleedin' coat ... Oh now don't laugh, girls, the story's true. Sure as Gawd made little apples."

The woman with the card of collar studs finally left satisfied, and the market settled down to normality. The hustle and bustle of the place contrasted with the peace and quiet of the little backstreets. Conner Street though had its fair share of activity. The 'Eagle' and a small hatter's shop occupied the corners at the market end, and then the row of houses continued on each side until they were halted by the two factories: the leather works and a small custard powder factory.

At the Kent Road end were two small corner shops. The one on the left was owned by a little old lady who sold sweets and tobacco, whilst the shop opposite boasted a multitude of things, from vinegar and hearthstone, paint and putty, to tin-tacks and shoe leather. Behind the counter, hanging high from a large hook in the ceiling was a bundle of canes. They had crooked handles and were looked upon with awe by the visiting children.

On this Sunday, the shops were closed and shuttered and the stalls and barrows stored away in a backstreet shed. The only one to be seen was the shrimp and winkle stall that stood outside the hatter's shop. On the stall was a white cover, nailed in place over the wooden boards. An aproned lady with a ruddy face scooped up a pile of winkles into a pewter pot and dropped the pint-worth into a brown paper bag. A customer waited while the lady scooped up a pint of shrimps. The ice cream man had just arrived and was tightening the red and white canopy above the four brass poles that stuck out of his barrow. He then opened up a box and stacked up columns of wafer cones ready for the children, two of whom were already waiting, copper coins held tightly in their sticky palms.

There was a strange tension in the air on that warm Sunday morning. Everyone felt it, as women snapped at their children and men stood in small groups talking quietly. It would soon be eleven o'clock and the waiting would be over. The suspense had grown during the past few months when signs and posters began to appear on hoardings, walls and lampposts. The signs pointed out first-aid posts, gas mask fitting stations and gas cleansing stations; the air raid shelters and the wardens' posts, which were set up inside sand-bagged and strengthened buildings. The posters issued terrifying instructions, 'What to do in the event of an air raid or an invasion'.

The past few months had also heralded in a new sound; the air raid siren. There had been demonstrations of this new, frightening device that screamed out a warning from the roofs of police stations and public buildings. The tone of the siren rose from a low pitched moan to an ear-splitting scream and, although broadcasts and leaflets had warned them what to expect, the sound still struck fear into the hearts of everyone who heard it. Bridie Flannagan called the siren a "scream from hell". Her husband Patrick used somewhat earthier adjectives to describe the noise.

The periodical 'try-out' of the air raid warning was sure to awaken the Flannagans' baby, and as soon as Bridie had settled James again the long high-pitched sound of the all-clear would reverberate through the streets. James immediately woke up and made his own contribution to the cacophony.

The Spencer Street Primary School was a gas mask fitting station. Every day the people came with their children, the young leading the old. They came for their gas masks and they stood patiently in line as the uniformed workers fussed and instructed. The conversations were repeated daily: "No, Mrs Smith, you musn't worry over your hair

14

... That's right, pull the straps over your head ... I'll try you with a medium one ... It's only condensation, Mrs Smith ... Yes, put your chin right into it ..." So it went on. They brought out the children's masks, the red and blue ones with the two eye-pieces and the flat nose that rasped when the wearer breathed out. So it went on: "No, Johnnie, don't frighten your sister ... Don't pull the nose off, sonny ..." The 'Mickey Mouse' masks were not at all frightening and the children rushed to try them on. "That's all right, Mother. If he won't take it off, let the little dear walk home in it." And mother walked from the centre with little Johnnie still wearing his mask and terrified two old ladies on their way in. The frailer of the two clung to her sister as a rasping noise came from the 'Mickey Mouse' mask. Johnnie's mother cuffed his ear and a wailing sound came from inside the mask as she led her son away.

The Fletcher sisters entered the centre to be confronted with a strange scene. One of the workers was demonstrating how to place a baby in a large container that was then zipped up. A hand pump supplied oxygen to the infant, who could be seen gurgling happily through a large cellophane visor. "C'mon, Mother, let's see you use the pump ... No, not so fast! It isn't a bicycle pump ... That's better, a nice steady action." There was a tearful outburst, and a reassurance, "Look here, I don't suppose you'll ever need to use this, but it is as well to be prepared, isn't it?"

Maud Fletcher whispered to her sister, "I wonder if they have anything here for the parrot?" and was rewarded with a despairing look.

One morning, Mrs Jenkins walked into the centre and stood patiently in line until it was her turn. Someone put on a mask and adjusted the strap over her head. When they had picked her off the floor they tore the mask off and applied the smelling salts. Later they tried again. Mrs Jenkins was picked up once more and eased into a chair. She sat ashen-faced for a while; then, when the colour had returned to her cheeks, they made towards her with a mask. Mrs Jenkins was adamant, "If you think I'm goin' ter put that bleedin' contraption on again, yer got another think comin'. Take it away, an' if there is a gas attack I'll piss on my 'ankey an' 'old it round me face. They say it's just as good!"

Mrs Brown nudged Mrs Jones, "That won't worry 'er much, she's always pissed anyway."

Nan Roberts sauntered into the centre and fluttered her eyelids at one of the male workers. She was soon attended to and left the centre with a gas mask case slung casually over her shoulder. Mrs Jones nudged Mrs Brown "Did yer see that?"

"See what?"

"Didn't yer notice? 'Er gas mask box. It was marked 'large'. I always said she 'ad a big 'ead."

Having decided that there was little more to interest them, Mrs Lizzie Brown and Mrs Emmie Jones left the centre. Both were carrying a gas mask in a box, and on the side of each box the word 'medium' was stamped with indelible ink.

Soon after, the Fletcher sisters left the centre and slowly made their way home to Conner Street; Minnie stern-faced, Maud tearful. Like everyone who collected their gas masks, the sisters were worried, and they knew better than most about the effects of a gas attack. Their younger brother had been gassed during the Battle of the Somme and had never fully recovered. They would never forget the silence when, a few years ago, the laboured breathing from his blistered lungs had finally ceased.

Each day people came and went. The mothers left the centre with large cartons resting on their prams, and the youngsters with small cases slung over their shoulders. Everywhere the preparations went on ...

As the sun rose higher in the sky, the tension mounted. In Conner Street, as with other streets in dockland, the inhabitants gathered around their wireless sets. The tension was mounting too in the Flannagans' home, but for a different reason. "I'm goin' to be late, woman, where's my boots?" the big Irishman said as he glanced at the clock.

Bridie puffed and handed him a pair of elastic-sided black boots from under the table. Patrick Flannagan took a brush and started to apply some polish to the dull toecaps. Two-year-old Terry grabbed one of the brushes and threw it at the cat who darted under the table. Patrick retrieved the brush and Terry kicked his foot under the table in an effort to get at the cat. "Terry, you leave that cat alone," screamed Bridie, her shrill voice waking up little James. The baby started to cry and Bridie cooed to him as she rocked the pram. "You naughty boy, now see what you've done."

The seven-year-old twins, Sheena and Sally, played in one corner, watched closely by Patrick junior, who waited his chance to poke at the doll's glass eye. At five years old Patrick junior was beginning to feel the urge to take everything to pieces, and he wondered what his father would say when the dismantled alarm clock was found.

Maureen came into the room, placing her hands on her hips. She puffed at Terry who immediately scuttled away to the scullery. Maureen was the eldest of the brood and at ten she felt sufficiently grown up to scold the children. Maureen was Patrick's favourite, although he would not admit to it. The child had her mother's colouring, with raven hair and very deep blue eyes. She had her mother's mannerisms too and the children knew when Maureen was angry with them. Bridie spoke to her daughter, "Will you see what Terry's up to, darlin'?"

The two-year-old was standing on a chair in the scullery, watching the goldfish as they swum lazily around inside their glass bowl. He imitated their mouth-gaping movement for a while before his eyes lightened on the iron wringer. In his wisdom he knew why the fish were so sad. Anyone would be sad if they had to stay wet all day he reasoned. He'd seen his mother put the dripping wet clothes from the boiling copper into those wooden rollers and had seen how dry the clothes had become at the other side. If only ...

"Terry, you naughty, wicked boy," Maureen shouted. Terry removed his hand quickly from the bowl and the

17

fish settled back to their lazy swim. The girl tucked Terry under her arm and carried him along to the parlour. Terry was crying. "Terry dry fish," he sobbed.

Patrick was nearly ready. He scooped up a pat of brilliantine and rubbed it between his palms to soften it, then plastered the grease over his dark wavy hair.

Bridie was watching the operation, "Don't be late, Pat, promise me you won't be late."

The man looked puzzled. "I'll not be late, woman," he answered.

Patrick Flannagan let himself out of the house and walked quickly along the street. The 'Eagle' did not open until noon on Sundays but the conniving Irishman would taste his first beer well before then. He had struck a deal with Florrie Braden, the 'Missus' of that pub, and he smiled to himself as he recalled the incident.

It had been a quiet night in the 'Eagle' as he stood against the bar counter listening to Florrie's protestations. "Do you know, I have to do everything here," she was saying. "I've got to stack the shelves, empty the drip trays, polish the counter, and everything else before I open. He's become absolutely useless. The drink's killing him, so the doctor told him."

The subject of Florrie's tirade stood at the far end of the bar. He was trying to roll a cigarette, watched by the only other customer, who was leaning on the bar counter. Florrie glanced at him, her eyes showing her disgust. "Look at him, doesn't it make you sick. He's like that first thing in the mornings, can't keep still. It wouldn't take me long to get out."

Patrick nodded in sympathy. "Why don't you get some help in, Florrie?" he asked.

The woman shook her head. "I wish I could afford it, but I already pay the two girls for the evenings, and the cleaner. This is only a small pub remember."

Patrick was thinking hard. "What you need is a little unpaid help."

Florrie looked puzzled, "Now where on earth am I going to get ..."

Patrick cut her short, "You need look no further," he

said quickly. "Why, I could help out on Sundays at least. If I got here at around eleven o'clock I could stock the shelves, polish the bar and have everything ready by the time you open up. What d'ya say?"

Florrie Braden thought hard. On the surface it sounded a good idea, but there had to be a catch somewhere. "I couldn't let you work for nothing, Pat," she remarked.

The Irishman was ready to deliver the 'coup de grace'. He leant forward, "I wouldn't consider payment, but I'll tell you what. If I should get a little thirsty, then I could open a bottle of beer, now couldn't I?"

Florrie became wary. She was well aware of the man's liquid appetite, and the bottle he mentioned could become a crate full. She cupped her chin in the palm of her hand, the little finger toying with her bottom lip, as she glanced again at her husband. John Braden was in trouble with his cigarette. He was trying to twirl the paper around the strands of tobacco but his hands wouldn't stop shaking. The other customer got tired of watching the performance, "'Ere, give it to me, John," he said, and the landlord gave him a cross-eyed stare, "S'alright, I can manage, it's my fingers, they're a bit stiff," he slurred.

Florrie's mind was suddenly made up: "Okay, Pat, it's a deal," she said quickly. She poured the Irishman a tot of her best whisky, and a double gin for herself. "This one's on the house."

Patrick's mouth was already dry as he rang the bell of the pub. It was a few seconds away from eleven o'clock on that Sunday morning, and the impending war was not in the Irishman's thoughts. Flannagan's war would start the night they bombed the 'Eagle'.

At number 22, they were getting ready for the broadcast. Joe Harper switched on the wireless set and it started to crackle. He checked the terminal leads on the square glass accumulator, cursing to himself as he tightened the caps. The oscillations became louder as Joe twiddled with the tuning dial. The sound of Big Ben boomed out the hour and a voice came over the air, saying that the Prime Minister would speak at eleven fifteen. Joe turned off the wireless to conserve the accumulator and sat in silence, hands clasped, his thumbs revolving round and round each other. No one spoke as the minutes ticked away. Joe stared at the floor and occasionally glanced up at the clock on the high mantleshelf. Slowly, very slowly the minute hand crept toward the quarter hour. Finally, Joe got up and turned on the wireless again. The oscillations sounded louder than ever in the quiet room. Joe cursed under his breath and gently adjusted the tuning dial. There was a crackle, then the announcer's voice introducing the Prime Minister.

The Prime Minister's voice sounded tired and deflated as he began: "I am speaking to you from the Cabinet Room at 10 Downing Street. This morning the British Ambassador in Berlin handed the German Government a final note, stating that unless we heard from them by eleven o'clock that they were prepared at once to withdraw their troops from Poland, a state of war would exist between us. I have to tell you that no such undertaking has been received and that consequently this country is at war with Germany ..."

His voice was interrupted by Bridie who burst into tears. Rosie Harper went pale and put her hand up to her face. Skipper stared down at the floor, his pipe held unlit in his hand. Joe shook his head sadly as the voice on the wireless continued.

"You can imagine what a bitter blow it is to me that all my long struggle to win peace has failed. Yet I cannot believe that there is anything more or anything different that I could have done and that would have been more successful ..."

Joe turned the volume down and said, "Well, we expected it, didn't we?"

"Holy Mary Mother of God, Holy ..." started Bridie, only to be cut short by Rosie. "Now stop that, luv, you've got the children to think of. It's no good lettin' 'em see you upset. War or not, I've got a shoulder of lamb to cook, an' the spuds ter peel."

"Holy Mother..." sobbed the little woman as Rosie put her arm around her shoulders and led her out of the room.

20

Joe Harper turned up the volume in time to hear the Prime Minister's concluding words, "Now may God bless you all. May He defend the right. It is an evil thing that we shall be fighting against. Brute force, bad faith, injustice and oppression, and persecution and against them I am certain that the right shall prevail."

Joe turned off the wireless set and turned away. "Where the 'ell 'as she put it," he puffed as he bent down to look in the cupboard. He brought out a flask of brandy from the back and placed it in the middle of the table, the contents pale-looking in the light of the sun's intruding rays. He found two glasses and, pouring a measure into each, handed one to Skipper.

The old man downed his in one gulp, and immediately started to choke. Joe slapped the seaman's back, making him gasp. With his eyes streaming and his voice coming out in a cracked whisper, Skipper said, "Gawd a'mighty, Joe, that stuff's bloody strong."

"It's good brandy, Skip. I got it when Rosie 'ad that bad turn last year. Anyway, 'ere's to us all," Joe said as he put the glass to his lips. Skipper looked dolefully at his empty glass and then at the brandy flask. Joe smiled and filled the old man's glass.

"Gawd bless us all, son," said Skipper as he sipped the drink.

Joe Harper looked through the parted curtains and caught sight of a tall, stooping individual who carried a service gas mask pack and steel helmet slung over his shoulder, and wearing an armband on his right arm. Joe recognised the long-striding individual and watched him stop by the shelter. It was just like Bob Bowman to have volunteered as the Street warden.

At the shelter the warden opened the gates and secured them. Best to be ready, Bob thought, we don't want any panic. Like Tom Carter, his pal who lived at number 34, and many of the men in the Street, Bob Bowman worked in the docks, which meant that he was exempt from call-up. He had been a docker for most of his working life in the Pool of London. His father, who was a stevedore, had first taken him along to the Pool when Bob was a tall, thin youth of eighteen. He was accepted for work with some reluctance due to his frail appearance, but he soon showed he could work with the best of them. On his twenty-first birthday Bob was made a 'ganger' in charge of a team of dockers. He had developed physically, growing to well over six feet in height. His hawkish features were dark and accentuated by large pale blue eyes. His shoulders were rounded, and his black hair was brushed back and parted in the middle. His strong, white teeth were gapped at the front and his bottom lip was inclined to droop over a dimpled chin.

On Bob Bowman's twenty-second birthday his father was killed in a dock accident. Bob was heartbroken, and when the chance came to him to train as a crane driver he took it. It was to be in a different wharf in the Pool and away from the place where his father had met his death. Now, at thirty-five, with lines forming around his mouth and eyes, he looked even older. Bob had one hobby; an abiding passion for growing flowers, and in particular, geraniums, which he grew in his back yard. As he secured the shelter gates in the open position, though, geraniums were farthest from his mind. There was a war to fight and Bob Bowman was determined to do his share.

The taste of brandy was still hot on their tongues when the wail of the air raid siren filled the Street and reverberated through the houses. Joe Harper and Skipper looked at each other for a second or two then Joe grabbed for the old man's coat. "Quick, Skip, get it on! I'll get the women."

Rosie came running into the room accompanied by the terrified Bridie. "O my Gawd, Joe!" she gasped.

Joe shouted at her. "Bridie get yer kids over the shelter!"

Bridie ran out and Joe went to take Rosie's arm. "Wait, the gas! I've got ter cut the gas!" she yelled.

Conner Street became alive, as everyone rushed from their homes. Joe held on tightly to the old man and Rosie as they joined the crowd. Down the street they came, like a scene from the *Pied Piper*, urged on, not by the sound of melodious pipes, but by the horrendous wail of the siren.

The Davis boys were holding on to their aged father, Bridie was clutching her baby close to her, and the twins held on to her coat. Maureen held the two youngsters' hands as they hurried to the shelter entrance. At the gate Bob Bowman and a policeman waved them in, and Bob called out, "Now don't panic. That's right, nice an' easy".

As Bridie came down the shelter slope the warden gave her a wink. "C'mon, Bridie, where's Pat?"

The little woman gave him a wicked stare and the warden winced.

The Conner Street folk filed down the two tunnels, into the dark, musty smelling place that they had prayed they would never have to visit. They screwed up their eyes in an effort to get accustomed to the dim light that was supplied by two bare electric light-bulbs hanging from the damp ceiling. They staggered over the duckboards that covered the stagnant pools of oily water and sat down on the rows of wooden benches that were placed along the walls and down the centre. The room was cramped and airless and the reek of carbolic from the toilet compartment filled the shelter.

Outside, the Street was deserted, except for one couple hurrying along; a big elderly woman and a shuffling idiot who held on to her arm. They reached the shelter and the policeman ushered them inside quickly. He then walked back to the gate and looked up and down the now quite empty street. Overhead, a flight of pigeons in ragged formation swooped low over the roof tops and a lone dog appeared from an empty house. It chased its tail for a while, then stopped to look along the Street, before trotting back inside. The faint sound of a tug's whistle echoed briefly from the direction of the river, and then it was quiet.

Bob Bowman ambled up casually to the policeman and gave him an enquiring look before placing his hands behind his back and walking back down the shelter slope and into the dark cave.

Conner Street was at war ...

Chapter Three

Bobbie Wilkins was an idiot. He had become a victim of children's ridicule, and an object of comparison by adults. If a child from Conner Street was caught pulling faces in the mirror, then the child would be scolded with, "D'you want to grow up to be like silly Bobbie?" If the recalcitrant youngster skipped his lessons, then the same comparison was applied. None of the Street's children wanted to grow up to be like Bobbie, so they went back to their lessons, and they tried hard to stop pulling faces in the mirror. But the children just had to pull faces at someone, and that someone was usually Bobbie Wilkins.

Bobbie wasn't born an idiot, and it didn't just happen overnight. The idiocy simply grew on him. It would be more correct to say that the sickness had been beaten into him, because Bobbie had a father who went to sea and a mother who tired of the long separations. There were nights when his mother found solace in the company of available men, and on such nights the little lad pressed his face deep into the pillow as the woman writhed and moaned in adulturous adventures. There were times when the seaman came to his home port and sought out his wife.

As the boy grew older he began to fear his father, and often threw his puny weight against the enraged man to protect his mother. In a drunken frenzy, the father would attack the woman, and cuff the boy out of his way. The screaming and fighting became more frequent, and so did the beatings. One heavy cuff around Bobbie's head made his nose bleed, and put him into a daze. The boy was just nine years old. From that moment on, the boy was changed. He became absent-minded and dull at his lessons. He would wander off for no apparent reason. His speech became slurred and he developed a tic. They sent him to a special school where the boy became worse, and where the headmaster believed in the cane as the finest therapy. The treatment failed, so they sent him to the kind nuns at St Mary's School.

When Bobbie was fourteen his mother had become very ill and had been taken from her home screaming and raving. She had met a seaman who not only gave her a share of his shore time, but also left her with a memento of his one-time visit to a Far Eastern whore-house. Bobbie's father was repulsed by the boy, who now dribbled incessantly because of his partially paralysed tongue. He decided to get rid of the idiot, and spoke to the parish priest about finding a home. Word got around the Street and reached the ears of Lizzie Brown, who became outraged by the news.

Lizzie Brown was treated with caution, and a good deal of respect, by the Conner Street folk. Although she was well into her sixties, and stood barely five feet in height, Lizzie was a veritable giant. She held her ground against any and everyone. Her frail appearance belied her strength, and it was said that she could fight like a man, and often had when her husband was around. Lizzie now lived alone at number 17 and was often seen in the company of Emmie Jones, a younger and much larger woman, and Ada Dawkins, a large red-faced widow who lived at number 4. Lizzie Brown had a sharp tongue and many a shopkeeper and market trader had taken a verbal lashing from the diminutive lady. Everyone knew Lizzie, and everyone was aware that she had a heart as big as the Street.

On the day that Lizzie heard the news about Bobbie Wilkins her faded grey eyes watered. She had walked back from the market and stopped in a doorway to re-tie her garter string which had slipped from above her knee to around the ankle. As Ada Dawkins greeted the bent figure, Lizzie straightened up with a sigh.

"What's all this about that poor little Wilkins boy, Liz?"

"I tell yer, Ada. That dirty tyke's goin' ter put the poor little bleeder in an 'ome. Breaks me 'eart it does. Never known a day's lovin' 'e ain't, not from the day 'e was born."

Ada shook her head. "Poor little sod, where's 'e at now?"

Lizzie Brown knew. She had made it her business to find out. "St Mary's are lookin' after 'im, at least fer the time bein'. They'll get 'im into one o' them places, you see," she said, with a knowing nod of her head.

Ada knew of those places. "It's a cryin' shame. If my Charlie were alive, Gawd rest 'is soul, 'e'd 'ave sorted that bastard out," she said, her fist clenched to emphasise the point.

Lizzie Brown looked up and down the street, to make sure that they were quite alone. "You 'eard about 'is mother?"

"Whose, Bobbie's?"

"Yes, Bobbie's," said Lizzie Brown impatiently. "Took 'er away they did. Last night it was. Screamin' an' callin' out. Gone to 'er kidneys it 'as."

"What 'as?" asked Ada.

"Why the syphilletics of course," answered Lizzie Brown.

Ada went home and stood for a long while in front of a picture of her Charlie. She had never yet made a decision without first consulting him. The tall guardsman stared out of a sepia photograph that was framed in carved ebony, and below the picture was a display of medals mounted on green beige and framed in the same type of wood. Ada spoke softly to the photograph, and felt the uncertainty flowing from her. "Gawd bless you," she said, then left her home to see the priest. The next day, two nuns walked into Conner Street and knocked at number 4. The children watched with curiosity as the two long-robed figures walked back along the street, their hands tucked demurely in their sleeves, rosaries swinging from their waists and supporting the large crucifixes.

A week later, a big black car drove slowly up Conner Street and stopped at number 4. It was driven by an old nun who had hairs sprouting from her chin. Two younger nuns climbed out from the back, one holding the hand of a scared boy, and the other, a large suitcase. The children gathered around the car and one young lad, bolder than the rest, moved forward to touch the gleaming headlight. The nun with the bristling chin sounded the horn making the boy jump back. The two younger nuns went into the house and later emerged without the boy.

"Did you see who it was?" asked one of the little girls.

"Course I did, it's silly Bobbie," another answered.

"'E's been in a silly school," the first girl said.

"I don't care if 'e 'as, 'e can still play wiv us, can't 'e?" replied the other girl.

The young lad who tried to touch the car stepped forward once more. "I don't s'pose 'e knows 'ow to play marbles anyway," he said with a grin.

"Don't you be so wicked, Albert Conlin," the second girl said. "If your dad kept 'ittin' you on the bonce, you wouldn't be able to play like normal children, so there."

Albert grinned. "Did you see 'is tongue? Kept pokin' out, it did. I s'pose it's cos 'e's firsty."

The second girl folded her arms and swung her head away from Albert, who stuck out his tongue and shuffled along the street. "I 'ate you Albert Conlin," shouted the girl, and Albert laughed. The big black car finally drove off down the narrow Conner Street and turned into the Tower Road, leaving the idiot boy behind in the care of Ada Dawkins.

Bobbie Watkins settled in with the kindly Ada, and he found some much-needed love for the first time in his young life. Ada Dawkins fed him, clothed him and protected him as best she could from the taunts and jibes. Bobbie was happy growing up in the close, friendly atmosphere of a small dockland street. The children eventually accepted and tolerated him as he tried to join in their fun. He grew to manhood physically, but remained a child in his mind, his mental development having been clubbed to a permanent standstill. He walked the street as a man because he was told to do so, but loved to watch the pretty marbles as the boys rolled them in the gutters. He tried to talk like a man because he was expected to, but he was only happy with the children. He wanted to sit with the boys as they played cards, and threw the ball at a tin can with sticks crossed on top, but he did not do so. He knew he was supposed to feel like a man and act like a man, and he tried. He watched the men as they smoked cigarettes and wore their caps on the side of their heads. When he tried to wear his cap at an angle it fell off, and the one time he had tried a cigarette, it made him sick. He tried hard to become like the men, but his head hurt and his body was clumsy. He found peace in his little room at Ada's with his comics, and with the pretty marbles that he found in the gutters of the street. When his head hurt bad, he went to bed and watched the patterns that danced on the ceiling, formed by the moving shadows that the coal fire created. Sometimes, the pictures formed by the glowing coals would frighten him and he pulled the bedclothes over his head, as a child would do. Sometimes, the pictures formed reminded him of things half-remembered, half-forgotten, and his head ached.

The events of that Sunday morning didn't mean anything to Bobbie, until that terrible noise made his head buzz. He had seen Ada crying earlier, but that was not so very unusual. Ada often cried when she looked at the man in the photo, and when her wireless played hymns on Sunday evenings. The mounting tension over the last few weeks was beyond his comprehension and he went about his simple tasks in the market in his own innocent way.

As the wail of the siren sounded and Ada grabbed his arm and hurried him out of the house, Bobbie became scared. His idea of war was from the pictures in his comics, with the enemy shaded green and the guns that fired beams of light. He could shut bad things from his mind by closing the comic, but the sight of everyone hurrying along the street and that awful noise frightened him. The box that was slung over his shoulder frightened him too, but Ada grabbed the gas mask and told him to take it with him when the siren started up. Bobbie felt he could not breathe when he tried it on and hid it under his bed. Ada had found it and told the idiot to keep it in a safe place and as they both hurried along Conner Street the box bounced about on Bobbie's back.

When the two reached the shelter the policeman ushered them inside, where most of the seats were occupied. They made room for Ada on a bench near the door, but Bobbie had to stand. Outside on the concrete patio the men stood talking, and Bobbie signalled to Ada that he wanted to join them. The woman was worried. "Stay under cover, Bobbie, for Gawd's sake, keep with the others."

The idiot nodded and shuffled out from the stuffy tunnel.

"'Ello, Bobbie, what you doin' 'ere? Come out for air?" remarked Ginger Davis as he nudged his brother. Bobbie grinned and stood against the wall, his gas mask box hanging down in front of him. Ginger's brother Fred leered at the idiot. "See you've got your mask all ready, does it fit?"

Bobbie nodded and pointed to the box, "Small one, Bobbie got small gas mask, lady said it fits."

"I don't know about that, Bobbie boy," Ginger said. "I reckon you should 'ave a medium, what d'ya say, Fred?"

Ginger's brother rubbed his fingers along his chin. "Yeah, I reckon so, that small size ain't no good."

Bobbie started to shuffle about in his agitation, and Ginger grinned at the group of young men standing around the entrance.

"Why don't you try it on, Bobbie? Let's see 'ow it looks," he said.

The idiot shook his head vigorously. "Bobbie don't like gas mask, makes me sick," he whined.

Joe Harper was sitting on a wooden bench by the wall watching the performance. Skipper, who was sitting next to Joe, spat out a stream of tobacco juice and said, "Tricky little snapper, that Ginger Davis. One of these days some-one's goin' to take 'im down a peg, mark my words."

Ginger made a grab for Bobbie's box and succeeded in

removing the mask. The idiot snatched it away from his tormentor and backed away. Joe Harper had seen enough. "All right, Ginger, you've 'ad your fun, leave 'im be," he said quietly.

Bobbie's tongue hung out as he backed towards the shelter door.

Big Albert Conlin sidled up to Joe. "What's 'a matter, Joe? The boys are only 'avin' a laugh."

"Yeah, well the laugh's over," replied the signalman.

Ginger Davis came up towards the idiot and Skipper shouted to him, "Why don't you leave 'im alone, you flash little monkey."

"Shut up, Grandad," Ginger sneered.

"If I get up off this seat ..." began Skipper, but Joe interrupted him by grabbing Ginger's coat lapels. "Talk to 'im like that an' I'll tear your 'ead off your shoulders," he spat out.

"Now what's goin' on," the warden called out, "you two tryin' to start your own war?"

Bobbie seized the opportunity to dart back inside the shelter. He still had the gas mask in his hand and as he entered, Lizzie Brown screamed out, "O my Gawd, it's a gas attack!"

People began to panic, and some of the children started to cry. Bob Bowman heard the noise and he rushed in. "Calm down, it's okay, it's all quiet outside, take it easy."

Ada grabbed Bobbie and pulled him down beside her. "Sit 'ere an' don't move, you've frightened everybody."

Bobbie tucked the mask back into the box and held it tightly on his lap. The shelter returned to the quiet mumble of anxious conversation and some of the children started to congregate around Ernest Jacobs, a fat boy clutching a tin box.

"Come on, Ern', show us your pitchers," said one little lad.

"No fear," replied Ernest. "Them's me stakes."

"Wot, fer pontoon?" said the little lad.

"Pontoon or brag," replied Ernest in an authoritative tone.

"Can't play brag, but I can play pontoon," said the

little lad hopefully. "An' I've got some cigarette cards too," he chirped.

Ernest Jacobs looked at the group, a gleam crystallising in his eye. Here was a chance to build up his supply of cards. He addressed the group of children, "Anyone want to play pontoon? Cigarette cards is stakes."

Four of the lads fished out some tattered cards, and one little boy took a bag of marbles from his pocket. "I've got these," he said as he rattled them in front of Ernest.

"Them's no good, only cigarette cards," replied the 'card-sharp' of Conner Street.

The game began in a deadly serious mood as the boys placed their stakes in front of them. Granny Flint was trying to take a nap and she clicked her tongue, aggrieved at the noise.

"I'm banker, cos' them's my playin' cards," announced Ernest.

Bobbie Watkins was sitting quietly beside Ada when he heard the rattle of the marbles. He saw the boys gathering and decided to investigate. He edged his way down the row of benches and stood in front of Granny Flint to get a view. The old lady gave him an icy stare and closed her eyes once more.

"Busted!" shouted one of the lads, and Granny Flint half-opened her eyes and clicked her tongue at the children.

"Can Bobbie play?" asked one lad.

"'E's got no cards," said Ernest in a tone of disgust.

Bobbie slowly put his hand into his top pocket and pulled out a few tattered cards. A grin spread over his round face.

"Okay, but no dribblin' over the cards," said Ernest.

Bobbie put the little pile of cigarette cards down in front of him and folded his coat-ends under his legs. Ernest licked his thumb and dealt one card to each of the lads. The card that he placed in front of himself was deftly manipulated from the bottom of the deck. The stakes went down and the idiot rubbed his hands together. "You got to bet more than one card," shouted Ernest, and the lads laughed. Bobbie took the pile in front of him and placed them all, with the exception of one card, in the centre of the game. The fat boy dealt the next card to each of them, and one to himself, again from the bottom of the pile.

"Stick," said the first boy, and then the second boy.

"Twist," said the third lad, then quickly picked up the card dealt to him. "Busted," he said sadly.

"Buy one," said the remaining lad as he laid down his stakes.

Ernest eyed the boy with caution as he dealt him a card.

"I'll stick," said the lad with satisfaction.

"Buy one," mumbled the idiot.

"Do what?" shouted Ernest.

"Bobbie buy one."

"'Ow can you buy a card wiv' no stakes?" sneered the card-sharp.

The little lad next to Bobbie nudged him. "Go on, Bobbie, put your card down," he said loudly.

"Buy one," repeated the idiot as he laid down his last dog-eared cigarette card, grinning as he did so. He held two pretty pictures in his hand and he wanted to buy another.

The little lad next to Bobbie had caught a glimpse of the two queens in his dirty grasp. His face took on a look of horror. "No, Bobbie, you mean stick," he said urgently.

"Bobbie buy one," the idiot repeated.

"No no, you can't buy one with them cards," said the little lad.

"If 'e wants to, let 'im buy one," Ernest butted in. He put a card face down in front of the idiot, who laid his two pictures down for all to see. A gasp went up and Ernest leered. "Turn your card over," he said with scorn.

Bobbie slowly turned the card to reveal an ace. The boys stared for a second then erupted in laughter. Granny Flint nearly hit the roof as the noise woke her up, and fat Ernest snapped his tin box shut. "I'm not playin' anymore," he said in disgust.

"Twenty-one! Bobbie's got twenty-one!" they cried.

The little lad nudged Bobbie, "Pick yer winnin's up," he said with a grin that spread from ear to ear.

The idiot made his way back to Ada and sat down next to her. His tongue hung out of his mouth as he felt for the winnings in his pocket. The little lad was sitting near him and he grinned at Bobbie as the victor felt his pocket. Bobbie grinned back, and the lad beamed. A stream of saliva ran down the idiot's chin and dripped onto the floor. His tongue hung out as he felt once more for the cigarette cards. Bobbie looked again at the lad and they grinned at their secret joke. The look that passed between them was for the world of children; the doors had long been closed on the adults for all their sage understanding. The exchanged smiles were innocence, a pure feeling that reflected their thoughts, an acknowledgement so open that for an adult it would be betrayal. The smile, that turned into a chuckle from the lad as Bobbie hunched up his shoulders in delight, was not understood by the adult mind of the boy's mother. She was talking to her neighbour when she heard him and promptly slapped the boy around the head. "I've told you before, an' I won't tell you again. Stop laughin' at silly Bobbie, you know 'e can't 'elp it."

The little lad stared at the floor, his eyes misting. The idiot's doleful eyes seemed to mist too and he searched for the cards in his pocket.

The long, even wail of the all-clear sounded and the people broke into spontaneous cheering. Feet clattered over the duck-boards as they hurried for the door. Bobbie found himself standing next to the boy as they waited their turn to move out into the sunlight. Bobbie tugged at the lad's sleeve and saw the tear that had traced a line down his cheek. As they walked up the sloping path to the street, the idiot pressed a handful of cigarette cards into the boy's palm. The lad looked fearfully in the direction of his mother before giving Bobbie a huge grin.

The Conner Street folk went home to cook their Sunday meal and talk of the day. They feared for the future and their fate, and they waited. Bridie waited too and, long after the all-clear, Patrick Flannagan staggered home for his meal.

Chapter Four

The cold, wet, mid-November evening settled over a blacked-out Conner Street, with a gusting wind that lashed the rain against the little houses and along the near-deserted turning. It had rained non-stop throughout the day and the gutters were running with water that poured down into the dark drains.

The homeward-bound folk held their heads down and their coat collars up against the weather. One or two late workers trudged into the back street, holding their torches low, the beams of which were diffused by tissue-paper discs affixed to the glass. The late folk looked forward to a hot meal and roaring coal fire, and later they would listen to the nightly broadcasts, as did the rest of the Street. They would hear of the occasional skirmishes, and the sporadic shelling on the Western Front. The news was very limited from that area, as was the information about fighting at sea. The war was two months old, and there was a lull on the continent as the armies faced each other. It was different on the oceans, where battles raged. A regular toll of merchant ships and their cargoes went to the bottom, together with a large part of the crews.

The nightly broadcasts did not name the doomed vessels, although sometimes a whole street already had news of the disaster. They knew of the men, and the ships they sailed in and they kept count. Conner Street knew Alf Morgan, for he was born in the Street and lived there until he decided to see the world. Alf Morgan thought that the merchant service was the answer, so he joined as a stoker. He saw a good many ports and harbours, one of which was Halifax, Nova Scotia. It was from there one dark night he boarded an old coal-burner, and set sail for London.

The ship joined a convoy, but started to lag behind with engine trouble. Four nights out, a U-boat attached itself to the convoy, and singled out the old coal-burner; the torpedo was straight and the aim was true, and the ship was caught foursquare in its boiler room. Halifax, Nova Scotia, was the last port Alf Morgan ever saw.

On that cold November night, a telegram boy pedalled into Conner Street on his red bicycle and stopped at number 5. The buff-coloured envelope had an official heading and the boy sighed as he rat-tatted on the door, the telegram held tight beneath his coat against the rain. The Morgans were startled as only the collectors and policeman rat-tatted in dockland, and it was too late in the day for the collectors. The dread on Mrs Morgan's face turned to horror as she saw the boy. The *Southern Star* had gone down, and the whole Street knew it. Mrs Morgan understood only too well the news the telegram boy brought.

The lull was having effects, since the dreaded bombs had not fallen, and apart from the first day of war, the shelter had not been used. Some of the evacuated children were brought home, and there was even talk of a swift end to hostilities. The market traded as usual and there was plenty of food in the shops. Of course, some things had changed, such as the now closed cinemas, and certain new laws that were strictly enforced; petrol was rationed, and exotic fruits became non-existent. People who broke the 'blackout' regulations found that heavy fines were imposed, and sometimes even imprisonment.

The blackout regulations brought with them a few problems for the odd trader. The man who sold black material from his stall in Tower Road market could not satisfy his customers' demands, and one day he upset Lizzie Brown. "I'm sorry, luv, but I've 'ad a run on the stuff. There's only wot you see."

Lizzie looked at him in disbelief. "This all you got?" she snorted, holding up a small piece of cloth. "This wouldn't even cover me carsey."

Another who was on the receiving end of Lizzie's acid

tongue was the man in the hardware store. "Tin tacks? Sorry, lady, sold out."

"Sold out of bloody tin tacks?" Lizzie choked. "'Ow the bleedin' 'ell can you run out of tin tacks?"

"I'll 'ave some in next week," said the man helpfully.

"Next week's no bleedin' good. I wanna get me blackout up this week."

"I've got some nails," he suggested.

"Nails is no bleedin' good," ranted Lizzie Brown. "I'll never get me bloody winders open."

"Sorry, luv, it's the shortages," he said apologetically.

Lizzie Brown hammered the counter. "I tell you what," she shouted. "If you ain't got 'em in by next week, I'll get me vinegar an' me 'earthstone somewhere else, so there!"

"I wish you would," mumbled the man under his breath.

"What did you say?" said Lizzie, her eyes popping.

"I said it's understood."

"Well, that's all right then," said Lizzie as she stormed out of his shop.

On the same cold November night that the telegram boy knocked at number 5, something happened to Albert Conlin that made him wince every time he thought about Florrie Braden.

Albert was a big man who sold salads from a stall in the market, and at the end of that particular day Albert Conlin was soaked through. He had the beetroots to cook for the next day and he had to get up early the next morning to go to the Borough Market for fresh supplies. So he was feeling a little sorry for himself as he carried the beetroots into his lodgings at number 15. Nell Jones, his landlady, had the copper boiling ready and, as soon as Albert had finished, she started to serve up his supper.

"Keep me meal in the oven, will you, Nell? I fancy a pint," he said.

Nell Jones puffed. "Don't be long then, Albert, it'll get all baked up."

Albert hoped it would, as he hated mutton stew with

the same passion that he loved a pint of ale. He put on his still damp coat watching as Nell placed the covered dish into the iron oven, next to the open coal fire.

The 'Eagle' was busy on that night as Albert slid through the heavy blackout curtains and entered the smoky bar. He recognised a few of the traders who were playing darts and the old man who stood talking to Florrie, a clay pipe hanging from the corner of his mouth. "'Ello, Skip, 'ow yer doin'?" he asked.

"Okay, son, just bin askin' Florrie if she fancies a night out wiv me."

Florrie laughed and slapped the old man's hand playfully.

"'Ow's the 'arpers?" Albert asked.

"They're all right. Joe's on nights this week," Skipper replied.

Florrie looked at Albert. "What'll it be?"

"Give us a pint of ale, luv," answered the big man.

"I 'eard the Davis boys got called up," remarked Skipper.

"Last week, gone in the infantry," Albert said.

Skipper remembered the episode at the shelter. He tapped the clay pipe on the bar counter and started to refill it. "Do 'em good if you ask me," he remarked.

Albert grinned and took a gulp from his glass. "God I needed that."

Florrie was watching him. She had a soft spot for the big man who sometimes helped her with the barrels. Florrie had a good understanding with the traders. She would often ask them to help her move a barrel onto the stillion or carry up a crate or two from the cellar. She especially liked it when Albert was available. She liked to watch as his muscular arms strained against the weight and his neck muscles tightened as he lifted the barrel. There was always a pint at the end of the chores and the traders were happy.

Florrie waited until the man drained his glass. "Another?" she asked, and the man nodded.

"Bad day, Florrie," he said.

The woman filled his glass and placed it down in front

of him. "Looks like you've got a thirst on."

"Well, I've been wet outside all day, might as well get soaked inside," quipped Albert.

"What you need is a nice warm bed, luv," smiled Florrie.

The remark was lost on the man as he took a large draught from his beer. He put the glass down satisfied, and lit a cigarette. The man standing next to him vacated his stool and Albert gratefully sat down.

Skipper waved goodnight as he left and Albert stared down at his half-smoked cigarette.

Wheezy Morris called over, "Fancy a game, Al?"

"No thanks, I'm dead beat," Albert answered.

Florrie Braden was serving a customer, her eyes glancing in the direction of the big man. Wheezy Morris noticed this and he nudged his partner, "See Florrie lookin' at our Albert? Fancies 'im, she does!"

Wheezy's darts partner was having trouble sighting the board, and his eyes crossed as he tried to follow the speaker's gaze.

"Sad I calls it, wot wiv 'er ole man in 'orspital," went on Wheezy.

The customers were leaving, and Florrie came over to where Albert was standing. "Al, be a dear, can you move a barrel up on the stand ready for tomorrow?" she asked sweetly.

"Okay," the man replied, and drained his glass.

Wheezy Morris had left his partner, who was having trouble finding the exit, and propped himself at the bar counter near Albert. He watched as the big man walked behind the bar and down the narrow stairs into the cellar. Wheezy looked at Florrie. "Good 'earted our Albert, Florrie."

The 'missus' ignored the remark, but Wheezy was not to be beaten. "Shame about Albert," he said, looking into his empty glass.

Florrie Braden looked puzzled. "What about him?" she asked.

"Well, 'e gets these funny turns."

"What do you mean, funny turns?" Florrie queried.

"He seems okay to me. Never noticed anything when he's been in here."

Wheezy rubbed his hands together below the counter. He had Florrie on a hook and he wasn't about to let her go. "'Aven't you wondered why 'e never got married?" he asked in a low whisper.

"I've never really thought about it," lied the 'missus'.

Wheezy glanced behind Florrie to make sure that Albert was still in the cellar. "Women make 'im violent. 'E gets sort of over passionate. Gets a bit rough wiv 'em, 'e does."

"You don't say?" Florrie said in mock disgust. "I'd never have thought it. Not our Albert." The woman was secretly intrigued, the thought of Albert Conlin taking her in those massive arms of his and crushing her to him gave Florrie shivers of pleasure. She looked at Wheezy, who was savouring the conversation.

"O, 'e's 'ad a few girls in the past but when they find out wot 'e's really like they soon ditch 'im," he said, trying hard not to betray himself. "All the dollies round 'ere won't 'ave nuffin to do wiv 'im."

Florrie wanted to lick her lips, but shook her head instead.

The sound of Albert climbing the cellar stairs stopped Wheezy in his tracks. "Well, I must be orf," he said quickly.

The last of the customers had left and Florrie ran a wet cloth over the bar counter. Albert was just about to leave when the woman spoke to him, "Al, slip them bolts over and we'll have a nightcap."

Albert wasn't sure whether he needed a nightcap but he did as she bid.

Florrie placed two glasses on the counter and filled them both to the brim. "Taste a drop of the best, Al," she said with a wink.

The man took his glass and took a swig. The feeling of heat went from his throat down to his stomach and his eyes watered.

Florrie drained her glass in one gulp. "That's my best Scotch, I keep that for my friends," she said pointedly.

"Look, Al, I've got some cheese and pickles upstairs, why don't you come up for a while?"

The pints of ale were having an effect on the big man and the last drink seemed to set his insides alight. Albert realised that it was hours since he had eaten, and the thought of that mutton stew in the oven at his lodgings did not seem too objectionable now. He looked at the clock. By now, that stew would no doubt be in Nell's dustbin. His stomach was sending him messages. "Okay, Florrie, that sounds good," he said.

Florrie waved him round the counter. "Turn the lights off then, Al, and mind your head," she warned him.

The stairs spiralled up to the small flat above the 'Eagle' and Albert had to duck low as he went through the archway at the foot of the flight. At the top of the stairs three doors led off and Albert entered the room facing him. The small sitting room was lit by a table lamp and the glow of the brightly burning coal fire. There was a large armchair in front of the fire and Albert slumped down into it with a contented sigh. He stretched out his legs and yawned. He could hear Florrie moving about in the next room and closed his eyes. The heavy veil of sleep was beginning to descend over him when the door opened. He opened his eyes quickly and saw Florrie standing before him. She held two drinks in her hands, "Get this down you and I'll bring in the supper," she said.

Albert took the drink and looked at it, then nodded his thanks. As Florrie tripped out of the room Albert suddenly realised she had changed into a dressing gown. He drained his glass in one gulp, his thoughts racing. It was almost identical to the one that the Embankment woman wore, and he shivered as the thoughts came back of that night on the foggy Thames Embankment.

It had been loneliness that took him up West. The desire to be with a woman sometimes caused him to ache inside, and he would walk the busy, well-lit streets until he saw the women. They stood in doorways, and smiled at passers-by. Albert Conlin wanted to seek their company and made toward the shadowed figures, only to walk quickly by as they smiled at him. He would make for the nearest pub and reflect over his beer, and then stroll down to the Embankment to catch the last tram home to dockland.

Women had not figured in Albert's life since his early days, when his widowed mother frightened girlfriends away. Her hold on Albert tightened during her last years, and when she died he found it impossible to carry on living in the dreary old house. He moved into lodgings, and very soon realised that he had hardly any friends of the fair sex. His easy ability to talk to the young available maidens faded quickly over the last dominating years of his mother's life, and now Albert had completely accepted his position. The occasional need was sometimes drowned at the 'Eagle', and sometimes repressed by his fear of those shadowy figures who smiled from the doorways.

He recalled that night with the bitter cold and fog. Yellow, sulphuric fumes had settled down over the town and he decided to hurry down to the Embankment before the last tram left. It was hopeless, with the swirling fog much more dense by the river, and he missed the tram.

He started to walk the long journey home when suddenly the woman appeared out of the fog. She was dressed in a fur coat with a scarf tied around her piled-up hair. Her face was heavily made-up, with spots of rouge beneath her eyes that made her look doll-like. Her lips were scarlet-painted and thin and her eyes watery and sunken. She smiled at him; a grin that made him start. "Ello, dearie, nasty night ain't it?"

Albert stared, his mouth hanging open.

The woman winked at him. "I'll give yer a nice time an' you can stay the night, wha'dya say?"

The big man nodded dumbly and the woman took his arm. "It's only a couple of minutes from 'ere, luv."

They crossed the tramway and took a narrow, rising street that led away from the river. Halfway along the street the woman stopped and took her key from the large handbag hanging from her shoulder. "Listen, dearie, I don't usually bring me fellas 'ome 'ere, but it's a terrible night, an' it's quiet."

41

Albert wondered where the woman usually took her men. He had visions of her selling her body against the cold statues that lined the Embankment.

"First floor, luv, an' keep quiet." She opened the front door which led into a dingy hall. The stairs creaked as they climbed to the room above. The open fire had died down and the woman threw a large knob of coal onto it. Without wiping her hands she poured a colourless liquid from a bottle into two glasses that stood on the table by the covered window. "Cheers, dearie," she said and swallowed the contents.

The smell of gin made Albert heave but he gulped his drink down and shuddered.

"Give me a minute," said the woman with a wink as she disappeared behind a Japanese screen. Albert took off his coat and started to unbuckle his belt.

"Put the money on the table, luv, it's custom," came a voice from behind the screen.

Albert felt foolish sitting in that cold room clad only in his underpants. The fire was beginning to pick up and the lump of coal started to spit out its gases.

The woman came around from behind the screen. She wore a dressing gown that gaped open at the front. It had a fluffy collar and cuffs and was adorned with large red roses.

The recollection of that night in the cold room off the Embankment made Albert wince as he felt again those clammy hands on his back. He remembered the giggles from the woman that turned to disbelief, as she realised that her ample charms were being lost upon the hulking man at her side. He remembered the effect of the gin and the sickly smell of her cheap perfume. "God Almighty," she said incredulously as he retched into the bowl. "Don't I just pick 'em!"

Albert remembered the early morning tram ride home to dockland, the clackety-clack that said over and over again, "Don't worry, luv, you'll do better next time."

His train of thought was interrupted by the door opening and Florrie entering again, carrying a tray which she set down on a small table.

"There we are," she said as she pulled up another chair to the fire. The tray contained buttered rolls, a large square of cheese with a knife pressed into it, a dish of pickled onions and two mugs of tea.

Albert gratefully started into the food and Florrie smiled at him.

"You didn't mind coming up with me, did you, Albert?" she asked. "I simply can't abide being here alone."

The man was staring at her dressing gown, with its fluffy collar and cuffs and the large red roses. "Course not," he replied.

"John will be away for a couple of days, they're giving him some treatment," Florrie went on. "The days are not too bad, it's the nights I can't stand. It's the being alone, although we've not slept together for over a year," she hastened to add.

The meal was eaten and the fire burned low. Florrie stood up, her large breasts standing out beneath the flimsy nightgown. She reached out and took his hand, steering him out onto the landing and into the darkened bedroom. Heavy drapes over the window were pulled back and the weak light from the moon shone down on the bed. Florrie pulled the covers over the window and lit a candle.

Albert sat on the bed and took off his shoes with deliberation as the woman watched him. She smiled and stretched and in the same movement let her dressing gown fall from her shoulders. Her thighs were heavy and her hips rounded, contrasting with her narrow waist and slender shoulders. Her breath came in gasps as she bent over him and tore at his shirt. Albert moved back but the woman smothered him with her open mouth, her fingers searching and probing. She finally managed to get him derobed and into the bed, her fingernails biting into his back as she fought against his immobility. She gasped "O my God, Albert, take me, do it, for God's sake do it!"

The man was drowning, immersed beneath the raving woman, whose breath was coming in screams. He fought for supremacy, as her nails bit deep into his perspiring body and drove red lines from his shoulders down to his waist. He was terrified. She was an animal, savage-like in her desires. Albert felt he was losing consciousness and he heaved upwards with his arms and threw the woman from him. She rolled from the bed and fell backwards onto the floor. Albert sat up and grabbed at his side where a trickle of blood had started to flow, dripping onto the sheet. He looked down at Florrie and saw that she remained still.

She lay on her side, her head by the washstand. Albert gasped and went from the bed to where she lay. He felt her head, gently turning her over as he did so. There was no blood but he could feel a large bump forming behind her ear. He wet a towel and pressed it to her forehead and the back of her neck. She moaned and her eyes flickered.

"Thank God," he said aloud as he picked Florrie up and placed her on the bed. She groaned and turned onto her side. Albert quickly dressed, glancing at her as he did so. The candle flickered and burned bright again as he opened the door. With a last look at Florrie, the man hurried down the winding stairs and into the bar. The night air hit him through his open shirt as he made his way quickly to his lodgings in the street.

In the small bedroom above the 'Eagle', Florrie turned onto her back and gazed up at the shadowy ceiling. Her head hurt and her body ached, but she felt a warm feeling inside. She called his name, then closed her eyes, her hand searching the empty space beside her.

Chapter Five

Christmas was only a few days away when certain things happened to brighten up the lives of the dockland folk. Cinemas started to open up again, and some of the theatres too. The big West End stores advertised that they would stay open late for the Christmas week and they promised to put on their usual treat for the kids, a Santa Claus complete with reindeer. People started to breathe a little easier, for they reasoned that it would be unlikely for any bombs to fall on London, at least until after Christmas. Children who had been evacuated were to be allowed a visit from their parents, and special trains were laid on for this purpose.

The Carters had two youngsters who had been evacuated to the country and their letters were giving Tom Carter and his wife Mary a few worries. It seemed that Reg, who was ten years old, and his sister Marjorie who was seven, were having to do certain chores for the local squire and his wife with whom they were billeted. One letter said that Marjorie had to make beds and do housework and Reg was helping on the farm with the animals.

Tom Carter was a docker who had little in common with country squires, and knew nothing of country life, but it seemed to him that his children were a little young to be put to work, especially by "them dung-caked landowners", as he put it.

"We'll write to 'em an' arrange a visit," Tom said to his wife Mary, "an' if there's anythin' untoward goin' on then they'll 'ave Tom Carter to deal with."

Mary looked at her broad-shouldered husband and winced as his massive clenched fist pounded the table. She dearly hoped that all would be well, else the dung-caked landowner would probably become even more

45

dung-encrusted. She tried to put her fears to one side as she hunted for presents to take to the children. After all, they may be with kind people, she thought. The children were probably very happy at the farm. But her doubts still nagged as she tied up the presents in their coloured wrappings. Mary had also managed to find a bottle of real Scotch whisky, which they would take as a present for the squire and his wife. Tom had his reservations, but as he said "Oh we'll give 'em the whisky, even if I break it over 'is 'ead."

Mary hushed him quiet. "Now don't go jumpin' to conclusions, let's wait till we get there, Tom."

They took the early morning train from Paddington during the Christmas week. Mary wore her best coat and hat and her smart shoes. Tom Carter refused to wear a tie. Instead he chose his white silk scarf which he knotted over his blue and white striped shirt. He wore his best blue serge suit and his brown button-up boots, and his check cap set at a jaunty angle.

Paddington station was crowded with waiting servicemen, who sat around with huge piles of equipment. More uniformed men and women milled around the RTO hut seeking instructions. A few others sat back on the seats, trying to snatch a few minutes' sleep. Red-capped military policemen patrolled in pairs, watching the servicemen and answering questions. The atmosphere in the station breathed confusion and uncertainty, currently aggravated by families trying to find the trains which would take them to their children. Tom and Mary were also confused as they approached the ticket barrier, for their experience of trains was confined to the very rare day trip to Southend. Mary carried two paper bags of presents, and Tom held the tickets.

They spoke to the ticket collector. "Does the train stop at Gloucester?"

The man merely raised his arm toward the train.

"Miserable git," remarked Tom, and Mary squeezed his arm.

Eventually the train pulled out of Paddington and the couple settled down in the smart compartment with its fold-away armrests, its carpeted floor and white linen head-squares. Mary snuggled back into the deep cushioned seat and smiled contentedly at Tom. An army captain occupied the window seat opposite the couple, and in the far corner an elderly cleric sat twiddling his thumbs. Facing him sat his wife, in her tweeds and gold-rimmed spectacles.

Presently Tom pulled out his pocket-watch and looked at it. They had been travelling for one hour. Mary also glanced at his watch and decided it was time to have something to eat. She pulled out a pack of sandwiches from a zip-up bag, which she held on her lap.

She leaned over and tapped the captain on his knee. "Care for a fish-paste sandwich?" she asked softly. The officer declined and buried his face in a copy of *John Bull*. Mary looked at the vicar and his wife, who was twitching her nose like a rabbit. "Would you care for one?" she asked. The tweed-dressed lady looked over her spectacles at Tom's wife and shook her head. "No thank you," she said coldly. The vicar declined with a slight smile that must have caused him some pain because he quickly reverted to his serious observation of the carriage roof. In fact, Mary had disturbed his contemplation upon the coming Sunday's sermon. He had considered the 'feeding of the five thousand', but the dreadful smell of those fish-paste sandwiches had changed his mind.

Tom Carter took a sandwich and munched it, occasionally wiping the crumbs from his lap onto the carpeted floor. The vicar's wife looked at the crumbs, at Tom, then returned her gaze to the rolling countryside. Tom finished his last mouthful, and was wiping his hands on a red spotted handkerchief, when the door slid open. A tall, stooping ticket inspector entered the compartment and held out his hand. The captain showed the man his pass and went back to his copy of *John Bull*. The vicar held out his tickets and the inspector clipped a chunk out of them.

Tom Carter was searching his waistcoat pockets for the tickets when Mary nudged him. "Your back pocket," she whispered.

Tom jumped up and accidentally knocked the inspector's hat from his head. The man stooped to retrieve the hat, noticing as he did so the crumbs on the carpet. He sighed as he remembered that feeling he had experienced when he woke up. It was going to be one of those trying days when it may be an advantage to turn over and switch off the alarm. The man had decided against it, and was beginning to think that all would be well, until he entered this compartment with its odour of fish.

Tom had now found the tickets and smiled at the stooping, mournful representative of the Great Western Railway. "'Ere we are, mate, knew I 'ad 'em somewhere," he said cheerfully. Mary's eyes went up in anguish as the train lurched and Tom stepped on the inspector's toes. The man winced noticeably and almost snatched the tickets. His face took on a look of pained authority as he said "These are third class tickets, sir, and you are in a first class compartment," the word 'sir' delivered with sarcastic intonation.

"Oh, is it?" replied the docker with an air of innocence.

"This way if you please, sir," said the inspector, standing back for safety. Mary gathered up her parcels, her face flushed in embarrassment. Tom grinned sheepishly and the vicar's lady looked at the pair over her gold-rimmed spectacles. The captain muttered, "Good God," and buried his face in his magazine.

The inspector led the way to a part of the train that had no carpet on the floor, and no white linen head-squares. He was determined to see to it that the cockney sandwich-eaters would cause him no more tribulation between Paddington and Gloucester. As he returned to punch more tickets, he tried to recall the last time there had been fish-paste sandwiches consumed in the upper section. Meanwhile, the occupants of the upper compartment were taking their own measures to combat the lingering odour. The captain lit a 'Gold Flake', and the cleric's venerable lady took out a lace handkerchief impregnated with toilet water and dabbed at her nose. The cleric gave her one of his holy smiles, and continued to twiddle his thumbs as he contemplated the ceiling of the carriage.

The train finally puffed into Gloucester station. The

Carters bade farewell to their cramped, third class fellow travellers, and hurried from the train out onto the forecourt. Mary gave her husband a look of disgust. "I felt a proper fool. Didn't you know it was a first class carriage?"

"Course I did," Tom replied. "I always wanted to travel in one o' them posh carriages!"

The day was fairly mild with a slight wind. Tom took a deep breath. "Beats Conner Street, luv, you can smell the country."

Mary just wanted to get to the children. "Let's ask that man the way," she said, pointing to an aged driver who leant against his battered taxi.

Tom took out a letter and looked again at the address, then sidled up to the ancient man. "I say, me ole mate, d'you know this 'ere place?"

The man gave Tom an icy look. He did not particularly want to be a mate of this man in his blue suit and brown boots. He'd seen the pictures in the papers of those London louts, as they stood on street corners during the strikes. He looked at Tom's cap and knotted scarf and knew that the man before him was definitely a troublemaker. He looked at the address at the top of the letter in Tom's hand. "That's the squire's house, be up Church Lane, off'n village," he said slowly, wondering what the townie wanted with the squire. Then the ancient driver remembered the scruffy children he'd seen that day in Comstead Village. "Your children be stayin' with the squire then?" he asked.

Mary nodded. "'Ave you seen 'em, are they all right?" she asked urgently.

"O, they be fine, you want me to drive you there?" asked the man.

Tom grinned at the driver, "That's right, me ole mate."

The Conner Street couple, sitting with their bags of presents, held on tightly as the driver pulled away from the station forecourt, and very nearly knocked the post-mistress off her rusty old bicycle. The village of Comstead was three miles from the station, although to Mary it seemed much more. The driver turned left just past the village pump and took a narrow lane hedged by tall bushes. The lane continued for a quarter of a mile then opened out into a wider road that was laid with cobblestones. A hundred yards along the road, the driver stopped by a short drive that led to a stone-built house. "Taxis are not allowed on squire's drive," said their chauffeur curtly.

"Right you are, me ole mate," said Tom cheerfully, unaware of the ancient man's look of disgust.

The two hurried up the drive, Mary holding on tightly to the parcels. The stone house was three-storied, with flint stones placed here and there on the façade. Two stone columns supported a balcony over the large oak front door. Tom looked at his wife, "There's no bleedin' knocker," he exclaimed.

"They've got no bleedin' curtains up either," remarked Mary.

Tom hammered on the door with his fist, but the sound was evidently not heard within. Then Mary noticed a knob poking out on the door lintel. She pulled on it and the sound of a distant bell reached their ears.

"Don't like this place, Tom, it gives me the creeps," Mary whispered.

"Them kids better be all right, luv, or I'm goin' to 'ave a few words wiv mister squire."

The door suddenly opened to reveal a tall, gaunt man in tweeds. His coat was belted and he wore a brown cravat over a green shirt.

"Mr and Mrs Carter I take it?" he asked in a cultured voice.

"'S'right, guv, we've come to see the kids," answered Tom.

"Won't you come in," said the squire as he stood aside.

The couple entered the hall and looked around. There was a wide staircase leading from their right, up and round to the landing above. The floor was marbled, and at the bottom of the stairs stood a grandfather clock in dark wood. Facing the clock was an ugly suit of armour, the metal arm crooked around a wicked-looking axe. Doors led off the hall on all sides, and one that was opened by their host led into a warm study. Books covered the walls, and brass statuettes were placed about the room. There was a large settee in the middle of the floor space, with a small table in iron and marble placed nearby. The large bay window was without curtains, and a huge table filled the alcove. On the centre of the highly polished oak table an aspidistra sprouted from an unglazed pot. The leaves were limp and brown. A log fire burned in the massive grate, and by the side of the fireplace stood a set of brass fire-tongs and pokers.

"Nice place you've got," Mary said.

"Yeah, very nice," agreed her husband.

"Won't you sit down. I'll tell my wife that you've arrived."

"Are the kids okay?" Mary asked him impatiently.

"Yes, they're fine," replied their host. "Can I take your coats with me?" He added, as he made for the door.

Mary handed him her coat and scarf but Tom preferred to keep his coat on. "'S'okay, guv, I'll just undo it," Tom answered.

The man left the room and Mary nudged her husband. "For goodness' sake take your 'at off, Tom," she implored him.

The docker removed the cap and ran his fingers over his hair.

The squire entered and announced that the children would be down in a few minutes. Tom studied the man and noticed that he had a habit of frowning, a pronounced movement magnified by his bushy eyebrows, which seemed to sprout outwards. The squire looked ill at ease, his hands continually going in and coming out of his coat pockets. "Would you care for some tea?" he asked.

Mary nodded her thanks and the tall man went over to the door and pulled on a tassel. After a few seconds the door opened and a tired-looking woman appeared. She had dark hair that was pulled to the back of her head in a tight bun. Her eyes were deep-set and her face was thin, with a nose that bent round from the bridge to the tip. She wore a dark dress with a white apron tied around her waist.

"Will you serve tea for two, Anna?" The man asked loudly.

The woman watched the man's lips, then left.

"Deaf as a post," remarked Tom to his wife in a whisper, and Mary gave him a meaningful look.

The host walked to a cabinet in one corner of the room and took down a cherry-wood pipe which he started to fill. "You had a good journey down, I take it?" he asked, and Mary nodded affirmatively and glanced wickedly at her husband.

"Yeah, we 'ad a comfortable ride, at least most of the way," Tom said, a ghost of a smile playing around his mouth.

The man looked at the door impatiently. "Where's the wife got to?" he muttered and Mary looked at Tom.

Footsteps sounded outside and the door opened. A large woman stood framed in the opening. She held the hand of a girl and rested her other hand on the shoulder of a boy. "Say hello to your parents now, children," she prompted.

The couple looked at their youngsters in astonishment. Reg was dressed in a pair of trousers that were sizes too big. His hair was unkempt and his pullover had holes in places. Marjorie hugged a small doll and stared at her parents, hardly able to believe that it was really them. She wore a dress that was meant for summer, and her grey-looking socks barely covered her ankles. Her shoes were dirty, and one of the straps flapped undone.

Mary sobbed as she tried to greet them and Tom felt a lump rising up in his throat. A cold feeling gripped at his insides and he gritted his teeth in rage.

The children stood for a few seconds, then the girl ran sobbing to her mother. "Mummy, Mummy, are we goin' 'ome?" she sobbed.

The boy walked bravely toward his father, holding back his tears, and the broad-shouldered docker swept him up in his arms.

The woman who stood in the doorway gave her husband a look of disdain and she closed the door behind her.

Mary was holding the sobbing Marjorie to her breast. "It's all right, luv, it's all right," she whispered.

The large woman walked over to her husband and stood by his side. The door opened again and the maid came in bearing a tray which she put down on the marble table. She sniffed and left the room silently. There were two cups of insipid looking tea and two plates, each of which had a tiny scone sitting in the centre.

Reg looked up at his father, "Are we goin' 'ome, Dad?" he asked, tears welling up in his eyes.

"You bet you're goin' 'ome, son, you're not stoppin' 'ere, that's for certain," Tom said with venom.

Mary looked at the woman, who stood impassive. "Where are their winter clothes? They brought plenty wiv 'em," Mary asked, a look of dark anger showing in her eyes.

"These are only the children's working clothes. They have their work to do you know. Daily tasks, in fact," answered the large woman.

Tom Carter nearly choked with temper. "Work? Tasks?" he spat out. "You mean to tell us you work these kids?"

"They have to earn their keep. Marjorie makes the beds and keeps the house clean – I mean she helps the maid with sweeping up and suchlike," replied the woman.

The gaunt man butted in, "Reg is learning how to care for the animals, isn't that so, Reg?"

"Animals? What animals?" screamed the infuriated Tom.

"The animals out at the back," ventured the man.

Tom reached out and gripped the man's arm in a vice-like hold. "'Ere, show me them animals, mister squire," he said through gritted teeth. He made the squire lead the way out of the study and out through a door at the back of the hall.

Mary meanwhile was looking hard at the large woman. "You 'eard what my Tom said, missus, you'd better get their cases packed, an' leave out their warm coats."

As Tom reached the courtyard the smell hit him like a blow. "Gawd Almighty, what's that stink?" he uttered.

The man felt his fingers going numb and tried to wrestle himself free of Tom's grip.

"Don't try, me ole son, you're likely to break your arm," Tom said, looking at the man with hate smouldering in his eyes. They walked over to the corner of the courtyard and there Tom saw the pigsty. Mud covered pigs fought to get at the swill. They pushed and shoved and slithered in the filth to get to the trough. Tom felt sick. "You mean to tell me you got my little lad to clean out this?" he shouted at the man.

"They're only pigs, they wouldn't hurt him," the man protested.

Tom's self-control snapped completely. He grabbed the squire by the seat and collar of his tweeds, and heaved him bodily into the filth of the sty. The man's face went deep into the swill and, in trying to get up, he only slipped deeper into the mess. Tom turned and walked back to the house.

Mary was waiting for the woman to bring down the cases. "What you done wiv 'im, Tom, you ain't killed 'im 'ave you?" she asked fearfully.

"No, luv, just sorted 'im out, nuffin ter worry over," he winked.

Presently the woman came down the stairs and put two cases by the front door. She held the children's coats over her arm. "Where's my husband?" she demanded.

"Wiv the pigs," answered Tom, and the woman gave him a funny look. "Come on kids we're goin' 'ome," Tom announced.

The youngsters grinned from ear to ear and Mary picked up her bag of presents. Tom grabbed the cases and walked out of the house. Behind them, they could hear the woman shouting, "Cyril, come here at once!" As the little party marched down the drive, the woman appeared at the front door. "If you've harmed my husband I'll call the police."

"Don't worry, luv," Tom replied. "'E's all right. Better run a bath, though!"

The London-bound train stood ready to leave as the tired but happy family reached the platform. The guard was ready with his green flag and whistle. Tom opened a carriage door and threw the cases in. "C'mon, this'll do," he shouted as he bundled them all into the compartment. The whistle sounded and the train puffed out of Gloucester station. Tom nestled back into the deep cushioned seats with their white linen head-squares and pull-down arm rests. He looked at Mary, and she gave him a huge smile. The two youngsters sat by the windows. They looked tired out but happy, and Tom, watching them, felt a lump in his throat.

Mary put her arm on his. "What's the matter, luv?"

"Dunno, got a bit o'grit in me eye I reckon," Tom said quickly.

An hour later the compartment door half-opened, then shut quickly. The representative of the GWR hurried down the corridor, mumbling to himself as he tried desperately to put as many coaches between him and his tormentor. As he went on his way he bumped into a ruddy-faced old colonel from Much Deeping in the Fold. The mumbling ticket inspector caught the colonel's shoulder and knocked the monocle out of his eye. The old officer's face went even redder. "Good Lord," he gasped as he polished his eyepiece. "Fish-paste and brown boots?" he repeated incredulously. "The man's a raving bloody lunatic. Whatever's the GWR coming to?"

Chapter Six

The Christmas holiday passed peacefully, with no air raids and very little news from the land front. Broadcasts did, however, tell of the continuing battles that raged at sea. The telegram boy pedalled around dockland on his red bicycle, slipping into the back streets to knock on doors with a rat-tat, then handing over the buff-coloured envelope with its official heading. But the boy on the red bicycle had already completed his business with Conner Street, at least for the time being. The only seafarer from that backwater had gone and would never return.

The 'Eagle' had been very busy during Christmas, with John Braden returning to contribute his dubious talents. The Bradens were particularly busy during the New Year's Eve celebrations, as Conner Street toasted in 1940 very loudly, but with some trepidation. In the new year, as in every year past, hangovers and headaches assailed the jollificators.

Early on New Year's Eve, Patrick took his tiny wife to the 'Eagle' and sat with their neighbours the Harpers, Joe and Rosie, and their lodger, Skipper. Joe's friend and workmate Fred Harris and his wife were also in the merry group. They joined in with the rest of the customers to sing their favourite songs, accompanied by the rusting tones of a battered old piano which in its long life had more pints of beer tipped into its innards than had Patrick Flannagan!

Early in the evening a young woman entered the 'Eagle' public house and hesitated at the door before walking up to the counter. She put down the small attaché case she was carrying and fumbled in her hand-bag for her purse. Florrie Braden was busy pulling a pint of ale and did not immediately notice the newcomer, but a few pairs of lecherous eyes coveted the slim figure of the woman, whose blonde hair barely reached her coat collar, and whose shapely calves were accentuated by her fashionable high-heeled shoes.

When Florrie Braden looked along the bar counter and saw the young woman standing there, her eyes suddenly widened and her face broke into a huge grin. "Well I'll go to the foot of our stairs! Is it really Julie?" she exclaimed, spilling beer over the top of the pint mug.

The young woman's white, even teeth flashed a smile and her pale blue eyes lit up. "That's who I was when I woke up this morning, Florrie. How are you and John?"

Florrie reached across the counter and clasped Julie's hand in hers. "You're the last person I expected to see in here. Where are you staying?"

Julie blinked back happy tears. "I'm staying at the Women's Hostel in New Kent Road. Just for a couple of nights. I'm looking for regular lodgings," she replied, putting a half-crown down on the wet counter.

Florrie straightened up and shook her head. "It's really you. I can't believe it."

John Braden shuffled past at that moment, holding two pints of beer in his unsteady hands. His wife blocked his path. "Look who's just walked in, John."

It took the man a second or two before he reacted. "My God! It's young Julie?" he gasped.

"Oi! John. What about our beer then?" an irate customer called out.

John Braden pulled a face and shuffled away with the beer to placate the solemn-looking individual, who leaned on his elbows at the end of the counter.

"He's not altered," said Florrie, jerking her head in her husband's direction. "Still upsetting the customers." Her eyes looked down at the half-crown. "Put your money away, girl. What you having?"

Julie felt embarrassed. People were looking at her and customers were waiting to be served. Florrie ignored their entreaties and grinned happily at the young woman before her.

Julie's cheeks flushed red. "Let me come round the counter and give you a hand. I haven't forgotten how to pull a pint you know."

Florrie waved her plump, ring-bedecked hand in the air. "You don't need to do that. You stay where you are and enjoy yourself."

"No really, Florrie. I'd sooner help. I'd feel more at home. Honestly."

"O all right then, luv. Don't stand no old nonsense from this crowd though," Florrie laughed. "We'll have a nice chat later. I might just know someone who's looking for a lodger, fingers crossed though."

Julie felt uneasy at first, but a pub atmosphere was not alien to her and soon she was laughing and joking as she helped the Bradens to deal with the ever increasing flow of customers. The piano melodies stirred the past for the young woman but the trade was too brisk for her to dwell on it.

"'Ere, darlin'. G'is a pint o' Best fer Dinky. 'E's gotta be kept oiled," said Skipper, jerking his thumb over his shoulder in the direction of the pounding keys, and at the same time rewarding Julie with a huge wink.

Julie placed the beer on the counter and watched as the little old man weaved an unsteady path towards the piano. She sighed and swallowed hard. It seemed like she was home at last.

'Dinky' Richards the pianist was blind. His sightless eyes rolled around as his skilful hands found the introductory keys, then closed as the melody rang out. It was as though the blind man wallowed in a love affair, raptured by every note, as his head tilted to catch the passing chords. His face often took on a pained expression, when his highly sensitive hearing caught a flaw in the already part-oxidised piano string. And his face took on yet another expression when his hearing picked up the vibrations caused by the placing of a full pint of ale upon the piano top. A wide grin would flash over his countenance for an instant. Then, like a snake delivering the fatal bite, Dinky reached out a long, thin arm and his hand closed perfectly around the glass. The operation was covered with his other vamping hand and the tune struggled on without the 'Eagle' choir being any the wiser. Even when the ensemble were in top key and the melody vibrant, Dinky could hear the soft tap if one of the customers bought him a pint and placed it to hand.

That night Dinky Richards was playing a selection from a popular musical show that was appearing up West. One of the customers was thrilled by the blind man's performance, and stood near to Dinky to watch his fingers as they caressed the keys. As the chorus rang out the man put down his glass, which was still three parts full, to join in the singing. The top of the piano, being the most convenient place to stand his glass, was also convenient for the pianist. After an hour or so, the customer came to the conclusion that the quality of the ale in the 'Eagle' left a lot to be desired. He'd calculated that he had drunk seven pints of beer, at twice his normal speed, and ended up being as sober as when he walked in the place. Not only was the ale losing its potency but the pianist too seemed to be flagging. Five minutes after the customer walked out of the bar, Dinky Richards did an unusual thing. He fell forward and played the last few notes of the song with his forehead.

"Get 'im a drink," someone shouted, "it must be the 'eat."

The last thing that Dinky wanted right then was a drink.

It happened on that merry occasion on New Year's Eve, 1940, that Patrick Flannagan also got a little more inebriated than the rest. The next morning, the Irishman found it impossible to raise his head from the pillow. "Jaysus," he croaked, "the room's spinning round." Bridie provided him with black coffee and a headache powder, then warned the children of his condition. Maureen put her hands on her hips, because she was the eldest, and she also raised her eyes in disgust, as her mother would do.

A short while after the medication had been administered, Patrick entered the parlour to state that he felt somewhat better, but not so that he could go to work. "If

I should fall down, woman, then I may end up in hot water." The statement was probably true, for Patrick's job was to stoke the boilers of the local bagwash factory.

Bridie gave the man his breakfast and, as he sat, eating implements held in shaking hands, eyes glued to his plate, his two young sons climbed onto a chair at the other end of the table to watch. Two-year-old Terry knew that if he licked his lips and stared hard enough at the egg on his father's plate, he would get a 'dip' on a piece of bread.

Terry tried licking his lips. In fact he tried two or three times, but the 'dip' was not forthcoming. It was not that the Irishman's behaviour was unreasonable, it was just that he could only barely focus his eyes on the plate. Anything further away was a blur. But the results of his father's over-indulgence the night before could not be understood by the two-year-old Terry and he went off in disgust to get the toy pistol that made a loud clacking noise, so he could shoot his father.

The sound of the toy pressed to the back of his head as the trigger was pulled, gave Patrick the agonising feeling of nuts and bolts being shaken beneath his skull. He groaned, his head in his hands and Bridie, coming into the room, got Maureen to carry the protesting Terry from the parlour, and Patrick junior settled down again on his chair to watch his father's discomfort. The man was still trying to find a way to eat his breakfast, but without much success, for he felt very sick. Young Patrick watched fascinated as his father, after checking that Bridie wasn't looking, slowly cut the rind from his bacon, then slid the rasher over the edge of the plate and into his lap. Patrick roared and thumped the table, and Patrick senior groaned once more. Bridie grabbed the boy, and spoke to Maureen, "I need to go to the market, I'll take this one with me," she said, giving the boy a stern look.

The weather was cold but bright on that first day of the year, and the market was in full swing, although some of the traders looked the worse for wear. Bridie finished her shopping at Albert Conlin's stall. She had taken her time so that the house would be left reasonably quiet. She knew that it would be around ten minutes to eleven before Patrick returned to the state of partial mobility. He would then announce that he would wash, shave and get a "breath of fresh air ..."

As Albert Conlin weighed up the tomatoes, Patrick junior's eye was caught by a shuffling figure that worked away behind the stall. The man's tongue hung out as he levered at a box of fruit. A stream of dribble ran down his chin as his face contorted with the effort. The boy watched closely as the idiot fought to get a case-opener under the lid of the box. The tongue slid around toward his cheek, then dropped to lick his chin as the operation became more and more difficult.

The young Patrick grinned at the idiot and poked his own tongue out. Bobbie realised that he was being watched and decided that he must show the little lad the best way to open a case of apples. He put the case-opener down while he turned the box round, then he picked up the implement and decided to turn the box round again. Patrick junior could see, even allowing for his tender years, that all was not right.

Albert too saw the mess the idiot was creating for himself. "Bobbie, for Gawd sake leave it alone. 'Ere, take this an' get me a mug o' tea," he said, handing the unfortunate a tin mug and two pennies. "Bridie, that poor bleeder'll be the deaf of me, you see if 'e don't."

As he spoke, Albert tipped the tomatoes into a brown paper bag and flipped it over so as to twirl the ends. The bag split and some of the tomatoes spilled onto the pavement. Bobbie saw the mishap, and quick as a flash he dropped the mug and picked up the fruit, some of which had squashed. When he had a handful he threw them into Bridie's shopping bag. Unfortunately, it happened to be the wrong bag, and the tomatoes landed on top of a half-dozen new laid eggs!

"Not that bag, you heathen," Bridie screamed. "Will you look at my eggs? They're all smashed," she wailed.

Bobbie was not to be beaten. He dived his hand down into the mess and pulled out a handful of egg shells, broken yolks and squashed tomatoes.

"Holy Mary, Mother o' God, take him away!" Bridie

61

cried, and Albert Conlin burst out laughing, his eyes watering, and his shoulders shaking violently. Bridie screamed at him, "You big pudden, what you find so funny?"

"I'm sorry, luv, I couldn't 'elp it. I tell you, 'e'll be the deaf o' me for sure."

Bobbie ran to the safety of a pile of boxes and peered over the top of them, his deep-set, dark eyes staring in anguish, his tongue licking the box as he watched Albert replace the tomatoes.

At ten minutes to the hour of eleven, Patrick spoke to Bridie, "You know, I feel a bit better, I'll get a wash and a shave, and then I'll take meself off for a breath of air."

Bridie puffed and got on with her washing, and the twins put their dolls' clothes onto the pile of dirty linen which was awaiting the copper.

At ten minutes past the hour, Patrick called out to say he was taking his stroll and Bridie grumbled to Maureen, "As far as the pub is all the stroll your father will take, darlin', and that's for sure."

Patrick reached the 'Eagle' and realised that he felt a little weak. This walking is tiring, he thought, I'd better sit down somewhere for a spell. The fact that the pub was at hand, he put down to sheer coincidence. After all, thought the Irishman, it could just as easy have been the undertakers.

By the time Patrick had consumed a few pints of ale he felt much better. His headache had left him and his thirst had returned.

The pub was fairly packed, with most of the traders who were regulars coming in for their 'liveners'. One or two people waved at the big Irishman, and one old character came over to ask about the rebel song. "You know, 'bout the bloke wot's goin' ter git shot at dawn or somefing?"

Patrick scratched his head. He knew the song well enough, but he had no recollection of ever trying to sing it. He bought the old fellow a drink and the two got into conversation. The man had spent a lifetime in the docks, and Patrick enjoyed his company. They drank a few more beers and then the old man asked him again about the rebel song. "Yer gotta sing it, Pat. Yer good lady stopped yer last night. Kept on treatin' the pianer player, so's 'e wouldn't play yer song. I's always got me eyes open, spot fings I do."

"Well, if you want to hear all about *Kevin Barry* I'll sing it, Pop," announced the swaying Irishman, as he banged his empty glass down on the bar counter.

The piano player was recovering from the night before, and the instrument stayed silent. Nevertheless, Patrick went over to stand with his arm resting on the top of that battered, scarred old upright and he started to sing. His hands waved and gestured and tears came into his eyes as the song rolled from his lips. The crowd in the bar were listening to the rendering when a little man pushed his way through. He carried a bar stool by its leg, and when he got within range of Patrick he promptly laid the Irishman out with one swift blow across the head.

They quickly bundled the assailant out of the pub, and then carried the unconscious man into the street. They propped him against the wall of the 'Eagle', to the chagrin of Florrie Braden. "I'm not having him lying there giving my pub a bad name. You'll have to take him home."

An emergency meeting took place and it was decided to commandeer Sammy Israel's fish barrow, which had been parked outside the 'Eagle' for the past two hours. Sammy brushed a few fish-heads off the barrow with the back of his hand and said, "Now him I don't mind on my barrow, but to push it down the street is too much. What if the Rabbi saw me, an' me a good Yiddisher boy? With a Catholic on the barrow would be too much."

Wheezy Morris had an idea. "Let's get Bobbie Wilkins, 'e'll push 'im 'ome fer a few coppers, I bet."

Sammy Israel looked much happier. "That's okay, but just don't ask me ..."

Wheezy cut him short, "Don't worry, Sammy boy, we won't tell the Rabbi, will we, lads?"

Sammy threw his hands in the air. "You please yourself, but just don't ask me ..."

"Sammy, fer Gawd's sake stop whinin' an' do somefing useful, go an' get Bobbie!"

They made Patrick comfortable on the barrow, with his head propped up on a kipper-box and they fetched the idiot. Wheezy borrowed a cloth money-bag from Florrie and slyly placed two metal washers inside. "C'mon everyone, 'ow about a whip round fer good ole Bobbie?" He shook the bag and Bobbie grinned in surprise.

Sammy put a couple of pennies in and Albert Conlin, who'd followed the idiot over to the pub, dropped a silver threepenny bit into the bag.

"C'mon, let's get Bobbie a nice collection, folks," sneered Wheezy.

Someone found a fish-head and an apple core, a few more washers, and a nut and bolt, all of which found their way into the bag.

Patrick was coming round as Bobbie pushed the barrow away from the 'Eagle'. The customers cheered and the shuffling figure grinned back, his tongue rolling around his face and his dark eyes shining.

It was tea break in the leather factory, and the girls sat in the window to drink their tea and watch the people as they walked by. As they chatted and giggled together, Sally Jones's eyes became like organ stops. She suddenly screamed out and pointed to the street. The girls fought to get a better view and, as the idiot passed by, straining against the weight of the barrow, the girls burst into a frenzy of cheering. Patrick heard the row through his befuddled senses. He sat up and saw the girls waving through the open window. He waved back and nearly fell off the cart. Then Bobbie decided to join in and he put the barrow down on its legs so his hands were free to wave. The girls cheered back and waved their arms in the air and Bobbie grinned, his face contorting with pleasure.

As suddenly as it had started, the cheering stopped and the girls' faces disappeared from the window. In their place was a stern old martinet, who looked at the scene with disgust. Bobbie did not want to wave to that face; he liked the girls' faces better, so he picked up the barrow and turned the corner, then marched the few yards to number 30, where gently he set down the legs once more and wiped his face on the back of his sleeve. Patrick meanwhile had regained his senses to a degree and tried to get off the barrow. But he chose the wrong end and, before Bobbie could help him, Patrick tumbled on to the pavement.

Bridie had been doing her wash and heard the cheering. She peered through the lace curtains of her parlour to see her husband struggling to get up from the floor, with Bobbie standing over him grinning like the devil. Bridie clenched her fists in anguish and asked the saints for guidance. As if they obliged, the pail of soapy water caught the woman's eye. She grabbed it and opened the door. Patrick was trying to sing to her, and Bobbie moved away, the broken eggs still registering in his mind. He saw the woman draw the bucket back and smartly dodged out of range.

"You drunken heathen, and to come home on a fish barrow!" cried the tiny woman as she threw the contents of the bucket over the unfortunate Irishman, who stood shaking before her. "And you," she screamed, pointing to the idiot, "you're haunting me today, begone with you!"

Patrick meanwhile had decided to give up the drink. He would go in his house and keep well away from the 'Eagle', for it was getting dangerous to even sing a song in there, he thought.

As the shuffling figure of Bobbie came into sight, his landlady and guardian Ada Dawkins was cleaning her doorstep. She looked puzzled as Bobbie approached her grinning widely, his hand holding a bag.

"What you doin' 'ome this time, Bobbie? Ain't they got no work fer you to do?"

"Bobbie pushed drunk man in cart, Sammy's fish cart."

"Who the bleedin' 'ell you talkin' about, Bobbie?" urged Ada.

"You know, man who speaks funny. Firty, number firty," said Bobbie.

"Oh my Gawd," moaned Ada. "You didn't push

Patrick Flannagan 'ome in a barrow, did you?"

"Bobbie don't mind. Men gave Bobbie money," he grinned.

"Money, what money?" asked Ada.

Bobbie held up the bag for Ada to see. "Bobbie got money, look."

Ada snatched the bag and peered inside. "Gawd Almighty, they 'ave 'ad 'ad a whip round, ain't they?" she said, with cold malice in her voice. "Who gave it to you, Bobbie?"

"Wheezy gave it Bobbie," the idiot said grinning. "Can Bobbie 'ave it?"

Ada tipped the money out and handed it to the grinning Bobbie.

"I'm goin' to take the bag back, you wait 'ere," she said, her eyes flashing furiously.

The 'Eagle' was getting ready to shut as Ada Dawkins walked in. Albert Conlin saw her and spoke, "'Ello, girl, want a quick 'alf a pint?"

"Thanks, Al, I'm lookin' fer someone," she said.

Albert got her a drink and handed it to the woman, whose gaze was resting on the foxy figure of Wheezy Morris. The man was laughing and joking with a couple of traders and he held a fresh pint of ale in his hand. Ada beckoned to Florrie and the woman came over.

"Hello, Ada, what's wrong, luv?"

"Florrie, do us a favour, girl. There's a woman outside, won't come in 'cos she's scared o' pubs, said she wants to speak to Wheezy. Looks a bit funny to me," Ada said, making a circular motion over her stomach with her hand.

"Okay, Ada, I'll tell him on the quiet."

Ada Dawkins watched as the landlady of the 'Eagle' called Wheezy to the counter and spoke in his ear. The foxy little man put his beer down and left the bar. As soon as he shut the door behind him, Ada sidled up and dropped something in Wheezy's glass of ale.

"C'mon now, time, gentlemen please. Drink up now," shouted John Braden.

Wheezy dived back into the bar. He looked relieved.

"Couldn't see anyone, Florrie, must 'ave gone."

"C'mon now, drink up," John urged again, and Wheezy picked up his glass. The ale disappeared into the man's stomach, and as the glass drained, a fish-head floated up, staring balefully at the man.

"Oh my Gawd," screamed Wheezy, as he threw the glass away from himself. "I feel ill, a stinkin' fish-'ead! I bet that Sammy Israel 'ad somefing to do wiv it."

Albert Conlin glanced at Ada, who was just leaving. She gave him a huge wink, and strolled back along Conner Street as though nothing had happened.

Chapter Seven

The early weeks of 1940 were very cold, with east winds that rattled doors and windows and whistled through draughty houses. The wind blew down trees, lifted slates from roof-tops, and performed other ominous tricks. It blew under front doors and lifted the passage mats so that they seemed to float like magical carpets. It took the chimneypot from the roof of 24 Conner Street and nearly caused the demise of old Granny Flint.

The chimneypot landed in the almost empty street, just missing the few passers-by, but pieces from the crumbling stack fell into the hole and down into Granny Flint's fireplace. The room became filled with soot and smoke which enveloped the old lady, who was snoozing at the time. As she remarked later, "I thought I'd died an' gone down to 'old Nick'!"

The reason Granny Flint didn't go downstairs, or even upstairs to escape, was Maureen Flannagan, who happened to be passing the old lady's window. She saw the smoke and heard Granny Flint screaming. And, with Bridie and Rosie Harper, carried the old lady out, still sitting in her armchair. They covered her in mounds of blankets while they tidied up and aired her parlour.

Skipper managed to find the brandy flask and gave the old lady a tot. The old seaman grinned at her. "I gotta say it, girl, but you look like one o' them there music 'all minstrels, what wiv that soot all over yer face."

With a look that spelt out 'be careful', Granny Flint held out her glass toward Skipper, who drained the brandy dregs into it. "Pity this is the lot, Gran, one more o' these an' you'd be able to sing us all a song," said the man.

"I'm sure," puffed the old lady. "Would yer like me

68

to do *Swanee River* an' tap-dance down the street?"

Skipper laughed and old Granny Flint waved her stick at him. "Be off wiv yer or I'll put this across yer shoulders yer young bleeder."

The early months of 1940 remained quiet except for the continuing battles at sea. The German U-boats were picking off the convoys, and the cost of getting food and supplies into Britain was very high both in lives and ships. Food supplies were low, and rationing laws were tightened up. The ration book became a way of life for everyone, and it caused quite a few headaches for the shopkeepers. The paper work was a gigantic task, with forms that had to be sent to the Ministry, and registration of all customers. Coupons, cut from the ration books, were counted and used to get further supplies. The one-man business became a round-the-clock operation and many of the solo shopkeepers had to find assistants to help them.

Stanley Nathan ran a little one-man business. He had mixed feelings about food rationing, for although it caused him many headaches, it also brought a new woman into his life.

The Nathan Provision Store stood at the Kent Road end of the market, and had been there as long as anyone cared to remember. Stanley's father had founded the shop, and when he died Stanley took over the business. He was now forty years old, fat, short and balding. He had a rosy face that beamed at the customers, and a manner that was charming. Stanley had tact, guile and personality, and he needed every bit of it with some of his customers. They marvelled at his cheerfulness and his memory. He never forgot to ask after his clients' ailing family members, and how little Johnnie's cold was. He was admired especially for the way he coped when his wife upped and left him, preferring the more ambitious man, as she put it, to the staid, contented Stanley Nathan.

When he had brought his new wife with him to help in the shop, the customers seemed to change. It was as though they resented her coming between them and their favourite shopkeeper. The woman did not have Stanley's personality, nor his tact, and many times she fell out with the more difficult customers. She finally stopped helping in the shop and everyone, including Stanley, breathed a sigh of relief.

Things were starting to go wrong, and the letter awaiting him one night as he got home confirmed his suspicions. He sat in his little house in leafy suburbia and read the contents over and over again. His wife had left him for a businessman who was someone in the fish trade. He puzzled, as he read and re-read the letter. Should he have taken that next-door property when it was available? Should he have expanded, and taken on assistants, and enlarged his store? He already knew the answer. He was happy, as his father was before him. Stanley did not see himself as an employer, paying out the wages and sitting behind a desk, instead of sweet-talking the acid-tongued Mrs Brown. He knew he was happy and he intended that it should stay that way.

The months that followed were very lonely, and he tried not to let the customers see pain in his face. He did not take into account the fact that they were dockland folk, people who were born into a tightly knit community. They were masters at reading faces. The chances of anyone fooling them with lies and deceit were very small indeed. Those rough diamonds stared at the eyes, the open gaze, daring the person to lie, and they knew. They did not sympathise with empty words, but shared the pain; the eyes said it, and the open faces absorbed the ache. It had always been that way; from the raw times when tall-masted schooners tied up at the docks, and the women waited on the wet, foggy jetties for their men to come home. They sometimes stood outside the brightly lit pubs with their children hugging their skirts and the baby wrapped around in the end of the woman's shawl. They pleaded with their drunken men for money for food and were slapped into the gutter, or abused with a drunken tongue that flayed them with barbed nautical obscenities. Their life was hard and the area was bleak, with cold, foggy streets that led to the wharves and docks, and damp verminous tenements that festered and ate away at the very soul.

The reformers worked hard in dockland. They got the worst of the tenements pulled down. They founded the

Seamen's Homes and the welfare organisations, and they planted trees along some of the soulless byways. They cleaned the filthy streets and altered the course of the open sewers. The reformers changed the lives of the dockland folk, but the image that was etched on their souls had descended from generation to generation. The look of suffering still lingered in their eyes. They recognised the symptoms, and saw them in their fat, balding shopkeeper.

Stanley Nathan often wondered about his wife, how her fortune fared with the ambitious businessman in the fish trade. He was to find out one sunny day during the summer of '39, when the 'Eagle' held their annual outing to Southend. Stanley often used the pub during his lunch hour, and he joined the party which strolled along the sea front for a bowl of jellied eels and a smell of real sea air. The friends joked and jostled each other, and they pointed out the pretty girls. They stopped at a stall that sold bowls of fresh jellied eels, together with hunks of bread. A tired little man served the portions, his face a picture of misery. The woman who washed the bowls behind the counter looked even more miserable. The dirty apron tied around her skinny waist, and the head-square tied over her hair, seemed to define her face, and it became imprinted on the mind of Stanley Nathan. His wife had sought her fortune with the businessman who was someone in the fish trade. Stanley turned away quickly when he recognised her, but he need not have bothered. The woman worked away as an automaton, neither seeing nor hearing. She would, no doubt, finally leave the man for someone with more ambition. Or would she? Stanley wondered.

The rationing had become a nightmare for the shopkeeper. So one morning in January he took a piece of cardboard and a black crayon and drew up a notice which he pasted in his shop window. He realised that he must get some help, and hoped the assistant would get on well with the Lizzie Browns and the rest of his customers. He looked at the notice and pondered on what she would be like. Now the young woman who had just passed his window would be ideal, thought Stanley. She looked fine, with her honey-blonde hair tied back with a thin black ribbon. He was suddenly jerked back into reality as the girl turned and came into the shop. She walked up to the counter and gave him a sweet smile. "Please, I've come about the job in the window."

Stanley stared open-mouthed for a second. "I'm . . . I'm sorry," he said hesitantly. "Didn't you just walk past?"

"Yes I did," replied the girl. "Is the job taken then?"

"No, no," replied Stanley, staring into her pale blue eyes.

"I have references, and I did work for the Bradens – from the 'Eagle', when they had their last pub in Kent!" the girl exclaimed, holding out some letters. "I worked as a barmaid, but I've done shop work," she added.

Stanley looked at her open, rounded face that flushed slightly as she spoke, and her dimpled cheeks, and he liked what he saw.

"Okay, when can you start?" he asked with a smile.

"Don't you want to see the references?" enquired the girl.

"Oh that's all right, I can see you'll do fine," said Stanley, shocked by his own outspokenness.

"I can start tomorrow, if that's okay?"

Food rationing was not the only thing that upset the dockland folk. Their beer was being tampered with. Apart from the fact that it became dearer, it also got weaker. The locals noted it and when they spoke to Florrie about it she lied to them by saying that it was the hops, which seemed to satisfy them, for they still came in for their pint and a chat.

A few of the regular customers were missing. The Davis brothers were already drafted and others were getting their papers. Wheezy Morris was one, but he walked into the medical centre holding his back. "Your back, you say?" asked the doctor. "What's wrong with your back?"

"Twisted it years ago, I did," answered Wheezy. "It ain't bin right since."

"Okay then, we'll just have a look, old man," said the doctor.

Wheezy gave him a funny look, and the medic pointed

to a chalk mark on the floor, "I want you to stand here and drop your trousers."

The little man did as he was bid.

"Now raise your hands over your head," said the doctor, pressing a bell as he spoke.

Wheezy had been making it seem a major operation to drop his trousers, and as he stood there with his hands held high he winced convincingly at the doctor. The door opened suddenly and a nurse walked in. Quick as a flash, Wheezy dived down to hoist up his trousers, and the medic raised his eyes. "Seems fine now, Mr Morris, doesn't it?" he said, pointing to the offending part.

Wheezy bit his lip. He'd been caught out by one of the oldest dodges in the medical profession. As far as the army was concerned, Wheezy needn't have worried, for the doctor looked at him and said "I'm sorry to tell you that you have a perforated ear drum, old man."

"You mean I can't go in the army an' do me bit?" asked the little man, trying hard to muster up a look of disappointment.

"Sorry, old man," said the medic as he stamped a card.

Wheezy hurried back to the 'Eagle' and got into conversation with Sammy Israel, who was going for his medical the next day.

"I tell yer, Sammy, I was disgusted. Pleaded wiv the doc' I did. Let me go, I want to do me bit, Doc', I says. Can't yer ferget me wonky ear 'ole?"

"What did 'e say, Wheezy?"

"Wouldn't 'ave it. Said a sharp noise in me ear could kill me."

Sammy Israel was beginning to get an idea. "'Ow did the doctor find out about yer perforation, Wheezy?"

"Put great big lights in me ear'ole. Though I don't fink they know what they're lookin' for. They didn't find out what was wrong wiv me bruvver."

"What was wrong wiv 'im?" Sammy asked.

"Stone deaf 'e was, but the doctors couldn't find a fing wrong wiv 'im. I could 'ave told 'em. It was 'is bleedin' wife wot caused 'im ter go 'mutton'."

"Yer bruvver's wife, 'ow come?" asked Sammy.

"Well, 'e liked a drink, did Alf. Trouble was 'e couldn't get up in the mornin' an' Mona, 'is wife, kept screamin' in 'is ear 'ole. Not only did it send 'im deaf, it sent 'im round the bend. 'E tried to cut 'er froat one mornin' an' they carted 'im orf to the looney bin."

Sammy had it all worked out when he presented himself to the army medical board.

"Shut the door behind you, Mr Israel," said the doctor, and Sammy walked right in.

"The door," barked the medic, and Sammy grinned.

"You have a problem with your hearing then?" queried the doctor.

"Do what?" said Sammy.

"You can't hear too well?"

"I'm sorry I can't ..."

"Never mind," cut in the doctor, "we'll examine the rest of your anatomy anyway."

Later, when the doctor had finished, he said to the yiddisher boy, "I'm glad to say that apart from your hearing, you're a perfect specimen."

"What yer say?" asked Sammy.

"It's okay," said the medical man as he stuck a probe into the unfortunate one's ear. "Looks perfectly okay to me," mumbled the doctor.

"Do what?" asked Sammy.

"I said okay."

"Pay?" queried Sammy.

"Good God," moaned the nerve-wracked doctor, as he beckoned the nurse over. "I've filled the form in, nurse. I want you to give Mr Israel his expenses, and a half-crown for his dinner. Sign this form please, Mr Israel."

Sammy picked up the pen, then threw it down in disgust.

"Strange," remarked the doctor. "Shall we take one more look in your ears, Mr Israel?"

The yiddisher boy went home to await his call-up, and to tell Wheezy Morris of his impatience to get into uniform. The subject was discussed at length in the ale bar of the 'Eagle'.

"You can't fool them panel doctors. Sharp as me ole mum's carvin' knife they are."

Sammy Israel nodded, "'S'right. You can't pull the wool over their eyes."

Skipper sat at the table, listening. He took out his tobacco pouch and proceeded to fill his clay pipe. "It depends 'ow much yer wanna swing the lead," he remarked.

"Wha'd'ja mean?" asked Wheezy.

Skipper took out a Vesta and struck it on the table top. Clouds of smoke enveloped him and Sammy coughed. "Are you still there?" he asked through the fog, and Wheezy laughed.

"Well, it's a question of 'ow far yer prepared ter go, ain't it?"

"I don't get yer," Sammy said.

"I knew of a chap once," began Skipper, "who got out o' the last lot. The '14 war I mean. This chap was fit as a fiddle, but 'e was determined 'e wasn't goin' ter get put into a uniform. When 'e got 'is papers fer the medical, 'e tore 'em up. Course they sent the police down. Found 'im wiv 'is 'ead in the gas oven."

"Was 'e dead?" asked Wheezy.

"Course 'e wasn't. There was a smell of gas, an' the police broke in an' saw 'im layin' there wiv 'is 'ead on a cushion. Couldn't a bin there more'n five minutes. Must a seen 'em comin' down the turnin'. Took 'im to 'orspital an' checked 'im over, then they sent 'im 'ome. Couple a days later, down comes 'is medical papers. Anyway, this chap, I'm tryin' ter fink of 'is name, Woods, that's it, Billy Woods. Well Billy ain't goin' an' that's fer sure, so 'e outs an' dives under a tram."

"Was 'e dead?" asked Wheezy again.

"Course 'e wasn't. They got grids at the front o' trams, ain't you ever seen 'em?"

"What 'appened?" asked Sammy.

"Tram was stoppin' anyway," went on Skipper. "'E got cuts an' bruises, an' a bit of a shakin'. The tram pushed 'im fer a few yards that's all. Anyway, back 'e goes in the 'orspital again, an' they look 'im over. Out 'e was, in under a week. Missed 'is medical, so they decided to send 'im some more papers."

The seaman paused in his narration to re-light his pipe. Sammy Israel and Wheezy Morris were eager for Skipper to go on.

"Well, what then?" asked Sammy.

Skipper wasn't satisfied with the performance of his pipe. He tapped the bowl on the edge of his chair and started to re-pack it, pressing the strands of tobacco carefully into a tight wad before putting a match to it.

"Go on, Skipper, what 'appened next?" asked Wheezy impatiently.

"Well, Billy Woods gets these papers," went on Skipper, "an' 'e gets a bright idea. 'E's got some sleepin' tablets, an' 'e decides ter wait till the police come fer 'im again. When 'e sees 'em comin' 'e swallers two tablets. The rest is already down the closet. Well, the police see the empty bottle, an' Billy Woods out like a light. Anyway orf they go to 'orspital again. Give 'im a stomach pump, an' a good talkin' to an' send 'im 'ome."

"What about the papers?" asked Sammy.

"I told yer, Billy tore 'em up like all the rest."

"No yer never."

"Well 'e did anyway," Skipper said with a shake of his head.

"What next," said Wheezy, who was desperate to get to the end of the story because his glass was nearly empty.

Skipper cleared his throat. "By this time, the 'orspital's gettin' fed up wiv our Billy Woods, so the doctor writes a letter to the army panel, sayin' that Billy's a lunatic, an' the panel send Billy a grade four card, which means that 'e's not needed. Anyway, when poor Billy sees the envelope, 'e don't open it. 'E already knows who it's from by the look of it. Well, 'e runs out of 'e's house, down the street, like the devil's after 'im, an' straight across the road. Didn't even look. Straight under a dray 'e went. Trampled by the 'orses an' crushed by the barrels."

"Was 'e dead?" asked Wheezy.

"Well, they never sent 'im any more medical papers," grinned Skipper.

Chapter Eight

The early spring of 1940 was very mild, with the winds coming from the south. The season's flowers opened their petals atop air raid shelters and between sandbags. They sprouted from sand-filled fire buckets and from every window box in Tanners Alley. The profusion of colour helped to tone down the ugliness that was war-time dockland.

Bob Bowman was pleased with his geraniums. They were budding well and he was looking forward to a good show this summer. The little back yard of the street warden's house was full of small earthenware pots. They stood crowded together on the scullery windowsill and on the cracked concrete floor of the yard. More pots stood in a row on a rickety wooden shelf that Bob had nailed up on the wall beside the lavatory door and each of the potted plants reached out for the restricted sunlight that shone grudgingly down into the yard.

Unlike Bob, his wife Grace was not very pleased with the way things were out back. It wasn't so much that she had to tread warily when she hung up the washing or when she used the wringer. It wasn't the fact that she had to be careful not to open the lavatory door too far in case the pots went flying. What Grace could not abide was "The awful pong of that bleedin' 'orseshit."

Bob just laughed it off. "Let me tell yer, woman, that's the finest fertilizer yer can get, 'specially if it's fresh."

Grace became resigned and just shook her head every time her husband disappeared from the house with a bucket and shovel and then returned carrying a bucketful of steaming geranium food.

In the early spring Bob Bowman was sure he would get

a nice show. "I'll stick a couple in the front winder soon as they flower, pet."

"Not wiv that bleedin' 'orseshit on 'em yer won't," vowed Grace.

May began with warm spells, which helped to add to the complacency that abounded. The news was the same from Europe, with the large armies facing each other along hundreds of miles of fortifications. There was renewed talk of a swift end to hostilities, and people prayed that it would be so. They offered up prayers from Spencer Street Methodist chapel in Thursday evening's bible class, and it was as if the prayers were heard as an urge to get the war moving. Which was precisely what happened.

On the next day, as the dawn broke, thousands of German soldiers and machines by-passed the defended front and swept through the Ardennes. Parachutists landed in Holland, Belgium and Luxembourg. The real war had begun.

In dockland, little groups gathered around to talk about the developments. They read the evening papers and heard on the wireless how the Prime Minister had resigned, and they were informed of the new leader, Winston Churchill. They discussed the events. "I tell yer, it'll be a long, drawn-out affair," remarked Skipper to Joe Harper.

"I tell yer, Skipper, we've got ter be grateful for that little strip o' water. If it wasn't fer that, we'd be fightin' 'em in the streets right now," said Joe.

"Yeah, they might be good soldiers," said Skipper, "but they can't walk on water yet awhile."

Joe Harper shook his head. "They seem to be goin' through the Low Countries like a dose o' salts. It's frightenin'."

"Them bastards wiv them parachutes, that's what's causin' the panic," Skipper said, with a shake of his head.

"Yeah, it must be frightenin' seein' 'em floatin' down," Joe agreed.

"I don't trust Germans. We 'ad one aboard ship. Officer 'e was." Skipper stated.

Joe sensed a story, and he made excuses, "Sorry I can't stop, mate, I've promised to slip over to see Fred Harris. Bin orf sick 'e 'as."

Skipper reached for his tobacco pouch as Joe stepped out of the house.

The sun had set, and the long spring evening was turning to dusk. Joe walked slowly along the turning toward the Kent Road. As he neared Fred's house at number 8, he saw his daughter Mary walking in his direction. She saw him and smiled. "Hello, Dad, I'm just on my way round to see you and Mum."

Joe kissed her. "You go on down, I'll be along in a minute, just poppin' in to 'ave a word wiv Fred, 'e's bin under the wevver."

Mary's eyes were red and puffed. "I'm on nights this week, Dad."

"Yeah, I can see, or 'ave you bin cryin?"

"Well, I'm worried over Bob now that it's all blown up out there."

"Don't worry too much, luv. Bob knows 'ow to take care of 'imself. 'E'll be okay, you'll see."

The tall, slim woman walked on down the street, and Joe went into Fred's house, where he stayed awhile talking.

Lizzie Brown had a few comments to make on the day's events. She stood by her front door in Conner Street, hands tucked into her apron. Emmie Jones stood with her in the gathering gloom. "I tell yer straight, if them parachuters land in this street they'll get wot for."

Emmie shuddered. "O I'd die if I saw 'em floatin' down, I'm sure I would," she said, looking over her shoulder as if one of the parachutists were standing there.

"Die nuffink," thundered Lizzie Brown. "I tell yer wot I'd do. I'd tie me carvin' knife on the end of me broom 'andle, an' I'd rip the bastards up afore they touched the ground, that's wot I'd do, mark my words."

Emmie Jones shuddered again, and tucked her hands into her apron like Lizzie. The conversation was beginning to scare her.

"I saw Joe 'arper's eldest girl a while ago. Looked

worried she did. 'Er feller's out there at the front."

Lizzie nodded. "Nice girl. Works in an army 'orspital, so Rosie 'arper told me."

Emmie Jones caught sight of Mrs Smith, who was hurrying along in the dusk. The two watchers screwed up their eyes in an attempt to see what the woman was carrying.

"Is that one of those tram sheets?" Emmie asked.

"Looks like it," agreed Lizzie.

Betty Smith reached the two women and set the bundle down on the pavement. "Gawd, that's bleedin' 'eavy," she gasped.

Lizzie and Emmie stared at the bundle.

"I carted that all the way from me sister's over on Spencer Street. Me arms feel like they're droppin' orf."

Despite the fact that Betty Smith was concerned about pieces of her aching anatomy, she looked pleased with herself. Tram sheets were now prized possessions in dockland, and increasingly difficult to come by. There was a time when the ageing destination sheets got thrown out for the dustmen, until some enterprising soul found that a good day or two's soaking in soda-water loosened the black paint. The linen sheets could be picked clean, then split, seamed and ironed, to produce a pair of high quality bed-sheets.

For a while the tram depot became seiged with applications for the sheets, until they realised why. From then on signs went up advertising old sheets at seven-and-sixpence a time.

Betty Smith picked up her bundle. "I'm goin' 'ome an' put this in to soak wiv a nice knob o' soda. I'll leave it in the bathtub. My 'arry'll 'ave to wash in the sink."

"Your 'arry's goin' ter give yer a black eye if yer not careful," remarked Lizzie, with good reason. Harry Smith was a heavyweight coalman with a well-known short temper. Mrs Smith's plan looked in jeopardy.

The knowledgeable Mrs Brown was usually consulted regarding the happenings around the dockland community, and Emmie Jones was aching to find out about Stanley Nathan and his new assistant. "'Ere, Lizzie, I know what I was goin' to ask yer. Is our Stan courtin' 'is shop girl?"

Betty Smith's bundle was getting heavy, but she decided to wait around for Lizzie's pronouncement on the matter.

"Well, it's funny you should mention Stanley an' that girl of 'is. Seems that she used to work as a barmaid for the Bradens, when they 'ad their pub down in the 'op fields. Tom Carter's wife was tellin' me. Got it from 'er 'usband's mates. Turns out there was a bit of a scandal. Can't get the rights of it, but this 'ere barmaid runs orf. Now she turns up workin' for ole Stanley Nathan of all people."

Betty Smith decided to get her heavy bundle home to the bathtub, and Lizzie Brown thought it time she went in out of the blackout.

"I 'ope our Stan's a little bit more careful this time," she said to Emmie as a passing shot.

The subject of the ladies of Conner Street's concern was at that moment sitting in the ale bar of the 'Eagle'. His assistant Julie Brett was with him. She had a serious look about her face, and Stanley was talking. "I don't understand, Julie. You've settled in nicely, and the customers have taken to you. Why, even old Lizzie Brown gives you a smile now and again."

Julie smiled at the joke. "Stan, it's difficult, and you've made it worse."

"I still don't understand," repeated Stanley. "You say you're thinking of leaving, because I asked you to walk out with me?"

"Let me try to explain," said Julie. "You hired me without even knowing my name. You didn't even look at my references, and now you want us to get serious?"

"Yes, yes I do," said Stanley. "We work well together, don't we?"

The girl nodded. "You don't know anything about me, it wouldn't be fair to you, and besides, I . . ." She stopped suddenly, and began instead to move her finger around the rim of the tumbler.

"Look," said Stanley, taking her empty glass. "I'll get us a refill and then we're going to have a serious chat, okay?"

It was early evening and the pub was quiet. John Braden served Stanley with the drinks.

"How's Florrie, John?"

"Okay, Stan. She's got some work upstairs," he answered.

Stanley Nathan took the drinks back to the table and put the gin and orange in front of the girl. He sipped at his whisky and soda, watching the girl as she put the glass to her lips. "Enough orange?" he queried.

"It's fine," replied Julie, as she took out a silver cigarette case from her bag.

Stanley glanced at the case. "That's nice. Unusual in fact. I bet it was expensive."

Julie wished she had left the case at home. "Yes, it was a present," she said quickly.

Stanley did not proceed with the conversation. He sipped at his drink thoughtfully.

Julie studied the man. He had a kind face, and his eyes were soft. He had proved nice to work for, but the thought of becoming his girl awakened her pain and suffering, and she found it very hard to come to terms with it. If he persisted, he would have to know, and the telling would mean the end for her as his assistant. She looked into his eyes and saw the concern there. She knew that she must tell him everything, and if that proved to be the end for them, well it would just have to be. There could be no other answer. The woman knew it deep inside her.

"Stan, I'm going to tell you something, and I want you to listen," she said as she picked up the glass, looking at it for a second or two before downing the contents in one gulp. She then lit the cigarette she had been toying with and exhaled a cloud of smoke.

"You remember when I first walked in the shop, I told you about me working for Florrie and John as a barmaid? Well, it was a few years ago. I was just eighteen and very innocent. There was a chap who used to come in very often. He was smart, and had all the right answers for a girl like me. Well, I thought I was in love with him. I couldn't wait for him to show up. If he didn't make an appearance one night I'd be really upset, that's how bad it was. Anyway, one night he asked me out, and it soon became the usual thing for me to be with him on my nights off, and even after work. He told me about himself. It seemed that he was waiting for a divorce to come through. He said his wife had got herself another man. I felt sorry for him, and it wasn't long before I'd become his mistress."

Stanley put his hand on hers, "Look, I don't want to hear, Julie," he said, his large eyes soft and pleading.

"You've got to hear it all, Stan," she said sadly. "If there's going to be any future as far as you and I are concerned, then you must listen. You can guess what happened next; I became pregnant. I was happy at first. I saw it as the thing that would bind us together. I didn't realise how wrong I could be. The man changed completely the moment he found out. It was then he really told me about himself. He had a devoted wife and three lovely children. He said that I should get an abortion. Money was no problem, and he knew of someone who could perform the operation. God, I felt as though I wanted to die."

Stanley squeezed her hand until she winced. "I'm sorry, Julie, but I don't need to know about it. What happened was in the past. It doesn't matter."

"But it does. That's why it does matter. Don't you see? There's always ghosts that come up to haunt you. Someone from the past who comes on the scene and spoils everything. No, Stanley, it's important that you know everything there is to know."

"Okay, Julie, but you know it won't make a scrap of difference to me," Stanley said softly.

"I couldn't stay where I was," said Julie. "I went to stay with my sister in North London. It was a bad decision, because my sister was on the streets. I hadn't seen her for some time and I didn't know. She looked years older than she really was, and every penny went to her keeper. He was a monster, a sadist who liked to beat women. I know, because I saw him attack my sister more than once while I was there."

Julie sighed, and fingered the silver cigarette case. "It was a couple of months later when I lost the baby. My sister was shopping and I was cooking a meal for the three of us. Her man tried to get familiar and we started to fight. I remembered scratching his face, then he knocked me down the stairs. I can just about remember falling, then waking up in hospital. I'd lost the baby. The terrible thing was that her pimp was there in the ward, waiting for me to come round as though nothing were wrong. He had a bunch of flowers, and an evil grin that dared me to say what really happened.

"I was terrified for my sister as well as myself, so I kept quiet about what happened. That man was capable of anything. I was determined to get away as soon as I could, but when I got out of the hospital nothing seemed to matter. The rush to leave wasn't important. I suppose if you live with evil and degradation, then some of it is bound to rub off. Anyway, I started drinking. Then I frequented the places my sister used. It wasn't long before I was taking men back home. Yes, Stanley, I became a prostitute."

The man dropped his gaze. He did not want her to see the tears that welled in his eyes.

"You wanted to walk out with me, Stanley. I had to tell you, surely you must understand?"

"Yes, I understand," replied Stanley. "But as I said, the past is the past. God Almighty, woman, we may never live to see the end of this war. Do you really think that because you've had a rough time it gives you the right to take it out on anyone who walks into your life?"

Julie gripped the cigarette case. "Do you know how I got this," she said, holding it out towards him. "It was for services rendered, do you understand?"

"I understand," replied Stanley. "Tell me, why do you carry that case around with you. Is it to punish yourself? A penance, so that every time you reach for a cigarette, you remember the life you led and the men you slept with?"

Julie's eyes filled with tears, and she made to leave. Stanley gripped her arm and spoke. "Now listen, girl.

Listen good. I'm not a priest in a confessional box. I can't issue you with so many Hail Marys. I'm a fat, balding man who's gone through a shambles of a marriage, with a woman who thought it was more exciting to sell jellied eels on Southend pier than spend her married life in Stanley Nathan's shop. Yes, Julie, my wife ran off with another man. I've had pain and suffering. I wanted to cut my throat, but somehow things get put into a different light when you least expect it."

The woman looked at him, and saw the soft eyes that stared back at her. She saw the pain reflected there, and she gave a deep sigh.

"I opened my shop as usual the next day," went on Stanley. "I was missing her, and it must have shown on my face. Do you know who my first customer was that morning? It was Lizzie Brown. She came in and looked at me. It was the only time I can remember her actually smiling. What's more she even said 'good morning', would you believe?"

Julie smiled, and Stanley was encouraged.

He winked at her, and went on. "When I weighed up her bacon, she even said, 'Thank you, Stanley'. I tell you, girl, the whole community helped me through that period. They ached for me, if you can understand what I'm trying to say. They're lovely people, and I'll never forget them. They didn't try to judge me, they helped me. They taught me something, Julie. You don't judge people, you accept them, with all their faults. Yes, like the Lizzie Browns and the Emma Jones of this world. Christ, Julie, can't you understand what I'm trying to say? I want to walk out with you! I want to stroll along the riverside, and watch the sun dipping over the wharves. I want to see the ugliness of the place, and think that it's the most beautiful sight I've ever seen. I can only do that with you, girl. Now do you see?"

Julie reached out for his hands and clasped them tightly. She laughed through her tears, "I see, Stanley, I see," she sobbed.

"You're staying on then?" he asked.

"What do you think?" she replied.

Chapter Nine

Throughout May 1940 the news got steadily worse. The British army was being squeezed back onto the French coast, into a pocket around a place called Dunkirk. The news bulletins were all very grave, describing the struggle to keep the Dunkirk area open for the eventual evacuation of the army.

By the end of the month, an armada of small boats had been assembled ready to leave for France. In fact the evacuation was under way during the last days of May. Thousands of wounded, soaked, exhausted troops were lifted off the beaches, under constant enemy fire, and taken out to where the large ships lay at anchor. Many of the small craft struggled all the way back across the Channel, laden to the gunwales with human cargo.

Two people in the local community were immediately concerned with the progression of events. Joe Harper's daughter Mary was one. Her husband Bob was somewhere in France. Mary listened to all the bulletins with a dread that became almost unbearable. Alberto Vitelli was the other. He also listened to the news with a deepening sense of futility and fear. He knew that very soon his country of birth would be at war with his country of adoption. The signs were all there and the inevitability was burning into his mind as the days wore on.

On the evening of June 11th 1940, Alberto Vitelli locked up his greengrocery shop in the Tower Road market and climbed the stairs to his small flat above. Maria, his wife, was visiting her cousin and would not be home for quite a while. Alberto sat in the quietness, his head buried in his large hands. He was unaware of the changing shades as the warm evening's sun dipped down in the reddened sky. The lengthening shadows darkened the room until it was night. Still the man did not move. A train whistle drifted across from the freight yard, with the sounds of shunting wagons as they were assembled for the night journey. The vague note of the steam whistle roused old memories, unlocking the door to the past. The man reviewed the fleeting thoughts from his supine position. He allowed himself to drift along with those memories beneath a feeling of despair that was an agony.

It was hot. Stifling hot, with the smells of the drains and the swill-bins at the rear of Leonardo's restaurant vying for supremacy. The stench rose unnoticed around the young boy as he crouched down behind the swill, waiting for the danger to pass. His hand gripped a fat wallet of pig skin, and his fingers traced the pattern as he waited. He crouched very still, allowing his breath to become normal and his heartbeats to slow to a boyish rate. He listened to the sounds of screaming and shouting as they became more distant. Still he did not move. They might return and he had to be sure.

It had been easy, except for that old witch Caterina. He had sidled up to the large foreigner with the cane and the white covers that draped over his shoes. He saw the bulge and reached it without the slightest slip. He removed the wallet and had started to back away when that crone called out. The foreigner spun around and shouted to the boy, who darted into the maze of alleys. Old Caterina pointed the way, her hand held out for a reward, only to be brushed aside.

It was hopeless, as the trail led nowhere in the dark by-ways. The boy had taken them in a wide arc, away from his abode, so that he would not be recognised by someone who would betray him for a silver coin. He had shaken off his pursuers and now he waited. He had learned to be patient, to trust his intuition, and that way he did not starve, and he remained free.

At last he moved. The wallet was in the swill-bin but the contents, lira and foreign notes, were hidden about the boy as he carefully picked his way home. Home, where his mother lay ill, and where his sister Carla brought the men who would pay for her services. He entered the street and climbed the dark stairs, two at a time. He sensed something was wrong before he pushed open the door. His mother had gone, and a priest stood comforting his sister. Carla sobbed, as the man of the cloth held his arm about her thin shoulders.

"Mamma, where's Mamma?" cried the boy.

The priest spoke, his deep voice ringing around the stone-walled apartment, "The suffering soul who is your mother is very ill. She has consumption, Alberto. She must have care, so we have taken her to a hospice of the Daughters of Christ. There she will be properly cared for. We must pray for her often, my children."

Alberto cried bitter tears. The money that Carla had earned in her room across the hall, and the lira he filched from the pockets of the rich, had now become enough to pay the price of a bed in the green-painted wards of the Daughters of Christ.

Carla was troubled about the boy, and she sought her answers at the church after mass that evening.

"I know of someone, Father, who will help me to get the boy away from here. There is a family in England related to our dear mother. The one who will help me has agreed to pay Alberto's fare on the ship to England. I want you to see the boy. Talk to him, Father. He must go from here before he ends up in the prison."

"Do not trouble yourself, my child. I will talk to the boy, and we will see to it that he starts a new life. Come now, let us pray."

It all worked for Alberto, and he found himself standing on the quayside, looking up at the great ship that would take him to the country where everyone became rich and famous. He was nearly sixteen, almost a man; so he could not cry. His eyes blinked back the tears as Carla brushed her cheek along his. "You must write often, and you must learn to speak the English tongue, Alberto. You must come home to see us when you are rich and famous."

Alberto kissed his sister and she fled, too heartbroken

to watch her little brother depart, maybe for ever.

The arrival at Liverpool was a relief for the boy. He did not like the dipping ship and the food that his stomach would not hold. He felt better as he walked down the gangplank and into the customs and immigration shed.

"You are from Naples, young man?" asked the tall man in Italian.

"Yes, and I have a letter of introduction, and my documents here." He held out the bundle of papers to the smiling man, who spoke to his companions.

"I see that you are sixteen today," said the man, and Alberto smiled proudly.

"There is your passport, you must guard it very well. Come, I will show you where to get the train for London."

The young man walked hesitantly along the platform and glanced once more at his ticket. He was tall for his age and already the grey suit that he wore was beginning to come apart at the seams around his shoulders. A soft cap was pulled down tightly on his head but did not hide all the black curly hair. Dark eyebrows stood out on the lad's pallid face and large brown eyes stared out in awe at the bustling scene. His black pointed boots squeaked as he walked beside the stationary train searching for an empty compartment. The young man carried a brown paper bundle under his arm and occasionally felt his breast pocket to reassure himself that he still had his documents.

Soon Alberto was seated alone in a compartment that reeked of cigar smoke and stale perfume. He glanced idly through the window as the train slowly moved out from the station and quickly gathered speed. He sighed, looked down at the parcel on his lap, then up at the luggage-rack. He was loath to part with the bundle. Although it contained little of value, the contents were his only possessions and he was determined to guard them with his life. Carla had warned him about the dangers of being alone in a big city, but for Alberto London held no fears. He'd run the back alleys of Naples and learned to take care of himself at an early age. Besides, there would be someone

89

to meet him who would show him the ways of London.

The lad's thoughts were interrupted by the compartment door being slid open and two men entering. They laughed loudly as they threw their small suitcases onto the luggage-rack and flopped down facing him. For a time they talked together but the lad could not understand what they were saying. Once or twice they talked to him but he could only smile and raise his hands in a friendly gesture. The men were looking at his bundle and obviously talking about him, he could sense it. He became uneasy and averted his eyes to the autumn landscape that flashed past the window. Later the two men became silent and presently drifted off to sleep. Alberto studied the sleeping men. They were both heavily built. The taller of the two had massive hands that rested in his lap. The man's hair was ginger in colour and close-cropped. His suit looked expensive and his button-up boots were of the sort Alberto had seen in the smart shops back home. The sleeping man's face was flushed, with a small, livid scar just below his left cheekbone. His thick lips hung open and occasionally his face twitched. His companion was a foot shorter, with wide shoulders that slumped down as he slept. His face was pale, with tiny blotches of blue veins on both cheeks. His hair was fair and thinning and was combed back. He wore metal-rimmed glasses that looked too small for his face. Alberto noticed that both men wore the same colour ties; a red and black design of vertical stripes. He wondered about the ties.

The train thundered on towards London and soon Alberto's eyes started to droop. The changing landscape had levelled out and could not hold his attention. Sleep overtook him and he dreamed of Carla. He saw her standing on the quayside, her small lace handkerchief held to her face. She was waving but he could not raise his arm in answer. He awoke with a start to find that his arm had become numb. Alberto rubbed the circulation back into it and put the parcel onto the seat beside him while he stretched. He could hear someone calling out along the corridor and the sound got louder. A white-coated figure passed by and the two men awoke. They stretched and the taller man nudged his companion, "Shall we eat?" For an answer the bespectacled one stood up and straightened his tie. The two glanced at Alberto as they left the compartment.

The lad put the bundle back onto his lap. Now that he was alone he would eat. He carefully unwrapped the paper and removed a small, crinkled parcel. Making sure that his possessions were secured once more, he took out the food. It consisted of a hunk of black bread, a thick slice of salami, an apple and a screw-top bottle containing cold tea. The food tasted good and he washed it down with the tea. His stomach stopped complaining and he stood up for a while to stretch his legs. Away across the fleeting fields he could see the spire of a church and his thoughts drifted back to his home. He wondered about his sick mother and Carla. Soon he would earn money and then, when his mother was well again, he would send for them both.

In the dining car, the two subalterns of the King's Own Light Horse sat sipping coffee. Second Lieutenant Rodney Fallon addressed his companion, "I'm willing to wager a few pounds, Cyril, the regiment will be ordered overseas before Christmas."

Second Lieutenant Cyril Nunn looked up over his metal-rimmed glasses. "I hope you're correct. Egypt wouldn't be a bad proposition this time of year. It'll beat the blasted climate in Scotland."

Rodney Fallon nodded. "These past months have been hell, haven't they? What with the rain during all the training, and the Old Man kicking up about the standard of discipline."

Nunn winced. He'd been on the receiving end of the Colonel's acid tongue on a couple of occasions. "Let's try to forget old 'Cannon Balls'. We've got the ladies to concentrate on."

That suited Rodney Fallon. He was beginning to enjoy his leave. It had started the previous day when they both stopped off in Liverpool to spend a day and night in living it up before pressing on to London. Rodney licked his lips eagerly at the thought of the big city.

With their coffee cups refilled once more the two sat idly watching the changing view. Tall chimneys replaced open fields, and large factories emitted sulphuric smoke clouds that hung over the industrial heart of England. Presently, Cyril Nunn turned to his companion. "You know, Rodney, I'll be glad to get in a spot of overseas. This country of ours is slowly going to the wall. It's becoming a dustbin for all of Europe. We've had the Irish, the European Jews, and now we've got the rubbish from Italy flooding in," he said.

Rodney nodded in agreement. "It's this Mussolini. Seems he's organising everyone, and the peasants don't like it. They're mutinous, Cyril. Can't wait to leave the country."

"Quite. Take that blighter in our compartment. I'd wager a month's pay he's from Italy. Shifty-eyed. Can't trust the blighters. Give him a few months and he'll be selling hot chestnuts on a street corner."

Rodney laughed. "I'll tell you something more. Give him a year and I wager he'll put some young woman up the duff."

Cyril roared with laughter and a few heads turned in their direction. "I'd like to know just what he's got in that parcel he's holding on so tightly to, Rodney. He hasn't let it out of his sight."

"Probably a supply of chestnuts," joked Rodney.

The two subalterns laughed loudly and there was a tut, tut, from two elderly ladies sitting nearby.

"I think we'd better return to our compartment, Rodney. I do believe the ladies are offended."

The autumn sky was leaden and let no sun through. Alberto could only guess that it was past midday. London would be reached in about an hour or so according to his reckoning and there he would begin his new life. He leaned back in the seat, allowing the rhythm of the train to lull him into a semi-slumber. His eyes were heavy from the continuous lack of sleep during the journey from Italy, and he was only vaguely aware of the two men coming back. The mention of the name

Mussolini immediately jerked Alberto back into alertness. He tightened his grip on the bundle and feigned sleep. Something warned him that he must be careful. His early training in the slums of Naples had made the lad's senses razor-keen and he was ready.

Cyril Nunn leered at Alberto. "Our dago friend appears to be sleeping peacefully, Rodney. What say we take a peepums at that parcel?" he suggested.

"I shouldn't, Cyril. You've got to be careful with that sort. Probably got a stiletto tucked down his breeches."

Cyril eased himself onto the edge of his seat and adjusted his glasses. He leaned over and gently prodded the parcel. Alberto remained perfectly still. Cyril looked at his companion and put a finger to his lips in a sign. Rodney mouthed the word "careful" as the bespectacled one stood over the young Neapolitan. Just at that moment the train gave a lurch and Cyril tipped forward. He put out his hands to save himself and fell against the seated figure.

"Awfully sorry, old chap. Just about to go to the closet," he mumbled.

Alberto's hands had reached out suddenly to contain Cyril and as the two became untangled the lad uttered the only English he knew, "'S'okay."

Cyril kept up the pretence by leaving the compartment, while Rodney stared out of the carriage window, his interest in the bundle now dissipated.

For the rest of the journey, Alberto kept a tight grip on the parcel. When the train reached the London terminal, he waited until the two men left the compartment before he made any move himself. He felt safe now that he was alone. At last he was in London. Presently he stepped out onto the platform and joined the milling crowds. Alberto felt strangely elated and his thoughts raced. First he would become rich. He would learn good English and maybe one day marry a beautiful woman from England. He would then ... His thoughts were interrupted by a voice talking to him in his own tongue, "You are the little one, then? The boy they call Alberto Vitelli?"

Alberto spun around to see the large man facing him.

There was a white flower in the buttonhole of his coat.

"You are Gino Campanari?" the boy asked.

"Yes I am Gino Campanari."

The young Neapolitan reached into his coat pocket. "I have a letter for you. It is from my sister, Carla. I have a letter from the priest as well."

Gino smiled, his thick moustache twitching. "I can look at the letters later. First we will go to my home. You must be hungry, and you must be in need of a bath." He slipped his arm around the lad's shoulders. "Come on, we'll get the bus. The journey's not long."

Outside the station entrance two men, who both wore ties of the same pattern, hailed a taxi, "New Bond Street, old man, and step on it, we've got a rather important engagement."

The London cabbie was not in the least impressed, but he weaved his way quickly through the traffic and turned into Shaftesbury Avenue. The fog was thickening and a dampness settled on the cobbled streets.

"Soon as we get to the club we'll grab a bath, then a bite to eat, what say? I'm feeling positively famished." Rodney suggested.

Cyril nodded and tapped on the driver's window, "I say, old chap, step on it. We're rather late."

The cabbie spat a stream of tobacco juice from the corner of his mouth and gave the horn a squeeze, although his path was clear.

"This'll do, driver," shouted Cyril presently, reaching for his wallet. Suddenly his face changed dramatically. "Good Lord, it's gone!" he said incredulously.

"Gone?" repeated Rodney. "Gone?"

"I say, Rodney old chap. I suppose you couldn't loan me the price of the fare?"

"Sorry, old bean. Haven't a brass farthing till I get to the bank."

The cabbie looked around and then spat another stream of tobacco juice into the gutter. "Where will it be now, gents? The bank, or the police station?"

Chapter Ten

When young Alberto Vitelli left the empty wallet under the carriage seat, he made a vow never to steal again, though he felt the two men had brought the punishment upon themselves, or at least upon one of them, by their actions. Alberto was going to become rich and famous. But he would have to change from the swift-footed little thief he had been back in Naples.

As he rode the top deck of the bus to Clerkenwell, Alberto looked down on the foggy London scene. He was aware that his long journey was almost over. Here in this big city he would find work. He would then be able to take care of Carla and his sick Mamma.

Gino Campanari sat beside Alberto, pointing out a few items of interest as they bounced over the cobbles. Alberto thought that the area was exciting. The streets were wider and cleaner than in his home city. He would surely become very rich here in London.

"We get off the bus here, Alberto," Gino said, pressing the red button on the ceiling.

"There are so many of our people's names here above the shops," said Alberto in wonderment.

"That is so," replied Gino. "Our countrymen call this place 'Little Italy', and you can see why."

The lad looked up at the shop signs. There were names from all over Italy. Famous Roman, Neapolitan, and even Sicilian names on greengrocer, hardware and butchers' shops. The names were everywhere, and Alberto grinned happily.

The boy was given a room at the Campanaris'. Gino's wife, Rosanna, took to him and treated Alberto as her own son.

The Campanaris' daughter Maria was a year younger than Alberto, and her natural curiosity slowly turned into an adoration of the young, good-looking boy from Naples. She was very careful to hide her feelings from her parents. Gino and Rosanna were very strict in such matters. Maria felt that her God-fearing Mamma and Papa would treat her feelings as sin in one as young as sixteen. But to harbour such thoughts, sinful as they were, was very exciting, and one day her parents would know.

Maria could speak English with hardly any accent, and she taught Alberto so well that very soon he could hold a limited conversation in his adopted tongue. He wrote home to tell Carla of his progress, and of his plans to become a rich man. He told Carla of how he worked in the business of Gino Campanari, and of the daughter who taught him the English. He wrote of the girl who one day would be beautiful, but was now a nuisance to him because she was always getting under his feet in the shop.

When Alberto was seventeen, he went to the market with Gino in the man's battered old Ford van. Gino showed the boy how to select the produce and how to barter with the traders. The two men returned, Alberto sitting proud as a peacock beside the older man. He learned very fast, and soon took on the responsibility of ordering the goods. Alberto also learned how to drive the Ford van, and from then on went alone to the market.

Gino was getting on in years and the young Neapolitan took more and more of the responsibilities upon himself. He buried himself in the running of the shop and the days flashed by. Slowly he began to become more aware of the young Maria. She had blossomed into a beautiful woman. Her rounded breasts and slender thighs, her flowing hair and dark, smouldering eyes stirred the young man. He began to watch her as she walked in and out of the shop. He missed her when she stayed away and tried to ignore her when she hung around him. His eyes gave away his thoughts, and as their glances met she saw the need and it warmed her.

A few days before Alberto's eighteenth birthday, a

cable came from Italy. It told of the death of his mother. Alberto was distraught and shut himself away from the family. He had planned it very differently. He was to go home and buy the very best house for his mother and Carla. Now his plans were shattered. It took a very long time to become rich. The ache stayed with him, and he took to walking alone. The ageing Gino was troubled by the boy's attitude and he noticed the effect it was having on his Maria. He talked to Rosanna of this and the woman smiled. "You mean that you have only today noticed that our Maria is a woman? You have only today seen the glances, the looks they share, Papa? You must be blind," she said, her hands held up to the sky.

Gino smiled and kissed his wife. "I too have seen the looks they share, Rosanna. I too have seen the way they are happy together. One day I think they will get married, or one day Gino Campanari will become very angry."

Maria was determined to talk to Alberto. She knew that he took an evening stroll, and tonight she would meet him. She would tell him of her feelings toward him and ask of his. She would try to make him feel less sad, and tonight she would pledge herself to him.

The thoughts running through her head made her feel breathless as she followed the young man. He walked slowly, hands in pockets, with his head held low. He stopped by the old churchyard and gazed at the flaking headstones that leant against the wall. Maria reached him and, as he turned, she slipped her hand into his and looked up into his eyes. She saw the pain there, and she nestled her head against his arm.

He squeezed her hand and smiled at her. "I know that I have cut myself off from you, Maria. It is the pain, the knowledge that I could do nothing to help my mother. That I could not pay the doctors who would make her well."

The girl looked into his eyes. "The pain is one you can share. The guilt is not yours, Alberto. Your mother had consumption. She could not have lived, even if you gave a million pounds. She was a victim of the poverty, the misery that is turning Italy into a country the people run

97

from. Your sister Carla knew that when she made the arrangements for you to come to England. She knew, Alberto."

Alberto put his arm around the girl's shoulders and kissed her clumsily on the side of her mouth. She responded by lifting her mouth to his and throwing her arms around his neck.

As the months went by, Alberto put more and more time into the shop. Gino had become ill with heart trouble. His wife Rosanna nursed him constantly. She was younger than her husband by twenty years, but the strain imposed on her turned her into a prematurely old woman. There was also the worry of the business. The local landowner had been putting pressure on the shopkeepers. Land prices were rising as industry moved into the area. Shop rents were pushed up until it became a struggle to run the business profitably. Pressure was applied to frighten the shopkeepers. Flashily-dressed characters appeared. They spoke of the terror of the gangs and the protection only they could offer.

Johnnie Arpino was sent to talk to Gino Campanari. He warned of the dangers of not paying for protection. When Gino tried to throw him out, his poor body succumbed to a terrible heart attack. Alberto was at the market when the racketeer called; he returned to find Rosanna bending over the prone figure of Gino. The man was very ill and Alberto knew that he had to act quickly. He picked up the old man and placed him in the cab of the Ford. Rosanna squeezed in to hold her husband's head against her as Alberto raced to the hospital.

The young Neapolitan returned to the Campanaris' alone. Maria was waiting for the news.

"Your father is in a coma, Maria. Your mother is beside him. There is nothing we can do now, except pray."

Alberto climbed back into the Ford, his face set hard. Maria ran to him but Alberto pushed her aside. "You must wait," he said quietly. "Your mother will need you. I have something that I must take care of."

The boy drove westwards. He knew of Johnnie Arpino

and of his gambling club in Soho. The cold feeling in his stomach persisted as he drove through the theatre traffic and over into the seedy area off the Charing Cross Road.

Johnnie Arpino sat behind his desk. One of his henchmen stood by the door. "Come in, Alberto, I hear you want to speak with me," he said.

The boy walked to the desk and put both hands down, fingers spread on the linoleum top. "Your visit today, Arpino, put Gino Campanari into a hospital. It is doubtful that he will ever come out again. You have gone too far this time. If I see you in my part of the city then you will have to answer to me."

"You are a brave boy," grinned the gambler. "But you are only a boy. You do not threaten Johnnie Arpino." He nodded to the heavy man who stood by the door.

The man walked over to Alberto and grabbed him by the collar. The boy's hand closed over a large glass ashtray that stood on the desk, and as he was pulled round, he brought the heavy object down on the man's head. Blood spurted from the man's skull as he folded up in a heap on the carpeted floor. Alberto backed away as Arpino stood up, a wicked-looking knife in his hand. There were sounds of footsteps and voices in the hall. Alberto grabbed a chair and wedged the backrest under the doorknob. Arpino crept toward him, the knife flashing under the light.

"I'm going to cut your heart out, little man," sneered the gambler.

Alberto crouched down, his hands wide apart. He feinted a jump at the gambler, then stepped to one side. Johnnie Arpino lunged at him, the knife held waist high. Alberto's toe flashed up and into the man's groin. As Arpino went into a heap, screaming in agony, Alberto grabbed the knife and a searing pain shot up his arm and blood ran down his fingers. He realised that he held the knife by the blade and it had laid his palm open to the bone. Arpino tried to rise but the boy kicked out at the man's head and felt the thud as his toecap caught Arpino's temple.

The men in the passageway hammered at the door and

Alberto looked around him desperately. It would have to be the window he thought, grabbing up the heavy chair by the desk. The chair took the window frame with it as it went through, and Alberto followed, landing on all fours in the alley. He heard the men coming after him. They were shouting and calling for assistance. He ran up the alley, out into the glare of Soho's lights. He found his van and quickly drove away from the area, his badly cut hand clenched to stem the flow of blood.

Gino was still unconscious. Maria told Alberto how the traders had gathered together when they learned what had happened. There was to be a meeting at Morrelli's the next evening, and everyone would be there. The boy was relieved. Now that he'd tangled with the racketeers there were bound to be repercussions.

Alberto's wound was stitched, and the next night the traders met. The meeting started by the boy telling of the fight with Johnnie Arpino and the possible reprisals. He spoke of Gino and the debt he owed the man for taking him in as a son.

One by one the men spoke. They vowed to form a group to fight the gambler and his mob. The meeting drew up a declaration that was to be delivered to Johnnie Arpino. In short, it said 'keep out'. Just as the meeting was about to break up, a messenger hurried to the front of the gathering and spoke to Alberto. The news was that Gino had died.

The days and the months that followed were sad for the Campanaris and their adopted Alberto. The business had to be conducted and a watchfulness had to be maintained. There was a depression settling over the country, and the traders suffered with the rest of the community. Money was in short supply. Unemployment reached terrible levels, and existence for most was little short of starvation.

Rosanna could not get over the loss of her beloved Gino. She became a recluse. Maria and Alberto tried to take her out for walks, and sometimes for rides in the Ford, but it was no use. The woman had given up her will to live. Maria talked to her mother about Alberto and of her desire to marry him, but the woman only stared at the girl, not hearing what was said, and not caring. Maria was heartbroken. Something would have to be done.

"I will have to write to Mamma's cousins. They have business far from London. She will be better away from this place. There are too many bad memories to bury the good ones, Alberto."

"You are right," the boy said. "I will speak to your Mamma. It is time that we thought about the marriage, too. We must talk to the priest."

On Alberto's twentieth birthday, the couple were wed. Mamma Campanari sat impassive as the service took place in the little Italian church in Clerkenwell. The ceremony that followed was subdued, but the couple were greeted by all Gino's friends, who were now also friends of Alberto. They were grateful for the way he had taken on the racketeers and worked to strengthen their group. They bade the couple good weather and Godspeed as they left for their honeymoon at a little seaside resort.

The early days of marriage was a happy time for Alberto and Maria, marred only by their concern for Mamma Campanari, who was staying with her cousins. The woman was clearly brokenhearted and, even when the two young people visited her, her eyes never lost their glazed look. It was as though Rosanna were waiting to join her beloved Gino. She sat listening to the news from her daughter, but would suddenly tilt her head as though she heard something. He face would then relax, become more serene, and it frightened Maria.

The business progressed. Neither Maria nor Alberto could forget the early days, when he first met her and brushed her aside as a nuisance. They both smiled at memories as they looked around and saw the changes. It was not the happy place it had once been, and they spoke about it: "I would like to leave here, Maria. Sell this shop and move south of the river. There are shops to buy, I've seen advertisements in the papers."

"I feel the same, Alberto. The memories sometimes tear my heart out. I want to start somewhere new, away from the past."

The young man grabbed his Maria and kissed her. "I will go to see about it tomorrow. We will start afresh and become very rich, no?"

Maria laughed as she recalled the plans they had made, on those long summer evenings that seemed ages gone.

Six months went by. Maria and Alberto were beginning to get restless when the offer came, via an old friend of Gino. He knew of a business that was going up for sale in the Tower Road market. It was south of the river, a good, homely place to begin again. The people were friendly dockland folk who would make a newcomer welcome, the man said.

The room above the greengrocer's in the Tower Road market was warm and dark on the evening of June 11th, 1940. The curtains were opened, and no breeze came in through the raised window, only the muted sound of the whistle from the freightyards. Alberto Vitelli sat very still, his head resting in his hands as he pondered. There was much to do and time was short. Maria would soon be home. He must write the letter, it was very important to explain.

Alberto reached for a writing pad and pen. There was ink in the drawer of the sideboard, he remembered. A late tram rattled past as he drew the curtains and lit the gas mantle. He sat down at the table and removed the stopper from the ink bottle. A small blob of ink dripped onto the white linen tablecloth and spread out from the centre of the stain like a searching octopus. Alberto stared hard at the mark and shivered violently, the pen shaking in his grasp. There were many words he must put down on paper. He owed it to himself and to Maria, and to all those who had left a troubled and violent Italy, to begin a new life in England. The words must tell of the love he felt in his heart for his country of adoption, even though he, and many of his people, had encountered much ill feeling since the outbreak of war. He must write of his despair, his heartache, now that all his dreams, his visions of the future, had been destroyed. There was much to say, much to put down on paper, about the plight of those of his people who had escaped a tyranny, and who had come among friends, to become as brothers and sisters, now to be seen only as the enemy. He rose and lowered the open window and drew the lace curtains. Seated once more at the table he studied the nib of the pen and the drying inkstain. There was much to say, but he found he could not begin. The events of the day came crowding in, blotting out everything else. It was as though a black curtain had descended. Some minutes later the clock on the mantelshelf struck the hour and Alberto Vitelli began to write.

Chapter Eleven

At number 14 Conner Street five young men sat around an improvised card-table. They drank beer which they poured from quart bottles, and they played cards with a dog-eared pack. They passed copper coins to and fro over the blanketed surface, and they grumbled over the snores and grunts of old man Davis who sat slumped in his armchair.

The night of June 11th, 1940 was warm and still. Blackout curtains kept out what little air there was, and caused the tobacco smoke to hang in dense layers about the room. The gas-light splayed down on the table and on the white faces of the men. It illuminated the scorch marks in the grey blanket, impressed there by the flat iron, and it shone down on the crates of ale by Jack Davis's armchair.

Wheezy Morris had 'cleared the board' and as he swept up the stakes of copper coins he gave a little chuckle, "Me luck's in ternight, boys!"

"Yeah, we can see that," agreed Ginger Davis. "Keep it up an' I'll 'ave ter ask me old sarge fer a sub."

"'E'll give yer a sub all right. The only fing 'e'll give away is about nine inches o' baynit," remarked his brother Freddie.

The men laughed and old man Davis grunted.

"You awake, Pop?" asked Ginger. "Wanna drink?"

The old man shook his head and settled down in his chair.

"Who's fer a top-up?" asked Albert Conlin, leaning across the table to reach the bottles.

"Turn the wireless on, Freddie," said his brother. "Let's get the news."

The cards were forgotten as the men listened to the reports of violence against the Italian population around London. Windows had been smashed, people attacked and fires started in some places. Feeling was running high against the Italians at the news of Italy's declaration of war on the side of the Germans. It had been a topic of conversation all day at the market.

"Bloody treacherous lot," growled Wheezy. "Yer can't blame people fer givin' 'em a pastin', can yer?"

"Serves 'em right," mumbled old man Davis.

"'Ello, Pop, you awake, fancy a drink?" asked Ginger.

The old man licked his lips, and sat up straight.

"'Ere we are, Dad," said Freddie, handing over a glass of brown ale.

The man gulped the beer down and wiped his mouth on the back of his hand. "I ain't bin asleep. Bin listenin' ter the wireless. Serves 'em right I say. Fink they're clever, linin' theirselves up alongside them bleedin' Germans. Wait till our boys git at 'em wiv the old cold steel. Don't like the ole cold steel, they don't."

"I wouldn't fancy a baynit up me arse either," grinned Wheezy.

Jack Davis wagged his finger at Wheezy. "We used ter put the fear up them Germans in the last war, mark my words. When them bleeders 'eard our orficer call out 'fixed baynits' they shook in their boots, I tell yer."

"All right, Dad, take it easy. You'll start your ticker orf again," said Ginger.

"Ticker nuffink. I seen the whites o' their eyes, I 'ave. Stuck a few as well, let me tell yer."

"Yeah, I bet yer did, Pop," laughed Ginger.

The old man stood up and took his tobacco-pouch down from the mantelshelf. He slowly filled his clay pipe, then lit it from a rasping Vesta, sending clouds of smoke ceilingwards.

The fourth man in the room sat thoughtfully tracing his finger along the pattern made by the flat iron in the blanket. Then he spoke for the first time. "Well, I reckon they was right ter 'ave a go at the wops. It's all right them politicians sayin' about keepin' calm. They ain't got ter live wiv 'em, 'ave they?"

"Yeah, but it's bad when they turn on people they've known all their lives. People like Vitelli, and ole Giuseppe the ice cream man," remarked Albert Conlin.

"Accordin' ter the news, they're gonna intern 'em all," said Freddie.

"Don't you believe it," interrupted the fourth man. "They won't intern 'em all, not English natrilised wops."

"Wot worries me is that these wops can carry on tradin', an' all the time keep their ear 'oles open fer scraps of info', an' Bob's yer uncle. Straight ter the uvver side," remarked Freddie.

"'E's dead right," shouted the fourth man, banging the table.

"I reckon a little bit o' rough stuff wouldn't 'urt none. It might warn 'em against tryin' anyfing funny."

"You're not suggestin' we go an' duff ole Vitelli up are yer?" exclaimed Albert Conlin. "Old Alberto is as much of a cockney as me or you."

"Yeah, well I wouldn't trust 'im wiv a bit of info', like a convoy sailin' time, that's fer sure," said Ginger Davis.

"I'm fer goin' round an' put the fright'ners in, what say you?" the fourth man asked.

Big Albert Conlin stood up and looked hard at the man. "Listen, 'Oppy. I don't go a lot on wot you're suggestin'. I reckon you're gonna cause a lot o' trouble. In fact duffin' the man up is more likely ter send 'im over ter the Germans, so yer can count me out."

Hoppy Dyke stared down at the little pile of coins in front of him as Albert put on his coat and bade good night to the old man.

Jack Davis had been listening to the conversation. He thought that it was time he gave the boys the benefit of his experience. He stood up, placed his pipe carefully upon the grate, and rolled up his shirt-sleeves over bony arms. "'And it over," he said suddenly, pointing to the corner.

"'And wot over?" asked Wheezy, perplexed.

"The bleedin' broom in the corner," shouted the old man.

Wheezy complied, standing back quickly, and the old

man pushed the chair back to make room. "Now I'm a Tommy, an' you're a bastard German," he said.

"Am I?" asked Wheezy.

"C'mon, let's be 'avin' yer," the old man said, pointing the broom bristle foremost at Wheezy.

"Now c'mon, Pop, sit down, you'll 'ave an accident if you're not careful," said Ginger, waving to the armchair.

"It's all right, son, c'mon yer bastard, come an' get me."

Wheezy Morris wasn't too keen to get within range of the old man's weapon, even if it was only a broom. In the old chap's hand, even the bristles looked menacing.

"C'mon then, yer cowardly git!"

Wheezy sighed. He would have to humour the old man. "Okay, yer English pig-dog," he screamed as he jumped forward.

"Got yer, yer bleedin' cabbige 'ead," shouted old man Davis, as he prodded the broom into the face of the advancing Wheezy.

"Gawd Almighty, wot yer got on that broom," Wheezy screamed, his face blackened by the bristles and contorted in disgust.

"Sorry, son, I fergot. I 'ad ter sweep the yard down yesterday. That bloody cat shit everywhere."

"Why, you silly ole bleeder," ranted Wheezy as he rushed out to the scullery, his hand held over his mouth, and the echoes of the men's laughter ringing in his ears.

A few minutes later Wheezy made an appearance, his face scrubbed clean with the aid of the old man's carbolic soap. He sat down sheepishly as Hoppy Dyke gathered up the playing cards and spread them out before him. "I take it we're all in this, ain't we boys?" Hoppy said.

"Yeah, we're in," they all said in unison.

"Right then. 'Ere's the shops," Hoppy said as he pointed to the line of cards. "We'll go down the alley by the pet shop, okay?"

The three men nodded. They were quite content to let Hoppy take charge. He usually did, from the time he first made an appearance in the Street.

It was a long gone summer when the days were warm and balmy, and the only people who knew about blackout were Patrick Flannagan and Mrs Jenkins. It was during the hot spell that the boys of the Street became restless. They were looking around for something now to amuse themselves with, when young Bernard Dyke moved into the precinct. He hobbled into the circle of boys and announced himself. They looked at his club foot and listened as he told them of a new game. The circle of hunched shoulders and bent heads opened up like a sunflower, the faces were beaming.

They found an old cap, then they sat like sentries, waiting for the first horse to fertilise the cobbles. When the deed was done, they surrounded the lad with the club foot, who proudly carried the cap full of steaming horse manure along Conner Street. The cripple had volunteered to climb the lamppost with the cap and the boys were curious. They had never seen a boy with a club foot climb a lamppost, and they had never seen the feat accomplished with a cap full of horse-shit.

The sun beat down on the pavement as the little boy stood alone at the base of a Victorian gas lamppost. He looked distressed and held his head in his hands, occasionally peeping to see if any person tall enough were walking in his direction. He waited alone, patiently, until an ideal candidate appeared. He walked tall and proud. He carried a wooden cane that was silver-tipped, and the man looked kind.

"Well, well, now what seems to be the matter, little boy?" asked the good Samaritan.

"Th-the big b-boys put m-me cap up-up there, mister," sobbed the boy, moving his shoulders up and down, the way he'd seen Jackie Cooper do it at the Tower Road Kinema.

"Now stop that crying, d'you hear," said the man, owner of the local leather factory. "I'll get your cap down for you, you shall see." And he raised his cane to the cap which was perched on the ladder-arm poking out from beneath the lantern.

"Good Lord," gasped the man as he staggered back,

covered in fresh horse droppings. "I'll tan your hide, you little guttersnipe!" he raved, shaking the manure from himself.

They appeared from everywhere, from behind dustbins, out of doorways, from corners, and out of houses. They appeared like a ravening hoard, screaming out "Shit-finger Dick, old shit-finger Dick!" They danced around him, just out of reach, waiting for him to react.

The man was enraged. He looked for a victim, and thought he'd found one in the shape of Bernard Dyke. By the gods, he thought, here was a laddie that would feel the cane across his shoulders. "Stop, you little swine," the man shouted as he took off in pursuit of the cripple.

The boys of Conner Street were shrewd in their selection of a lamppost for the plot. The one that stood outside the Flannagans' house was ideal because it was near the Tanners Alley, and Tanners Alley afforded an extra escape route. It was this route that Bernard Dyke chose, and as he hopped along his pursuer realised that he was not making any headway. The cripple had perfected a movement which led from a hop onto the club foot to a skip with the other leg, then onto the club foot again, a movement that carried him over the ground at a remarkable rate. The factory owner was soon outstripped, and he returned to his office to recover.

The grinning, leering doorknockers might have looked down on the scene, seeing one of their own, a misshapen thing that grimaced as it hobbledegooked through their domain, with the figure of outraged virtue hard on its heels. It was a singular spectacle which would no doubt be discussed at the next coming-together of the night-people, when the church bell peals the midnight hour, and the rusty chimes drift down the narrow path, when the lion on the door would shake his flowing mane, and roar his approval, when the grinning devil would turn to watch the mailed fist give the Roman salutation. The ashen figures would rattle their delight on their plates without disturbing the sleepers in the cottage bedrooms, summoning the creatures of the night who would marvel at the events, and slink away before the going down of the moon, and the coming of the human dawn.

The fomenter of the nocturnal whisperings had swaggered from the alley, and had taken a roundabout route home. He was met with backslappings and words of praise, "Cor, 'e never got near yer," said one.

"I bet 'e stinks like a drain," said another.

"Serves 'im right. 'Is factory's bin stinkin' our street out long enough."

A little boy with a wheezy cough spoke up, "I fink we oughta call 'im 'Oppy. 'E 'opped down Tanners Alley like a grass 'opper."

"Wot's a grass 'opper?" said a boy with a running nose and large ears that stuck out like sails.

"It's wot's down 'oppin'. There's fousinds of 'em down 'oppin'."

Hoppy Dyke ran his finger along the line of playing cards. "We walk up 'ere, stop to see if it's all clear, then slip into the alley, an' creep along to the Vitellis' back yard. Okay?"

The trio nodded.

"We chuck a dustbin over 'is wall, then when 'e opens 'is winder, we pelt 'im wiv the rotten fruit an' cabbiges," Hoppy expounded.

Ginger Davis slapped Hoppy on the back, "We're wiv yer, ain't we, Freddie?"

"We sure are, 'Oppy," said Ginger's younger brother.

"I 'ope we can get 'old of some rotten fruit," remarked Wheezy.

"Don't be stupid," said Freddie quickly. "There's always piles of it in the alley every night."

"Right then. We'll 'ave another drink, then orf we'll go," said Ginger.

"I'm comin' too," said Ginger's father, squaring up like a prize-fighter. "I can still 'ave a go," he said, thumping Wheezy in the back of the neck with his clenched fist.

"Gertcha, silly old bleeder," moaned the victim of Jack Davis's right hand.

The four men walked purposefully up Conner Street

and over the deserted Tower Road. They walked along past the shuttered shops until they came to Silas Cornbloom's pet shop. There was an alley beside the shop which the four entered, their torches shining a dim path before them.

It was a black night, with the thick cloud blanketing off the moon and stars. A slight breeze had got up and it threatened rain. A dog barked in the distance as the men crept along the dark alley. The path ended in a T-junction and the four turned left.

"It's the last but one," whispered Ginger Davis.

"This is it," said Hoppy. "You get a dustbin, Ginge. You 'elp 'im, Wheezy, me an' Freddie are gonna get some spunky apples."

Ginger Davis and Wheezy returned carrying a dustbin between them. They placed it up on the wall and gave it a shove. It toppled into the Vitellis' back yard with a loud clatter.

"Who's there?" shouted a voice as a window was thrown up.

A woman's voice answered the man's, "Yer silly bleeder. D'yer fink anyone's gonna answer yer?"

"Might be a cat," the man said meekly.

"Oh that's different, 'course a cat'll answer," mocked the woman.

"Put that light out," screamed someone else, and the window slammed down to the sound of "cobblers".

It was quiet once again in the alley. The sound of the dustbin did not seem to have disturbed the Vitellis.

"Tell yer wot," said Hoppy. "Let's aim a cabbige frew 'is winder."

Wheezy grinned and let fly. The sound of breaking glass carried up the alley.

"What the 'ell's goin' on out there?" shouted a man's voice.

A dog barked somewhere, and the woman's voice exploded, "What is it, them cats again? Started jumpin' frew winders now 'ave they?"

"Put that bleedin' light out," shouted another.

"Yer muvver wasn't married," screamed the woman as

she slammed down the window.

"There's nobody in," said Wheezy.

"I'm goin' over the wall," announced Hoppy. "Watch out fer me."

"I'm wiv yer," said Ginger as he clambered up and into the Vitellis' back yard. Freddie followed them and Wheezy sat up on the wall, watching out.

"Try the door, it mightn't be locked," whispered Hoppy.

Ginger lifted the latch and pulled on the door. It creaked open, letting light from the landing gas mantle flood into the yard. It lit up the passage and the patent-leather shoes that were suspended about a foot above the floor.

Hoppy Dyke joined Ginger and the pair stood, eyes popping as their gaze travelled up the figure, from the shiny black shoes to the bulging, grey waxen face. They held each other's hand, like young children, as they looked on death for the first time. They shook as they slowly backed out into the yard.

"Is it 'im?" asked Freddie in a whisper.

"Wot's wrong?" muttered Wheezy as he jumped down from the wall.

"It's the wop," said Hoppy. "Strung up wiv red cord 'e is. 'Ung 'imself from the bannisters."

"Gawd a'mighty, wot we gonna do? We've gotta tell someone. We can't go ter the cops, can we?" wailed Wheezy.

"Right, over the wall quick. We'll tell the priest," said Hoppy.

"I bet 'e's asleep," mumbled Wheezy.

"Well we'll 'ave ter wake 'im up, won't we?" answered Hoppy.

The double funeral stopped the market. The shops shut for two hours in respect, and the stalls did not appear at all. The dockland folk from the little backstreets lined the Tower Road as the horse-drawn carriages trotted up to the Vitelli Greengrocery. Sad-faced women watched as the two coffins were slowly carried out and placed on the highly polished chromium dais. They put their handkerchiefs up to red eyes as the cortège slipped slowly along past the shuttered shops. The sleek black horses wore their tall plumes and dipped their noble heads as if in respect.

The trio, Hoppy, Ginger and Wheezy, stood silently together. They were among the first to arrive and they hardly took their eyes from the goings-on across from where they waited. They talked in whispers, as though the dead souls might hear, and they crossed themselves with feeling.

Further along the road three women stood paying their last respects. When the procession had passed, they turned to face each other.

"I bin finkin', Lizzie. Where they goin' ter put 'em?"

Lizzie Brown gave Emmie Jones a quick look. "What d'ya mean?"

"Well, 'e done away wiv 'imself, didn't 'e? I didn't fink they buried 'em in 'oly ground."

"Well I don't know about 'im," interrupted Betty Smith, "but they gotta do the right fing by that poor little bleeder, ain't they?"

"That's right," agreed Lizzie Brown. "'E might 'ave done 'imself in, but that poor little cow never. She 'ad 'er froat cut."

Chapter Twelve

July 1940 was very hot and during those long, dry midsummer days the news of war got steadily worse. France had capitulated and the German armies were massing along much of the continental coastline facing England. The narrow strip of water was the only factor that prevented an immediate invasion. More British ships had been sunk, and the German airforce had started to bomb English coastal towns. Papers were making gloomy reading. There were items on what to do in the event of an invasion, an announcement that there was to be no more ringing of church bells and, most depressing of all, the horrendous news that the English habit of tea drinking was to be interfered with. Papers carried the news that tea was to be rationed at two ounces per week, per person.

As usual, the folk of Conner Street had something to say about the latest round of news. "Why 'ave they stopped them church bells, Lizzie? I love to 'ear 'em on a Sunday mornin'. It makes me feel all sort of peaceful, it does really."

"Well you better 'ope you don't 'ear them bells any more on a Sunday, or any other day for that matter, 'cos if yer do it means we're being invaded, Emmie."

Betty Smith looked up the street and saw the two women talking. She put on her clean apron and trotted out to join the discussion. "I saw that bit about the tea bein' rationed an' I was really shocked. Why, my ole man drinks a potful before 'e goes ter work of a mornin'. Gawd knows what I'm gonna do now," Betty complained.

Lizzie looked up and down the street to make sure there was no one listening. "Save the grouts, put 'em in a bag an' add 'em to the pot, next time yer brew up," she urged conspiratorially.

"Gawd, Lizzie, if my ole man caught me doin' that he'd give me a back-'ander, I'm sure 'e would," said Betty with a horrified look.

"Well, if my ole man tried that on me I'd open the tyke!" exclaimed Emmie.

The concern of the dockland folk for the safety of their children was reflected in the sudden increase of those sending their youngsters out of London. Many children left their homes for the first time, though there were others who had already been evacuated once and were going for the second time. Other families were worried by the stories from parents who had visited their youngsters and found them not being properly cared for. The Carters' account was instrumental in Bridie's decision to keep her brood under her wing. "I'm not letting them chicks out of my sight. If the Holy Lord wants to take us, then He can take us all together," she said in a hushed voice.

On the domestic scene, there were a couple of events that helped to brighten up the depressing atmosphere which seemed to be slowly absorbing everyone. The engagement between Stanley Nathan and Julie Brett was announced, and Albert Conlin started to visit the 'Eagle' once more. The two items were of course discussed by the 'Ladies of the Street', a description formulated by Skipper, who had the good sense to utter the words in a confidential manner, and only to his trusted confidants. Even the old seaman realised that the wrath of the ladies would be too terrible to contemplate, should they hear that their immaculate behaviour was being questioned by such a scurrilous sobriquet.

These paragons of virtue gathered outside Emmie Jones's house to hold council. She had cleaned her windows, changed her curtains, hearthstoned the front doorstep, and served her Arthur with his tea, "a nice piece of 'addock, fresh out the water," she'd told him. Emmie had earned her rest, and she stood with her hands tucked into her apron, listening to Lizzie Brown.

"Well all I 'ope is 'e's doin' the right fing. 'Specially after the last turn-out. Made 'im ill fer weeks when she run orf," Lizzie was saying.

"She wasn't much good to 'im, Lizzie," Emmie pointed out.

"That's wot I'm sayin'. Mind you, this one seems all right. Yer can't take much notice o' wot people are sayin', after all, she works 'ard in that shop of 'is, an' she gets on wiv people," Lizzie said to her nodding friends.

"By the way," Emmie said. "I saw Albert Conlin come out o' the 'Eagle' last night. Drunk as 'old 'arry' 'e was, could 'ardly keep 'is feet."

Lizzie cupped her hand around her chin and pursed her lips. "I thought 'e stopped usin' the place. Didn't 'e 'ave a set to wiv Florrie Braden?" she asked.

"Well, that's what my bruvver-in-law's wife told me, an' she ought ter know, Albert lodges there," answered Emmie.

"Well, I 'eard 'e was usin' the 'Crown' in Spencer Street. Rough 'ole that is," remarked Lizzie.

"You're tellin' me, I ..." A shout from inside the Jones' house interrupted Emmie's conversation. "I'd better get in, Lizzie, it's Arfur. 'E's 'urt 'is back. Twisted it down the ship's 'old. I gotta rub it fer 'im."

"Wot yer usin'?" asked Lizzie. "I always use that Wintergreen. Luvvly stuff that is," she remarked, as the voice rang out again from inside number 7.

There was another little affair which punctuated that hot July. It became known as the 'spy business', and the leading character might easily have jumped out of a boys' magazine. He was long, thin and wore a dark beard. He was dressed in a black suit, with a black cape that hung from his narrow shoulders like a dust sheet. He wore black shoes with patent toe-caps and a black trilby hat that rested upon his large ears. He seemed to drift along rather than walk. His feet danced over the cobbles like a ballet dancer, fleeting across the stage during some grand performance.

"'E's like some bleedin' fairy," pronounced Hoppy Dyke.

"Well, we'll 'ave ter watch points. See if 'e shows up again. 'E might be a bleedin' spy," said Wheezy.

The man did show up the next afternoon. He stopped outside the leather factory and took out a dog-eared notebook from inside his coat. He started to write, flipping over the pages, wetting the tip of the pencil with his tongue. He growled at young Maureen Flannagan and made little Terry cry. Then as speedily as he entered the turning he departed, observed by a worried Bridie.

"I'd like ter know wot 'e's puttin' in that bleedin' notebook," grumbled Wheezy Morris.

"Well, we'll 'ave ter catch 'im. 'E must be up ter somefing," said Hoppy.

"I tell yer wot we can do," said Wheezy. "It's 'arf day termorrer. When I put me stall away, we'll 'ave a couple o' pints in the 'Eagle', then we'll 'ang about the Street. See if 'e shows up."

"Okay, I'll meet yer in the ale bar, 'bout one o'clock," arranged Hoppy.

The next day was warm and sunny, with the Conner Street folk bathing in the lazy atmosphere. Flies buzzed in the heat.

Good as their word, the two friends kept watch in the street. They strolled back and forth, eyeing the folk who used the turning as a short-cut. They were beginning to think the 'spy' would not show when Hoppy spotted him. "Look, there 'e is! Comin' past the alley."

Wheezy chuckled. "Looks a right eighteen-carat character, don't 'e?"

The two men watched as the 'spy' walked up to the custard powder factory and stopped. He got out his notebook and proceeded to take particulars, dabbing the stub of a pencil on the tip of his tongue. He then crossed the street and started to address the lamppost that stood outside the Flannagans' house.

"What yer doin', mate?" asked Hoppy, trying to keep a straight face.

The man tapped his notebook. "It's all down in here," he said in a cultured voice. "I have to write it all down and then assess it."

"I don't get yer," Hoppy said, scratching his head.

"Sizes. Doors and windows, They all have to be put down you know."

"Oh, I see," lied Hoppy. "Gotta put 'em all down, 'ave yer?"

"Of course. Building regulations. Heavy penalties involved if the regulations are not complied with."

"What about the lamppost then?" asked Wheezy. "I see yer talkin' to it. Is the lamppost okay?"

"O, it's fine. We don't need to move that."

Wheezy nudged his friend. "'Ere, I've bin finkin', what's 'e dressed up like that for? It's a bakin' 'ot day, an' 'im dressed up like it's the middle o' winter."

"I dunno, p'raps it's cold in Germany in July," grinned Hoppy.

The caped figure circled the lamppost and returned to where the two friends stood. "Carpenter's the name, Benjamin Carpenter. How do you do?"

The two men grinned at the 'spy'.

"Me an' me mate was wonderin', d'yer feel the cold then?" asked Hoppy.

"Cold, of course it's cold," said the caped intruder, rubbing his hands together and walking off.

"Take no notice, the man's a loony, nutty as a fruit cake," observed Hoppy Dyke, struggling to keep a straight face.

The cripple's diagnosis proved correct, for the next day Benjamin Carpenter was apprehended as he read the riot act out to a pair of dray-horses. The law, represented by PC Smith, arrived in the nick of time, for Benjamin Carpenter was about to receive a severe cuff around the head from the outraged drayman, who took umbrage over his steeds being lectured to by this "bloody lunatic".

"Take 'im away, mate, or I'll smash 'is bleedin' 'ead in," said the foaming drayman.

Benjamin Carpenter was taken away, back to the hospital from which he had absconded. All in all though, he was not too sorry to be back home. He hadn't cared much for the places he had seen while he was out, and it felt nice to be back in the peace and comfort of the familiar surroundings.

The Street settled down once again to gloom and despondency. The days were long and became longer because the government decided to play tricks with the clock. They introduced 'Double British Summertime', which meant that the nights got shorter and the days began with folk going to work in the dark mornings. It was as though a piece of the early night had been lopped off the front and stuck on at the end. It was a good idea as far as throwing the enemy into fits of hair-pulling at the antics of the mad English, but it had a tiring effect on the worker, who now had to try to get to sleep while it was only just getting dark, and who had to go to work holding a torch to light the way.

Tempers were getting short-fused and there were incidents.

"Wha'd'ya mean 'e kept yer ball? 'E's got no right ter keep it."

"Well 'e did, Dad. Said we shouldn't kick a ball in the street."

"Oh 'e did, did 'e?"

The man's wife joined in. "Now don't go getting all upset, Tom."

Tom Carter did get upset, and he stormed along the street to number 7. He knocked on the door and when Emmie Jones answered he demanded to see the man of the house.

"'Fraid 'e's at the 'Eagle'," said Emmie.

"Well, I'm gonna 'ave a word wiv your ole man," said Tom Carter.

The fuming docker pushed his way into the smokey ale bar, and found Arthur Jones holding a pint glass in his massive fist.

"I want a word wiv yer, Arfur," said Tom.

"Wot yer drinkin', Tom?" asked the man.

"I'll 'ave arf o'mild," said Tom.

"'Arf's no good, 'ave a pint."

"Okay, Arfur, give us a pint."

"News is bad, ain't it, mate?"

"Yeah you're right, 'nuff ter drive yer round the twist."

"Wanna fag, Tom? Got 'em orf the ship, they're Senior Service."

Back in the Street Mary Carter sat worrying and watching the clock.

Young Reg looked at his mother. "Is Dad gonna fight Mr Jones?"

"Course 'e's not. Dad's only goin' ter get yer ball back. Now drink yer cocoa an' get in ter bed."

"But Mum, Mr Jones is bigger than Dad."

"I don't fink that'll worry yer farver, Reg. Now are you gonna drink that drink an' get ter bed?"

"Mum, why ain't Dad bin called up like Jimmy Bennett's dad?"

"'Cos yer farver's too old ter fight, that's why."

"Well what's Dad doin' sortin' Mr Jones out then, Mum?"

"You ask too many questions. Now look, you've got skin on yer cocoa."

Two hours later, Mary Carter put her coat on and walked along to number 7. Emmie answered her knock. "Emmie, 'as my ole man bin 'ere?"

"Yeah, I sent 'im up the 'Eagle', luv. 'E wanted Arfer, an' that's where 'e is."

"Did 'e say what 'e wanted 'im for?"

"No, Mary, 'e just wanted ter talk wiv Arfer."

Mary nodded and turned away.

"By the way, Mary, I got your Reg's ball 'ere, 'e wouldn't knock fer it."

"Fanks, luv, g'night."

"Night, Mary."

Two men sat in the 'Eagle' sharing a joke. One of them had a nagging feeling that he had omitted to do something. The warm glow inside and the convivial company put Tom Carter at his ease. There would be time tomorrow. He would surely remember then what it was he had to do, he thought.

The 'Eagle' was doing a fast trade during those hot summer days and nights. The regulars from the Street and the market came in and discussed the latest news bulletins over their ale, and they became more and more fearful for the future. Little groups sat around the tables to debate on what exactly went wrong in France. They planned the future battles, and the more knowledgeable of the group terrified the rest with their pronouncements. If the speaker was an optimist then everyone went home happy, but if his tone was pessimistic, then the sense of fear prevailed and the customers went home feeling miserable.

As there seemed to be more pessimists than optimists among the pub's customers, the listeners of the group soon sought to insulate themselves from doom. They were fed up with pronouncements upon the future bombing of London, the use of poison gas and the date of the invasion. They turned to the storytellers. They sought the pedlars of the adult fairy tale, the orator who could relate strange happenings and amuse them. The listeners desired to be transported to some eastern market-place, to hear the soothsayer at work. They longed for the spinning of old tales, of kings and princes, yarns that could be bought for a coin or two. The listeners would hear of hot nights filled with the wild scent of jasmine and dotted with silver points of light shining down from a sky of deep blue velvet, and where the yellow orb-like moon hung low, casting its powdery glow upon the stage.

There was no soothsayer in the 'Eagle', but there was an able storyteller. There were no eastern carpets that could whisk the listeners off to a Persian harem; the carpets in the 'Eagle' were holed and dirty, although their origin may have been further east, perhaps even as far as the end of the Mile End Road. As to the perfume, the modest 'Eagle' could not boast jasmine, but it had a fine scent of 'Nosegay' and 'Goldflake'. There was also a full moon on the night the 'Eagle' storyteller wove his tale, although it was hidden from view by the blackout curtains. There was no dish for the listener to drop his coin into, but a glass of dark liquid to quench the speaker's thirst throughout the saga of the *Damselfly*.

"Well it must 'ave bin '94 or '95, if me memory serves me right," said Skipper as he packed his old clay pipe. "I was up in Liverpool lookin' around fer a ship when I saw it. It loomed up out of the fog like a great sea monster. Docked an' still it was, although it appeared ter be breathin', strike me if it didn't. Anyway, I saw the name, the *Damselfly* it was called. Funny name, I remember finkin' ter meself. The lines was all slimy an' wet, an' the plankin' looked sort o' greasy, like the ship 'ad travelled in a sea of oil. Very strange it was."

The audience watched the old seaman as he deliberately lit his pipe, blowing the smoke upwards. When he was satisfied that the bowl was drawing well he continued. "I was young an' ready fer anyfing, an' I signed on fer a trip. The *Damselfly* was bound fer the Orient an' it suited me. You could reckon on bein' away fer a year or more when you signed on fer such a trip. I'd 'ad enough of Liverpool an' I fancied the noise of the wind in the canvas. I liked the windjammers an' the *Damselfly* looked a challenge. Ter be honest, I was a'feared of that ship but, as I say, when yer young the fear is a prod in the back."

The listeners, sitting around the table in the little ale bar nodded their agreement and motioned for Skipper to go on, but the old mariner had spotted Joe Harper coming his way with a frothing pint of ale held in his hand.

"There we are, Skip," said Joe as he put the glass down in front of the storyteller.

"Gawd bless yer," grinned the seaman as he sipped at the froth. When he had taken a large gulp, and wiped his mouth on a red handkerchief, he continued with his tale.

"Well, as I was sayin', I signed on an' went ter me lodgins ter make preparations. The ship was leavin' on the evenin' tide next day so I decided ter get well an' truly drunk so's I'd get a good night's sleep. I went in a pub I know near the docks 'cos some of me ole chums was there most nights. Anyway, I was beginin' ter enjoy meself, an' the rums was comin' up fast, when I spotted this ole seaman. 'E 'ad a patch over 'is eye an' a gold earin' in one of 'is lug-'oles. I don't know what it was but 'e seemed ter look strange. Couldn't put me finger on it, but I just 'ad a funny feelin' about 'im. I must 'ave bin starin' at 'im, 'cos 'e nodded an' asked me if I was sailin' on the *Damselfly*.

Gawd above knows why 'e should ask that question, there must 'ave bin nearly a 'undred people in that pub, an' 'e asks me that. Anyway, I says yer, an' we get inter conversation. We must 'ave bin talkin' fer a decent while when I suddenly felt funny, like I was gettin' 'ot. I started ter sweat, an' I felt really ill. The ole seaman with the patch reckoned I'd caught a dose of the Mersey fever. I felt really rough, so I decided ter get back ter me lodgin's. I remembered gettin' under the blanket's an' goin' from 'ot ter cold. Well, I must o' dropped orf ter sleep. I was 'avin' this dream. It was a terrible dream, not a nightmare. Nightmares are mumbo-jumbo ter me, but this dream was real.

"I was aboard the *Damselfly*, an' we was in the tropics. The sun was beatin' down an' I was ill. They 'ad me laid out on a plank up on deck. I was sweatin' an' me mouth was parched. I couldn't speak 'cos me tongue was too swollen, an' I jus' laid there. Two o' the crew were talkin'. 'Dyin' 'e be,' one of 'em said. Then the captain comes up. 'Fetch me the sailmaker,' 'e says in a deep voice. The sailmaker turns out ter be ole 'one-eye' from the pub. 'E looks at me wiv a wicked grin spreadin' all over 'is face, an' 'e rubs 'is 'ands tergevver like 'e was enjoyin' me sufferin'. Then the captain opens a bible an' starts sayin' the burial service. Gawd I was scared. I looks at the sailmaker an' I nearly 'as a fit. There 'e is, large as life an' twice as ugly, stitchin' the canvas inter a shroud fer me. 'E was leerin', an' d'yer know what? I saw 'orrible 'orns startin' ter sprout from the top of 'is 'ead. 'E was the devil 'imself. Then I see the tail growin' from behind 'im. It 'ad a tip like a snake's tongue, terrible it was. Anyway, I'm layin' there 'elpless, when I spots the large darnin' needle e's usin'. It seems ter be doin' the stitchin' all by itself. The needle was shining like it was made of silver an' it really glistened in the sun. The captain finished the service an' then they came over ter put me in this canvas shroud. As they picked me up I woke up.

"I found that I was soaked in sweat. The blankets felt like someone 'ad poured a bucket o' water over 'em. I 'ardly 'ad the strength ter lift meself up in the bed. I looked out an' I could see it was daylight. I got up an' washed an' shaved, then I went down fer me breakfast. The landlady was surprised ter see me up. She told me I'd bin in a fever fer more'n two days. The doctor 'ad bin in an' 'e was due ter call back. Course, I'd missed me ship, an' I 'ad ter kick me 'eels up in Liverpool til anuvver chance come along.

"A couple o' days later I felt better, an' I went fer a drink in the pub I used the night I got took bad. I asked the landlord if 'e remembered me, an' 'e said 'e did. 'E also remembered me gettin' took bad. Funny fing was, 'e 'ad no recollection of the seaman wiv the patch who was talkin' ter me. It seemed strange ter me. I kept on finkin' about that ole one-eyed seaman, an' that silver darnin' needle that sewed by itself. Sent shivers down me back it did. Still I 'ad ter pull meself round, so I got anuvver berth an' I was away fer over a year.

"It was next year, '95 I believe, when I was in Liverpool. I 'appened ter go in that pub I bin tellin' yer about. There was a couple o' seamen talkin' an' I got ter 'ear-wiggin'. 'Yeah, went down wiv all 'ands,' this seaman said. 'In the China Sea last year,' 'e went on. 'Must o' copped a typhoon, there was some nasty storms out that way last year.' Well I pricked me ears up an' I 'eard the seaman mention the ship: it was the *Damselfly*! Gawd, if I 'adn't bin taken bad, I'd 'ave bin feedin' the fishes by now!"

Wheezy Morris broke the silence. "Funny ole world ain't it?"

Skipper nodded. "Yer can say that again. 'Cos the strangest part of all 'appened years later. I was shippin' out wiv a seaman whose 'obby was paintin' small pitchers of butterflies an' insects, an' the like. Well, I saw this paintin' 'e done of a damselfly, an' underneath 'e'd printed a name in Latin. I asked 'im what the inscription meant. Know what 'e said? It means 'devil's darnin' needle'. 'E told me that they sometimes called damselflies by that name. Well, I don't 'ave ter tell yer 'ow I felt. I stayed cold fer a bleedin' week. Funny fings dreams is, funny fings ..."

Chapter Thirteen

On Saturday morning, August 7th, 1940, Maureen Flannagan put on her mother's apron and busied herself about the house. Her father was at work and her mother was shopping in the market. James the baby slept peacefully in his pram outside the front door, and beside the pram the twins Sheena and Sally played 'five-stones'. The two boys Terry and Patrick junior were constructing a deadly trap for their feline pet, who watched their endeavours from a safe distance, its green eyes unblinking.

The morning was warm, and along the Street the usual rituals were being performed. Women hearthstoned their front door steps and cleaned their windows. The menfolk stood with thumbs tucked under their braces, and with clay pipes burning orange as they conversed. They blew clouds of tobacco smoke into the air and sent the aroma of 'Nosegay' and 'Old Returns' drifting down the Street. The men wore worried frowns that morning as they spoke of the impending invasion. They tried to appear unruffled in the presence of their wives, but the women knew how they really felt, and gained no comfort from their conclusions.

Only the children remained unaffected, and they went about their usual Saturday pleasures. They got under the feet of adults, and upset the peace of Conner Street with their requests: "No you can't 'ave me 'ammer, you'll smash yer fingers wiv it."

"No, yer can't borrer me chopper, yer farver'll box yer ears."

"Don't chop up that box outside me front door, I've just done that step."

The youngsters of dockland were adept at making a

few coppers from their labours, and the sale of good dry firewood provided them with the means to see the latest films on show at the local 'bug-hutch', as they named it, or the opportunity to consume a plate of pie and mash at Cuthbert's pie shop. The problem was obtaining a weapon to decimate the large orange or apple boxes, and then packing the fragments in such a way that their customer would believe he or she was getting a bargain in domestic fuel. The children of Conner Street were expert at foraging for boxes and selling the produce. They worked in small groups, and enlisted the aid of a tiny helper who would be responsible for the sale.

"'Ello, son, wot yer want?"

"Wanna buy some firewood, mister?" puffing heavily.

"Wot yer puffin' for, son?"

"It's the bag, mister, ain't 'arf 'eavy," said the tiny tot.

"'Ow much?"

"Only sixpence, mister, an' yer git tons o' wood."

The angelic features swayed the customer, and another sixpence found its way into the pocket, along with the usual assortment of string, bubblegum, and a fold-up knife with its instrument for removing stones from horses' hooves.

On Saturday August 7th, the Solomon brothers, Ron and Ernie, went into the firewood business. They obtained an egg box and an apple box and they looked around for a tool to break up the wood. They sneaked into their house and removed the chopper from its resting place under the stairs, and broke up the boxes, selling the sticks to Mrs Jenkins. They also sold the bits of wood to other people in the Street, for they made sure there was plenty of wood to go round.

"Look, don't go puttin' in that much, Ern, watch me."

Ron Solomon placed three sticks upright in his canvas bag and then laid a sprinkling of sticks on the top. He then demonstrated how to walk along as though carrying a heavy burden.

"Yer gotta puff, Ern, an' let 'em see yer can't 'ardly carry it."

The young one grinned and tried the technique on

Mrs Jenkins. "Cor blimey, lady, this bag ain't 'arf 'eavy."

"I s'pose it is," agreed the bleary-eyed lady, and rewarded the budding actor with a South African sixpence.

Maureen Flannagan enjoyed Saturdays too. She usually took the twins to Cuthbert's on most Saturdays and she tried to dodge meeting silly Bobbie there. Bobbie slurped when he ate his pie and mash, and liquid ran down his chin and onto his coat. He pulled faces too and made the twins giggle, which prompted the forthright Maureen to ask Bobbie to "stop being so silly".

"Gawd 'elp us, luv," laughed the owner of the pie shop. "You might just as well ask the Thames to stop flowin'!"

Bobbie liked Saturdays too. He got paid on Saturday morning, and he liked to wander along to the pie shop. He stood and watched the slithering eels in the galvanised tanks outside the shop. He enjoyed watching the shop-owner grab an eel and quickly cut off its head. A deft flick of the knife and the eel was gutted. A chop, chop, and the inch-long pieces were ready for the boiling pot. The man cleaned the chopping-board with his knife and then repeated the process, but the idiot had seen enough and he went inside.

Patrick Flannagan had finished his shift at the furnace and he had reached the 'Eagle' in time to consume a few pints of ale. He now sat in the backyard with his feet up on the window-ledge. The chair in which he sat spewed out its contents of horsehair stuffing, and one leg was missing. It remained usable though with the placing of two house-bricks under the seat. The big man sat comfortably with his cap pulled down over his face. His steady breathing moved the cap up and down as he slept in the warm afternoon.

In the scullery, Patrick junior stalked a buzzing blue-bottle that had got itself trapped behind the curtain. The boy carried a pint glass that he sought to drop over the 'buzzer'. He looked through the window at his father and grinned at the moving cap, then went on with his hunt. As the bluebottle flew away a roar filled the air. It came from

127

the police station roof and screamed out its stark message of fear.

Joe Harper sat in his signal-box at Bermondsey Crossing and waited. He had received a call to hold the signal at red. He thought about this and wondered. There might be a raid on down in Kent, or maybe only a mishap down the line. He lit a cigarette and waited. The war was getting to be bad for everyone, he thought. Bad for his daughter Mary, who had seen her husband wheeled into her hospital ward exhausted and with shell fragments in his arm and leg. The war was bad for his daughter Josie, whose husband Brian had been called up, leaving her to manage the two young children. Joe ran his fingers through his hair and stared down at the floor.

The noise seemed to start from way down the track. It rushed along the rails and enveloped the signal cabin, and at the same time the phone rang.

Silly Bobbie sat in his quiet bedroom while Ada Dawkins sat downstairs listening to the wireless. Strains of *Old Monterey* drifted on the warm air and Ada's head dipped down onto her chest. It was late afternoon as Bobbie reached under his bed and took out a square wooden box. He opened it and leaned down to smell the varnish. The box was about nine inches long and wide and just a fist deep. It was well made, with strong brass hinges and a bone catch that looped over a brass stud to secure the lid. The top of the lid was inlaid with a paler wood than the mahogany from which the box was made. The whole casket was highly polished, with a shellac that lifted the grain and colour to a reddish brown. The box was made to hold something valuable, as indeed it did.

Bobbie smiled as he took out the contents of the box. There was a small bag tied up with a bootlace. The bag contained Bobbie's complete collection of marbles. In one corner of the casket there was a pile of money. The idiot took out the coins and started to count the smooth, worn pennies. He never reached more than eleven or twelve before he tired of concentrating, and today it was too warm to count all the coins. In the box there was a knife that had many gadgets. Bobbie cleaned the knife with his shirt sleeve and then inspected the blades. There was a large blade that was very sharp and a smaller one which Bobbie used to cut string with. The rest of the gadgets were a mystery to the idiot, although some of the children had told him of their uses. Bobbie opened up the long curved prong which he had been told took stones from horses' hooves. There was a corkscrew that one of the children said was used to pick up twisty worms in the garden. Bobbie shut the corkscrew quickly when he remembered what the child had told him. There were a couple of old army badges and a few broken pencils, a dice with a few counters and a folded up piece of paper. Bobbie carefully unfolded the square and looked at the coloured picture with interest. It showed an Indian elephant. The beast was adorned with the glorious silk and satin trappings of a maharajah, and its tusks were encased in silver tubes with jewels encrusted along their length. Atop the beast there was a seat made of padded velvet and covered with a sunshade. On the seat sat an evil-looking prince, who held a stick aloft. Bobbie stared at the half-naked figure of the mahout, who sat at the elephant's ears. He seemed to be beating the animal with a bamboo cane and Bobbie frowned. He hoped that one day that man who beat the elephant would fall off and be crushed beneath those massive feet.

The idiot carefully replaced all his treasures and slid the box back beneath the bed. He handled the casket very carefully. He had owned it for as long as he could remember. In fact the box had been given to the boy by the kind nuns when they left him with Ada Dawkins. The box was very old and had been made to hold a ship's sextant. For years the box had kept the instrument safe and dry beneath the tight-fitting lid. It had lain on the railed shelves in the cabins of tall-masted schooners and ships of the line. Later, when the owner of the box left service, it rested forgotten in dark cupboards. Hard times caused the box to see the light of day once again as it passed through the doors of an establishment that advertised its benevolence with three brass orbs hanging from chains above the portals.

The box with its sextant was never reclaimed, for the owner now travelled in fluffy cloud schooners across the heavens in the company of his nautical ancestors and had no need for such a piffling instrument of mortals. So the box remained on the dusty shelf. The romance and mystery were lost on the scrawny pawnbroker; he made his living on a thousand such treasures left and sometimes never claimed back. He looked at the sextant and decided it would sell if properly exhibited, and on the glass shelf it went, in pride of place in his large window. The box remained, as the buyer of the instrument did not need the case. It stayed until the unromantic pawnbroker was touched by the pleas of the visiting salvationists who asked for gifts for their charitable ventures. The box passed through the hands of godly people and into the grimy hands of an idiot, who lavished as much love on that box as it had ever known in its long existence. It was now placed back in its cache, and as the idiot slid out from beneath the springs he heard the roar start up. It filled the room and Bobbie quaked.

The wail of the siren sounded unreal on the soft warm afternoon. It seemed so improbable and impossible on that lovely day with the few wisps of cloud hanging high in the azure sky. It grated on the relaxed folk of Conner Street and they rushed out into the sun to stare skywards with disbelief. The wail diminished into a dying moan, but before it stilled the sound of a heavy drone reached their ears. Machines flying high and following the ribbon of twisting water approached in tight formation. Among them tiny pieces of cotton opened and expanded as shells burst but the aircraft still flew on.

"Gawd Almighty, there's fousands of the bastards, they're everywhere," screamed Emmie Jones.

"Get yerselves in the shelter quick," shouted Bob Bowman the warden, his face red from running.

"The bleeders are after the docks, they're after the

Surrey," Skipper said as he hurried across the street on the arm of Rosie Harper.

The sky became streaked with vapour trails and the black smoke of exhausts as the aircraft went into their bombing run. The streaks widened and drifted over the virgin blue canvas as the picture dissolved in nightmarish apparitions.

"Look, they've got one, 'e's goin' down!" screamed Wheezy Morris.

A bomber left the formation and turned. It dipped earthwards and dived down toward the Kent hills, one of its engines billowing smoke.

Most of the inhabitants of Conner Street did not enter the shelter but stood instead on the pavement totally transfixed. They saw the formation turn and make their return run. Flashes could be seen over the chimneypots and explosions rocked the homes. Here and there a window shattered from the blast, and a couple of slates rattled off the roofs. Pigeons flew round the houses and settled for an instant, before flying off again in stark terror.

"Gawd 'elp them poor bleeders down town, they won't 'ave a chance," moaned Lizzie Brown, her hands tucked in her apron and carpet slippers on the wrong feet.

As the flying armada bore down on its target once more, the bombers could see that down below the whole of dockland was burning. Their excitement showed in their voices as they spat out instructions to their pilots. They pressed the buttons with their gloved thumbs and sent more bombs screaming down into the inferno. From high above, the docks were like a grate that was ready laid and waiting for the spark from the devil's tinderbox.

On that first run the spark was dropped among the docked piles of Russian fir and Finnish pine. The blazing mass spread to Norwegian spruce and Canadian cedar. The whole of the timber burned, and sap and resin flowed in sticky, red-hot streams. It dipped into the water and set the Thames alight. The timber sheds crumbled. The galvanised panels blew outwards and the girder skeleton melted and took on frightening shapes. Sparks crackled and leapt skywards, and water turned to steam as white-hot iron sank down into the mud. All of the docks were ablaze; a mammoth smoke cloud rose up in the sky and was visible for miles, the indiscreet pall of a funeral pyre.

The engines of destruction had flown away and now the all-clear sounded. Fire engines roared to the Surrey Docks from all over London. There were whole streets by the Surrey that were burning. Hoses melted but the exhausted firemen battled on, their faces grey with shock and emotion. The wall of the dock threatened to collapse on the fire tenders but the firemen would not move. Oxygen-starved, they had to be pulled away bodily as they fell over the hoses and were too tired to pick themselves up again. Their desperate battle against the roaring flames was witnessed by the families who were trapped in the streets adjoining the docks. They waited quietly, the women sometimes crying silently until a path out of the inferno was made safe. The red-eyed inhabitants marched away carrying pitiful bundles containing few of the smaller, and most treasured possessions.

A fire tender rushed along the traffic emptied road and turned into a side street. Chief Fire Officer Smart sat beside the driver, a lad of twenty, who drove like a demon. He shouted encouragement as the driver steered the tender over fallen debris. The heat was intense as they skidded to a halt and started to set up their hoses. The flames had spread into the houses in the street, and a fire engine that had arrived earlier had its paint scorched black.

"Are they all out?" shouted Officer Smart above the din.

"They're all clear," answered a blackened fireman.

"Let it burn, that wall's goin' any minute," the fire chief shouted. "We'll get into the next turnin' see if we can contain it."

There was a roar as the dock wall collapsed, sending a sheet of flame outwards and completely enveloping the tender. Officer Smart saw his driver sitting upright in the cab, his hands gripping the steering wheel, his body taking up a posture of death on his funeral pyre. There was nothing that could be done for the man and Officer Smart turned back round to the fireman he had just shouted to, shaking. The man lay prone across the fire hose, with his uniform smouldering. There was no time to lose, the whole street was about to be swallowed up in the engulfing flames. The fire officer grabbed the man and struggled painfully to get him up onto his shoulder. A burning pain ran down the length of his back as he staggered along to the end of the street. His breath came in gasps and his legs started to give out. Gawd don't let me drop him, he prayed to himself.

"C'mon, mate, let's 'ave 'im," a voice said, and Officer Smart fainted.

Earlier that fateful Saturday, a scruffy individual was strolling along by the dock wall holding a paper bag. He looked through the locked gates and saw the duty dock policeman leaning against his office door and talking to a colleague. The man's befuddled brain managed to deduce that it must be afternoon if the gate was locked. He knew the dockers all rushed out at twelve noon on Saturdays and then the gates were locked. Then a thought struck him. It might be Sunday, in which case it could still be morning. The man's brain reacted against the pressure put on to it and it refused to respond. It decided it must be Saturday because there were too many people about in working clothes for it to be Sunday and, after that great piece of detective work, it went back to working at its usual pace.

The man was used to sleeping rough, and recently he had found a very nice place way inside the Surrey Docks. It was easy to get in, all that was needed was the knowledge of the exact spot. The tramp found the place by watching a young boy squeeze through some loose planking near the jetty and retrieve his ball. Later the tramp gave the spot a hefty kick and sure enough the bottom of the board gave way from its nailed joint. Carefully replacing the board, the tramp waited until it was dark, then made his way into the docks to find a safe, warm place to lay his head. The only danger was the dock police. As long as he was quiet and kept out of sight he was sure he'd be all right. That night the tramp found the perfect bed on a stack of veneer. The wood smelt pleasant, and it held his warmth. The tramp had found some sacks which enhanced his comfort and there he stayed. The place was tucked away down by the most quiet part of the docks where even the dock police hardly deemed it necessary to venture.

The tramp walked past the gate and down towards his secret spot. He stopped and taking out a quart bottle of ale from the paper bag took a large swig. He had scrounged the price of the beer by helping to push the laden fruit barrows from market, and having drunk most of his wages the tramp felt unusually tired. The day was very warm, and the sun beat down relentlessly on his tattered old overcoat making him long for his veneered bed in the shade. He staggered in the right direction and upon finding his private place he lay down at full stretch, his heavy eyelids dropping down to shut out the light. It was peaceful, he thought, listening to the gurgling water and the far away sound of a steam engine as it pulled out of the station. He heard the chatter of the starlings that rested high up in the shed girders and the creaking sound as the barges strained against the mooring ropes. This was perfect, thought the tramp as he took another swig from his quart bottle.

"How do you plead?" asked the magistrate.

"Not guilty, your worshipful."

"But you took the shoes from the shop without paying for them," said the tired-looking beak.

"Well, your 'ighness . . ."

"Sir will do," said the stern man in the lofty chair.

"Well, your 'ighness, I mean sir, I meant to pay, but I was tired an' I just forgot."

"Is the man ill, or without all his faculties?" asked the beak of the solicitor.

"Arnold Thomas has been a model of good behaviour recently, sir, and I think it was just an oversight on this occasion."

"An oversight, an oversight," repeated the magistrate.

"Yes, sir," said the tall skinny-looking solicitor. "You see, the defendant was trying the shoes out by walking around the shop when someone called him from outside. My client states that as the shoes were so comfortable, he didn't realise he was wearing new ones and he just kept walking."

"What about his old shoes?" asked the beak.

"He left them in the shoe box," said the solicitor meekly.

The magistrate sat bowed in his high-backed chair, his head resting upon his two closed fists. It was time to speak his words of wisdom to the unfortunate soul before him, and he took a deep breath. "It appears to me that you, Mr Arnold Thomas, sought to deprive the owners of the shoes, the company of Messrs Comfywear, of those said shoes, without due and proper payment. I am loath to consider what may have happened should you have succeeded in your evil scheme, when at a later date some person asked for a pair of shoes and was shown a pair of singularly shabby boots, minus the soles and parts of the uppers, minus the laces, and smelling of Billingsgate fish market, the place where I understand you earn money by pulling laden fish barrows. No, Mr Thomas, I cannot permit this situation to arise in the future by allowing you to walk out of this court unpunished. You will go to prison for fourteen centuries ..."

The tramp woke with a start. He had dreamed he was back in Wandsworth and he felt his heart pounding. He sat up and observed his tattered footwear. He knew that he would have to think of another, less dangerous way of replacing them. The thought of exchanging his new-found bed for the hard prison cot was abhorrent to him and he shook his head. It was peaceful here, and the distant drone made him feel sleepy again. He closed his eyes but the drone became louder. It now sounded directly overhead and the tramp opened his eyes.

The first explosion knocked him off his resting place. The pile of timber some distance away had turned into a burning mass. He saw the timber shed opposite his position billowing smoke and flame. The tramp started to run, wishing he was back in Wandsworth right that minute. He heard the clatter as more bombs landed, his ear drums perforated by the first explosion. He had to get out of here fast, he thought as he made for his secret entry spot. The way was barred by a sea of flame that made him gasp for breath.

He retraced his steps to his hideout and took another path. In front of him he saw the dock gate that he had passed earlier that day. It was burning. He heard a shuddering noise that hurt his ears, then a flash that swept away the gates. He ran for the opening and saw a policeman fighting to free himself from a pile of logs that had been blown down from their stack. The policeman saw the tramp and screamed at him to help.

Arnold Thomas ran past. He knew he was trespassing and he wanted to put distance between him and the law. He reached the opening by the street and stopped for breath. The policeman's cries rang in his ears and he hopped about in agitation. I can't leave him to roast, he thought, and he went back. The pile of logs was burning and the flames would soon envelope the trapped man. The tramp grabbed a short log and used it as a lever, prising at the rest, straining until he trembled with the exertion. The pile moved and the policeman dragged himself from underneath. He moaned and then fainted, and the tramp saw that his leg was crushed. He would have to carry him out, but he knew he would never make it. Already the fire was filling the dock and sweeping toward him. He left the policeman and ran for the opening once more. Halfway there he stopped and looked back. The policeman lay perfectly still. It was no use, the tramp knew he couldn't leave him there. He hopped around again in panic as he tried to think. His gaze caught sight of a wheelbarrow propped against the burning logs nearby. The tramp grabbed hold of it and hurried to the fallen man. He managed to roll the policeman onto the barrow and lashed him tight with his belt. The flames were licking at his heels as the tramp trotted out of the dock, the moaning policeman gritting his teeth from the pain of his shattered leg.

Late in the evening, the sky was coloured red from the still burning docks. Two exhausted firemen stood by a canteen van and sipped tea from large enamel mugs.

"I've never seen anyfing like it," said one. "I turns round an' there 'e is, pushin' this wheelbarrer out wiv a copper tied on it."

"Go on," said his mate.

"Yeah, I tell yer, I couldn't believe me eyes. This feller looks like a tramp, proper scruffy 'e is. 'E wheels the barrer up ter me an' says, 'Don't say anyfing about me, I've already bin in trouble over me shoes.' I ask yer, fancy worryin' over 'is bleedin' shoes. 'E 'ad the clothes scortched orf 'is back an' the flames lickin' round 'is arse an' 'e's worried over a fing like that."

The fireman set down his mug and put his arm around the shoulder of his friend. "I reckon the 'ole world's gorn bleedin' crazy, Bert."

Chapter Fourteen

As the blood-red sun dipped down behind the chimneys of dockland, the sky took on a dark, smokey tinge. In the east, flames still spurted up from the savaged Surrey Docks. A smoke cloud rose high into the heavens. It seemed unreal to the Conner Street folk as they watched the spectacle. Fire bells rang out almost continuously as reinforcements hurried to the blazing inferno. People stood in their doorways staring up at the flashing, reflecting sky. They looked on in disbelief and in horror. It was as though the war had only just started. And for most of them it had.

Fire tenders were arriving from many areas around London. They came to relieve exhausted, grey-faced men who were dropping with fatigue and the lack of breathable air, their lungs almost bursting with the pressure created in the cauldron that had once been the peaceful last resting place for the produce of the vast North European forests. Fir and spruce, pine and cedar had lain in huge piles about the docks, seasoning and drying to become tinder for the bombers.

Inside the Surrey Docks the floor space had become a molten lake of treacle as sap boiled and ran from the logs. It was like volcanic lava, and certain death to any living thing in its path. It ran down into the river, turning the water into liquid fire. It ran up against sheds, setting them alight. The whole scene was one of weird, twisted shapes that shifted and changed as the girders buckled in the heat. The planks of wood piled up inside the sheds generated terrific heat and blew out the corrugated walls with tremendous force. Firemen were pulled back, for it was impossible to combat the blaze at its source. It was becoming hard to save the surrounding streets from destruction.

The loop of land that pushed out into the Thames contained not only the docks, but many wharves and small factories. It also housed the local workforce, in tenements and small terraced houses. That Saturday night saw the end of many of these homes, and the exodus of refugees continued all evening. Pitiful groups of tired, sad-faced folk trudged from their destroyed homes down town to rest centres and church halls which had been hurriedly made ready for them. They used horse-drawn carts, barrows and manpower to transport the salvaged pieces of their possessions, their prized flotsam that no amount of money would induce them to part with. There was Granny's photo, and the old jug, now chipped, which had once stood on a wash-stand, the wedding present from a departed. Bales of soaked bedding balanced on a kitchen table, alongside a chiming clock that only 'donged' the half-hour. Tired children sat on carts and barrows, a girl cuddling her doll, and a boy stroking a terrified pet tom-cat. They came away from the hell to kindly solace from helpers and allowed themselves to be herded into rest centres. They muttered their thanks as hot soup and mugs of tea were handed out. As they trudged along to safety they passed fire tenders on their way to the scenes of destruction. They sometimes waved, and the firemen waved back shocked at what they saw. The firemen shouted encouragement to the homeless stream of folk, then held on tightly as they were rushed to the mouth of the inferno.

That night, as darkness drifted in slowly, the fires were still out of control, lighting up the sky. Sparks shot up from the crumbling sheds and wood-piles, night being turned into day by the magnitude of the blaze. It caused the pigeons to fly at midnight, and the children to believe it was still too early to go to sleep. The size of the inferno increased until the whole of the docklands were burning.

In Conner Street the folk were out on their doorsteps.

They looked up at the sky, some in silence, some in earnest conversation.

Lizzie Brown stood with hands tucked under her apron. "The bastards 'ave done the Surrey in," she said bitterly.

"Gawd a'mighty, Gawd," Emmie cried out. "Whatever's ter become of us?"

"We'll be all right, yer silly mare," Lizzie said reassuringly.

"My Arfur's gone ter see if 'is mates are okay. Some of 'em live downtown."

"It's no good us 'avin' blackout up, no bleedin' good whatsoever," remarked Mrs Jenkins, a glass of ale held in her shaking hand.

"All I 'ope is the bastards don't come back ternight," said Lizzie. "All London must be lit up."

"Gawd 'elp us if they do," Emmie Jones said, shaking her head.

The initial shock had passed, but now the dread of what might come filled the Conner Street folk as they sought the company of their neighbours. Each individual handled the fear in a certain way.

Ada Dawkins found that it helped to talk to her dead husband Charlie. She told him of the day's events and the eyes that stared down at her seemed to fill her soul with calm. Bobbie sat up in his room. He could not understand the reason for the sky to be so red, light enough for him to read his comics without the gaslight being turned on. He did not want to see the pictures of war. Instead he looked at the animal pictures. He grinned at the matchstick men and the talking duck. He liked the pictures of the farmyard, where a huge sun smiled down on cows, and sunflowers with shy, drooping faces that looked down on frolicking lambs. He wished he and Ada could be there, where Ada would not cry any more and he would sit in the sun, watching the animals.

Patrick Flannagan had his own way of coping with his fears; he got drunk. Bridie cuddled her baby close to her and kept her brood near by. Joe Harper and Rosie sat with Skipper in their parlour. The wireless set emitted soft music, and the old seaman puffed away at his brown stained clay pipe. He was lost in his thoughts of a better time, long gone, where men battled the storms at sea and not each other. He thought of his days before the mast, listening to the rising wind in the rigging. He reminisced of the days in far off ports and in rusty old tramp steamers, and occasionally he sighed deeply.

Lizzie Brown had her two friends in for a chat. She shared a few bottles of stout with them as they sat in her parlour, among the glass ornaments and ebony-framed pictures hanging on the walls. Lizzie talked of her departed husband, who had one day walked out and never came back.

"Real right bastard 'e was," she said. "Never any good from the day I married the tyke."

"'Ow long's 'e bin gone, Liz?" asked Emmie.

"Winter it was, Guy Fawkes night, 1936," answered Lizzie Brown.

"Still, yer better orf wivout 'im, gal," said Betty Smith.

"I should say so," Lizzie laughed. "I reckoned someone claimed 'im fer a guy."

The two women laughed, and Lizzie filled their empty glasses. "You know, I never could remember 'im doin' a full week's work all the time I was married ter the bleeder. Wasn't as if 'e didn't 'ave a trade. Tanner 'e was, worked in the leavver market, when 'e was sober. I've seen 'im lose many a good job over the booze, an' uvver poor sods scratchin' aroun' fer work."

"Bleedin' shame," said Betty Smith.

"Well at least my ole man don't piss all 'is wages up the wall," said Emmie. "Good ter me is my Arfur, never sees me short 'e don't."

Betty Smith glanced at Lizzie, a trace of a smile showing on her face. "Well it's all right if yer got an ole man in steady work," she said with envy.

"My Arfur's 'ad it bad in the docks," Emmie answered quickly. "'E 'ad ter fight fer a decent day's pay. Bin frew a lot o' trouble 'as my ole man, wot wiv the strikes, an' the 'black-leggin'. Many a time I 'ad ter take 'is suit over uncle's ter get the price of a loaf o' bread."

Betty Smith snorted. "You was lucky, Emm. My ole man didn't 'ave a best suit till lately. Tell a lie. 'E did 'ave one, till 'e 'ad ter take it ter work when the arse fell out of 'is working trousers."

Lizzie Brown took a draught from her glass. "I fink we've all 'ad our share of the pawnbroker. Trouble wiv my ole man, 'e used ter sleep in 'is Sunday best when 'e came 'ome pissed. I 'ad ter press the bleedin' fing afore I could take it over uncle's."

"I tell yer one fing," said Emmie Jones, looking at Betty Smith. "I bet your ole man wuz the smartest coalman round these parts. Fancy deliverin' an 'undred-weight 'o nutty slack in yer Sunday best."

At the 'Eagle' conversation was flowing. Everyone discussed the bombing. Wheezy Morris and one of his darts partners leaned on the bar counter talking to John Braden the landlord. Big Albert Conlin sat on a bar stool smoking a cigarette and staring woodenly at the empty bottles lined up on the bar. Florrie Braden had been too busy to remove them; she was fussing between customers, giving her husband wicked glances. Occasionally, she looked over in Albert's direction. Florrie still had a warm feeling for the man and often thought about renewing the liaison. John would never be any the wiser, she thought. Most nights he went to bed in an intoxicated condition and it would be so easy. She sighed as she cleared the glasses and the line of bottles in front of Albert. Recently Florrie had dropped the odd hint or two, but it seemed to be in vain. Her words were falling upon deaf ears. Albert was determined to stay clear of any emotional entanglements with the hot-blooded Florrie. There was an element of pity in her attraction toward Albert. Florrie knew that he lived alone and that he was a lonely man. He had told her that, when he was not sitting in the 'Eagle', he spent his time reading. She felt that warm glow deep down inside as she looked at him on that Saturday night, and she sighed again.

At the warden's post a few streets away, Bob Bowman sat with two other wardens. The men wore armbands and carried tin helmets that were strapped to canvas gas mask cases. They spoke of the bombing of the docks and the destruction that was surely to continue.

"They've bin puttin' anti-aircraft guns in Southwark Park all week," said one.

"And on the factory roofs," said another.

"Well I tell yer wot," informed Bob Bowman, "they better not try an' put anyfink on the factories in our Street. The bleedin' lot'll cave in."

The conversation was interrupted by the entry of a messenger, bearing a sealed envelope.

"Wot yer got there, son?" asked one of the men.

"It's from headquarters," announced the pink-faced youth.

"Give it 'ere then," beckoned the man.

The youth stepped forward and handed the message over, then stood back.

The warden read the sheet of paper and signed the receipt.

"Okay, son, on yer way," he said.

"Anyfing wrong?" asked Bob Bowman.

"It's a 'red alert' warnin'," replied the controller. "The bastards are due back."

Conner Street's warden ran his hand over the back of his head. He stood up and stretched, his long angular frame arching as he did so. Bob was tired. The river traffic had been very heavy recently, with the cargoes being unloaded late into the evening. He had also noticed that the strain showed on the ships' crews who moored their vessels and went about their business in the Pool. The oceans of the world were getting progressively more hazardous for shipping, and more and more seamen's lives were lost to the lurking U-Boats.

Bob Bowman looked around the warden's post as he slipped his arm through the strap of his service pack. He felt he was at last going to be able to do something useful. He had not had much to do so far, apart from keeping an eye on the shelter and checking that the Street was fully

143

blacked out during the hours of darkness. He was beginning to wonder if he had been right in volunteering for the job of warden. His wife Grace had shed a few tears when he first walked into his home and put the steel helmet on the table. Funny thing about that, he thought. It was the first time he had seen her cry. She hadn't cried when the doctor told her she could not have any more children after young Brenda was born over five years ago. She hadn't cried that time they sent for her when he fell down the ship's hold and they thought he'd broken his back. Grace wasn't one to create a fuss.

A telephone bell startled Bob and jarred his thought back to the business in hand. "I'd better get back, they've bin pumpin' water out o' the shelter. It's seepin' in from somewhere."

The controller was speaking into the phone. As Bob was leaving the man put his hand over the mouthpiece and shouted, "I nearly forgot. There's a bike there. Take it, it might come in 'andy."

Bob looked at the rusted frame and worn saddle. "You sure you can spare it? It looks like it came out of a Salvation Army sale."

The controller ignored Bob's comments. "There's some bicycle clips on the 'andlebars."

Bob Bowman put on the clips and pedalled back to Conner Street.

Fred Harris walked down Conner Street and knocked on Joe Harper's door. "Can't stop, Joe, just ter tell yer, ole Jerry the rag-an'-bone man copped it. 'E lived by the docks apparently. Dragged 'im out awhile ago, so one of the lads told me. Burnt to a cinder 'e was, poor bleeder."

"Gawd a'mighty," gasped Joe. "We're gonna miss 'im comin' round on Sundays. I loved to 'ear 'im call out."

"Take my tip, Joe," warned Fred Harris. "Keep yerself 'andy ter get in that shelter. It's odds on the bastards'll be back ternight. The bloody 'ole o' London's lit up fer 'em."

Further along the Street, Mary Carter sat in her

parlour looking at her husband Tom as he read the evening paper. "Tom, do you think there'll be another raid ternight?" she asked.

Tom Carter didn't answer right away. "If yer like," he said.

Mary puffed and spoke sharply, "Tom Carter, did you 'ear what I said?"

Tom put the paper down and smiled at her. "Sorry, luv. I was readin' a funny bit in the paper. What did yer ask me?"

Mary ignored the question and looked down at her knitting. "I can't seem ter get started on that pullover of Reggie's. Fair put the fear inter me, that bombin'."

"Now it's not worth upsettin' yerself, Mary. Yer don't want the kids ter see yer upset, now do yer?"

Mary picked up her knitting. "I was talkin' ter Lizzie Brown a little while ago an' your mate Bob came past. Went ter look at the shelter. Ridin' a bike 'e was."

"Ridin' a bike? Bob Bowman ridin' a bike?" Tom laughed.

"Rusty ole thing it was. Wobblin' all over the place 'e was."

Tom laughed even louder. "If ole Bob was on a bike it 'ad ter be rusty, 'cos 'e'd never buy one. Someone must 'ave give it to 'im."

Mary was infected by her husband's laughter. Her face relaxed as she remembered something. "Bike clips. 'E 'ad bike clips on."

"Well that's not unusual. People usually wear bike clips when they ride a bike," Tom remarked, looking at Mary as she burst into loud laughter.

Mary took some time before she could answer him. She dabbed at her eyes and swallowed hard. "It made me notice 'is socks. They were odd ones."

Tom Carter shook his head. "It's that warden's job. Drivin' 'im round the twist it is."

Mary regained her composure and started on her knitting. Tom picked up his paper as the children came into the room. "Now don't get all them games out, you've got ter get washed soon."

"Just five minutes, Mum."

"All right. Just five minutes."

For a while Mary knitted. Then she stopped and looked at the back of Tom's newspaper. Her face had taken on a stern look again, her eyes reflecting her worry, and her young son, who was playing snakes and ladders with his sister, clearly noticed. The boy's eyes kept glancing in his mother's direction and his sister became impatient.

"For goodness' sake, will you frow them dice," she pleaded, her hands propping up her tiny pink face.

"Okay, fusspot," laughed her brother, and he threw two sixes.

"I'm not playin' wiv you, you're cheatin'," she complained.

"Now come on, kids, put that game away, it's time you got washed fer bed," Mary ordered.

Marjorie yawned and left the table, while young Reg gathered up the counters. "Will there be any more bombin', Mum?" he asked quietly.

"We don't know, son," answered his mother. "If the siren goes in the night, I want you ter get yer sister up, but don't frighten 'er. We'll 'ave ter go over the shelter, okay?"

"Wot, over that stinkin' place?"

"Yes, over that stinkin' place, Reg," Reg's father butted in. "It may not smell very nice, but at least we'll be safe there."

"Okay, Dad," said little Reg, and he walked out of the room.

Presently the children came in to say good night, and when they were at last alone Mary confided to her husband. "I'm scared for their safety, Tom. I wonder if we did right in bringin' 'em back inter this."

Her husband put down the paper and stretched his legs out. "Now look, luv, it's no good you gettin' yerself all worked up about it. We couldn't leave 'em wiv that pair o' carrot crunchers, now could we? Besides, if we'd 'ave found 'em new people, 'ow could we be sure they were bein' looked after properly?"

146

Mary nodded agreement. "I only 'ope it don't get too bad," she sobbed.

Tom reached out and took her in his arms, cuddling her head to his chest. He could feel the softness of her body and her sweet response as she nestled in to him. The trace of cologne from her hair was pleasant in his nostrils, and his hands gently stroked her back.

"Wait, Tom," she whispered, as she pulled the curtains tighter.

"Close the door, case the kids come in."

The evening wore on, and in that little parlour in Conner Street two bodies joined together to forget the carnage and destruction for a few precious moments.

The news of the bombing reached the Davis brothers as they sat in their billet in an army camp in Cambridge. They cursed the Germans and feared for their old father who was now living alone. The ginger-haired Davis boy put down his army boot and cleaning brush, and spoke to his younger brother, "I'm worried over the ole man, Fred. They didn't say 'ow bad the damage was, only mentioned the bleedin' docks."

"'E'll be okay," his brother said reassuringly. "Our street's a couple 'o miles from the Surrey."

"S'pose you're right," Ginger said. "Trouble is, yer feel so 'elpless stuck in this bleedin' God-forsaken 'ole."

"D'yer fink ole four-eyes'll give us a pass ter get 'ome?" Freddie said.

"No chance," replied his brother. "Mister Second-left-bleedin'-tenant wot's 'is name ain't got no 'eart. We've got about as much chance of gettin' a leave pass orf of 'im as gettin' a pork chop out of a synagogue."

"Well I'm goin' over the canteen, want any fags?" asked Freddie.

"Yeah, can yer get me five Woodbine?" Ginger replied.

Ginger lay full stretch on his camp bed and stared up at the ceiling. Above, on the dusty beams, a small spider hung from a delicate strand of web. The sound of snoring came from the corner of the hut, farthest away from the door. The only other occupant of the room was in the land of dreams and, from the happy expression on his face, Ginger guessed rightly that the soldier was back home doing something much more suitable for a Saturday night. Ginger cursed and aimed his boot brush at the spider, who ran up the strand and disappeared into the dust on the beam. The brush travelled in an arc and landed on the sleeping soldier. He turned over, grunted and started to snore once more, his face now wearing a miserable expression. By an unhappy coincidence, the brush hit his back at the exact moment that the girl in his slumbers rejected him.

The billet was quiet except for the snoring. Most of the men were either in the canteen or in town. Ginger was due for guard duty the next morning, and there were brasses to polish and boots to shine. He felt depressed without any knowledge of his father's welfare, and helpless at being so far from Conner Street. Ginger paced the room; if he could slip out of camp without being challenged, he could maybe hitch a lift to London, and scrounge the fare back in time for the guard mounting at 8 am. It may work, he thought. He would have to be quick. If he couldn't make it back in time and Freddie was with him, then they would both be in trouble. It would also be easier to hitch a lift if he were alone. His mind was made up. There was no way he would be able to dissuade his younger brother from accompanying him. So he had to leave before Freddie got back from the canteen. Grabbing his small pack and gas mask, Ginger slipped out of the billet and sauntered down to the main gate. He held his breath as he reached the guard post. If he was asked for his pass he would have to make some excuse and hope for the best. As it happened there was a truck waiting to enter and the duty sergeant was deep in conversation with the driver. Ginger walked past casually and got a nod from the soldier on guard. It was easy, he reflected as he walked swiftly up to the main London road. Twenty minutes later, he was sitting in a meat lorry that rattled on toward London.

The driver was a man in his fifties, a Londoner whose

firm was based at Kings Cross. He whistled tunelessly as he crashed through the gears and wrestled with the large steering wheel. Ginger sat back and stared at the ribbon of dark road. The beam from the screened headlights gave only a limited view ahead, and Ginger marvelled at the driver's ability to travel at such a speed.

"Slippin' 'ome fer a weekend then, son?" asked the man.

"Yeah, mate," replied Ginger. "I'm gonna see me ole man, 'e lives near the Surrey Docks."

"Whereabouts?" asked the driver.

"Conner Street, orf the Tower Road," answered Ginger, taking a drag on a cigarette that the man had given him.

"'E should be okay," said the man reassuringly. "The bombin' was round the dock area, 'cording ter the news. 'Eard it when I stopped fer a cuppa. So I wouldn't reckon that Conner Street got touched."

"Gawd I 'ope not," said Ginger. "Me ole man's bin on 'is own since me an' me bruvver got called up."

"Ain't yer got no muvver then?" asked the friendly driver.

"Died when I was a kid," replied Ginger. "Me young bruvver don't even remember 'er."

"Christ, that's 'ard luck," sympathised the driver. "Ne'mind, son, the ole man'll be all right, mark my words."

The two men lapsed into silence, and Ginger started to doze off. He was awakened by a jolt and found that the lorry had stopped.

"Time ter get orf, son," said the driver.

"Fanks, mate, all the best."

"That's all right, 'ope yer find the ole man 'ale an' 'arty."

The driver turned his lorry into the depot gates and Ginger felt in his pockets. He just about had the bus fare from Kings Cross to Bermondsey. It wouldn't be long now, he'd be home soon. Better get across the road to the bus stop. Hope I don't have to wait long, he mused.

He started to move away from his position near the

railway station entrance when he spotted two military policemen walking out of the forecourt. They strolled along in his direction, their boots sounding loudly on the cobbles. Ginger held his breath and started to walk across the wide road.

"Just a minute, soldier," one of the men called out to him.

Ginger didn't wait to find out what they wanted. He took to his heels and darted over the road and into a dim side street. The two policemen followed hard on his heels.

Ginger felt his breath coming in gasps as he tried to put space between them. It was no good, they were gaining on him. He turned into a dark alleyway and realised his mistake. It was a dead end! He turned and crashed into one of his pursuers. The military policeman hit the ground with a thud and Ginger ran off, the other man following closely behind him. Ginger gained a few yards and darted into another side street. He spotted a dark doorway and jumped into the recess. It was now or never, he thought as the policeman turned into the street. Ginger stepped out into the man's path and aimed a blow at him. His lashing arm caught the pursuer between the eyes, and the man's headlong running magnified the force of the blow. He went down hard, completely stunned.

Ginger took off along the darkened street, not daring to look back. The street led out into the Kings Cross Road, and Ginger noticed a bus some distance away, moving in his direction. He ran the few yards to the bus-stop and leaped on board before it had even stopped.

"Bit of an 'urry, son, ain't we?" the conductor asked him.

Ginger grinned sheepishly at the man and glanced out of the rear window of the bus. There was no sign of the two military policemen. Ginger ran up the stairs and sat down gratefully on the nearest seat, his heart still pumping furiously.

As the bus crossed the Blackfriars Bridge, Ginger Davis looked along the river eastwards. The night sky was red with the fires that were still raging at the Surrey Docks. The bend of the Thames made the glow seem as though it were emanating from way inland. Ginger knew the river well. The twisting, turning lifeline of the metropolis ran very near to his part of town. He loved the smell of it, the mud, the fresh fruit, as cranes hoisted the boxes on to the quayside. He loved the tang of the air and the empty coconut-carrying barges that he used to climb into so that he could gather the broken husks that lay on the deck. He remembered his boyhood; slipping past the dockers and stevedores as they toiled on the incoming cargoes. He would sit on the quayside watching the big ships spewing forth their wares, from the Orient, from Cape Town and northern ports, as slings of yellow timber emerged from the depths of the holds. Ginger gritted his teeth as he realised that much of the area he loved was now disappearing in the inferno. He looked away from the east, tears welling up, and he heard the wail. It rose above the sound of the bus engine. The scream increased until the slumbering pigeons awoke and flew away from the rooftops. It sent a shiver of fear through the young soldier.

The bastards had come back.

Chapter Fifteen

The air raid siren had hardly stopped before a salvo of gunfire from the factory and park emplacements vibrated through the twin caverns of the Conner Street shelter. People were still spilling into its evil-smelling interior, cursing and crying out against the alien air fleet above. They glanced up fearfully as searchlights pencilled the sky in white, converging to criss-cross and hold the odd invader in the glare. Guns were trained on the mechanical moth and shells flew upwards. The local guns in the Southwark Park and on the jam factory roof opened up and the sound rattled the shelter doors and hurt the eardrums. The exploding shells puffed around the aircraft, like little balls of cotton wool. Jagged shrapnel fell to earth, still glowing red as it fell in pieces to lie on the pavements.

As the air armada reached their overhead position above dockland, they unleashed their deadly cargoes. Bombs fell to earth, whistling down as the air rushed the tailfins. Heavier high-explosive bombs fell with a juddering sound, like the ire of some unimaginable fiend who shuffled sheets of corrugated iron. The bombs fell down river at first, then more locally. Explosions rocked the shelter and seemed to lift it off its foundations. Bombs fell through roofs and tore buildings apart in one almighty flash; the blasts lifted chimneypots and threw them streets away; explosions tore up huge chunks of roadway, then spat out mangled metal into the craters. One bomb blew up a small home and snatched up a policeman sheltering in a doorway, dropping him on a rooftop many yards away. The man was dead, and still completely unmarked.

In the shelter, the terrified Conner Street folk prayed to their particular gods with some token sign; the clasping of hands, the twiddling of rosary beads, shaking gestures resembling the sign of the cross. The people sat huddled together for comfort, and one old woman dozed off to sleep.

"Gawd a'mighty! 'Ow the bleedin' 'ell can she sleep?" someone cried out.

"She's stone bleedin' deaf, that's why," cried another.

"Gawd in 'eaven, I wish I was deaf right now," cried Lizzie Brown.

The raiders flew on, choosing new targets. They aimed for the railways, the wharves up river, and large buildings, all choicely illuminated by the still burning Surrey Docks. Guns fired at the aircraft, and bombs continued to fall. Stockpiles of shells became low at the gunsites as the gun barrels got white hot. Crews swivelled their weapons round in an arc to face a new flight of bombers that appeared down river. In the park a bomb fell through the bandstand roof, hit the floor and rolled down the few steps on to the dry, yellow grass. It lay there grey and daunting, and was seen by the gunnery sergeant some distance away. He calmly walked towards it and then dragged it by the tailfin away from his men. As he started back, a bomb landed on his gun emplacement, enveloping the site in flame. When the sergeant picked himself up he was aware of hot blood trickling on to his chin. Of his crew, there was no sign.

The gunfire flashes lit up the deserted Conner Street and illuminated the way for a crouching figure who ran, head held down in a futile gesture of self-preservation. He stopped at number 14 and banged on the door. There was no answer. The figure cursed, then saw that the doorstring had been left out. He pulled on it and entered.

"Well I'll be striped!" gasped the old man inside. "It's me boy, Ginger, ain't it?"

"Well it ain't the bloody tallyman, Dad," the soldier laughed.

"Wot yer doin' 'ome?" Jack Davis asked.

Ignoring the question, Ginger looked closely at the

hunched figure of his father who sat in a chair by the empty grate. "Why ain't yer in the shelter?" he asked.

"If yer fink I'm gonna sit down that bleedin' deaf trap wiv all them women, listenin' ter Lizzie Brown an' 'er cronies, well yer got anuvver fink comin'."

"But, Dad, the bleedin' bombs a' fallin' like rain. Yer can't sit 'ere."

"Oh can't I? You jus' watch me. Listen, son. Yer muvver died in that room upstairs, an' if I'm ter go 'ere, wot's okay fer yer muvver is okay by me."

"But, Dad," implored Ginger.

"There's no buts, so don't stan' there lookin' all mean an' 'orrible, go 'n put the kettle on."

Ginger did as his father bid and noticed that the gas jet was very low. "Kettle'll take a while, Dad, the bastards must 'ave caught a main," he shouted.

"Can't 'ear a word yer sayin', wot wiv the noise. 'Ow long's the kettle gonna take?" asked the old man.

Suddenly there was a rumbling explosion and the house shook.

"Gawd above they must 'ave 'it the gas works," the old man croaked.

Ginger came running into the parlour, and stood by his father.

"T'ain't the gas works, the gas jet's still alight," Ginger said.

"I 'eard a sound o' glass, I bet the upstairs winders 'ave all broke. There'll be glass all over me bleedin' bed now," his father moaned. "I told you an' that bruvver of yours ter tape 'em up."

Ginger ran upstairs to the tiny front bedroom. The whole of the window frame lay across the old man's bed. There was glass everywhere.

Ginger ran down to his father, who was pouring the boiling water into a teapot. "It's a right old mess up there, but don't worry, I'll clear it all up in a minute," he said reassuringly.

"It's a good job we've got those shutters on the down-stairs winders," Jack said. "I'd 'ave 'ad the 'ole bleedin' street lookin' in."

Father and son sat sipping the steaming tea. The sounds of the bombing now seemed farther away. The local guns still kept up the bombardment, and every now and then the house rattled.

"'Ere, I never asked yer, wot yer doin' 'ome, anyway?"

"Got a weekend pass, Dad," lied the soldier.

"I 'ope yer ain't deserted. They shot deserters in my time," croaked the old man.

"Course I ain't deserted. I told yer, I got leave."

"By the way, 'ow's young Freddie doin'? 'Ope yer takin' care of 'im? Always a little mite wild was our Freddie."

"Fred's okay, Dad," replied Ginger.

"Why couldn't 'e get a weekend pass?" asked Jack suspiciously.

"Cos 'e's on guard," said Ginger, looking away.

"I remember when I was courtin' yer muvver. Went over the wall ter see 'er. There was this colour-sergeant. Tricky bit o' goods 'e was. Anyway, I ups an' belts 'im, I did. Put one on 'is chin. I see yer mum fer a few 'ours, but they got me. Twenty-eight days in the glasshouse I got. If it 'ad bin wartime, I'd a bin shot."

The guns kept up their pounding as the raiders tired of their game and turned for home. Behind them they left a wake of destruction. Homes were destroyed. Wharves and factories were burning. The Thames was alight from the spilling oil. Firemen battled desperately as water mains burst, and their hoses ran dry. The carnage was widespread throughout London. Fire tenders rushed along debris-strewn streets and quickly turned away as their path was blocked. Gas mains flared, and water shot upwards in fierce jets from fractured pipes. Buildings burned and homes lay in ruins, with rescuers delving into the piles of rubble. They often stopped their digging and were silent, listening for the sound of a voice that would tell them there was someone alive beneath the ruins.

A merciful dawn broke, and light lifted over the chimneys. With the dawn came the even wail of the all-clear, and the folk of Conner Street emerged from their place of refuge. Ada Dawkins wore the beginnings of a black eye.

It had happened some time during the height of the bombing, and as the idiot's landlady and protector walked up the slope of the shelter to the street she felt stiff. Her hair was hanging down, and there were scratches on one side of her face. Beside her, the shuffling figure of Bobbie looked diminutive as they made their way to number 4. It was not all due to the cramped night inside the shelter. Ada had become involved in a fracas.

Earlier that night Bobbie had been sitting beside Ada, and facing them were the Flannagans. Bridie held the baby tightly and little Terry slept, his head resting on her lap. Maureen had her arms around the twins and Patrick junior sat beside them. Bobbie was getting fidgety. He wanted to be back in his cosy room away from the noise that frightened him. When the guns sounded and the bombs exploded, the idiot felt sick. His ears were paining him and his back was aching from sitting so long in one position. He wanted the noise to end. When the bombs stopped he would be able to get his box out and look at his treasures. He shifted his position and felt the one treasure he had carried with him to the shelter. It was a marble, green in colour, with a milky streak running through the centre. Bobbie took the marble from his pocket and held it in the palm of his hand. Across the space between the benches, Patrick junior watched the idiot's actions. When Bobbie looked up, Patrick poked his tongue out and Bobbie replied, his own tongue rolling round his chin. A stream of saliva ran down onto the idiot's coat-front and Patrick abruptly burst out laughing.

Ada looked round and nudged the idiot. "Keep still, Bobbie," she said irritably, kocking the marble from the idiot's palm as she prodded him.

Bobbie watched horrified as the glass marble rolled down the aisle and disappeared under the bench where Granny Flint slept. Bobbie gasped. He couldn't bear to lose his best marble, and he decided to fetch it before forgetting where it had gone to. He shuffled down the aisle, ignoring Ada's plea for him to come back. Bobbie went down on all fours and felt under the bench. His fingers touched the marble, but he only sent it farther along under the bench. Impatiently he grasped the old lady's ankle to move it out of the way. Granny Flint awoke with a start and saw the dribbling idiot kneeling at her feet. She let out a piercing scream and Bobbie jumped back.

"Get 'im away," Granny Flint shouted.

"Bobbie Wilkins grabbed Granny Flint," someone said.

"What's goin' on?" asked another.

"Bobbie Wilkins attacked the old lady," someone else shouted.

"The idiot tried ter rape old Granny Flint," the first one said to the woman sitting next to her.

The fat figure of Dolly Mason stormed up and slapped the idiot hard around the face. Bobbie reeled back, his eyes watering.

Ada jumped up and tore into the fat woman, grabbing her hair as she lunged. The two staggered back and fell in a heap between the benches, tearing and scratching at each other. They were finally pulled apart, with Ada sobbing in her anger.

Bobbie, meanwhile, had retreated to his place on the bench, his face scarlet from the slap.

Patrick Flannagan began to cry, upset at the idiot's sad expression, and Bridie held the boy against her. "It's all right, darlin', it's all right," she said quietly.

"Poor Bobbie," sobbed the boy. "That 'orrible lady 'it poor Bobbie."

The noise of the incident carried outside, and brought Bob Bowman in. "What the bloody 'ell's goin' on in 'ere? I could 'ear you lot above that bleedin' mob," he shouted, pointing with his thumb to the roof.

"She 'ad no right ter bash my Bobbie, 'e was only tryin' ter get 'is marble," Ada sobbed. "If she comes near him again I'll do fer 'er, so 'elp me I will."

Bob Bowman turned to the idiot. "Where's yer marble, son?"

"Dere, over where lady sleepin'. Bobbie only get 'is marble."

"Okay, son, I'll 'ave a look."

The warden felt under the bench and fished out the cause of the trouble. He handed it to Bobbie, who quickly put it back into his pocket.

Later, as the Conner Street folk emerged, they smelt cordite fumes, and smoke from the nearby fires. A smell of gas also hung in the chill morning air, and the folk shivered. They were relieved to see that their Street had remained intact. Most of the little homes had wooden window shutters that had been closed tightly. The upstairs windows were, in most cases, taped against blast, and they were still intact. A few untaped windows had been smashed, and here and there a roof tile lay in the street. Half of a red chimneypot lay outside Bridie's house. Beside it was a jagged piece of shrapnel. Almost stately above the minor debris, the Street had survived.

The Sabbath morning was like no other as the early morning sun climbed up over the chimneypots. The rays shone blood red through the filter of smoke that hung in the sky, and lingered heatless and troubled. The sun climbed higher and became hotter as it lifted over the wall of smoke. The Street remained almost empty. For the most part, the inhabitants were catching up on their sleep. They tried to get the cramped, stiff feeling out of their bones and sighed with pleasure to realise they were still alive. It was a miracle that no bomb had fallen in the Street. From the flames and smoke, they knew how lucky they had been.

In the Davis's house Ginger was sipping a cup of tea. "I'll 'ave ter get back soon, Dad. They 'ave a roll call early mornin's an' I'm gonna be missed."

"I knew it," the old man said. "I knew yer bunked 'ome. Gawd, son, wot yer go an' do a fing like that fer, don't you fink yer ole dad can look after 'imself?"

"I was jus' worried, Dad. We 'eard all about the first bombin' on the wireless in the canteen."

"Yer better 'ave a bite o' breakfast an' get on yer way back. If the bleedin' red-caps come round 'ere snoopin' they'll get me boot up their backsides, you mark me words."

Ginger grinned and placed his arm around his father's bony shoulders. "I'll fry a rasher an' put it between a couple o' slices then I'll be orf."

"'Ow yer gettin' back?" asked Jack.

"Don't yer fret," replied Ginger. "I'll get a 63 bus ter Kings Cross an' see the RTO. Tell 'em I've lost me travel warrant. I'll get back all right."

The soldier slipped a couple of slices of streaky bacon into a frying pan and while it was sizzling he cut two thick slices of bread. He spread a dollop of butter across the bread and, when the bacon was starting to blacken, he made the sandwich.

"I knew yer bunked 'ome when I see yer bruvver wasn't wiv yer. You look after 'im, Ginge. Freddie's not as steady as you."

"Yeah I know, Dad, that's why I didn't let 'im know I was comin' ter see yer."

"Is there any news of where yer bein' posted to?" the old man asked.

"Gawd knows," replied Ginger. "Could be anywhere. I wouldn't mind Buckin'am Palace," he joked. "I could get 'ome every night then."

The sun had risen overhead as Ginger stood at his front door. "Now don't ferget, Dad, if it gets bad, get down the shelter, d'yer 'ear me?"

"Okay, boy, I will. Might even sit next ter old Lizzie. I used ter fancy 'er a few years back, though it was 'er tongue put me orf. Proper ole gas-bag. Mind yer though, a few o' these would soon tame 'er," he joked, raising his hand in a threatening manner.

Ginger grinned and walked a few yards before his father beckoned him back. "'Ere, I almost fergot, put this in yer bin, I got a bit put by."

Ginger started to protest at the proffered ten-shilling note.

"Don't argue, put it away in yer pocket," his father insisted.

"Fanks, Dad, I'll pay yer back."

The slight, hunched figure of Jack Davis watched his son reach the elbow of Conner Street and turn back to wave before he disappeared from sight. The old man closed his door and walked into his parlour. "Sod the rent, they'll 'ave ter whistle fer it," he said with conviction.

As midday approached, the smell of cooking drifted out onto the Street. A few children appeared and played close to their own front doors. They were under strict orders not to stray far. They played five-stones, and drew hopscotch lines on the pavement. They stopped at the sight of the police car that drove into Conner Street. They gathered around as the man next to the driver got out and hammered on the door of number 14. Two red-capped army men sat impassively in the back seat of the car. The policeman hammered again and Jack Davis's voice barked out from within, "All right, all right I'm comin', can't yer wait a minute?"

The door opened and Jack Davis confronted the policeman. "Wot yer want?" he asked in an aggressive tone.

"We want to have a word with Private Ronald Davis. He was reported 'absent without leave'."

As he spoke to the old man, his two companions got out of the car and walked up to the door.

"Yer can't come in 'ere. I don't allow any ole Tom, Dick or 'Arry in my 'ouse," protested Ginger's father.

"I've got a warrant, Dad. You can't stop us, and I warn you, if you try, I'll take you down the station. Now c'mon, stand aside."

The old man muttered as the three men went into his home. "Bleedin' comin' in ter peoples' 'omes. Kick up the jacksey, that's what they need."

The men ignored Jack Davis's muttered threats and searched the house.

Finally they emerged and drove away.

As the Conner Street folk prepared their Sunday midday meal they listened to the wireless broadcasts. The news was bad. There had been widespread damage with many lives lost. Fires were still burning, although the Surrey fires were now under control. A lot of the backstreets near to the docks were destroyed and thousands of people had been made homeless. The broadcasters issued repeated warnings, urging families to allow their children to be evacuated and to take precautions against bomb blasts. Instructions were issued advising that windows should be taped, pails of water made ready to fight fires, and gas masks placed in a handy position. People were also requested to board up windows and make some of their rooms blast-proof. All the news was depressing that bright Sunday noon.

Conner Street's warden had been very busy during the past week. There were food supply ships sitting in the Pool, and their vital cargoes had to be discharged as quickly as possible. The docks and wharves were a prime target for the German Air Force, and the river men were working at a tremendous pace to get the berths vacant for incoming vessels. Bob Bowman had his own special responsibilities as warden for Conner Street. There was the shelter to take care of. Sand and water buckets had to be kept filled. Kerosene lamps had to be primed and made ready for emergency use, and then there was the Street blackout. Twice every night Bob Bowman patrolled Conner Street to make sure that no light shone out from the houses. More and more the inhabitants came to rely on their good-natured warden. Bob was asked about how to get sandbags, how to board up windows, and once he was asked how "'er tom cat could be dissuaded from pissing in my back yard." Nan Roberts also required Bob's services. She called him in one night to have a look at her leaking tap. Miraculously, the tap had stopped of its own accord by the time Bob arrived. Nan Roberts offered the warden a drink and Bob was tempted. But after rubbing his hand over his stubbled chin he politely declined her offer. Bob didn't want to get too comfortable, and he didn't want Grace to hear about his nocturnal visit to the Street's own siren.

As the sun climbed up over the chimneys and its rays pierced the parlour window they shone on the resting warden. Bob's eyes were closed, his mouth hung open, and his long legs stretched across the small room. Grace came in quietly and was obliged to step over his legs to get the box of Swan Vestas from the mantleshelf. She was worried about her husband. Already he was beginning to show signs of exhaustion. His thin features were white and drawn. Grace realised also that last night was only the start of a terrifying time, and she went quietly out of the parlour.

Although the Conner Street folk were still suffering from the experience of the previous night, their cockney humour won through.

"I told me ole woman ter get down those stairs fast. Know what she said? 'I'm lookin' fer me clean drawers.' I told 'er, the bastards 'ave come ter bomb yer, not rape yer. Sod yer drawers I told 'er."

"My ole dutch went ter church," someone else piped up. "Jus' got back she 'as. When the vicar said 'Let us all pray', she shouted out, 'Wot yer fink we've bin doin' all night?'."

"I 'eard one o' the German planes got shot down," related yet another. "Anyway, the pilot baled out. Sailin' down all peaceful like, when 'e sees ole Lizzie Brown beneath 'im. 'Oldin' a carvin' knife she was. Couldn't face 'er. Turned round an' went back 'e did."

"Did yer 'ear about that fight in the shelter last night?" asked another man as he strolled up to the 'Eagle'.

"No," replied his drinking partner. "Wot was it all about?"

"Well, I 'eard silly Bobbie Wilkins took a shine ter that ole biddy Flint. Gits up, an' away 'e goes over ter see 'er, so I 'eard. The ole gal's out like a light. Snorin' 'er bleedin' 'ead orf. Well, young Bobbie strokes 'er leg. Up she sits an' screams out, 'Don't stop!' Everyone gits the wrong impression. They all fink she's sayin' 'Don't! Stop!' Gawd, she should be so lucky. Must be ages since anyone's stroked 'er leg."

The storyteller's companion laughed. "I reckon she didn't mind 'im strokin' 'er leg, it was 'im dribblin' all over 'er feet she didn't go a bundle on."

Chapter Sixteen

Early on that Sunday morning, John and Florrie Braden came up from their place of refuge in the cramped cellar of their pub. They looked around and saw the bar was a complete shambles, with glass and debris everywhere. All the windows facing the Tower Road were smashed and the frames hanging out. A strong smell of alcohol came from behind the bar, and the large, flower-etched mirror on the wall behind the counter had a crack running the length of it.

"Gawd," moaned John, "seven years' bad luck."

Florrie gave him a disdainful look. "Sure it's only seven years?"

From their shattered bar, the Bradens could see the origin of the blast damage. Along the Tower Road, on the other side of that debris-strewn thoroughfare, they could see the bombed shop of the late Alberto Vitelli. Where not so long ago the Vitellis had served their customers with cheerful smiles, there was now a pile of smoking rubble. The shops on either side had miraculously escaped destruction, though their shutters had been blown right off.

Florrie dabbed at her eyes as she stared at the ruins. "It's terrible. Just terrible," she cried. "Look at that wood sticking out on top of that heap."

John Braden's eyes were bleary and he squinted in an effort to follow the direction of Florrie's pointing finger.

"There's a lump of wood sticking out in the shape of a cross. It makes me go cold looking at it. It's like a memorial," she said.

"Makes you wonder," John Braden said. "First bomb in the street and it lands on one of their own."

"Alberto wasn't one of them, nor was Maria. They were as much English as you or I. Alberto was beginning to talk like a cockney," Florrie sobbed.

John Braden went to a small space behind the bar and emerged holding an unbroken bottle of brandy. His face was glowing. "Here's one they never got," he grinned.

"Don't stand there grinning like an idiot, pour us a drink," Florrie demanded.

The two sat among the dust and broken glass sipping their drinks. The sun was beginning to rise up in the sky and early morning rays shone on the bar, faintly lighting up the dust that lay on its beams.

"Heaven knows how we're going to get this lot cleared up by opening time," wailed John as he put his glass of brandy to his lips with a shaking hand.

"Well, we're going to have a good try, that's for sure," asserted Florrie.

John Braden blinked his bleary eyes and sighed. The previous night he had taken his last spare bottle of whisky into the cellar, and during the terrible bombardment had drunk the entire contents. Florrie had taken her small brandy flask with her, and she too had taken a tot or two, her mind concentrating on her warm, intimate bedroom, and a certain big man who had once shared that room with her.

"Come on then, John. Let's make a start," said the woman, getting up and fetching the broom.

As the couple set about the task of removing the broken glass from the bar, a voice called out, "Are you two all right in there?" The figure of Patrick Flannagan stood framed in the place where there had once been a window.

"Come on in, Pat, and mind yourself, there's glass everywhere," warned Florrie.

"Holy Mary! What a mess," Patrick remarked.

"Sit yourself down and have a drink," invited John, waving his hand at the bottle on a dusty table.

"Look at it all," moaned Florrie. "We'll never get cleared up in time for twelve."

Patrick poured himself a large tot of brandy and

surveyed the damage. He looked up at the windowless gaps which let in the insipid light, then gulped up his drink. "I'll not be long," he announced, and was gone.

Florrie glanced at her husband and shrugged her shoulders.

As the two toiled away they heard the sound of wheels on the cobblestones outside, and the voice of Hoppy Dyke, "Push the bloody fing then, Wheezy, lost yer strength?"

"Wot yer fink I am, a bleedin' 'orse?" moaned Wheezy.

The Bradens looked out and saw a barrow parked in the kerb. It was laden with planks of wood, and they saw the puffing figure of Wheezy Morris leaning on the load, mopping his brow. Hoppy was already sizing up the frames. "Don't worry, folks, me an' my mate'll 'ave yer winders boarded up in no time."

The Bradens dared not ask where the makeshift workmen got their timber, but John whispered to his wife, "I bet the bleeders pulled a fence down somewhere."

"I'm not worried where the wood came from, so long as we can open come twelve," said Florrie quickly.

Albert Conlin left his lodgings and walked up Conner Street. He saw the work going on and he offered his help. Hoppy Dyke grabbed a saw and handed it to Albert. "'Ere, Al, you do the sawin'." He pointed to Wheezy. "'E can't do anyfing straight, not even a saw-cut."

"If you was ter take yer bleedin' coat orf an' do a bit o' work 'stead o' jus' measurin' we'd get a bit more done," Wheezy moaned.

"It's no good you goin' on," Hoppy said with a grin. "Some of us was born ter work, an' some ter supervise. It's the way of the world, me son."

Wheezy carted a plank of wood to the window frame and started to nail it in place. Patrick Flannagan came along and spoke to Hoppy. "It's okay. The watchman said we can have more, as long as he gets his drink later."

"Right y'are, Pat. I'll tell the Bradens it'll cost 'em drinks all round, 'ow's that sound?"

"Good lad," said Patrick. "Now I'm away to get meself ready. I've still got the stacking to do, to be sure."

Hoppy waved as the Irishman sauntered down Conner Street, then he found a piece of board and wrote the words, 'Business as usual'. When he had hammered the board to the door of the 'Eagle', he called his workmen together.

"Now listen, men," he said in a whisper. "Ole Percy only wants a drink fer this lot o' wood. We'll tell the Bradens it came ter firty bob, okay?"

Wheezy rubbed his hands together and Albert Conlin just grinned. "Okay then, chaps, let's get a drink."

The announcement of 'Business as usual' was not strictly true, for there was one character conspicuous by his absence. Dinky Richards did not make an appearance at the lunch time session. The battered old piano stayed silent and was used in its secondary capacity as a stand for pints of ale. It also served as a place to lean against when the beer started to take effect. The blind piano player was not forgotten however, and he was toasted in his absence. The 'Eagle' clientele hoped that Dinky would show up for the usual sing-song that evening.

Dinky Richards had every intention of getting to the 'Eagle' as usual that Sunday lunch time. He left at his usual time and made good progress from his home in Spencer Street. Dinky used his stick as usual to feel his way along, but today he suddenly felt an obstruction in front of him. He could tell that the pavement was blocked. There was no option but to go round it. He stepped out into the road and immediately fell headlong into a crater. Luckily his fall was broken by the soft earth and a pool of filthy, muddy water. Dinky spluttered as he found his feet and the water stung cold as he wiped the mud from his face. Although soaked through, he was unhurt, apart from a few sore places. Standing up to his waist in the pool, he cursed. He cursed the German airforce, the cold water, and the whole filthy war. Dinky did not curse his blindness. For him it was a condition he'd lived with since birth. He knew the area and found it easy to get around. At certain times, when he waited at the kerbside for assistance to cross the road, there was always a hand that touched his arm, and a few kind words as someone helped him across to the other side. On this particular morning, however, there was no one about, and Dinky realised that he could quite well remain in his present position all day if he didn't do something about it.

Police Constable Smith strolled along the debris-strewn backstreets until he came upon a hoarding that had been blown down by the blast. It lay across the whole of the pavement, and PC Smith put his hands on his hips and considered the situation. As he stood there he heard a voice call out. It cried for help, and the custodian of the law bent down and tried to lift the hoarding. He managed to move it up slightly, but it was too heavy for him. As he let it go that faint cry for help was repeated. "Christ, there's someone underneath," he said aloud to himself. "Don't move, I'll 'ave yer out in no time," PC Smith called out.

"'Urry up, I'm gettin' cold," the voice shouted out.

PC Smith knelt down and tried to see beneath the hoarding. "Are you 'urt?" he shouted.

"Don't fink so, jus' soakin' bleedin' wet an' bleedin' cold," replied the faint voice.

PC Smith scratched his head. The morning was warm and there was no sign of water beneath the hoarding.

"'Ow comes you're wet?" he asked.

"Gawd a'mighty, wouldn't you be wet, up ter yer waist in water?" said the now frantic voice.

PC Smith turned round and looked at the crater.

"Of all the people round 'ere, the first one on the scene's a bloody idiot," wailed Dinky. "Over 'ere, sod yer! Over 'ere!"

The long arm of the law finally reached into the crater and hauled Dinky out, setting him down on top of the hoarding. He was then taken to the hospital, where he was given a bath, a change of clothes and, to the delight of Dinky, a promise to get him to the 'Eagle' in time for the evening session.

One of the shops that adjoined the destroyed green-grocery was the provision store belonging to Stanley Nathan. He had been informed that his shop had been damaged and was already at the scene, working to replace the broken shutters. Julie Brett joined him later, and the two began to replace the tins and packages that were strewn over the floor. They worked hard right through the morning and by lunchtime the task had been finished. The shutters were secured and the shelves tidied and restacked. Stanley fitted a new padlock and winked at Julie. It would be 'Business as usual' for the Nathan store as well.

In the 'Eagle' trade was brisk. Tired, shocked men stood quietly talking of the night's bombing, and their normal quick humour was tempered with anguish. The usual faces were there: market people, folk from Conner Street and the few regulars from neighbouring streets. There were always one or two strange faces that popped in, and normally they merely got an inquiring glance, but the stranger who walked into the 'Eagle' that Sabbath mid-morning received slightly more than a casual look.

He was tall, with thick, greying hair that was brushed back carefully. His face was wide, with a few lines around the corners of his pale blue eyes. The man carried himself with confidence, his walk was almost a swagger. The suit he wore was expensive, and the shirt was obviously silk. He walked up to the bar and ordered a beer.

"I can see you've received some damage," he remarked in a cultured voice.

John Braden handed the man a pint of ale and nodded. "Wasn't too bad, mainly glass. The windows," he said, pointing to the planks at the window frames.

The man glanced around the bar as he sipped his drink. Hoppy Dyke studied the man and whispered to Wheezy Morris, "Mind wot yer say, that feller there's a tec."

"Is that wot 'e is? Looks more like a pox-doctor's clerk if yer ask me. Look at the gear 'e's wearin'."

Sammy Israel was enjoying his leave from the Rifle Brigade and was determined to get drunk before he returned to his camp the next day. He had seen the stranger walk in and he sidled up to Hoppy and Wheezy.

"That's a nice bit o' 'schmatter' 'e's wearin'," Sammy

said, nodding in the man's direction.

"I tell yer 'e's a dick. Look 'ow 'e keeps clockin' everybody. Lookin' fer you, Wheezy, I bet," grinned Hoppy.

"I ain't touched a bit o' stolen since Gawd knows when. Strickly straight I am," Wheezy said, hooking his thumbs through his waistcoat.

Florrie Braden was busy at the other end of the bar and did not immediately spot the stranger. When her husband had finished serving him, she turned and started sharply. For a second she stared as though not sure. The man had aged somewhat, but it was definitely him.

She called John over. "Didn't you recognise him?" she asked.

"Recognise who?"

"The stranger you just served."

John looked over at the man, trying to focus his red-rimmed eyes.

"It's Alan Denman. What's he doing round here? As if I didn't know," said Florrie with concern.

At that moment, the door opened and Stanley Nathan walked in with Julie Brett. He ushered her into a corner where there was a vacant seat and then went up to the bar to order his drinks.

While he waited to get served, Julie fumbled in her handbag and took out a mirror which she studied, touching her hair with the palm of her hand. Julie did not relish the thought of going into what she considered a man's domain on Sunday at lunch time. But Stanley had persuaded her, saying that they had both earned a drink. She felt uneasy and looked around to see how many other women were there. She could only see two. One old lady sat near her, who had a drink in front of her and was staring down at her clasped hands. Julie saw the troubled look in the old lady's eyes as she twiddled her thumbs endlessly. The other woman sat near the door. She was heavily made up, with blobs of rouge on her cheeks. She was joking with the market men, prodding at one of them as she spoke. Julie cast her eyes in the direction of Stanley who was just getting served.

Two men on Stanley's far side took their drinks and walked away from the bar, affording Julie a sight of the tall stranger. The first sight of him hit her like a hammer. Her body started to tremble, and her breath came fast. It was him! He looked much older, and his hair was now streaked with grey, but he was still very much the same as when he had first walked into her life. What was he doing here after all this time? Julie wondered. The dread of meeting someone from her days on the streets was one thing that was often in her thoughts, but this was totally unexpected. She never dreamed she would meet Alan again.

The shock hit her hard, and when Stanley returned to her table with the drinks he noticed that something was wrong.

"Julie, you're as white as a sheet, is there anything wrong?" he asked with concern.

"I'm okay, Stan," Julie replied, trying to gain control of herself.

Stanley took her hand and said, "I'm sorry, love, I must have worked you too hard."

"Of course you didn't. I'm just feeling a bit shaken after last night."

Stanley patted her hand. "Now I want you to listen to what I've got to say. There's plenty of room at my house. It's far enough away to be a lot safer than living round here. When we've finished our drinks I want you to go to your digs and pack. We can get to my place before it's dark."

Julie shook her head. "I can't move just like that, Stan. It was very good of the Morgans to let me have their son's room. I can't just leave them, not after getting on with them so well."

Stanley's face looked a picture of disappointment, and Julie squeezed his hand. "It's not that I don't thank you for offering, and I know you'd be the gentleman, but I just can't leave them, not just now. When I first went there, the Morgans were still trying to cope with their boy's death. I felt like an intruder. There were times when I bundled in on Mrs Morgan and saw her sobbing over

170

her son's photo. Slowly I managed to ease her grief by talking to her. She still sits in her little room with that photo nearby, and we talk about her son. She says it helps to ease the pain. They treat me like a daughter, Stan. I just can't leave her, not yet anyway."

Stanley sighed and gave her a grin. "Okay, Julie, I understand. It's just that I worry over you."

He picked up his drink and took a swig. Over his shoulder Julie saw the tall figure from her past put down his empty glass and turn to leave. As he did so their eyes met for an instant. The spark of recognition showed in his eyes before he looked away and walked to the door.

An hour later, Stanley and Julie left the bar and walked the short distance to the girl's lodgings. She held on to Stanley's arm, her troubled thoughts hid from him. He must never know. It was going well for both of them and Julie felt happy with the kind Stanley. He had taken her to his heart, and the knowledge of her past did not make any difference to him. Julie often wondered if he was pained by it. He never spoke, nor hinted. It seemed that he had denied the very existence of her dark past and never discussed it, and Julie was grateful.

The sun was high in the heavens as the two people stood by the Morgans' front door. Stanley kissed her gently on the lips and looked hard into her eyes. "Don't forget what I said. There's plenty of room, and there's a lock on the bedroom door."

Julie smiled. "Stanley, the way I feel right now you'd need one to keep me out."

The shopkeeper raised his eyebrows in mock reproof, and his assistant looked down at her shoes. "Stan, you don't mind if I stay in tonight, do you? I don't feel very well, I think I've got a chill coming."

Stanley Nathan squeezed her arm. "You get an early night. I'll see you tomorrow."

Julie kissed the man gently on the cheek and watched as he walked out of the Street. As she turned to enter her lodgings she saw Alan Denman. He sauntered along across the Street, walking away from her. He must have spotted her, and now he knew where she lived. Julie went inside quickly and ran up to her room. Her heart was pounding and she felt faint.

"Julie, is that you?" called out Mrs Morgan. "Dinner'll be in five minutes."

"I'll be down right away," the girl answered in a voice she hardly recognised.

Later that afternoon, Julie found herself sitting on her bed. The Sunday meal was over and she had helped Mrs Morgan with the washing up. The elderly couple were sitting in their parlour listening to the radio. Julie could hear the strains of *La Cumparsita* drifting up from below. The violins, stringing at the tango, evoked a feeling of melancholy within her heart and she threw herself down onto the bed. She laid her head on the cool pillow and thought about Alan Denman. Why did he suddenly appear out of her past? What was the significance? He would be aware that in presenting himself at the 'Eagle', Florrie would recognise him. He expected the news of his visit to be passed on.

Julie twisted fretfully on to her back and stared up at the flaking ceiling. He saw me at the door, she thought. Even if the visit was just a twist of fate, he now knew of her presence in the dockland area. If he intended to get in touch, he would only have to drop a letter through the door. Her breath was quick and shallow as she contemplated his move. She felt strangely frightened, a feeling that was mingled with excitement. The girl also experienced a feeling of guilt at the prospect of a letter. It was as though she were betraying the kindness of Stanley, but she could not shake off the feeling of expectancy. She closed her eyes and allowed her thoughts to drift back in time, then she turned and buried her face in the pillow as she sobbed softly.

When the 'Eagle' shut on that Sunday lunch time, three characters remained loitering outside. Hoppy Dyke leaned on the pub wall, as he found it easier to keep his feet that way. Wheezy Morris stood beside him, listening to the cripple's oration. Sammy Israel sat on the kerb, his army uniform unbuttoned and his beret and belt pushing through the lapel of his tunic. Sammy was on leave from the Rifle Brigade, and he was determined to get drunk at least once more before he turned his attention to bayonet practice. He held his head in his hands as he listened to Hoppy's scheme. It sounded all right, and what did it matter? In two days he would be back at Winchester, well away from any repercussions, and with a few shekels in his pocket.

"I tell yer, it's easy as taking a tanner from a blind man," Hoppy was saying. "I went up the alley last night to 'ave a look. The fencin' looks like it's ready ter fall down on its own. We can get in an' lever up the winder. There's a nice few quid's werf of 'ats in there. Top 'ats, bowlers, an' even wimmin's straw 'ats. Ole Solly Goldberg said 'e'll take the lot. Said 'e'll pay us right away. Come on, wha'd'ya fink?"

Sammy Israel looked up at Hoppy, disbelief showing on his face. "I've never known Solly Goldberg ter pay anybody right away. Good business man is Mr Goldberg. Even keeps me waitin' for the 'errin's I sell 'im, an' me one of 'is own."

"I tell yer 'e's promised ter pay up sharp," Hoppy insisted.

"Well I'm not so sure," went on Sammy. "I've known Solly fer years. 'E was at my Schmickling, an' that's ages ago."

"Gawd blimey, Sammy boy, can't yer speak the King's English," Wheezy complained. "Wot's 'Schmickling'?"

Hoppy Dyke laughed. "It's when the yiddishers get circumcised."

"Gawd 'elp us," moaned Wheezy. "You lot 'ave ter get an audience, even when yer gettin' the top o' yer dingle sliced orf."

"It's custom," said Sammy proudly. "We 'ave a party fer the child."

"Don't they frow all nuts an' raisins over yer as well?" asked Wheezy.

"Silly git, that's a Barmitzvah," corrected Hoppy.

"A wot?"

"It's when we come of age," said Sammy.

173

"Well I still fink it's stupid," insisted Wheezy. "Wot did they do when yer got called up, all get pissed did they?"

Hoppy got impatient with the trend of the conversation. There was more pressing business to decide. "Well, wot about it? Are yer in?"

"Yep," said Wheezy.

"Sammy?"

"Okay. Long's Solly coughs up sharp."

"Right then, now listen. We'll wait till it's dark. 'Ave a couple o' pints, then Bob's yer uncle, in we go."

The three strolled off in an unsteady manner; Sammy to his flat in Spencer Street, Hoppy to his house at number 21 Conner Street, and Wheezy to the buildings in the Kent Road.

Chapter Seventeen

Orange streaks showed across the evening sky, fading to violet with the setting sun and the folk of Conner Street became anxious. Night was approaching, and with it the dread of another air raid. The children were shepherded from the Street and given an early supper. It might be another night in the shelter, and with that in mind the youngsters were hurried off to bed for a few hours' sleep. The long summer evenings were not conducive to sleep however, and the cry of the toffee-apple man, peddling through the Street late in the evening, caused a few problems.

"Mum, I can't sleep."

"Well try."

"But, Mum, it's still light out."

"Listen, Johnnie, they've altered the clocks ter trick the Germans. It's really late."

"Mum, I can 'ear the toffee-apple man. Can I 'ave a toffee-apple?"

"No yer can't. I'm not gettin' toffee all over me bed-clothes, now get ter sleep."

"But, Mum, Reggie Carter's dad lets 'im 'ave a toffee-apple in bed."

"Now listen 'ere, yer little tyke, if yer don't get ter sleep this minute, I'll go up the 'Eagle' an' fetch yer farver 'ome. 'E'll give yer wot for."

"O all right then," puffed Johnnie.

As if to justify her actions, the boy's mother added, "Anyway, those apples are all rotten. They've got worms in 'em."

"Cor."

"An' they'll rot yer teef."

"Wot, the worms?"

"No, the toffee. Now will yer get ter sleep?"

The lad lay twisting in his bed, thinking of a nice, juicy, sweet-tasting toffee-apple on a stick. It wasn't fair. Reggie Carter ate toffee-apples in bed. Reggie Carter even had a scooter with real ball-bearings. Perhaps if he ran away they would realise a little old toffee-apple wasn't much to ask for. It would be different if he asked for a scooter with ball-bearings. He would run away in the morning. Then he could have lots of toffee-apples, and eat them all in bed. He could stay up till it was black as ink, and stand outside pubs like Reggie Carter, and eat arrowroot biscuits, and drink gallons of lemonade. Just wait. He would show them. A drummer boy in the army, that's what he'd be, or a cabin boy on a large ship.

The sandman called, and the little lad's eyes shut. He saw the toffee-apple man in front of him, holding out huge treacle-covered apples on sticks. The man wore a candy-striped suit and a top hat dotted with jelly beans. The lad took a bite from the sweet toffee-apple, and saw the man grinning evilly at him. The lad saw that the bite had exposed a worm-eaten core and he awoke. He tried to look down at his tongue. It was dark in the room, and he heard a voice that seemed to come from a long way off. "You, Johnnie, get yer clothes on quick, it's the bloody siren."

At the corner of Conner Street, a shaft of light hit the pavement and a voice shouted, "Watch that light."

The 'Eagle' was full. Three young men, one in a uniform, sat in a corner.

"It's no good goin' yet. The bleedin' Street's full o' people." Wheezy moaned.

"We'll wait fer an hour, it'll be quiet by then," said Hoppy.

"Wot we gonna put 'em in?" asked Wheezy.

"Don't worry, I've already seen ter that. Yesterday I lobbed a couple o' sacks over the wall," answered Hoppy, tapping his head meaningfully.

"All I 'ope is Solly pays up sharp," said Wheezy,

sipping his beer.

"So do I," added Sammy Israel.

Joe Harper walked into the bar accompanied by Rosie and Skipper. The old seaman winked at Florrie, his faded eyes drifting down to the woman's ample bust.

"A few years ago I'd a bin over that counter," Skipper muttered out of the corner of his mouth to Joe.

"A few years ago I'd a bin wiv yer, Skip," grinned Joe.

"You two goin' ter stan' whisperin' all night," piped in Rosie.

Skipper licked his lips in anticipation and he fished in his coat pocket for his pipe. "I likes 'em wiv a bit o' meat on 'em," he went on. "Can't stand a skinny lookin' woman."

"Wot yer mumblin' about, Skip?" Rosie asked.

Joe got the drinks and the three sat at a table next to the conspirators.

"When yer goin' back, son?" Skipper asked Sammy.

"Termorrer," answered Sammy, wishing the old man hadn't asked.

Joe Harper looked at the uniformed Jew. "Got many yiddisher boys in your lot, Sammy?"

"Cor not 'arf, Joe. Most of 'em come out o' the Mile End Road."

Joe picked up his pint of ale. "Well 'ere's to yer, son."

"Cheers, Joe," Sammy said with a wink.

Skipper was looking at his pint with a frown.

"What's wrong Skipper?" Rosie asked. "Don't yer fancy it?"

"It's either me mouth, or that bleedin' landlord's bin waterin' it down," Skipper said with a glance in John Braden's direction.

"I wouldn't fink so," Wheezy piped in. "'E never touches the stuff."

Florrie Braden was busy serving. She could not help thinking about the visit from Alan Denman. She had noticed the look of horror on Julie's face when she had spotted him. After all the trouble he had caused her, why should he appear again? Florrie had liked Julie and was upset when she decided to leave Kent. For a while the two

177

women had kept in touch, until Julie went onto the streets. What was the reason for Alan Denman to come to the 'Eagle'? She hoped it was just a coincidence. Even so, what was he doing in London? Perhaps he had heard from someone about Julie, and had decided to try his luck again. In any case, she was determined to have a quiet word with the stranger if he showed up again. Julie seemed happy with Stanley Nathan, and Florrie aimed to keep it that way.

Dusk was slipping down like a cloak. For the past hour the half-daylight had stayed unchanged. Blackout curtains had been drawn and lights lit, although it was still possible to see the length of the Street. Now suddenly it was black. Stars winked down from the velvet sky, and a full moon appeared over the chimneypots.

"C'mon lads, we can't wait no longer," said Hoppy.

The three conspirators waved goodnight to the Harpers, then slipped quickly out of the pub.

"Funny," observed Joe Harper. "Either they don't like our company, or they've gorn orf beer."

Rosie grunted. "I can't abide that 'Oppy feller. I bet they're up ter no good."

"Wouldn't be surprised," remarked Skipper. "First time I've seen Wheezy leave without Florrie 'avin' ter shoo 'im out."

The three young men walked quickly up the alley that led off from Tower Road. They moved silently, until Sammy's foot made contact with an empty tin can. The rattling noise over the cobbles clattered loudly through the quiet Street, and the three stopped.

"It's no time ter play bleedin' football," hissed Hoppy.

"Got no consideration, some people. Fancy frowin' their rubbish up bleedin' alleys," moaned Wheezy.

Sammy was silent. The escapade did not seem such a good idea now. Sammy was a born costermonger who, like most of his faith, had a shrewd business brain. He had recognised that anything was saleable, but the thought of Solly fencing top hats and straw bonnets in wartime made him shake his head.

The alley ran along the side of an empty, boarded up

shop. Hoppy pulled on a part of some corrugated fencing and it bent outwards. "Quick, lads, in yer go," he whispered.

The three were soon inside and standing in the yard. There was a six foot wall that separated them from the hatter's. Hoppy spotted the outline of an oil drum, which he moved to the foot of the wall. "It's empty, lads. This'll make it easy," he said.

The three men clambered one by one on to the drum and slipped over into the hatter's yard. Hoppy worked on the window catch using a kitchen knife. Soon he grunted with satisfaction and gently slid the window frame up. The men climbed over the sill and stepped into a dark room. The moon had risen, but its pale beam barely reached into the room. What light there was enabled the three to pick out a few wooden crates, and a door in one corner of the room.

"C'mon, lads, upstairs we go," hissed Hoppy, his heart pumping fast with excitement.

"Where's yer torch, 'Oppy?" whispered Wheezy. "I can't see a bleedin' fing in front o' me!"

"Can't shine it 'ere. Too risky. Wait till we get upstairs," answered Hoppy.

The three men started to climb the stairs when Hoppy, who was leading, suddenly stopped.

"Christ! The sacks! We fergot the sacks!"

Sammy was last in line. "I'll get 'em," he volunteered. He climbed back into the yard and scrambled over the wall into the next yard. He went to the fencing and felt around in the dark. The sacks were lying near to where they had entered. The corrugated sheeting was gaping outwards and, as Sammy retrieved the sacks, he saw a light shining up the alley. The sound of slow, deliberate footsteps reached him and he quickly threw himself face down among the rubble. A beam from a torch shone over his body and Sammy held his breath.

PC Smith had been on duty along the Tower Road and found the urgent need to relieve himself. When he had finished, PC Smith buttoned up his trousers and sighed with contentment, then he walked back out of the alley.

Sammy stood up and looked down at his uniform trousers. The bottom half was soaked in urine.

"My God!" he mumbled aloud. "To be pissed over, and by a gentile!" The insult made the yiddisher boy grit his teeth. He quickly clambered over the wall and rejoined the two men.

"Wot kept yer, Sammy?" asked Wheezy.

"Will yer just look at me uniform?" moaned Sammy. "'E pissed all over me. 'Ow 'e didn't spot me, I'll never know."

"Who the bloody 'ell yer talkin' about?" asked Hoppy.

"PC bloody Smith, that's who. What a place ter 'ave a riddle. I couldn't move, 'e'd 'ave seen me," wailed Sammy.

"Well I'll be blowed. Yer mean ter say yer just lay there an' let a cozzer piss all over yer?" Wheezy said in mock horror.

Hoppy interrupted them. "Never mind about that now. Fill these sacks quick as yer can, an' let's get goin'."

The room at the top of the stairs was both workroom and showroom. Hats of all descriptions were lined along shelves. The light of Hoppy's torch picked out top hats, brown Derbys, straw bonnets, bowlers, and fine, flower-bedecked creations.

"Cor, look at those," whispered Wheezy, pointing to a row of lace bonnets. "Wonder wot me ole mum would say if she could wear one o' those."

Hoppy was busy stuffing the loot into the sacks. "Them ain't fer the likes o' me an' you. Up West. That's where this lot was goin'. Look at the label."

The three peered at the stitched label inside the brim of a top hat. The light of Hoppy's torch shone on the words, 'La Parisienne'.

"Yer lords an' ladies an' the rest o' the toffee-noses buys this stuff. Bloody idiots. Buy a brick o' shit if yer stuck a fancy label on it," Hoppy said with feeling.

Wheezy was filling a sack with ladies' bonnets. "I fink me ole mum would look good in one o' these," he said.

"We told yer, they ain't for the likes o' the people round 'ere," remarked Sammy.

"O, an' why not?" asked Wheezy. "Nuffink wrong with cockney people. Least they got manners. I seen some of them there dooks an' earls. Seen 'em at Epsom once. Bleedin' carry on it was. The gippos on the Downs 'ad more decorum. I saw ..."

Hoppy stopped him. "We gonna 'ave a lecture on manners, or are we gonna piss orf while we can?"

The three men made their stealthy exit from the hatter's shop without being seen; each carrying a sack of loot slung across his shoulders, they turned into Conner Street. Their plan was to stow the sacks behind the shelter, in a small recess that afforded an emergency exit. They reasoned it would be safe there until Solly called around next morning. Down the Street they went, in single file and bent forward with the bulkiness of the sacks, like extras from *Snow White*, unseen, until PC Smith turned the corner by the 'Eagle'.

Sammy was trailing, and he turned to make sure they were not being followed. He saw the beam of light from the policeman's torch. "It's the cozzer!" he cried.

"Quick, run!" shouted Hoppy.

The beam of light flashed along the Street. "What's occurrin' then?" shouted PC Smith.

In the light of the torch, PC Smith saw what looked like three hunchbacks disappearing around the corner. He stood and scratched his head.

"Must be goin' crackers," he said aloud. Voices coming out of holes was one thing, but hunchbacks running abroad in the neighbourhood was too much. PC Smith longed for the end of his spell of night duty.

The three ran towards the shelter. "Quick, get inside!" shouted Hoppy, thinking the policeman was following them.

"Blimey!" gasped Wheezy. "'E would 'ave ter show up."

Into the stuffy-smelling shelter went the three. They sat in the darkness, the sacks stowed by the door.

Wheezy lit a cigarette and puffed out a cloud of smoke. "That was close," he muttered.

"Shush!" barked Hoppy. "'E may be outside."

181

The men were silent, listening for the sound of the policeman's tread outside. It remained quiet, and Wheezy stamped out his cigarette.

"C'mon, boys, let's get them sacks stowed," said Hoppy.

As they stood up, the moaning wail of the siren started. It picked up in sound until it turned to a scream.

"Cor blimey," moaned Wheezy, shuffling around in agitation.

"Quick!" shouted Hoppy. "There's no time now. Put 'em right in the corner."

The three sacks were hidden just in time. Into the shelter came the folk from the Street. White-faced and hurrying they came; wide-eyed and scared, but some still managing to crack a joke.

Granny Flint tottered in, puffing and panting with the effort. "Gawd a'mighty Gawd, this'll be the deaf o' me."

"Shut up, Gran, that bastard 'Itler can't kill you," said Lizzie Brown, sitting down heavily beside her.

The three conspirators sat wooden-faced, watching the Conner Street folk pile in.

"Wot you free doin' 'ere?" asked Lizzie Brown. "Ain't you s'pose ter be outside watchin' out?"

"I'd sooner be inside watchin' out, Liz," joked Wheezy.

"Not so much o' yer cheek," said Lizzie sharply. "Piss orf out there an' leave room fer the wimmin an' kids."

The three left the safety of the shelter and joined the rest of the men in the covered area at the front of the refuge. Inside, the women were talking quietly. Children sat yawning, miserable at being dragged from their warm beds. One lad, ignored by his mother who was talking to her neighbour, started to pick at the string on one of the sacks.

Suddenly the guns opened up, and a loud explosion rocked the shelter. It was followed by another loud salvo of gunfire and another explosion. Dust fell from the concrete roof and the lights flickered.

"Holy Mary," muttered Bridie Flannagan, cuddling her baby close to her.

Maureen had her arms round the two boys and the twins sat on each side of Bridie, their heads leaning on her. "It's all right, children, it's only the guns," she said reassuringly.

Granny Flint gave Bridie a cold stare. "She said that last night."

Lizzie Brown patted the old lady's hand. "She's only sayin' it fer the kids' sake, they're all scared."

Granny Flint sniffed. "Shouldn't be 'ere. Should all be 'vacuated," she said quickly.

Yet another explosion and another roar of gunfire rocked the shelter. With the drone of planes came a whistling sound as a bomb fell earthwards. There was a dull thud, but no explosion.

"Did you 'ear that? Must o' bin a dud," said Lizzie.

"Bastards!" Emmie Jones cried. "If this keeps up we'll 'ave ter start sleepin' 'ere."

"Gawd ferbid," said Granny Flint. "I couldn't sleep a wink in this stinkin' place."

Lizzie Brown grinned. Granny Flint soon nodded off to sleep and her head tilted to one side and her mouth hanging open.

It had suddenly gone quiet. The droning of the planes diminished and the gunfire ceased. The lad in the corner had untied the knot on one of the sacks and was delving inside.

"Cor, look wot I got!" he said loudly, holding up a top hat.

"Where did yer get that?" asked his mother.

"Look, Mum, there's lots of 'em in the sack."

The boy's mother fished in the open bag and removed a lady's bonnet.

"Turn the sack up, let's 'ave a look wot's inside," someone said.

"'Ere, gi's one," said someone, and "Pass us one," said another.

Within minutes, the loot from the hatter's shop was on display. Even Granny Flint wore a bonnet. Joe Harper heard the laughter and popped his head inside.

"Wot's goin' on in there?" asked Bob Bowman, the Street warden.

"Well I'll be!" said Joe. "They've all got party 'ats on. Gawd knows where they got 'em from."

Someone from the adjoining shelter heard the laughter, and came in to see what was going on.

"'Ere, take a few next door," said the boy's mother, passing a sack to the woman.

Outside, the three men responsible for the hilarity sat with downcast faces as the woman ran past them and into the next shelter.

"Wonder who put them 'ats in there?" grinned Joe, looking directly at the three.

"Gawd knows," said Hoppy.

"Solly Goldberg's goin' ter be pleased," groaned Sammy.

"I'm not too 'appy meself," moaned Wheezy.

"I wouldn't 'ave minded if we'd 'ave earned a few shekels," said Sammy, his face registering disgust. "I've bin pissed on an' not earned a penny. I knew it wasn't a good idea from the start."

"Well yer didn't 'ave ter come wiv us, did yer?" snapped Hoppy.

"'Ere, Sammy, d'yer know wot yer smell like? That piss-'ole in the pitchers," Wheezy cracked.

Sammy ignored the remark and sat glumly, his head resting against the wall behind him.

Overhead the droning started again as the night raiders turned for home. The guns started up and explosions sounded in the distance. The drone became louder and the explosions got nearer. Above the din came the rising sound of singing from within the shelter. Lizzie Brown's voice could be heard. "There's an old mill by the stream," she shrieked, and the chorus answered her, crying out, "Nellie Dean!"

"Where I used to sit and dream," she sang. "Nellie Dean," they cried.

The adjoining shelter, not to be outdone, started up with their own chorus.

The gunfire was deafening, and pieces of shrapnel

184

clattered down the cobbles. The full moon was high, and the pale, cold light was changed to a pink glow from the nearby raging fires. Flashes of light followed by loud bangs went on for the next hour, as the anti-aircraft guns in the park aimed at the new flight of bombers overhead. The raiders spewed from their bellies of death and turned over the edge of London to make their return run. Buildings collapsed. Fires started and roared out of control. Hospitals were hit, and everywhere craters gaped, smoking and filling with sewage. Firemen found their hoses ran dry as water mains were hit. Factory walls fell outwards, down onto the firemen below. Ambulances ran a gauntlet to and from the hospitals. Doctors and nurses worked on, almost out on their feet, and police and rescue squads delved into the rubble for sobbing, terrified survivors.

It continued through the night. Shrapnel and shell cones fell, still glowing hot. Tower Road was cratered; in Spencer Street, an oil bomb fell slap in the middle of the tannery. The place burned fiercely, threatening the adjoining houses. Little Dixon Street was hit by a landmine and wiped out. A high-explosive bomb landed in Conner Street and made a hole in a back yard. Conner Street was lucky that night; it suffered a few cracked windows.

At the height of the bombing, a strange and unreal incident was taking place. Inside a cavern of concrete, an old lady and an idiot were facing each other. The lady wore a bonnet, tied under her chin, and the idiot wore a top hat. The old lady held her skirts high, and the idiot stuck out his chin. They were dancing a jig to the accompaniment of a mouth organ. The audience clapped and laughed as the two performed. Lizzie Brown was light on her feet and danced in tune to the music. The idiot dribbled onto his chin and shuffled on the spot. The woman locked arms with the man and spun him around to the delight of the bedecked audience. It might have been a scene from a Victorian music hall, with the top hats and flowered bonnets, and a dancer showing a glimpse of her pink, knee-length drawers. Instead, the light came from an electric light bulb, and the thunderous applause came from the guns in the park and the bombs from the sky.

The old docker shook the mouth organ and wiped it on his coat-sleeve. Lizzie Brown kissed the idiot on the cheek and sat down heavily on a bench. Bobbie shuffled along to where Ada sat, a top hat resting uneasily on his ears. He sat beside her, a happy light showing in his eyes. Ada squeezed his arm and gave him a warm smile.

Later, as the bombers flew out over the sea and the all-clear shrilled out, they emerged. Tired, thankful, and still wearing their fancy headgear. They went in their houses to brew tea, to get some sleep, and for one young lad, to make a discovery.

Reg Carter slipped into the back yard of his home to see if his rabbits were all right. Two dust-covered pets were out of their cage. They were sniffing around a hole that hadn't been there a few hours ago. Reggie peered down and saw the fins of a bomb sticking out of the rubble in the crater.

Chapter Eighteen

Not all the inhabitants of Conner Street used the shelter. Old man Davis refused to budge from his home. The Morgans stayed together in their parlour and Julie Brett sat with them. Mrs Morgan had a philosophy about the bombing. "If yer number's on it, love, it won't matter a scrap where yer at, it'll find yer." As for old man Davis, he fully expected to be found, but he was adamant: "My ole dutch died upstairs, an' when I go I wan' it ter be in this 'ouse. Wot was good enough fer 'er is good enough fer me."

Patrick Flannagan hardly ever used the shelter. When the siren wailed out its eerie warning, he gathered up his tribe and despatched them all across the Street to the refuge. For himself, the house was shelter enough. When he wasn't on night shift at the bagwash factory, he would be snoring the moment his head hit the pillow. With help from the 'Eagle', Patrick slept well, and even the German night raiders could not rouse him. There was only one person who could waken the big Irishman, and that was Bridie. She'd gently touch his shoulder, and say a few words such as, "Pat, the 'Eagle's' open", and he'd be wide awake.

Early on Monday morning, when young Reggie Carter discovered the unexploded bomb, the police and air raid wardens moved in to arouse the Conner Street folk. Everyone in the Street was moved to a nearby rest centre, hastily prepared by volunteer workers. The Street was roped off, and a notice was placed at each end of the turning. It said simply, 'Danger, Unexploded Bomb'. A policeman patrolled by the rope, and only lifted it when an army lorry drove up. The vehicle had a sign over the cab with a red flag flying both sides of the notice. Royal Engineers of the Bomb Disposal Squad hurried into the Street and set about shoring up the bomb. They worked through the morning, and by mid-afternoon the officer and a sergeant climbed down into the enlarged hole. At five o'clock that evening the safely defused bomb was loaded on to the back of the lorry. As the policeman lifted the rope for the vehicle to leave, Florrie Braden ran from her pub bringing the last bottle of whisky with her. Each man was given a huge tot, and Florrie spoke loudly enough for the policeman to hear, "If I get summonsed for serving outside of hours then it'll be worth it."

The policeman turned away to look down the Tower Road.

When Julie Brett returned to her lodgings that evening, she found an unstamped envelope propped against the china soap dish that stood on the washstand. The envelope was addressed, 'To Julie'. With trepidation the girl opened the letter and read the contents.

Dear Julie,

I'm sorry if I upset you by my presence at the 'Eagle' on Sunday. I refrained from talking to you as I noticed that you were with someone. I expect you are wondering why I should suddenly appear after all the time that has elapsed. Well, it was no accident. After all that happened between us, I just had to see you again.

When you left, I tried to pick up the pieces and repair my marriage, but it was no good. From the day you left I have not shared the same bedroom as Elaine. We still live together, but there is nothing there anymore. She has taken the two children to her mother in the West Country to get away from the bombing and I have a flat in the East End which I use during the week. The reason for this is that I have opened another factory in London, and we are doing war work.

It was Percy my manager who saw you at the 'Eagle'. You don't know him, but he knows you by sight, and in fact often covered for me while we were together. Percy has been with me a long time and he was on some business for me when he went into the 'Eagle' by chance. I feel that it was fate that our paths should cross once more.

I don't expect that you want to see me any more, Julie, but for old times' sake I would dearly like to talk to you to discover what you have been doing since we parted.

Say that you will meet me. I will be in the 'Boatman' at Greenwich on Wednesday of this week. I will be there at 8 o'clock and I will wait till 9. Please try to come.

Yours,
Alan Denman.

Julie Brett sat on her bed. Her hands were shaking, and her eyes misted. Boldly scrawled words on the sheets of paper flowed together as she tried to re-read the sentences. A large tear slipped down her cheek, and she threw herself face downwards into the pillow. It was impossible. She could not meet him. In any case, Stanley always took her out on Wednesdays. She could not deceive him after all he had done to help her rebuild her life. She dare not consider the meeting. Slowly she turned over onto her side and looked at the letter once more. A strange feeling of excitement made Julie shake. The old flame of passion had not quite burned out, after all.

Julie clenched up the letter and threw it to the floor. She knew that once she spoke to Alan Denman again there would be a danger of a new involvement. She simply could not trust herself. She bent down and retrieved the crumpled letter and straightened it out on her lap. Putting it behind the clock, she went down to talk to the Morgans.

Florrie had made up her mind to talk to Stanley Nathan. Ever since the first time her young barmaid had walked out with Alan Denman, Florrie had predicted trouble. There was only one way for it to end for the girl, and that was for her to get hurt. When Julie had lost the baby and

189

ended up on the streets, Florrie's dislike for the man responsible turned to hatred. When he walked into the 'Eagle' on Sunday, Florrie knew that unless she did something shrewd, Julie was going to get hurt again. And this time, more than one person was involved. Stanley Nathan was a good man. She could not stand back and see the new object of Julie's affections upset by what might happen. She would go to see him. Now would be the right time, she knew that every Monday evening Stanley worked late in the shop. It was his practice to work on his rationing forms and to update his ledgers. Julie would not be there in the shop, so it would give her the opportunity to warn him.

Stanley Nathan was just finishing off filling in a large form when Florrie knocked on the shutters. Stanley pushed aside a huge pile of papers and went to the door. Florrie repeated her banging before he reached the front of the shop.

"Sorry to trouble you, Stan, but I knew you'd be here late," said Florrie.

"That's all right, Florrie, come on in."

He led the way to the back of the shop and beckoned Florrie to a chair by the table. "I was just about to make a cup of tea, care for one?"

"Well it would make a nice change to the stuff I've been drinking lately," joked the landlady.

Stanley lit the gas and placed a small tin kettle over the flame. "What can I do for you?" he said as he tipped out the contents of a brown china teapot into the sink.

"Well, it's about Julie that I've come, Stan," Florrie began.

"She's okay, isn't she?" the man said quickly, concern showing on his face.

"She's fine, Stan, it's just that I'm worried."

"Worried?"

"Alan Denman has shown up," she said, watching for the reaction on his face.

Stanley showed no surprise. His mouth creased into a serious smile. "I know."

"You know?" queried Florrie. "You saw him?"

Stanley did not answer right away. Instead he walked over to the table and spooned some tea leaves into the teapot. Florrie watched his broad back, surprise showing on her face.

"He was in the pub yesterday, wasn't he," remarked the man.

Florrie nodded. "I didn't think you knew him."

"I didn't, until then. Somehow I knew, the moment I saw Julie's reactions. O, I made out I hadn't noticed anything, but Julie went white. I just knew that it had to be him," said the shopkeeper.

"Have you spoken to Julie about it?" asked Florrie.

"No. If she wants to talk, then I'll listen. It may be too painful for her, so I'm not going to ask her," Stanley said.

The kettle started to boil, and the man filled the teapot with the water.

"Do you think he'll try to contact Julie?" Florrie asked.

"I think he will," replied the shopkeeper, "but for his sake, he'd better stay clear."

Florrie looked at the man, a surprised frown causing her eyebrows to arch. She had known the shopkeeper for some time, and it was the first instance she could recall when he had spoken so grimly. She noticed the way he emphasised the sentence, his jaw muscle knotting as he spoke.

"I've been turning it over in my mind, Stan. I know that Julie has told you all about her past, but I expected her to try not to let on that the stranger was him. She was too scared of your reaction. You might have done anything. Julie loves you, Stanley. She's really happy now, and I know the girl. I think she's terrified of the past. What it might do to both of you. She's trying hard to bury her memories, but when he walked in my place yesterday it was like a bad dream come true. Don't let the past destroy your lives, love. I think a lot of both of you, and I wouldn't want something like what happened yesterday to spoil it all for you."

Stanley gave her a friendly wink. "You take sugar?"

"Two, please."

He poured out the tea into two large mugs, and added the milk and sugar.

The two sat facing each other across the desk. Florrie sipped her tea, and Stanley studied her. The woman was aware of his gaze and she put down the cup. "Does it worry you, Stan?" she said quickly.

"You mean about Julie's past?"

"Yes."

Stanley looped his finger through the handle of the cup and moved it around on the desk top. His forehead creased into deep lines as he answered. "There are nights when I lay in the dark and can't get to sleep. I try not to dwell on it but I can't help it. I see those men, buying her body, and I break out in a cold sweat. I find it hard to take sometimes. The problem is, I think so much of her, I can't bear to think of her with anyone else."

"Listen, Stanley Nathan," Florrie began, "I've been around myself. When I first met John I was not exactly altar-pure. He knew it, and he wouldn't let me forget it. There would always be remarks and jibes. He never, ever talked about it openly. I think he tried to bury the memory of it, and his way was with the bottle. There was this fellow that he knew about, and the only time my John would mention him was when the drink was saying it for him. We never tried to sort out the problem, and I suppose I was as much to blame as he was. Anyway, the drinking got worse, and now there's only the pub that keeps us together. We've only got a business relationship now. What I'm trying to say is, don't make the same mistakes. Forget the past, it doesn't matter. She's yours now, and when you get married make sure you're happy. I'm going on a bit, but I hate to think what might happen if you don't accept the past, then cast it out. Think of the two of you. The way things are now, we've all got to grab at happiness. Just you make sure that you don't miss the opportunity."

As Florrie left the shop, Stanley kissed her lightly on the cheek. "I thank you for being concerned, and don't worry. I'll sort my problem out, and we'll be okay, Florrie."

"Course you will, Stan. See you soon."

"See you soon," he repeated as he watched the landlady cross the road.

As she reached the other side, she turned and gave him a wave before walking along to the 'Eagle'. She felt better for the chat with Stanley, although the feeling of something bad still persisted inside her. She was aware of her serious face, and she paused at the door of the pub to compose herself. It would not do for the landlady of a pub to be miserable. She looked up at the evening sky. The setting sun stained the clouds red. Streaks of a 'shepherd's delight' would soon pale, and the full moon would rise high into the heavens. A bomber's moon they called it.

The pub was filling up, and Florrie went behind the bar. John Braden gave her a quizzical stare and got on with serving a customer. Wheezy was leaning on the counter. Hoppy stood beside him.

"Where's Sammy?" Florrie asked.

"Gorn back early," replied Wheezy.

"I fink 'e prefers the sergeant major to us," said Hoppy, grinning at his friend.

"I hear the hatter's shop got broken into last night," Florrie said.

"Yeah. Whoever done it dumped the stuff down the shelter," answered Hoppy, a look of angelic innocence sweeping over his countenance.

"The police were asking questions today, although it was awkward, what with that bomb in the Carters' back yard. They'll be back tomorrow though," Florrie predicted.

"Well I don't know who nicked them 'ats, but it livened up the shelter. Silly Bobbie 'ad a top 'at on. Dancin' wiv ole Lizzie Brown 'e was. Looked a proper card," said Hoppy.

"Looked like a pox-doctor's clerk, if yer ask me," added Wheezy.

An old man who was leaning against the bar straightened up and faced Wheezy. "I tell yer wot. 'E may not 'ave all 'is marbles, but 'e 'ad that shelter in stitches.

While they was all laughin' at 'im they was fergettin' the bloody bombs, son."

Hoppy nodded. "Bobbie Wilkins is okay by us, Dad. You gotta agree though, 'e did look eighteen-carat."

The old man returned to his pipe and ale, and Wheezy went over to the dartboard. Hoppy leaned dejectedly against the counter. His crippled foot was aching, and he placed it on the foot rail. Hoppy watched Florrie's rear as she walked along to talk to John. He picked up his glass and drained the contents. There were better things to do than just standing here drinking, he thought. Florrie figured in those things. He ogled the woman as she came back along the bar. Her large bosom bounced as she walked and Hoppy sighed to himself. He missed Sammy, and now Wheezy was playing darts. He looked around the bar. He saw Albert Conlin walk in, and noticed Florrie's eyes light up. The woman leaned on the counter, her bust spread on the oaken wood. The big man grinned sheepishly as Florrie jested with him.

"Hello, Al. Come in just to see me, have you?"

"I 'ad ter get out o' the 'ouse. Nell's sittin' there snorin' an' there's nuffink werf while on the wireless," Albert complained.

"So you've decided to take me dancing or something, have you?" Florrie joked.

Albert Conlin fumbled for some coins. "Give us a pint o' usual, Florrie."

The landlady pulled on the pump handle and filled a pint glass to overflowing. "A pint o' best for the best," she said, a gleam in her eye.

Wheezy Morris was waiting for his turn to throw the darts. He ambled over to Hoppy. "See Florrie? She really goes a bundle on 'im, don't she?"

Hoppy nodded, and Wheezy went on, "The man's too dopey ter see it. Wish it was me. I'd give 'er wot for."

Hoppy looked at his friend in disgust. "She'd smuvver yer wiv 'em," he cracked, nodding at the woman.

"Wot a way ter go," answered Wheezy, lighting a Woodbine.

Time was weighing heavily on Hoppy and he felt

194

restless. He looked around the little bar and saw the Harpers' old lodger sitting alone by the door. The man was puffing away at his pipe, a near-empty glass in front of him. Wheezy had gone over to take his turn at the dartboard and Hoppy felt the need to talk to someone. He ordered two pints of ale and carried them over to the table. Skipper looked up and stared at the beer.

"There we are, Pop, 'ave a drink on me," Hoppy said.

"Cheers, lad. I was just about ter get meself one."

"All right if I sit 'ere?" asked the cripple.

"Sit yerself down, son. I expect yer miss Sammy, don't yer?"

"I tell yer, Skip, if they'd 'ave me I'd be orf termorrer."

"Fink yerself lucky, lad," said the old seaman, tapping his pipe on the table leg. "There's gonna be a lot o' fightin' ter be done afore this war's over. A lot o' young blood's gonna be spilt. Don't be too anxious ter put yerself in the way of a bullet."

"Yeah, I s'pose yer right, but d'yer know I really envied Sammy when 'e left. At least 'e ain't sittin' around 'ere waitin' fer a bomb ter fall on the Street."

"Well I'll tell yer wot," Skipper began. "Sammy's okay fer the present, but mark my words, there's gonna come a time soon when young Sammy's gonna be wishin' 'e was in your shoes. A PBI is the worstest job in the army."

"PBI?"

"Poor bloody infantryman, that's wot," Skipper went on. "Up the sharp end every time, cor blimey."

Hoppy took a sip from his glass. "It ain't much fun sittin' in that bloody shelter every night, waitin' ter see if one o' them bombs is gonna find yer. Fair gives me the creeps it does."

Skipper looked at his pipe and decided that it needed re-lighting. He struck a match and puffed hard on his brown-stained clay briar.

Hoppy watched him drawing on the pipe, and noticed how gnarled the seaman's hands were.

"Yer don't fink you're the only one who's scared o' the bombin', do yer? I've lived a few years, an' I want ter go on fer a mite longer yet." Skipper said, through a cloud of

195

tobacco smoke. "I tell yer, I used ter 'ave a sayin' when I was a young stripplin'. I used ter say that I'd like ter live till I was ninety, an' die in a brothel, on the job. Long as I didn't kick the bucket in the waitin' room I'd be 'appy. I'd still like ter reach ninety, though I don't worry too much about the brothel. Wot I do fink about is goin' under a pile o' rubble."

Hoppy laughed. "I reckon you could still make them dollies know wot's wot."

Skipper burst into a fit of coughing. When he had regained his breath, he looked at his pipe. "Bloody fing wants a good pipe-cleaner, it tastes like the inside of a tram driver's glove," he moaned.

Hoppy finished his drink. "D'yer fink the bastards'll be back ter night?" he asked.

"Gawd knows. I 'ope not. I ain't 'ad a good night's sleep fer a week," the seaman complained.

"It's the waitin'," said Hoppy. "Just sittin' without bein' able ter do anyfing. That's wot I can't stand."

"We're all in the same boat, son. All we can do is just sit there, bein' scared. I remember bein' scared at sea, but it wasn't as bad as now. I was scared when the wind got up, an' the waves almost swamped the ship. I was scared when I 'ad me first woman, but nuffink beats this."

Hoppy grinned. "I bet that was a long time ago, Skip?"

"Wot's that?"

"Yer first woman."

"Blimey, it must be donkey's years ago", agreed the seaman. "Big ole Bertha up in the Pool."

"Wot's the 'Pool'?" asked Hoppy.

"Liverpool. That's wot us seafarers call it. Got some big uns up there. Never ferget it. Me first trip it was. Down ter Aussie we went. Anyway, back I comes, wiv money in me pockets an' feeling like a dog wiv two dicks an' the waves almost swamped the ship. I was scared lookin' around. Didn't 'ave ter look far, I can tell yer. I spots 'er in the pub. Built like a brick carsey she was, an' enough paint on 'er face ter cover all the rust on our ship. It didn't stop me buyin' 'er a drink. Never ferget it. Stout she wanted, an' a pint at that. I've never see'd a tart drink like it. Gulped the stout down like soap suds down a drain-'ole. Well anyway, she takes a shine ter me, an' orf we goes to 'er 'ouse. She jumps inter bed, an' she's shoutin' fer me ter 'urry up. I was wearin' those 'igh buttoned boots at the time. I 'ad a bleedin' knot in one of 'em, an' there's 'er screamin' fer me ter get a move on. In the finish, I gets on the bed wiv one boot left on."

"Cor, I bet that was uncomf'table?" remarked Hoppy. "Fancy sleepin' all night wiv one boot on."

Skipper gave the cripple a disdainful look. "All night! Blimey, son. Under ten minutes an' I was back out on the cobbles. 'Arf a crown it cost me. Wouldn't even let me give 'er a kiss. Said it'd spoil 'er make-up. Bloody make-up! Anyfing yer done ter that face would 'ave been an improvement. She 'ad a dial like Big Ben."

Hoppy laughed and for a few minutes forgot the war, his aching foot, and the fact that very soon the air raid siren would most certainly scream out again.

Distressed by the nightly blitz, the Conner Street folk were coming together. Lizzie Brown spoke to Nan Roberts in the market one day, the first time the two women had done so for years. 'Cheap-Jack' sold Mrs Jenkins an article even though she was a penny short in her purse. Someone had even seen the old hawker in Tower Road attempt a smile. It was a time to come together in the fact of adversity, and the folk of Conner Street did it in their own special way.

Chapter Nineteen

Nightly, and without pause, the bombing blitz went on. During the hours of darkness the folk of Conner Street became shelter-dwellers. They sat cramped and miserable, young ones asleep in their parents' arms and older children leaning exhausted against their mothers' bodies. They spent the terrible nights fitfully sleeping, or crying silently. The menfolk stood outside under the concrete canopy, taking turns to sit on the two benches that spread end to end between the two caverns. It was exhausting for everyone, and to add to the misery children in particular began to suffer from skin eruptions. Boils and sores started to appear. Scabies spread from child to child, and head lice were discovered on the cleanest of children.

It was into the second week of the blitz and, miraculously, not another bomb had fallen on to the Street. Spencer Street was not so lucky. They had a second bomb that knocked down a row of houses and made the whole Street homeless. The folk of Conner Street heard about the two families that were killed and felt helpless with rage. Spencer Street was only two turnings away, and it was reasoned that the bombs were getting nearer. Conner Street was getting desperate and, although the danger was being driven home to them, some families decided they could take no more. They spurned the safety of the shelter and stayed in their frail homes. For those who continued to go to the shelter nightly, something had to be done. Some of the men brought back doors from the bombed houses and placed them down in the gangways. They propped them on bricks to keep the wood away from the smelly, dark water, and the children slept more peacefully. For the parents the continuing agony of trying to catch a few hours' sleep sitting up on the hard benches remained. Legs and feet started to swell and backs developed cricks that were hard to get rid of. As the bombing got heavier and the nights longer, so the torture became worse. Mrs Jenkins got sick, and Granny Flint developed pneumonia. They put her to bed in her little home, and Lizzie Brown and Emmie Jones took turns to sit with her. The men boarded up the old lady's windows, and piled sandbags outside to catch any blast.

Not far away from the Street was the jam factory. Its owner, a benevolent soul, opened the gates of his factory to give refuge at night. The woeful manager tried to warn him of the consequences, but the paragon insisted. In they came, carrying their bundles of bedclothes, people who were desperate for a night's sleep in safety. They climbed up on the huge piles of sugar that were stacked in the ground floor warehouse. In the warm, stuffy atmosphere, they slept well. The thick walls deadened the sounds from without, and soon the morning came. They told their friends and more came. They climbed even higher on the stack to find a spare space, and trampled over the already established refugees of the night. Arguments broke out as children were trodden on. A fight broke out between two large women, who rolled over and over to the bottom of the pile. It was getting impossible to control the situation, and more people came.

The authorities learned of the jam factory and its teeming sleep-seekers and they spoke to the owner. The following night the people were turned away as they arrived. A hastily printed letter told of the dangers in case of fire. Sugar would run like treacle. Panic would mean loss of life. The letter told of the new incendiary bomb that was being used in the blitz. It was a small, silver-coloured tube that ignited on impact and burned with a white hot ferocity. One incendiary device on the factory would be an unmitigated disaster.

The people read the letter and trudged away. The manager rubbed his hands together.

"They've been pissing over the sacks, sir. Actually

urinating over the sugar, sir."

The owner of the jam factory sighed deeply and walked away. That night the warehouse was quiet, scoured of ragged foundlings and left to the rodents, and other creatures of the night.

There was a strange fatalism developing amongst the dockland folk. The news of someone's death by bombing did not raise their emotions so greatly now. Death in some violent form was expected and accepted. The living shook their heads and went about their day. The night was spent clinging to the thin strand of life, waiting and hoping. The grace between walking out of the shelter or a fragile home next morning and being blown into eternity during the night lingered like a candle flame, flickering and spluttering in a draught, burning brightly, then suddenly extinguished. Such was acceptance of the terrible times; exhaustion and physical weakness produced the only respite, the overriding need to sleep. Folk began to sleep through the most violent of nights. They began to lose their comprehension of events. The thought of a warm bed, and being enveloped in soft, clean white sheets, was paramount. Brutal death, even when witnessed, was no more such an awesome thing.

"Johnnie, run up the top an' get yer Granny a pinch o' snuff." Johnnie grasped the sixpence. "Up Catchpoles?"

"Yes," replied his mother, "and hurry up, Granny don't feel very well."

The little lad skipped up the street, dodging the broken glass on the pavement and the pieces of window frame that littered the place. He danced around a pile of sandbags and turned the corner. 'Catchpoles' was not open. Johnnie, being rather young, did not know anywhere else he could buy snuff. He did not recall having seen the brass scales hanging from brass chains, and the little weights that were put into one of the scale pans. He could not recall having seen those large, brown earthenware jars where snuff was kept. Only 'Catchpoles' had those things. It must be the only shop in the whole of London that sold snuff, he concluded.

"No good you standin' there, son. 'E's not open," a voice said.

Johnnie stepped from the doorway, and stopped twisting the sixpence around in his palm. He looked up at the tall man, a question written across his jam-streaked face.

"Why, mister?" he asked with all the innocence of youth.

"'E's gorn. Killed 'e was, last night," replied the tall man.

"Cor," was all the boy could say.

The man nodded at a pile of red-dotted sand on the pavement nearby, and walked off. The boy twisted the sixpence around in his palm again, and walked away from the doorway. As he passed the sand, Johnnie kicked it curiously. A cold, dead eye, attached to red strands, stared up at him, and the boy ran all the way home.

During the early days of the blitz, Julie Brett found herself faced with a heartrending decision; whether or not to meet Alan Denman. She had not confided in Stanley about the man's reappearance. She did not wish to hurt him by reminding the man of her past. Stanley had accepted her without question and she wanted it to stay that way. Julie knew in her heart that if she did not keep the appointment, she would never know for sure if she would have been able to go through with their marriage had she met Alan again. This way, by keeping the appointment, she would know what her feelings were once she had spoken to him. She wanted to be sure in her mind, to know that it was possible to turn away, and to finally bury the past once and for all.

It was Wednesday evening, and a fresh wind was rising. A few leaves dropped from the grimy plane tree near the tram stop as Julie waited. She pulled the collar of her coat up against the wind and sorted some copper coins from the depths of her handbag. The tram rattled up and stopped. As Julie climbed aboard, two young people ran up and jumped on just as the tram accelerated away from the stop. The young couple sat on the seat in front of her. The man, dressed in a naval uniform, sat staring ahead. The girl held his arm tightly, her head resting on his shoulder. They did not speak, simply sharing the intimacy of the moment. Julie sighed and held out the fare. The grey-haired conductor flipped out a ticket and punched it on his tin ticket machine. The couple were wrapped up in each other, not noticing the collector. As the man passed back along the aisle he winked at Julie, and glanced back at the lovers.

Presently the church spire came into view and Julie got off the tram. She walked along by the little shops and turned into a narrow street. At the end of the turning Julie saw the sign 'The Boatman' swinging in the wind. She entered and looked around in the smoke-laden air. The ceiling beams were low and the bar smelled of stale beer. The girl felt uneasy at entering the pub alone. A few faces stared at her, then resumed their wooden expressions. She could now see Alan Denman. He stood some way down the bar, his fist clenched and resting on the counter. His hair looked even greyer than she'd remembered. He did not look her way until she had almost reached him. When he turned, Julie saw the pale blue eyes, and the thin, clipped moustache. He looked older; less ruddy, but more lined.

"I knew you would come," he said, a ghost of a grin on his face.

Julie gave him a cold smile. The man was so sure of himself. In that department he hadn't changed one bit, she thought. He still stood in the same relaxed manner, still conducted himself with an air of confidence. Somehow though, he was different. Julie could not fully understand it, but there was something that puzzled her. Perhaps it was the passing years. The picture of him, his manner, never completely shut out from her mind, was a picture of the past.

"What can I get you?" he asked.

"I'll have a port and lemon," the girl replied.

He placed the order, and while the barman poured the drinks, Alan Denman looked hard at Julie. "You've hardly changed. In fact, you look even better than I remember you," he said.

The drinks were paid for and Alan motioned Julie to a vacant table. "It's better here," he remarked.

"How are you?" Julie asked, fishing for words.

"Fine, fine. You know I just knew you would come," Alan Denman repeated.

"Well I almost didn't," Julie said, annoyed at his manner. She was thinking of when she had lied to Stanley not more than two hours ago. Her excuse of a severe headache, and the man's cheery wave as he walked down the Street made her cringe inside. God, she thought, he is so trusting, so innocent. Instead of being in her man's company, she was here, rekindling the past. Alan had spoken to her but the words passed unheard. She was aware that he had asked her a question.

"I'm sorry," she said quickly, noticing Alan's eyes staring at her, waiting for an answer.

"I said, is the man I saw you with on Sunday your steady?"

"We're going to be married. We've set a date for November," Julie answered.

Alan toyed with the half-empty glass in front of him. His lips parted slightly in a faint grin. "Shopkeeper, isn't he?"

"That's right," said Julie quickly, her eyes on his face.

"Do you love him?" Alan Denman asked, taking the empty glasses to the bar before Julie could answer.

Julie watched his self-assured saunter to the counter, and she gritted her teeth. She was aware of her face getting hot and she opened her handbag and took out a small mirror. She could see the two red blotches on her cheeks. By the time Alan Denman returned to the table, Julie had composed herself somewhat.

The man sat down and looked at her, his eyebrows raised as if begging the answer to his earlier question.

"I'm very fond of him," Julie said.

"I asked you if you loved him."

"Yes," answered Julie.

203

"You don't sound too convincing," replied Alan.

The red blotches were appearing again. Julie looked down at the drink in the middle of the table.

Alan Denman passed it toward her. He could see that the girl was uneasy.

"Are you sure you love him?"

Their eyes met. "I love him," repeated Julie. "Though not in the way I was with you. It's a quieter, more settled thing. With you I felt on edge half of the time. Up in the air one minute, then down in the depths the next. With Stanley it's even, no upsets. We just feel good together."

Alan Denman smirked. "I bet you sometimes wish it was a little more exciting, Julie, eh?"

The girl looked at him and noticed his smirk. She caught her breath. It was wrong for her to have come. He was acting like a hunter, with all his traps set, and his prey coming head on. Well it wouldn't work. She would spring the trap, from the outside.

"Did you know about the baby?" she asked suddenly.

The man winced noticeably, his eyes dropping down away from her gaze.

"Yes, I heard," he said.

"Did you hear about me after that?" Julie asked quietly.

"No. I tried to contact you, but I heard that you went to live with your sister. In fact I pestered Florrie Braden, but she insisted she didn't know your address."

Julie caught his eye and held his gaze. She wanted to see his reaction when he heard the next bit.

"I was a prostitute."

"What!?"

"I went on the game. The streets."

"You mean you . . ."

"That's right. I went to bed with men. For money."

"God Almighty, Julie. D'you mean you was like a common tart?"

"No like about it, Alan. I was a common tart. Paint and powder, high heels, black stockings. Believe me, I was as much a tart as you'll ever see. Are you shocked?"

"I don't believe it. You! No, you're just saying that."

Julie watched Alan closely. Gone was the suave, cocky manner. In its place was a look of disbelief. The man's eyes were popping and his mouth hung open. Julie almost felt sorry for him.

"No, it's not true. It can't be true! You wouldn't do it. You couldn't," he spluttered.

"I could, and I did," replied the girl, revelling in his discomfort. The roles were now reversed. The man was on the defensive.

"I took their money and they took me. It was simple. At least they all paid for the pleasure. You used me, and when I needed you most you cut me off, running back to your wife with your tail dragging the floor. You know, I feel sorry for your wife right now, 'cos if I'd have agreed, you'd be making plans right now, wouldn't you?"

"Julie," he protested, but Julie wasn't finished.

"You told me about your wife in the letter. Was it true? Are you sleeping apart?"

"I already told you, Julie. My wife is away with the children."

"I mean did you sleep apart before she went?"

"Yes, I swear."

"Then knowing you, there must have been other women."

"I've not been celibate. But they don't mean anything, none of them. You're different. I need you, Julie. I make no secret of the fact. Come and stay with me. The flat is nice, you'll be happy there, I promise."

Julie shook her head, then reached for her handbag from the chair beside her. "I must be off. I knew it was foolish to come, but now I can be happy. No wondering, no troubled thoughts about whether or not I could turn my back on you and walk away."

"Julie, you must give it time. Think about it for a while. You'll come to realise. You couldn't be happy for the rest of your life being the partner of a shopkeeper, you'd go insane with boredom."

Julie smiled and got up. She looked down at him, her eyes glinting. "You know you're so different, Alan. You're poles apart, the two of you. There was a time when I'd have gone to the ends of the earth with you. But I've changed. We've all changed, and there's a war on. None of us know how much more time we've got. I'm going to leave now, and I'm going to get back to Stanley as quick as I can. I'm going to tell him of this meeting, and if he still wants me, I'll gladly marry him tomorrow. As for you, I wish you well, Alan, and I hope you will get back with your wife."

Julie walked quickly to the door of 'The Boatman', her heels clicking on the wooden floor. Alan Denman watched her go and sighed.

She did not turn, but walked out into the dusk. Her heart beat fast as she made her way to the tram stop. Birds were singing in the trees which lined the pavement. Dark clouds gathered and blotted out the early stars. Few people were about, and those who were on the thoroughfare did not linger. They all seemed to be making for somewhere, using the limited amount of time for their calls, then hurrying to their own places which offered them safety. For some it was the deep shelter of the Underground: the train-free stations that had become a nocturnal home. For others, it was the surface shelter, or the 'Anderson' shelter, a corrugated affair sunk in the little town gardens. For many, their own home provided them with frail safety, and they refused to leave for a more substantial haven.

Stanley Nathan shut up his shop that evening and walked across to the 'Eagle'. It was usually his night out with Julie, but tonight he was at a loose end. He didn't feel like going straight home. Instead, he walked into the bar, and bumped into Lizzie Brown who was coming out.

The old woman carried a jug of beer. "'Ello, Stan. No Julie ternight?"

"She's not feeling too good, Liz. I'm having a quick'un then I'm off home."

Lizzie Brown nodded and walked off along Conner Street, her stockingless feet encased in huge, fluffy slippers. She went a short way, then turned to make sure that Stanley really did go into the 'Eagle'. It was Lizzie

Brown's way. She took salt with everything, including anything she was told.

Stanley really did go into the pub. He ordered a pint of ale, then sat with his back to the partition that divided the bar from the off-sales. The night was cool, with a hint of a storm. Dark clouds were gathering over dockland, and the darkness was deepening. The fears of another blitz still lurked. Although the pub folk laughed and joked as usual, their laughter was becoming more forced lately, and the jokes were old hat. Conversation was strained and staccato; now and then men's eyes darted up to the bar clock. Perhaps the threatening storm would come, perhaps it would pour all night, they thought, and the bombers would stay grounded; better still, it might even get foggy. Now that would really be something; clean sheets, and a good night's sleep. Even during a storm the bombs could fall, but a pea-souper would be really nice.

Stanley was deliberating. He did not want to stay too long. The trains to suburbia were erratic, with long hold-ups and diversions. Lots of the track had been targetted by the German Air Force. Stanley did not relish the idea of sitting in a stationary train if the raids started. He would have one more drink, then go home.

"Give us a tot o' whisky, Florrie, 'e's not well at all!" Mrs Morgan said.

"There we are, luv. I hope he's better tomorrow."

"Takes 'im days ter pull round a bit. Dicky 'eart the 'orspital told 'im. 'E's never been right since we lorst our lad."

"Never mind, luv. He'll be okay. Mind how you go."

"Yeah, I've gotta be careful meself. Nearly went down a 'sender' crossin' the Street. It's me bloody knees. Keep givin' way they do."

"You shouldn't have come out. Julie wouldn't have minded popping over for you."

"I would 'ave asked 'er, but she 'ad ter go out. I do 'ope she gets back afore it gets blackout."

"Night, Mrs Morgan."

"Night, Florrie."

Stanley had allowed the conversation to drift over him,

until Julie's name was mentioned. He felt the vibration as Mrs Morgan closed the off-sales door behind her, and he took his back off the partition. He sat up straight. Julie had not wanted to be taken out that evening, and now she was out somewhere. It was strange, he thought. Had the man in the pub contacted her? Perhaps she was going to meet him. What did it mean? Stanley did not order the other drink. Instead, he walked out into the dusk, his mind turning over the possibilities. He felt ashamed of the thoughts that raced through his head; he walked on, not realising the direction he was taking. He ignored the few cheery "hellos", lost in suspicion.

The huge, imposing mass of Tower Bridge loomed up in front of him, the white stonework standing out against the blue-black clouds. The lone, tall figure of a City policeman stood motionless on the centre span of the bridge, his hands clasped behind his back. The policeman gave Stanley a quick glance then resumed his down-river gaze, motionless except for his thumbs that twirled over each other behind his back.

Stanley walked on to the bridge and stopped to look down at the black, cold water. A snub-nosed little tug chugged through the centre of the river, passing between the twin bastions. It tooted twice, a spurt of steam emitting from the whistle on the funnel each time it sounded. The toot was answered by a booming, bass sound from a cargo ship at anchor. A hawser dropped over its side and splashed down into the river. The tug turned in its own length and made for the tow-line. The cargo ship was no doubt anxious to get out from the Pool on the evening tide, down to the estuary, and obscurity. The tug fussed and snorted, eager to assist, and the ship eased away from the quayside, slowly and deliberately.

Stanley turned back to re-cross the swirling river, his mouth set firm. He walked slowly toward the Tooley Street junction, not able to cast out the terrible thoughts that plagued him. He should have been more firm, more aware of Julie's needs. He should have insisted that she went with him, instead of staying at the Morgans'. He had been wrong to try to bury her past for her. Her need was for him to listen and to understand. His reluctance to talk to her had been his downfall, and now it was too late. He slowed down his pace, cursing his prejudgement of her. God! If only he knew where she was, who she was with, why she should slip out to keep an appointment. He cursed his thoughts again. How easy it was to think the worst. She may have gone out for some air. To do what he was doing right this minute. That was it! She wanted to be alone with her thoughts. To walk in the quiet evening and think.

The tram stopped at the junction and the conductor jumped down. He pulled on the lever and the points clanked into place. As the tram started off, the conductor jumped nimbly aboard. The rattling contraption slowly took the right-hand turn and she saw him; the heavy, sure step, the broad back, and the distinctive gait. Julie jumped up and pulled hard on the bell string. The tram eased up as the driver automatically shut off the power handle.

"Silly little mare," shouted the conductor, but Julie neither heard nor cared. She ran across the road and turned the corner. Stanley was some way ahead, his long stride taking him away from her. Julie ran faster, and Stanley heard her steps. He turned and saw her, his eyes lighting up and his face splitting in a huge grin. The girl ran to him, her arms outstretched. Stanley swept her up into his bear-like grasp, her body crushed to him, her face buried in his heaving chest. They embraced, without asking for reasons, not realising the improbability of their paths crossing at that time. They hugged. Julie cried and Stanley grinned, his flushed face resembling a harvest moon.

"Take me home with you, Stanley darling, I need you so much."

Chapter Twenty

By the end of the second week of nightly, non-stop bombing, the folk of Conner Street were utterly exhausted. The ritualistic ordeal began with the air raid siren screaming out its warning, drawing the people out of their homes and into the dark caverns of concrete. The people came and sat in the evil-smelling place of refuge, and whispered together beneath a dim electric lamp. They waited for the worst, nervously conditioned by the awful wailing.

It was inevitable that some character would give the siren a more appropriate name, and that name was borrowed from one of the Fletcher sisters. It was Tom Carter who renamed the siren 'Moaning Minnie', and he told his wife that the only difference between the two noises was that Minnie Fletcher made the most. Tom Carter swore that the old spinster kept up the racket longer than the siren, and it would have been a good idea, so he maintained, to have tied Minnie to the top of the police station and let her give the warning.

The Fletcher sisters had both been jilted early in life, or so the story went, and were now quite content to live with their memories and a profusion of stuffed birds and china ornaments. They were happy to clean daily the china and glass domes that covered the birds, or rather Maud was. Minnie was the task mistress, watching out for any speck of dust that the more timid Maud overlooked. Minnie would tut, and give her sister a scathing look, then Maud would go over her cleaning to Minnie's satisfaction. The younger Maud was totally dominated by the elder, and at times harshly treated. Minnie was a stern-faced woman with dark piercing eyes, while Maud had a hooked nose and soft, sleepy eyes. The dreamy Maud was quite content to submit to Minnie's domination and the elder took advantage.

The day started very early for the spinsters, and Maud would begin her tasks by polishing the brass fire-tongs and stand. Then with loving care she would gently wipe and polish the many little china ornaments and glass trinkets. It was then the turn of the stuffed birds to receive the younger sister's attentions. The birds were glued onto wooden perches and housed beneath thin glass domes. The glass covers glistened brilliantly from the stroking of Maud's duster, but Minnie would still tut-tut and remove an imaginary speck of dust that irritated her. Maud merely sighed, and carried on dusting and polishing.

After Maud had prepared the midday meal and they had eaten in their grossly over-adorned parlour, the sisters parted company. Minnie went upstairs, and Maud took her nap in the hard leather-bound chair. Minnie did not sleep. She spent the afternoons at the upstairs window, looking down on the passing folk, and sometimes calling out in her high-pitched voice to a young lad below, "Come 'ere, boy!" and the lad obeyed.

It was the custom among the lads in Conner Street that on no account was Minnie Fletcher to be ignored. Many times a youngster would half-slide, half-creep past Minnie's window, hoping to avoid having to run errands for the frightening old lady, and sometimes the strategy worked. When the old woman called out however, the lad would pick up the thrown message and run to the shops. It was usual for Minnie to wrap her shopping list around a half-crown, and woe betide the lad who did not bring back the correct change. Minnie would scream out a tirade of abuse at the terrified lad then send him back to the shops. It was something that all the youngsters of Conner Street dreaded, bringing back the wrong change.

Minnie Fletcher knew which lad to select for her errands, and she hovered in the upstairs window like a bird of prey, waiting and watching. She owed her success to her sister Maud, for the dreamy-eyed woman had inadvertantly terrified one of the lads and from then on the sisters had become witches to the more impressionable youngsters. Minnie's bidding was invariably done, and the lads weaved tales around the strange happenings at number 10.

211

Young Joey Solomon started it off. "The one wiv the funny nose was talkin' to 'er parrot an' it dropped dead! Honest it did, I see'd it."

"Cor! Did she put a spell on it?"

"Yeah. Mumbled somefing, an' it plonked down wiv its eyes still all starey."

"Cor! What did she do then?"

"She didn't bury it like me dad done when our rabbit died. She got glue an' stuck it back on its pole."

"Cor! I fink she's a witch or somefink."

Joey nodded. "My dad said they're both spinsters."

"Wot's spinsters?"

"Spinsters is worster den witches. Spinsters can fly ter der moon, an' turn people inter frogs an' fings."

"Cor!" said the little lad, who was even younger than Joey's six years.

Not being conversant with the skills of the taxidermist, and not daring to risk being turned into frogs or worse, the lads did Minnie's bidding.

Joey's impressionable young friend went home and that night he dreamt about terrible spinsters. He awoke screaming out their names and his mother shook her head, mystified.

The lads of Conner Street suffered Minnie's commands, and even bragged about it. If the errands were quickly done, and the change was correct, and if Minnie Fletcher had not needed to scold her sister too much that day, the lad received a silver threepenny bit for his troubles.

"Cor, did Minnie der witch give it yer?"

"Yus, an' I see'd 'Arold."

"Who's 'e?"

"'Arold's 'er parrot. Talks to it she does, and it stares at 'er."

"Cor."

The older children often played 'tin-can Tommy' in the Street and if the game happened to be beneath Minnie's window, the participants of the game received the sharp end of Minnie's tongue. The verbal explosion was such that her neighbours winced noticeably from the old spinster's vibrating tonsils. Tom Carter wilted from one

212

verbal exchange with Minnie. It concerned his son Reg, and it all started when Tom found out that his lad had been sent across the Tower Road for errands. The final result was that Tom Carter discovered a new name for the air raid siren.

It became 'Moaning Minnie'.

It was Saturday night, and two weeks after the first bombing raid. As usual 'Moaning Minnie' wailed, and the shelter quickly filled up.

Ada Dawkins stayed in her bed that night. She had a heavy chill and was running a temperature. Poor Bobbie sat by her bed and refused to budge. He had his box of treasures with him, which he placed on the foot of Ada's bed.

"Bobbie, it's no good you sittin' there. I'll be okay. Now get yerself orf down the shelter."

"I stop 'ere, Ada. Bobbie look after Ada."

Bobbie's landlady sighed and shook her head. It was no use arguing with the idiot. Ada could see by the set of his mouth that his mind was made up.

"Well if yer gonna stay, don't sit there starin' at that box. Put the kettle on, we'll 'ave a cuppa,' Ada croaked.

Granny Flint did not go to the shelter either. She was too exhausted to leave her home, and Lizzie Brown sat with her. Jack Davis too remained obstinate and sat nightly in his front parlour, protected from flying glass by the planks of wood nailed to the outside of his windows. The Fletcher sisters said that they would not be seen dead in the shelter, or rather Minnie said. The Morgans, Frank and Mabel, had stopped at home for the past couple of nights. Frank had been feeling ill. Tonight, however, the couple had decided to go to the shelter. The bombing seemed to be getting worse and Mabel was worried. It seemed that even the vibration from the guns in the local park was threatening to bring their little house down around their ears. Mabel packed Frank's medicines and a blanket to put around his shoulders and left early to get a seat in the already cramped and overcrowded shelter.

As the siren wailed, and the guns opened up, the china crockery rattled on Granny Flint's dresser and a spoon tinkled against a medicine bottle.

213

"Is them bombs I can 'ear?" asked Granny Flint, and Lizzie reassured her. "Only guns, Granny."

The barrage continued and the sound of aircraft became louder. The bomb run had started. The drone became a roar as the planes wheeled and turned above. The whistle and clatter of falling bombs and the explosions that shook the small homes in Conner Street were getting nearer. Each bang was louder than the previous, and each explosion shook the homes more severely. Jack Davis cursed the Germans and put his cap on. Granny Flint was snoring, and Bobbie and Ada looked up at the ceiling, half expecting a bomb to come through the plaster. Flashes lit the Street and something fell through the Carters' roof. A fire started in the bedroom upstairs.

"Quick lads, it's an incendiary! Get the sand!" Bob Bowman shouted.

Men ran from the safety of the shelter. The warden crashed through the Carters' front door, his momentum carrying him half-way up the stairs. Men followed him, each one holding a bag of sand. The bedroom was ablaze, and lying on the bed was a silver tube, burning with a phospheric glow. The smoke was choking the men as they dumped the sand onto the bomb. Joe Harper threw a chair through the window and the bed was thrown out onto the pavement below.

Shrapnel fell, and another incendiary hit the cobbles, bounced along the Street and stopped outside the Flannagans' home. The silver tube did not flare, but white smoke was pouring out from near the fins. Hoppy Dyke did not stop to get a sandbag. He darted across the Street and grabbed the incendiary by the fins. As he was momentarily bent over it, the device exploded in flames. Hoppy screamed in agony as a sheet of white hot fire ran up between his legs melting his flesh and setting his clothes alight. Men close behind him ran up and quickly doused the flames. Hoppy lay in a heap by the Flannagans' door, moaning pitifully, only half-conscious. They strapped his legs together and carried him gently into the Flannagans' passage. Wheezy Morris took off his coat and laid it beneath Hoppy's head. The lower half of the cripple's body was soaked in blood and sand and his club foot was twisted at a grotesque angle. Wheezy went out into the Street and vomited against the wall. Men ran back from the Carters' house and someone sent for Bob Bowman.

"The telephone at the post!" he shouted. "I'll phone fer an ambulance." The warden jumped on his rusty bike and pedalled desperately along the glass-strewn turning. Half a mile along the Tower Road stood the Wardens' post, reinforced with sandbags at the entrance. Inside, two ashen-faced men wearing steel helmets dealt with constant messages. "I've got another one 'ere, Fred. The bloody picture palace is alight. Two bodies by the door!"

Bob Bowman charged in. "Quick get an ambulance ter Conner Street! We've got a bad 'un! Poor bastard's 'ad 'is legs burnt off 'im!"

"Christ! They're all out, Bob. Even got the emergency cars runnin' ragged."

"Well, get someone there quick as yer can, or 'e's gonna die!" shouted Conner Street's warden.

Two men stayed with Hoppy, and the rest went back into the shelter entrance. A shell cone bounced along the turning and slithered down to the men's feet. Joe Harper noticed Skipper by the shelter door.

"C'mon, Pop, let's get yer inside, there's not much you can do."

Skipper protested but Joe gently led him by the arm into the dark, stuffy interior. Rosie saw her husband's blackened face.

"You okay, luv?"

"Fine. Don't worry, we'll be all right. Keep yer eye on Skipper."

The old seaman was grumbling. "Treatin' me like a child. I'm as good as any of yer."

"'Ave a rest, Pop. Come out later," whispered Joe.

The old seaman sat down heavily by the door and Joe returned to his post.

The guns were sounding off and overhead searchlights pencilled the night sky with their white lances. The bomb run was beginning again. A loud clatter echoed along the Street and an oil bomb hit the leather factory. Within seconds the factory was a burning hulk. Chunks of flaring debris dropped down over the wall onto the roofs in Tanners Alley. Fires started along the pretty cottages, and the factory wall fell outwards into the alley. The few inhabitants who were still in their homes managed to clamber over their back gardens and along the waste ground to Kent Road.

The Carters' home next to the factory was set alight once more, and the roof fell in. One of the men ran to get the firemen, and Tom Carter had to be restrained from trying to enter his fiercely burning house.

"Gawd Almighty! All we've ever 'ad is in there, Joe."

The signalman had his big arms wrapped around the sobbing docker. "It's not true, son. Everyfink yer got that really matters is in the shelter. Yer wife an' kids. That's all that matters right now."

Tom Carter relaxed and Joe Harper allowed the man to break away from his grasp.

A battered car pulled up at the Flannagans' house and two men quickly untied a stretcher from the roof of the makeshift ambulance. Hoppy was carried out and gently placed onto the car. He had ceased moaning, and now lay very still. As the ambulance car pulled out of the turning, an explosion ripped out some shop-fronts along the Tower Road. The car rocked to one side, swerved around a fallen lamppost and continued on its way.

High above dockland, a parachute billowed out and fell gently earthwards. On the end of the silk cords hung a wicked-looking object. The parachute almost cleared the Street, then sailed back. Down it fell, directly above the shelter. The intense heat from the burning leather factory caused the chute to rise up and drift. Once clear of the upward current of air it started to fall again. Directly below was the row of little houses that stretched from the shelter to the Kent Road. The drifting landmine went through the Morgans' roof exploding instantly. The row of houses collapsed and the Morgans' clock stopped at half-past midnight.

As the landmine fell to earth the folk in the shelter were trying to get some sleep. One little child whispered to its mother, "Mum, can I go 'ome?"

"You are 'ome, luv, go back ter sleep."

On another bench sat the Solomon boys with their mother. Joey leaned his head against his mother's arm and dozed fitfully. The rest of the Solomon family stared ahead. Rachel Solomon was a proud woman. Her shoulders were square and upright. Her raven coloured hair was pulled across her head, plaited in a thick rope that came down to the middle of her back. Bernard Solomon her husband worked at the fire station as a controller. That night, as the counters and tiny marker flags closed in around Conner Street, he worried more than ever. A messenger pedalled in, and a new counter was placed directly on Conner Street. Bernard Solomon turned deathly white and answered the phone for the umpteenth time.

As the bomb exploded the shelter seemed to lift up. Dust fell from the roof and the lights went out. There was no warning. No clatter or scream from the falling bomb. The explosion violently surprised everyone. People stood up in panic and trampled over some of the younger children sleeping on makeshift beds between the rows of benches. Men were knocked off their feet, and in a tremendous swirl the blast tore off the shelter doors, sucking them out into the Street. A huge chunk of concrete fell over the entrance, bringing down a pile of earth with it. The shelter entrance was sealed. A smell of gas drifted across to the men who were picking themselves up. Water from a ruptured main poured along the Street. The water seemed to absorb the gas vapour, and it started to run down the sloping entrance to where the pile of rubble lay.

"Quick! Gi' us an 'and!" Joe cried, grabbing a shattered bench.

The men levered away at the concrete.

"It's no good, we'll 'ave ter get some of the dirt away!" the warden shouted out.

Wheezy Morris clambered up to the top of the pile, his slight frame squeezing into the gap near the roof. Working like a scratching dog, he gradually made some space. Another figure ran down to help the men. He was dressed in a dust-covered black suit and wore a steel helmet. A

217

white collar stood out against the flames and flashes. Reverend Leslie Weston did not have time to pray to his chief as he battled away with the men.

At last, the concrete slab was prised away and cool air rushed into the shelter. Someone inside had found the emergency oil lamp and lit it. Reverend Weston poked his head and shoulders into the hole.

"It's all right, folks. You are safe. Shall we all offer up a short prayer?"

"Cor blimey!" exclaimed Mrs Jenkins. "Wot d'jer fink we've all bin doin' all night!"

With the oil lamp held high the Conner Street folk bowed their heads.

"Holy Father, we thank you for our deliverance..." began the reverend.

The light from the oil lamp shone down on a still figure near the door. Rosie Harper's hand went quickly to her mouth. She eased herself towards the figure. A small blue mark had appeared on Skipper's temple. His clay pipe, held between his stiff fingers was pointed towards the floor.

"From the valley of the shadow of ..."

The prayer was halted by Rosie's scream.

"Skipper! Talk to me, Skipper!" screamed Rosie, pulling on the old seaman's shoulders. Skipper's body toppled over and fell down between the benches.

Emmie Jones and Bridie rushed to comfort the sobbing woman, and the reverend squeezed through the small gap. Outside it had become quiet. The bombers had left and the guns were silenced. The white-collared man knelt down and administered the last rites to Skipper, his mumbled words resonating around the cavern.

The hush was broken only by a tiny voice that said, "Mummy, why is that man asleep?"

The mother's tears dripped down on the fair hair of her child.

" 'Cos 'e's tired, darlin'. 'E's very tired."

At number 4, Ada Dawkins was twisting and turning in her bed. Bobbie's head was drooping, and at each gun

218

report he jerked back. The explosion brought most of the ceiling crashing down on to Ada's bed. The window frame fell in, showering broken glass everywhere. Both Ada and Bobbie were cut about the hands and face. Bobbie was whimpering at the foot of the bed, his cut hands still holding on tightly to his box of treasures.

A voice called out, "You all right up there?" The tread of heavy feet sounded on the stairs and big Albert Conlin barged in.

"Gawd, Ada! The bleedin' Street's a right mess. Yer better get dressed, there's big cracks along yer wall, the bloody lot might cave in any minute."

Ada pointed to the washstand. "Give us that towel, Albert. Pour some cold water on it."

Disregarding her own cuts, Ada bathed Bobbie's face. The cuts were not deep, but the blood ran down in lines along the idiot's white features.

"'Elp 'im down the stairs, Al. I'll be down in a few minutes."

Albert Conlin stepped back into the Street, the idiot by his side. The smell of cordite hung in the air, and high in the heavens cold stars twinkled down. Albert could feel Bobbie's arm shaking as he gently steered him toward the shelter.

Bob Bowman had organised the men into groups and they were sent to check on the rest of the Conner Street folk who were not in the shelter. Men came running up to Albert Conlin. "Are they all right?"

"Few cuts. Nuffink serious. This poor bleeder's in a state o' shock," he replied.

Jack Davis was okay, but old Granny Flint was in a bad way. Lizzie Brown was trying to comfort her. Granny was unhurt but the blast has smashed the windows and broken almost everything in the old lady's home. The shock of it all had caused her to go into a fit. Her lips were blue and she shook uncontrollably. One of the men ran to try to get the doctor in Kent Road. Doctor Mason usually got very drunk after his evening surgery and was very rarely to be tempted out at night.

Tom Carter and Patrick Flannagan, who had rushed

home from his night-shift when he heard of the Conner Street explosion, went to check on the Fletcher spinsters. The front door of number 10 was hanging from one hinge. All the windows were shattered, and the interior was a terrible mess. Thousands of pieces of china and glass ornaments lay broken around the room. The glass domes were also broken into small pieces. Poor Harold had fallen from his perch again and lay in a stiff position on the dresser. The two men called out and faint voices answered them.

"Where are yer?" cried out Patrick.

"Under the stairs," answered Minnie in a strangely quiet voice.

"C'mon out, it's all right," said Tom Carter.

The two old spinsters appeared from beneath the stairs, their clothes covered in dust. Maud was sobbing, but Minnie had a stern look. "If them ornaments are damaged I'll ..." she started, but Patrick interrupted.

"Never mind the bloody ornaments as long as you've been spared, ladies."

The two women suffered the destruction with differing reactions. Maud cried bitterly; her lifetime's work of cleaning and polishing the pieces of china and glass had ended on that Saturday night. Minnie, on the other hand, stared stone-faced.

"Shut yer snivellin', Maud. Don't let them see yer cryin'."

Maud caught sight of the stuffed parrot lying on the dresser. "Oh Harold, poor Harold," she sobbed, clutching the bird to her.

"Stop it, Maud, stop it this minute," shouted Minnie, giving Patrick a despairing glance.

"C'mon, luv, let's get yer down the shelter. It ain't safe ter stay 'ere."

Maud shook off Patrick's attempts to coax her from her shattered home. "Poor Harold," she cried.

"Well bring the bloody parrot with yer," shouted Patrick.

The fire at the leather factory had been brought under control. The flames were still licking up from the ruins, and everywhere the Street was littered with broken glass and rubble. Fire hoses ran along the turning, but the exhausted firemen were taking a breather. The night sky was red with fires, and the dust pall over Conner Street glowed with a pink tinge.

The men watched the approaching figures with sad eyes. They walked slowly, with Patrick Flannagan holding the sobbing Maud Fletcher's arm. Maud held the dust-covered parrot like a child, close to her body. Minnie scorned the assistance of Tom Carter. She walked proud and upright. Behind them came Bobbie, a pathetic figure, his face still blood-stained. Big Albert Conlin walked beside him, talking to him in a quiet voice. Jack Davis had been persuaded to leave his damaged home and was already at the shelter gates, talking to the men.

"The bastards 'ave finally done it. They've got our Street," he said in a choked voice. "More'n forty years I've lived 'ere. Brought me kids up 'ere an' lost the ole lady while I lived 'ere. Gawd Almighty, the bastards ain't gonna get away wiv this. You wait. You'll see. We'll give 'em back double, mark my words."

Someone handed Jack Davis a small, flat metal flask. He put it up to his lips and took a swig. The men had started to gather round at the shelter gates. It had gone very quiet. Footsteps could be heard running in the Tower Road end of the turning. The runner appeared from around the corner and stopped breathless at the shelter gates. Two haunted looking eyes stared out from a blackened face. He pointed to the bend of the Street.

"They got the 'Eagle'!"

Around the elbow of Conner Street, and up on the corner, another bomb had fallen during the height of the raid. It had narrowly missed the 'Eagle' but hit a gas main. The explosion had brought down the little pub and below, down in the cellar, two bodies lay side by side. The pathetic heap of rubble still exuded whiffs of smoke, and as the men from the Street reached the place of the tragedy, they saw a strange sight. From the heap of stones and timbers a marker stuck out of the ruins. It was the wooden pub-sign.

Bob Bowman pulled some of the eager volunteers back, saying, "If they're still alive, too many pairs of feet treading over the top of 'em won't 'elp much. Just stand by, we'll call yer if need be."

The warden, Joe Harper and Patrick Flannagan started to remove some large timbers. Bob Bowman beckoned to Harry Smith and Arthur Jones to help with the smoking joists. Gently they eased away the timber and some of the larger stones and bricks. The progress was slow and hard. The rest of the men stood silent and white faced. In the middle of the pile of rubble Arthur Jones was reaching for a chunk of stone when a disconnected timber joist fell on his hand. "Christ! Get it orf!" shouted the docker.

The men who waited rushed to help. They heaved on the timber, and Arthur was finally freed. He sat down, ashen-faced, clutching his crushed hand. Someone produced a bottle of iodine and bandages. Arthur Jones nearly passed out as the contents of the bottle were poured over his wound. While the first-aider was bandaging Arthur's hand the men made progress. They had removed enough debris for Wheezy Morris to squeeze down into the cellar. He disappeared like a ferret going into a rabbit warren, only to emerge again almost immediately. His shocked face said it all. Bob and Joe hauled him out and Wheezy vomited into the gutter.

"Crushed! Pair of 'em! 'Oldin' 'ands they are!" he spluttered.

Joe Harper sat down heavily on a timber joist. He mopped his forehead with a red handkerchief. "Bloody shame. First young Dyke, an' poor old Skipper, an' now Florrie an' John. They've done it proper ternight," he said bitterly. "Wiped out good people, an' finished orf our Street."

The survivors of the night's bombing stood around the ruins of the little pub, half-reluctant to leave. Joe Harper stood up and walked away down the Street. He looked up at the cold, white stars and at the eerie reflection of the fires. He saw the broken, shattered turning and he choked back tears. As he turned the corner he could see the pathetic little group of homeless folk who stood by the shelter gates. Anger boiled up within him as he crossed the Street and entered his home.

Chapter Twenty-One

The stars were blanketed by the smoke-laden sky. The first dawn light crept into the heavens, mercifully changing the blood-red night into an orange-coloured day. The all–clear had sounded, yet still the Conner Street folk did not leave the shelter area. Some people were emerging from the stuffy interior, rubbing their eyes in total disbelief. They stared hard through red-rimmed lids at the desolation around them. They stared pityingly at the few dust-caked homeless who sat on makeshift seats at the shelter gates. Empty, ragged cameos of utter despair and complete dejection, the folk from within sorrowed with the rest.

Already a small band of volunteers was arriving. A mobile canteen with steam coming from inside was parked opposite the shelter. Tea was being issued in large mugs, biscuits were being passed around, and a few cheery words from the Salvation Army ladies and WVS workers helped to muffle the shock of the night. Scalding hot mugs were clasped in shaking hands and tears dripped into the steam. Bowed heads reached down to the hot tea, as though their hands could not be trusted to bring up the mug to their lips. The drink helped to steady their jagged nerves and some folk were smiling their thanks. Bobbie Wilkins sat slumped on an upturned dustbin. He was shaking violently and big Albert Conlin stood by his side, his large arm around the idiot's shoulders. Albert's other arm was crooked towards his face, a steaming mug clenched in a massive fist.

The morning was strangely cold, the wind rising sharply. The northerly gusts blew over the glowing embers that once was the leather factory, and warmed as they swirled along the Street. The winds carried the sweet, sickly smell of scorched, charred leather and brick dust. The flurries whipped up dust and rattled at the loosely-hanging doors. It took the remaining pieces of glass from shattered frames and whipped off loose slates from insanely leaning roofs. Smoke curled in the sky and in the Street the growing group of red-eyed people stared. They were witnessing the end of their Street; for some of them the Street that they were born in, set up home in, and had hoped to die in.

The wind dislodged a door from its broken hinge and it clattered on to the pavement. Bobbie jumped in fright but Albert Conlin reassured him, "It's okay, son, drink your tea."

Bobbie bent his head and sipped noisily. Ada Dawkins sat by his side, her hair covered in white dust. Next to her sat the Fletcher sisters: Minnie, proud and upright; Maud, head bowed, her hands clasping her coat tightly around her frail body. Occasionally Maud would peer furtively beneath the folds of her wrap and smile sweetly to herself. Harold must be kept warm, she mused, and gathered her coat tightly against her. Minnie gave her sister a sideways glance and pursed her lips. God knows what will happen to her if she's ever left alone, she thought. One thing is certain, that flea-bag of a stuffed parrot will have to go. Better wait though. Let her get over the shock of the bombing. For the moment there was other pressing business to be taken care of. Minnie looked around her and spotted a likely candidate.

"Young man," she shouted, and the young man jumped. "Will you help me? I've got some things to gather together." The virago stormed off, her recruited vassal trailing in her wake.

The Conner Street folk were beginning to overcome the initial terror of the destruction around them. The first shock that numbed their senses and made their blood turn to ice was now quite dull, and the stranger shock of deliverance was refracted into cold fury at the German Air Force and the German race as a whole. Tears of anger welled up in the eyes of the Conner Street folk, and rolled down Ada Dawkins's face.

224

"The bastards. They've finished our Street. I 'ope the tykes rot in 'ell, an' that whoreson 'Itler dies an 'orrible deaf."

Bobbie stared at Ada, his eyes reading the anger, but his befuddled brain unable to grasp the reasons for the things that were happening around him. He sat hunched in the cold early morning, his grease-stained cap pulled down around his ears and his old tattered coat buttoned up incorrectly against the wind.

Bob Bowman came up to the group, his dust-covered tunic flapping open. "All this side of the Street's gone. The roofs are all ready ter cave in. There's not 'ardly a stick o' furniture werf savin'." He sat down heavily on the kerbside, his feet in the gutter. The events of the night had left him utterly exhausted. He remembered that only last week he had pleaded with his wife Grace to go to the shelter with Brenda instead of their preferred refuge under the stairs. If he had not been so persistent they would both be dead by now. The cold sensation of the closeness of death, in trembling fingers of ice that gripped his vitals, made the warden shudder violently. He held his head in cupped hands and closed his eyes.

Joe Harper saw the tired figure sitting there in the gutter and felt a wave of pity. The warden had taken on the job and had assumed the responsibility for the Street. He had never spared himself since the blitz had started. Each night he had organised the men and regularly patrolled the turning. He had stopped the squabbles in the shelter and made sure that the old folk were looked after. He had hardly slept in the two weeks of non-stop bombing, and the exhaustion was evident.

"You okay, Bob?"

The warden looked up at Joe Harper through red-rimmed eyes. He did not answer but nodded faintly, then resumed his sad looking position.

Rosie Harper had emerged from inside the shelter with Bridie holding her arm. Rosie held a handkerchief to her face and sobbed loudly. Behind Bridie came her brood: Maureen, who carried the baby, and the twins, Sheena and Sally. Patrick junior held the two-year-old Terry's

225

hand and Terry was struggling to get himself free. The Flannagans walked up the shelter path onto the Street, to be met by Patrick.

"It's no good, you can't go in," the Irishman said quietly.

Bridie looked at him. "I've got to! There's the children to feed, and the baby's bottle ..."

"I tell you it's no good. The gas is off, an' the ceiling's all over the floor. I tell you it's not safe."

Bridie started to cry. "Holy Mary, Mother of God, what am I to do?"

Patrick held his hands up to the heavens, and one of the volunteer women came over. "Don't worry, my dear, we can get the bottle made up in the mobile, then we'll get you to the rest centre."

Bridie sniffed her thanks, and Terry started to cry. Maureen handed the baby to her mother and then comforted her young brother.

"If you stop cryin' Pat'll give you some of 'is marbles, won't you, Pat?"

"Nope."

"Yes you will," asserted Maureen, and Patrick junior appealed to his father. Patrick shook a fist at him and the boy reluctantly fished out two coloured marbles. Terry took the gift and tried to put them into his mouth. Maureen sighed the way she'd seen her mother do on such occasions, and slapped his wrist. Terry threw the marbles into the gutter and started crying again. Patrick junior tried to retrieve them from the broken glass and debris, but his sister hauled him away. The twins laughed at Patrick junior, and he kicked out. It looked like the Flannagans were starting a war of their own when, suddenly, Bobbie fell off the dustbin. The tears turned to laughter at the idiot's misfortune and the war was forgotten. Bobbie picked himself up and proceeded to dust his tattered coat, a sheepish grin spreading over his grimy features, and Ada Dawkins shook her head in despair.

The early morning wind was getting up, with the promise of a cold spell in the northerly gusts. A figure appeared in the Kent Road end of the turning, walking briskly towards the shelter, and from the other end of the Street the local policeman, pushing his bicycle around the debris, picked his way to the group of homeless folk. PC Smith stopped by the shelter gates and bent down to remove his cycle-clips. His face was red from his exertions and his eyes were watering.

"We've got ter get 'em all in the centre, Bob. No good 'em 'angin' around 'ere."

The Street warden had got up from the kerb and was resuming his usual role of Conner Street's guardian. He cast a worried glance over the milling group and started to get the exodus under way. The other newcomer to the group was in conversation with Joe Harper and the Irishman.

"I've roused 'im, bloody ole goat. Pissed as a pudden 'e was. I told 'im, get yerself round ter Granny or I'll send some o' the boys along ter see yer."

Nan Roberts was listening to the conversation. "Who's 'e talkin' about?" she asked of Betty Smith.

"Why that there Docter Mason. Poor old Granny Flint's 'ad a fit. 'E went ter get 'im. Looks like 'e's put the fear o' God inter the drunken ole bastard, " Betty Smith said with venom.

Nan Roberts nodded her agreement. " 'E was a good doctor once. Saved my Bert's life 'e did. Ole Doctor Moore was treatin' 'im fer indigestion. Bloody great ulcer 'e 'ad."

"I grant yer, 'e was a good doctor years ago, till the booze got 'old of 'im," admitted Betty Smith.

The messenger was talking, his thumbs tucked through his braces. "Couldn't rouse 'im at first. 'Ad ter pour a jug o' cold water over 'im. Soon woke 'im up it did. Should 'ave 'eard 'im goin' orf. Anyway, when I told 'im I'd get the lads round if 'e didn't 'urry up, 'e soon changed 'is tune."

The exodus had started. Women with young children were helped on to the back of a battered old removal van that had somehow been found by one of the volunteers. The driver sat glumly in the cab while Bob Bowman and the red-faced PC Smith sorted out the passengers. Bridie Flannagan was helped up on to the van with her brood. The Solomon boys with their raven-haired mother were next, then little Ernie Jacobs and his large mother, who found difficulty in climbing aboard. The operation was expedited with the helping hand, or rather shoulder, of Patrick Flannagan, who was rewarded with an icy stare from an ungrateful Mrs Jacobs.

"C'mon now, folks," urged Bob Bowman, "let's get yer in the warm."

The mums with their young children waited patiently.

"Don't worry, folks, we'll send the van back," announced the warden.

The driver looked even more glum and he slumped over the wheel.

It was one thing to be working on Sunday morning, but to have to make a return trip to the Street on what was supposed to be a day of rest irked the employee of Watson's Cartage Contractors. He mused over his bleak chances of a drink before closing time and his face took on a scowl.

While the loading was taking place, the swaying figure of Doctor Mason appeared in the Street. He carried a small black bag in his hand, and blinked his bloodshot eyes as he picked his way gingerly through the debris-strewn turning. The medic's hair was dishevelled from his impromptu cold shower, his blue nose twitched, and his unshaven chin moved from side to side. He cursed the war, the young popinjay who nearly drowned him, and the old lady for having the temerity to throw a fit at such an inconvenient hour. God! he thought, how he needed a drink. He could feel his tongue swelling and he swallowed with difficulty. Perhaps old Granny Flint would have a tot of the good stuff lying around! He quickened his pace and almost fell through the front door of his patient, which was suspended from one hinge, with the iron knocker broken in half. As he picked his way along the passage, the voice of Lizzie Brown rang out, "We're in 'ere!"

The doctor entered the tiny bedroom at the back of the

house, and saw the pale figure of Granny Flint propped up against a pile of pillows. Lizzie Brown and her friend Emmie sat at the old lady's side; Lizzie stroking the patient's bony hand.

Doctor Mason realised that the possibility of obtaining a drink in the present circumstances was nil. Better get the examination over with as soon as possible, he thought, opening his black bag and fumbling for the thermometer. He finally found it and wiped the biscuit crumbs from the glass. The doctor's attempts to lower the mercury were unsuccessful, for after two shakes, he dropped the instrument under the bed.

Lizzie and Emmie looked at each other, and Granny Flint opened one eye. The bleary-eyed doctor got down on all fours and searched among the plaster and broken glass, under the chunks of window-frame, and around the old lady's chamber pot. Finally the thermometer was recovered and wiped on the sleeve of the medic's coat.

"Can you hear me?" croaked Doctor Clarence Mason, holding Granny Flint's chin between thumb and forefinger. The old lady opened one eye, decided she didn't like what she saw and immediately shut her eye again. It was going to be hopeless to take the woman's temperature, especially with her pursing those lips so tightly. Better settle for the pulse, he thought. This proved to be more of a success, except for the fact that the hands of Doctor Mason's pocket-watch seemed to be spinning round at a terrific rate. When the hands slowed down, and the doctor regained his control over his vision, he realised that he had forgotten the count. Never mind, he thought, let's do the heart bit. The stethoscope is here somewhere, sure it went into the bag. He fumbled around among the bottles of pills, biscuit crumbs, and grimy prescription pads.

Lizzie Brown got impatient. "You lookin' fer yer sounders? They're in yer pocket. I can see 'em stickin' out."

Doctor Mason almost got the earpiece of the stethoscope rammed up one nostril, but finally found both ears.

Granny Flint opened one eye again and decided there

and then that she didn't fancy being prodded with a cold sounder. "Tell 'im ter breave on it first," she hissed at Lizzie, who grinned widely. It was the first words the old lady had uttered since the bomb fell. Emmie patted the old lady's hand, and the doctor completed his exacting examination. One thing puzzled the man. He couldn't be sure whether or not the rushing sound was coming from Granny's chest. He had experienced a similar sound inside his head ever since the cold water episode. It was becoming very confusing. The doctor extended his white-coated tongue, then meaningfully licked his dry lips. The meaning was lost on the ladies of Conner Street, and the venerable Doctor Mason clicked his tongue in an irritable fashion as he removed the prescription pad from his black bag.

"Give her two, night and morning. She'll be running around in a couple of days."

Granny Flint did not intend running anywhere, and what was more, she didn't care for the black bag resting upon her bunion.

"Oi, yer bleedin' bag's on me foot," she yelped.

The doctor mumbled his apologies and stepped to the foot of Granny's bed to retrieve the bag. The movement of his foot caught the handle of the chamber pot, and it spilled over. The medic raised his bleary eyes to the plasterless ceiling and cursed all chamber pots. The cold, wet feeling in his right shoe made him even more irritable and he made for the door. Some plaster trickled down from the shattered ceiling and found its way down the considerable gap between Doctor Mason's collar and neck and he left as quickly as his shaky legs could propel him.

Out in the Street, the evacuation was well under way. The van had left for the rest centre at the Tanners School. Some of the menfolk had formed a patrol in the Street against possible looters, and the rest of them were coming back later. Bob Bowman was already organising the men into a recovery team. Everything of value, anything that could be saved was piled outside the shattered homes. The heap did not look very impressive: a broken armchair, a rickety wardrobe, and an even more rickety table. Here and there along the devastated turning appeared a small bundle of bedding, a few worthless but priceless heirlooms, and the odd timepiece. There was a table outside Ada Dawkins's home. On the table stood a faded photograph in a glassless frame. A tall guardsman stared down the Street, as though waiting for his Ada.

Those of the homeless who did not hitch a ride on the van had decided to walk to the rest centre. It was situated in a back street off the far end of the Tower Road, and the band of volunteers had some of their group making the old school hall a little more accommodating. The children's benches were spaced out to section off areas. The tea urn was steaming, and hot soup stood in a large stewpot above a simmering gas flame. There were blankets piled neatly on the benches, and clean, crisp towels, with a small bar of white soap beside each towel. Around the walls were the efforts of the schoolchildren. Water colours of bright yellow suns, and deep blue skies. Black-haired men, and red-haired women with scarlet lips. There were also paintings of less translatable ideas; strange fits of colour, and nightmarish brush-work that reflected the troubled minds of the young.

The morning wore on, and the van had returned to load up the treasures of Conner Street. Carefully, with due reverence, the vases and the clocks were placed on the bedding bales. The wardrobes and tables, the washstands and the tallboys were packed on the van until there was no more room. The motor growled into life and the irritable driver crashed in the gear. Slowly the van moved off down the Street. Over the bricks and rubble, crunching the glass beneath its tyres, the vanload of treasures went on its way to the warehouse for the homeless. There the furniture, the bric-a-brac and timepieces would join the huge pile of belongings, to remain until the lucky folk reclaimed their treasures, or until the firebombs destroyed them.

It was quiet, almost too quiet on that fateful Sunday morning, a war-time Sabbath when the church bells could not ring, when the rag-and-bone man ceased to call, when the ice-cream vendor and the winkle stall did not appear at the corner of Conner Street. No more could the 'Eagle' open its doors, defying the German Air Force to take away what was an age-old custom; to walk through the doors of a public house on the stroke of twelve noon on a Sabbath, to order a glass of beer, and to dwell on the events of the week. To sit in the company of one's own and to smell the dampness of the bar, the tang of ale on wood from the overfull pints that dripped on the polished counter and imbued the air with the smell of hops and wax. The silver-blue smoke of Nosegay and Goldflake. To sit in the bar and drink in the company of the docker, the carman and the coster. To dwell with one's kin, in a sharply-creased serge suit and highly polished boots. The white silk scarf that twirled around braces, and the loud checked cap, worn at a cocky angle. To pick up a pint glass with work-scarred hands, and to toast one's neighbour. To hell and beyond to the foe, and welcome to the folk of dockland, was once the message as the doors swung open. There would be no welcome this Sunday to the shuffling few; the Conner Street coalman and the dockers, the Irishman, and other grim-faced characters as they stood in silence, looking at the pile of rubble.

Down the Street, the drama continued. Granny Flint would not allow herself to be persuaded out of her wrecked house. Lizzie Brown pleaded with her, and Emmie Jones remonstrated with her, but to no avail. It was an hour since the doctor had left, and the two helpers had only just managed to get Granny dressed. The old lady sat in the cane chair beside her bed and pursed her lips.

"It's no bleedin' good. The ole cow won't move," hissed Lizzie.

Emmie shook her head in despair. "Well she can't stop 'ere. There's no water, no gas, an' the bleedin' roof don't look none too good. If we don't get 'er round the rest centre, she's gonna 'ave anuvver one o' them there turns."

"Keep yer eye on 'er, Em. I'll 'ave a word wiv Bob," Lizzie said.

As Lizzie ducked under the hanging front door, she spotted the Street warden talking to Joe Harper. The men were standing by the shelter gates, and they looked over in Lizzie's direction.

"'Ow's the old gal, Liz?" asked Bob.

"Bright as a new pin. Trouble is, we can't get 'er out o' the place. She just won't budge," Lizzie moaned, hands spread to the sky.

Bob Bowman's face was serious. "Give us a few minutes, Liz. We're expectin' the 'earse for poor ole Skipper any time now. Soon's 'e's bin I'll see what I can do."

Almost as soon as the warden had uttered the words, a van turned the corner and pulled up outside the shelter gates and two men got out. Joe Harper waved them in the direction of the cavern which contained the body of his old friend.

Lizzie looked hard at the plain grey van with whitened rear windows, and then at Bow Bowman. "Never seen an 'earse like that before. Must o' bin a few poor bastards copped it last night."

The two men appeared with the stretchered body carried between them. Expressionless and casual, the men slid the stretcher into the rear of the van and banged the doors shut. Lizzie Brown's face suddenly brightened and she winked at the warden. "'Ere, mate, where yer takin' the ole chap to?"

"Got a mortuary set up in the Drill Hall," answered the doleful driver.

"Ain't that near the Tanners School?" Lizzie enquired.

"Just round the corner," said the driver.

Lizzie took the man's arm and steered him away from the rear of the hearse.

Minutes later, Granny Flint came out of her house, with Emmie and Lizzie both holding on to her. The warden and Joe had removed the hanging door and Granny Flint strode through the opening like a queen. There was a look of serenity upon her aged face and a sweet smile on her lips. Eagerly she made her way to the hearse and allowed herself to be placed beside the driver. Emmie squeezed in beside her, and the driver's mate got into the back of the van beside the body of Skipper.

As the van drove slowly away around the corner Joe looked at Lizzie with a puzzled frown. "What made the ole gal change 'er mind, Liz?"

Lizzie Brown put her hands under her apron and grinned a toothless smile. "I just told 'er the Lord Mayor o' London sent a special moter car for 'er. I told 'er it was 'cos she was ninety terday."

"Well I'll be," gasped Joe, and the warden laughed aloud.

"Is it really 'er birfday?" asked Bob.

"Gawd knows," grinned Liz. "She finks it is, that's all that matters."

"Well, I 'ope she don't find out she's bin in an 'earse. If she ever does, your life won't be worf livin'," chuckled the warden.

Joe Harper swallowed hard and stared down at his feet.

"Ter tell yer the trufe, I don't fink she will mind," Liz said quietly. "She always 'ad a soft spot for the ole chap. She won't mind sharin' 'is last ride."

Chapter Twenty-Two

Early on Sunday morning, Stanley Nathan was awakened by the local police and told that his shop had been extensively damaged by blast during the night.

He and Julie arrived at London Bridge Station at lunch time and walked the mile or so to Tower Road. The extent of the night's bombing was apparent as they neared Conner Street. Tower Road itself was closed to traffic as there were at least two large bomb craters that spread across the road from pavement to pavement. Workmen had already sealed off the fractured gas main, and other men were busy boarding up the damaged shop fronts.

Tower Road curved slightly, then straightened out for its last half-mile to the junction with Kent Road. The lovers picked their way carefully through the curve and came face to face with a horrifying sight. Every shop had been damaged, every roof had shed tiles, and every inch of the pavement was strewn with broken glass, bricks and rubble. Just short of Conner Street was a large crater, caused by the gas explosion. The ruins of the 'Eagle' spread out to the lip of the hole and some of the large timbers had ended up standing upright in the concavity, like giant markers. The smell of destruction was all around the two as they walked slowly, unbelieving, up to the entrance of the Street. Burnt wood mingled with brick-dust. A sickly sweet smell of cordite and gas fumes lingered in the air, and from the ruins of the 'Eagle' came an aroma of sour beer.

A lorry was pulling slowly out of the turning. It turned left to dodge the crater and then drove along to Kent Road. Stanley and Julie saw the battered pieces of furniture piled up on the lorry and tied with rope. The two men sat holding on tightly to the swaying load as the vehicle bounced and shuddered over the debris-littered roadway. The Street warden was replacing a rope that had been stretched across the turning and he greeted the two with a solemn face.

Julie did not need to be told that the Bradens were dead. She could see that no one would have survived beneath the ruins of the pub. Her nails bit into Stanley's arm as Bob Bowman recounted the events of the night. Her eyes glazed with tears and the warden's features swam before her as she listened. She tried to speak but the words stuck in her throat. Two of the people she really cared for and loved were dead. Florrie had been like a mother to her, and helped her when she most needed it, and now she was gone. John too had always treated her with kindness and understanding, even though he himself was often muddled and confused. Julie sobbed loudly and buried her head into Stanley's chest. The shopkeeper gently stroked her hair and held her close. There was nothing he could think of to say that would ease her pain. He knew only that time could heal the hurt, and he steered her away from the ruins and into the silent Street.

The two walked reverently along the turning, Stanley holding Julie's arm tightly. Slightly behind them, the tall, stooping figure of the warden moved in their wake, like an unwilling guide whose job it was to point out the ugly results of the past few hours. Bob Bowman felt he should walk with them. It was his Street and the responsibility still weighed heavily on his shoulders. As they passed the burned-out leather factory and turned the corner Bob kicked a piece of brick from the pavement in a futile gesture.

Stanley did not know why he steered Julie into the Street. He thought about it as they came up to the flattened row of houses. It seemed to him that they had to look at it for the last time. The old backstreets of the East End were disappearing with the relentless bombing.

The day was cold and damp as the two slowly and painfully made their way along the damaged Tower

Road. Julie wanted to talk to the Conner Street folk. She felt the need to be with them, to share their sorrow and compassion, and almost without thinking they wended their way toward the rest centre. They went to meet their friends, refugees from a place of chaos and confusion.

Only a few houses at the Tower Road end of the devastated little backstreet were still habitable, and even in these the water and gas had been turned off. A water main had been damaged in the Tower Road and the gas works along Kent Road had sustained a direct hit during the night. No roast meals were cooked in the area on that cold Sunday. Emergency water tankers were moving around the backstreets dealing out one bucket of water to each person. For the kids it meant that they had to go without a wash, which did not seem to trouble them too much. As for lighting, kerosene lamps were brought out, cleaned and trimmed, then placed in the small parlours in preparation for the coming darkness.

Conner Street on that cold Sunday afternoon seemed to have become a graveyard, quiet, devoid of life. The adjoining Tanners Alley was desolated, hideous in silence. The wall of the leather factory had fallen into the cobbled path, and the damage caused by the heat of the fire had left the cottages blackened and shell-like. Gone were the autumn flowers, gone were the dainty window shutters and the little window-boxes, and gone too were the inhabitants, who had made their escape over the back gardens. Very few of them had left their homes for the shelter the previous night, but the caprices of Providence had dealt kindly with them, and everyone who lived in the once pretty alley was safe.

One thing remained the same, although it now seemed to lean a fraction more from the perpendicular. The Crimean cannon had heard the rumble of war once again and now bore a new scar on its iron carcass, a deep indentation caused by a bomb fragment. It had been warmed again, not by the speeding ball-shot through its core but by the terrible searing heat of the factory fire. Now in the cold, dull afternoon, the Crimean cannon that had changed into a hitching post cooled. Northerly winds whistled around it and gusted along the Street, creating eerie sounds in and about the forsaken homes, as though lamenting the departed.

In the old school hall, the refugees from Conner Street ate their Sunday lunch and then resumed their places on the low benches. They felt the enormity of the night's events now, and they sat hunched, with few words passing between them. The children in their innocence were more vociferous as they sat in a group at one end of the hall.

One of the refugees was missing. Wheezy had slipped out early that afternoon to visit his pal, Hoppy Dyke. Hoppy lay propped up against a mound of pillows in a small converted storeroom. Guy's Hospital was full of blitz casualties; the less severely injured were resting in corridors, or in any odd corner that could accommodate them. They lay quiet and shocked, drugged against the pain and sleeping fitfully. Wheezy gave one or two of the casualties a cheery wave as he followed the nurse's directions to the storeroom. He found his friend and pulled up a chair at the bedside. An iron frame beneath the bedclothes kept the linen away from Hoppy's burnt legs, and by the bed, covered with a white cloth, was an instrument trolley. Wheezy looked hard at Hoppy, hardly recognising him. The casualty from Conner Street was wincing with pain, his face drained of colour, and he looked much older than his years.

" 'Ow's it goin', mate?" Wheezy asked cheerfully.

Hoppy's face screwed up in pain. "Bloody legs are givin' me 'ell."

Wheezy lifted the white cloth from the trolley and peered beneath. "Wot's this, yer dinner?"

Hoppy screwed up his face again and his eyes closed for a second or two. Wheezy now sitting by the bed felt at a loss for words. He looked up at the ceiling and around the windowless room. A nurse appeared and went over to the bed opposite. She leant across the patient and listened to his breathing for a few moments before taking his pulse. Wheezy's lecherous eyes never left the nurse until she disappeared from the room. The white of her thighs above the black stockings had aroused him and he turned to Hoppy. "Did yer see that, mate? Cor! I bet yer get an eyeful in 'ere!"

The patient's singed legs sent their painful ciphers along his nervous system and he grimaced.

"'Ere, yer ain't burnt yer ole plonker, 'ave yer?" Wheezy asked suddenly.

This time Hoppy managed a weak grin. "It's only singed, fank Gawd."

The pretty nurse appeared again and walked up to Hoppy's bed. She placed a thermometer in his mouth and took his wrist, looking at a watch that was pinned to her apron front. Wheezy watched until the nurse was finished, then he gave her a crooked smile. The reply was a cold stare from the nurse as she walked from the room.

"Cor! I bet they drive yer mad in 'ere," Wheezy said, screwing up his face for effect.

The pain was getting worse and Wheezy's conversation irked the patient. He wanted Wheezy to leave and the nurse to hurry up with his painkiller.

"Never mind. Give it a couple o' days an' you'll be up an' at 'em, mate," Wheezy went on.

Hoppy managed a tired grin. His eyes closed again and he bit his lip. The nurse walked over to the bed and looked down at Wheezy. "I'm afraid it's time to go," she said coldly. "He must get some sleep now."

The swirling fog seemed to be getting worse as Wheezy Morris made his way back to the rest centre. The early evening was cold and damp, with condensation glistening on the cobbled streets. If it gets any worse they won't be coming tonight, he thought, and he whistled tunelessly as he reached the centre, crossed the deserted playground, and entered the stuffy interior.

It was tea-time at the Tanners School Rest Centre, and Granny Flint was causing a minor stir. "It's no good, I can't eat yer bleedin' cake. It's stone 'ard I tell yer."

The volunteer gave Granny Flint a forced smile and persisted with the cake.

Granny Flint pulled a face. "Now listen 'ere. I ain't eatin' that lump o' brick yer call cake, so there. An' I tell

239

yer somefing else. I ain't drinkin' that bloody cocoa, 'cos I don't like cocoa, so put that in yer pipe an' smoke it."

Seeing that it was hopeless to persist, the helper left Granny Flint.

The rest of the women of the Street sat around Granny, their faces tired and strained, but their spirits still high.

"Wiv that fog comin' down outside, I reckon we'll get a rest from the bastards ternight," said Lizzie Brown.

"As long as that wind don't get up," said Emmie.

"Well I don't know about you lot, but I'm stoppin' 'ere ternight. I couldn't face that shelter again, not after seein' poor ole Skipper's face as 'e lay there," Nan Roberts joined in.

Mrs Wallace got up and beckoned her ailing husband to follow. "Well we're goin' back ter the shelter, ain't we, luv?"

George Wallace coughed loudly and nodded.

As the couple got to the door, Mrs Wallace turned and looked at Nan Roberts. "Yer know the old sayin', lightnin' don't strike the same place twice."

Granny Flint gave out a wicked chuckle. "I didn't know it was lightnin' wot knocked our 'ouses down."

The Wallaces left the centre, the women's laughter ringing in their ears.

Lizzie Brown watched them leave and turned to Granny Flint. "Granny, you're a wicked ole lady," she said with a sly grin.

Granny Flint shrugged her shoulders and the women laughed, except for Emmie Jones. She wiped a tear from her eye and sat with her head bowed.

"Cheer up, Emm, it could be worse," said Lizzie.

Emmie looked at Lizzie Brown and the tears started to fall. "Gawd, Liz, you make me so mad sometimes. We've lost our 'omes, an' we've lost good neighbours, an' wot's more the bastards will be back ternight."

The women went quiet, and Granny Flint started to doze.

Lizzie Brown looked at the little group for a while, then got up and stood before them, hands on hips. "You lot make me sick, sittin' there as though it was the end of

240

everyfing. We're alive, ain't we? The Almighty smiled on most of us last night. We're warm, an' dry, ain't we?"

The group looked at Lizzie in silence.

"Well, ain't we?" Lizzie said more loudly.

The women nodded.

"When I say fings could be worse I mean it," Lizzie went on. "Just imagine that door openin' an' that ole tyke o' mine strollin' in. Yes, my ole luvs, fings could be worse."

The evening wore on and the fog swirled around the school building. From the interior, sounds of a harmonica and singing drifted out into the haze. A sudden breeze caught a sweet wrapper and sent it across the school playground. The wind freshened, and above an early star winked down. The fog was clearing.

Epilogue

A high flying jet plane was tracing a thin line across the azure sky. The sun was climbing and there was just a ghost of a breeze. June flowers were blooming in the public garden as the old man walked slowly along the gravel path. He stopped once or twice to admire the gardener's efforts and to rest his tired and aching legs. He leaned heavily on a stout walking-stick, for his arthritis had been paining him of late. Today, however, he felt much better. The prospect of an early summer cheered him and it would certainly help his stiffening joints.

The public garden allowed a short cut to 'The Bargee', which was only a few minutes from the park exit. If he had timed it right they would just be opening by the time he reached there. The old man usually left his ground floor bedsit at ten thirty am and stopped to buy a morning paper and tobacco at the corner shop. Weather permitting, the old man's journey to 'The Bargee' was a daily occurrence. The riverside pub was the popular haunt of managers from local firms, and more than one contract had been finalised in the little saloon bar. Tourists as well found 'The Bargee' on their itinerary, and the pub's manager and his wife had by now become quite used to appearing in the tourists' family snapshots, usually taken on the pub's veranda overlooking the Thames.

That veranda was the old man's destination, and he liked to get there before the lunch-time flow of impatient, harassed businessmen. On this particular morning, with the heat already rising up from the gravel path, the prospect of a pint of bitter made him lick his lips. As he left the garden the old man turned to his right then walked a few yards before crossing the street. Since the

242

wharves had closed there was not much traffic using the riverside route through dockland. The only vehicles he encountered were a slow-cruising police car and the milk float that whined along on its way back to the depot. At the entrance to the pub the old man leant on the wall and glanced up at the clock face on the tower of St Mary's Church. The hour hand pointed to the six and had been in that position since the Blitz, when a bomb had blown the minute hand away and shattered the clock's mechanism. Still leaning against the wall the old man pulled up his sleeve to look at his thick wristwatch and realised that he hadn't wound it lately. Must get one of those new-fangled watches that don't need winding, he promised himself.

The sound of sliding bolts came from inside the pub and the door swung back.

"'Ello, Bob. You're bright an' early this mornin'." The speaker was a pretty young girl who served behind the bar. Her hair was fair and cascaded over her eyes as she bent down to fasten the door back.

"Nice mornin'. Gonna be a scorcher, mark my words," Bob commented as he walked into the pub.

The girl trotted in behind him and walked around the counter. She adjusted her yellow smock, then waited while Bob Bowman went through his usual ritual. First he doffed his greasy cap and stuffed it into his coat pocket. Then he hooked his walking-stick over the back of a bar chair, his clenched fist placed on the bar counter for support. Next he took a handful of silver from his pocket and dropped the coins in a heap in front of the girl. Molly Wright smiled and counted out the price of a pint less ten pence. While she was pulling on the bar pump Bob looked around him. There was only one other person in the saloon bar, a young man who was filling up the cigarette machine.

"There yer go, Bob," Molly said as she placed a foaming pint of beer at his elbow. Conner Street's ex-warden took a long swig from the glass and then put it back on the counter. He pulled out a large red spotted handkerchief from his coat pocket and shook it furiously before wiping it across his mouth. He gasped and burped loudly, his face still flushed from the effort of his walk.

"Cor I needed that," he gasped as he wiped his watery blue eyes on his handkerchief.

Molly leaned on the counter facing him, her large brown eyes looking at him fondly. "Where yer goin', Bob, on the veranda?" she asked.

"Yus, I reckon I will. A bit o' sea air will do me ole chest good," Bob replied, with a grin spreading over his bony features.

Molly followed him out on to the veranda and placed the pint of beer by his hand. Bob settled himself and proceeded to fill his pipe.

Molly sat on the edge of the table facing him. From her position she could see into the bar. "The river looks calm, Bob. It's 'ardly movin'."

The old man squinted up his eyes and looked up river to the distant Tower Bridge. "Tide's on the turn. Looks calm I grant yer, but them currents is bloody treacherous. If yer fell in yer'd be swept down river quick as lightnin'."

The cigarette man popped his head around the door and winked at Molly. "All done. See yer next week, babe."

Molly bared her white teeth in a forced grin, then pulled a face at the disappearing figure.

The gesture was lost on Bob. He was scanning the river, his eyes narrow slits. He noticed that a few of the wharves were coming back to life. Here and there a pane of glass replaced a loophole, and a few brightly coloured window-boxes had appeared, suspended over the water.

Molly followed his gaze as she sat with her arms folded over her small breasts. "We're getting quite a few new customers in lately. Some of 'em are dressed real funny. Lovely people they are though. Ever so friendly."

Bob Bowman took another swig from his glass. "I've seen a few changes on that river, girl. I was only a pup when I started workin' in the docks, an' I packed up in '65. Took me severance I did. I'm eighty come August, please Gawd."

Molly smiled at him. "Well you don't look a day over

sixty, Bob."

Bob snorted. "Go on wiv yer, yer cheeky little mare."

Molly Wright ignored his remark. "Can I get yer a refill before the crush starts?"

"One more. I gotta bit of a dry froat, luv."

While the barmaid was filling Bob's glass a customer came in. He was elderly and straight-backed. Molly served him a Guinness then carried Bob's drink out on to the veranda. "Mr Fred'ricks 'as just come in," she said.

The old man pulled a face. "'Im. Bloody ole moaner. What wiv 'im an' that Miss Cavendish. Right pair o' neighbours they are."

Molly frowned, and Bob continued, "'E's bin complainin' about me geraniums. Said they gave orf a smell o' cat's piss. I tell yer. If them flowers do smell it's 'is bloody ole tom cat wot's done it."

Molly watched him take a sip from the glass, her eyes wide and smiling.

"There's 'er. Scatty mare." Bob snorted.

"Who?"

"Why, ole Miss Bloody Cavendish. She reckons they're spyin' on 'er."

"Who is?"

"Why the council. Told me last week. Said they're peepin' in 'er letter-box."

"No."

"'S'right. Told me they're watchin' ter see if she takes in men friends."

"Really?"

"Sure as I'm sittin' 'ere. Sure as Gawd made little apples. Bloody 'ell, who in their right mind would fancy ole Miss Cavendish?"

Molly laughed heartily. "Bob, you are a one. If your Brenda could 'ear yer carryin' on like that she'd 'ave somethin' ter say."

Bob Bowman looked up at Molly. "That reminds me. Brenda an' Joe are coming up ter take me out fer a drink come Saturday. I s'pose they'll tell me all about their new 'ouse."

Molly's eyes became sad, and she looked at the old man

245

fondly. "Didn't yer want ter go ter Sevenoaks wiv 'em, Bob?"

"O' course I didn't. I like it 'ere better. I've got me flowers an' me privicy. Can't ask fer much more, can yer?"

Molly noticed that some customers had walked in. She excused herself and Bob was left alone with his thoughts.

Presently a tall stranger walked out on to the veranda. He was broad-shouldered and wore a sand-coloured suit. Around his neck hung a large camera, and he carried a small bag with the letters TWA stamped on the side. For a time he stood looking at the river.

Bob followed his gaze. A lone sculler was battling against the ebbing tide, and a pleasure boat was passing under Tower Bridge, heading in their direction. Apart from the two craft the river was empty.

The American started to take some snapshots, his camera clicking and whirring. When he was satisfied with his efforts, the American sat down facing Bob Bowman and gave him a friendly grin. "That's some river, isn't it?"

The old man wanted very much to tell the tall man about the river. His river: the ships moored at anchor, awaiting a berth, the tugs hauling clusters of laden barges up into the Pool, the cranes, dipping and swinging over the quays, the shouts of the river men, the laughter and the curses. Instead he bit his tongue and said simply, "It's pretty quiet terday, mate."